THE LAST DAY

THE LAST DAY

Glenn Kleier

Hodder & Stoughton

First published in Great Britain in 1997
by Hodder and Stoughton
a division of Hodder Headline PLC

10 9 8 7 6 5 4 3 2 1

British Library Cataloguing in Publication Data

Kleier, Glenn
The last day
1. Pseudo-Messiahs – Fiction 2. Thrillers
I. Title
813.5'4 [F]

ISBN 0 340 71242 2

Typeset by Hewer Text Composition Services, Edinburgh
Printed and bound in Great Britain by
Mackays of Chatham PLC

Hodder and Stoughton
A division of Hodder Headline PLC
338 Euston Road
London NW1 3BH

To all who confront the peculiar
physics of dogma,
piety and self-righteousness

Acknowledgments

My heartfelt gratitude to Ms Jillian Manus of Manus and Associates for the extraordinary level of enthusiasm, expertise and intelligence with which she has so skilfully agented this project. You are a remarkable lady, Jillian. You made the entire process an absolute delight.

Special thanks to vice-president and executive editor at Warner Books, Mr Rick Horgan, and to his superb team of professionals. Rick, your keen insights and thoughtful suggestions were dead-on accurate and fostered many a valuable refinement. Senior production editor Bob Castillo and copy-editor Fred Chase, thanks for your unfailing attention to detail. Working with all of you was a truly rewarding experience.

Special thanks to George Lucas and Philippa Pride at Hodder and Stoughton for all your hard work and contributions.

Ryan and Sean, thank you for your patience over the last several years in putting up with an often distracted dad. While it wasn't always easy typing with one or other of you climbing into my lap, I wouldn't have had it any other way. I miss those days; they are special memories for me. (But you still have to wait till you're older to read this book!)

There are no words to express the debt of gratitude I feel towards my father and mother, Gene and Mary Rose Kleier. Thanks for putting up with a skinny, hyperactive, lippy little kid; and for planting inside him those core beliefs that have sustained him through all these years. I could not ask for more loving and generous parents than you.

And I save my deepest appreciation for my beloved wife, Pam, who is not only beautiful and brilliant, but infinitely understanding. You remain the most consummate human being it has ever been my privilege to know, and without your unflagging support, patience and assistance, this little allegory would not exist.

My love to all of you, always.

Glenn

THE LAST DAY

1

'Jesus Christ!' the first man exclaimed.

'More or less,' the second responded.

The two well-dressed TV executives sat alone in a World News Network editing suite as a series of bizarre, silent scenes played out on the huge video wall before them.

Towering on the screen was the face of a grinning, feverish-eyed, middle-aged man with a scruffy beard. He was dressed in a tattered robe. His long stringy hair was matted with blood that trickled from a laurel wreath of rusted barbed wire on his head. As the camera pulled back, a heavy wooden cross became visible across his shoulder. Behind him, a street sign read 'Via Dolorosa'. A title font on the screen identified the man as 'Douglas Bandy, former stockbroker from San Jose, CA'.

The first executive nodded appreciatively.

Emerging next on the large screen was a young family of five, also shabbily dressed, seated on the worn cobblestones of what appeared to be an ancient market bazaar. The family extended their upturned palms to every passer-by, and ultimately to the camera taking the video. The font read: 'The Étien Dubois family, formerly of Orléans, France'.

The video then cut to a wide scene of a highway choked with cars, buses, bicycles and animal-driven vehicles. Beyond, the contorted skyline of Jerusalem loomed in the distance.

'Here's where we come in with the historical material,' the second executive explained in a genteel English accent.

Obligingly, the video screen presented sweeping footage of a beautiful, elaborately embroidered wall tapestry. As the camera moved in to migrate slowly down the full length of the mural, an epic story unfolded.

'The Catastrophic Millennium Pilgrimages of AD 999', the title font described it. The sequence began with wealthy, medieval European families giving away their belongings to the poor and setting off for the Holy Land. On their journey, the travellers soon fell victim to terrible hardships. The tapestry depicted graphic scenes of marauders waylaying, pillaging, raping, enslaving and murdering the pilgrims. Those fortunate enough to survive the trek were then shown arriving, destitute, in the forbidden Jerusalem of the Muslims, left to starve in frustrated desolation.

'We'll add the voice-overs next week,' the Englishman commented, 'and that will finish it.'

'An outstanding piece,' his cohort acknowledged, an expression of admiration spreading across his face. 'It looks like your Millennium Eve special will be a huge success. Airtime's selling well all over the globe.'

'Was there ever any doubt?' the Englishman said, feigning surprise.

His associate emitted a short, snorting laugh. 'I'll tell you what, Nigel, when you first proposed this whole idea, a lot of us here in the States thought you were crazy. I mean, forming special news teams, sending them all over the world at such expense to chase after a bunch of religious fanatics! I honestly thought Corporate was going to take a bath on this one. But once again, you've shown your knack for creating news. You developed this millenarian craze into a major international story. Hell, if things go as well as we anticipate, maybe we'll run it again next year for the *real* turn of the millennium!'

'To be quite honest,' Nigel confessed, 'it falls short of my expectations.'

'What do you mean?' the fellow executive protested. 'The set-up couldn't be more perfect! Your coverage of the millenarian movement over the last six months – the growing insanity in the Holy Land, Rome, Salt Lake City. All the crazy speculation about what's going to happen when the world odometer ticks over to the year 2000. The TV audience can't get enough of it! You were light-years ahead of the other networks, Nigel. You had the foresight.'

The Englishman remained unconvinced, wagging his head slowly. 'The story lacks substance. These zealots may be entertaining, but they have no true credibility with our audience. They're a sideshow. A curiosity. I was hoping we'd eventually find something with a harder edge.'

'Like what?' his associate wondered.

'If only we'd been successful in getting one of the heavyweight religions aboard. A choice, apocalyptic statement from the Pope would have been nice. Or perhaps the discovery of some ominous new Dead Sea Scroll. What our report needs is a jolt of drama. Something to give the evening a little more . . . impact.'

2

Mount Ramon Observatory, Negev desert, southern Israel, *11.57 P.M., Friday, 24 December 1999*

At this late hour, four Japanese astronomers were hunched over an assortment of infrared monitors, spectroscopes and optical instruments, gazing skyward from the open deck of Israel's only celestial observatory. Bundled against the cold, the men were special guests of the Israeli Ministry of Science, on leave from Kyoto University, Japan. The latitude and dry atmosphere of the southern Israeli desert were ideal for studying this, the largest meteor phenomenon in two thousand years, as the earth passed tonight through the Geminids asteroid belt. Already the astronomers had recorded hundreds of encounters.

'With all this activity, you would think a few might survive the descent,' one colleague commented in Japanese to no one in particular.

'Yes,' another replied. 'It would be exciting to collect a fresh specimen.'

In fact, at the very foot of Mount Ramon lay the scars of several ancient meteorite craters, the only such sites in the Middle East, stretching for miles across the great rift of the Negev Valley. But the scientists were uninterested in things terrestrial. Their eyes were fixed firmly on the heavens.

Quite unexpectedly, the most senior fellow of the group noticed in his instrument one meteor far brighter and larger than typical. Lips trembling, he rose slowly from his chair to confirm the sighting with unaided eyes. Certain of himself now, he blurted out in exhilaration, 'Gentlemen, I think we have an impact!'

He and his associates gaped with fascination as the light grew rapidly in size and intensity. It hurtled directly towards them on a flat trajectory, from approximately thirty degrees above the eastern horizon. The younger men remained spellbound only long enough for the danger to register, then abruptly abandoned their posts for the questionable cover of a near-by table. The senior astronomer, however, stood his ground, avidly absorbing every detail as the object passed well overhead.

In its flight across the Negev, the fiery mass illuminated a large swath of craggy mountains and rambling desert valleys. Its brilliant passing scattered the livestock of bewildered nomads, frightened an elderly Bedouin couple travelling in a donkey-driven cart, and roused various camps of millenarian pilgrims paused on their way to the Holy City of Jerusalem to celebrate the New Year 2000.

Nor did the meteor elude the detection of Israeli Air Defence. Coincidental with the astronomers' first sighting, an image was captured on radar at an Israeli military airfield, located near the southern side of the mountain.

'God damn!' a stunned sentry shouted in alarm, jolted out of his complacency by a conspicuous blip emerging on his screen. His fellow sentries were at his side in an instant, squinting closely at the object, each finding it hard to accept that the peaceful state of Jordan was the seeming point of origin.

'Code D, hostile.' A telemetry specialist made the call. But having never seen the likes of this, he couldn't identify it. 'Too small for a plane,' he decided, 'too fast for a cruise missile, too low to be a Scud.'

The officer of the watch, frantically trying to determine the exact source and direction of the invader, sounded a full-scale alert, scrambling aircraft and enabling batteries of Super-Patriot missiles. But there was no time for an intercept. The object was already across the border and rapidly losing altitude.

3

Negev Research Institute, Negev desert, southern Israel,
11.59 P.M., Friday, 24 December 1999

Rising up stark and indifferently out of the weathered rock and red sands of a secluded desert canyon, an imposing glass-and-steel structure lay directly in the path of the meteor. As if to direct the oncoming visitor, there were two wings to the complex which converged in a large V. At their intersection sat a huge geodesic bubble, its one-way bronze glass reflecting multiples of the oncoming fireball.

'Israeli Negev Research Institude', the installation proclaimed itself in bold Hebrew and English signage. For years, the Israelis had professed this to be a biotechnology laboratory, but the centre was known to be affiliated to the Israeli Defence Force and considered by neighbouring countries and US intelligence to be a major military research and development facility. Fully fenced and guarded by motor patrols, the institute was aglow with activity.

Inside the dome was a multi-tiered laboratory of dazzling complexity. The huge infrastructure was composed of seven separate levels, each suspended from a central supporting shaft. Set well back from the dome, each floor afforded an open, cinemascopic view of the night sky.

The institute was staffed by scores of preoccupied technicians tending a vast, layered network of cybersystems. Lengthy arrays of electronics at the top level fed downward into banks of computers on the next, which interacted with lower levels of endless coiled tubing. These, in turn, percolated clear fluids into ever-descending substrata of processors, filters, auxiliary systems and convoluted bionetworks.

Eventually leaching its way to ground level, the refined alchemy met up with the sole recipient of all this mass science: a virtually motionless, naked human figure, submerged in dark amber fluid in a transparent sealed rectangular vessel. The still form lay on its side, doubled up in a foetal position, legs tucked, arms drawn into its chest.

But the figure was much larger than a foetus. The physique was slight, adult and female.

The body floated pale and free in soft spotlights, attended by assorted monitors and scholarly men and women. Its entire head was encased in a helmeted Medusa of electrodes and spiralling wires. These attachments fed into a port in the back of the holding tank and continued upward in spreading branches to unite with the various technologies above. A larger tube, the thickness of a garden hose, meandered its way from the gut of the body, out of the top of the vessel to disappear in a tangle of connections overhead.

Beyond the figure, separated and off to one side like a couple of abandoned prototypes, were two identical female forms in similar support vessels. Their heads were also encased in helmets but only partially linked into the labyrinth above. Each, however, bore umbilical hoses which tapped into the grand placental network.

To the other side of the showcased subject, the scientists were focusing their attention on monitors displaying three-dimensional, holographic images of a human brain. Visible within the brain were thirteen distinctly non-organic devices. Thin square wafers less than a millimetre in size, the objects were distributed deep within the cerebral hemispheres.

Originating from each device were wisps of ultra-fine fibres which collected into tiny threads. The threads travelled up through the brain tissue, penetrated the skull, then migrated under the scalp to a central gathering point in a larger wafer attached to the back of the skull. From here, a single, coiled wire emerged from the scalp and through the helmet to join the mechanisms and monitors beyond. Next to the monitors were other displays, including EEG screens, which recorded wildly active readings.

'My God, look at this one!' A gratified administrator summoned his charges, and they converged to marvel at the progress of their work. 'This is an historic moment, ladies and gentlemen,' he crowed, taking full advantage of the euphoria to squeeze an attractive female assistant next to him. 'We're about to steal a page from the Book of Genesis!'

Inside the central vessel, the slumbering form would twitch occasionally, reminiscent of an infant's startle reflex. Hunched down, observing this closely, was a frail, elderly, white-haired gentleman in lab coat and tie. The vessel's glass reflected his troubled frown. 'What have I done!' he reproached himself softly. 'God forgive me, what have I done!'

Just before the fireball impacted, there was a synchronized moment when all in attendance sensed the ominous presence, suspended operations, and turned in spellbound unison to fathom the approaching spectacle of their doom.

Steadily disintegrating in its fiery descent, sloughing off hot chunks of itself to the desert floor below, the core mass of the object was still sizeable as it plunged into the swollen dome of the complex. Tearing through layers of whirring cybernetics, it penetrated deep into the pulsing tubes and electronic ganglia.

There was a pause as if the entire structure were sucking in its breath, and then the top of the dome erupted in a white napalm concussion. The upper four tiers, and any person stationed there, vaporized instantly. As air defence sirens bellowed belatedly in the distance, a series of smaller explosions in the lower levels began to issue thick black smoke.

Miraculously, the substructure containing the human forms remained, for the moment, intact. The frail white-haired man, struggling desperately in the acrid fumes to free his imprisoned subjects, staggered against a chamber and collapsed.

Abandoned by the other attendants, their support systems disastrously interrupted, all the encased figures were showing escalating movement; particularly the main subject, which was becoming frantic, grappling clumsily with its helmet and kicking against the sides of its vessel. Reacting to a more intense electronic burst from the circuitry above, the figure underwent a grand mal convulsion, arched its back and exploded the sides of its container with a powerful thrust of its legs.

Outside the inferno it was the chaos of the dead and dying. Frustrated security patrols held well back beyond the perimeter fence, unable to do anything but watch as the terrible drama played itself out. Over the mournful tremolos of the sirens, the first interceptor jets could be heard arriving overhead, too late to do anything but make wide, futile circles over the stricken installation.

From within a ruptured wall of the building, a struggling, naked, bleeding female form was thrust out on to the ground. The thin white arms that made the deposit hesitated, then quickly withdrew back inside.

Left sprawled in the dust, the abandoned escapee, driven on by the fumes and heat, desperately began to claw and lurch itself forward. It had scarcely dragged itself out of lethal range when the last of the infrastructure gave way and a final explosion atomized the greater part of the installation, hurling the terrified victim violently across the ground. The battered form recovered quickly and immediately resumed its crazed flight. Without apparent knowledge of its direction, it writhed its way onward, unobserved, through the main gate and out into the night.

4

Ben-Gurion apartment complex, Jerusalem, Israel,
1.05 P.M., Saturday, 25 December 1999

The phone jangled Jonathan Feldman out of the last truly undisturbed sleep he would ever have.

Groping in the dark for the receiver with one hand, his wire-rimmed glasses with the other, he sent a half-eaten bowl of yesterday's cereal tumbling from cluttered nightstand to floor.

He snapped on the light and squinted near-sightedly down at Cheerios and milk sloshing in his Nikes. Swearing profusely, Feldman cradled the phone between ear and shoulder and wrestled on his glasses.

'What?' he croaked, pouring cereal from shoes to bowl.

'Jon, get over here. Jordan just hit a military installation in the Negev!'

It was the familiar, if unusually excited, voice of Breck Hunter, a videographer and close friend with whom Feldman worked as a World News Network Middle East TV correspondent.

'What?'

'Just about an hour ago. I can see the glow in the sky from here.'

'Jordanians?'

'That's the buzz over the military radio band,' Hunter explained.
'Let's get out there.'

At a relatively young thirty years of age, Feldman's crisp reporting
style and disarming on-camera presence had already caught the
attention of the World News Network hierarchy. It had helped net
him this prestigious assignment, his first outside the US. Yawning,
Feldman pushed up his spectacles, rubbed unfocused, pale grey eyes
and began gathering his resolve. 'Okay. See if you can get us clearance.
I'll pick you up in five minutes.'

Checking his clock, he was doubly glad he'd left WNN's dull
Christmas Eve office party early. But his hopes for tonight's
more promising US embassy function, he realized, might now be
jeopardized.

Journalistic instincts began taking over. *Why Jordan?* he wondered to himself. *Why would a poorly armed, moderate Arab state
risk war with a military power like Israel?* He shoved papers
around his desk, searching for his keys. *And wouldn't a surprise attack be more effective over Rosh Hashanah? This is a
Jewish state, for Chrissakes. Not exactly Washington at Valley
Forge.*

He pulled on his sneakers, stopping only long enough to swear
at the wetness, grabbed his worn leather jacket from a chair and
bolted out of the door. Once again, he was thankful he'd slept in
his clothes.

Although he'd only been on assignment here a few months, the
newsman had come to learn his way around Jerusalem quite well.
Firing up his rented all-terrain Land Rover, Feldman hustled away
from his downtown apartment complex, heading south. The dust
in the streets was kicked up in turbulent swirls with his passing,
the result of a severe drought that had begun long before his
arrival.

He found it fascinating the way the night transformed this strange
city. The bright gleaming lights misrepresented Jerusalem's antiquity,
and obscured its truth. To the passing eye, the artificial illumination
cast shadows, disguising the Holy City as a stable, thriving metropolis.

But as Feldman knew, sadly, the reality was otherwise. Beneath Jerusalem's veil lay the ancient origins of three very proud religions with a history of violent opposition to one another. Jew, Christian and Muslim lived grudgingly side by side in segregated sections of the city amid continuing tension and distrust. Locked in an eternal struggle that dated back to before the Crusades, they competed in a three-way ideological tug-of-war over control of the city's sacred shrines.

Despite their intense political differences and animosities, the three religions were surprisingly similar. They were, after all, born of the same God, tracing their theological descent back four thousand years to one common source – Abraham, the grand patriarch. To their lasting frustration, the three faiths were inseparably commingled in the dust of Jerusalem's past, each playing an integral part in the Holy City's celebrated, historic encounters with divinity.

As Feldman picked his vehicle's way through the narrow corridors of the downtown district, he had to be careful to avoid yet another kind of religious encounter. With the calendar inching relentlessly towards the year 2000, Jerusalem was inundated with thousands of millenarian visitors. Comprised of hundreds of bizarre cults, the millenarians had burdened the intolerant city with their own peculiar brands of religious fanaticism.

Drawing near Hunter's apartment block on the outskirts of the city, Feldman at last got an unobstructed view of the horizon. Due south he spotted the red shimmer of what he assumed was the Negev disaster. Shrugging off a spell of déjà vu, he rolled up to the courtyard where Hunter awaited him, video camera and travel bag in tow.

Above average in height and powerfully built, Hunter was dressed in fatigues left over from headier days covering Operation Desert Storm. A respected, hard-story video journalist, he looked at the world through alert, squinty blue eyes.

Before the Rover could slow to a halt, Hunter slung his gear into the back, slid in beside his colleague, slapped the dashboard hard twice and they barrelled off towards the glowing sky.

'So what did you find out?' Feldman wondered.

'Nothing more than I told you,' the cameraman replied. 'It looks like an isolated attack. Nothing else hit so far.'

'Did you confirm it was Jordanian?'

'No. But that's the intelligence read.'

Jonathan Feldman, the wordsmith of the two-man team, was athletically lanky with clean features, a long, straight nose and bright grey eyes that stood out boyishly under unkempt dark hair. Slightly older, Hunter was rugged, outdoorsy, with light hair and blond-tan complexion.

Their relaxed familiarity underscored a strong friendship they'd developed over the past year as members of a WNN field unit crew. They'd worked closely together covering some of the many millennialist movements that had sprung into prominence across the US.

As both reporters had soon learned, many of these millenarian sects had been in existence in America and throughout the world for decades, patiently anticipating the new millennium. But most had only come into being within the last few years.

The majority of these millenarian cults had religious orientations, ranging from the uplifting, whose adherents saw the twenty-first century as the beginning of a holy reign of Christ, to the doomsayers, who perpetually envisioned Armageddon. Some groups were secular, others more metaphysical. Still others were merely social or political. And many remained as yet undeclared, but found the millennium an exceptional excuse to drop out and reinvent the 'live for today' hedonism of the mythical 1960s.

From groups numbering in the thousands to single voices crying in the wilderness, there was a millennial philosophy for every inner calling, with more than 297 separate millennialist organizations currently listed on the Internet.

It had been obvious to Hunter and Feldman early on where most of the important millenarian activity would end up. Requesting to be included in WNN's Israel operation, the two men had manoeuvred themselves into the Jerusalem post. It had been a timely move. With each passing day, numbers of these cults all over the world, like so many colonies of lemmings, would reach critical mass and converge on the Holy Land. And while the greatest concentrations were clustering around Jerusalem, other famous biblical sites, such

as Nazareth, Bethlehem, Mount Sinai and Megiddo, also had their
advocates.

5

Somewhere in the Negev desert, southern Israel, 1.20 A.M., Saturday, 25 December 1999

Three excited Japanese astronomers tore across the desert floor in
hot pursuit of the fallen star. Already they'd forgotten their poor
associate, who, having the least seniority, had been left behind to
finish their experiments.

From their mountaintop vantage point, the men had clearly
witnessed, in horror, the meteorite's collision with the research
institute. They immediately set off in their car, making their way
across the rugged rift of the valley floor, the huge orange glow guiding
them like a beacon. Along the way, they were treated to an on-going
light show of meteors, jet fighters and helicopters criss-crossing the
night sky with regularity.

Hardly a half-kilometre away from their goal, however, and completely without warning, a thin, bearded, weather-beaten Bedouin in a
hooded robe suddenly rose up in the beam of their headlamps, waving
desperately for them to stop.

Narrowly avoiding him, the car spun out of control, rotated twice
and careened to a dusty halt. The nomad, seemingly unaffected by his
close call, jabbered at them excitedly in Arabic. The old man pointed
alternately to the flames of the destroyed facility beyond and to a
nearby gully.

The astronomers grew excited with the assumption that the Bedouin
had found a piece of the meteorite. But their excitement quickly gave
way to shock. As they hurried in the indicated direction, their panning
flashlights revealed a nomad woman crouching over a motionless
human form curled naked on its side in a foetal position.

6

Somewhere south of Jerusalem, Israel, *1.42 A.M., Saturday, 25 December 1999*

In the convoluted topography of southern Israel, there were few direct highways to anywhere. And although the research institute was only about seventy-five kilometres due south of Jerusalem, Hunter and Feldman had to take a roundabout route. The first legs went quickly with Feldman's aggressive driving.

'So, you still thinkin' of quitting WNN when all this is over?' Hunter rehashed a dead topic.

Feldman smiled, turned and raised an eyebrow at his friend. 'Hey, if you'll recall, "quitting" isn't exactly the operative word here. My contract ends when this millennium story's over.'

Hunter shook his head, knowing better. 'Hell, Bollinger told me he's asked you to be a part of our East Coast special assignments crew. Party time, man! We'd kick some ass together back in New York!'

'Tempting,' Feldman said, laughing at his friend's enthusiasm, 'but I can't pass up this deal in Washington – a chance to cover a presidential election. An opportunity to do some really serious reporting. WNN's too crazy for me. You know I'm too conservative to make it in showbiz news.'

Hunter shrugged his big shoulders. 'I just hate to see us break up a good team. It's been fun.'

Feldman nodded his agreement. 'Yeah, it's been great working with you, Breck. I'm going to miss you and all the gang. Hard to believe I'm coming up on my last day.'

As they zigzagged south, the terrain became increasingly rugged, the vegetation sparse. In the crisp, clear night air, the reporters could make out the beginnings of the scabrous Negev Mountains, massive sandstone formations thrust up in ever-higher, primeval slabs. Soon,

they had to exit the transit highway at a small desert kibbutz town
marked 'Dehmoena' on the map, but spelled 'Dimona' on the road
sign. A common situation in this country, which has no uniform rules
of spelling. Hunter and Feldman were used to these inconsistencies,
but regardless, the beacon of the glowing fires told them this was
the place.

Concealed on three sides by a box canyon and sunken slightly,
the remains of the installation were virtually impossible to see
from any angle but due east. And at ground level, even that angle
was unsatisfying. Particularly since the Israeli military, which was
everywhere, was ensuring that bystanders kept their distance. The two
journalists were not surprised to see more than a hundred vagabond
millenarians drawn to the disaster.

'Shit, we're not going to get anything from way out here,' Hunter
fumed, watching the Israelis holding the curious onlookers well away
from the front gate area.

'No,' Feldman concurred.

'And the militia will never let media through.' Hunter spoke from
experience.

'Especially if this is a covert military facility,' Feldman added. 'But
we have to try.'

Hunter nodded in agreement. 'Why don't you see what you can learn
from some of these onlookers while I check out the equipment. Then
we'll drive up to the front gate and talk with the field commander.'

One group of about twenty men and women looked as though they'd
been here a while. Next to their old faded-blue school bus, they had a
small camp stove with a blackened pot of coffee percolating. Feldman
walked up and introduced himself to a scraggy-bearded man in worn
blue jeans and sandals, seated on the ground with an old US Army
blanket around him. Despite his bedraggled appearance, the man
had a ready, pleasant smile, and he responded in German-accented
but excellent English.

'Friedrich Vilhousen, from Hamburg,' he said.

'Tourist or pilgrim?' Feldman began with his standard millenarian entrée.

'We are Sentries of the Dominion,' Vilhousen explained, 'one of
the largest new orders in Europe.'

Feldman had never heard of them.

'We've been in Tangier and are travelling to Jerusalem to meet up with our main group for the Arrival. We are called to make ready His Way, and to His purpose—'

'Sorry, Friedrich' – Feldman had no interest in yet another take on the Second Coming – 'right now my only concern is to learn more about the air strike here. Did you see it happen?'

'Air strike?' The German looked puzzled. 'No air strike! It was the Hammer of God, the First Sign!'

Feldman started to nod and back away.

'It was no air strike,' the millenarian insisted. 'We see it come out of the eastern sky, a bright burning star, and it light up the whole desert. And then it strike this laboratory of evil. Righteous, man!'

A missile, then, Feldman concluded to himself. *Probably a cruise missile. So how did the Jordanians get ahold of one of those?*

'Okay, thanks. And, uh, good luck with the Arrival and all.' Feldman was not a particularly cynical person, at least not as bad as Hunter. But the past months of evangelical barking had jaded him somewhat. Now that he was on to something far more meaty, he wasn't about to muck up this story by giving it a millenarian spin. He took one last look at the Sentries of Dominion and turned to go. They were all so alike, these millenarians. Yet each different. At least this group seemed a bit more subdued than most. Of the thirty-odd sects he'd reported on, he least liked the hell-and-damnation crowd. The doomsayers. Zealots whom Feldman found less than sane and more than scary.

While generally lumped into the millenarian classification too, these doomsday militants, Feldman realized, weren't certifiable millenarians. To be precise, as he had discovered through thorough research on the subject, true millenarianism included only those who subscribed literally to the New Testament Book of Revelation, chapter twenty. This scripture proclaimed that Christ would return, physically, to subdue Satan and rule on earth in peace, harmony and happiness for a thousand years.

And of these true millenarians, there were further sub-classifications: the post-millennial optimists, who held that Christ would bring peace on earth at the Last Day through His Church. And the pre-millennial pessimists, who believed peace would come only through a decisive battle between the forces of Christ and the forces of Satan.

While also adhering to the Book of Revelation, the doomsdayers

– or 'Apocalyptics', as they were more accurately called – tended to see the millennium not as a beginning but as an end. Their vision was one of earthly annihilation in which all who did not subscribe verbatim to their narrow interpretations of scripture would perish miserably in hellfire. The faithful, on the other hand, would be escorted triumphantly and corporally to heaven by Christ Himself. These were generalizations on all accounts, of course, because there was a broad spectrum of ideologies at work. Feldman had come across many subtle distinctions separating the different eschatologies – those formal branches of theology that dealt with the end of the world and/or the Second Coming.

Leaving the Sentries of Dominion to their millennium preparations, Feldman returned to the Rover, where Hunter was fitting a video camera with a fresh battery.

'What they saw strike the research centre sounds like either the righteous hand of God or maybe a Tomahawk cruise missile,' Feldman reported.

Hunter smiled thinly and grunted.

'So now,' Feldman proposed, 'what say we try the direct approach?' And they headed over to the main gate for a chat with the presiding officer.

'It doesn't look like they're letting anyone but military personnel through,' Feldman remarked as they approached, observing the clot of spectators at the entry area.

As the reporters worked their way towards the front of the crowd, they noticed an IDF guard rousting a millenarian from behind the temporary barricades. The unfortunate man had crept undetected to the perimeter and had sneaked a snapshot of the inferno through the chain-link fence.

If anything, a photograph from the vicinity of the fence was actually worse than one taken farther back, owing to the proximity of the tall protective embankments surrounding the institute inside. Nevertheless, the intolerant guard confiscated the man's camera, smashing it on the ground with the butt of his rifle before rudely ejecting the trespasser.

Hunter prudently lowered the video camera from his shoulder and the two newsmen slunk quietly back into the crowd. They decided to retreat to a hillside to see if a telescopic shot might work. It didn't. The facility had been cleverly placed. There was simply no vantage point anywhere around that could afford them a view of the ruins. The two were about to pack it in when, through his video camera zoom lens, Hunter noticed a small line of vehicles approaching along one of the access roads. Zooming in even closer, he identified in the orange light of the flaming ruins six wide-bodied Jeep-like Humvees and two Land Rovers carrying more Israeli militia and technical support personnel.

'Jon, I've got an idea!' he exclaimed, not taking his eyes off the convoy, unconsciously pushing Feldman towards their vehicle.

'Wh – what?' Feldman sputtered as he staggered forward, ill prepared to move in the precise direction Hunter had suddenly chosen for him.

'I'll drive and you just do exactly as I say . . .'

In the dust and difficulty of working their convoy through the milling spectators, the military detachment didn't notice another Land Rover slipping deftly into place behind them. Scrambling into his Desert Storm fatigue jacket as he drove, Hunter narrowly skirted a careless millenarian.

Swearing, the cameraman pulled a GI-issue hat from his bag, plopped it on Feldman's head and pushed a clipboard of papers at him. 'Now,' he said, 'when we get to the gate, you look real assertive and official-like. I'm gonna blow by the guard and if he gives you any shit, you wave this clipboard at him and shout "Containment team!" in Hebrew. Got it?'

Feldman grinned and nodded his head. 'Sure, but I don't know any Hebrew.'

'What do you mean, you don't know any Hebrew?' Hunter shouted. 'You're half Jewish, aren't you? I've heard you speak it before!'

'All I know are a few Yiddish curse words.'

'Then just say it in English, for God's sake. There are plenty enough transplant Jewish consultants working around here. They'll just have to think we're a Jewish-American containment team.'

The vehicles ahead were slowing down. The guards looked each car over before waving them quickly through, preoccupied with holding the civilian onlookers at bay. Feldman was on the passenger side closest to the gatehouse. Not at all optimistic about this, he sure as hell didn't want to get detained or arrested out here in the middle of the desert on what was supposed to be a relaxing Christmas Day.

Hunter slowed the Rover, taking Feldman right up to the guard. Feldman looked stern and held up the papers while the guard narrowed his eyes at the meaningless forms. Hunter accelerated, the guard opened his mouth to object, Feldman shouted 'Containment team!' and they roared off.

'Don't look back,' Hunter warned, watching a befuddled guard recede in the rear-view mirror.

If Hunter was as surprised at their good fortune as Feldman, he didn't show it.

Feldman smiled to himself. While he preferred to do things by the book, he appreciated Hunter's brash but effective style. Now they could turn their attention to the billowing black smoke, the source of which was coming into view.

'Pull around the berm, up that hill,' Feldman pointed. 'Let's get a look at this sucker.'

Taking the Rover to the top of a rise inside the grounds, they finally had a good view of the entire disaster. The devastation was massive. Typically, Israeli desert installations were basic and spartan. But this facility had been impressive. Except for its shattered windows, the V arms of the laboratory were intact. The once enormous dome, however, was reduced to a fractured shell, still smoking and belching hot gas into the night sky.

Feldman turned to see Hunter already scanning the scene with his video camera.

'Let's do a quick take right here,' Hunter suggested, motioning Feldman into position in front of the ruins and running off some fast footage. 'I want to stash at least a background tape in case we get noticed.' Finished, he shook the cassette loose from his camera and wedged it under the front seat.

As he began shooting the second tape, an Israeli guard team caught sight of the camera, scrambled a vehicle up the hill and confronted them. The reporters were held at gunpoint for an hour and a half and passed back and forth between uncertain field officers while their press papers were checked and rechecked. Finally convinced that the two were nothing more than media nuisances, the Israelis confiscated what they thought was the only videotape and escorted the newsmen in their Rover out of the compound, directing them to a point well beyond the fence.

'No problem.' Hunter grinned at Feldman once they were safely out of reach. 'We'll just shoot your sequence from out here with the fire in the background and let the editing team cut back and forth to the footage we stashed.'

Creeping back as close to the perimeter fence as they dared, Hunter switched on his camera and lights, and rolled tape as Feldman, framed by the smoke and flames, delivered an overview of the devastation.

'This is Jon Feldman for WNN reporting from just outside the Israeli Negev Research Institute in southern Israel where a surprise, early Christmas morning missile strike has destroyed a reputed military research installation . . .'

They had the package to WNN's Jerusalem office in time to make the noon feed. And thanks to a slow news day, Feldman's ruffled, unshaven good looks and reflective, almost shy delivery were served up with Christmas dinner all across the globe.

7

Vatican, Rome, Italy,
4.37 A.M., Saturday, 25 December 1999

So far, it had not been a good day for Pope Nicholas VI. Tired and alone in his chambers with his thoughts, the Holy Father had been up since well before midnight, roused from his sleep by a distressing nightmare of fire, death and destruction that had left him with severe heartburn.

Frowning, the paternal-looking, grey-haired pontiff drew aside the drapery of his balcony window to peer out once more at the multitudes gathering in vast St Peter's Square. The unrelenting rain, he was certain, had significantly reduced the numbers of faithful come to receive his annual Christmas Day blessing. Unfortunately, this left him with a disproportionately larger crowd of the peculiar millenarian sects that, for weeks now, had been making the Vatican their personal Mecca.

The diminished number of faithful was a disturbing development. For this sacred holiday, Nicholas had been depending on a large turnout of supporters to deflect attention from the millenarians and to help obscure the provocative banners and chants of doomsdays and Second Comings.

Indeed, the media had encouraged the siege by giving the 'Romillennians', as the Roman contingent had come to be known, what they desired most – worldwide exposure. Each news service sought to upstage the other by ferreting out the most outlandish and heretical characters they could find. As a consequence, the media were attracting to Rome the oddest element of fringe-dwelling millenarians Europe had to offer.

Although Jerusalem was a vastly larger centre of millennialist activity, most reporters preferred the comforts of Rome. Meaning the Romillennians enjoyed far better access to a far greater number of reporters. And to Nicholas's great chagrin, as he was the most prominent religious leader in the world, the media and the millenarians had carried this foolish, disruptive brouhaha directly to his doorstep.

After much soul-searching, the pontiff had reluctantly cancelled a trip to the Middle East during which he was to hold a dramatic convocation on Mount Sinai with Jewish and Muslim hierarchs. Worse, he'd had to postpone the unveiling of his Millennial Decree, a condemnation of materialism which Nicholas hoped to make the defining achievement of his new papacy. This urgently prepared ecclesiastical document, with which Nicholas intended to fulfil a very sacred obligation and usher in a more promising new millennium, was to be unveiled on 1 January. Now it would have to wait for a more receptive climate, such were the frustrations posed by the strange current events.

The situation was only tolerable because the Pope and his College of Cardinals were fully aware that this bizarre religious hysteria would be short-lived. Just like the very similar phenomenon that had occurred in AD 999.

This time around, however, with the wisdom of hindsight, the Church was unconcerned about a lasting problem. When the second millennium turned into the third, and 1 January had passed, this current millenarian plague – these one-thousand-year locusts – would disappear as efficiently and completely as its predecessor.

The new year could not come soon enough for the weary Pontiff.

8

US embassy, Tel Aviv, Israel,
9.13 P.M., Saturday, 25 December 1999

The US embassy in Tel Aviv was an impressive government building in the Roman style, with six large columns at the top of expansive sandstone steps. A spotlessly uniformed valet reluctantly accepted Feldman's Rover from him, put off by the dirt and sand that Feldman never noticed.

There were accolades awaiting inside where the two newsmen arrived unintentionally but fashionably late. Having slept through WNN's evening newscast, neither was aware that their Negev Institute report had made lead story. Their first major scoop.

Ascending the grand staircase to the main hall, Feldman and Hunter worked their way through warm greetings from familiar associates and new faces alike, who congratulated them on their freshly achieved stature. A genuinely renowned affair, the US embassy Christmas celebration was originally held in appreciation of Christian consulate members and staff detained in the Jewish state over the holidays. But the Christmas party had grown to include Israeli politicians and government officials, as well as connected media, prominent business people, and many of the area's well-to-do. A gathering of the élite. Even for the resourceful and persistent Hunter, obtaining two invitations had been no easy feat.

Feldman was not here to dispel any homesickness. Nor was he here for the outstanding cuisine and excellent news contacts. For both Feldman and Hunter, the sole appeal of this event was the prospect of meeting the available young women reputed to make their appearance here. And to the newsmen's complete gratification, the office scuttlebutt, for once, proved accurate. Among the hundreds of elect guests in attendance tonight were some of the most chic and beautiful women the two reporters had encountered since arriving in this foreign land.

Feldman smiled and shook his head with a slight twinge of envy as he watched his friend assimilate himself promptly into the crowd. It was so much simpler for Hunter. Feldman's love life in the Middle East had been less than satisfactory. It was partly owing to his hectic lifestyle, where spontaneous news opportunities and pressing deadlines allowed little time for sociable activities or meaningful encounters. But mostly, if truth be told, it was simply because he was far more discriminating than Hunter.

In leaving America, Feldman had left no special love interest behind. Not for lack of candidates – his honest, handsome features, affable nature and appealing wit having always attracted a fair amount of female interest. It was that he harboured a stubbornness about making serious personal commitments, a perspective he had acquired at a young age witnessing the turbulent unravelling of his parents' marriage.

Consequently, while he very much enjoyed the company of bright and attractive women, he ultimately avoided lasting entanglements. Before he'd allow a promising new relationship to take off, he invariably did so himself. Not maliciously or intentionally to inflict pain, but as a form of self-protection. And tonight, Feldman was ready to start the empty cycle anew.

It should prove far easier for him this evening, now that he'd be-come an instant, if somewhat uncomfortable, celebrity. The Negev installation attack, of course, was the hot topic, and the young reporter was in constant demand. Speculations and rumours abounded to the effect that the installation was some secret military complex where strange and extraordinary research had been taking place. Everyone wanted more information and no one would accept the fact that Feldman was sharing all he knew.

But Feldman was currently more interested in some extraordinary research of his own. A quick visual survey of the crowd couldn't confirm if an interesting young woman he'd once met was here. It was a long shot. She was a graduate student in journalism, he presumed. This intriguing individual had come to Feldman's attention during a guest lecture he'd given at the University of Tel Aviv a month ago.

In his concluding question-and-answer session, Feldman had experienced a short but rather lively exchange with an attractive, dark-eyed woman with a slight French accent. It amounted to a difference of opinion regarding how much personal slant a reporter should reasonably interject into a story.

In her opinion, the West's 'male-dominated club' of journalists was so obsessed with being objective in their reporting that they sanitized the truth out of stories. She had proposed that journalists not be afraid to take moral stands in their coverage of important issues, and that they play more active roles in promoting positive political and social change.

Feldman had responded with the standard line that facts must be allowed to speak for themselves, and that a reporter's job is merely to report, not to interpret. Unintentionally, he'd allowed this spirited woman the last word – an offhand remark about 'the fraternity of journalism not having enough collective testosterone to really get firm on any given issue'.

But there had been no venom in her delivery. Rather, there was a not-so-subtle flirtatiousness to it, catching him off balance and completely sidetracking his train of thought. In the pause before he could collect himself, audience laughter segued into applause, he was summarily thanked by the presiding professor, and his female counterpoint had dissolved into the dispersing crowd.

Feldman had not been embarrassed so much by the affront to his masculinity in front of a hundred students and professors. No, he'd been flustered mostly because this outspoken woman had playfully pinched him on his journalistic ass. To Feldman, that had made things considerably more personal. And challenging.

With one eye out for Mystery Woman, he basked in what he knew only too well would be a brief limelight. More talk about the attack. More rumours about what the Negev installation had really been. More opinions about who was responsible for the missile strike and how the Israeli Defence Force, which never let any aggression go unanswered, might retaliate. And on.

Only one thing could have improved this exceptional day, and suddenly she materialized. For the briefest moment before she was blocked from view, Feldman caught sight of his fantasy. In an adjoining reception room, talking and laughing. Even more beautiful than he remembered.

Her hair was different now. Instead of the long cascade of soft dark curls he had admired previously, it was a raven's nest of wild ringlets. But those eyes and that perfect olive complexion were unmistakable. Before she was again obscured from sight, he appreciated that she was tall, slender, and impeccably dressed.

Impatiently, Feldman worked his way in her direction. He experienced an unfamiliar sensation of mild panic when, amid the frustrating distractions, he realized she was no longer in the side room. But a quick reconnaissance found her off in a hallway, in intimate conversation with an affected, self-important-looking Middle Eastern business Turk. The newsman positioned himself to catch her eye, but she was absorbed in her conversation.

Feldman waited patiently in idle chat with a few fellow reporters, then, sensing the moment, he uncoupled perfectly to exchange glances with Miss Mystery.

He knew exactly how he wanted to handle this. In feigned anger he stood with hands on hips, pressed his lips tightly together, squinted one eye while arching the opposite brow, and then pointed an accusing finger at her. 'You!' he mouthed, widened both eyes in stern recognition, held it for just the right amount of time, and then lapsed into a disarming grin.

She returned the smile. Full of white teeth and self-assurance. She moved towards him and offered her slim right hand. It was a signal of dismissal for the Turk, who faded bitterly away.

Feldman grasped her by her elbow and her smooth, cool fingers, drawing her firmly to him in a manner that said he had something personal to convey. She did not resist.

To overcome the din of surrounding conversation, he brought his lips to her ear. She smelled fresh and wholesome, without perfume. He whispered, 'I've just had my testosterone level all topped up, so you have to be nice to me now.'

She laughed appreciatively, but offered no apologies. Standing on tiptoe, she whispered back into his ear, 'After today, I should think your ego's all topped up as well!' Again, there was no bite. Her voice was playful, and the hint of a French accent captivating. She *was* teasing him, he decided.

Realizing he was still holding her arm with both hands, he self-consciously released her. Yet she paid no apparent heed and didn't retreat.

'What's your name?' he asked.

'Anke Heuriskein.'

'And you're a graduate student at Tel Aviv University?'

'Working on my master's in international law.'

'Law? I should have thought journalism.'

'No. Journalism was my major as an undergraduate. Fun, but there's no real future in it.'

This came out matter-of-factly, and Feldman couldn't tell if she was really sincere this time. It must have shown in his face, because she gave him a sideways smile and poked him in the ribs with an elegantly tapered forefinger. He realized she had a knack for catching him off guard and resolved to be more alert in the future. Turnabout was also fair play, he vowed to himself.

'So,' she said baitingly, 'do you still think journalists should be nothing more than word processors, impersonally recording events?'

'You mean am I still an advocate of impartial, unbiased, fair and honest reporting?' He'd been ready with this answer for a month.

'No. I mean don't you feel that a journalist should have a social conscience? Bear some responsibility for the societal consequences of a story?'

'I don't believe it's a reporter's place to influence news, slant news or make news, if that's what you're asking,' he responded stolidly. 'It's a reporter's job to report. Pure and simple.'

'But things are not always so pure and simple, now, are they?' she purred, and averted her eyes mysteriously.

Feldman was more than charmed. As he loosened his crumpled tie for manoeuvring room, his focus was interrupted by the reappearance of Hunter picking his way towards him from across the room. Feldman interpreted his partner's serious look and groaned audibly.

Hunter was at their side now, leaned close to Anke and hooked a thumb towards Feldman. 'Sorry to intrude, but Mr Celebrity here is wanted back at the shop.'

Turning, he gripped Feldman by the right biceps. 'I just got a call from headquarters. Things are heatin' up.'

Feldman bit his lip, nodded and turned to find an amused look on Anke's perfect olive face. 'Can I—?' he began.

'I'm out a lot,' she interrupted, 'why don't I call you?' and she proceeded to take Feldman's number in a small black phone book she produced from the pocket of her jacket.

Reluctantly departing with his colleague, Feldman watched helplessly as another slick-looking Don Juannabe promptly moved in to fill the void.

9

WNN news bureau, Jerusalem, Israel, *11.56 P.M., Saturday, 25 December 1999*

Hunter and Feldman rolled back into WNN headquarters to find the cramped offices humming with activity.

Area news director Arnold Bollinger spied the two reporters immediately and motioned them aside. In his mid-fifties, Bollinger was the earnest type, a black man with superb news instincts, a stocky, sound build and short, greying hair. He had an open, honest face, with large, sincere eyes. While he may have considered Feldman and Hunter a bit too cavalier and undisciplined for his tastes, Bollinger nevertheless appreciated their work as intelligent and substantive. Hunter had a deserved reputation for risk-taking. Feldman was a stabilizing influence, if too easily tempted astray.

But Bollinger was ecstatic with their report on the desert installation attack, and he was more than willing to let them run with a major story that appeared to have legs.

'We're getting some interesting feedback, guys,' he explained, handing Feldman a selection of data sheets. 'Especially this one.' He isolated one page in particular, pointing at two names.

'Dr Kiyu Omato . . . and Dr Isotu Hirasuma?' Feldman struggled with the note. 'Japanese?'

'Two astronomers from Japan, running some sort of study out at that big observatory in the Negev,' said Bollinger. 'We checked them out and they're legit. Strong credentials. They saw your newscast and they've been waiting here to see you. Claim they're eye-witnesses, and they'll only talk with you.'

'Actually,' Feldman wished aloud, 'I'd like to find someone from *inside* that research centre. And learn what the hell was so important that the Jordanians would risk war to take it out. Any new info, Arnie?'

Bollinger shook his head. 'Not even US intelligence sources have anything definitive. At least that's what they claim. Best anyone knows right now, it was a biotech lab. And though the Israelis are screaming it's the Jordanians, the State Department won't confirm it.'

Hunter joined the speculation. 'Well, the Jordanians, or whoever, sure as hell weren't out to Scud some new improved carrot. Has to've been a military installation – chemical or biological weapons development.'

An irreverent voice behind them intruded. 'Yeah, and you boys were out there just padding around in the contaminated debris, all exposed and unprotected.' It was Cissy McFarland, WNN project co-ordinator, overhearing the conversation as she passed by. She was always ready with an overdue payback jab at the two reporters. 'Sassy', Hunter used to call her. Full of herself for a twenty-three-year-old, Cissy was one of Arnold Bollinger's protégées, with a brilliant summa cum laude mind and a promising future with WNN.

Meant as a joke, her comment about contamination nevertheless opened an unpleasant door.

'Not entirely exposed,' Hunter returned as she blew by, ignoring him.

'Yep, you're sure two dedicated, *dumb* news jocks,' she tossed back over her shoulder, red-blond hair bouncing, hips rolling smartly as she turned a corner in her pleated skirt, leaving them in a wake of mock scorn.

Hunter grinned, Feldman looked reflective.

'Okay, Arnie,' Feldman said, adjourning their meeting and heading off with his partner towards their offices. 'Let's talk with these eye-witnesses before we call it a hell of a day!'

Feldman only wanted a moment to shed his sports jacket, take a breath and settle in at his desk, but the two Japanese men awaiting him were too insistent. They recognized him on sight and, elbowing Hunter aside in their haste, began bowing and rattling at the TV reporter in a flurry of unintelligibility.

With difficulty, Feldman got their identities: Kiyu Omato, a senior professor at Kyoto University, and his assistant, Isotu Hirasuma.

The elder man could contain himself no longer. 'Not missile!' he declared to Feldman in a thick accent. 'Meteorite!'

Feldman closed his eyes and dropped his chin to his chest in disappointment. He'd been anticipating insightful revelations into the attack on the laboratory. He looked up, first at Hunter, then back at the two very serious astronomers anxiously awaiting his response.

'Thanks, guys, I appreciate your professional opinion, but I don't think anyone, least of all the Israelis, is going to buy your meteor theory.'

'Not theory.' The earnest face showed concern, perhaps alarm. He pulled from his pocket a white handkerchief, opening it to reveal a blackened chunk of misshapen rock about the size of a baseball. 'Meteorite!' he said again, shoving the object at Feldman while his assistant vigorously nodded his affirmation and held up a handkerchief of his own. 'Not attack – accident! No war now!'

With that, the second astronomer also produced a satchel filled with more such fragments and explained, in much clearer English, 'Four of us see meteorite from observatory. With own eyes we watch meteorite strike laboratory. On our way to impact site, we find survivor in desert.'

Feldman's eyes widened. Hunter looked up from a random meteorite chunk he was inspecting. 'Survivor?' they asked in unison.

'Yes. Young woman from desert laboratory.'

Hunter and Feldman had already decided that the junior astronomer with a better grasp of the King's English was the preferred interviewee. Feldman pulled out a microphone and Hunter switched on his camera.

Clearing his throat, Hirasuma began again. 'Three of us leave observatory to follow meteor. But just outside laboratory grounds, we come across desert people—'

'Bedouins?' Hunter suggested.

'Older man and woman – with injured survivor.'

'So you actually saw this meteor hit the centre?' Feldman backed them up to re-examine their story.

'Yes.'

'How close were you?'

'Maybe fifteen kilometre away, but night very clear. We see through binoculars big explosion and follow in car.'

'Tell me more about this survivor,' Feldman said.

'She young woman. Maybe twenty year old.'

'She bleeding bad and in shock,' the older man interjected. 'Clothes blown off. She smell like smoke. Not talk, not walk, just make horrible sounds. Eyes not focus.'

'What did you do with her?' Feldman wanted to know.

'We give first aid,' Hirasuma said. 'Man and woman not let us take her to hospital. We help put her in cart and cover with blanket. We give man and woman first aid kit, food, money. They leave and we go look for meteorite sample.'

'When we see you on TV news,' Omato added, 'we know we must tell you facts.'

'Dr Omato expert,' the younger astronomer insisted. 'He not make mistake. Meteorite, not missile. No war!'

'Do you think you can find again the location where you discovered the survivor?' Feldman asked.

'Yes,' both men answered.

Feldman and Hunter took addresses and phone numbers and thanked the two scientists, promising to get back to them tomorrow.

Apparently not satisfied that they'd convinced the reporters, the two astronomers were slow to leave. 'You tell world?' the older man was compelled to ask one more time.

'We'll see,' Feldman replied non-committally, shaking their hands and returning bows as they backed away.

He held his thoughts until the two astronomers were out of sight, then turned to his partner with a sceptical expression. 'What do you think?'

Hunter, who'd been staring vapidly into space, tossing a chunk of meteorite in the air, shrugged his big shoulders and replied non- chalantly, 'I think it makes for a hell of a follow-up story. I'd love to get a crack at their survivor – anyone who knows what was going on inside that installation.'

10

Meeting chambers of the IDF Command Centre,
UVDA Israeli military airfield, southern Negev,
1.37 A.M., Sunday, 26 December 1999

At an Israeli Defence Force centre located approximately forty-five kilometres south of the destroyed Negev laboratory, the troubled high command had convened to receive debriefings about the incident. The IDF chief of staff, Major General Mosha Zerim, a distinguished, straight-shouldered man of sixty-four, had been listening in sober silence as the last officer finished his report.

The general then cleared the room of all but a handful of his confidential advisers, sat back in his chair and crossed his legs. 'Gentlemen, I don't have to tell you how serious this is,' he opened. 'Defence Minister Tamin is absolutely furious. If the Prime Minister or the Knesset find out what was going on in that lab, it will be our heads. *All* of our heads!'

After a long pause, he asked of one colleague, 'Ben, you've heard the reports, what do you think caused the explosion?'

Brigadier General Benjamin Roth looked up from his notepad and sighed audibly. 'It has to have been an attack, Mosha.'

'But there's nothing to prove that, Ben,' argued Intelligence Commander David Lazzlo, a trim, middle-aged man of medium height, with neatly combed, short, greying-blond hair and blue eyes. 'There is no explosives residue. No missile or bomb casing fragments. Our intelligence systems and American reconnaissance satellites can confirm no launchings, no aircraft in the vicinity. Nothing.'

'We have post-launch radar intercept,' Senior General Alleza Goene interjected. 'The missile was probably remote-launched from an attack bomber. And it's too soon to know if there's any bomb residue. Besides, the devastation was so complete any evidence may have disintegrated.

Hell, almost the entire site was vaporized!' A veteran and hero of the '67 war, Goene was a large, powerful, intimidating man of fifty-seven. He was red-faced and visibly impatient with the conservative bent of this group.

Lazzlo appeared uncomfortable with this evaluation. 'How do we explain the large quantities of raw iron ore debris, then?' he questioned. Having spent most of the day at the ruins supervising the investigation, he was steadfast in his opposition to a retaliatory strike. 'Granted it sounds unbelievable, but we can't rule out the possibility of a meteorite impact, as evidence suggests. We're in a period of meteor shower activity!'

'There are just too many damned convenient coincidences,' Goene retorted. 'For months, Syria and Iran have been making formal enquiries about the nature of the facility. Even the US has suspicions of our purposes there. And the odds of such a perfectly timed and targeted impact, striking absolutely dead centre of the installation during the final phases of activities, is beyond calculation! Then there's the trajectory of this "meteorite" – entirely too flat and sustained to have been unpowered, as you claim.'

'Goene is right on all but one count,' Roth concluded. 'We were attacked not by missile, but by a super-cannon, such as Iraq was developing before Desert Storm. The Jordanians, we presume, discovered what was happening at the centre and then, under cover of a meteor shower, propelled an iron ore projectile from a hidden super-cannon to destroy it. A cannon would explain the lack of a self-propulsion system. And the Jordanians would have the implausible but defensible argument that we suffered a meteorite hit.'

'All very convincing, gentlemen,' David Lazzlo countered, 'except that this projectile is estimated to have weighed over a quarter of a ton at impact. What possible technology exists to hurl an unpowered object of that size over thirty kilometres at such a trajectory?'

'A technology no more incredible than what *we* had created and what we *lost* at the laboratory!' an angry Goene snapped back with a forceful logic that shut Lazzlo down completely.

Allowing a moment for claws to retract, presiding General Zerim rendered his judgment. 'Reluctantly, I must agree with Ben and Alleza. The meteorite theory is simply not credible. Like it or not, we must support the position of Defence Minister Tamin. The official IDF line, and our preliminary determination, is that this was an unprovoked attack. We'll continue investigations and determine the source, at which time we'll inflict an appropriate counter-strike. Our forces will stay on full alert until further notice.'

11

Israeli Negev Research Institute ruins,
Negev desert, southern Israel,
9.46 A.M., Sunday, 26 December 1999

With Bollinger's blessings, Feldman and Hunter had returned to the desert the next morning to meet their Japanese eye-witnesses. Outside the perimeter lines of the laboratory ruins, there was nothing more to see in the daylight than had been apparent earlier. Most of the millenarians were gone, but the Israeli military were as entrenched and unyielding as ever. The rival media were also on the scene now.

The morning papers added nothing to what Feldman and Hunter had already known, either. As before, the official word of the Israeli Defence Force was that a hostile missile strike had taken place and that no one as yet had claimed responsibility.

'And that damned defence minister, Shaul Tamin, will never hold a press conference when it comes to Israeli security matters,' Hunter complained aloud to Feldman. Watching the Japanese scientists driving up, the cameraman tossed his newspaper in the back seat and swung out of the Rover to meet them. 'We need more than a rehash for our follow-up story. Let's see what our scientist friends here can show us.'

Joined by all four astronomers this time, the reporters formed a hasty caravan and, before the other news teams were on to them, motored out into the desert heading due east.

In less than fifteen minutes, the Japanese identified the ravine where they claimed to have discovered the survivor. True to their account, there were discarded bandage wrappers and gauze, trampled brush, tyre and cart tracks and footprints in the gravelly sand. But no sign of the survivor or the Bedouins.

Another hour's sweeping search of the vicinity turned up only a few bands of pilgrims and about twenty more kilograms of what the astronomers claimed were meteorite fragments.

'The couple that picked up the survivor are probably headed towards the main highway and Jerusalem,' Hunter conjectured, and alerted the Japanese that they were breaking off the search.

Still unsure that their evidence had convinced Feldman and Hunter, the scientists were anxious. 'Now you go on TV and tell truth?' the older man pleaded once more.

'You've been very helpful,' Feldman told them all. 'We'll give it serious consideration.'

The astronomers thanked both men profusely and headed off to search for more fragments.

After they had left, Hunter suggested, 'How about we return to the ruins and set up our camera in the same spot as before to cut our follow-up?'

'Fine,' Feldman agreed, 'only I don't know exactly how we should handle this. You don't buy into the meteorite crap, do you?'

'Hell, no, but I think it's a godsend of a follow-up. The Jesus freaks are gonna have a field day with the news.'

Feldman was not convinced. 'I got real problems with that, Breck. That's *National Enquirer*-level stuff. If we come out with this meteorite garbage we're just legitimizing the apocalypse cults. We might as well blow Gideon's trumpet.'

'It's not like we're creating the story here, Jon,' Hunter reasoned. 'Those astrologers aren't millenarians, man, they're *professionals*! And eye-witnesses, no less. Bollinger checked them out. We're only reporting their expert opinion!'

'Astronomers,' Feldman corrected him, although he found the slip of tongue interesting. 'I don't know, Breck, we really need to be responsible here.'

Hunter shook his head. 'Okay, look. Let's go ahead and tape two cuts, including a meteor version. Then when we get back, we'll have these meteor samples we found checked. If they test out as fresh, we go with the story. Or at least let Bollinger rule on it. Fair enough? Hell, what if it does check out? We might be preventing a war here!'

Feldman shrugged. 'God, I hate to take what amounts to the only hard news we've covered in three months and turn it into tabloid journalism.' He rose from his seat in the Rover, stretched and looked out at the smoke still emanating from the smouldering ruins. 'I want to know what was going on over there. I want to find that survivor.'

12

Dyan IDF military base, Jerusalem, Israel, 10.00 A.M., Sunday, 26 December 1999

Alone in his private office, General Goene's sombre mood was interrupted by a knock at the door. An adjutant entered to announce that WNN was telecasting a new development in the Negev Institute story. Swearing, Goene dismissed the assistant with an irritated wave and snatched up his remote control.

Materializing on his TV was a handsome, dark-haired, clean-shaven young man. He was standing in front of the main gate of the shattered Negev installation, a large black rock in his hand, thick smoke twisting up into the sky behind him.

'. . . substantiated reports from two independent authorities,' the man was saying, and photos of a Tel Aviv University geologist and an Oriental-looking scientist appeared in boxes at the corners of the screen. 'The reputed attack on this Israeli research centre yesterday may actually have been a natural phenomenon, the impact of a large meteorite.'

The general glowered as the special report cut to taped interviews with the two authorities, who documented their claims with more large specimens of blackened ore.

'In their search for these meteorite fragments,' the reporter continued, 'the team of astronomers also came across what they believe to be the only person to survive the disaster. A young female in her early twenties, short in height, slight build, dark hair, suffering from multiple injuries and possibly in a state of shock. She was last seen early yesterday morning near the explosion site, in the care of a Bedouin couple.'

Cursing loudly, Goene smashed the remote control to his desk and grabbed for the phone. 'Get me Lazzlo!' he shouted into the receiver, staring at the next news story without seeing it.

A minute later, the voice of Intelligence Commander David Lazzlo came over the speakerphone.

Goene disregarded Lazzlo's greeting. 'I presume you caught the TV broadcast?' the general fumed. 'They've gotten on to your meteor bullshit, and now they're talking about a survivor. A shell-shocked woman. God knows what information she'll spill! Where are we on a body count? If there is a survivor, I want to know who the hell she is and I want her found. *Now*, goddammit!'

13

WNN news bureau, Jerusalem, Israel,
9.17 A.M., Monday, 27 December 1999

'You struck a nerve, guys!' Bollinger congratulated Hunter and Feldman at the staff meeting. 'The IDF is all hot over your meteorite story! And the survivor thing? Denying it so hard it's gotta be true!'

They'd never seen the bureau chief this enthused.

'We just got an official cable from the defence minister, Shaul Tamin himself,' Bollinger gloated, 'personally demanding an immediate retraction. Tamin's releasing official government figures showing that the odds of a celestial object striking their facility are over six billion to one. He's threatening reprisals against Jordan. And Jordan's accusing the Israelis of self-sabotage as a ploy to derail the peace talks.'

'Is there any word from US intelligence on the cause of the explosion?' Cissy asked.

'Nothing,' Bollinger replied. 'So far, the allies can't come up with a better explanation than the meteorite. No one's claimed responsibility. Even the Hezbollah and Hamas plead innocent, for once.'

'I thought you might like to know' – Feldman offered up another tidbit – 'I got a fax from Dr Omato and his colleagues complaining that the IDF is attempting to revoke their visas.'

'I'll call our contacts in the Knesset and see what I can do,' Bollinger offered, frowning. 'But the good news is,' and the bureau chief resumed his beaming, 'WNN viewership is soaring. Our ratings are through the roof and we're getting additional funds and personnel to expand our investigations.'

While gratified by the turn of events, Feldman nevertheless couldn't overlook the global effects the meteorite story was having. Increasingly, predictions of a Second Coming were receiving worldwide attention and, for many people, a significant credibility boost. Millennial fervour was intensifying.

But there was yet another, more subtle change occurring in the collective millenarian psyche. The carefree attitudes once commonly held for the coming New Year had transmuted into a more sobering realization. Suddenly, the promise/curse of the new millennium was more tangible. And now, each night in Jerusalem, there were more and larger rallies, lasting later around blazing bonfires, stoked by equally fiery sermons. For the millenarians, the Last Day was rapidly approaching. And the world was watching.

14

National Ministry of the Universal Kingdom, Dallas, Texas, *10.30 P.M., Wednesday, 29 December 1999*

The Right Reverend Solomon T. Brady, DD, a short, thick-set, red-faced man with a perfect white pompadour, was furious at WNN. He loathed the sensationalistic media attention freely bestowed on the ludicrous millenarians while his legitimate ministry had to pay thousands of dollars per minute for its vital broadcast time.

More to the point, he was peeved at the increasing allure the millennialists were exerting on his own flock. Brady fully recognized that his evangelistic followers were vulnerable to this type of apocalyptic appeal. But, while his own message may have traded somewhat on the fears of a Second Coming, he wasn't so opportunistic or obvious as to exploit the issue simply because the millennium was at hand.

Nor so short-sighted. While these millennialists might be having their day in the sun now, nightfall was rapidly approaching. Reverend Brady's lost sheep would quickly return to the fold come New Year's Day, more loyal and giving than ever. Finally, they'd comprehend what he'd been insistently preaching all along: that the Cataclysm would occur at a time no mortal man could foretell. Just as Christ had stated.

Meanwhile, however, the Right Reverend had to endure the most difficult period of his ministry. His congregation, which had once numbered just shy of eight hundred thousand, had contracted substantially of late. Today's news was worse. Reverend Brady knew this in advance, looking up from his broad mahogany desk to find his chief accounting officer standing before him, shifting annoyingly from one foot to the other. The accountant had arrived in Brady's office as inconspicuously as an undertaker, to reluctantly present a report of the Universal Kingdom's latest contribution figures.

Reverend Brady impatiently flipped to the last pages to discover that receipts were off yet another seven per cent from last week's depressing five-point decline. He angrily thrust the document back across his desk, sending a twenty-nine-dollar 1998 Universal Kingdom commemorative ashtray to its ruin on the marble floor. Without a word, Brady turned to scowl out of his window at the bustling campus far below.

15

The Mount of the Ascension, Jerusalem, Israel, 5.30 P.M., Friday, 31 December 1999

The Mount of the Ascension was the highest elevation in Jerusalem, its summit rising about four hundred metres above the city. Also known as the Mount of Olives, at its base lay the sacred Garden of Gethsemane, where Christ last meditated prior to His arrest and Crucifixion. Between Gethsemane and the Golden Gate of the city was the deep and narrow Cedron Valley, a large Jewish cemetery.

Jewish tradition had it that when the Messiah came to Jerusalem on Judgment Day, He'd pass over the Mount of the Ascension/Olives, gather the dead buried in the Valley of Cedron and enter the Old City of Jerusalem through the Golden Gate. In defiance of such notions, however, the Arabs had sealed up the gate with stone many years ago.

This was the afternoon of the Day. Hunter, Feldman, Cissy and a full WNN crew had set up their equipment in a second-storey apartment near the top of the mount. They were fortunate to have acquired these headquarters, as there were few residential areas and commercial structures here. The majority of buildings on the sparsely developed mount were religious sites, scattered among the Aleppo pines, olive trees and wizened scrub. They included sacred shrines, tombs, churches, temples and various ruins dating from the time of King David up through those of the Crusades and the Knights Templar.

WNN had rented out an entire flat for the night, paying an outrageous sum to dislodge its residents temporarily. From the vantage point of the apartment's balcony there was an unobstructed view of the highest point on the mountain, the imposing Tower of the Church of the Ascension, about fifty metres to the left. It was precisely at this tower that Christians believed Jesus made His triumphant Ascension into heaven. Logically, then, it was here that most millenarians felt Christ would return.

From the courtyard area at the base of the Ascension Church and Tower, the assembled multitudes of millenarians spilled down the slope directly in front of the WNN apartment, across the Cedron Valley and all the way to the ancient city gates below. The crowd also included a considerable number of Muslims – Christians and Jews holding no monopoly on the terminal significance of this mountain. Islam also predicted that Judgment Day would occur on this spot.

'Not exactly Times Square, is it?' Hunter quipped as he trained his video camera on the crowd.

'No,' Feldman responded, 'more like Apocalypse Central.'

Earlier in the day, Feldman and company had been down among the pilgrims, sending candid footage of millenarian interviews via satellite back to hungry audiences all over the world. Now, as the crowd grew too dense for comfort, Feldman had elected to retreat to their apartment above the fray to set up for the 'climactic' evening.

Even before the godsend of the Negev laboratory disaster, WNN had been steadily priming its worldwide audience, shrewdly building towards this moment. And for tonight, WNN's executive producers had fashioned a special programme. Cleverly, the coverage would be co-ordinated with the time zone changes. Once midnight had uneventfully passed in Jerusalem, the WNN coverage would shift to Rome for a live telecast of the Millennium Eve happenings there. Then, after doomsday failed to materialize in Rome, coverage would jump to New York, and on to Salt Lake City, where the last bastion of millenarians would be crossing their fingers. By capitalizing on the time changes in this way, WNN would ensure itself a rotating, worldwide, prime-time audience.

All of which had given Feldman butterflies. The prospect of hosting potentially the largest live audience ever was intimidating. This surprise honour had been bestowed on him abruptly this morning when the intended announcer, who'd flown in yesterday from New York, had come down with a sudden flu. Honour or no, because Feldman was reasonably certain nothing apocalyptic was going to happen tonight, he had to contend with the fact that he'd be presiding over the largest theatrical let-down of all time. A hell of a send-off for his last official day with WNN.

'Worse than Geraldo Rivera and his Al Capone vault,' Hunter insensitively suggested.

But, as WNN had calculated, the magnitude of the inevitable disappointment would itself be newsworthy. There'd be ample back-pedalling, rationalizing millenarians to keep the story interesting. Irrespective, Feldman could content himself with the knowledge that, shortly afterwards, he'd be off to Washington, DC, and a whole new life in the pre-eminent world of US political news coverage.

Outside WNN's rented apartment, it was beginning to drift into evening. Looking beyond the balcony across the mountainside and off into the ancient land of the Israelites, Feldman was taken with how quickly this harsh, drought-stricken country softened in the pink and purple twilight. If ever there were a night for a religious experience, this would be it. But not for the destruction of the world. More for a quiet, divine social visit.

Except for the gathering of a few clouds far off to the south-west, the sky was clear, starlit and still. Peaceful but for the singing, chanting and sermonizing of the millenarians attempting to solidify their positions with God.

Feldman donned a sweater and returned to the balcony with a black coffee. Inside, their preparation work finished, Hunter and Cissy were making sport of one another again while Bollinger talked with the home office and the rest of the crew wandered downstairs for a break. Yawning and stretching, Feldman couldn't be sure he'd heard someone call his name.

There it was again. It came from somewhere below. Leaning over the second-floor balcony, he scanned the crowd, finally double-taking on the alluring, upturned visage of Anke Heuriskein.

'Am I disturbing your final meditation?' she called up.

'Wait there, I'll be right down!' he shouted back, and he was gone, depositing the coffee cup so hastily on the rail it spilled over the side on to a turbaned, semi-toothless man below. The poor victim, his black, angry eyes searching the mysteriously vacant balcony above him, swore profusely in an acerbic Middle Eastern tongue.

Feldman was thrilled at his good fortune. Although Anke had taken his phone number at the embassy party, he hadn't heard from her.

So he'd impatiently searched for her number in both the Tel Aviv city phone book and the Tel Aviv University directory, to no avail. Finally, with the help of a university professor friend, he'd found what he'd been looking for. Only to be greeted by the beep of an answering machine.

He'd left three messages: asking her to call; asking her to dinner; asking her to meet him this evening for the televised finale, given that Millennium Eve would be his last official day with WNN and he'd be leaving for the States shortly. His last invitation was days ago and he'd heard nothing. Yet he'd sincerely believed he'd made a favourable first impression. He'd *felt* the chemistry.

His feet were in no way as light as his heart as he tripped over squatters in the stairwell, nearly taking a nasty fall. Undaunted, he pressed his way out into the square, fearful he'd lost her in the crowd. But there she was, waiting for him, smiling with those appealingly full and sensual lips. He reached through the last barrier of people and drew her safely to him. Wrapping his arm snugly around her shoulders, he worked their way back to safety, shielding her protectively from the buffeting crowd.

Struggling once more past the loiterers in the stairwell, at last reaching the sanctuary of the makeshift WNN newsroom, he closed the door on the noise and turmoil behind them. Turning to her, his eyes were aglow with delight and adrenalin.

'I didn't think you'd got any of my messages,' he said, still out of breath from his exertion.

'I hadn't until yesterday,' Anke explained. 'I live in Jerusalem, you know. I was here all week.'

This was good, Feldman concluded. She hadn't been ignoring him. 'It's great to see you, Anke, you look wonderful!'

And she did. Her thick hair was straight now, pulled back loosely and held up with a simple clip. It didn't appear as if she were wearing make-up, not that she had any need. Hers was that exceptional complexion with the healthy gleam of a natural tan.

It intrigued Feldman how each time he saw her she looked so different and yet so gorgeously the same. There was a versatility to her beauty that slipped dimensions. Tonight, she exhibited a more casual, girlish demeanour. As he looked into her face, he saw a sweetness, almost an innocence, that made her seem far

more familiar than their brief acquaintance gave him any right to
feel.

'So you live here in Jerusalem?' Feldman confirmed. 'Where?'

'On the North Side, but I keep an apartment in Tel Aviv when I'm
attending classes.'

A rather expensive arrangement, Feldman surmised. 'How did you
find me here in this crowd?'

'When I got your messages' – and she laughed at this, perhaps
finding Feldman's somewhat awkward invitations amusing – 'I tried
to reach you at your office and they told me you'd be out all day.
They were kind enough to give me your location here.'

From over Feldman's shoulder came the mischievous voice of Breck
Hunter. 'So, Anke, you decided to come spend the last hours of planet
earth with us?'

Anke looked past Feldman and smiled. 'Sure. You seem to have
the best seat in the house.'

'Catered, too,' Cissy McFarland added, and was introduced holding
a bulging paper sack. She invited their new guest to join them in some
kosher box dinners.

On the way to the dining room to join the rest of the crew, Cissy
held back, elbowed Feldman's side and whispered up to him, 'She's
gorgeous! Where did you find her?'

Feldman just shrugged his shoulders nonchalantly with a sly smile.

Over bagels and sandwiches, and thanks to Hunter and Cissy's
unrestrained curiosity, Feldman was able to fill in some important
gaps about his new acquaintance.

'So tell us a little about yourself, Anke,' Cissy suggested. 'Where
are you from originally? Do I detect a French accent.?'

'I'm from Paris,' she said. 'My mother's French, my father
American.'

'So what brought you to Israel?' Hunter asked.

'I came here in '97 to take an assistant professorship at Tel Aviv
University. I'm working on my graduate degree.'

Hunter stole a quick, sideways glance at Feldman. 'Let's see now,
Anke,' he said, 'what I can't figure out,' and he gestured with his
coffee spoon towards Feldman, 'is what you see in this underfed,
underpaid, diehard news geek!'

Bollinger and the other crew members burst out laughing.

Nodding slightly, pursing her lips to restrain a smile, Anke regarded the uncomfortable man next to her. 'Well,' she teased, 'I should think he has promise as a reporter, if only he'd show a little more social conscience.' She paused at the look of objection on his face. 'But then again,' and her eyes locked into his, 'there was the wonderful report he did about that meteorite destroying the Negev Institute. Now *that* was worthy journalism. Who knows, Mr Feldman' – she smiled at him admiringly – 'you may even have prevented a war.'

The timing and sincerity of the compliment caught Feldman quite off guard. He felt his cheeks grow warm.

As they finished their meal, Bollinger had one final question of Anke. He wanted to know if she was unduly concerned about the prospect of the world ending in the next three hours and thirty-five minutes. She replied that she was not.

Outside on the mountain, however, it was an entirely different story. Escalating noise drew Feldman and his associates on to the balcony where they observed increasingly strange activities under way.

The rising tensions and close quarters had apparently pushed several incompatible cults into open opposition. In some instances, what began as civil disagreements in theology had degraded into shouting matches and even fist fights, pitting zealot against zealot in a battle of the self-righteous.

'There, I think God likes that guy's style.' Feldman facetiously pointed to an open circle of fighting where one defender of the faith had run up and smashed a folded lawn chair over the head of another.

'Yeah, skull-cracking for Christ,' Hunter snorted, and Anke looked disapprovingly at both reporters.

'Oh, over here!' Hunter shouted. 'Where are the field glasses?'

To their right, a small group of men and women had shed their clothes and were prancing before a bonfire to a poorly played pan flute.

'Yes,' Hunter intoned in a bad W. C. Fields imitation, 'naked unto the Lord!'

The Israeli police were kept busy trying quietly to extract the troublemakers without aggravating conditions, and more than one millenarian would experience the rapture of jail tonight.

As the sweet smell of marijuana came wafting up to the balcony, Bollinger clapped his hands and announced, 'Okay, gang, let's get some of this on tape, shall we?' The crew, who'd been standing around entranced by all this, snapped to and hustled off to gather their gear while Hunter, way ahead of them, was putting a telephoto lens on his camera to zoom in on the nudists.

Feldman scanned the turbulent assembly, feeling better about the evening's potential newsworthiness. 'Well, Anke, this should be a New Year's party unlike any we've ever seen!' She looked down on the crowd with a wry smile and shook her head disbelievingly.

16

Mount of the Ascension, Jerusalem, Israel, *10.00 P.M., Friday, 31 December 1999*

Promptly at 10 P.M. Jerusalem time, live from New York City, WNN International began their worldwide news segment, *Millennium III*. As Hunter readied himself and his camera crew for the impending signal to go live, Anke and Feldman moved over to one of several TV monitors positioned just inside the balcony.

The WNN International news team in New York opened with a brief overview of the current millenarian saga, effectively conveying with selected news clips the worldwide scope of the phenomenon. Next, they went to a historical background report.

At 10.30 P.M. Jerusalem time, the newscast turned to the rise of the neo-millenarian movements in the US and abroad, from the early 1990s to the present. Feldman noted with special interest a report on one of the longer-standing millenarian creeds, the Watchtower Bible and Tract Society.

Also calling themselves the Jehovah's Witnesses, and known for their fervent door-to-door preaching, these particular millenarians appeared to have a great deal at stake that night. The most crucial dogma of their faith revolved around the prediction of an imminent Second Coming. This prophecy was based on complex biblical calculations derived in the 1870s by founder Charles Taze Russell. In concert with a special passage in the Gospel of Matthew, it had been foreseen and declared that the generation of Jehovah's Witnesses alive in 1914 would 'not pass away' before Judgment Day occurred.

With the youngest of that generation now in their upper eighties, the millennium had become an all-or-nothing event to justify their faith and very existence. Indeed, their current spiritual leader and head of the governing board, Joshua Milbourne, who had been born in 1914, was in failing health with a serious heart condition. One way or another, for over six million adherents of the religion, the end was nigh.

The WNN report included a live bedside interview with the ailing Joshua Milbourne, who was watching the telecast in his private hospital room. In the course of his interview, Milbourne mentioned that he had several delegate Witnesses present at the Mount of the Ascension. They were there, on his behalf, to ensure that Milbourne was one of the 'biblically designated 144,000', the chosen few who would reign in heaven as 'kings and priests' over the new nation of God on Earth.

Bollinger immediately dispatched two of his staff to search for Milbourne's delegates.

The interview with Joshua Milbourne was especially noteworthy because the elderly Witness was one of the few established church leaders to proclaim officially that Judgment Day would commence at twelve o'clock that night in Jerusalem. WNN would keep a reporter at his bedside and intended to cut back to Mr Milbourne later for a follow-up 'eating of the crow' segment.

Time elapsed quickly, and Bollinger soon cued Feldman to take his position on the balcony to ready himself for the live signal switch. A red light began flashing and there was a call for quiet.

Feldman made for a striking presence on camera, out in the night air of the Holy City, overlooking the dark sky and the fires and candles of the unsettled assembly. His lean, boyish face was slightly flushed with emotion, his appearance casually masculine in an open Oxford shirt and dark cardigan. He kept his commentary short for this first segment, introducing the strange scene below him as the camera swung by to take in the bedlam and nervous tension of the teeming masses.

Quickly, Feldman's time was up and the live signal was passed back to WNN International for a comparative glimpse of Rome, New York City and the Great Salt Lake. As the red on-air light went out, the crew relaxed and Feldman stepped in from the balcony to a round of congratulations.

The breeze was picking up slightly, and the clouds Feldman had noticed earlier off to the south had apparently collected into a squall. It was too far away to affect the telecast here, but would perhaps create enough of a wind to add some drama.

At Feldman's suggestion, Hunter would begin the final segment with a tight camera zoom on the storm. Flashes of lightning were developing in the distance and Feldman could make good use of the metaphor. As the clock came up on 11.45, he again took his position on the balcony, Bollinger cued the camera on the squall, and Feldman smiled quickly at Anke, who responded in kind.

'There's a storm brewing over this ancient Holy Land tonight,' Feldman began, as the camera zoomed back from the angry clouds to include the young reporter in the shot. 'As you've witnessed over the last few months, a great spiritual movement is taking place across the globe in anticipation of the coming new millennium, only minutes away now. There are an estimated two million people assembled in this vicinity who firmly believe that, in less than fifteen minutes, we are about to experience a climactic end, or perhaps a new beginning, to our world as we know it.'

The camera pulled back, panning to the right to include in the picture a frumpy, middle-aged woman.

'One of these people,' Feldman continued, 'is Allissa Bateman from Trenton, New Jersey. Ms Bateman is a member of a religious sect who believe they are in communion with the Archangel Gabriel, the spiritual harbinger who will herald the Judgment at midnight with a blast from his golden trumpet.'

Bollinger switched to another camera angle to better frame the smaller woman with the tall Feldman. The developing storm sat nicely behind and above the woman for the perfect dramatic touch.

'Miss Bateman, you've travelled thousands of miles from home to be here tonight. Can you tell our audience what you previously did for a living, and why you're here?'

'Yes, I'm forty-three years old, married with two children, Bill and Tommy, and my husband, Frank, he had to stay home with the kids and his job, of course.' Ms Bateman babbled on about a personal spirit messenger for a few more moments and Feldman wrapped her up quickly, not to lose momentum.

Cutting away between guests, Bollinger switched to cameras surveying the masses below, which were getting truly emotional now as the final moment neared. The rising wind had had a chilling effect. The majority were kneeling, praying, crying, singing, fainting. The fighting and antagonism had ceased.

Bollinger checked the clock twelve minutes till. He cued the next guest, a tall, gaunt young man with shaved head and black robes. Very much like a monk, except he wore upside-down crucifixes from his earlobes, and his eyelids were tattooed to resemble open eyes. Very Sodom and Gomorrah, Feldman decided. He was going to have a hard time playing it straight with this guy, but the audience would love it.

'And this is Mr Astarte. Am I pronouncing that correctly?'

'Just "Astarte",' the man answered solemnly. 'Yes, I am of the Second Realm.'

'And what's the Second Realm anticipating here tonight, Mr Astarte?'

'Only "Astarte",' he insisted. 'We are here for the changing of the realm, the new time in which the natural cycle will occur and Lord Lucifer will ascend to His throne to rule for the next two thousand years.'

'And will this transition be a peaceful one,' Feldman wanted to know, 'or will we be confronting Armageddon here?'

'We do not yet know,' Astarte informed the world. 'We must be prepared for resistance, but the Lord Lucifer comes into his realm by divine right, and nothing can prevent it. If we must fight to safeguard his passage, so be it!'

With that there was a significant roll of thunder from the distant storm, and Feldman took full advantage of it. 'Exactly when and how will this transformation take place, Mr Astarte?'

The 'Mr' was deliberate, and Astarte looked annoyed. He answered patiently. 'It will occur at midnight, of course, and the signs, as you can see' – he gestured to the storm with his head – 'are already upon us. We do not yet know the manner of the transition.'

'All right, we thank you for your time and we'll let you get back with your group in time for the transition.'

Astarte closed his eyelids to the camera, made a stilted bow and exited. No doubt, Feldman thought to himself, this last guest would hold the Christians in their seats long enough for them to ensure that good triumphed over evil.

More crowd shots. 'And we're coming up on five minutes until the turn of the millennium,' Feldman announced. The wind had picked up only a trifle more and, unfortunately, Feldman realized, the squall seemed isolated and still too far away to bring any real fire and brimstone to their melodrama.

Into his earphone came the breathless voice of Bollinger. 'Jon, we got one of those Witness delegates coming up. He saw our broadcast on a portable TV and found his way over here. We're gonna put him on, get ready.'

Beyond the blinding camera lights, Feldman made out the form of a short, shaggy-haired man being led towards him. Without skipping a beat, he announced to the camera that WNN had been successful in locating one of the Jehovah's Witnesses mentioned earlier, and the delegate was ushered on to the balcony.

'Your name, sir?' Feldman enquired.

The small, bearded, serious-looking Witness, who reminded Feldman of a miniature Rasputin, squinted up at the reporter and said in a surprisingly deep voice, 'I am John Jacob Maloney of the Watchtower Bible and Tract Society governing board, and official delegate to the Second Coming of Christ!'

'Mr Maloney, I understand you're here on behalf of Joshua Milbourne representing the Jehovah's Witnesses. Can you tell our viewers exactly what you believe you'll be witnessing here tonight?'

Maloney stepped forcefully towards the camera and glared into its lens with the feverish expression of a certified fanatic. 'The hour has come, O ye of little faith! The Judgment of God is at hand and it is too late to save yourselves. You would not listen, you would not repent, you would not make ready the way of the Lord. And now the Hand of God is upon you. It is the Last Day!'

His eyes bulged and his hands flitted wildly above his head. 'It is the Abomination of Desolation and ye shall be smitten and marked and damned for ever to the bowels of hell! Praise be the Name of the Lord! Praise be the Paraclete of Kaborkah! O Lord, in Thy glorious Name—'

So frenetic was his delivery, Maloney unintentionally expectorated on the camera lens, which forced the production team to cut away to a side shot. The view of him raging into an inanimate machine removed much of the sting of his comments and gave the whole encounter a ludicrous perspective.

Taking back control, Feldman placed a firm, calming hand on the doomsayer's shoulder as the smaller man looked around, bewildered, for a live camera. 'Thanks, Mr Maloney. I'm assuming you'll make yourself available later for some follow-up commentary?'

Maloney was guided off the balcony, still railing and spouting. The production crew could hardly contain itself. This was precisely the mania the New York headquarters had been wanting to showcase.

Feldman repositioned himself in the centre of the balcony and initiated the final sixty-second countdown to the new millennium. As the cameras and searchlights panned over the uneasy scene, he considered what a sweet touch it would be to have played a little 'Auld Lang Syne' from loudspeakers. Everyone could certainly do with a little forgiving and forgiveness tonight. But he knew the humour would be lost on this sombre gathering.

The crowd picked up the count. And suddenly it occurred to Feldman, with midnight less than twenty-five seconds away and all the cameras and crews occupied with the crowd, that he now had the perfect opportunity to steal a kiss from Anke. At the stroke of the new millennium, an indelibly romantic occasion!

When the clocks struck midnight and the cameras explored the crowd reactions, Feldman would have the opportunity to catch *her* off guard for a change! He unhooked his lapel microphone and started to move towards her. Anke was unaware of him, her eyes intent on the world outside, searching curiously.

It was the sacred moment. As if on cue, the wind subsided. For the first time since their assembly, the crowd of irrepressible millenarians held its breath. The world held its breath. And all over Judea there was a deep and solemn silence, culminating at the stroke of midnight with a large clap of thunder in the distance. Simultaneously the Church of the Ascension's bells peeled, along with a dozen other counterparts throughout the Holy City, tolling in the twenty-first century.

Feldman was perhaps the only person present whose mind was on other things. This was *his* personal, sacred moment. As he approached Anke, he appreciated how truly beautiful she was. So fresh. So unsuspecting. It must have been the emotion of the moment, but he was feeling light-headed. Awkward. He was losing his balance. As was Anke and the whole production crew around him. The entire apartment began to spasm and shudder violently.

Cameras and lights on tripods went hopping, rotating, toppling. The electricity was cut off and there was an ungodly eruption of screams and panic from the throngs on the mountain. In a horrific return to reality, a revelation of fear gripped Feldman unlike anything he'd ever felt.

17

Mount of the Ascension, Jerusalem, Israel,
12.02 A.M., Saturday, 1 January 2000

Feldman was hopelessly disoriented. It had taken every ounce of his concentration to reach out and snare Anke as they collapsed to the apartment floor. He had cradled her on top of him, wrapping his arms around her, placing his cheek tightly against hers.

And then, just as suddenly as the violent tremors had begun, they ceased.

The earth was still again. In the darkened room, above the screams of the crowd, no one was stirring. Feldman, in urgent tones and short of breath, repeatedly asked Anke if she was okay. She didn't answer him, but he could feel her rapid breathing and she squeezed his arms, which were still wrapped tightly about her. He was afraid to lessen his grip lest she detect him shaking.

'Everyone okay?' It was the quavering voice of Bollinger. One by one, the entire crew checked in.

Feldman determined from their voices that there were several people still on the balcony. 'You'd better move inside,' he warned, 'it may not be safe out there.' Making a valiant effort to calm himself, he sat upright, still holding Anke in his lap, and began stroking her hair.

'What's happened?' she asked finally, sounding small and anxious.

'Earthquake,' Hunter declared. 'We've lost our power but we're okay now.'

'Earthquake my ass!' It was one of the production crew members from over near the balcony. 'Any Christian worth his soul better have the fear of God in him right now!' A number of voices concurred and someone began the Lord's prayer, with several people quickly joining in.

Another of the production crew flipped on a cigarette lighter, but Hunter warned against gas leaks and it immediately clicked out. A few moments later, someone ferreted out a flashlight, which helped locate a battery-powered halogen flood lamp. The dusty room was reilluminated with an eerie blue light.

Feldman could see two of the crew near the balcony, another at the window, and others scattered about the room. Bollinger was under a table, Hunter and Cissy were crouched together in a corner.

Sounds of sirens and emergency vehicles came filtering in from outside, mixed with the unceasing din of the crowd. Inconsolable screams of hysteria, anguished crying and fearful prayers joined triumphant choruses of hymnals and psalms amid the reinvigorated caterwauling of the doomsayers.

'What's going on out there?' Bollinger called over to the crew at the balcony.

One of them stopped praying and responded, 'I can't see a whole lot. The lights are out all over. Lots of people moving around, plenty of commotion. But only a couple of buildings on fire that I can see.'

Anke's hair had come undone from its clasp and Feldman drew long, soft strands from her face. She looked up at him, her brow troubled, her lips pressed firmly together, her hold on his arm undiminished.

One by one, the prayers in the room ceased and a few decided it was safe to stand. The apartment was in disarray, but Feldman noticed that while there were cracks in the walls and ceilings, none seemed serious. He helped Anke rise, and with him supporting her against his side, together they worked their way over to the balcony for a look outside.

At least in the darkness, the damage appeared limited. 'Maybe it was just a warning,' the born-again Christian crew member hoped, his voice still trembling. 'Maybe that's all there is for now.'

'This is just too unbelievable!' Bollinger stammered.

'To say the absolute least,' Cissy underscored. She rested her head against Hunter's chest, closing her eyes. She'd been crying. Watching her, Feldman raised his eyes to meet Hunter's pensive, unwavering gaze. They traded questioning looks until Hunter shrugged his shoulders, shook his head in denial and looked away out over the balcony again.

A crew member announced that the phones were dead. Cellular phones were still functioning, although the range appeared limited to the immediate vicinity.

'God, I bet the whole world is going apeshit right now,' Bollinger said. He was beginning to recover his journalistic senses. 'I wonder if any of the networks here are back on line yet?' He pointed to an engineer. 'Jimmy, see if we can get some battery power to the satellite link and let's try to get some updates out of here. Joe, where are you?' Joe's faltering voice emanated from the stairwell. 'Joe, go up on the roof and check the dish. Somebody see if Israel Radio is alive and has anything on this.'

'Israel Radio is dead,' someone quickly reported back.

'The dish is fine,' Joe called down from the roof a few minutes later.

Whether by managerial brilliance or rote instinct, Bollinger's firm commands to his crew were remedial. Everyone, including Anke, pitched in to reassemble the operations. Patched together with batteries and cables, the WNN team was once more the first to get the story out. Their transmission lacked any video, and the audio quality was poor, but amazingly they were back on the air to the WNN European Bureau by 12.42 A.M.

To rejoin a world in uproar.

Hunter had succeeded in nursing a satellite TV monitor back to life, and as the team crowded around, a fuzzy picture and squawking audio relayed the tale. For forty-one minutes and forty-eight seconds, all anyone outside Jerusalem knew was that, at the designated hour of the new millennium, some supernatural calamity had struck the Holy Land. Just as had been predicted for so long, by so many. Forty-one minutes and forty-eight seconds was time enough to foment mass hysteria, suicides, heart attacks and assorted insanities on a global scale.

Everywhere, cathedrals, churches, synagogues and temples were breached by stampeding mobs seeking refuge from the wrath of God. Many were trampled or crushed to death. Random violence, lootings and rioting ignited spontaneously and unpredictably in major cities worldwide.

In Times Square, New York, the throngs of assembled revellers had panicked in the streets as they watched Jerusalem tremble, scream and fade to black on the giant Jumbotron video screen above them. In the ensuing onslaught on the subways, hundreds of hapless people were forced off the congested platforms on to the electric tracks and in front of oncoming trains. (Later that evening, inexplicably, the illuminated globe high atop Number One Times Square would short out all its lights and refuse to descend to the New Year.)

Feldman, his eyes fixed on these unsettling scenes of chaos, made a valiant effort to restore reason to the world. Suppressing pent-up emotions, in a calm and soothing voice, he sent his desperately awaited message of reassurance crackling out across the dark skies. Frantic engineers at WNN's European Bureau cobbled the audio together with file footage of the Holy City, rushing the report out to a rampaging world.

18

Mount of the Ascension, Jerusalem, Israel,
2.27 A.M., Saturday, 1 January 2000

Feldman and crew maintained their transmissions until the batteries expired at approximately 2.30 A.M. Middle East time. Two of Bollinger's men had been able to make limited scouting expeditions out into the city. They confirmed by cellular phone that damage was extensive in many areas. However, given the apparent magnitude of the quake, casualties were relatively light. This had all been dutifully transmitted to the European Bureau.

After they'd done everything they could, after all the gear had been packed and stowed in the vans, Bollinger gathered the exhausted team and asked for their attention. Looking at their tired faces, the news director shook his head in reflective disbelief. 'Gang, I can't stand here and pretend that I understand what went on tonight any more than you do. Maybe tomorrow, in the light of day, this will all make more sense.

'After twenty-six years in this business, I guess I'm not a particularly religious sort of person, but I have to confess that this whole thing has truly spooked the hell out of me, too. One thing I do know is that you were extraordinarily professional and calm during all of this, and I'm extremely proud of all of you.'

He looked over at Feldman, who was slouched wearily on the end of a couch with Anke. 'And I don't know where you found this amazing young lady, Jon, but she's been a real trouper tonight, and we all thank you, Anke.'

There was a simultaneous murmur of agreement, to which Anke responded with a weak smile.

'A few things before we break camp,' Bollinger concluded. 'I'm confident that at least some of our transmissions have been successfully received. Either way, there's no doubt headquarters is, at this very moment, rushing up additional support from Cairo. While the phone lines and electric are out, let's all stay close to our mobile phones, but use them sparingly so you don't waste the batteries. If repair crews re-establish communication links outside the region, I'll get word to you on what's happening in the world. Otherwise, plan on a staff meeting at the office at eight A.M. sharp.

'And Jon.' Bollinger called Feldman aside for a moment. 'Since it looks like your departure for the States might be delayed a bit, maybe you'd consider sticking with us a few more days to help us sort through this new development.'

'Fine,' Feldman graciously agreed. 'I don't start until next Thursday, anyway.' Besides, he didn't mind an excuse that would buy him a little more time with his new acquaintance.

Hunter stood next in line to talk to Feldman. 'So, you're hangin' with us a while longer, eh? Great! We're gonna need you until all this dust settles!'

'Only for a few days,' Feldman confirmed.

Hunter nodded. 'Look, you go ahead in the Rover and get Anke home, I'll take Cissy in her car. And, uh, I may be late to the meeting tomorrow.'

Feldman thought he understood and nodded. He'd noticed for some time the coalescing relationship between Hunter and Cissy. And he loved the way they teased one another mercilessly with underlying affection.

But there was more behind the intent, introspective look on the cameraman's face. This was not about Cissy.

It took Feldman over an hour to drive Anke the two and a half kilometres to her home, picking his way carefully down the mount through the throngs and around fallen debris in the streets.

He was continually impressed with this remarkable woman. She had recovered quickly from her initial alarm and had worked relentlessly with the rest of the team in whatever capacity asked of her to get them back on the air. Now she sat quietly, interrupting her private thoughts occasionally to give a brief smile and point directions.

Fortunately, there appeared to be little damage to the northern section of town. When they arrived in front of her contemporary white villa, it looked untouched.

Anke turned to him in her seat and put her hand on his. 'Jon, please don't take this the wrong way . . .'

Here it came. He felt his gut knotting as he looked into that exquisite face. This sounded like the intro to a permanent farewell. It wasn't often that he'd been on the receiving end.

'But' – she dropped the other shoe – 'I live by myself and I'd just prefer not to be alone right now.'

He was travelling the wrong wavelength and her words didn't register right away. He said nothing and she felt compelled to elaborate. 'You see, there's a loft upstairs, and if you don't mind a pull-out bed, I'll wake you in time for your meeting and fix you a nice breakfast, and you can leave whenever—'

Feldman was up to speed finally, and so was his pulse. 'Oh, absolutely, I wouldn't consider leaving you alone right now!' he insisted, quickly bolting from the car and slinging his carry-all over his shoulder.

19

Somewhere in Jerusalem, Israel,
3.41 A.M., Saturday, 1 January 2000

Out in the disrupted city streets, Hunter had no thought of sleep. He'd dropped Cissy off at her apartment, resisting her persistent, tempting offer that he stay and ride in with her for the eight o'clock meeting. Instead, he'd decided to fight the impossible road conditions back to WNN headquarters, alone, promising Cissy to return with breakfast and her car in time to make the meeting.

After several hours, he arrived at the WNN offices to find the building relatively undamaged but the electricity out. Switching on emergency back-up batteries, he sat at an editing bay reviewing his videotape of the moments leading up to the earthquake – particularly the segment featuring the interview with the odd Satanist, Astarte. Hunter's interest focused on the electrical storm in the background, and he used the special Advanced Definition Optics of the editing system to zoom in on the vicinity and enhance the image.

In his opinion, the storm was peculiar. Very intense and very concentrated. Stationary over one location for an extended period. Yet, while he hadn't been paying particular attention at the time, he could recall no trace of the storm after the earthquake. It was as if it simply vanished with the tremors. All this stirred unreconcilably in his mind as he carefully inspected the video footage.

Finally, as the first light of morning arrived, it dawned on him. He slapped the table. Pausing the tape, flashlight in hand, he hustled over to a large map of Israel suspended on the far wall of the room. Locating the Mount of the Ascension, he attempted to orient the view he'd had from the villa balcony. Before he could accomplish this, he was distracted by the gradually increasing sound of pounding on the door of the front office.

Hunter tolerated interruptions poorly. But his irritation evaporated quickly as he opened the door to a very striking young woman flanked by two seemingly unworthy male companions. It was one of the WNN support teams, hurriedly arrived from Cairo, he learned. They'd come in style, travelling in a fully equipped, self-sufficient, forty-foot mobile video RV.

20

Romema Ilit housing development, Jerusalem, Israel,
5.50 A.M., Saturday, 1 January 2000

In his dream, Feldman was a child again. He was studying his catechism with his beautiful, dark-haired mother. But try as he might, he couldn't remember any of his lessons, and it disappointed her greatly. He sighed and stared down at his text once more, but it had changed.

Instead of catechism, it was the Talmud. He looked back up into his father's face this time. His father was frowning, speaking to Feldman sternly in Yiddish, but Feldman couldn't understand. He closed his eyes, crying, and he heard his mother's voice, soothing now, comforting. 'Jon, Jon, it's okay, shush.'

He opened his eyes and the face was now Anke's. Her hair was down around her bare shoulders, a thin-strapped nightgown falling delicately across her breasts. She was smiling and whispering. 'You were having a nightmare, Jon. I heard you all the way downstairs.'

The moon was up now and half full, infiltrating the room with a creamy light. Feldman was embarrassed. 'What did I say?'

Anke laughed softly. 'You were calling for your parents. First "Mama!" Then "Papa!"'

Feldman smiled ruefully and shook his head, attempting to dislodge the uncomfortable, long-buried emotions his dream had resurrected. 'My mother was Catholic and my father Jewish,' he explained. 'They each wanted me raised in their own faith and it used to create a lot of tension between them. I was reliving an episode, I guess.'

'So how did your parents resolve their conflict?' she asked, sitting next to him on the side of the bed.

'They didn't,' he answered. 'They divorced when I was nine.'

'You were an only child?'

'Yes.'

'That must have been terribly hard on you.'

He stared out of the window towards the divided moon. 'For years I felt totally responsible. My legacy from being the offspring of the two most guilt-inducing religions on earth.'

'So what faith did you end up?'

'Neither. I finally gave up both religions and went independent. Agnostic, actually. But I wonder what triggered these memories tonight. It's the first time I've thought about this in a decade.' And the first time, he realized, that he'd ever discussed this issue anywhere other than on his psychiatrist's couch during his difficult adolescence.

'I had troubled dreams, too,' Anke whispered, tenderly smoothing his hair as he had done for her hours earlier. 'With what we went through last night, it's any wonder we slept at all.'

Feldman sat up, more awake now, but still very tired. Anke's warm, lithe presence close to him in her slight gown was distracting. He fought for a gentlemanly comment to counter his thoughts. 'I'm . . . I'm sorry I woke you.'

'Not at all,' she said in a way that convinced him she meant it. She stood. 'It's about time to get up anyway. Why don't you go ahead and shower. I've laid out some clean towels for you, and I'll fix you some breakfast.'

Feldman agreed, threw back his covers and rose, only to realize that all his clothes were in a pile on the floor. He promptly retrieved the sheets, embarrassed once more in front of this disorienting woman.

Anke turned to go as if nothing had happened. But he heard that sweet, soft laugh of hers as she descended the stairwell.

He sighed. She always seemed to catch him in an awkward moment.

It was growing lighter outside when, after a rejuvenating shower, he sat down in his same wrinkled clothes to a superb breakfast of ham and eggs.

She sat across from him with some toast and juice and poured him more coffee. 'So what do you really think happened last night, Jon?'

'You tell me.' He avoided answering her, wanting to shrug off this topic right now. Ever since he'd abandoned religion in his youth, blaming it for his parents' divorce, he'd felt an emptiness inside him. A hole in his soul. Assuming he had a soul. Consequently, he found it difficult to confront the underlying question of what might or might not have occurred the previous evening.

Anke leaned back in her chair and deliberated for a moment. 'Well,' she ventured, 'I honestly don't know what I think right now. But what if God – that is, if you believe in God – really is communicating something to us?'

'How do you mean?'

'I mean, there's just too much coincidence to what happened last night for it all to be simply a natural occurrence, wouldn't you agree? Whether I like it or not, that's a very real possibility. What if, after all these centuries of silence, God is finally talking to us again? Maybe there's a message in this. Or the beginnings of a message. Maybe last night was a wake-up call.'

'So, God was just clearing His throat?' Feldman needed to lighten this up, but not yet knowing Anke's sensibilities, he feared he might have come across as sacrilegious.

She wasn't offended, and smiled. 'Maybe. All I know is that I've never been so scared in my life. And I can't simply disregard what happened. Can you?'

Feldman surrendered to his real feelings. 'Hell, I'm not sure what to think, Anke. For a while there, I thought maybe all those millenarians, whom I'd always considered idiots, might end up being right after all. Meaning that I, this lost, ignorant soul, would be doomed to eternal damnation for having no religious underpinnings.'

He suddenly understood the roots of his nightmare, and the realization hit him full force. Never before had he attached any relevance to his dreams. Finding a significance now presented an overtone that disturbed him.

Anke screwed up her face. 'I don't know that I'd go so far as to accept any of those millenarian theologies,' she said. 'But you can't just dismiss last night out of hand, can you?'

'Maybe not,' he replied slowly, still somewhat distracted by his new awareness, 'but I find it hard to believe that any intelligent deity would mark His return by terrorizing His public. I guess I'll do as Bollinger suggested. I'll just wait and see how it all looks in the light of day.'

His wait was over. The dawn was breaking. Feldman glanced at his watch and realized that, with the streets in such poor shape, he might be hard pressed to drop by his apartment for a change of clothes.

Anke was already on her feet. 'I understand you'll be leaving Israel soon, permanently?'

He shrugged his shoulders. 'Yes, I'm afraid so. This was just a temporary assignment with WNN. I've got a new job waiting for me back in the States.' As he stared into her eyes, his promising new position was losing some of its allure.

She nodded, a fleeting look of disappointment showing on her face. 'Well, Mr Feldman' – she smiled again – 'this was one New Year's Eve I don't suppose we'll soon forget!'

Feldman rose and walked towards her. This time he wasn't thwarted in his designs. The kiss was long, and long overdue. He felt the earth moving again. And left feeling more reinvigorated than his hour and a half of sleep warranted.

Driving was tedious, hampered by toppled walls, fallen utility poles and electrical lines. He stopped briefly at his apartment for fresh clothes. There was no newspaper on his porch. He opened his door and noted with dismay his slovenly, unkempt quarters, which compared poorly with Anke's tidy, well-appointed town home. He shrugged and made a firm commitment to purge the place at the earliest opportunity.

Peeling off his shirt, he tossed it near a laundry basket in the corner and pulled on a fresh shirt from a pile of clean clothes near his bed. As he picked up his shoulder bag, his cellular phone rang. It was Hunter. Bad reception, but no disguising the excitement in his voice.

'Goddamn, I've been trying to get through to you for an hour!'

'Well, my phone's been open,' Feldman confirmed. 'The cells in the area are probably overloaded.'

'Listen carefully in case I lose you,' Hunter said, panting. 'This is incredible! One of the WNN Cairo teams came in early this morning and we all drove down to Bethlehem. You got to get down here right now! We missed it, pal!'

'Bethlehem? What's going on in Bethlehem?'

'This is where the epicentre of the quake was. The same place where we saw the lightning storm hit last night. There's some really weird shit going on down here and I'll tell you all about it, but get here quick before we lose this scoop.'

'Okay, okay, but what about Bollinger and our meeting?'

'I couldn't get through to him. Tell him we got him one hell of a follow-up story to last night. Get everybody and everything down here, now! There's a second mobile unit on its way from Cairo that should be at headquarters soon. We'll need it, too. When you get down here, look for a WNN RV with a satellite dish parked near David's Wall in the open area between King David and Manger streets on the north side. If we're lucky, we'll be the only media operation here. Bye!' He was gone.

God, does this guy never sleep? Feldman thought as he phoned Bollinger from his car. But the circuits were hopelessly tied up. Slowly wending his way through Jerusalem, the reporter was surprised to see so many buildings with severe damage. The darkness had certainly masked the destruction. Passing by the Old City, he could see major cracks showing in the walled-up entranceway of the ancient, sacred Golden Gate. Shaking his head at the destruction, he turned off on a south highway and impatiently made his way out of the city.

Bethlehem was ordinarily a very short drive from Jerusalem, virtually in the suburbs, only about ten kilometres south. But in the aftermath of the earthquake, the trip was prolonged. Feldman had ample time to work the redial button of his cellular phone. Finally, he got through to Cissy.

'Where are you?' she wanted to know. 'We've been trying to reach you all morning!'

'I'm on my way to Bethlehem,' he told her.

'Where? Have you heard from Hunter?'

'Yeah, he's in Bethlehem now.'

'What the hell's he doing there? Jimmy said he took off with one of the new Cairo mobile unit teams early this morning. He's got my car and he was supposed to pick me up for the meeting, the bastard!'

Feldman heard her talking off-phone with someone and Bollinger jumped on the line. 'Jon, what's going on?'

'Arnie, Hunter called me a while ago from Bethlehem. He's down there with one of the teams from Cairo. He wants the entire crew and equipment down there right now. Says we've got the chance for a real scoop if we hurry.'

'What's the story?'

'He didn't have time to give me details, but he said Bethlehem was the centre of last night's quake and that thunderstorm. He said there's some really weird shit going on down there.'

That seemed to have Bollinger's attention, but he sounded irritated at the last-second fire drill. 'This had better be good, Feldman,' he warned. 'I'd like a little more detail to go on than "some really weird shit" before we all just haul ass out of here in the middle of a story.'

'That's all I know, Arnie, but he was pretty insistent.'

Bollinger signed off, still grumbling. Feldman switched on the car radio. Finally, Israel Radio was back on the air. He had to wait for the English version before he heard more appalling news of the night before. The widespread, global panic. The violence, the destruction, the death. This only reinforced in his mind his earlier argument to Anke.

Underscoring Hunter's claim, Israel Radio also confirmed Bethlehem as the epicentre of a major earthquake measuring seven point one on the Richter scale. With the exception of a mild tremor reported in Rome, apparently none of the other millenarian stronghold cities around the world had suffered like disasters.

21

Bethlehem, Israel,
9.35 A.M., Saturday, 1 January 2000

Arriving in Bethlehem from the north, Feldman overlooked a picturesque hillside town of about twenty thousand inhabitants, primarily Christian Arabs whose families had lived here for hundreds of years. Other than in the ethnic origin of its residents, Bethlehem had changed little since the birth of Christ. From rolling, sparse pasturelands that surrounded the town, shepherds still drove flocks of sheep and goats along worn, narrow, cobblestone alleyways into the central marketplace bazaar. Side by side with ancient, historic structures, newer construction had been randomly squeezed in over the centuries. But built of the same indigenous stone, most were hardly distinguishable from their predecessors.

Interspersed among this maze of densely packed dwellings were the elegant white-sandstone spires of a dozen churches. Including the centre-most focus of the town, the fourteen-hundred-year-old Church of the Nativity, located in Manger Square over the grotto that Stephen Martyr had identified in AD 155 as the precise spot where Christ was born.

Feldman was amazed there was no visible damage from the previous night's violent quake. Instead of a disaster zone, he found the town swarming with millenarians. Shops and cafés were bustling and there were no signs of interrupted municipal services. No cordoned-off areas for utility repairs, no emergency crews digging through rubble.

The crowds were densest not near revered Manger Square in the centre of town, as Feldman had anticipated, but at a large, park-like common on the north side. The common was encircled by the connecting loops of Sderot King David on the north and Sderot Manger on the south – *sderot* being the Hebrew word for street. Near where the two loops of the boulevards met, Feldman spotted the WNN RV, parked behind a row of stucco buildings.

He knocked at the door, a bolt was drawn back, and he was greeted by an unfamiliar, bookish-looking, middle-aged man in a tie and horned-rim glasses who, conversely, recognized him instantly.

'Mr Feldman, we've been expecting you.'

Feldman was still not used to his newly acquired celebrity status.

'Good, you made it!' Hunter's voice came from somewhere out of the darkness inside.

Before the door shut and enveloped him in temporary blindness, Feldman spied Hunter seated at a small table next to a very attractive young woman in glasses. She wore a pin-striped business suit with a scoop-neck blouse. Her intelligent face was framed with a straight, dark, banged hairstyle cut at the nape of the neck and set off with the perfect make-up of a runway model. Behind her was a wall of flickering TV monitors.

His eyes adjusted quickly to the blue light.

'Jon,' Hunter began, 'let me introduce you to Erin Cross, WNN's expert on Middle East religious history and antiquities, and Robert Filson, senior news editor, who you just met.'

Feldman smiled and shook hands. Robert's was soft, damp and weak. Erin's was cool and firm. As she stretched across the table to Feldman, the low-cut neck of her finely tailored blouse effected a rather unavoidable presentation of cleavage.

'It's a pleasure to meet the famous Mr Feldman,' she said in an interestingly textured voice, smiling, her dark lipstick contrasting sharply with her milk-white skin.

A phone on the wall lit up and Hunter warned everyone to ignore it. 'It's Bollinger again,' he snorted impatiently. 'We'll fill him in when he gets here, but no more interruptions for now.' He snatched the plug from its socket.

Filson arched an eyebrow, but Hunter was oblivious and launched immediately into his explanation. 'Last night, after I dropped Cissy off, I went back to headquarters to work on a few things. Like everyone else, I guess the weight of all this wasn't sitting well with me and I wanted to review the footage we shot at the beginning of the quake. I was trying to pinpoint the location of that lightning storm when these guys and their team-mates' – he gestured to Erin and Filson – 'showed up a little after daybreak.

'They've got a ham radio in here, and on their ride up from Cairo they got a report out of Turkey about the epicentre of the quake being here at Bethlehem, exactly where I'd figured on a map to be the site of that electrical storm.'

Feldman interrupted. 'Well, where's all the damage around here? I didn't see a thing coming in, and Jerusalem's a mess.'

'That's the least of the weirdness,' Hunter replied. 'Once we connected both the lightning storm and the quake to Bethlehem, we made the unanimous decision to check things out. And it's paid off. Big. Look at this.' He gestured towards a monitor and everyone turned.

'This is selected footage from a bunch of stuff we shot earlier this morning here in King David Square,' Hunter explained. 'We're in the process of editing it down right now.' He picked up a remote control from the table and started a video clip. 'Okay, now take a look at monitor C.'

There appeared on the screen the remains of an old, rock-walled enclosure, about waist high, rectangular, approximately fifty metres long by twenty-five metres wide.

'This is an archaeological *tel* known as David's Wall,' Hunter explained, using a Hebrew term for 'excavation site' that he'd picked up earlier from Erin Cross.

Feldman did not quite understand, but he didn't want to interrupt.

'David's Wall is about a stone's throw from here on the west side of the plaza,' Hunter went on. 'There are all kinds of excavations going on around this area.'

The camera turned a corner and arrived at an open entranceway into the enclosure. Isolated in the middle of the courtyard was a water-filled cistern carved from solid rock, about two metres in diameter, from which people were carefully ladling water into jugs and bottles and miscellaneous containers. 'Okay, now we're inside the wall,' Hunter narrated, 'and you're looking at the ancient, sacred Well of David.'

Feldman had been expecting something with a little more drama to it, and he shifted impatiently in his seat. But Hunter was not to be rushed.

'Erin,' he addressed the young woman at his elbow, 'tell Jon about the well.'

Erin, who had perhaps the best posture Feldman had ever seen, turned her swan-like neck towards him and smiled coquettishly. 'I'd be happy to. Mr Feldman, both the wall and the well are the oldest historic landmarks in Bethlehem, dating back to about the year 1000 BC. The well still supplies potable drinking water to the residents here. Legend has it that three thousand years ago, a young shepherd filled his goatskin with water from this well and went off to watch the army of the Israelites do battle against Philistine invaders.

'This shepherd boy, who was born in Bethlehem and whose name was David, and who would later become the greatest king of ancient Israel, supposedly drank the water from this well before engaging and slaying the Philistine giant, Goliath.'

Hunter interrupted. 'Not a bad little anecdotal beginning, eh?' He beamed with self-satisfaction. 'Now look at monitor E, Jon.'

With the punch of a button Hunter brought up a wide shot of the common. The camera was looking east, away from the well. Standing about thirty-five metres directly across from the entranceway of David's Wall was a large, partially excavated mound in which a flight of stone steps had been exposed. The steps led up to a flattened area at the top of the mound on which the remnants of massive stone columns could be seen.

Feldman surmised that these were the remains of a once-magnificent structure, like much of Israel its glory days long behind it. He could see little else with the hordes of millenarians swarming about it.

Erin continued her archaeological exposition. 'These are the ruins of the ancient Israelite Temple of the Messiah,' she said, 'almost as old as the Well of David. Built by King David, legend has it, to anticipate the coming of another great ruler who would also drink the waters of this well.'

Hunter turned back to Feldman. 'Last night, according to hundreds of eye-witnesses – and we've interviewed dozens of 'em – during the storm and earthquake, an incredible event took place here.

'At the time, there were only a couple of thousand people around these shrines, primarily overflow from the capacity crowds at Manger Square. The crowd here was mostly under the control of a millenarian order known as the Samaritans. The Samaritans' deal was to set up paid trips to Bethlehem for sick and invalid people from all over the world, with the idea that the poor suckers could get cured at the Second Coming.'

He leaned towards Feldman and placed his hands palm down on the table. 'So, among the Samaritan followers, there's this one crippled Bedouin boy of about fourteen or fifteen. Supposedly, the kid and his parents were picked up in the desert by a group of Samaritans travelling up from the south. The boy was brought to David's Well yesterday on a stretcher, all bandaged up, he couldn't walk or feed himself, couldn't see, hear or speak. Or so everyone swears, anyway.'

Feldman was hoping this wouldn't turn out to be some sort of religious miracle story.

'After they baptized him,' Hunter went on, 'he and his family stayed near the Well of David for the evening ceremonies and the boy just lay there on his stretcher, apparently sleeping.

'Later in the evening, remember, the storm came up. Close to midnight, there was a lot of lightning and wind – it never did rain, though – but everyone scrambled for shelter near the buildings around the sides of the plaza. That's when several people noticed that someone had forgotten the boy.'

'They'd left him lying out in the storm?' Feldman gasped, incredulously.

'Yeah. Apparently with the sacred hour of midnight approaching and in the throes of the storm, everyone panicked. As the lightning got really bad, a number of people saw him illuminated out there, but before anyone summoned the courage to go out and get him, he suddenly stood up, shook off his bandages, walked into the enclosure, calmly drew water from the well and drank it. Then, with everybody yelling for him to get the hell out of the open, he began to walk slowly towards the old temple.

'Meanwhile, there was a big countdown to midnight going on from a large part of the crowd that didn't notice what was happening with the boy. But he just kept on walking, right up the steps, turned around at the top and raised his arms high.

'Then a shout went up celebrating the new millennium, yelling and cheering, and suddenly there was this shock of electricity. A bolt of lightning must have struck really close. Everyone claims it hit the boy and radiated out into the square. At the same time, as if the lightning set it off or something, the earth began to shake and you can see what happened.' Hunter brought up monitor G, which delivered a tight zoom on the base of the well.

Feldman saw the beginnings of a jagged fissure on the ground. The camera followed it away from the well, the fracture yawning as much as a foot wide in some places as it wandered along.

'They claim the ground just opened up as you can see here,' Hunter explained, 'from the well clear to the base of the temple, up the steps, splitting them all the way to the top, right between the feet of the boy.'

'And you see what's carved there on the top step?' Hunter could hardly restrain himself. The camera continued to travel along the fissure, up the stairs to close in tightly on the very last riser.

Worn, but clearly visible, were ancient Hebrew letters carved into the face of the step. The first two letters were bisected by the very end of the fissure, but were still legible, if indecipherable, to Feldman.

'Exactly where the boy was supposedly standing.' Hunter leaned forward and touched the screen with his forefinger. 'There, that's the ancient Hebrew word for "Messiah", right, Erin?'

'Correct,' Erin confirmed. 'The letters read right to left. The Hebrew pronunciation is "Moshiach".'

'And to top it all off' – Hunter slapped his hands on the table – 'there were over two hundred and fifty alleged infirm and handicapped people present who now claim to have been cured of their afflictions when the lightning struck. I tell you it's voodoo, Jon, but it's perfect. We've got a follow-up to end all follow-ups! The climax everybody's been looking for!' He sat back, luxuriating. 'We've got ourselves a genuine, bona fide Messiah figure!'

Erin Cross anted up additional support. 'I have to tell you, Mr Feldman, it looks pretty good. We talked to a lot of people here who claim to have been cured of everything from cancer to blindness. And some of the evidence is rather convincing. It'll make for a sensational feature.'

Feldman had sat silent through most of this, elbows on the table, chin resting on the heels of his thumbs, fingers laced and pressed against his mouth. But his eyes had betrayed a growing fascination.

'This is completely incredible, Breck,' he finally whispered. 'Absolutely unbelievable. This boy, where is he? Have you seen him? Have you spoken to him?'

'No,' Hunter admitted. 'The Samaritans are hiding him, protecting him, they say. We don't even know if he's in Bethlehem any more. But we're working on it.'

Filson, who'd added nothing to the conversation so far, finally contributed. 'That presents a nice element of mystery to all this, of course,' he said in the flat voice of a third-generation accountant. 'But without the boy, we lose the crux of the story. And we lose our scoop if and when some other network finds him first. I think we should sit on this development and allow ourselves more time to find the boy. Otherwise, we risk putting every other newshound on the scent.'

Feldman and Hunter exchanged glances. It was unclear whether Filson was attempting to assert himself or simply offering his opinion.

But while they didn't yet know what authority Filson might or might not exercise over this operation, they were not about to let an interloper threaten the momentum.

'I've enough confidence in our team to move forward with this story right away,' Feldman replied in a straight, certain tone. 'Particularly with the addition of your two crack WNN teams.' He was patronizing Filson, but Filson, apparently, was unaware.

'Not to worry, Filson,' Hunter assured him, 'we've got the man-power, the nose and the inside track to get the job done.'

They didn't wait for approval. As they rose from their chairs, Feldman clapped Hunter soundly on the back. 'Brilliant work, buddy. Now why don't you show me around outside and tell me how you see us putting this story together.'

Erin rose with them, and Filson, who appeared to have an objection, finally closed his mouth and said nothing.

Hunter grinned at Feldman. 'All this is starting to make that ol' presidential election look a tad tame, now isn't it?'

Feldman just smiled.

By the time a furious, anxious Bollinger and his crew arrived with the second Cairo team, Hunter and Feldman had worked out the sequence of shots and storyline for the newscast. Rather than allow the fuming bureau chief any sort of explanation, they simply sat him in front of a monitor along with as many of the crew as could squeeze into the RV, and played him a rough cut of their newscast.

With Feldman providing live commentary, the videotape methodically unveiled the entire bizarre tale. The final segment of their story focused on the beneficiaries of the miracles alleged to have occurred when the lightning struck. Especially poignant was one series of photos showing a paralysed young girl from southern Alabama, the victim of a car accident some years before. The selected photographs showed the wreckage of the car in which she was injured, shots of her in a body cast, and in a wheelchair.

And now, after the events of Millennium Eve, she was seen slightly older, her fresh face beaming as she walked haltingly on two wasted, but obviously functioning legs. The joy and religious rapture of her parents were extremely moving. Entirely convincing.

To counter any end-of-the-world misinterpretations this 'miraculous' happening might have fostered, Feldman had crafted a secular ending to the story. A positive message of hope and faith, and the extraordinary power of the mind to heal. A refreshing optimism that disavowed the Samaritans' claims of miracles and the arrival of a new Messiah. But Hunter had insisted that the story close with a slow zoom into the chiselled word 'Moshiach'.

There was a momentary pause in the cramped RV, then a growing murmur of amazement, followed by an outburst of applause that included even Filson. Feldman bowed, extended his arms towards Hunter and deferred to his associate, who accepted the praise with a gratified grin.

Bollinger, his anger completely quashed, looked as relieved as he did pleased. 'Breck,' he said, exhaling deeply, smiling broadly, 'WNN has been on my butt all day for details on our follow-up, and all I could do was promise them "something big". Thank God you delivered, you asshole.' He had obviously known that Hunter had been ignoring his calls.

'Now,' the bureau chief said, rubbing the palms of his hands together briskly, 'let's see if we can find that boy!'

22

Bethlehem, Israel,
7.17 A.M., Sunday, 2 January 2000

In a café early the next morning, Hunter and Feldman didn't even touch their breakfasts. They were absorbed with sections of that day's and the previous day's London *Times*, electronically transmitted by satellite link directly to a copier in the WNN RV.

In an article from the bottom half of the previous day's front page was a story entitled 'False Alarm Breeds Doomsday Panic', with the subhead 'Jerusalem Earthquake Heralds New Millennium'.

In that day's paper, however, the story had graduated to top front page: 'World Jolted by Reports of New Messiah!' It was accompanied by lengthy accounts of religious unrest and sidebars detailing the strange developments in Israel and around the globe. Feldman was relieved to find that at least no major rioting or violence had re-erupted.

Virtually the entire main news section was devoted to the story. Religious organizations everywhere were in a state of confusion. Official responses differed widely, from outright denunciation by the Catholic College of Cardinals in Rome, to complete embracing by such denominations as the Seventh Day Adventists and Mormons. Most religious leaderships, like the Jewish Rabbinical Council, took a wait-and-see approach.

An interesting anecdote, Feldman noted, was a report of a mild tremor in Rome with minor damage to a priceless Michelangelo fresco in the Sistine Chapel, and a fracture in the main altar stone of St Peter's Basilica. There had been, however, no such 'supernatural' occurrences reported in Salt Lake City.

Another small notice caught his eye and he called Hunter's attention to it. Joshua Milbourne, spiritual head of the Jehovah's Witnesses, who had been viewing the WNN Millennium Eve programme from his hospital bed, had died that night of a massive heart attack. Death had occurred, the article said, at one minute past midnight Middle Eastern time as Milbourne witnessed the beginning of the climactic earthquake.

'Well,' Hunter observed dryly, 'I guess you can say he made it to the Second Coming and fulfilled the old prophecy. That ought to keep the Jehovah's Witnesses in business a while longer!'

As Hunter and Feldman arrived at the morning staff meeting held outside the WNN RV, they made the nodding acquaintance of a familiar-looking executive in an expensive European suit and tie, standing at Bollinger's side. Bollinger, oblivious to their arrival, continued his monologue to the crew. But the new visitor detached himself and approached them around the edge of the gathering.

Feldman finally recognized who this was, and he gripped the firm hand of Nigel Sullivan, WNN's European bureau chief. Though they'd never met, Feldman knew and respected the man largely responsible for WNN's millenarian coverage and Feldman's current position. 'It's a pleasure to meet you, Mr Sullivan.'

Sullivan smiled warmly. He motioned the sleepy-looking newsmen to the last row of chairs. 'Please, no need to be formal with me. I'm Nigel to you and to everyone else, as well,' he said with the aristocratic accent of an English nobleman. But there was no stuffiness or distance to it. 'I'm delighted to finally meet you lads. As I've been telling Arnie and your associates, you've done an outstanding job here. Simply outstanding.'

'Thank you, sir,' they both responded, neither quite able to drop the formality yet.

'Have you heard how the world's responding to last night's newscast?' Sullivan asked.

'Just what we've read in the morning papers,' Feldman answered.

Sullivan sat back in his chair and looked them squarely in the eyes. 'For the last two nights, I'm pleased to tell you, WNN, with your team's outstanding contribution, has dominated world news ratings beyond anything ever achieved. A seventy-one per cent share! And that's global, gentlemen. A seventy-one per cent share! Not only unprecedented, virtually inconceivable!'

Feldman and Hunter looked at each other in disbelief, and then broke out in wide grins.

'This has happened so quickly, and become so large,' Sullivan continued, 'it's caught everyone quite by surprise. At this time, no other network is even within shouting distance of us. But believe me, gentlemen, after the last two nights, every one of them is mounting a major thrust to catch up.'

That much was obvious. From where they sat they could see as many as twelve competitive network vehicles queued up around the quadrangle where there had been none ten hours ago. A number of news helicopters, Sullivan's among them, rested in a pasture nearby.

'Jon.' Sullivan turned to Feldman and placed a hand on the newsman's shoulder. 'I understand you've accepted a new position back in the United States. And while I realize it may be too late, I'd like to persuade you to reconsider. I'm prepared to offer you a new contract with an open term, quadrupling whatever compensation package you've been afforded.' He turned to Hunter. 'And I'll be extending the same provisions to your current contract, as well, Breck.'

The two reporters looked at each other and blinked.

'We want to expand our coverage of this development,' Sullivan explained, 'yet we wish to preserve the unique chemistry and style that your team has created here. We'll put several additional teams at your disposal for developing the lead story on the boy Messiah. And we're turning the Jerusalem office into a regional news centre, expanding operations into three additional wings of office space and conference rooms. I'm here to see that you gentlemen get what you need – everything you need. It's one bloody big story, lads. Handled properly, it could well be the story of the century. The millennium!'

Twenty feet beyond them, Bollinger had just been delivering commendations to his troops and now he called over to Nigel Sullivan to address everyone.

Sullivan rose and the two journalists followed suit. 'We'll have lunch together today, if you're available, gentlemen, and we'll continue our discussion then.'

They nodded, thanked him, and he strode to the front of the meeting area to extend his congratulations and encouragement to the rest of the crew. Turning towards each other, Feldman and Hunter were mirror reflections of restrained enthusiasm.

'Holy shit, Feldman!' Hunter whispered.

'Holy shit, Hunter!' Feldman whispered back.

The potential measure of his circumstances was finally dawning on Feldman. He'd stumbled into a world-class opportunity. A place where Pulitzers and legends were made. A place that generated books and speaking engagements and professorships with honorary degrees at hallowed Ivy League colleges. This was heady stuff. There was simply no way he could refuse this break, despite the embarrassment of having to renege on a plum position he'd fought so hard to win.

And yet, while he decided to accept Sullivan's generous offer, in the few seconds it took for all these grand permutations to ricochet through his mind, from somewhere he found the foresight to focus on the larger picture. Whatever his good fortunes, he knew he must not lose sight of his need to *understand* what was happening here in the Holy Land.

He was yanked from his reflections by a tug at his shirtsleeve. A flushed and elated Cissy McFarland had stolen up on the two reporters from behind.

'I'm glad I caught you bozos before you had a chance to slink off,'
she deadpanned. 'Guess what?' She pulled a pink telephone slip from
inside the neck of her shirt and waved it in their faces.

'Your hooters have a message for us?' Hunter ventured.

She gave him a withering look and turned to a grinning Feldman
as the only semi-rational alternative. 'I've got confirmation from the
Samaritans. They'll meet with you in one hour at the Bethlehem Star
Hotel. Here's the room number and the names of the leaders there.
Maybe you can finagle an exclusive with the Messiah boy and we'll
have ourselves another scoop!'

23

Bethlehem, Israel,
11.28 A.M., Monday, 3 January 2000

Three pompous-looking Samaritan disciples had met with Feldman
and Hunter for nearly an hour. Things were not going well for the
two reporters. The main obstacle was the head Samaritan himself,
the First Reverend Richard Fischer.

A dogmatic, arrogant, portly man with wavy grey-brown hair,
bulbous nose and acne maculations on his face and neck, the Reverend
had done most of the talking. He took obvious delight in the attention
he'd been receiving, and in the power he now wielded as custodian of
the hottest media property on earth.

'Boys,' he addressed the frustrated reporters, 'while I'll grant you
WNN may be the best-followed network covering this particular story,
as directors of the Samaritan movement, we, the Leadership Council,
must refrain from showing any partiality. All we're able to tell you at this
time is that the Messiah *will* be making a public appearance in the near
future. Where and when I'm not disposed to say, but you and all your
fellow media people will be apprised in due course.' He rose, extended
his damp, fleshy hand, and summarily dismissed his guests.

Once the reporters had left, one of the disciples turned to the First Reverend and exclaimed in a chagrined voice, 'Reverend Dick, I don't get it. You let Brother Leroy sell our videotape of the Messiah to WNN an hour ago. Why did we have to keep that a secret? And you sold it for a pittance! If we'd just waited, I bet that Feldman would've paid us a fortune!'

Fischer presented his cohort with a knowing smile. 'Brother Gerald, you miss the tactics entirely. Leaking the tape to WNN is the best investment we could make. No one must know it came from the Leadership Council. As long as WNN believes they finessed it from one of our lower-level brethren, we preserve the tape's credibility. You've got to appreciate the cynicism of the media, Brother. They're a suspicious lot and will surely question the tape's authenticity anyway. If it came directly from us, that would only deepen their scepticism.'

Reverend Fischer was getting through to his less savvy associate. 'Consider the fact that WNN now has the greatest world audience of *any* network,' he continued. 'Once they air that tape, the Messiah is assured of a global congregation. We'll have no problem interesting commercial sponsors in our upcoming venture. And we'll be guaranteed maximum compensation here on out from all the networks, each of which will be forced to bid generous contributions for access. That, Brother Gerald, is precisely what will give us the finances we need to properly expose the Messiah to the world!'

As the two reporters pulled out of the hotel carpark, Cissy called on their car phone and urgently summoned them back to the RV. Feldman informed her of their failed mission, but she wasn't disappointed. 'Forget it,' she consoled him. 'Wait'll you get a load of what we just got our hands on!'

Met by Bollinger at the door, Feldman and Hunter were ushered into the RV to view a freshly acquired amateur video. 'This,' Bollinger announced with unabashed excitement, pointing to a dark picture appearing on the largest wall monitor, 'is our next exclusive.'

Secured at minimal expense, Hunter and Feldman were told, this unique prize had been secretly furnished by an underling from within the Samaritan camp. Not of great quality, the tape had been taken at night in the light of pole mercury lamps. But both reporters knew instantly what this was. Shaky, shadowy, grainy, then turning completely white in response to sporadic lightning strikes, this was a video recording of the Millennium Eve phenomenon at the Bethlehem common.

Shot from a distance of some thirty feet, the figure in the video was of slight build, robes thrashing wildly in the wind at its back, face impossible to discern. Each time the lightning flashed, the image bloomed white and the camera operator was momentarily blinded, lost his framing in the viewfinder, then awkwardly regained it.

As the form reached the stone steps of the temple and began its ascent, the camera zoomed in. Off screen you could hear the crowd above the screeching wind, counting down the seconds towards the twenty-first century. Topping the steps, the figure turned towards the camera, into the wind, raised its slim arms heavenward and faced the Well of David across the courtyard. At last there was a brief, vital moment of fulfilment when the face was illuminated by lightning and finally visible to the camera.

At that instant, the crowd countdown reached midnight, a tumultuous cheering began, and then the video was purged by a violent shock of bright light that shorted out the image, leaving only a blank, snowy screen. The audio, however, continued unaffected, a hellish uproar of shrieking wind, terrified screams and resounding thunder. And then a deep rumbling, which Feldman judged to be the earthquake.

'Rewind a bit and go to the ADO Plus,' Hunter requested, pointing to an instrument cluster of special effects on the video control board. 'Isolate on that shot of the face, ADO in and enhance the image.' But he couldn't restrain himself long enough for the editing engineer to enact his instructions. Excitedly, he pressed forward to take the controls himself.

Feldman shared his enthusiasm and watched intently as Hunter skilfully located the exact frame he was searching for – the moment when the face was at its best angle, turned about three-quarters to the camera, the instant before the image was lost to the lightning flash.

Through the magic of electronic manipulation, Hunter magnified the image and a whisper of awe escaped the lips of the viewers. Although the enlargement blurred the face at first, it was still discernible. Very pale and alien-looking. With each adjustment, the visage became sharper and better defined until, at last, all the features were reasonably distinct.

The eyes were bold and dark and unwavering. The nose was prominent, Romanesque. The cheekbones high, the jawline strong. The dark hair was of medium length and splayed wildly in the wind.

There was a wrath-of-God intensity here. An intimidating, anguished, judgmental sternness. Yet, while the brow was furrowed, the eyes were almost sorrowful. The lips were parted and full. This was a youthful face, but there was an aged wisdom to it. It was noble, intelligent, authoritative.

'Holy shit!' Hunter exhaled. 'There's a Messiah figure for you!'

And Feldman had to agree.

24

Ben-Gurion apartment complex, Jerusalem, Israel,
10.41 A.M., Tuesday, 4 January 2000

Feldman was sleeping well past his intended wake-up. He was having another dream. This time, he was skating out on a huge body of water, all by himself, racing along at a rapid clip with powerful, sure strokes of his long legs. It reminded him of winters at Ohio State when he used to ice-skate with friends out on the large pond near his dormitory.

Only in his dream, it was warm and balmy and the lake wasn't frozen. He was skimming across the surface of an open sea – the Sea of Galilee. Although he'd never been here before, somehow he knew. He was heading for shore. Skating on his bare feet. The wind in his face, the sun glowing brilliantly above. It was exhilarating. Skidding sideways, spinning, turning, sliding, magically flinging himself across the swells. Until he almost casually sensed the presence of a rising wave behind him. Dark, ominous, rumbling and surging towards him.

He straightened out his heading and quickened his pace towards the shoreline. But the wave was growing, towering behind him, gaining on him. It was a tidal wave! A tsunami!

Feldman was tearing frantically over the swells now. He dared not look back. He need not look back, because he was now engulfed in the dark shadow of the wall of water and enveloped in a deafening roar. He was scant yards from the shore and safety when the deluge crashed down on him, rolling him, twisting him in his bedclothes.

He sat up with a start, breathless, sweaty, but so relieved to be rescued that he broke into a smile.

Until he noticed the clock on his nightstand. He'd wasted precious hours of the one day he had available to spend with Anke.

25

The Vatican, Rome, Italy,
6.06 P.M., Tuesday, 4 January 2000

His Eminence Alphonse Bongiorno Litti, one of the Pope's trusted cardinal advisers, depressed the massive bronze lever of a huge carved mahogany door and entered the resplendent anteroom of the Papal Palace Apartments. Awaiting him in large, overstuffed, seventeenth-century French settees, were Pope Nicholas VI and Antonio di Concerci, prefect of the Congregation for the Doctrine of the Faith of the Catholic Church in Rome.

Litti was an affable-looking, unimposing man, five feet eight inches in height, olive-skinned, heavy-set, in his late sixties. His large brown eyes were naturally sad, burdened by prominent dark bags, separated by a protruding nose. His hair was a wiry salt-and-pepper. The click of his heels on the marble floor attracted the attention of di Concerci, who looked up, nodded briefly at his approaching colleague and returned to paperwork he and the Pope were examining.

Di Concerci, on the other hand, was large of frame, but agile, elegant and deliberate in his movements. A vigorous seventy-one years of age, he had a long, dignified face, with high cheekbones and deep-set, penetrating, dark brown eyes. His white hair was full and wavy underneath his bright red cardinal's skullcap.

Too late for di Concerci to notice, Litti returned the nod in an equally reserved manner, and greeted his pontiff with a respectful 'Your Holiness'.

'*Buona sera*, Alphonse,' Nicholas acknowledged, and waved him to the empty chair on his right.

'You look tired, *Papa*.' Litti noted with concern Nicholas's surprisingly pale and drawn appearance.

The pontiff managed a thin smile and patted his associate's arm reassuringly. 'These are tiring times, Alphonse.'

As was their custom, an acolyte delivered cognacs to the room in long-stem glasses. Nicholas accepted his glass, but immediately set it upon the intricately carved ivory coffee table before him. He placed his elbows on his armrests, his chin in his left palm, and focused on one of the sculpted figurines whose heads supported the tabletop. 'Do we have a full damage assessment from the tremor?' he asked.

'Yes, Holiness,' Monsignor Litti replied. 'Nothing more than the fresco in the chapel and the High Altar in the basilica.' Litti was referring to Michelangelo's *Last Judgment* on the rear wall of the Sistine Chapel, and also to the main altar of St Peter's Basilica.

'Have you inspected the damage personally?'

'Yes.'

'And?'

'The crack in the fresco is about two and a half metres long, perhaps three centimetres across at its widest. Deep, but surprisingly not a structural problem. The altar, however, has split entirely in two, but did not collapse. The weight of the two marble slabs against one another managed to hold it upright. As a precaution, we've temporarily shored it up in the middle.'

'That is the extent?'

'That's all that the engineers and I have been able to discover.'

The Pope fell silent and leaned back in the massive chair, pressing two fingertips of his left hand to his cheek. 'So what do you make of all this, Alphonse?'

The cardinal didn't know quite how to answer. He was not comfortable in di Concerci's presence, an acute conflict of personalities having established itself many years before. He took a sip of his drink and stalled, searching for a non-committal response.

'Don't make it difficult for me tonight, Alphonse,' Nicholas pressed gently. 'I want you to speak your mind.'

Litti glanced at the Pope's face and perceived an earnestness he could not disappoint. 'I find it very peculiar, all of this, Holiness,' the cardinal had to admit. 'From the strange events in the Holy Land to the tremor here in Rome, I confess, I feel a certain preternatural quality at work here.'

He waited for some sort of reaction from either man before continuing, but di Concerci was looking away towards the window, and Nicholas had resumed his fixation on the figurine. Not wishing to be difficult tonight, Litti continued.

'I simply cannot reconcile as coincidence the timing and location of the storm and quake in Bethlehem, Holy Father. Not to mention the appearance of this Messiah figure, or all the alleged miracles.

'Or even the odd occurrences here at the Vatican – the conspicuous crack in the chapel wall, appearing, of all places, in the image of Michelangelo's *Last Judgment*. Extending from the feet of the triumphant Saviour in the sky down to the earth where the souls of the resurrected dead are being judged. With no other visible fractures elsewhere in the mural.

'And then the High Altar of the basilica, foot-thick marble, splitting cleanly and precisely in the middle. With far more delicate objects near by completely unaffected!'

Deliberating over the totality of these seeming miracles, Litti's voice softened to a faint, reverent whisper. 'Holiness, I believe the Church must examine these circumstances seriously and with great care. With every assumption that most, perhaps all, of these extraordinary events are true signs from God!'

Litti fell silent and the Pope allowed a considerable interlude, displaying no reaction to the cardinal's position, but continuing his unblinking introspection.

At length, and without altering his gaze, the Pope asked his prefect, 'And your analysis, Antonio?'

Di Concerci rose slowly from his chair, took several steps towards the large leaded-glass window near him, and looked out over the broad expanse of St Peter's Square at the multitude of millenarians below. He spoke without turning. 'While I can fully appreciate Cardinal Litti's impulses, and I'll grant you these events are certainly peculiar, I must take a more pragmatic posture, *Papa*.'

Litti could feel his face reddening. This was precisely why he had wished to defer his comments until after the prefect. He had never understood the Pontiff's regard for this man.

Di Concerci turned and moved around to Nicholas's side, to the subtle exclusion of Litti. 'I agree that these events are worthy of examination,' he continued, 'but not with the assumption that they are signs from God. Throughout the past century, Holy Mother Church has correctly approached all such alleged miracles and signs with deserved scepticism. And that approach has served us well. In this particular instance, there are any number of alternative explanations that *do not* invoke divine intervention.'

This last statement finally re-engaged the Pope. He examined the prefect's stolid face.

Di Concerci continued his argument. 'That a quake could occur here coincident with one in Bethlehem is not so implausible. The entire Mediterranean, after all, is one giant tectonic basin. Perhaps one quake triggered the other.

'It's also a well-documented scientific fact that electrical storms can be generated by, and often accompany, such geological disturbances as volcanoes and earthquakes.

'Then there is also the feasibility that these quakes, both here and in Bethlehem, were the result of a deliberate well-orchestrated scheme. An elaborate plot involving underground explosions detonated by certain millenarians desperate to preserve their cults and insure themselves against embarrassment.'

Litti could not contain a short, derisive laugh. Di Concerci gave him a forgiving, tolerant look and posed a question. 'Cardinal Litti, can you demonstrate beyond any reasonable doubt that the damages to the chapel and basilica were not man-made?'

The cardinal would have liked nothing better than to muzzle his rival, but he had no effective defence to this challenge. Instead, he countered with a pointed question of his own. 'How then, di Concerci, do you explain the transformation of the invalid boy at the Well of David? The fissure that opened at his feet along his path to the temple? The many miraculous cures experienced by hundreds of afflicted bystanders at the very stroke of the millennium? Surely you cannot so easily dismiss these phenomena!'

Di Concerci remained composed. 'I must confess, Alphonse, I found the dramatic television newscasts of the so-called Messiah quite impressive, too. But then I had to let reason take hold. Much of what was reported must be discounted as speculation and hearsay, greatly magnified by impressionable witnesses and an opportunistic media. What substance remains is still vulnerable to scrutiny.

'For example, the question of the boy Messiah: given the great emotions and expectations these millenarians have invested in a Second Coming, would it not be inevitable that at least one of them might succumb to some sort of messianic manifestation? This is a common psychological disorder even in the most normal of times.

'Or, more likely, could all of this have been simply a grand, elaborate hoax? Perhaps the boy was never afflicted at all. A well-coached impostor. What better mechanism than a new Messiah to guarantee extended life for an otherwise doomed religious fringe element?'

Di Concerci's supreme self-assurance was gnawing at Litti, who saw through the prefect's conscious efforts to appear reasonable and wise in front of Nicholas. 'But the fissure?' he objected. 'The many people cured of substantiated ills? You cannot rationalize away everything, di Concerci!'

'I'm sorry, Cardinal Litti, but did you not notice that the alleged fissure at the well was undetectable in the night video? It was only visible in daylight, in video taken many hours later. Plenty of time for the Samaritans to trench an artificial opening. Or perhaps the fissure was constructed prior to the boy's presumed transformation, with everything simply a cleverly executed special effect.

'And as regards the miraculous cures that occurred, again, it could all quite feasibly be part of an elaborate fraud. Nevertheless, let us assume for the moment that some of the claims are valid. That some of these individuals were truly disabled and truly cured.

'Psychosomatic illnesses aside, you'll note that many of the alleged cures seem to centre around motor and neurological difficulties. Medical history is replete with incidents involving victims of accidental high-voltage charges – including lightning strikes – instantly and inexplicably cured of afflictions such as these.

'However, Cardinal Litti,' the prefect allowed, 'I'll admit to you that there is one aspect in all of this for which I find a logical explanation elusive. My quandary lies with the timing and location of the earthquake in Bethlehem. Although I wouldn't rule out the possibility of a hoax, I frankly don't believe such an occurrence could have been man-made.'

Litti lightened somewhat, wondering if di Concerci might actually be opening his mind for once. But his hopes were immediately dashed.

'Nevertheless,' di Concerci redressed himself, 'granting that the timing and location of the quake would be an amazing coincidence, it is not out of the realm of natural possibilities. In any given year, there are more than one million separate, measurable seismic occurrences that take place across this planet. *One million!* And the Holy Land is squarely within one of the more active fault zones in the world.'

'Your knowledge of science is remarkable,' Litti interjected sarcastically.

'I confess, Alphonse,' di Concerci offered in a soothing tone that smacked of condescension, 'I, too, have been troubled by the implications of recent events. And as a consequence, I've devoted considerable time to researching the circumstances. As I first stated, there *are* viable alternative considerations which should be explored before we risk further alarming the faithful and propelling more of our followers into the ranks of these irrational millennialists.'

This last point registered visibly with Nicholas.

Di Concerci again addressed the Pope directly. '*Papa*, if there's a sign in any of this, it's certainly not a clear one. We must be extraordinarily careful in how we respond or we could find ourselves overreacting to one of the most embarrassing, albeit well-crafted, hoaxes ever perpetrated upon the Church. I fervently believe that we must take a strong stand, and I highly recommend that we issue immediate reassurances to the public elaborating upon the contentions I've just made. To delay further is highly dangerous and threatens the solidarity of our congregation.'

Litti sensed the influence di Concerci's arguments were having. In desperation he rose to his feet and appealed to his pope. '*Papa*, surely after two thousand years of anticipation and preparation for an event of this nature, the Catholic Church, above all others, *must* recognize the signs of God! This young boy could well be a John the Baptist, come to prepare the way for—'

The Pope froze him with an outstretched hand, leaned back in his heavy chair, closed his eyes tightly. At length, he turned to di Concerci. 'You are right, Antonio. I, too, have allowed my emotions to over-whelm my reason. Please, move quickly on this. I ask that you prepare a papal letter to be submitted to me for release by tomorrow afternoon.

'Alphonse, I'd like you to initiate repairs immediately on the fresco and altar. Supervise the work personally and have it completed as quickly as possible.'

Litti was appalled. 'But Holiness, what if the damage is truly a sign from God? Should it not be preserved, at least temporarily—'

'*È finito*, Alphonse!'

Nicholas's look and tone of suppressed anger were manifestations Litti had never witnessed in his pontiff before. Shaken and embar-rassed, the cardinal bowed his head, both in acquiescence and to avoid what he presumed would be the triumphant expression of his opponent.

A fatigued and troubled Pope Nicholas VI dismissed his advisers and retired to his chambers. Before preparing for bed, he sat himself in his study at his large, ornate desk. The same desk from which his predecessors had directed the course of nations and kings, launched crusades, rid the world of evil apostasy and heretics.

Cupping his chin in his hand, the Pope lost himself in his thoughts, reflecting on the reassuring points of di Concerci's argument. Neither di Concerci nor Litti could have known how close the Pontiff had come to sharing with them a very sacred, long-standing secret. A grave confidence passed down to him from many decades before. How he longed to unshoulder the great burden he'd been carrying. But the prefect's words of hope had given him cause to reconsider. Perhaps di Concerci was correct. Perhaps Nicholas hadn't the need to break faith with this inviolate trust. Not yet. It might not prove necessary.

He fished his spectacles from his pocket and positioned them on his nose. From a braided chain attached to his waist, he located a large, intricate gold key. He carefully inserted it into a lock on a side door of his desk, feeling it smoothly turning the heavy turmblers inside. The door unlatched and from within the dark vault the Pope withdrew a faded leather-bound portfolio secured by leather thongs. He laid the parcel on the desk in front of him.

Releasing the strings, he opened the case to reveal three collections of yellowed documents. Removing the third collection and holding it reverentially between his fingertips, he drew back into his chair, reading it closely, his brow deeply furrowed by its terrifying contents.

26

WNN news bureau, Jerusalem, Israel,
11.15 A.M., Wednesday, 5 January 2000

The rumours had been filtering in since early morning, and by now Bollinger was convinced they were accurate. Direct from the millenarian grapevine, it was said that the Messiah would finally be making a long-awaited public appearance. Having fasted and meditated for four days and nights in the deserts north of Jericho, the Messiah would give an address near the resort town of Tiberias, on the western shore of the Sea of Galilee. Tomorrow morning, at dawn.

Feldman, Hunter, Erin Cross and a production crew were dispatched immediately to Tiberias by WNN helicopter to prepare for whatever eventualities might develop. Sullivan, Bollinger, Cissy, Robert Filson and more crew were to fly up in a second helicopter later, to join them.

27

Tiberias, Israel,
3.30 A.M., Thursday, 6 January 2000

Feldman was up early, breakfasting on fresh dates, figs, pomegranates and orange juice. He was accompanied by Arnold Bollinger, Nigel

Sullivan, Cissy McFarland and the swarthy, gregarious lady of the farmhouse where WNN had been extremely fortunate to find quarters.

He hurried his meal and excused himself to wander outside in the fresh ocean air. Shoving his hands in his pockets he walked out along the footpath that overlooked the Galilee, alone with his thoughts. Directly, he heard someone calling his name and he trotted quickly back up the path to where a crew member was summoning him. The helicopters were idling, ready for the morning's reconnaissance.

Feldman ran into the house for his shoulder bag and dashed back out to join Sullivan, Bollinger, Hunter and Erin in the passenger compartment of the first chopper. The engine throttled up and they tilted off into the pre-dawn sky with the second chopper close behind.

Below them were the lights of thousands of boats moored at the edge of the sea. And along the shore, tens of thousands of campsites stretching out for miles. They'd hardly begun their surveillance, however, when the crowd showed signs of general commotion. Lights were coming on everywhere. Horns and shouting could be heard even above the staccato of the helicopter blades.

'What's happening down there?' Bollinger wanted to know. It was a few moments before a decipherable pattern emerged, but as evidenced by migrating headlights, it appeared that the masses were inclined in a northerly direction. Many boats had pulled up anchor and were making off hastily up the coast.

'Radio back to the mobile units and see if they know anything,' Sullivan directed.

The report came back: the Samaritans had made a public announcement on Israel Radio that the Messiah would be appearing about thirteen kilometres to the north, on a mountain known as Beatitudes, located directly off the highway that followed the shoreline.

As the pilot pivoted the helicopter in the desired direction, Hunter left his seat and zipped open an equipment bag. He withdrew a large, bulky Steadicam, a special gyroscopic camera that enabled smooth video to be taken even aboard a jarring helicopter. Placing it on his shoulders, he flipped on a light, illuminating Feldman. 'Ready whenever you are,' he signalled.

Feldman cleared his throat, adjusted his tie, and reeled off a brief update on the situation. After he had finished, Hunter motioned the

pilot to descend and then augmented their bulletin with amazing video
of the endless car lights below: more than a million millenarians,
they estimated, in a mass crusade towards a rendezvous with their
Messiah.

28

Mount of the Beatitudes, Israel,
4.46 A.M., Thursday, 6 January 2000

Visible from more than five kilometres away, the mount was more a
tall hill, easy to spot, lit up with huge halogen lamps. As Feldman and
company approached overhead, they could make out an enormous,
elevated, altar-like stage setting at the summit, upon which the bright
lights were focused.

If there were any questions in their minds as to where the Samaritans
had found the capital to produce such an elaborate event, they were
soon answered. Plastered across the front of the stage and at strategic
points all around were insignias of proud sponsors: IBM, Coca-Cola,
Sony, Ford, Nike.

Separated by about forty feet from the sizeable crowd that had
already assembled, the altar was protected by a tall electrified fence.

'Do we put down, or do we stay in the air?' the pilot wanted to know.
Other aircraft in the vicinity seemed to be holding their distance.

'Let's keep the other helicopter aloft to cover crowd scenes and
panoramic shots of the stage,' Sullivan suggested, 'and let's try to
set down inside the fence. We'll see if we can get clearance for some
close-ups and maybe even an interview.'

They picked a space as far removed from the centre of the
stage as possible, concerned about overhead wires or that the
downdraught of the blades might topple some of the lighting towers
or staging equipment. But that was the least of their problems. Once
the Samaritans discovered what was about to happen, a dozen

burly men scurried out from beneath the stage brandishing heavy nightsticks.

The pilot pulled up and looked back at Sullivan for instructions.

Glancing around at everyone and shrugging his shoulders, Sullivan exclaimed, 'They can only tell us to leave! Let's try a landing, shall we?'

The pilot defiantly set the chopper down virtually on top of the guards, sending them scattering. With the helicopter safely on the ground, Feldman realized that the angry security force would hold back only until the blades had slowed. But he had an idea.

'Nigel,' he shouted in Sullivan's ear, 'keep the rotors close to lift-off speed. Meanwhile, let me go out and talk to them while Hunter takes some footage, just in case.'

Sullivan hadn't a better idea, so they popped open the door and Feldman staggered across the neutral zone like a man in a hurricane. He was hopeful that his newfound celebrity status might gain him an entrée here, and he did detect a note of recognition in the eyes of at least one guard, whom he approached.

'Jon Feldman, WNN News,' he bellowed in the wind and flashed his media credentials. 'I'm here to meet Richard Fischer.' This was a gamble. For all Feldman knew, Fischer wasn't even here.

'Nobuddy's allowed in here,' the big man countered in a thick, American Dixieland drawl. 'Nobuddy. We waved all the other choppers off, but y'all set down anyways.'

'Well, I talked with Reverend Fischer by cellular phone patch not fifteen minutes ago,' Feldman lied, 'and he said he'd see me if I could get here right away.' Turning back to the helicopter, Feldman signalled for the pilot to cut the engine, pointed to Hunter and waved for him to come over.

The guard blinked and looked at a fellow guard, who was no help.

'Y'all stay right here and I'll go ask Mr Fischer,' he decided, and started off.

Feldman quickly grabbed Hunter, directed his camera on the second guard, and in his most pronounced stage voice shouted, 'Okay, we're here live at the Mount of the Beatitudes broadcasting worldwide an interview with the official Samaritan security detail. Take it, Breck Hunter!'

The video camera and prospects of worldwide exposure momentarily froze the guards. Hunter picked up immediately on the ruse and launched into a barrage of flattering personal questions as Feldman slipped off, tailing guard number one under the enormous stage.

There was a labyrinth of framework and modular scaffolding under the twelve-foot-high platform above them. Within the maze were a number of mobile trailer units, one of which, Feldman presumed, held the reclusive Messiah.

He caught up with the guard just as the panting man arrived at a trailer and rapped at the door. 'First Rev'rend Fischer,' he called out, 'I think we got us a problem!'

The door opened and Richard Fischer's portly shadow filled the entranceway. 'What is it, Mr Granger? We're busy.'

'I'll represent myself, thank you, Mr Granger,' Feldman asserted, and moved out into view.

'What are you doing here, Mr Feldman?' Fischer frowned in surprise. 'No media's allowed behind the fence!'

'I need to talk to you, Reverend, it's important!'

Fischer nodded to Granger, who stepped aside, but he neither left his post at the door nor invited Feldman in. 'Make it quick, Mr Feldman, I've only got a few minutes.'

'We want to video the appearance, Reverend Fischer. This is an event of international importance and it deserves a better representation than images taken fifty feet away through a chain-link fence!'

'We've already made arrangements for complete, professional video, Mr Feldman. We hired our own private production crew. This time, if you want a good look at our Messiah, you'll have to acquire it from me and not some amateur. Our costs will be reasonable, of course.'

'If it's compensation we're talking about here, sir, be assured, we'll not only pay for the footage we shoot, we'll make complete copies available to you for your unlimited use. Besides, I didn't see any video crew outside. What if they don't show, or what if their work doesn't turn out? At the very least, wouldn't it be wise to have professional back-up?'

Fischer had perked up at the mention of compensation. 'How much of a contribution are you suggesting, Mr Feldman?'

'I'd need to get authorization, but I think I could speak for maybe, uh, ten grand?' Feldman was fishing.

'This is the Messiah we're talking about here, Mr Feldman!' Fischer barked, insulted. 'No less than three hundred grand! And I want exclusive rights on all footage after your first telecast. Take it or leave it.'

Feldman scratched the back of his head and made a desperate decision. 'I tell you what, I'll take your deal on the three hundred grand, but give us a break on the video rights. If we can't have full use of the tapes, they're worthless to us.'

Fischer looked at his watch. 'Okay,' he decided. 'But I want a written contract to that effect before you shoot a single frame. Deliver it to Mr Smead in trailer number seven. And keep your people out of the way. No closer than fifteen feet to the Messiah. And absolutely no questions or conversation! Understood?'

'Perfectly.' Feldman shook Fischer's hand.

'Granger,' Fischer instructed his guard, 'you go with Mr Feldman and mind that he does *exactly* as we agreed. Any slip-ups and you take his camera and videotapes and eject him and his crew!'

'Yessir, Mr Fischer.' Granger gave Feldman a hard look, and Feldman quickly jogged back to the helicopter.

Granger followed close behind, out of breath and red-faced, to assume watch over the WNN operation. He ordered his men back to their posts, charging them to use their handguns, if necessary, to ward off any other landings.

Feldman trotted up to where Sullivan and Bollinger were anxiously waiting.

'I hope I didn't overstep my bounds,' he explained, 'but I committed us to a buyout exclusive of this event for three hundred grand.'

Bollinger gasped, 'You did *what*!'

Sullivan waved him off. 'You did fine, Jon. It's worth ten times that amount to us. The closest any competitor is going to get is the fence!'

However, for the other unfortunate media on hand, even that second-class vantage point was unattainable. The steadily massing, elbow-to-elbow crowd was packed right up against the yellow warning barricades to within a few feet of the electrified chain link, jealously guarding their space. WNN's frustrated competitors were relegated to hovering helicopters or the rooftops of distant cars.

Behind him, Feldman noticed a rosy pallor creeping along the eastern edge of the mountain range. Dawn was only minutes away now. He took up his position on the stage just below the altar.

There were metal stairs starting at the very back of the stage, at ground level, and rising steeply in the direction of the audience. Passing through the centre of the main platform, the flight extended all the way up to the elevated altar. At this time, a dozen individuals began filing up the steps towards the seating section on Feldman's level. These officiants comprised the Samaritan Leadership Council hierarchy, including a beaming Richard Fischer, who nodded airily to Feldman as he passed. The Messiah was not among them.

From loudspeakers, music began to play. Softly at first, then louder. A heavenly, glorious aria from some obscure opera Feldman had heard before but couldn't identify. While he realized this precisely timed and elaborately orchestrated performance was a contrived effort to instil awe and wonder, he nevertheless had to acknowledge its effectiveness. The entire atmosphere was charged and eminently supernatural.

Hunter assumed his primary camera position on the ground, head-on with the stage, capturing the altar in silhouette against the increasing dawn. Bollinger gave Feldman the high sign and the reporter called down over his headset, 'Okay, let's go live and set the scene.'

Hardly had he begun his intro, however, than the huge halogen floodlights illuminating the hillside were abruptly switched off and the volume of the music increased. The crowd became hushed as the sun suddenly broke the jagged crest of a distant mountaintop behind the stage, casting a single, golden beam directly upon the back of the altar.

As if ascending into a tunnel of light, a small, slender figure rose steadily up the centre stairway, continuing all the way to the top where it halted and stood motionless behind the altar.

Feldman held his breath.

The Lord is come!

29

Mount of the Beatitudes, Israel,
6.21 A.M., Thursday, 6 January 2000

The massive audience was absolutely immobilized by the ethereal scene, and remained so for a full sixty seconds while the celestial music crescendoed to its finale.

The slender Messiah was dressed in a loose, hooded, full-length white robe, trimmed with red and purple piping. The head was bowed, the face completely shadowed by the hood in the dawning sunlight behind.

Feldman, the TV crew, and the millions of breathless spectators watched, spellbound, as the mysterious form appeared to unfurl itself slowly. The head tilted back. The slim arms rose steadily from its side, upward to the sky. The sleeves slid gracefully down to unveil thin, opalescent arms. Arms that extended to small, clenched fists which petalled open to display fine, outstretched, alabaster fingers.

And at last the hood dropped away, revealing the unearthly, radiant, alluring, upturned face of an angel. Innocent, unpretentious, childlike and beautiful. Yet purposeful and wise. The eyes were closed and the mouth opened wide, exposing straight and perfectly white teeth.

Feldman was taken aback, then charmed to realize that this transfixing, commanding display had been, in actuality, nothing more than an early morning stretch and yawn. Although, because of the contrast of sunlight and shadows, and the distance of the crowd, he doubted that anyone but he could tell.

While this was most certainly the same arresting face Feldman had seen in the crude Millennium Eve video, its impact on him now was entirely different. There was no semblance of the pain, rage or anguish that had exuded from the dark TV monitor. Perhaps it was the inexactness of the computer enhancement, but this face had none of the intensity. It even appeared less angular now. Softened. Sweetened.

Yet it had lost none of the otherworldliness that gave it its divinity. This was an amazing creature. The skin was so completely smooth, unblemished and literally vibrant in its pure, radiant whiteness. The face was perfect in its symmetry, with large, wide-set dark eyes rimmed with long black lashes. The jawline was chiselled, firm. The nose prominent, Roman-godly. Entirely appropriate.

The only physical imperfection to mar this compelling, flawless visage was the appearance of odd red welts that were visible in small, scalped patches in the Messiah's unruly raven hair. A very bad haircut.

But if this were indeed the face of a Messiah, God had played a cruel joke on His anointed one. This strange and surreal appearance wasn't that of a boy, but of a young woman. And when Feldman heard her speak, he was certain of it.

Looking over the crowd, the Messiah called out in a clear, engrossing, authoritative but entirely feminine voice.

'*Vasheim aboteinu tovu lisanecha*,' she announced in perfect Hebrew, which Feldman did not comprehend.

'*Bism Elah atty Laka*,' she intoned in perfect Arabic, which was also lost on the reporter.

'In the Name of the Father, I come to you,' she said in perfect English, and Feldman realized that the Messiah was repeating the same phrases in a variety of languages.

'*Au Nom de Dieu notre Père, je viens à vous*,' she continued in French.

She repeated the process in German, Spanish, Russian, Chinese, Italian and Japanese, picking up the pace in a rhythmic chant that physically moved the crowd. Ten separate languages in all, recorded on tape, and her accent, in each instance, was perfect. Finishing one circuit, the Messiah began a new phrase, starting the rhythmic translation process all over again. She punctuated her oration with decisive movements of her arms and body.

The world received its first sermon from the new prophetess. A short speech that came to be known as the New Beatitudes:

In the name of the Father, I come to you.
In the name of Truth, I come to you.
In the name of Revelation, I come to you.

Blessed are you who listen, for you shall understand.
Blessed are you who see, for the New Light shall shine upon you.
Blessed are you who resist convention for the sake of righteousness,
*   for you shall be vindicated.*
Blessed are you who seek the Answer within you, for you shall
*   know the mind of God.*
Blessed are you who defy the powerful in My name, for you shall
*   be called courageous.*
Blessed are you who are selfless, for your compensation shall be
*   immeasurable.*
Blessed are you who are tolerant, for you shall attain Unity.
Blessed are you who safeguard the defenceless, for you shall gain
*   life everlasting.*
Blessed are the secure of heart, for you shall find comfort in
*   yourself.*

Rejoice and exult, because your reward is great in heaven; for
*   so did they persecute the prophets who came before.*
*   (Apotheosis 4:6–19)*

There was one point near the end where the Messiah, in her sweeping scope of the crowd, brought her eyes to rest on Feldman's. Only for an instant, only in passing, but there *was* a contact. And even in the briefest of glances, her dark, serene, multi-hued blue eyes penetrated him unnervingly.

He felt simultaneously dizzy, confused and invaded. But he had no opportunity to reflect on the experience. The Messiah's hands rose to the heavens as if bestowing a blessing upon the crowd. And then the slender figure turned abruptly, arms dropping, and calmly descended the steps as the crowd erupted.

The massive audience was in ecstasy. Laughing, crying, praying, fully sated and taken with the rapture of this religious moment. Feldman was fearful that at any second the insensate, joyous mob would surge forward and shock divine sense into some of the more unfortunate faithful near the electric fence, providing Hunter with a little anecdotal footage. But the assembly remained respectful of itself and there was never any danger.

Feldman believed that most of the crowd had been prepared from the onset to accept this Messiah figure as their Saviour, regardless of her newly revealed sex. That she did such an effective job surpassing expectations, however, was what sent her audience into this prolonged state of euphoria.

But not all her audience. There were some here who did not come to welcome a new religious icon. Particularly a female one. And they left this encounter with scepticism, scorn and displeasure.

Yet, to all who personally witnessed this unprecedented event, there was no denial that *something* very extraordinary had happened here.

30

WNN headquarters, Jerusalem, Israel,
8.06 A.M., Thursday, 6 January 2000

'There you are!' an aide called out with relief, spying Feldman at a coffee cart. 'We've been looking all over for you. Sullivan's called a special strategy session in conference room four.'

Leaving his coffee mug behind, a tired-looking Feldman hustled off down the corridor, only to be interceped by another staff member who stuck her head out of a door and called hesitantly to him.

'I – I don't know if I should even bother you with this one,' she second-guessed herself, noting the harried look on Feldman's face, 'but I have a long-distance call from Japan – some guy who insists he knows you and has some important news. I can barely understand his accent.' She looked at the scrawled message in her hand. 'A Dr Omato?'

'I'll take it.' Feldman braked, stepping inside the door to accept the phone from her outstretched hand.

'Hello, Dr Omato, how are you? You're back in Japan now?'

'Hello, Mr Feldman. Fine. Yes, IDF deport us after we appear on TV.'

'I'm sorry to hear that, sir.'

'No problem. Our work finished. But I have more important news for you now. About Messiah!'

Feldman had been jotting unrelated notes on his pad, but now the astronomer had his full attention.

'You have new information about the Messiah?'

'Yes, Mr Feldman! Messiah is woman!'

Feldman sighed inwardly, returning his mind to his notepad. 'Yes, that seems to be the consensus.'

'No, Mr Feldman, I mean, Messiah is woman from meteorite crash. She survivor in desert!'

Feldman's pen point tore the page and he jolted upright.

'What!'

'Yes, we see her on TV. She survivor we help after meteorite crash.'

'Are you certain, Dr Omato? It was dark. You said the woman was injured.'

'Yes, positive. Dr Hirasuma also agree. Dr Somu also. We positive.'

'Okay, excellent. That's a great help. You've been *very* helpful. Can I have someone from our Japanese bureau get a statement from you?'

'Yes, of course.'

'Excellent, thank you. Hold for my assistant, please!'

Feldman passed the phone back to the staff member, leaving her with instructions, and headed off to the strategy meeting, his mind churning.

'Good, Jon, you're here!' Sullivan addressed him as he joined the session in progress. 'Just to let you know, we're trying to arrange another appointment with Richard Fischer. He returned to his hotel with the Messiah in a rental helicopter a short while ago.'

Feldman found a place at the table between Cissy and another female staffer.

'The Samaritans control the entire hotel grounds now,' Sullivan continued. 'It's fenced and heavily guarded and they're not letting anyone enter. If we can get a message through, we're going to offer a handsome sum for a private interview with the Messiah, which we'll want you to conduct, naturally.'

Feldman nodded.

'Right-o.' Sullivan switched topics. 'Now let's get back to our concepts for an alternative back-up story tonight. If everyone prefers the idea of developing an analysis of the Messiah's sermon, I'd like to suggest, Jon, that you consider a co-anchored report with Erin Cross. As our expert on religious issues, Erin has some nice angles to suggest.'

'Sure,' Feldman agreed.

'Let's get to work, then.' Sullivan rubbed his palms together. 'Any questions before we begin?'

Feldman raised a hand slightly. 'Maybe this is a moot point now, Nigel, but are we all in agreement, the Messiah is a she?'

Sullivan shrugged his shoulders above a wave of bobbing heads and murmured affirmatives. 'There doesn't seem to be much argument about that.' He smiled. 'And quite attractive, to boot! Perhaps a trifle eccentric, but striking nonetheless, wouldn't you say?'

'But who is she and where in heaven's name did she come from?' Bollinger posed the core question.

'I think I know where she came from,' Feldman offered, and all eyes quickly focused on him. 'I got a call a few minutes ago from Dr Omato, the Japanese astronomer who assisted us before. He and his colleagues are convinced our little Messiah is the missing survivor from the Negev disaster, the injured woman they found in the desert. I'm having our Japanese bureau get their statements.'

'Damn!' Hunter broke the stunned silence. 'A shell-shocked, mad scientist with a messiah complex!'

'Or,' Bollinger had been following a similar train of thought, 'possibly an amnesia victim caught up in the millenarian brouhaha.'

'Or,' Cissy extrapolated, 'an amnesia victim, manipulated by the Samaritans.'

'I think we're on to something here,' Sullivan concurred. 'Well done, Jon. Let's resurrect the investigation of the Negev laboratory. Put both teams three and four on it together. And let's keep a lid on the Messiah/survivor story until we see what we can turn up, shall we?'

'Try for a list of personnel working at the institute that night,'

Bollinger suggested. 'Names, ages, description. Anything to help us identify her.'

'Cock your ears,' Sullivan urged. 'Surely someone who knows her true identity has recognized her face from the newscasts by this time. She's not exactly common-looking, now is she?'

There was no disagreement on that score.

'Okay, now on to the matter of a follow-up report on yesterday's sermon.' Sullivan turned to Erin Cross. 'Erin, would you be so kind as to share some of your key insights with Jon?'

'Gladly, Nigel.' Erin accepted the floor, fixed her bright smile on Feldman, and approached a pull-down screen on the wall behind her.

'I spent the better part of last night doing a comprehensive comparison of the New Beatitudes with the originals,' she explained, scrolling open the screen to reveal a large side-by-side print-out of both sermons. 'For now, I'll spare you some of the more technical evaluations, of which there are many—'

'Thank God!' Cissy hissed under her breath, loud enough for it to register with most of the table.

'—and summarize what I consider to be the essential underlying points.

'It's important to note how these New Beatitudes differ in their intent from the originals. Christ's Beatitudes are designed to inspire and comfort the downtrodden and to promote passivity, humility. The New Beatitudes, however, appear to lead us in a very different direction. The New Messiah encourages open-mindedness, independence, self-reliance, assertiveness and selflessness. A more proactive stance, I would say.

'If there is a key to where the Messiah is going with all this, I believe it occurs in the third line of her introduction.' She pointed to the screen and read the verse aloud: '"In the name of Revelation, I come to you."'

'It's the use of this word "Revelation" that I find so intriguing. It's possible that in using this term, the Messiah is referring to John the Apostle's Book of Revelation, which, of course, contains the apocalyptic messages describing the end of the world and the Second Coming of Christ.

'On the other hand, by "Revelation" the Messiah could simply be implying that she intends to reveal something of special, spiritual significance in the future. If so, what this special "Revelation" might be is also left unclear.

'Despite the title the Samaritans have given her, it's impossible to determine yet what this woman actually considers herself to be. Does she really believe she's a true Messiah – that is, a spiritual leader personally anointed by God? Or does she merely think herself a prophetess, inspired by God to provide insights into the future? In any event, there's no denying that she has convinced herself she's some sort of an emissary from God.'

A staff assistant timidly raised her hand. 'I know this is going to sound ridiculous to everyone, but should we really rule out the possibility that she might be a genuine Messiah, a holy person sent by God?'

Hunter nearly choked on his coffee.

Sullivan was quick to shut him down. 'None of that! We'll respect all points of view at this table!'

The cameraman apologized and Erin addressed the question.

'If we make the assumption that she's a true Messiah, then we have to ask ourselves why. What purpose would it serve a supreme being to send a female envoy to convey His message? And why would God allow her to mimic the life of His Son? To parallel the origins of Christ with a birth in Bethlehem, a Sermon on the Mount? It confuses Christ's message; it doesn't make theological sense, if you ask me.'

'But maybe God has a separate message for women?' the female staff member suggested.

'Yeah! Or maybe God's looking to balance the scales with women?' someone else volunteered.

'Right!' Cissy snorted, contemptuously. 'God's going politically correct on us!'

Sullivan raised his hand to bring the proceedings under control. 'I suggest we leave the philosophizing to the philosophers and stick to the issues at hand. Let's turn our attention to developing a substantive report on these controversial New Beatitudes, shall we?'

31

The Vatican, Rome, Italy,
11.00 A.M., Friday, 7 January 2000

Nicholas had heard so much about the previous day's controversial New Sermon on the Mount that he'd been eagerly looking forward to viewing it. There was a sense of relief in him now. The universal consensus that this purported New Messiah was female had removed any of his subconscious fears that the world was experiencing the Second Coming. At best, she could be no more than a prophetess.

Nonetheless, the Pope had had a background examination run on the Reverend Richard Fischer. It had revealed him to be a one-time carnival barker, alcoholic, drifter and sometime Bible salesman before finding his niche as an evangelical. This would add credence to the conventional Vatican wisdom that yesterday's Sermon on the Mount II media sensation was nothing more than a clever marketing scheme concocted to exploit the current millenarian fad.

Nicholas had asked his respected confidant, Prefect Antonio di Concerci, who'd already seen this video, to join him. Meeting in the anteroom outside the palace's small movie theatre, they entered together, walking midway down the aisle, taking seats next to each other in the otherwise deserted room.

'What is the status of your millennial decree, Holiness?' di Concerci asked, making conversation as they awaited the start of the tape. The cardinal was referring to Nicholas's long-awaited encyclical on materialism.

'It's finished, Tony. I've merely been awaiting the appropriate time to issue it. I didn't see how it could receive the attention it warrants under recent conditions. However, now that we seem to have safely crossed this bothersome millennium barrier, I believe I shall have it released next week.'

The theatre darkened and the video began. The Pontiff was unconsciously drawn forward in his seat as the picture opened on a breathtaking, distant pre-dawn shot of the mount crowned in glowing lights and cloaked with vast crowds that spilled down the slopes into pockets of lingering fog.

Nicholas frowned. Not with displeasure, but with deepening wonderment as the first rays of morning broke the horizon, irradiating the stage from behind. He folded his hands tightly together as the stirring music crescendoed and the Messiah began her transcendent march to the altar.

The first clear image of the New Messiah took him quite by surprise.

'She is an angel!' Nicholas exclaimed in full appreciation, and di Concerci glanced at him, nodding gravely.

The Pope absorbed the rest of the video engrossed, in silence.

At its conclusion, after a period of quiet reflection, di Concerci finally spoke. 'Wouldn't you agree this is a female, Holy Father?'

The Pope's eyes finally focused on his associate and he responded in a thoughtful tone. 'Oh, yes, yes. This is most assuredly a female. And with such a commanding presence!'

'She has a certain gift of oratory,' di Concerci conceded. 'What's your assessment of her possible authenticity?'

Nicholas looked back at the blank screen as if the answer lay there. 'I came here quite prepared to brand her a fraud, Antonio,' he admitted. 'Certainly, as a female, she cannot be a Messiah. But perhaps she could be a prophetess. I would like to understand better her affiliation with these Samaritans, who she really is, and where she comes from. There's an ethereal quality about her. We simply need to learn more.'

'What do you make of this "New Light" she speaks of, Holiness? This "new Revelation"?'

'Those are the two aspects of her Beatitudes I find disturbing,' the Pope asserted. 'The rest of her message, as far as I could tell, is benign and uplifting. It will be interesting to see how far she takes this and what, if anything, we hear next from her. We must keep a close eye on this situation, my friend.'

'I quite agree.'

'If this woman is the product of some duplicity,' Nicholas added, 'we must quickly root it out. The sooner we do this, the faster we can restore our world congregation to normality. I'm greatly concerned about the state of Holy Mother Church right now, Tony. Support around the world is down substantially, both spiritual and financial. No event in the last 100 years has affected the Church as severely as all these disturbing millennial phenomena.'

32

WNN headquarters, Jerusalem, Israel,
8.49 A.M., Monday, 10 January 2000

Erin Cross's audience appeal in the well-received telecast of her Beatitudes analysis did not go unnoticed by upper-level WNN officials. She was quickly assigned several follow-up opportunities during the coming week to offer her additional on-camera experience, another step in grooming her for a more visible future with the network. There was even talk that WNN International was considering a long-term pairing of Feldman and Cross as a highly attractive media couple.

News in the Negev laboratory investigations, however, was not so positive. The search teams continued to be thwarted in their efforts to uncover any pertinent data. Worse still, developments on the messianic front were also wanting. Nothing had been forthcoming from the uncooperative Samaritans, and nothing had been seen of the angelic young woman since last Thursday's electrifying Sermon on the Mount. For lack of a better alternative, the same TV coverage of the sermon and the popular Beatitudes analysis had aired repeatedly on WNN all weekend. Every possible significance of the new messianic appearance had now been explored on every network by every conceivable expert.

In desperation, at the conclusion of the morning staff meeting, Sullivan made the decision to finally break with the Japanese astronomers' survivor/Messiah story.

'Even if it eventually proves inaccurate,' he explained, 'at the very least it may apply pressure in the right places and shake some facts out of all this damned secrecy.'

33

UVDA Israeli military airfield, southern Negev,
9.16 P.M., Monday, 10 January 2000

Chief of Staff Major General Mosha Zerim was alarmed.

'This New Messiah person, one of our personnel from the institute!' he exclaimed to his colleagues. 'Is this possible?' He was joined in his military conference room by Senior General Alleza Goene, Commander Benjamin Roth and Intelligence Commander David Lazzlo. All three had flown in from various points in response to WNN's latest news report.

'No, Mosha,' Benjamin Roth assured him, 'we are virtually certain that this Messiah, as she's called, is *not* one of our laboratory personnel.'

'Correct, Mosha,' Alleza Goene agreed. 'We've gone to the extent of making electronic image comparisons of the woman with photographs of *all* female institute personnel, even those not on duty the night of the attack, and we have no matches. None. This Messiah appears to be younger than most of our female staff. Late teens or early twenties, perhaps. And none of the women at the institute were even close in bone structure, height, weight or complexion.'

'Who, then, is this mysterious Messiah?' Zerim asked.

'We don't know yet,' Roth admitted, and gestured to David Lazzlo, seated across from him. 'We put the Intelligence Department on it following a routine request of the Knesset even before the survivor allegation surfaced. So far, nothing.'

Lazzlo nodded to verify this and added, 'But if she's Israeli, we'll identify her soon enough.'

'The only witnesses claiming to have seen a survivor are those Japanese astronomers,' Goene reminded everyone, 'the same ones who started the meteorite rumour our intelligence commander here is so fond of.'

Goene stole a quick glance at Lazzlo and continued. 'We interrogated the Japanese thoroughly and believe that any victim they may have come in contact with must have been injured outside the institute grounds – a Bedouin woman perhaps. At any rate, we revoked their visas and deported them. They'll be no more trouble to us.'

Zerim was somewhat reassured. 'Defence Minister Tamin will be relieved to hear this. False allegations by the media are of no consequence, but we'll suffer severe repercussions from both the Prime Minister and the Knesset if we fail to contain every aspect of this accursed Negev operation.'

'Then there's still one more contingency we must cover,' Lazzlo warned, and all eyes turned to him. 'We must consider the possibility, however remote it may be, that one of the test subjects survived the explosion. Particularly one of the enhanced subjects.'

Goene scoffed.

'I must point out,' Lazzlo explained, 'that the apparent age of the New Messiah approximates that of the test subjects. The sex, of course, matches. If we intend to "contain every aspect of this accursed Negev operation",' he quoted Mosha Zerim, 'then we must ensure against the worst possible scenario. And proof to the outside world of the existence of an enhanced test subject would most surely be the worst possible scenario.'

Zerim looked back and forth quickly from Goene to Roth with escalating concern.

Goene drummed his fingers on the tabletop and turned to Lazzlo with undisguised contempt. 'Now you go beyond ridiculous. If you understood anything about the physical limitations of the test subjects, you'd know they were totally incapable of escape. Since the moment they were first gestated, none of them, especially the enhanced subjects, were ever outside their vessels, nor taken off their umbilicals!

'The main subject of the infusion had never taken her first step nor crawled, for that matter! She was in the final stages of an extremely delicate, totally uncertain experiment with far greater odds of failure than success. We don't even know if she could see, hear, speak or function with any degree of normality.

'Even assuming that one of them could have survived the initial explosion, how could she have escaped her sealed tank? How could she have found her way out of the facility? And done so in the few seconds remaining before the entire laboratory was vaporized? There were no close exits to the bottom level. There wasn't enough time!'

'General,' Lazzlo responded calmly, 'we know from eye-witnesses in patrol details outside the perimeter fence that there was a delayed explosion after the initial impact. Technicians on the bottom level, if not immediately overcome by toxic fumes, may have had enough time to release one of the test subjects. Wouldn't a scientist's instincts have been to rescue the end product of five years of development and millions of shekels of investment?

'Perhaps this technician dragged the subject outside through a rupture in the wall of the structure, then returned to help others, only to die in the final explosion. Bedouins investigating the accident could later have come across the survivor, just as the Japanese astronomers claim.'

Despite himself, Goene was taken aback by this scenario. 'Surely you aren't suggesting that this Messiah character is the infusion subject?'

'No,' Lazzlo answered, and then quickly countered, 'Although it isn't outside the realm of possibility. No one living knows what the test subjects looked like. As you are well aware, this was a highly classified project. Few researchers at the institute even knew the true nature of the operation. And those who did weren't allowed to take work home with them. Whatever records there were, they were all destroyed in the explosion.'

Mosha Zerim, who, intentionally, had never had more than a rudimentary connection with the project, was growing increasingly nervous. 'Alleza, you and Ben were at the facility several times to review operations. Didn't you examine the subjects?'

Goene shrugged. 'All of them were wearing cranial monitors whenever I toured the facility.'

Zerim was aghast. 'You mean we have no mechanism for identifying a subject, if indeed one of them has survived?'

'Yes, there's a way.' Benjamin Roth finally rejoined the conversation.

'At least there's a way to identify the two enhanced subjects, and they're the only ones who could expose the operation, anyway. If you'll recall, there were originally four test subject embryos. Three of them had the Leveque biocircuitry chips implanted in their brains during their fifth month of development. The remaining foetus was left unaltered to serve as a control. One died as a result of the implant procedure, the rest survived, at least until the attack on the installation.

'To identify an enhanced subject, all that's necessary is to X-ray or CAT-scan the cranium. The enhanced subjects were the only ones carrying Leveque biomicrochips, which would easily show up on X-ray. The one control subject had no such devices and would appear normal and pose no threat to us.'

Lazzlo, staring reflectively at the table through all this, turned towards Goene and Roth. 'Both of you saw at least the bodies of the subjects. You must have some idea of their apparent height, weight, shape.'

'They were all encased in tanks of dark-coloured fluid,' Goene explained, 'on their sides, their limbs doubled up. It would be impossible to estimate with any accuracy.'

'Then answer me this,' Lazzlo said, 'is there anything you saw in those vessels to rule out the possibility that this New Messiah *might* be a test subject?'

Goene wasn't ready to concede his position. 'Lazzlo, you saw the broadcast. The woman on that stage spoke a dozen foreign languages. Fluently. With perfect accent. How could someone born yesterday, quite literally, accomplish such a feat?'

Lazzlo levelled his gaze at Goene and replied in an even voice. 'Easily. If the infusion process was successful.'

There was a dead stillness, and then Zerim folded his hands, placed them on the table in front of him and bowed his head. 'Alleza. Ben. Did either of you see anything in those containment vessels that would rule out the possibility that this Messiah might be one of the test subjects?'

Goene looked long and hard at David Lazzlo. 'No,' he said softly.

And Benjamin Roth concurred.

'Then we have no choice,' Zerim declared. 'As soon as it can be arranged, I want this Messiah person located and discreetly transported to Hadassah Hospital in Jerusalem for immediate X-ray. Alleza, you take charge of this operation and make damn sure it's carried out in absolute secrecy. Obviously, with all the media attention and publicity this woman is receiving, you must take great pains to acquire her quietly. If you find she's one of the enhanced subjects, you will hold her in confinement until further directions from Defence Minister Tamin.'

A tired Mosha Zerim pushed back his chair and rose. The others rose with him.

'You can rely on me,' Goene answered.

Zerim took some relief in knowing that there was no more efficient or capable a soldier.

'One more thing, Mosha.' Benjamin Roth raised a last, disturbing issue. 'If this Messiah does prove to be one of our enhanced subjects, she carries the only Leveque neurochips in existence. The technology is priceless, to say the least. Recovering the microchips would help offset some of the staggering toll we're suffering from the loss of the institute.'

Zerim acknowledged the point and they filed out of the room.

The last to leave, Lazzlo placed his hand on the shoulder of Benjamin Roth in front of him and the older officer turned. 'Tell me, Benjamin,' he asked, 'can these microchips be removed without seriously injuring or killing their host?'

Roth stared into the earnest eyes of his subordinate. 'I don't know, David.' His face grew troubled. 'I honestly don't know.'

34

WNN headquarters, Jerusalem, Israel,
9.46 A.M., Tuesday, 11 January 2000

A disgruntled former Samaritan underling named Thomas Brannan contacted Feldman's office with privileged information to offer. A good piece of intelligence these days would quickly go to the highest bidder, and WNN had cultivated a reputation for top dollar, promptly paid. But surprisingly, in this instance, the ill-at-ease, dishevelled Samaritan that Feldman confronted wasn't interested in money. This was a moral issue with him.

'It's all a sham, Mr Feldman,' the anguished man cried. 'The Messiah's gone.'

Feldman was stunned.

'She's been gone since the Friday after her sermon. They had Her locked in a room, kept away from everyone. No windows, always guarded. And then they go in Friday morning to give Her breakfast and She's disappeared. Not a trace. They don't know how She got out. The security camera shows She didn't come through the door. I think She was broken-hearted at all the greed and evil, Mr Feldman. I think She just gave up on all of us and went back to heaven.'

'Tell me, Mr Brannan,' Feldman said, 'did you spend any time with the Messiah? Talk to her? Get to know her at all? What's she like?'

The man looked up and his eyes seemed to enter another world. 'Oh, Mr Feldman, She was wonderful. Incredible. No two ways about it, She was *divine. Heavenly!* But no, I didn't get to talk to Her or even see Her much – mostly just in passin' as they took Her here and there. But She was so *beautiful.* Her skin just *glowed.* Mostly though, it was what She did when She looked at you!

'This one time, the most special one, I really got close to Her. She was bein' brought down the hall to the van for Her Sermon at the Mount, and I saw Her comin' and I knelt down and She looked over at me as She passed by, and She looked *right through me,* Mr Feldman. Her eyes bore straight into my heart and She laid open my soul, wide and naked and defenceless. And in that split second, She purged me clean, I swear to God. I was tremblin' and weak and scared and full of bliss, all at the same time.

'After She disappeared, they tried to cover things up. They said not to tell anyone. That She'd come back. That She'd told Reverend Fischer to carry on for Her. And then they changed that story and said She was still here, but invisible, and only the Reverend was worthy enough to see Her. I'm just so afraid I won't see Her again. I swear, I'd soon die to be with Her if She's gone back to heaven. I'd soon *die*!'

'Mr Brannan, what can you tell me about the Messiah video that was taped the night of the earthquake? Were you there? Is it genuine?'

'Yes, sir, I was there. But I didn't see who took the video, and I didn't even see the Messiah. I was back in the crowd under an awning just tryin' to survive the storm, you know? But I seen the video, and it looks exactly like what was goin' on there. And I can tell you, I was standin' on those old temple steps earlier in the day with my friends, and there was no crack in the ground then. I felt the earthquake and I felt the lightning. The next day when I come back, there's the crack runnin' from the well to the top of the steps. It was real, all right.'

'Where was Reverend Fischer when all this was going on?'

'The Reverend Fischer wasn't even in Bethlehem at the time, Mr Feldman. He was stayin' in a hotel suite in Jerusalem, watchin' you on TV. 'Cause the phone lines were out, they had to come up and get him the next day to tell him what was goin' on. That's when the video turned up and Reverend Fischer moved his things down to the Star Hotel.'

'So he knew about the video before we aired it?'

'Oh yes. We all saw it, but the Reverend kept control of it.'

'Do you have any idea where WNN's copy came from?'

'No, sir.'

'Wasn't the Reverend upset when he saw our bootleg copy?'

'I really don't know. Nothin' much was ever said about it, as I recall.'

Feldman had video statements taken and Thomas Brannan departed with what appeared to be a somewhat lighter heart. Feldman felt a little stirring in his heart, as well. Perhaps when these new revelations hit the air, the Reverend Fischer might finally be provoked into a long-overdue interview.

35

WNN headquarters, Jerusalem, Israel,
1.17 P.M., Thursday, 13 January 2000

Once Feldman broke his story on the Messiah's escape from the
Samaritans, reports of Messiah sightings began popping up all over
Israel. In Nazareth at a synagogue. In Cana at a wedding. On the Sea
of Galilee – walking on the water, to be sure. Sometimes appearing in
more than one location at the same time. It was said that the Messiah
would surface somewhere, preach to a small gathering until it became
a large gathering, and then simply disappear again. Only to resurface
somewhere else.

And everywhere, miracles. Lots of miracles. Sight restored, lameness
cured, sins forgiven. Feldman put little stock in any of this. Most of the
incidents he'd investigated proved considerably less than credible.

'Hey, Hunter, maybe she could give you a brain,' Cissy sneered
across the table during the morning meeting.

Hunter continued the banter. 'Maybe the Messiah would like to
join Feldman's fan club!'

This was a sore subject with Feldman. Much to Hunter's amusement,
Feldman had begun to collect a sizeable following. Each day there were
loyal groupies – teenage girls, mostly – who hung out at the gates of
WNN headquarters, waiting to catch a glimpse of their furtive hero.
And whenever Feldman was out on interviews, a gathering of fans was
sure to ensue. Of late, he'd taken to wearing a hat and sunglasses.

Apart from the sideshow, however, there was an aspect to many
of these alleged messianic appearances which had been piquing his
curiosity. In addition to a handful of amateur photographs of the
Messiah, which were blurred and suspect for the most part, there
were other, more telling indications from purported witnesses that
something was going on. Always it was in their portrayal of the

Messiah's intense, sapphirine eyes. Or, more precisely, her 'look'. A riveting, penetrating, emotionally unsettling gaze that transfixed the recipient. Feldman knew that look first hand, which for him at least lent a certain amount of authenticity to the strange tales he was hearing.

36

National Ministry of the Universal Kingdom, Dallas, Texas, *9.30 A.M., Friday, 14 January 2000*

As his secretary brought him the morning mail, the Right Reverend Solomon T. Brady looked like a man about to have a stroke. His normally red face was more flushed than usual, and puffy. In just the last week, he'd gained back the twelve pounds he was so proud to have lost, and the cameras of his televangelical ministry made him look even heavier.

The Reverend stared at the bundle for a while and then absentmindedly flipped through the stack. This last week had been devastating, not just in the fact that contributions had slowed and he was having to cut back his TV ministries from eight hours to two per month, but also because, for the first time in the twenty-two-year history of his Church of the Universal Kingdom, he'd lost his way. He simply hadn't a clue about how to counter this vexing millenarian infection.

The Reverend was momentarily distracted from his depression by the insignia of the Church of Jesus Christ of Latter-day Saints appearing on an envelope. It was addressed to his attention from the Mormon Temple of Salt Lake City, Utah. Inside he found a form letter reading:

Dear Religious Leader:
As a duly authorized official of a nationally recognized religious

organization, your presence is respectfully requested at the First Convocation of Interdenominational Religious Faiths of the Third Millennium, to be held in Salt Lake City, Utah, at the Mormon Tabernacle Convention Centre, Friday, Saturday and Sunday, February 4, 5, and 6, in the year of our Lord 2000.

The important purpose of this assembly is to convene both national and worldwide religious leadership to address the controversial issues raised by recent occurrences in the Holy Land; events that hold significance for, and directly affect, virtually every religious establishment.

Issues which will be explored include:
- *an evaluation of the authenticity of a new messianic presence*
- *biblical correlations and prophetic fulfilment*
- *the impact of new religious dogma on congregational unity*
- *new potentials for interdenominational collaboration and associations.*

Each attendee is invited to submit, on the forms provided herewith, additional topics for discussion, which will be included on the agenda in the order received.

The letter went on to provide details for registration, accommodation and attendant charges, which struck Reverend Brady as inordinately high at $2,000 per head. Nevertheless, this was the first ray of hope, and perhaps the last opportunity he would have, to find desperately needed answers.

The ability to network with other religious organizations that were likely experiencing similar problems was alone worth the price of admission. The Reverend sent in his application, overnight delivery. The topic he submitted for the agenda: 'What a non-millennialist sect can do in today's unstable religious environment to sustain congregational interest and contributions'.

37

Nordau Towers, Tel Aviv, Israel,
5.50 P.M., Saturday, 15 January 2000

It had to happen eventually. Another network chanced to be in the right place at the right time.

Taking the day off, Feldman had been lying on the couch with Anke cradled in his arms, dozing, the television on, when he was jolted awake by a competing station's news bulletin.

'Captured on videotape a short while ago by a UBN news crew, an actual appearance by the reclusive New Messiah. We bring you this report now, live from the United Broadcasting Network's exclusive Messiah News Centre!'

Feldman clicked to full alert.

The UBN news crew had managed to catch on tape the final few minutes of what appeared to be a spontaneous visit by the Messiah to an Arab-section, lower-school playground in Jerusalem. The video opened showing the Messiah sitting on a low stone wall, next to an elderly schoolmarm in a chador. This time there was no question of authenticity. This *was* the Messiah, and she looked absolutely radiant in the afternoon sunlight.

Gathered about her, laughing and climbing in her lap, was a small group of young children, with others of like age sitting about singing and talking to her. A crowd was beginning to collect and the newsmen were shouting questions to her, but she was ignoring them. The camera zoomed in, angling for close-ups, getting jostled in the process by excited onlookers.

The Messiah, apparently disturbed by the encroachment, finally turned her attention to the cameraman, and in a clear voice intoned in perfect English: 'Why do you pursue me?' She extended a graceful hand towards the aged woman next to her: 'Here is a story better told – that of our vulnerable elders,' and she gestured to the children around her, 'and our helpless little ones.

'For I say to you: whosoever defiles the innocence of the young, whosoever preys upon the weakness of the elderly, so shall they be banished to the eternal abysses. Go, and send forth *this* word!'

Her dark eyes flashed, her eyebrows arched in stern warning. But a child pulled at a fold of her robe to get her attention, and glancing down, she became distracted and melted into a warm glow.

There was a murmur of approval from the crowd in response to her words, but the Messiah did not linger. She slid her legs over the opposite side of the wall, displacing from her lap the clinging children who protested vigorously. As she did so, the crowd behind the wall separated in front of her like the parting of a sea, and closed protectively behind her as she disappeared into it.

Feldman smiled. Perhaps time would prove this curious episode to be nothing more than the self-righteous, abstruse ravings of another delusional zealot. But for now at least, the resolute little prophetess was only adding more lustre to her image.

38

The streets of Jerusalem, Israel,
the third week of January 2000

Apparently, a French documentary film crew was next to confront the feisty young Messiah. They claimed to have stumbled across her as she was preaching to a small group of millenarian pilgrims at Wadi El Joz, Jerusalem, an ancient wellspring which had recently gone dry owing to the drought.

Unfortunately, the film in their cameras proved disastrously overexposed. The only hard evidence the Frenchmen could supply for their encounter was the surviving audio track. A French network aired the report, consisting of artist's renderings accompanied by a narrator and the audio.

According to the account, after the film crew had spotted the Messiah, they stealthily circled the gathering to come up behind her. One bold cameraman, searching for the best available vantage point, climbed up and seated himself, cross-legged, in the basin of the dry wellspring itself, only a few feet behind the unsuspecting prophetess. Switching on his camera, he grinned and called out brazenly to her in French, 'Hey, my pretty little Messiah, dance for the camera! Show us a little leg, yes?'

His fellow crewmates had snickered at this, but the Messiah apparently did not find his antics so amusing. She stopped her instruction, turned slowly, and folded her arms across her chest, stifling his leer with her penetrating gaze.

'I am the vessel which bears drink for the parched soul,' she responded sharply, in French, 'yet you would discard the water for the cup!'

Shaking off the effects of her accusing eyes, the cameraman tried to save face with his comrades. 'I am a red-blooded man!' he exclaimed. 'I like women. What is wrong with that?' He resurrected his grin.

She walked past him, studying him. 'You are like the man adrift at sea who quenches his thirst with salt water. At first, his body appears satisfied, but soon the thirst returns. And each time it comes, it comes sooner and stronger than before. Each swallow only leads to another, driving him to madness!'

What was relayed next was subject to a great deal of professional scepticism. The report claimed that, as the prophetess turned to leave, the spring spontaneously gushed back to life, dousing the cameraman's lap and *amour* with icy water. Again, there was no proof for this anecdote. It was true, however, that the wellspring was supplying clean, sweet water once again. And having drunk from the spring, the entire French crew, including a now subdued cameraman, attested to a dramatic spiritual and physical rejuvenation.

In yet another of these fleeting encounters, a female newswoman for an Atlanta, Georgia, TV station caught on video an enlightening new finding for the public record. The reporter was in a second-storey Jerusalem hotel room overlooking Salah Ed-din Square when she noticed the fast-paced Messiah leading a crowd through the street below. Leaning out of a window with her video camera in time to intercept the prophetess, the reporter called down frantically, 'Who are you? We don't even know your name. Do you have a name?'

Surrounded by a large, flowing, ever-growing entourage, the young Messiah paused, turned and shielded her eyes with her hand in the morning sun. 'Yes,' she said, almost hesitantly, dropping her hand after locating the reporter, 'I have a name. The name God has chosen for me is Jeza. My name is Jeza.' She turned and was gone again.

There was no universal agreement on the correct spelling of her name, as she didn't bother to clarify it. Hereafter it was often spelled 'Jeeza', 'Jeze', 'Jesa', or 'Gisa'. But there was no disagreement on the pronunciation. It was 'JEE-zuh'.

The next documented appearance was recorded by a London *Times* newspaper journalist. He happened to be strolling near the Hurva synagogue in Jerusalem's Old City Jewish quarter when a small crowd began gathering at the entrance to the temple. On a hunch, the journalist ran around to the back of the building and was able to enter through a door left unbolted.

He then quietly made his way to the congregational area of the synagogue where he spied the Messiah sitting cross-legged on the floor, speaking enthusiastically with ten elder rabbis. By now, hundreds of people were crowding at the windows outside for a glimpse.

Before being detected and ejected, the journalist was able to shorthand what became known as the first of Jeza's New Messianic Allegories, the complete text of which ran in the next edition of the *Times*. Later editions would appear in this form:

THE PARABLE OF THE INVENTORS' SONS

When Jeza had come into the temple, the chief rabbis recognized Her and welcomed Her saying, 'For what purpose do you honour us with your visit?' And She spoke scripture with them, impressing all with Her breadth and knowledge. Then they asked of Her, 'Are you truly the Chosen One, the New Messiah?' And She answered them saying, 'I am the New Messenger. I am the clarity amongst the din.'

'Then teach us,' they said, 'and we will listen.' So She taught them, saying:

'There were two inventors who each had a young son. Now each inventor created a great, complex machine that performed its tasks well and made the inventors much money.

'In time, the sons grew to manhood and both inventors retired, turning their machines over to their sons, saying, "Go now, use your machine properly and it will earn you your living."

'So the sons took their fathers' inventions and put them to work. And for a while, the machines performed as they should, earning each son his living. But then there came a time when the parts wore and failed, and the great machines would no longer function.

'So the first son went to his father and said, "Alas, the great machine is broken and my customers are angry. You must fix it or I will lose everything." So the father took up his tools and went out to fix the machine.

'The second son also went to seek his father's help, but his father refused him, saying, "You are a man now and this is your responsibility." So the second son, with great worry, went back and laboured on his machine alone, losing much business, but with time, restoring it to use.

'Yet, the first son never learned to repair his machine, and when the time came that his father died, the machine fell again into disrepair and the first son lost everything.

'But the second son taught himself how to keep his machine functioning. And, over time, he saw to make improvements that caused the machine to perform better than it had even for his father.

'Now I ask of you, which of these was the better father to the son? The one who generously helped? Or the father who made his son discover for himself the workings of the great machine?'

And the rabbis answered Her, 'Why, the second father who made his son discover the workings of the great machine.'

And Jeza said to them, 'So, too, must you no longer look only to the Father, but go forth and learn the functions of His Great Machine – and improve upon it.' (Apotheosis 12:5–16)

39

Palace of the Sanctum Officium, headquarters of
the Congregation for the Doctrine of the Faith of the
Holy Roman Catholic Church, Vatican City, Rome, Italy,
2.00 P.M., Friday, 21 January 2000

Thirty cardinals rose from their armchairs around the ornate long
table as Nicholas VI entered the room. The Pontiff deposited a sheaf
of documents before him, removed his spectacles from their case,
fitted them across his nose and took his place at the head of the table.
'God's blessings upon you,' he greeted them, and they responded in
kind, taking their seats.

On the Pope's immediate left was Antonio di Concerci, prefect of the
Congregation. Di Concerci placed several papers in front of Nicholas,
without comment, and then returned to examining documents of his
own. Nicholas gathered his up and skimmed rapidly through them.

Further down the table and on the opposite side of Cardinal di
Concerci sat Cardinal Alphonse Bongiorno Litti. A little flushed,
a little anxious, Litti turned to the elderly man on his right, but
the cardinal was occupied with his own papers. Litti rotated in
the opposite direction, but that neighbour was also busy reading.
Frustrated, Litti sighed, folded his arms and stared at the whorls in
the dark mahogany tabletop.

Litti had read this document before him numerous times, and his
reaction had never wavered. The report had been hurriedly prepared
at the Pope's request by the Congregation in secret session under the
auspices of di Concerci, sitting prefect. Its ponderous commission:
*A Preliminary Evaluation of the Purported New Messiah, with an
Assessment of the Current and Potential Repercussions of the Millenarian
Movement on the Stability and Welfare of Holy Mother Church and Her
World Congregation.*

The report was vintage di Concerci. Hopelessly dogmatic and closed-minded. To Litti, the final lines betrayed the prefect's mindset:

Given the cursory examination with which this Forum has been charged, it must be concluded at this time that there are no preternatural circumstances surrounding the appearance of an alleged Messiah in Israel. Granted that a number of surprising and perplexing incidents and coincidences have occurred, in each instance a reasonable explanation can be provided referencing natural or man-made causes.

However, we find the issue of unrest within the World Congregation to be very real and pressing, and we recommend an immediate, formal inquiry be conducted to examine these issues in specificity, and to render a vox veritatis *whereby these circumstances can be put in measured perspective for the faithful.*

After discussions with the Congregation, the Pope was to decide whether or not a formal *inquirendum*, an official, secret inquiry of the Holy See, should be undertaken. Such a weighty inquisition would likely result in recommendations for a papal encyclical, or decree, to clarify the Church's position in these consequential matters.

The Congregation for the Doctrine of Faith, the Catholic Church's stern defender of holy orthodoxy, was precisely the organization to undertake this mission. Its reputation and demonstrated abilities for uncovering facts and truths in moral matters could be traced all the way back to the 1500s when it was better known as the Congregation of the Inquisition.

There was little doubt around the great table that an *inquirendum* would, indeed, be authorized. The real issue was how quickly the *inquirendun* could be completed and an encyclical issued to restore order. And, not insignificantly, who would be entrusted with heading this important inquest.

It was Alphonse Litti's ardent hope that Nicholas would bestow the distinguished responsibility on him. To that end, the cardinal had already sent a long private letter to Nicholas listing more than eighteen solid reasons why Litti was the right choice to oversee this sacred undertaking.

But Nicholas, apparently, had little inclination for a prolonged discussion of the issue.

'Brethren,' he began, and the cavernous hall quieted in attention. 'This controversy surrounding a possible Second Coming, or the arrival of a New Messiah, genuine or otherwise, demands a calm and reasoned response from this Holy See as the one source most highly qualified in these matters. All of us recognize that the very existence of the Church is predicated upon the inevitable return of our Saviour. It is an eventuality we have been anticipating for two millennia. But sadly, as these recent occurrences have made evident, we seem surprised and ill prepared to authenticate it.

'While the Church traditionally moves slowly and cautiously in examining serious theological concerns such as these, unfortunately the recent events in the Holy Land require immediate and decisive response from this chair. I have prayed fervently over the past days for guidance and wisdom in these proceedings. I believe my prayers have been answered and I am now decided how we shall move forward.'

Litti inhaled.

'Effective immediately,' Nicholas declared, 'I order this Congregation to initiate an *inquirendum*, to be headed by Prefect Cardinal Antonio di Concerci, who has done an admirable job in the completion of this preliminary report.'

There was acclamation and applause from fellow cardinals in the hall, but not from Alphonse Litti, who sat quietly, stunned and crushed.

'Furthermore,' the Pope continued, 'I order that the inquiry receive the complete and uninterrupted attention of the entire Congregation, and that the final draft be completed and submitted for my review four weeks from today, 18 February.'

The hall grew immediately still again. This was an unheard-of deadline in an ecclesiastical domain where such substantive inquiries typically required years to reach their painstaking conclusions.

'I recognize the unreasonableness of the timeframe,' the Pope responded to the silence, 'but we must all recognize the unreasonableness of this crisis.' And in a quieter voice, almost to himself, 'I only pray that four weeks is not too long.'

'It will be done as you order, Holiness,' di Concerci assured him. 'I request your permission to dispatch delegates to the Holy

Land immediately for a first-hand investigation of the circumstances there.'

'Of course, Antonio,' Nicholas granted. 'I authorize you to do
whatever is required to arrive at the truth of this matter as quickly
and completely as possible. If this person, Jeza, is indeed a precursor
to the Second Coming as John the Baptist was to the First, we must
determine it without delay.'

'My fellow cardinals.' Di Concerci rose from his chair to address the
assembly. 'I ask the entire Congregation to remain here in counsel after
our audience with His Holiness. I would wish to make appointments
to chair the respective subcommittees and to establish the structure
for accomplishing our objectives.'

An ashen, depressed Alphonse Litti knew all too well that his
out-of-favour, conflicting voice would not be among the appointees.
He also knew that any window for salvaging his dissenting perspective
was rapidly closing.

Heavily, Litti stood and extended his hand to hold the proceedings
in abeyance. 'If I may,' he began, and the Pope displayed a fleeting look
of annoyance. 'As a means of advancing the progress of this important
inquirendum, I'd like to call to the Congregation's attention the fact
that a convocation of world churches is gathering in the United States
on 4, 5 and 6 February. The expressed purpose of this convention is
to address the very issues we're pursuing here.'

'Begging your forgiveness, Holy Father,' di Concerci broke in impatiently, 'but Cardinal Litti has raised the question of this conference
to me before and I have investigated it. It's being hosted in Salt Lake
City by the Church of Jesus Christ of Latter-day Saints, Mormon,
whose creed, as you know, is profoundly millenarian. The make-up
of the convention,' he added, 'will be predominantly millennialists
and fundamentalists. It hardly raises itself to the level of a world
convocation, and we should not legitimize the proceedings with our
attendance.'

'Holiness' – Litti ignored di Concerci and appealed directly to the
Pope – 'your words were that we should arrive at the truth as quickly
and completely as possible.' He gave di Concerci a pointed, defiant
glance before continuing. 'The prefect has unintentionally overlooked
the fact that the Presbyterian, Lutheran, Unitarian and Jewish faiths,
among others, will each be represented there. Even if there is little

new information to come from this conclave, what harm could it possibly do? The *inquirendum* would at least benefit from knowing the perspectives of these other denominations.'

The Pope shrugged his shoulders deferentially, and to di Concerci said, 'I see no harm in Alphonse attending this conference, Antonio.' Rising from his chair and with a patriarchal smile, he added, 'In any event, perhaps it will keep the two of you out of each other's way for a while!' There was appreciative laughter from the assembly, and the Pope retired, leaving the Congregation to its work.

40

WNN headquarters, Jerusalem, Israel,
4.47 P.M., Friday, 21 January 2000

'Everybody's eating our goddamn lunch,' Bollinger complained hotly to the entire staff at their end-of-week meeting. 'How come every other local TV reporter from Kalamazoo can run into Jeza and we come up empty for two damn weeks? Where the hell *are* you guys?' he shouted to the field teams who sat hangdog and tired. 'And we still don't know a damned thing more about that Negev laboratory than we did three weeks ago. We got *six* crews out here at an unbelievable expense and *nothing* to show for it!

'I want more reconnaissance, more spotters, more cell phone contact going on. And I want you guys to come back with something really big by Monday morning or some of you are going back where you came from. Do I make myself clear?'

After the dispiriting staff meeting, it was an especially pleasant diversion for Feldman to receive a phone call from Anke, who normally wouldn't disturb him at the office. It had been four long days since he'd seen her, and he was not looking forward to telling her he'd be working this weekend.

'Jon, I'm sorry to bother you at the office.'

'Not a bother. It's good to hear a friendly voice. How are you?'

'Actually, I'm doing very well – for the both of us. I've found you a contact with the Negev Research Institute. And it's a good one.'

Feldman bolted forward in his chair, ecstatic. 'You're kidding! I can't believe it! You don't know how badly we need a break like this! Who is it?'

'Not now. Come down tonight after work for a nice home-cooked dinner and I'll tell you all about it. We've got a meeting set up for tomorrow morning. Just you and me, and no cameras. And for God's sake, don't tell anyone. There's apparently a lot more to this than any of us realize!'

The drive to Tel Aviv was a short fifty minutes, and an eager Feldman arrived well before dark. Despite his persistence, however, Anke refused to discuss business until after dinner. They dined on the balcony in the refreshing salt breeze, enjoying steamed crabs and rock lobster that Anke had prepared to perfection. Later, snuggling together in a love-seat, a luxury liner plying the twilight sea before them, Feldman took his arm from around her, grasped her smooth brown shoulders and turned her towards him.

'All right now,' he commanded with transparent sternness, 'I've been frustrated long enough. You tell me immediately about this source of yours or I'm turning you over my knee!'

She laughed at the impatience in his eyes. 'Believe me, Jon, this is worth waiting for. I just wanted you to relax a little first.' Her face glowing with excitement, she grasped his hands in hers. 'When I got back to campus for classes last week I picked up a copy of the university paper to catch up on what had happened over the winter break. I was shocked and upset to read an article and obituary on Dr Jozef Leveque, who was a genetics biology professor at the university. I knew him and his wife, Anne, very well. Both of them being from France, like me, we had much in common.

'The article was peculiar in that it didn't give a cause of death, a date or anything. Well, I didn't make the connection at the time, but later I phoned Anne Leveque to offer my condolences. We talked for a while, and she finally confided in me that her husband had died in the explosion at the institute. She was terribly shattered over it, of course, poor thing.

'I tried to get Mrs Leveque to open up a bit, but she seemed very nervous, although I could tell she wanted to talk to someone. When I told her about us, who you were and all, she got extremely anxious and made me swear an oath that I wouldn't say anything to you. She made some excuse and hung up. I thought that was the end of it, but then today, she called to say she wanted to meet with you and me tomorrow morning and that it was very important. But only you and me and no cameras or tape recorders. She was calling from a pay-phone because she was afraid her home was bugged.'

Feldman looked off into the distance at the disappearing ocean liner and sighed appreciatively. 'You don't know how timely this is!' He gave her a vigorous hug. 'When do we meet?'

'Seven o'clock, tomorrow morning.'

He feigned a frown of concern. 'Then we'd better get to bed early tonight, wouldn't you say?'

41

Nordau Towers, Tel Aviv, Israel,
7.00 A.M., Saturday, 22 January 2000

Anne Leveque arrived promptly and nervously at the appointed hour. Anke invited her in and introduced her to Feldman, whom she immediately recognized. 'You're as handsome in person as you are on TV,' she complimented him in excellent English, and Feldman smiled graciously.

Mrs Leveque was a sprightly, dignified-looking woman, in her early seventies, Feldman guessed. Nicely dressed, with thick silver hair swept back and secured by a gold clasp. Although she smiled with her lips, her grey eyes and brow were in perpetual worry. Feldman reassured her that she could place her trust in Anke and him.

As if she'd finally resolved her inner conflicts, she stared closely at them for a moment, reached over to take their hands in hers, and whispered softly, 'You make such a wonderful couple. Jozef and I were much like you many years ago.'

Feldman glanced over at Anke, who was sitting close to him with large tears in her eyes.

Mrs Leveque attempted another half-smile. 'Yes, I know I can trust you both and I will do what I have to do.' She grew serious again and stared intently at Feldman. 'Jon, I want you to know that I love Israel dearly and would never do anything to harm it. What I am about to tell you is not a betrayal of Israel. It concerns a secret IDF operation unknown even to the Prime Minister and the Knesset. And that makes my situation all the more serious because the operation is outside the law.'

She could no longer look Feldman in the eye. 'I am ashamed to admit to you that I and my late husband played a major part in all of this.'

Feldman frowned and reclined slightly in his chair.

'As you know,' the woman proceeded, 'the IDF functions under the control of Defence Minister Shaul Tamin, who is directly involved in this operation. Tamin is a ruthless man, and what I say here will place me at great risk. Nevertheless, for the safety – and possibly the life – of someone . . . very important to me, I must do this. I must expose something I fervently believe is against all the laws of God and nature.

'But I must have your solemn oath that certain aspects of this story, which I will designate to you, will be held in the strictest confidence.'

They both solemnly agreed.

This seemed to satisfy Mrs Leveque and she settled into the couch.

'It's an involved story and I should start from the beginning.'

'Do you object to my taking notes?' Feldman asked.

'Not so long as you don't record names or those details that I will indicate as sensitive.'

Mrs Leveque opened her large saddle purse next to her chair and withdrew a worn, cloth-bound album. 'Because you will not believe what I am about to tell you, when I am finished I will share with you my husband's diary, which will substantiate everything. You understand, however, I cannot let you borrow it. It is all I have left of these last strange years with Jozef.'

Feldman nodded.

Mrs Leveque held the diary in both hands, as if drawing strength from it.

'First,' she began, 'let me explain to you that I met my husband Jozef at the University of Cologne in 1952 where we were both graduate students in biology. We fell in love, and after completing our degrees, Jozef received a professorship at the University of Tel Aviv. We married against my parents' objections – I'm a devout Catholic and Jozef is Jewish – and we moved here in the summer of 1954.'

Feldman noted with interest that, unlike his parents, the Leveques seemed to have reconciled their disparate religious persuasions.

'Jozef quickly earned a research position at the university and I was also offered a biology professorship there. Because of our careers, we decided to forgo having children. Our daughter, Marie, who was born in 1968, was a wonderful accident. It wasn't until we had her that we realized how much we'd been missing in our lives. Marie was the most loving, intelligent and happy child a parent could ever wish for. She completed perfectly the love Jozef and I shared.

'But then, in the early spring of 1992, my only child, my beautiful, bright, twenty-four-year-old Marie, was nearly killed in a senseless, brutal act of terrorism by the Hezbollah near the Western Wall in Jerusalem. My Marie was never a political person. She was kind, gentle, caring. Simply out on an innocent excursion in the wrong place at the wrong time.

'A car bomb exploded. A piece of shrapnel struck Marie in the back of the head—'

Feldman felt his stomach knot.

Mrs Leveque's eyes were misting, but she kept her composure. 'Today, my beautiful Marie lies as she has for eight years. In a coma, on artificial sustenance, in a special medical room at my home.'

She exhaled deeply before continuing. 'Marie was Jozef's greatest joy. He lavished his love on her and this senseless tragedy was devastating to him. But rather than let it destroy him, and rather than accept it as the will of God, he considered it a challenge. He resolved to conquer it. That was his nature.

'At first, Jozef felt he could possibly restore Marie – and now I am entering a subject that must remain proprietary.'

Feldman dutifully put down his pen and pad.

'Jozef's field of research at the university was bio-electronic circuitry, a hybrid field of science pursuing ways to integrate nerve tissues with microchip circuitry. His research team had developed a type of microchip on which nerve tissue would grow and mesh, creating artificial nerve pathways.

'Jozef's objective was to design, for lack of a better term, nervous system patches. These patches would be used to help restore motor function in cases of paralysis, such as in severe spinal column trauma. The idea was to insert the patches into damaged pathways to reconnect severed or damaged nerves.

'By activating individual, microscopic areas of the chip, the theory was, you could turn on or turn off various, random nerve pathways through the chip. Through trial and error, you would finally locate all the correct connections to unite the proper brain impulses with the proper muscles to make the limbs function normally again. It was brilliant and very promising research.

'But, as advanced as Jozef's work was, Marie's injuries proved far too extensive to benefit. There was no hope of restoring her faculties, even if she could be awakened from the coma, which was unlikely.'

She now allowed Feldman to resume his note-taking.

'Prior to Marie's accident,' she continued, 'a colleague and great friend of many years, Dr Giyam Karmi, had offered Jozef a department directorship at the Israeli Negev Research Institute to conduct advanced genetic studies on livestock. For reasons that only became clear to me later, Jozef felt this position would allow him access to specialized equipment and technologies that might be of some help to Marie. So, while maintaining his fellowship and research at the university, in the fall of 1994 Jozef took the position at the institute and began working closely with Dr Karmi.

'In merging their different fields of expertise, along with that of other brilliant scientists at the institute, Jozef and Giyam developed a number of ingenious processes for accelerating bovine growth.'

'Super-cattle?' Feldman suggested.

'No, not super-cattle. Not larger or stronger, necessarily. Just faster-growing. Much faster-growing. Reaching optimum size and weight far more efficiently and cost-effectively than with conventional animal husbandry. Their work was stunning. Light-years ahead of anyone else. You see, the cattle weren't raised in any way similar to the standard methods. No pens. No food lots. They were gestated.'

'Gestated?' Feldman questioned. 'Like incubating chicken eggs?'

'Well, no. They were maturated in artificial wombs.'

Feldman and Anke exchanged questioning glances.

'The process involved surgically removing the embryos from the host mother and transplanting them individually into special nurturing vessels, complete with artificial amniotic fluids and placental systems.

'The vessels were managed by a complex network of computers that would automatically monitor the developing foetuses and administer precise dosages of nutrients, vitamins, proteins and hormones, including specialized bovine and foetal growth hormones, stimulants to promote healthy, mature muscle development, and other compounds to force rapid growth. Unbelievably rapid growth.

'The maturing cattle embryos were kept tranquillized throughout the process and could be induced to develop to optimum adult size in less than five months.'

'Five months!' Feldman exclaimed. 'You mean two months in the mother's womb and five months in the incubator?'

'No,' she replied, with some pride in her voice. 'I mean a *total* of five months' gestation, including both natural and artificial womb. Jozef and his associates' process exploited the accelerated growth that all foetuses typically undergo during their final month of development. And magnified it sevenfold.'

'Holy cow!' Feldman blurted out, despite himself.

For the first time, Anne Leveque showed a full and genuine smile. 'Yes. A cow that could be raised entirely to adulthood in a virtually automated, efficient, completely monitored and controlled environment. Free of injury and infectious disease.

'With a little time and perfecting, Jozef and Giyam could have turned their process into a highly cost-effective operation. An ideal means for providing this country of limited pastureland with high-quality, wholesome, lean beef, at dramatically reduced production costs.'

'What happened?' Anke asked.

Mrs Leveque's face faded back into the familiar, anguished mask.

'I could never have imagined that Jozef had an ulterior motive for the relentless passion he poured into his work. To him, this great achievement was simply a means to restore our beloved Marie to us.'

'I don't understand,' Feldman interjected. 'If Marie's condition was irreversible, I don't see how this artificial gestation system, as miraculous as it sounds, would be applicable.'

'And now we come to the damnation of it all.' Mrs Leveque spoke this as if releasing a terrible burden. 'Jozef's intent wasn't to cure Marie. It was to *re-create* her!'

Feldman and Anke looked flabbergasted.

Mrs Leveque paused for a moment, stared down at her tightly clasped hands, and then continued.

'You are familiar with some of the recent experiments that have resulted in the successful cloning of higher-level mammals and primates?'

The couple nodded their heads.

'Well' – she looked up, the pride readily apparent in her eyes – 'Jozef eclipsed all of these remarkable accomplishments – and by more than a full year, I might add. His methods, however, were quite different. He utilized a procedure he developed called polar body fertilization.'

Feldman wrinkled his forehead in puzzlement.

'Let me explain. If you've ever taken a biology course, you may recall that during the early stages of egg formation in the human female, the immature ovum cell undergoes a change known as diploidy. That is, it doubles from forty-six chromosomes to ninety-two. Next, the egg cell undergoes haploid division. That is, it splits into two cells of forty-six chromosomes each. Finally, in a process called meiosis, it divides for the last time into four cells of twenty-three chromosomes each, all contained within one common membrane.

'Two of these four cells are larger, and one of them will win out over the other cells and eventually become a mature egg. The two smaller cells are known as polar bodies. These smaller cells also contain twenty-three chromosomes but very little cytoplasm – the substance that surrounds the nucleus and makes up the bulk of a cell.

'Without the cytoplasm, these polar body cells are quite similar in composition to male sperm cells. Under the right conditions, it is possible to reunite the polar body with the matured egg cell, producing a complete, fertilized egg.

'It's a process known as polar body fertilization, and the resulting offspring, if the pregnancy goes to term, would be female, and always identical to its mother. That's to be expected, because obviously the baby will possess all the chromosomes, exactly the same chromosomes, as its mother. A carbon copy.

'Jozef's strategy was to perform a polar body fertilization procedure with Marie's ova, without my knowledge, because he knew I would never agree to such a thing. On certain days when I was teaching at the university, Jozef would dismiss Marie's nurse to conduct his operations. He extracted numerous ova from Marie, separated out the polar bodies at the lab, and performed *in vitro* polar body fertilizations. Subsequently, in December of 1995, Jozef implanted numerous fertilized ova back into Marie's womb, four of which ultimately developed into viable foetuses. Later, he removed all the embryos in a Caesarean section and secretly installed them in special gestation vessels at the Negev Institute.

'Jozef attempted to explain away Marie's incision as an emergency appendectomy. But I saw through him and he finally opened up to me with the entire story. To my eternal shame, I must admit to you that, after my initial shock and disbelief, I, too, was lured into his madness.

'The thought of having my Marie back, of being able to look into her eyes, to hear her laugh, to hold her close to me, normal, healthy, happy again – my angel child – it was too much for me to resist! And I could not help but support Jozef in his plans. Although I must also admit to you that I lived in constant fear of God's retribution, which I feel is now coming to pass.'

'Excuse me, Anne,' Anke interrupted, 'but how could the same hormones and artificial gestation methods developed for cattle be used on human embryos? And wouldn't the laboratory personnel detect the difference between human and bovine foetuses?'

'Jozef had all that figured out, Anke. For his special vessels, he altered the endocrinology, changed the growth hormones from bovine to human, adjusted the nutrients, proteins and medicine contents accordingly. He substituted new computer programs modified specifically for human subjects.

'With his authority as a director of the institute, he was able to restrict access to the vessels. We knew we'd have to be extremely calculating to gestate even one of our developing daughters – or granddaughters perhaps – to adulthood without detection. But we were willing to take that chance.'

Feldman stopped her again. 'Did I understand you correctly – your husband used growth hormones and intended to artificially gestate your daughter's foetuses all the way to adulthood?'

'Correct.'

'But why? Why not simply remove the healthiest baby at the equivalent of nine months and raise her normally?'

'We were prepared to do that, if necessary, but we faced a problem that even Jozef's resourcefulness couldn't solve: time.

'I was thirty-seven years old and Jozef a year older when we had Marie in 1968. We were sixty-two when she was injured and sixty-six by the time Jozef introduced Marie's embryos into the gestation vessels. Jozef was not in the best of health. We were simply too old. There was not time enough left for us to raise a child safely to adulthood in the conventional manner.'

'But I should think,' Feldman persisted, 'you'd be faced with raising an infant in an adult's body.'

'That brings us to the next, most complicated aspect of Jozef's strategy. And here, we enter again into proprietary research areas that must be kept in confidence.'

Feldman set aside his pen and pad once more.

'This is where Jozef drew upon his greatest expertise. Not only did he wish to accelerate Marie's physical growth, he wanted to do the same for her mind.

'The idea and mechanism for doing this came to Jozef several years earlier from a series of experiments at the university. As I mentioned before, Jozef had been working with a team of researchers developing biomicrochip circuitry, a type of artificial bridge to carry nerve impulses across severed areas of the central nervous system, helping to restore limb movement in the treatment of paralysis.

'Independently, he'd also conducted tests on some alternative applications of this neurochip technology. Instead of neuromuscular cells, he focused on brain tissue, which is also a form of nerve tissue. However, he knew that regular brain cells – unlike nerve cells – would not grow on the artificial chip surface because, after birth, brain cells soon lose their ability to multiply.

'So, Jozef began experimenting with foetal subjects. Sheep. And the receptivity of foetal brain tissue proved to be even better than with neuromuscular applications. By implanting the chip early during foetal development, Jozef found that the brain cells would readily grow on the surface and integrate with its circuitry.

'More interestingly, he found that the neural brain cells would actually adapt to the circuitry and learn how to respond to it. The mesh of neural cells that formed on the chip would act like an informational placenta, allowing input to permeate between the chip and the neural passages of the brain. The brain could incorporate input from the chips as if they were a natural, organic, sensory element of the nervous system.

'All the circuitry of the neural chips was hard-wired. Micro-fine wires from the chip would extend from inside the brain and out of the skull, gather into one strand, exit through a port in the back of the foetus's head, and then out through the mother ewe's abdomen. By sending mild electrical impulses into select circuits in the neurochip, Jozef could artificially stimulate and precisely identify which areas of the brain were connected to each specific circuit.

'Depending on where the chip had been inserted, the electrical impulses could create, for example, isolated muscle responses in the tail, or the right forelimb. Through trial and error, Jozef would eventually learn exactly which nerves controlled what functions.

'Once, in a whimsical effort to demonstrate his results to me, Jozef played a tape of a John Philip Sousa march he dearly loved and made one poor little lamb dance a silly, repetitive step across his mother's womb.' Mrs Leveque hummed a few bars and the familiar tune was immediately recognizable to Feldman, if not by name.

'Wouldn't this type of procedure,' he enquired, 'implanting a foreign object in the brain and shooting electricity through it, damage the brain?'

'Not that we could determine. The brain is very tolerant to intrusive procedures during the foetal stage. Also, the brain functions on electrochemical impulses anyway, you see, as its natural means of transmitting messages. Sheep embryos that were allowed to go to term after the implantation seemed perfectly normal, healthy and active after birth.'

'What became of the experiments?' Anke asked.

'Sadly, it was just at this time that Marie's accident happened and Jozef abruptly discontinued his work. Of course, you can see how he would have hoped to have used this wonderful science to help Marie. But even if it were possible for her adult brain cells to integrate with the neurochip, so much of her brain tissue had been destroyed that, mentally, it was very unlikely she could ever be normal.'

Once more, the emotions welled in Mrs Leveque and her eyes brimmed with tears. 'But, God forgive him, my husband was an incredibly stubborn man, and simply wouldn't believe that Marie was lost to us. He wouldn't allow her to be disconnected from feeding tubes. And he wouldn't give up on his obsession that somehow, with all his resourceful ingenuity and miraculous technologies, he would some day devise a way to reverse our tragedy.

'It was this obsession that drove him to implant the neurochip devices into our daughter embryos. That was his answer to our time limitations. He would use these neurochips to transmit information from computer cybersystems directly into their developing brains. "Intelligence infusion", he called it.

'Jozef would build their knowledge as they gestated. Accelerate their minds to keep pace with the growth of their bodies. This was our best and only hope for preparing our girls in time to cope with a world that, in a manner of speaking, had already victimized them once before.'

'I'm a little fuzzy on how the artificial learning process works,' Feldman confessed.

'Unlike in his sheep experiments earlier,' Mrs Leveque explained, 'Jozef had devised new, far more sophisticated neurochips. When our daughter foetuses grew large enough, Jozef selected three of the four and implanted a dozen neurochips into the audio, visual, spatial and thought-processing centres of each child's brain.

'And in one of the girls, he also implanted a different type of neurochip into a separate, cognitive receptor site. This was a brand-new chip he'd developed. It included a unique microtransmitter-receiver, capable of both receiving and sending communication signals. The device was completely untested and was conceived as almost an afterthought. Jozef's intent was to provide this one special child with a continuing source of communication, input and output, even after birth. Through this chip, her intellectual capacities would be unlimited, powered by the unending source of natural chemical electricity of her brain.

'With the two daughters who had only the regular neurochips, you see, their input wiring would have had to be disconnected during the birth process. After which, their neurochips would no longer function.

'The last remaining embryo we decided to leave completely unaltered so that if anything went wrong with the highly risky procedures, we would still, God willing, be blessed with one healthy adult daughter. Infantile of mind, perhaps, but nevertheless healthy.

'In that way, we allowed the unaltered foetus to serve as a control in the experiment. Except for the intelligence infusion, she went through the entire process with her sisters. She wore the monitoring helmet and electrodes on her scalp – everything. Everything but the neurochips.

'Even though she would have been born infantile in intelligence, her brain would not have been infantile in its physical development. Hers would have been a full-grown, mature, adult brain, with far more capacity to learn than an infant's. Especially with the help of her artificially educated sisters, who could assist her even if Jozef and I were no longer able.

'But almost immediately, there was a problem. Shortly after the implantation procedures, one of our embryos suffered a cerebral haemorrhage. That night the monitors recorded internal bleeding in the occipital centre of her brain, and by morning, we'd lost her. Fortunately, however, our two other girls tolerated the procedures well and all three continued their incredible growth, at about seven times the normal rate.'

'Excuse me, Anne,' Anke broke in, 'but how could Jozef have possibly expected to infuse decades of normal, day-to-day learning through these ... these computer signals. Knowledge isn't just quantitative. It's qualitative. And it's tempered with things like emotion, interpretation and a host of cross-pollinated experiences too complex for me to even imagine.'

'That's true, my dear. We didn't expect the artificial education process to give them comprehensive knowledge about life and the world. There would be many gaps to be filled in after birth. Jozef's diary does a better job of explaining all this than I can, but, unfortunately, the diary contains none of his scientific records. They were all lost in the explosion.

'In any event, the multiple neurochips gave us the ability to synchronize input to many different brain centres at the same time – hearing, vision, thought-processing, and so forth. That way, our daughters could experience things three-dimensionally. Understanding how to crawl and walk, for example. And then we built upon that knowledge, training and instructing them bit by bit to understand speech and language. To identify images and spatial orientations. To grasp mathematics, geometry, and so forth.'

'Like virtual reality?' Feldman decided.

'Except that with virtual reality, you have actual physical stimuli working in concert with tactile, visual and audio cues. With Jozef's system, it all occurs in the mind. Probably much like having a very vivid dream. After birth, all these pre-learned capabilities would allow the girls to relate much more easily and faster to the real world.'

'Did you include religious instruction in your intelligence infusions?' Feldman asked.

'Yes,' the widow replied. 'The Bible, the Talmud and New Testament, of course. But also the books of the other great religions – the Koran, the Torah, the Avesta, and so forth. Realizing that it was religious intolerance behind the attack that injured our first Marie, we felt it important that our new Maries have an understanding of all the major theological doctrines.'

Feldman was about to ask Mrs Leveque another question when she raised a hand in the air to signal a hiatus. She placed the other hand to her heart and closed her eyes.

Alarmed, Feldman and Anke sprang up and moved towards her.

'Anne, are you feeling ill?' Feldman asked.

She waved her hand slightly in the air. 'Just . . . just a little tired, I think.'

'Can I get you some water?' Feldman offered.

'Perhaps a little something to eat,' Anke suggested.

The widow opened her eyes. 'Today has been a little stressful for me,' she said. 'I've never spoken of this to anyone before. Maybe if I could lie down for a moment. But only for a moment. It's important that you hear everything as soon as possible, so the world can know the truth. Before this tragedy grows far worse.'

42

Nordau Towers, Tel Aviv, Israel,
10.00 A.M., Saturday, 22 January 2000

It was an ill-humoured Bollinger taking Feldman's call. 'Where the
hell have you been?' the bureau chief railed. 'We've been looking all
over for you. Why weren't you at this morning's meeting?'

'I'm in Tel Aviv with Anke,' Feldman tried to explain, 'I'm—'

'Dammit, Feldman!' Bollinger exploded. 'You're off relaxing while
the rest of us are busting our humps trying to scare up leads!'

'Calm down, Arnie,' Feldman pleaded, 'it's not what you think. I'm
on to something really big down here. You won't believe it. Something
that just might vault us right back into the spotlight!'

Bollinger's tone switched instantly to one of apologetic curiosity.
'Oh yeah? Seriously? What have you got, Jon?'

'I've got the inside scoop on that Negev installation,' Feldman said.
'And it's mind-boggling.'

'Jesus Christ! No kidding! Wonderful! Well, damn, let's hear it!'

'I don't have the whole story yet, Arnie. I'm still working on it. But
I'll get back to you directly.'

'But—'

'Trust me. Gotta go!'

'But—'

Hanging up, Feldman left the phone off the cradle to ensure
that Mrs Leveque's rest would be undisturbed. But it was unnecessary. At that moment she emerged from the bedroom, looking more composed, to rejoin the reporter and Anke in the
living room.

'Are you sure you feel up to this, Anne?' Feldman asked. 'We can
postpone things to a better time.'

'No, no.' She smiled and patted his hand. 'I'm feeling better. Besides, it's vital that I tell you the rest of this now, for reasons you'll soon understand.'

Settling back in her chair, the widow picked up where she left off.

'For a little more than a year, Jozef was able to continue the gestation process with our daughters, undisturbed, in a restricted section of the Negev Research Institute. Over time, however, he began borrowing more and more heavily on the laboratory's enormous computer capacity. To develop and control the increasingly complicated and delicate infusion process properly, Jozef was forced to pirate increasing amounts of time and memory from the central computer system.

'Ultimately, this began interfering with the service platforms regulating the bovine gestation programme. And that, as a consequence, attracted the curiosity of Giyam Karmi. Giyam naturally wanted to learn what powerful addenda to the bovine procedures Jozef was working on.

'Finally, after Jozef exhausted every possible ruse, things turned ugly and Giyam literally had to force his way into the department. When he discovered the true nature of our work, he became hysterical, sacked Jozef immediately and prepared to shut down our systems.

'In desperation, Jozef appealed to Defence Minister Shaul Tamin. Jozef had met Tamin through the university, having consulted on several defence projects for him at one time. After Marie's accident, however, both Jozef and I had taken a solemn oath renouncing all military research. Jozef refused to assist Tamin further and we had not seen him in years.

'But we had nowhere else to turn. Tamin was the only person in a position to offer us help in time. So, despite our vows, we told the defence minister all about Jozef's infusion process and its military applications. And how Giyam's short-sightedness was placing the technology in immediate jeopardy.'

'Pardon me, Anne,' Feldman interrupted once more, 'but I fail to see any defence applications in Jozef's experiments.'

'As Jozef presented it, there were two major potentials: first, the ability to infuse legions of future Israeli soldiers with enhanced autonomic military training. In an emergency, even civilians, if they carried transmitter-receiver implants, could be automatically summoned up, infused with the latest technical schooling and combat training, and immediately activated.

'Second, and more important, each and every soldier would have instantaneous, silent, two-way communications capabilities, virtually anywhere, any time.'

Feldman nodded, beginning to comprehend.

'Needless to say, this would allow tremendous communications advantages. Instant mass troop mobilization and response to last-second field commands; mental maps by which every soldier could always be apprised of his or her position and direction; the ability for any soldier to immediately identify friend or foe; to instantly transmit exact co-ordinates for artillery telemetry, and so forth.'

She paused and lowered her eyes. 'In order to save our daughters, Jozef and I broke the sacred vow we'd made. We offered our technology to the IDF.'

Her brow creased and she appeared to be on the verge of tears. 'We were so possessed of our dream, Jozef and I, we could no longer pull back from it. We had watched our three beautiful Maries develop from infants into little girls, all in less than a year! We had stared daily through the glass into each of those dark chambers, gazing at our daughters as they slept, unable to hold them or caress them or kiss them.

'Because of their sterile environment, we dared touch them only when absolutely necessary. To perform quick maintenance functions, like replacing their cranial monitors, or shaving the little electrode patches on their scalps. That's the only time we could see their sweet little faces. Not the accustomed, sentimental moments a parent treasures with a child, perhaps, but precious to us, all the same. We loved them so much. We would have sold our souls to keep them.

'But instead, we did something far worse. And for this, God cursed us.

'Shaul Tamin made Jozef a wicked proposal. He said he would allow Jozef to continue the project on one condition only: that Jozef agree to alter the current infusion process for military applications.

'The idea was abhorrent and appalling to us. After the horrible violence our first Marie had been subjected to, it was inconceivable that we should now turn our innocent daughters into soldiers.

'We had to think of something quickly or all would be lost. In desperation, Jozef struck a deal with Tamin. A devil's deal. Jozef knew that the defence minister was most interested in our daughter who carried the special reception-transmission microchip. In order to save the others, he felt he had no choice but to offer her up to Tamin. We would give over this one special child, alone, to military intelligence infusion. And we would remove the other daughter from the infusion process and gestate her separately with her control sister. Tamin agreed to this.'

Anke and Feldman were stunned. No one said anything until Feldman finally broke the silence.

'Wouldn't removing the other daughter from the intelligence transfer halt her mental development?'

'Yes,' Mrs Leveque confirmed. 'At the time Tamin took control of our operation, she was perhaps seven years of age, intellectually. We'd have initiated her birth and that of her unaltered sister right then, except Tamin insisted they continue in the gestation process. That's how he kept Jozef tied to the project.

'Obviously, ending up with adult daughters with arrested mental maturity was a great concern to us, but at least we felt we'd have healthy minds to work with. Minds uncorrupted by Tamin's secret military schemes and conspiracies!

'As much as Jozef and I had been obsessed by our project, Shaul Tamin was possessed. To him, this programme offered Israel an area of tactical superiority no other military force could hope to equal. Not even the United States. He was completely taken by the infusion process and its seemingly limitless applications. He had the IDF assume complete jurisdiction over the operation, under the strictest confidence and security. The bovine experiments were discontinued indefinitely, and from that point forward, the huge Negev Research Institute in its entirety was devoted to his project.'

'What became of Dr Karmi?' Feldman asked.

'Because Tamin did not trust him, Giyam was removed from his directorship. It was a terrible blow to him and, I'm sorry to say, he succumbed to a heart attack not long afterwards.'

Feldman sighed. 'So how close did you come to completion before the explosion?'

'A week,' the widow said. 'Military encoding for our special daughter was to be completed at the end of last month. Birth for her and her two sisters was set for the first day of the new millennium.'

She shook her head forlornly. 'God allowed us to get that close, to come all that way, to be utterly convinced in the viability of our methods. And then, without warning, He brought down His hand upon us in righteous indignation, taking away everything in an instant!'

She paused and looked off into the distance for a moment of introspection, then returned her watery gaze to Feldman. 'But God does work in mysterious ways, and I never lost my faith in Him. Thursday morning, 6 January, in the most mysterious way imaginable, God restored some of what He'd taken from me. In your newscast at the Mount of the Beatitudes, Jon, I saw in the face of the New Messiah an undeniable resemblance to my Marie. Jeza, the lone survivor of the Negev disaster, is my daughter.'

This came as no surprise to Feldman. The moment Mrs Leveque had mentioned shaving small circles in her daughters' hair to attach electrodes, he had made the connection. He'd recalled the little circular welts he'd seen in the Messiah's scalp at her Mount of the Beatitudes appearance. But to have the widow confirm his suspicions still set his adrenalin coursing. Another incredible scoop. And the credit for this one went to Anke. He squeezed her hand.

'You said a "resemblance" to your Marie,' he observed. 'Isn't she identical to your original daughter? I thought they shared the same chromosomes.'

'They do. But even with identical twins, there are always differences. Sometimes very noticeable ones. In this instance, the distinctions were fairly pronounced. In the eyes, voice, demeanour.'

'Then forgive me, Anne, but isn't it just possible that this Jeza is someone who merely resembles your daughter closely?'

'I knew it was my Marie the moment I first saw her, as only a mother can know,' she responded with a calm conviction. The widow then placed on the coffee table the album diary she'd been clutching and opened it to photographs of a beautiful dark-haired young woman.

'These were taken before the accident, when Marie was approximately twenty-one years of age, the same age as her new siblings would be now.'

Feldman and Anke could certainly see the resemblance. The first Marie was most definitely an attractive woman. With features very close to those of Jeza. But the similarity was more familial than identical. The small young woman in the photographs looked more like a sister than an identical twin.

Not to be unkind, Feldman thought to himself, but Marie's eyes were not the least piercing or authoritative. She was a bit heavier, her complexion much darker. It occurred to him that perhaps the Messiah *was* this Marie, *only more so*. All the best qualities of the original Marie, but improved. Taken to perfection. Face, figure, eyes. And Jeza's skin. Absolutely angelic.

'Anne,' Feldman commented after examining the photos, 'I have to admit I see a strong resemblance, but in all honesty, I'd be hard pressed to identify them as identical twins. The eyes, the complexion. There's a questionable difference there.'

Mrs Leveque nodded her head in understanding. 'Beyond the often wide distinctions you will find in natural identical twins,' she explained, 'you must also take into consideration the effects our unusual gestation process would have on the body.

'The skin of all of our gestated daughters possessed an unusual lack of pigmentation. Remember, in their entire existence, they had never been exposed to a single ray of sunlight. That, coupled with the artificial amniotic fluid, affected the appearance of their skin and their eyes.

'Recognize, too, that any normally ageing person experiences the effects of gravity and the continuing erosion that life visits on physical features. These influences result in uneven distributions of body fat, and help accentuate an asymmetry of the face and body. These factors would account for any of the more pronounced differences you noted.'

'Still,' Feldman persisted, 'how can you be absolutely certain this Jeza woman is one of your daughters from the Negev lab?'

The widow Leveque beamed with pride. 'Because I met her.'

This took Feldman completely by surprise. 'You met the Messiah? When? How?'

'Friday a week ago, the fourteenth. I had to leave Marie alone at home temporarily that morning while I went to the market. I was only gone about half an hour, and when I returned I saw that our front door was standing wide open. I knew I had secured it before I left.

'I was so fearful, I just rushed inside without even considering that an intruder might be there. But when I got to Marie's room, I saw this young woman in a white robe, standing at the foot of Marie's bed, just staring at her. I knew immediately who it was. She turned to me and smiled a small, sweet smile – my Marie's smile – and she said, "Do not be afraid, for I come from the Father."

'It was such a shock, I couldn't contain myself and fell to my knees before her, my arms around her waist, and I cried out all the tears and anguish and pain I'd kept inside me through all my tragedies. She held my head to her and stroked my hair and brought me such great comfort and inner peace.'

The elderly woman closed her eyes and tilted back her head, revisiting the moment with an aura of complete serenity. 'After a while, she lifted me to my feet and I saw such wisdom and peace and grace in her eyes that I no longer felt the need to cry. My only thought at the time was to keep her there with me and just revel in the love of my newly found daughter.

'But she told me she had to go. I begged her to stay just one night. She simply said, "Woman, I must be about my Father's business." Then she touched my face once more, smiled again that precious smile, and left. I delayed following her for the barest second or two, I'm certain. But by the time I rushed out of the house to find her, she was already gone. Vanished.'

'Anne,' Feldman asked, 'do you have any idea how Jeza knew about you or where you lived?'

'I don't really know. Perhaps it was another of the many eclectic things Jozef implanted in her memory with the intelligence infusion. I have no idea of all the information Jozef provided her with. Then again, it could have been some sort of instinctive or spiritual cognition that led her home. I just don't know. There's a far deeper wisdom inside her than I can account for.'

The widow Leveque closed her eyes once more and fell silent, the tremendous emotional expenditure of her story an obvious drain. After a time she looked up and smiled.

'When you called me last week, Anke,' she said, 'of course I didn't know at first that you were involved with Jon. All of us who had connections with the Negev Institute had been warned by the IDF that the operations there were top secret, and that the consequences of divulging information would be severe. When you happened to mention Jon and WNN, I realized I'd said too much and panicked.'

'So, after you were visited by Jeza, you changed your mind?' Anke speculated.

'No, Anke. It was after I was visited by the IDF that I knew I had no choice but to talk to you.'

'The IDF came to see you?' Feldman asked. 'When?'

'Last Thursday morning. General Alleza Goene and some of his staff officers.'

'What did General Goene want with you, Anne?'

'I'd never met him before, although I'd heard his name from Jozef in connection with the work at the Negev. General Goene was in charge of security for the operation and would visit the facility on occasion. Jozef was mindful to have things in tight order. General Goene was one of Tamin's cronies, and a rather intolerant individual who took security issues very seriously.

'When he visited me, the general seemed kind at first. He offered his condolences over my losses and asked me a number of questions about Jozef and the operations at the Negev. First he asked about any records or notes Jozef might have kept at home. I told him that all such documents had been classified by the IDF and that Jozef was required to store all of them at the laboratory. I didn't tell him about the diary.

'But in particular, he was interested in my daughters. He wanted to know if they were viable enough to have survived outside the gestation chambers at the time of the accident; if they would've been able to see or walk at the time; what negative effects the explosion and short-circuiting of the infusion system might have had on them mentally and physically, and so forth.

'Naturally, I was on the alert, and I played ignorant. I knew that my daughter who survived – Jeza – had to have been the one chosen for the military infusions because of her advanced mental development. I knew Goene would want her back. And, of course, I'd move heaven and earth to prevent that.

'Next, Goene asked if I'd seen the "so-called Messiah" on TV, and if I thought she bore any resemblance to the Negev test subjects. I told him I saw no similarities whatsoever, but I could tell he didn't believe me.

'He started getting short with me, and asked for photographs of Marie, which I refused him. Then, he asked if he could enter Marie's room to view her, and if one of his men could take snapshots of her. When I refused, they went into her room anyway. I tried to stop them, but another officer restrained me.

'Then, as he left, Goene told me, under penalty of treason and loss of my pension and Marie's health care benefits, that I must say nothing about what happened and report immediately to him any information I had regarding the New Messiah.

'And that's when I decided to call you, Anke. Knowing the danger Jeza is in, I must protect her somehow. The best way I know is through Jon's strong, clear voice on the television.'

'Exactly what danger do you think Jeza is in, Anne?' Feldman asked.

Mrs Leveque fixed her eyes intently on Feldman's. 'I put nothing past Shaul Tamin, Jon. He is a very cold and ambitious man. Because Jeza represents the living proof of secret, illegal experiments, I feel she's in grave danger. Tamin doesn't want the truth to leak out. Worse still, she carries inside her a priceless technology Tamin badly wants.'

'And in breaking this story through us,' Feldman summarized, 'you believe Tamin will be pre-empted from doing anything to her?'

'Yes. I believe once the world knows about the connection between Jeza and the IDF, neither Tamin nor Goene will have the audacity to take any further action against her.'

'Then if I understand you correctly, Anne,' Feldman double-checked himself, 'you have no problem with us telling your story as long as we keep you and your family's identities confidential.'

'Yes,' she replied. 'Other than ourselves, I believe the only people alive who know the complete truth about what was going on at that institute are Shaul Tamin and the IDF high command. And while Tamin will certainly suspect me when your report breaks, if you protect my identity, there's no way he can prove anything.

'But there are other conditions I must also set:

'I must insist that you not mention the existence of the neurochips or the extraordinary science behind the intelligence infusion. Exposing these proprietary technologies could result in serious criminal charges.

'I must also insist that you conceal the military aspects and objectives of the experiment, which were, of course, classified. Simply identifying the IDF as sponsoring illegal research should be sufficient to protect Jeza. Nor do I think it would bode well for her were the public to learn she may carry inside her some secret military directives.

'But beyond that, I have a greater worry. You see, Jeza has no awareness about the source of her unique abilities – the network of neurochips implanted within her brain. I shudder to think what effects such a revelation might have on her. Confronting the harsh reality of her artificial intelligence and those foreign devices inside her, alone and unprepared, could be very devastating and dangerous for her.'

'I understand,' Feldman acknowledged. 'But Anne, I think it's important that we include *some* sort of reasonable explanation about how Jeza developed her extraordinary mental abilities. There are millions of frantic people out there who believe her knowledge is divine. They need to know the truth. Would you have any problems if we were to cover the intelligence infusion in general terms only, without mentioning the neurochips? Let's say we describe it merely as some sort of passive, memory-building process – like with pre-recorded audio tapes fed through earphones or the like – and we omit the details?'

'I appreciate your thinking here,' the widow replied, ruminating, 'but I need to be assured that this will indeed be handled in only the most general terms.'

He nodded his understanding. 'You can depend on me.'

Feldman paused before his next question, being very careful how he phrased it. 'Anne, there's just one more thing I'd like to clarify with you, please . . . In your mind, having met her, is there anything you saw or felt that might lead you to believe that Jeza could actually be a true Messiah, the promised one of the Old Testament? Or, in your opinion, is this messianic belief of hers entirely . . . delusional?'

Anne looked questioningly at him, and he feared he'd upset her.

'Are you asking me whether I think Jeza is insane?' She put it bluntly, but her tone did not suggest she was offended. 'That's a question, I admit, that I'm wrestling with myself. And I don't know that I have an answer quite yet. But I can tell you this: the young woman I met last Friday morning is not the Marie I bore and raised. Even with all the physical similarities.

'Apparently, Jeza believes herself to be a prophetess. And there are many, I'm certain, who consider that madness. Perhaps it is. How can we know what effect her unnatural development has had on her? What are the psychological results of extended isolation in those ungodly gestation tanks? All those hours of raw infusion and terrifying military encoding? What mental damage might she have suffered if her neurocircuits overloaded in the explosion? Any of these traumatic situations, I think, would have been enough to render her completely insane.

'I consider how all this must affect her. Here she is, thrust abruptly into the world. Born an adult, with built-in, but incompletely formed, memories. Displaying incredible, seemingly divine intellectual gifts. With no better explanation, why shouldn't she assume her special talents come from God? Perhaps that Samaritan cult implanted such thoughts in her impressionable mind.

'But then again, I keep thinking about all these amazing supernatural events that surround her. In meeting her, I myself felt something inexplicably spiritual and moving. So who is to say whether God reached out into that laboratory, in the midst of His just destruction, and touched this precious, innocent being to carry forth His greater purpose?

'As to whether she is mad or Messiah, Jon, I simply don't know. I pray to God she is neither. I pray that Jeza will return to me as simply a normal, sweet, caring child whom I can love and cherish.'

And a few more tears slipped from her eyes.

43

WNN news bureau, Jerusalem, Israel,
10.19 A.M., Saturday, 29 January 2000

Nigel Sullivan had made the gutsy decision to sit on the incredible revelation of Jeza's true identity in order that the story might be developed to its maximum potential. Even Feldman had thought him foolish at first, fearful that the facts about Jeza's origins might leak. But now, a week later, the brilliance of his plan was becoming obvious.

In order to preserve the secrecy of the project, the story had been scrambled into many pieces and disseminated to New York headquarters and to various WNN stations across Europe. No clues were given to the production staffs regarding sequence or storyline. All week long, as the many segments of the tale were independently developed, computer files, directions and information had been flying back and forth continuously across the Mediterranean via secret couriers to avoid Israeli Defence Force intelligence.

WNN's report would not contain any new video of the Messiah. However, thanks to the magic of electronic imaging, WNN's computer artists had created lifelike video footage. This was accomplished by borrowing real images of the Messiah from existing video and altering them to develop totally different sequences.

It would be a two-hour presentation, *The True Origins of the New Messiah*, an exclusive report by Jonathan Feldman and WNN News, the pieces to be assembled in final form at WNN's Jerusalem headquarters.

Under the tremendous deadline pressures, in the middle of a long-distance teleconference with the European bureau over missing graphic sequences, an annoyed Feldman and Hunter were interrupted by an insistent Cissy McFarland.

'Dammit, Cissy, this had better be good,' Hunter fumed, already irascible over the dispute with the Europeans. 'How in the hell do you expect us to get this damn thing done by tomorrow?'

'Well, you may not need to finish it, you big ass,' she shouted back, 'if we don't deal with a much bigger problem first. The IDF is here and they're demanding we show them what we plan to air or they're going to shut us down and impound our equipment!'

Feldman and Hunter were dumbfounded. 'Since when is Israel a police state?' Feldman wanted to know. 'They can't do that!'

'Those damn promos,' Hunter continued his rampage. 'Jon warned Bollinger not to reveal so much. Always gotta go for the big ratings,' he complained to no one.

'Forget it, Breck.' Feldman appreciated the seriousness of the situation. 'You and Cissy better sound the silent alarm and get any sensitive tapes and information out of the edit suites and stashed, just in case. And you'd better move fast!'

Feldman hurried down to the conference room to find Sullivan, Bollinger and Robert Filson facing off against four militia and General Alleza Goene himself.

Sullivan, red in the face, was furious. 'This is an outrage! Where's your court order? This is illegal!'

The general's brass nameplate and a chestful of decorations gleamed from the front of his taut, spotless military jacket. 'I need no authorization. In matters of state security, the IDF has complete authority,' he asserted, turning as Feldman entered the room.

'Excuse me, General, I'm Jon Feldman, lead reporter on this sto—'

'I know *exactly* who you are.' Goene cut him short.

Feldman blinked.

'*You* are the one who's responsible for this fanatical millenarian craze. *You* are the one who whips the masses into a frenzy over this false Messiah, with no regard for the consequences, solely to build ratings for your network. But *I'm* the one who's been made responsible for restoring order. And I will do so with whatever means necessary.' He turned back to Sullivan. 'Now, show me the programme.'

Feldman looked to Sullivan for a clue.

Sullivan, controlling himself, addressed Feldman without taking his eyes from Goene. 'The general here is under the impression that our upcoming newscast on the Messiah will reveal classified state secrets. But when I ask what prompts his accusations, he can't tell me.'

'General,' Feldman asked, trying to take the offensive, 'are you saying that the alleged Messiah is in some way connected to the Israeli government or the Defence Force?'

Goene's face darkened and the veins rose in his thick neck. 'You have exactly one minute to show me the programme!'

'Arnie,' Sullivan instructed Bollinger, 'I want you to call Levi Meir at the Knesset immediately and get a clarification on the general's request.'

'The Knesset has no say in this matter,' Goene retorted, livid. 'You have forty-five seconds.'

Bollinger, Sullivan and Filson had gone pale, but they held their ground.

'General,' Feldman tried again, 'you have to know that this story isn't being handled here. It's not a live report, it's a produced special, put together at our European headquarters and in New York to be broadcast worldwide. I recorded my segments days ago and the footage has gone to Europe. You need to take these matters up with our European headquarters.'

'Nonsense!' Goene reacted. 'Our intelligence has intercepted no relevant broadcast transmissions or satellite feeds to Europe. You're producing the report here!'

'If you'd like, I'll take you around and you can see for yourself.' Feldman continued his ruse. 'Our segment was finished and shipped by personal courier days ago. There's nothing to show you.'

Sullivan flashed Feldman a look of panic.

Goene wasn't backing off. 'Then I will at least view *your* segments. You show me now!'

'I'll show you that there's nothing here, but I'm not going to reveal the contents of the story,' Feldman replied calmly and evenly. 'And I'm the only one who knows the identities of my sources.

'Furthermore,' he added, pushing his luck, 'any actions you take against this office will most certainly be used by our international headquarters to substantiate our report – tying the IDF, Defence Minister Tamin and you personally to developments!'

Goene's face went purple with fury at this impertinent threat, and his four military guards instinctively assumed a more menacing posture. Sullivan grimaced at the riskiness of this gambit.

Nevertheless, despite his anger, Goene appeared to be considering this unanticipated downside.

Feldman sensed an opportunity to end the confrontation. 'General,' he said in a conciliatory tone, 'if you and your men will simply leave now, without further problems, I see no reason for us to acknowledge this incident. And you'll have our assurances there'll be no mention of you or this meeting in the broadcast. Agreed, Nigel?"

The general looked to Sullivan, who nodded supportively. Goene rubbed a hand roughly over his mouth, his eyes flitting about as if searching for a better alternative.

Feldman was gambling that the image-conscious Tamin had put Goene on a short leash. If the general had been given *carte blanche* to wield his force and was truly confident in his accusations, he'd likely have stormed the offices already, without notice.

Finally, Goene's eyes came to rest on Feldman's.

'I warn you, if WNN divulges any classified information or documents, or if there's any exposure whatsoever of sensitive government research in your broadcast, you'll answer to a higher authority than me. It will result in the immediate expulsion of all WNN personnel from Israel, and the confiscation of all WNN property in the state. Is that understood?'

Neither Feldman nor Sullivan said anything, and finally the general, with a surly scowl, signalled his men and stalked out of the room.

Back in the editing suites, Cissy and a relieved crew began emerging from their niches like woodland creatures after a storm, recovering tapes and other work-in-progress from hastily created hiding places.

A relieved Hunter pinched Bollinger's ample jowl. 'Bingo! Struck another nerve, didn't we, Arnie?' he gloated, only too delighted to see the military thwarted.

But unfortunately, as Bollinger explained, the phone call to WNN's sympathetic connections at the Knesset was not reassuring. With the rise of the increasingly unstable millenarian movement, the dynamics of Israeli politics were changing. The perceived threat to public safety and security had created a vacuum in which Shaul Tamin had been successfully manoeuvring. The defence minister had been quietly, steadily expanding his powers, asserting more independence, success-fully usurping civil authority from the Ben-Miriam administration. Word was, WNN could well be on thin ice if this new report proved destabilizing.

Sullivan gathered the troops for a quick meeting, related the circumstances and informed them of the possible consequences should the programme air as planned. The staff were unanimous in their support, with the exception of Robert Filson.

'I've got a bad feeling about all this, people,' Filson opined. 'If the real issue here is rating points, consider what happens if they close us down. No future Messiah coverage means *no* ratings. Not to mention the extremely unpleasant consequences of dealing with the legal system in a foreign country on *treason charges*! I seriously recommend we delay the broadcast in order to study the situation.'

There was dead silence in the room for a moment, and then Hunter stood, held up his arm and said, 'Everyone who thinks Filson is an anal-retentive chickenshit, raise their hand.'

Filson was the only one to abstain.

The crews went back to their work, continuing straight through the night, finishing up early Sunday morning. Tired but satisfied, Feldman, Hunter and Erin Cross returned to Feldman's apartment to rest fitfully and await the broadcast later that evening.

Despite her major contributions to the project, Anke, who drove in from Tel Aviv to join them, wouldn't be mentioned in the credits. Feldman, grateful though he was, didn't want to risk involving her, given the recent actions of the Israeli Defence Force.

Having viewed the report *ad nauseam* in editing, when the special programme finally did air, Feldman and Hunter tended to judge it more from a technical standpoint and had lost some confidence in it. It could have been the lack of sleep, but it struck them as contrived and absurdly unbelievable.

They couldn't have been further from the truth.

The newscast would ultimately win WNN a Pulitzer. The heavily promoted, anxiously anticipated programme would become the most watched, rewatched, listened-to, talked-about, studied, analysed, debated, deplored and praised piece of television newscasting ever aired.

When the lengthy broadcast ended, the couples collapsed in Feldman's living room, too drained and numb to make the trek to the bedrooms. Feldman switched off the TV with his remote.

After a few moments, Hunter whispered out into the darkened room, 'You know, if somebody was out to really mess up the world, he couldn't't've picked a better time than the millennium or a better vehicle than some pseudo-Messiah figure. Kinda makes you wonder, doesn't it? So what are we dealing with here, guys – Messiah, or Frankenstein monster?'

Maybe they were already asleep, but nobody answered.

44

Ben Gurion apartment complex, Jerusalem, Israel,
2.12 A.M., Monday, 31 January 2000

He stretched out his long tanned legs and looked down the narrow track at the sandpit beyond. A crowd lined the runway. The judges

stood at the end with their tape measures, awaiting him. He dug his
spikes into the asphalt for a secure grip and mentally anticipated his
approach.

Feldman knew this was a dream, but he couldn't get out of it. He
was back in college, in the middle of an athletic competition, about
to vent his youthful angst in the all-out sprint and explosive release
of the long jump event.

The crowd was getting impatient. Behind him, he heard Hunter's
voice urging him on. 'Hurry, Feldman, hurry!'

He felt uncharacteristically nervous as he started his approach. But
his legs, which carried him to college on a four-year track scholarship,
were as quick and strong as ever. They launched him into a spectacular
leap. Above him, low clouds roiled dark and menacing. Below him, the
sandpit had turned into a deep, wide abyss of flames and tormented
souls, and he flailed wildly in panic.

Feldman woke in a sweat. Curled next to him on the inside of the
couch, lost down among the pillows, Anke breathed slowly and evenly.
Her long, soft hair lay tousled in her face, only her mouth showing, full
lips parted slightly. Feldman smiled and lightly kissed those lips.

Carefully extracting himself, he got up to use the bathroom. But
as he crept past his phone it began to ring loudly, startling him. He
snatched up the receiver in an instant, hopeful of saving the others'
sleep. On the opposite end came a man's voice, serious, deliberate,
insistent.

'Jon Feldman?'

'Uh, yeah.'

'Please listen to me very carefully. You have only about thirty
minutes to clear out of your apartment. A detachment of militia from
the Defence Force is on its way to arrest you and your associates.'

'What?'

'Listen to me, you've got to clear out right away and you've got to
leave Israel now. Don't use the airports or the trains. Take Highway
1 to Route 30 east to Jordan. That's your quickest way out. Amman
is only about a hundred kilometres. With a little luck you should make
it in a couple of hours.'

'Who is this? How did you get my number?'

By now the others were stirring and Hunter was up, groping for
the light switch.

'I'm a friend and I'm trying to help you. Please listen to me. You haven't much time.'

'What about Nigel Sullivan and Arnold Bollinger and the rest of my WNN crew? What's happened to them?'

'They're going to be rounded up, too. *Don't* call them from your apartment. Wait until you're on the road and use your car phone. I can't do any more than I already have. Trust me and go. Good luck!'

'Wait a minute! Who are you, and how do you know all this?'

Feldman heard nothing more but the dial tone.

'Come on, guys,' he called to the others, 'we're gettin' the hell out of here, *now!*'

Gathering only their essentials, they bolted from the apartment into Feldman's Rover and tore off through the night. Hunter, sitting next to Feldman in the front, began punching in numbers on the car phone to pass along the alarm.

'Anke' – Feldman looked into her eyes in his rear-view mirror – 'you don't have to leave with us, you know. You're still in the clear. They don't have anything to connect you with me yet.'

She leaned forward and squeezed his shoulder. 'I'm too involved to quit now. I want to be with you to help, if I can. If you'll let me.'

Hunter interrupted. 'I got hold of Sullivan, guys. He says for everyone to stay calm and head for the Ambassador Hotel in Amman. He'll meet us there to decide what we'll do next. Probably send us all down to Cairo for a while until this thing blows over.'

He tried to reach Cissy next, but her line was continually busy.

'Something's wrong,' he decided. 'Turn around, Jon, we gotta go back for her!'

Feldman hit the brakes and made a sharp U-turn. Ten minutes later, the car was rolling slowly and quietly past Cissy's flat with its lights off.

They were too late. There, parked around the side, was an Israeli military jeep. Feldman slipped the Rover into an alley and pulled over to deliberate.

'Shit,' Hunter exhaled briskly. 'They've got her!'

'There was no one in the jeep,' Erin observed. 'They must still be up in her apartment.'

'Come on, Feldman,' Hunter urged, 'let's take a look.' And he got out of the Rover, fishing a loose tyre iron from the boot.

Feldman was right behind him, pausing only long enough to hand Anke the keys and suggest she move up into the driver's seat. 'If we run into trouble, you guys get the hell over to Amman and contact Sullivan. He'll know what to do.'

Outside the apartment building everything was quiet. There were no lights on upstairs.

'This is weird, Jon,' Hunter decided. 'It could be a trap.'

'Yeah, if her line's busy, why are her lights out?' Despite the potential threat, there was no talk of turning back. They made their way softly up the stairs that led to a small landing and Cissy's front door.

'I can't see shit,' Hunter whispered, cupping his hands over his eyes, face pressed against the glass of the sidelight. 'I'm gonna knock.'

'What?'

'Yeah, hell, let's do it! Here!' Hunter handed Feldman his tyre iron and Feldman flattened himself against the stucco beside the doorway.

Hunter rapped lightly at first and waited. There was no answer. A bit harder. Still no answer. Finally he smashed his fist hard against the wood and he heard a cry of complaint from inside. The porch light flickered on, the door opened and a squinty-eyed Cissy peered out over the chain-lock.

'Cissy!' Hunter whispered.

'Hunter, is that you?' Cissy called out. 'What the hell are you doing here in the middle of the night? Are you drunk?'

'Cissy,' he whispered again. 'Quiet! Listen to me. We're in big trouble. The military's after us. They've got warrants for all of us. We gotta split now! Right away!'

From inside the apartment, they heard the muffled, accented voice of a man. 'Hey, Cissy, what is it? Everything okay?'

Hunter looked baffled and Feldman stepped forward, lowering his weapon.

'Feldman?' Cissy was still squinting into the light. 'Are you in on this, too?'

'Cissy, listen to me,' Feldman whispered insistently. 'Hunter's right. We think the IDF is after us for the broadcast. We got to head out of here quick. Just grab a few things and let's go, please!'

Hunter was still mentally scratching his head as a large, shirtless, bristly-chinned young man unlatched the door and slipped an arm around Cissy. 'What's going on?' he asked. 'What do these clowns want?'

'None of your business, pal,' Hunter shot back. 'She works with us and this is confidential. Take a hike.'

The man wasn't backing off. 'You take a hike, asshole.' He reared himself up and pulled open the door, giving Hunter a threatening shove in the chest.

'Answer me one question, dude.' Hunter held his ground as Feldman fingered the tyre iron. 'Are you IDF?'

The man puffed himself up even more and announced proudly, 'Sergeant first class, asshole!'

Like a rocket, Hunter fired a short, devastating right to the chin and the soldier toppled backwards, landing in an unconscious heap.

Cissy was incredulous and kept looking back and forth between the two combatants, sputtering. Hunter grabbed her by the shoulders, looked her dead in the eyes and hissed forcefully, 'I'm not gonna say this again. Tamin's after our asses and we're gettin' out of here. Stuff some clothes in a bag and let's go!'

She screwed up her face at Feldman, who nodded emphatically, and then she quietly gave in.

Two minutes later, Hunter took her bag in one hand, her arm in the other and hurried her through the door. On her way out, she looked back mournfully over her shoulder at her fallen soldier, sighed, and hustled off with her two escorts into the night.

45

Ambassador Hotel, Amman, Jordan,
Monday morning, 31 January 2000

All but one of the WNN crew managed to escape Tamin's grasp. Arnie Bollinger had risked returning to his office to retrieve some important papers, but the IDF had been lying in wait and promptly arrested him.

Feldman, Anke and the remaining WNN staff, meanwhile, had made it safely to Amman, Jordan. *En route,* Feldman had thought to make a precautionary phone call to Anne Leveque. His warning, however, came too late. To his great anger and dismay, Feldman learned that the widow had already received another visit from Goene. The general had come armed with a search warrant this time, tearing apart her home until he found and confiscated her late husband's incriminating diary.

As tired as he was when he reached Amman, Feldman was unable to sleep. He felt a devastating guilt over the disastrous consequences of his *Origins* report. But there was to be no relief from the bad news, which continued dribbling in via Israel Radio news briefs.

It was apparent that Tamin was coming under increasing political pressure back in Jerusalem. In a rare live radio broadcast, the defence minister vehemently denied WNN's accusations regarding the nature of the Negev Institute experiments. He also defended his repressive police actions against WNN as necessary to safeguard nameless 'state security secrets'.

And then, in his most outlandish and brazen act yet, the defence minister announced an all-out manhunt by the IDF to take the elusive Messiah into 'protective custody'.

Feldman was beside himself. As the reporter was well aware, with the Leveque diary now in the IDF's possession, the only remaining evidence left to indict Tamin and Goene was embodied, quite literally, in the person of the prophetess herself.

Despite WNN's *Origins* report, the large majority of Jeza's followers remained fiercely loyal to her. Many denounced the report altogether, but most simply discounted its importance, believing that the Millennium Eve phenomenon at David's Well purified any possible spiritual contamination from the laboratory experiments; that the lightning strike atop the temple ruins was the pivotal moment when God anointed Jeza and imbued her with her soul and her mission. To Jeza's faithful supporters, then, this current threat to their Messiah was an intolerable outrage that demanded immediate and forceful action.

But then, at last, there came some good news. Perhaps as a token appeasement to the Knesset, the IDF finally released Bollinger later in the day without pressing charges. The exhausted, bedraggled newsman arrived shortly thereafter at the Amman airport to a hero's welcome. The large crowd that greeted him was led by a tired, but cheering, WNN news staff.

The message Bollinger bore from the IDF, however, was not good. WNN was barred from Israel indefinitely. All its properties seized under direct orders of Shaul Tamin. Sullivan had no choice but to relocate all operations and personnel immediately to WNN's regional headquarters in Cairo, Egypt, pending further developments in the Holy Land.

46

Mormon Convention Centre, Salt Lake City, Utah, *8.42 A.M., Saturday, 5 February 2000*

It was the second morning of the first convocation when, at last, the meeting got down to its most controversial topic of interest: 'An Evaluation of the Authenticity of a New Messianic Presence'. From an elevated lectern at the front of the huge auditorium, a tall, gaunt, bespectacled Mormon elder called to order the assembly of over five hundred religious leaders.

Delivering the day's keenly anticipated focal presentation would be a scholarly young Mormon theologian who was introduced as Brother Elijah Petway, a foremost authority on Old and New Testament correlations. Brother Petway was a small, lean, light-complexioned man with thinning blond hair, compressed face and pale blue eyes that blinked mechanically behind wire-rim glasses.

Eagerly taking the podium, he beamed at his attentive audience. 'My fellow Judeo-Christians, Muslim and Buddhist brothers and sisters,' he began, in a prim and precise voice as thin as his physique, 'I thank you all for the opportunity to bring before you the results of my exhaustive studies.'

After a somewhat tiresome explanation of the methodology and

thoroughness of his research, Petway launched into the gist of his
findings – a litany of both obvious and obscure parallels drawn
between scriptures of the Old and New Testaments and the recent
occurrences in the Holy Land. The bulk of his correlations consisted
of such things as a comparison of the alleged meteorite with the biblical
Star of Bethlehem; similarities between the Japanese astronomers and
the Wise Men of the Orient; the significance of the 25 December date
on which the institute was destroyed, and so forth.

He finished with a controversial pronouncement.

'Obvious to everyone now, in the light of the World News Network's
revelations,' he maintained, 'is the unique and biblically relevant nature
of Jeza's nativity. As you'll recall, Jeza was created through a process of
conception known as polar body fertilization. This process precluded
the introduction of sperm into the reproductive organs of Jeza's
maternal donor. Indeed, the procedure circumvented altogether the
need for male gametes.

'We have, therefore, a pure, virgin conception and virgin birth, in
the truest sense!'

There was a stir of rumblings from large sections of the audience,
but Petway's enthusiasm was unabated. He took a large, self-satisfied
breath. 'I feel there is an inevitable conclusion this assembly must
draw from the overwhelming body of direct and indirect evidence
just presented. I submit to you that it is irrelevant whether Jeza
be God-made through an immaculate conception, or man-made
through artificial fertilization. God works in strange ways. If it be
His decision to use man's folly to achieve His own objectives, who
are we to question?

'I also submit to you that it is irrelevant whether the New Messiah
be male or female. The apparent anomaly of Jeza's sex should not
diminish her message. We must search for the higher meaning in why
God has chosen a female to represent Him this time.

'And finally, I submit to you that, even if you agree with
but a portion of the amazing correlations I've just identified,
we must all of us now make the evaluation that this special
presence among us, this saintly, godly creature known as Jeza,
can be none other than the only begotten Daughter of God: Jeza
Christ!'

This resulted in diverse reactions from the assembly, ranging from caustic outrage through merely appreciative applause to tumultuous standing ovations and enthusiastic alleluias. Strong support emanated not only from the millenarian sections, but also from the Jewish contingent, which was made up of several excited rabbis, including the respected head of the ultra-Orthodox Hasidic Lubavitcher movement, Rabbi Mordachai Hirschberg, who held a hand over his fluttering heart.

Petway vacated the podium convinced of the persuasiveness of his arguments.

Certainly, for one quiet, inconspicuous gentleman sitting alone at a more distant table, Brother Petway had scored far more hits than misses. Carefully capturing every word on tape recorder, making precise entries in his notepad and feeling completely vindicated, was the revitalized Cardinal Alphonse Litti.

47

WNN regional headquarters, Cairo, Egypt,
10.03 A.M., Sunday, 6 February 2000

Other than Arnie Bollinger's safe deliverance from the hands of Shaul Tamin, there were few positive developments to help alleviate Feldman's growing frustrations with his exile. Over the last several days, removed from all the action in Israel, he and his associates had little to do but hang around Cairo headquarters, hoping for WNN to get their visas restored.

Trying to keep abreast of current events this morning, he and Anke sat in an empty WNN editing bay scanning a dozen TV monitors on the wall in front of them. Each set was tuned to a different channel, the volumes muted on all but the one that happened to engage their interest currently.

Abruptly, Anke gestured towards a particular screen. Feldman obligingly jumped to a programme where an earnest-looking man was reporting on the growing world prominence of two opposing millenarian sects.

'The startling arrival of the female mystic Jeza has had a polarizing effect on the hundreds of millenarian creeds around the world,' the announcer explained. 'In the light of recent events, most millenarian sects have split into two distinct camps of pro-Jeza and anti-Jeza factions.

'Among millenarians within the anti-Jeza bloc, a majority have been gathering under the banner of a rather vocal organization known as the Guardians of God. In the pro-Jeza coalition, supporters have been steadily migrating towards an evangelical sect calling themselves the Messianic Guardians of God. Although these two factions represent opposite extremes of the millenarian movement, surprisingly both sects were once one and the same.'

'Damn,' Feldman exclaimed, 'I've crossed paths with those Guardian weirdos before. They're a scary lot.'

'How so?' Anke asked.

'Hunter and I did a story on them shortly before Millennium Eve. They're a doomsday cult claiming to commune with the second order of the celestial hierarchy – the archangels. They consider themselves soldiers of Christ – self-appointed escorts of the Messiah for the Second Coming. Their thing is paramilitary training in preparation for the battle of Armageddon.'

On the TV monitor, a large group of men, women and children were shown holding a rally in front of a large bonfire. Many of the adults were bearing ceremonial swords and truncheons, waving them over their heads as they sang and prayed. The voice of the reporter announced over the footage, 'This group of celebrants represent one of the oldest surviving millenarian sects in the world, dating back more than a thousand years to the first Millennium Eve of AD 999.'

The footage on the screen was displaced by video of an ancient wall painting. The images on the painting were of men, women and children, clad in white robes, shown embarking from Europe on a pilgrimage to the Holy Land. 'Before journeying to Jerusalem,' the announcer explained, 'these earlier Guardians of God gave up all personal belongings, devoting themselves to spartan lifestyles, prayer and regimented military training. Their sworn objective was to serve as protectors of the Messiah upon His return on the Last Day. That this sect survived their perilous pilgrimage to the Holy Land was due in no small measure to their fierce militancy.'

The camera zoomed in on a section of the painting, targeting a pennant one of the pilgrims bore at the front of the procession. Emblazoned on the standard was a simple coat of arms: two human femur bones in the form of a T, flanked on each side by a sword and a battle-axe. Latin words were inscribed in golden arcs above and below the cross. The top read 'Custodes', the bottom 'Dei' – 'Guardians of God'.

The video then dissolved back to a modern-day Guardian, who was busy brandishing his sword in a mock fight against evil. As the Guardian fronted the camera, raising the sword high above his head, the image froze and the camera zoomed in to focus tightly on his chest, exposing an identical coat of arms embroidered on the man's robe over his heart.

'These present-day Guardians of God,' the announcer continued, 'like their predecessors, pledged themselves as soldiers of Christ for the battle of Armageddon. However, last month, with Jeza's appearance at the Mount of the Beatitudes, the Guardians became bitterly divided over her validity as a messiah. Unable to accept Jeza's sex, the main body of Guardians declared her a fraud. They created for themselves a leadership role among the general pool of anti-Jeza sects.

'In response, the pro-Jeza Guardians broke away to form a counter-movement, declaring their support for Jeza with an expanded name, the Messianic Guardians of God, complete with their own heraldry.' Up on the screen came a flag bearing the Messianic Guardians' new insignia – the initials MGG in silver on a yellow shield with palm leaf clusters. 'And at this time, the Messianic Guardians appear to have emerged as the popular standard-bearers for the entire pro-Jeza movement.'

Feldman and Anke shook their heads at one another and he jumped to yet another newscast. This one was reporting on how Israel's Ben-Miriam administration, blind-sided by Tamin's recent actions, was still reeling from the public relations fiasco. Worldwide, Israeli embassies had been picketed by pro-Jeza malcontents who saw dire biblical implications in any attempts to arrest their Messiah. The situation had deteriorated in many areas to actual attacks on the embassies and several fire-bombings, instigated by an increasingly militant Messianic Guardian faction.

'I can't understand how they can keep Tamin as defence minister,' Feldman complained to the TV. 'Eziah Ben-Miriam is a decent man – why doesn't he dump the bastard and rid himself of these problems?'

'Ben-Miriam isn't in a strong enough position,' Anke explained. 'His coalition government is too weak, and Tamin is powerful, with friends in high places. It will take an act of the Knesset to bring Tamin down, and Tamin's friends will fight that. There are rough times ahead for Israel, I'm afraid.'

'And all the while,' Feldman fumed, 'we're sidelined here on the damn bench, right in the middle of the championship game!' He tilted his head upward, calling out in exasperation to the heavens, 'Hey, Coach! If you're up there, it's time to put the first string back in!'

It was as if divine providence were listening. At this precise moment, on the opposite side of town, several members of WNN's number-three field crew happened to be shopping in one of Cairo's large open-air markets. Attracted by the noise of an excited gathering in the middle of the square, they elbowed their way through to find themselves suddenly in the presence of none other than the Messiah herself.

Jeza, encircled by a throng of exhilarated worshippers, was busy comforting a hyperventilating young mother and her crying baby.

The WNN crew was stunned. No one had had the slightest suspicion that Jeza was in Egypt. The crew rushed back to their van for their equipment and alerted headquarters. But by the time Feldman and company arrived, the Messiah had pulled her signature vanishing act. Feldman, however, was simply thankful for the impossible good fortune that had put him back into the contest. Jeza was in Cairo. And, once again, WNN had the scoop.

Although the crew was able to capture only the final scene of the episode on camera, the video they took was priceless. In it, Jeza was shown speaking in Arabic to an adoring audience, many on their knees, their foreheads touching the ground before them in complete devotion.

Through WNN's staff translator, Feldman learned from witnesses that what had transpired here was yet another Jeza miracle. Supposedly, a hysterical woman had come shrieking out of her home

into the marketplace carrying her lifeless baby. It was said that the
baby had died in his sleep. Sudden infant death syndrome, Feldman
presumed.

Quite by coincidence, the frantic woman ran right into Jeza, who
stopped her with an outstretched hand and said, 'Woman, why do you
weep?' The poor distraught mother, unable to answer, simply held out
the child, described as blue and limp. In the crowded market, a ring
of onlookers quickly collected.

Jeza was said to have taken the child in both arms, clasped it to her
breast and closed her eyes, praying. Then, abruptly, the child spasmed,
coughed and came back to life! The crowd, recognizing Jeza, fell to
its knees and declared her a prophetess of Allah. Jeza was returning
the child to its mother just about the time the WNN crew arrived on
the scene.

The rest of what happened Feldman was able to view right there in
the marketplace on videotape replay. He saw the now familiar glowing
face of Jeza turning to address the gathering. The translation of her
comments, from Arabic ran:

'Why do you marvel? What profits this child if his body is awakened
but his mind is asleep? I say to you, the Word is alive, but there are
those who would smoother it. Open your mind to the Word. For
inside each of you is a resurrection. The power and the glory and
the understanding!'

And then she slipped away into the crowd.

Vintage Jeza.

48

National Ministry of the Universal Kingdom, Dallas, Texas,
6.30 P.M., Sunday, 6 February 2000

The Reverend Solomon T. Brady returned home from the convocation with mixed feelings. He had, however, not come away dissatisfied.

He'd brought with him an intriguing idea that just might assist him in his struggle to shore up flagging contributions.

The concept was originated by a fellow evangelical out of Raleigh, North Carolina, during a seminar entitled 'The Impact of New Religious Dogma on Congregational Unity'. This gentleman, a radio talk show minister, had found success in dealing with the turbulent events of the moment by using the situation to continually challenge and stimulate his flock. Rather than fighting the growing distraction of the popular Messiah, he exploited it.

Via call-ins, the minister would solicit different perspectives about the prophetess and her message from his listeners. Taking no sides, he'd comment on the viewpoints and add a sense of moderation and authority to the topics discussed. The resourceful preacher found that his callers were also willing to contribute funds for the opportunity to vent their spiritual spleens, everyone seeming to have a strong opinion to share about the prophetess. Although this format was a radical departure from the standard evangelical approach, it nevertheless helped to keep the coffers full. It was a strategy the Reverend Brady thought he'd try.

This idea of a Messiah hotline was itself worth the cost of the convention. Not that Brady hadn't found the rest of the sessions interesting, if worrisome. After learning so much more about this Jeza person, he was nagged by suspicions that she just might be genuine.

There were some persuasive points expressed: Jeza *did* fulfil many ancient prophecies relevant to a Messiah and the Second Coming. She also satisfied many modern prophecies, both secular and religious, that had been proclaimed over the years regarding the new millennium. Nostradamus. Edgar Casey. The rabbis Menachem Schneerson and Haim Shvuli. All foresaw the appearance of a world religious leader at the turn of the twenty-first century heralding the end of the world. And Jeza was clearly the only qualifying figure on the scene at the appointed time.

However, at the end of the convocation, no consensus could be reached regarding the true nature of this unusual young woman. Brady consistently sided against a Mormon-sponsored proclamation to declare Jeza a true Anointed One. As did the majority of attendees. It was as if by voting against her, Brady might somehow help make Jeza go away. Or at least lessen her impact on him and his ministry.

The only thing the attendees could agree upon was to hold a second convocation to continue their work, four weeks hence, same place.

49

WNN regional headquarters, Cairo, Egypt,
9.00 A.M., Monday, 7 February 2000

Feldman received an urgent call at his desk and flew out of the door, stopping only long enough to snatch Hunter from his office. 'Jeza!' he shouted to everyone within earshot. 'She's about ten minutes away from here at the Eastside Christian Mission, preaching. Come on!'

Arriving in record time, Feldman and Hunter were flagged over by the meritorious female staffer who had called in the sighting.

'She's been in there about twenty minutes!' the beaming woman exclaimed, pointing through a tall wrought-iron gate behind her. 'And, uh, we owe this kid over here one thousand dollars for contacting me.' Next to the staffer, a young boy of about ten grinned and held out a grimy hand.

'Okay,' Feldman agreed, looking over at the high wall and stone buildings that bordered the mission grounds. 'Hang on to him and we'll settle up afterwards. Where is she?'

'In the courtyard inside, in front of that old stone church.' The woman pointed in the general direction.

'Fine,' Feldman said. 'But this time we're going to be clever about things. I don't want to frighten her off. Only Hunter and I are going in. I want the rest of the crew positioned at every gateway and door. When she does bolt, I want to find out where she goes – and how she manages to escape so easily.'

Selecting a light, inconspicuous camera and cordless microphone, the two reporters pulled the Rover next to the wall and used its roof as a step-stool. Hunter reclined on top of the wall with his camera while Feldman dropped down stealthily inside.

Jeza was speaking to a group of about fifty people in a small courtyard. Stealing his way casually through the crowd, Feldman donned his sunglasses and pulled his baseball cap lower to make himself less recognizable. Finally insinuating himself between a burly man and a large woman in a dirty apron, he found himself not five feet away from the elusive young prophetess.

A nun was asking the Messiah, 'Do you claim to be the Daughter of God and the Sister of Jesus?'

Jeza answered, 'Jesus is my Brother and God is my Father.'

'Do you only hear God, or do you see Him, too?' another nun asked.

'Mostly, God speaks to me. But when I meditate, and when I pray, I see Him.'

'What does He look like?' the same nun followed up her first question.

'He is all beauty and goodness and fills up my spirit with gladness,' the Messiah said.

Feldman stole a look back at Hunter and pointed to his ear. Hunter signalled with a thumbs-up that the audio was coming in loud and clear.

'Are you the Messiah of the Apocalypse?' a woman asked nervously, cradling a sleeping child in her arms. 'And is the end of the world coming soon?'

'I am the Messiah of the New Light,' Jeza responded, 'and an end is coming!'

'Armageddon or the Rapture?' the increasingly alarmed woman wanted to know.

'First there was the Old Testament,' Jeza told her, 'wherein man was taught to claim an eye for an eye and to see God in fear. Then there came the New Testament, wherein man was taught to turn the other cheek and to see God in love. Now there is a Newer Testament. A testament wherein man shall raise himself up to see God in a New Light.'

A quiet buzz of alarm spread through the crowd. 'The Rapture! The Rapture!' they concluded.

Although he knew it would be risky, Feldman could no longer

resist. He cleared his throat. 'And how shall we raise ourselves up?' he asked her.

Jeza turned slowly and laid her invasive indigo eyes on the reporter. Despite his being prepared for it, once again it was like a vacuum sucking the consciousness from him. He grabbed the shoulder of the burly man next to him, who, although annoyed, nevertheless tolerated the impertinence. Feldman steadied himself and quickly shook off the giddiness. The sunglasses had been no help.

Jeza still hadn't responded. She knitted her brow, studying Feldman, as the crowd turned to see the cause of the interruption. Feldman, fully recovered now, swore to himself, thinking he'd spoiled the session. But finally Jeza's brow smoothed.

'Describe for me your God,' she said.

Feldman was taken aback and searched through his mind for his early catechism training. 'Uh, God is all-knowing. He is, uh . . . He is all-powerful, all-good. Right?'

'Then go, and be likewise,' she directed.

'But how, Jeza? How do I become like God?'

'By all means,' she replied. 'If you strive to be all-knowing, all-powerful and all-good, you can violate no law of God in your pursuit.'

Feldman realized she was starting to back away, going into her disappearing act again, and he sought for a way to stall her. 'Yes, I think I understand, but can you be more specific?'

He appeared to be too late. She was off now, moving towards the front gate. But she slowed, stopped, turned to him and levelled that piercing gaze once more. 'You investigate, but you do not learn. You ask, but you do not hear. You knock, and when the door is opened, you turn away. Blessed are they who are given no answers, yet find understanding.'

It was not said with malice, but it still stung.

'Please,' he pleaded, 'there's so much more I want to know!'

'The time is not yet come,' she answered, and was off again, the audience following after her. Feldman called quickly into his remote mike to alert the staff. Over the heads of the people in front of him, he could make out a keeper swinging wide the front gate, with the WNN crew scurrying into position on the other side.

If the Messiah saw what was developing, she paid no heed. With a dozen cameras whirring at her, she marched steadily ahead, past them, through an alley, down a flight of stairs, headlong out into the rushing traffic of a busy thoroughfare. Feldman and crew were chasing pell-mell, trying to keep up, but the onslaught of cars, buses, trucks and bicycles was too menacing. It was suicide to follow. She was gone.

50

The Oval Office, Washington, DC,
9.00 A.M., Wednesday, 9 February 2000

The usually implacable Allen Moore, forty-third president of the United States, was nervous. Yesterday's New Hampshire primary had delivered him a totally unexpected setback.

Moore's official reason for delaying his entry into the presidential race had been to concentrate on the important responsibilities of his office and remain aloof from campaign distractions. The idea was to assume a detached, 'presidential' posture.

New Hampshire was a state his ticket had carried easily in the last election, and it had simply been assumed that Moore would fare well there in this primary, without any direct, personal involvement. The polls supported this thinking. Such a laid-back victory, the theory went, would have positioned him as confident and unstoppable in steamrolling towards his party's renomination.

So, on the advice of his manager, Moore had withheld himself from the presidential race until late January, and withheld himself physically from the state of New Hampshire, not campaigning there personally at all. This allowed a hard-running young upstart Democratic senator, Billy McGuire of Maryland, to set up camp in New Hampshire and earn many a pragmatic New Englander vote.

Not that Senator McGuire really won. He'd received only thirty-eight per cent of the vote to Moore's forty-three, with the balance allocated to various favourite sons. But even getting close to the heavily favoured Moore was a win for the ultra-right McGuire. The media were now casting Moore as 'vulnerable'.

'A goddamn fluke.' Presidential campaign manager Ed Guenther defended himself and consoled his president at the same time. 'We'll cut McGuire off at the knees in March on Super Tuesday and be rid of him!'

President Moore nodded, wanting to accept this scenario, but remaining keenly aware that the ill-timed Middle East instabilities could well work against him if events continued to influence the precarious US economy.

Brian Newcomb, Democratic Presidential Re-election Committee chairman, who had called this meeting, was less forgiving. He was well aware that the influential new phenomenon in his party, the rapidly growing millenarian bloc, was an unstable lot. 'Unfortunately, Ed, things aren't quite so pat. Now the millenarians are going to draw encouragement from this. And we can't risk another reversal. We've got to regain our momentum, which means now we'll have to commit some of autumn's earmarked campaign funds to these primaries. It's a disruptive, costly change in our game plan.'

Newcomb left an obvious political maxim unspoken: once lost, that special, magical aura of invincibility is never truly regained.

Moore, a moderate, was annoyed with this unexpected turn of events. After all, he was reasonably popular, he had been presiding over a stable economy – at least until the advent of this strange Messiah woman – and he was considered eminently re-electable by the majority of his party. The Republicans, on the other hand, had fielded a particularly unexciting batch of candidates this election year.

Moore realized that now, even if he sailed through the rest of his primaries, his New Hampshire 'loss' would certainly be resurrected by the media periodically to add drama to the race – a dark cloud that could follow him all the way to November.

51

Cardinals' chambers, Vatican City, Rome, Italy, 7.00 A.M., Thursday, 10 February 2000

Alphonse Litti pushed his chair back from his desktop computer and watched with trepidation as the final page of his report shuddered from the printer. He'd been up all night, but he defied his fatigue with the stubbornness of a driven man. Never in all his life had he felt so centred in his purpose. And so alone in his forlorn hope.

Since returning from the convocation, Litti had studied transcriptions of every known word or phrase uttered by the prophetess. He'd sequestered himself in his chambers, consulting and cross-referencing scripture against the Jeza record. At the end of the two days, the cardinal had developed what he felt was an emerging understanding of the young Messiah's message. Alphonse Bongiorno Litti saw a message that spoke forcefully and personally to him.

A message with the dual purpose of salvation and destruction.

The cardinal had laboured continuously, compiling his insights and preparing a document of provocative premises and frightful conclusions. In less than one month, he intended to present this document personally to the assembled denominations at the Mormons' second convocation in Salt Lake City.

But today, he'd present his report to Prefect Antonio di Concerci. And demand that it be included in the Congregation's draft *inquirendum*, due to be presented to the Pope in one week. Knowing his work's inflammatory composition, Litti realized the risk he was taking. Yet his conscience demanded that he see this to whatever end awaited him. He could only pray that God had given him the persuasive skills to put forth a convincing argument.

* * *

After waiting about twenty minutes in the prefect's anteroom, Litti was announced by di Concerci's secretary and admitted into a private, well-appointed suite. As he entered, it occurred to him that in his many years at the Vatican, he'd never once been inside di Concerci's office. And vice versa.

Spacious, with high, inlaid bronze ceiling, art-glass windows, heavy tapestry drapes, crystal chandelier, dark mahogany panelling, floor-to-ceiling bookshelves laden with ponderous volumes, exquisite oriental rug, large mahogany desk and matching high-back, throne-like chair, di Concerci's office was an imposing seat of authority.

'Cardinal Litti.' The prefect greeted his associate evenly, without standing. 'I have only a few minutes. I'm due to meet Cardinals Thompson and Santorini in the Museo Sacro.'

'I'm sorry to intrude without notice,' Litti apologized, 'but this is a matter of some importance. I have for you a completed report uniting my analysis of the Mormon convocation with the Congregation's study-in-progress – and with my own personal research. I believe you'll find the results quite eye-opening.'

'Yes, Alphonse, I am sure,' di Concerci responded dismissively. 'Leave it with my secretary and I will deal with it directly.'

Litti stood his ground. 'I've been up for three soul-wrenching days and nights on this, di Concerci, and I'll not have you brush it off like so much dust!' The tone in his voice was surprisingly harsh.

Di Concerci scrutinized his colleague closely and leaned back in his chair, caught off guard. 'Cardinal, you look terrible, if you don't mind my saying so. Are you feeling poorly?'

'Only in my heart, Prefect.' Litti stared unwaveringly at his associate. 'Only in my heart.'

Di Concerci rose and extended his hand to take the thick envelope. 'I assure you, this will receive my personal attention as soon as possible. Now, I must attend to my meeting—'

But Litti maintained a firm grip on the package. 'You and I have never seen eye to eye, Cardinal,' he said, staring up at the taller man. 'And I'm afraid there's not much friendship between us. Nevertheless, in the scores of years we've been acquainted, I've never once asked anything of you. I ask now. Postpone your meeting and read this document.' The unshaven Litti was flushed with emotion, his eyes feverish. 'Please!'

The prefect's brow creased and he searched Litti's face, reflected for a moment, then sighed. 'Very well. Have a seat outside and I will read your report.'

Litti released his envelope and left the office. As he closed the heavy double doors he heard di Concerci telling his secretary to cancel his appointment, not to disturb him, and to fetch Cardinal Litti a tall glass of water.

A little more than a half-hour later, the doors to di Concerci's office opened. Litti turned in his chair to see the prefect studying him intently, his brow still furrowed, his face sombre.

'Cardinal Litti, would you step inside, please?'

Di Concerci admitted his colleague, closed the doors, and without a word ushered him to a plush chair. He then seated himself behind his desk, folded his hands across the top of Litti's report, and stared down at it, still saying nothing.

Litti nurtured a small glimmer of hope. At the very least, it would appear that the report had the prefect thinking.

Taking a deep breath, di Concerci raised his eyes to Litti's. In a soft, surprisingly tender voice, he addressed his fellow cardinal. 'It's true, Alphonse, you and I have never seen each other as friends. But if you can overlook that unfortunate fact for a moment, I would like to speak to you now as if I were your truest friend.'

This startled Litti and he relaxed, unclenched his intertwined fingers, and sat back in his chair.

'What you've written here, Cardinal,' di Concerci said gently, spreading his hands out over the report, 'is, quite frankly, heresy. Unbridled heresy of the highest order. This document is a complete repudiation of your Church. It disavows your entire life, your vocation, your sworn commitment to God.'

Alphonse Cardinal Litti felt the weight of his worst expectations settle over him. He closed his eyes tightly, squinting back tears of emotional conflict, and rested his head against the back of his chair. He inhaled deeply and responded in a choked voice. 'Yes, Cardinal, you're quite right. It *is* a repudiation of my Church. And of my entire life.' He suddenly sat upright, his cheeks flushed, and glared into di Concerci's face. 'But *not* my commitment to God! It's because of my great love of God, my undying commitment to God, that I'm willing to sacrifice *everything* to open my Church's eyes, your eyes, to the truth! To the true will of God!'

'It is not too late, Alphonse,' di Concerci appealed. 'I will hand this document back to you and I'll erase it from my mind. You're obviously very tired and overwrought. You need some time away to rest. A vacation would do you worlds of good—'

'No, Cardinal.' Litti shook his head resolutely. 'You must submit this to the Congregation and to Nicholas, unaltered and in its entirety, as is required.'

Di Concerci tented his fingers and brought them to his lips, pausing, groping for an effective counter-argument. 'Litti, think for a moment. If you have me submit this, you'll be removed from the Congregation, if not from your cardinalship. And if you persist in these ravings, you will doubtless be excommunicated. You're throwing away your entire career. Everything. For God's sake, man, is it worth it?'

Litti's answer was calm, straight and deliberate. 'It's for God's sake that I do this. Just deliver my report to Nicholas and the Congregation, and I will make myself available should anyone wish to discuss it. I only pray that other eyes prove more open than yours.'

'You have opened my eyes to at least one thing, Alphonse,' the prefect replied soberly. 'You've opened my eyes to the reality that this self-proclaimed Messiah, this Jeza, is a very dangerous woman.'

Litti rose slowly to leave, his joints and his mind aching. 'Can you recall New Year's Eve of the millennium, Cardinal di Concerci?' he asked sorrowfully. 'The world's first vision of Jeza in the electrical storm? I quote you Matthew, chapter twenty-four, verse twenty-seven: "For as the lightning comes forth from the east and shines even to the west, so also will the coming of the Messiah be."'

Without saying a word, di Concerci leaned to his right and opened the bevelled-glass doors to a vintage cabinet. He withdrew a small, very old-looking bound book with a faded, wine-coloured cover.

'And let me quote to you from this, Cardinal,' he said, opening the book reverentially on the desk in front of him. 'Do you know what this is, Alphonse?' He didn't wait for an answer. 'This is an original Latin manuscript of the Gospel of St John. Copied by hand, by the monks of Domrémy, Lorraine, as a gift to Joan of Arc. It's been in the di Concerci family for hundreds of years and was a present to me from my father upon my vestiture as a cardinal.'

Delicately, he searched through the pages for a specific passage.

'Here, I read to you in Christ's own words, John, chapter ten, verses fourteen to sixteen.' He translated from the Latin:

'"I am the good shepherd, and I know mine and mine know me, even as the Father knows me and I know the Father; and I lay down my life for my sheep. And other sheep I have that are not of this fold. Them also I must bring, and they shall hear my voice, and there shall be one fold and one shepherd."'

He carefully closed the covers. '*One* fold, Alphonse. And only *one* shepherd. Jeza cannot be Lord.'

Resigned, Litti turned and moved painfully towards the door. 'You are wrong, di Concerci,' he said, looking back sadly over his shoulder. 'Jeza *is* a Messiah. A second Messiah. And She is come to fulfil the prophecies. To oppose Her is to oppose the will of God. In the end, those who defy Her will be destroyed. And the end is nearer than you know!'

52

The seaport of Said, Egypt,
6.32 P.M., Friday, 11 February 2000

With Jeza having departed the Holy Land, conditions in Israel had calmed enough that the way was now clear for Anke to return to her studies in Tel Aviv. And while Anke wouldn't be so far away that she couldn't visit on occasion, Feldman still found the idea of her parting difficult.

Tonight, Feldman had designed a special evening for her. He'd made reservations at a romantic little restaurant, Delta of the Nile, at the picturesque seaport of Said, on the shores of the Mediterranean.

Over a candlelit dinner, he found Anke unusually quiet, and offered her a shekel for her thoughts.

She looked up at him uncertainly.

'Go ahead,' Feldman prodded gently, 'it's not like you to be shy!'

She laughed. 'It's a subject I know you're not really comfortable discussing, that's all.'

'Tonight, anything goes,' he pledged.

She took a breath. 'Jon, I'd like to know what you really think about this woman, Jeza. Despite everything Anne Leveque has told us, I still can't escape the sensation that there's more behind her than can be explained by that neurochip science, as amazing as it may be. And I know you share some of my feelings. I can see it in your face with every report you do on her. It troubles you, too, doesn't it?'

This was not the romantic subject Feldman had hoped was on Anke's mind. He sighed and stared down at his entrée, which had suddenly lost its appeal. 'Okay,' he reluctantly honoured his pledge, 'okay.'

He paused, collecting his thoughts. Finally he looked her in the eye. 'I can't say I haven't considered the possibility that she might be, well, a real Messiah,' he admitted. 'It does trouble me . . .

'I mean, if you set out to design a person to look and talk and act just like some divine being, I don't see how you could come up with a creature more imposing than Jeza. So maybe she's the wrong sex, and maybe she's too petite. But then, with her, that doesn't seem to matter, does it? It doesn't seem to get in the way at all. In fact, quite the contrary, it only serves to *enhance* the whole divine shtick! It makes her even more divine overcoming those supposed obstacles. Yes, there's a power there, I agree with you, that seems to come from beyond the science lab.

'And I can't say that I have a plausible explanation for every miracle I've reported on – although there are certainly a good many I would question,' he hastily added. 'But I have to tell you, I find the whole Jeza experience rather off-balancing, even intimidating at times. I just don't know what to make of it all, Anke. I just don't know.'

She frowned at him in absorbed consideration. 'Jon,' she whispered softly, 'what if Jeza really *is* a Messiah? What if we really are entering into the Last Days?' Her chin was trembling.

Feldman reached across the table and took her hands in his. 'That's a path of thought I don't care to travel too far,' he told her. 'But even if I knew for certain we were facing Judgment Day, there's one thing I have to cling to. While you and I may not be perfect people, Anke, and while we may not live religion the way a good many people seem to out there, I'd still put our ethics up against the best of 'em – millenarians, clergy, whatever. And I don't think a fair-minded God could ignore that, do you?'

She exhaled and relaxed. 'But, in fact, you really don't believe in her, do you?'

'In all honesty?' He paused for a long moment, growing gravely introspective. 'No, Anke, I can't see it. Maybe it's that I don't want to see it, but at this point in time, I just can't accept it.'

Anke appeared to find some comfort in this, gazing into his eyes with a look of reassurance.

After dinner, strolling in the warm evening through the crowded, open-air marketplace bordering the harbour, Feldman and Anke held hands and leisurely browsed through the exotic shops filled with spices, bolts of colourful fabrics, crafts and tourist curios. As they walked, Feldman appreciated his companion out of the corners of his eyes, delighting in her intrinsic happiness, her goodness, wholesomeness and beauty.

This was all starting to feel so comfortable to him. Finally, for the first time in his life, he found himself settling into a loving relationship with a woman. Not kicking and scratching, nervous and sceptical. But willingly. At long last, perhaps he'd broken free of those irrational, constrictive, primal inhibitions a young boy and his therapist had once laboured so painfully over.

At a pavement counter, Anke stopped to pick up an intriguing little item that caught her attention. It was one of those novelty 'magic eye' children's books with the mysterious now-you-see-it, now-you-don't holographic images lurking inside computer-generated patterns. This particular book happened to contain hidden three-dimensional pictures of the prophetess Jeza.

Anke flipped the book open and, laughing, held a page up to Feldman's nose, drawing it away from him slowly until the jumbled dots magically materialized before his eyes into the arresting face of the Messiah. Abruptly, however, a strange surge of disorientation began to envelop the reporter. An unpleasant, disquieting sensation. He grabbed Anke for support.

Startled, she dropped the book, peering into his colourless face. 'Jon, are you all right?'

He staggered, inexplicably light-headed, as she anxiously attempted to support him. Fighting to regain his composure, he had a sudden awareness. He released her and spun quickly around. There, not twenty feet from him in the milling crowd, looking inside him with those deep, unfathomable eyes, stood Jeza, the Messiah.

No sooner was Feldman's view obscured by passers-by than she was gone. But there was absolutely no doubting it. This was no illusion. He had seen her. He had *felt* her.

53

The Papal quarters, Vatican City, Rome, Italy,
7.15 P.M., Friday, 11 February 2000

Nicholas VI was seated at his ornate desk, signing documents. He looked up as a knock came at the open doors of his chambers.

'Yes, Antonio, enter.' The Pope had been expecting his visitor.

Antonio di Concerci, leather-bound attaché case in hand, crossed the threshold and greeted his pope, but without his accustomed smile. Nicholas gestured him to a chair, removed his reading spectacles and turned in the prefect's direction.

'You look particularly thoughtful tonight, Tony,' the Pontiff observed, good-humouredly.

'And you look well, *Papa*.'

'How is the *inquirendum* coming?'

'On schedule, Holiness. And your deadline will be met without compromising the integrity of our work, I assure you.'

'Excellent. Then you wish to talk with me on another matter, I presume?'

'Yes. I'm struggling with a dilemma, Holy Father. It concerns Cardinal Litti.'

The Pope took a long breath, dropping his chin, shaking his head.

'I must speak to you in confidence, Holiness,' di Concerci prefaced his remarks.

Nicholas looked up, his face changing from annoyance to concern. 'Of course, Tony.'

'As you know, *Papa*, Cardinal Litti attended that interdenominational Mormon conference last weekend.'

The Pope nodded.

'And as you may have noticed, he was behaving rather peculiarly even before he left.'

'Yes,' the Pope agreed. 'I've been worried about him. He's not been himself of late.'

'I'm afraid he's deteriorated considerably since last you saw him. He came to my office early yesterday morning, unannounced, unshaven, unkempt, and he demanded an audience. When I informed him of a conflicting meeting I had with Cardinals Thompson and Santorini, he became belligerent and insisted that I cancel my meeting and immediately review his findings from the Mormon conference.'

'What did you do?'

'Quite frankly, I felt his state of mind unstable, and rather than provoke him further, I agreed to do as he asked.'

'Did that placate him?'

'He insisted on sitting outside my office while I read the document in its entirety.'

The Pontiff's eyes widened and he scratched his chin. 'And what was the content of his report?'

Di Concerci leaned back in his chair, his lips compressed, as if hesitant to continue further.

'Speak, Antonio.'

The prefect placed his attaché case on the corner of the Pontiff's desk, flipped open the locks and removed a multi-page document.

'Holiness, I don't know how else to describe this.' He laid the papers next to his attaché case. 'These are the ravings of a delusional fanatic. Litti has gone mad. He's renounced the Church. He recognizes this Jeza woman as the New Messiah and proclaims that our destruction is imminent.'

Nicholas sank back in his chair, stunned. 'Alphonse, a millenarian?'

'He demands that the Church recognize Jeza as the New Messiah and that we support her message and mission – assuming anyone can determine precisely what her message or mission might be. And Litti demands that this report be included in the *inquirendum*.'

The Pope remained slumped in his chair, his chin cupped in his hand, his eyes far away. Almost to himself he said in a voice filled with reminiscence, 'This is not Alphonse, you know. I remember so well, many years ago, when I first arrived here as a young, naïve graduate from the Pontifical Theological Academy. Alphonse was one of my first friends. He was very carefree and easy-going. Not at all like he is now. I fear for him. I wonder if it could be a stage of early senility?'

Then to di Concerci he added, 'I want Alphonse to see a physician immediately. A complete check-up. Will you see to this, Tony?'

'Yes, Holy Father, right away. But what about his report?'

Nicholas exhaled. 'Leave it with me. But I can tell you, it will *not* appear in the *inquirendum*.'

After di Concerci had left, Nicholas let his troubled thoughts wander for a while until they finally returned to Alphonse Litti's poor misguided effort, lying in forty-odd pages on the edge of the Pope's antique desk. In the very spot where once lay the marriage annulment petition from Henry VIII and the manifesto of Martin Luther's Ninety-five Theses.

The Pontiff reached over, gathered up the papers, and placed them in a plain envelope he marked 'A. Litti'. From his waist chain, he retrieved a large gold key and unlocked the side vault of his desk. Before depositing the envelope inside, the Pope hesitated, recognizing within the vault a faded brown-leather portfolio. Then, hurriedly, he tossed in A. Litti's report and shut the door.

54

WNN regional headquarters, Cairo, Egypt,
8.30 A.M., Monday, 14 February 2000

Over the weekend there was yet another Jeza sighting by the WNN crews. This proved to be a particularly revealing one. Cissy, who had already reviewed the video on Sunday afternoon with Bollinger and Sullivan, had the tape in hand at an editing bay, awaiting Feldman's and Hunter's arrival for preview and development of the day's newscasts.

Hunter slid into the editing room well ahead of Feldman, and braked hard when he spied Cissy sitting cross-legged on the edge of the table.

'Hey, Ciss,' he started, 'what's happenin'? I hear we got some more hot video footage—'

'I'm still pissed off at you, Hunter!' she hissed, crossing her arms to match her legs.

'Now what for?'

'What for? For punching my date's lights out, that's what for!'

'Your date? Hell, that was no date, Cissy, that was IDF. You know, the good folks who threw Arnie in jail?'

'Schlomo wasn't threatening me, he took me out to dinner, for Chrissakes!'

'*Schlomo?*' he mocked. 'I've got news for you. If you hadn't left with us, in a few more minutes ol' Schlomo and his pals woulda been tossin' your freckled butt in the brig! You oughta be thanking me.'

'I don't need you to look out for me, *thank you.*'

Feldman had arrived outside the door, but he came to an abrupt halt at the sound of elevated voices. He was used to the two of them bickering, but this went well beyond the pale. Unfortunately, he needed access to the room to view the new Jeza tape before he met with Sullivan and Bollinger. He looked at his watch, tapped his toes as the altercation intensified, then retreated back down the hallway a safer distance.

He found situations such as these extremely distressing. They revived difficult memories of his failed attempts to quell arguments between his parents. Nevertheless, something had to be done, and once again he felt responsible for refereeing two people he loved. He bit his lip, gathered his resolve and forced himself back down the hall towards the escalating volume. Anxious faces peered out at him from office doorways, offering silent support as he passed by. He acknowledged them, grim-faced, and continued on.

Approaching the viewing room once again, he could hear Hunter protesting feebly, but Cissy's enraged voice towered over him. Suddenly there was the sound of glass breaking and a squeal of alarm from

Hunter. Feldman feared he'd delayed too long. He scurried around the corner into the room, hoping he was in time to prevent the impending manslaughter. Hunter, cringing in a corner, greeted him with a look of pleading desperation, coffee from a shattered pitcher dripping down the wall behind him. Cissy stood over the imperilled cameraman, the latest Jeza videotape held high and threatening in her hand.

'You goddamn son of a bitch!' she screeched.

Feldman rushed over and wrapped the frenzied woman in his arms, rescuing both Hunter and the precious videotape. The mortified cameraman saw his chance and darted around Cissy like the all-state linebacker he once was, out of the office, down the hall, not to be seen for the rest of the day.

Restraining the enraged, sobbing woman in his arms, Feldman comforted her until she regained some composure.

'Breck doesn't mean to be so insensitive, Cissy. He's just a clumsy, rough old jock who never learned better. In his heart, I know he thinks the world of you. It was pretty obvious from the way he decked that soldier the other night. But maybe you two just aren't meant to be, you know?'

She grimaced in pain and despair, shuddered through another paroxysm, then finally composed herself again. 'Yeah, I know, I know. It's just going to take me a little time, that's all. I'll deal with it.'

'I know you will, Ciss. Come on now, let me drive you home. You take the rest of the day off and things will look a whole lot better tomorrow. You'll see.'

'No,' she said, 'you've got a meeting with Sullivan. I'm okay now, really. I'm going to step into the ladies' room for a minute and then I'll drive myself home. You go on. I'm okay. Really.'

Feldman was unconvinced, and wouldn't leave until he could coax a smile from her. Laughing and crying at the same time, she finally delivered.

'Go on, get out of here,' he commanded. 'I'll call you later to check up, okay?'

'Thanks, Jon,' she said in a calmer voice. 'You've always been good to me.' She grabbed his hands in hers, stood on tiptoe, kissed Feldman's cheek, and left.

Settling in with his filled coffee mug at the editing bay, Feldman called

Sullivan to let him know he was ready for their meeting. Before they began, Bollinger gave him the background on the tape they were about to view. 'This footage was taken Saturday morning, Jon, downtown at the University of Cairo campus. We got a call about nine-thirty that Jeza was on the grounds near the Student Union Centre. By the time we got there, a professor had come across her and invited her into an auditorium to address a class.

'Our crew was able to squeeze in and set up in the back of the hall while she was preoccupied answering questions. You're going to find this interesting. It's one of her lengthier exchanges ever.'

The video opened with Jeza standing behind an elevated podium at the bottom of a large, darkened, bowl-shaped auditorium. The Messiah was dressed in a long, simple, white cotton robe, trimmed in a red-and-purple band on the sleeves and hem. Illuminated in soft overhead lights, speaking comfortably into the microphone in front of her, she held the audience in rapt attention.

The class professor, a swarthy, animated, bearded man with dark, liquid eyes and a turban, was the only other person on the stage with the Messiah. He appeared to be moderating the symposium, selecting the questioners from the audience.

The videotape picked up on a question posed by a tall, thin, middle-aged clergyman in a dark cassock. 'Jeza, pardon me,' he said in a polite tone, 'but your teachings seem to contradict many tenets of the Holy Bible. Are you above the Bible?'

'Where I am,' she responded in that commanding, yet soft, soothing voice of hers, 'is by the hand and will of God. I bring you His Word as His begotten messenger.'

After each of her comments, the hall was abuzz with low-volume conversation, which quickly and respectfully abated with the next question asked.

'Jeza?' A black male student in a colourfully embroidered robe was recognized by the class professor. 'Your teachings would seem to follow Christian philosophy in that you have proclaimed yourself the Sister of Jesus Christ and the Daughter of God. Are you then God, and should you be worshipped?'

'None should be worshipped but God the Father,' she responded.

'Are you superior to Jesus?' he questioned.

'Is ice superior to water?' she answered matter-of-factly, without the slightest edge to her voice. 'Both are the same elements in different form, for different seasons.'

The class professor now posed a question of his own. 'Jeza,' he asked, 'are you proclaiming a new religion, or are you an adherent of a current theology?'

'I bring you insight into the will of God,' she responded. 'The New Light is the culmination of all religions. It is the natural goal to which all religions must aspire.'

'Then to what religion should we belong?' a young man in a bright yellow turban asked.

'The Lord will not judge you by your religion,' she answered. 'Nor does He favour one religion over another, nor one person over the next. Each man, woman, child will be judged only by how far that individual advances towards the fulfilment of personal perfection in the New Light.'

A leather-skinned, angry-looking man in Arabic garb sprang to his feet, his eyes flashing with emotion. 'But if you are the sister of Jesus, you are a Jew. Are you then not partial to the Jew over the Arab? What have you to say to the freedom fighter who has lost his homeland to the Jews!'

'I say this to you,' she responded solemnly, her face growing dark. 'The embittered divisions between Arab and Jew are an abiding source of anguish to God! As I am the Almighty's daughter, so also am I sister to Muhammad. Know you not that both Arab and Jew arise from the same root? That you share the same heritage in the patriarch, Abraham? The same deity whose name is both Allah and Yahweh? You are brothers in the eyes of God unlike no other peoples on the face of the earth, yet you hate and you shed one another's blood as mortal enemies!

'To you who pursue violence to regain your homeland, know this: your issues are worthy, but you yourselves are not! The acts of terrorism that you bring are abhorrent in the eyes of God. I say to you, let the persecution of the Jews – and of the Palestinians, and of all religions and peoples – let it all end now, for evermore. Until you forswear such acts of violence, God will turn His face from you. Until you and your brother Jews can come together with love and a true desire for reconciliation and unity, neither will know a peaceful homeland!'

The hall was stock-still. Taken aback, the befuddled Arab slowly resumed his seat.

After a period of profound silence, a young female student tentatively raised her hand. 'Lady Messiah, are you here to found a new religion?'

'The New Light is not a religion, nor is it a list of rituals. The New Light is the understanding by which each may strive towards God's will for humankind.'

The professor then asked, 'What is God's will for mankind? And what exactly is the New Light?'

'All is being revealed according to God's plan,' she replied. 'You must watch and you must listen.'

A young black man, raising his hand animatedly from far back in the audience, was called on and created a stir when he pleaded, 'Messiah, my mother is very ill. I beg you, please cure her!'

The professor immediately rushed to the centre of the stage and warned, pointedly, that any further attempts to seek interventions or personal favours from the Messiah would result in the removal of that individual from the auditorium. He then promptly called on another questioner. However, in an unsubstantiated report issued a few days later, a Cairo paper claimed that the young man's mother recovered that same hour, completely and inexplicably, from a purported terminal illness.

Another female student posed a question which brought about a rift of laughter. 'Messiah, is God male or female?'

Jeza showed no undue reaction. 'God is both male and female,' she said straightforwardly. 'And mankind is separated from God by its sexes.'

The same student followed up her question. 'You refer to God as "He" and to humanity as "man", or "mankind". Isn't that preferential and sexist? Particularly since you yourself are female?'

There were a few whistles and catcalls in the audience. But the professor stood with a stern face and the auditorium fell immediately silent.

Jeza did not hesitate with her response. 'It may be more correct to identify God as "It", and mankind as simply "humanity". But this is not the custom, and to depart from the traditional so late in the hour is more academic than purposeful. For you to dwell on these terms as divisive is to distract yourself from your purpose, which is unity. Nevertheless, if you wish to understand scripture as God intended it, it is wise to go back and remove the inequity, as I will make clearer to you in days to come.'

'You say "late in the hour", Messiah,' the professor noted with a catch in his voice. 'Are you foretelling the end of the world?'

There was a palpable suspension of breath in the audience.

Jeza herself grew solemn and pensive. 'A great change is coming,' she slowly answered. 'It will mark both the end and the beginning. You must be vigilant and you will come to understand God's plan.'

This caused quite a stir in the assembly and the professor had to stand again to restore order. He selected another individual.

'By what rules shall we live?' the student asked. 'By the Ten Commandments? The Talmud? The secular laws of our nation?'

'All of these and none of these,' she responded enigmatically. 'I say to you that through the ages, God's word has been revealed many times to man. It is the same word, spoken by many tongues, written by many hands. To some it is the Bible. To others the Koran. To still others, the Torah. And there exist many more forms.

'As the banks of your Nile are changed each spring by the recurring floods, so also does the full meaning of the Word change with each iteration and translation and interpretation. To know the way of the Lord, you must hear more than words.'

'But Messiah,' another clergyman protested, looking upset and confused, 'I have devoted my entire life to studying scripture and the great theologians. Are you saying that all my work has been in vain?'

'There is much to be learned from the scriptures,' the Messiah answered him, 'even if the translations be poor. But there is little that you will gain from the writings of the theologians, even if you understand them perfectly. For there are as many interpretations of the Word of God as there are religions upon the face of the earth. And none can tell you the separate truth that lies only within your soul.'

The clergyman persisted. 'Surely the great and learned religious scholars have better insight and understanding of the complex scriptures than the common man!'

Jeza did not seem put off by the man's tenacity. She turned to the general audience and, in a slightly elevated voice, imparted to them a metaphor that would later come to be known as:

THE PARABLE OF THE CHEF'S APPRENTICES

'Behold there was a chef who was master of a kitchen. One day he called to his apprentice cooks and gathered them about him saying: "For this evening's meal, I shall prepare a special banquet. Go to the well and collect a measure of water."

'Now the youngest of the apprentices hastened to the well and soon returned with a large pail filled with clean, clear water, which he placed before the elder apprentices.

'Upon seeing the pail of water, one of the elders said to the youngest apprentice, "This pail is not large enough. We will need more water to prepare such a banquet. You must return again to the well!"

'Another said, "The water from the stream is fresher, and will improve the flavour of the foods. You should draw the water from the stream!"

'And yet another said, "You have spilled water upon the floor and we cannot prepare the meal until you remove it."

'At this time the master chef returned to the kitchen, and hearing this, he took the pail of water and poured it out upon the floor, saying: "Before a banquet can be prepared, the kitchen must first be cleaned." And to the youngest apprentice he said, "Come while they do this work and I will share with you the arrangements for the feast."

'Amen, Amen I say to you: go forth and fill your pail knowing that the Lord God cares not about the volume nor the content, but will judge you by your intent. And none may judge but the Father Himself.' (Apotheosis 23:4–11)

Concluding her discourse, the Messiah blessed her audience and stepped back from the podium, accepting the outstretched hand of the professor as a fusillade of flashbulbs and applause erupted. The audience pressed towards the stage, and Jeza was quickly ushered out a back way, disappearing from view.

55

WNN regional headquarters, Cairo, Egypt,
9.30 A.M., Wednesday, 16 February 2000

There was good news at the morning staff meeting. WNN's latest report on Jeza's appearance at the university was a sensation, capturing record ratings.

And then, just as the meeting was about to break up, an excited cameraman from one of the field teams suddenly raced into the room. Breathlessly, he announced another Jeza encounter. Waving the prize video in the air, he explained that less than an hour ago he'd happened to catch the Messiah in a major engagement.

This latest development, by the sound of it, could prove to be one of the most amazing reports yet. If the advance billing was correct, at last WNN had caught on tape an apparent Jeza miracle. Possibly three miracles, the cameraman claimed, as they all hustled off to the viewing room.

By way of prefacing his video, the cameraman explained that he'd been stopped at a traffic light in one of the poorer sections of downtown Cairo. Sitting there, he'd noticed a little urchin with a rag in his hand bounding out into the street from across the intersection. The boy was heading for the cameraman's car, evidently to wash his windscreen for a handout. Sadly, in his haste to nab his customer before another competitor, the boy had dashed in front of an oncoming bakery van and was struck.

Compounding the tragedy, the bakery's name appearing on the side of the truck happened to be that of a Sunni Muslim company. An unfortunate circumstance in that this accident occurred in a predominantly Shiite Muslim district, igniting instant outrage. In moments, the vehicle had been completely surrounded and the luckless driver dragged from behind the wheel.

This was the point at which the alert videographer had swung his camera in action. The alarming scene materialized on the viewing-room screen, waves of people appearing magically from nowhere, rallying to the cries of the onlookers and rushing to the scene of the accident. Watching the drama unfold, Feldman was certain the poor delivery man was about to be pummelled to death. But as the mob descended upon him, there was an abrupt division at the crowd's far end and the angry throngs began separating and falling back.

The focus was off-centre for a few moments as the cameraman scrambled on top of the roof of his car for a better view. A hole had formed in the middle of the action now, and the camera zoomed in to show a small woman standing boldly before the downed and bloody driver. It was Jeza, of course, but over the noise, it was difficult to hear what she was saying.

Recognizing who this was, the crowd began quieting. It sounded as if Jeza were talking in Arabic, and she was pointing to the forlorn man at her feet. She then gestured towards the front of the vehicle and barked a command. The crowd parted again to allow an anguished man with a small boy in his arms to pass through. It was apparently the father of the child who had been struck by the vehicle. The boy's extremities dangled loosely, his face was buried in the crook of his father's elbow, and it was impossible to tell how badly he was hurt, or if he were even alive.

Jeza called out to the father, and he squatted on his haunches in front of her, rocking to and fro, howling, still holding the limp child. Jeza raised her arms skyward and the sleeves of her robe cascaded to her shoulders, exposing the vivid whiteness of her limbs. She called out loudly, presumably in prayer, ending with the only word Feldman recognized, 'Allah.'

Despite its unrestrained fury only moments ago, the crowd was now dead still, with only the ambient sounds of the city audible. Jeza, also silent, lowered her arms to her sides and watched the child intently. So did everyone else. They didn't have long to wait. The legs stirred. The head moved. The man holding the boy relaxed his grip and revealed the child to the astounded audience. The boy's eyes were open, flitting around, puzzled and scared.

A tumult overtook the crowd. 'Allah! Allah! Allah!' they shouted, and hands began moving out to touch the prophetess. But she halted them with both palms upraised, gestured down to the truck driver again, and motioned them back. Stooping, she took hold of the terrified man's wrist and helped him to his feet. She placed a hand on his shoulder, steadying him, speaking with him momentarily, and then turned with him back towards his vehicle.

Guiding him by his shaking arm, she was given a wide berth as they made their way to the side of the truck. It was a panel van, and Jeza grasped the sliding door by its handle, throwing it open wide. She pulled the driver carefully out of the way, then made another brief announcement to the crowd.

The mob paused for a moment, looked at one another, and then started to burrow full bore into the truck in a feeding frenzy. Hundreds of men, women and children pillaged its goods hand over fist, grabbing as much as they could carry. One man waddled by the camera with hard rolls stuffed down the sleeves and the front of his tunic and trousers to the point where his clothing was about to burst.

And then it suddenly occurred to Feldman that Jeza was missing. Even reviewing the tape again in slow motion, it was impossible to tell exactly when and what had happened to the Messiah. She was there, and then, quite implausibly, she had vanished, leaving the deserted driver to gawk nervously as his bakery truck was greedily relieved of its freight.

But if rescuing the driver and restoring the boy were two miracles, then there was yet another to behold. Astoundingly, the procession of scavengers went on for the duration of the video, at least twenty more minutes, until the camera ran out of tape. And still, the small van hadn't exhausted its cargo. Roll after roll, loaf after loaf, baskets of pastries, buns and all manner of baked goods flowed endlessly from its doors until it would appear that every last pocket, shirt front, box, bucket and apron was sated.

'The only thing lacking,' Hunter pointed out, 'is the fishes.'

While none of these three events could be conclusively demonstrated to be a miracle, the new video nevertheless presented some very powerful and fascinating images. The temptation to promote this extraordinary material as the *Miracles Tape* proved commercially irresistible. No sooner did the first teaser promo air on WNN's midday news than the public went wild with anticipation. Major sponsors descended on the network in a feeding frenzy of another kind.

*   *   *

Working late into the night to ready the *Miracles* video for a news special the next day, one by one the WNN team members gave in to their fatigue and retired for the evening. But an enthralled, motivated, wideawake Feldman continued to work well past midnight. In particular, there was one aspect of the new tape that had intrigued him all day, but he had been unable to devote any attention to it until now.

Alone in the darkened viewing bay, he played with the editing controls, trying to identify the precise moment when the Messiah seemed suddenly to vanish in plain sight. Perhaps there was a fourth miracle here. Concentrating on the segment of tape taken just before Jeza disappeared, he examined a wide shot in which the figure of the Messiah was continually in the frame, visible the entire time. She was conspicuously there, immersed in onlookers near the side of the truck, then suddenly she turned and seemed simply to evaporate.

He rewound the tape for the umpteenth time, magnified the image a bit more, zoomed in on the grainy image, and worked patiently with the controls to enhance the resolution of the Messiah's immaculate face. Frame by frame he advanced the tape until the final moments when she looked directly into the camera, just before she turned and melted away. After some effort, he succeeded in making the image clearer than in any of his previous attempts. Now he could view her ennobled, divine features with a relative degree of clarity. Those bottomless, enervating eyes. Drawn into them, once again he was suddenly overcome with that disquieting, swooning, paralysing sensation that he'd come to recognize so well.

As before, he regained his equilibrium quickly, amazed that a mere video image could affect him so profoundly. But suddenly the hairs rose on the back of his neck. His hands were trembling. The breath left him and he rotated slowly in his chair. There, silhouetted strikingly in the doorway, silent and motionless, stood the slender form and commanding presence of Jeza herself.

Feldman was transfixed. His heart and mind raced wildly. Back-lit before him, she had the aura of an apparition. Feldman could almost feel the waves of energy radiating from her.

'Come with me,' was all she said. And Feldman was up out of his chair, pursuing the quick-paced, earnest young lady as she quietly departed down the hall.

How she had eluded the security system and night-watchman on her way in, he was unable to fathom. She led him through the exit, down the steps and off into the deserted streets.

He questioned nothing, content to let her dictate the situation, following her closely for over an hour, out of the city, heading due west. Into the bordering desert they trekked, up a steep, winding path, which left Feldman panting, until finally at the top of a tall precipice, she stopped to face the first light of morning, dawning just now behind Cairo below them.

Jeza wasn't even breathing hard, and showed not a hint of perspiration. She turned to Feldman and, with a faint, appreciative smile, motioned him towards a large smooth stone. Once he'd settled, she sat cross-legged on a similar stone next to him and gazed out over the city in peaceful contemplation.

Feldman couldn't take his eyes from this extraordinary woman. He'd never before been so close to her. At this proximity, with the first morning sunbeams catching her face, she was more resplendent than ever. He marvelled again at her physical perfection. Not a single blemish, discolouration or wrinkle. Not one. Her features were all as finely chiselled as if by a master sculptor.

Gazing at her now in the cool morning stillness, and recalling the bizarre circumstances of her unnatural incubation, he was moved to sympathy for this strange and isolated woman.

Still she said nothing, and Feldman was determined to wait her out, to avoid anything that might disturb this curious relationship. He watched her incisive eyes as they flitted across the Egyptian landscape, taking in the architectural extremes of ancient pyramids and contemporary skyscrapers. And he wondered what was going on in that alien, prefabricated mind of hers.

As if wishing to answer his curiosities, she at last turned to him and presented a sweet, comforting smile. 'I seek your help,' she said straightforwardly, her eyes invading him, although this time without the vertiginous side effects.

Her gaze was still unsettling. It affected him like a visual truth serum. As if any thought he might have she could instantly read. In the middle of trying to cope with that distraction, yet another odd awareness struck him. She never blinked! At least, not that he'd detected. Her gaze was absolutely unfaltering.

He shook all of this off and tried to focus on her unanticipated question. 'My help? Um, certainly. Of course. How can I help you?'

She grew reflective. 'It is nearly time for me to leave this place. I must travel far from here for a short while and carry on the Father's work in other lands. Will you assist me?'

Feldman was not sure what she was asking.

'Assist you? How?'

'In arranging transport and lodging and audiences with those I must see.'

'Where do you want to go, when do you want to go there, and with whom do you want to meet?'

'My first journey is to America. In two weeks. To address the assembled religions of the world by the great salt lake.'

Feldman had no idea what she was referring to. 'Sure,' he promised, 'I can do that, no problem!' He could hardly contain himself. Here was an opportunity for WNN to establish a direct relationship with the most famous sought-after celebrity on earth. The benefits and the rating points would be incalculable.

'I wish to speak with all the representatives of the world religions on the last day of their assembly,' she added. 'Also, I would ask you to witness and record these events.'

Feldman grinned. 'Absolutely. I'll make all the arrangements right away. Now, how do I contact you? Where are you staying?' He was trying to look casual, holding his breath, hoping she'd reveal her hiding place to him.

'I will meet you here at dawn, one week from today, to hear of your plans.'

'But what if I should need to reach you in between?' He gave it one last try.

'I will not see you again until one week from today.' She stated this as a fact, not a decision. 'Now I must go.'

'Very well,' Feldman agreed, and they both stood. He extended his hand to her and she took it. Hers was so small in his. So warm, so smooth.

So strong. He tentatively tried to withdraw his hand, but was taken off guard by her leverage. She held him fast. Not threateningly, but to emphasize a point.

'You will return alone?' she asked.

'Of course.'

She smiled her kind smile once more and released him.

Feldman began his trek down the hillside, fully expecting to find her gone when he turned for a last look. She was.

56

The Vatican Gardens, Rome, Italy,
2.15 P.M., Friday, 18 February 2000

A pensive, lonely Cardinal Alphonse Litti sat at the edge of a carved stone bench in the Lourdes Grotto of the Vatican Gardens. At this precise moment, the Congregation for the Doctrine of the Faith was meeting with Nicholas VI, presenting their formal *inquirendum*.

Litti knew his report would not be among its pages. Four days ago he had received a courier-delivered epistle from Nicholas in response to his persistent requests for an audience. In the letter, Nicholas had expressed concern for his health and had commanded a complete physical by the Vatican medical staff, followed by an extended vacation. From the tone, it was obvious that Nicholas was aware of Litti's report. And had rejected it.

Neither would the Pope grant an audience, nor give his cardinal permission to attend the Mormons' second convocation, coming up in two weeks.

There was nothing in the formal *inquirendum* that would have surprised Cardinal Litti anyway. As the preliminary report had hinted, the Congregation's final determination was to discredit Jeza as a legitimate prophetess, much less a Messiah. Falling short of labelling her an outright fraud, the Congregation, in rendering the solemn judgment of Holy Mother Church, proclaimed

Jeza a false witness to God's will. At best misguided, possibly delusional.

The Pontiff approved the *inquirendum* document in its entirety, elevated it to encyclical status, and had it dispatched under his papal seal to all the Apostolic Churches for immediate dissemination to their congregations.

From this point forward, the faithful were hereby ordered to discount the teachings and messages of Jeza, and to abstain from further attention to, or acknowledgment of, her words and deeds.

57

WNN regional headquarters, Cairo, Egypt, *10.12 A.M., Saturday, 19 February 2000*

The news of Feldman's contact with Jeza had the WNN international brass breaking out the champagne and toasting the winsome young man who had single-handedly delivered them at least three weeks of guaranteed, unchallenged world news leadership.

All the big wheels of WNN were rolled in for this preparation. Now that they understood what Jeza was referring to by 'the assembled religions of the world by the great salt lake', no expense would be spared to ensure her safe passage to the Mormon convocation. Teams of attorneys worked on the legalities of international transportation for the New Messiah, since she had no official country of origin – no passport, no birth certificate, no medical records.

The attorneys would also have to contend with the raft of lawsuits from competing media that would surely ensue once WNN extracted from the Mormons a contract for exclusive coverage of the 'Holy Bowl', as Hunter had impiously tagged the event.

Security would be a nightmare of extraordinary proportions. With the millions of people who'd doubtless descend upon the city, getting

Jeza safely into and out of Salt Lake City, much less the convention hall, would be taxing.

And while WNN had hoped to delay disclosure of the event for as long as possible to avoid interference with their arrangements, there was no holding the lid on a story of this magnitude. Word leaked out quickly, and WNN was snowed under with calls, telegrams and messages from all over the world. One communication that did manage to escape the avalanche of messages was a cable from the White House. Presidential campaign manager Edwin Guenther requested a phone call from Jon Feldman.

Absorbed in a heated meeting thousands of miles away, Brian Newcomb, Democratic Presidential Re-election Committee chairman, was vocal in his opposition to the bold plan under discussion.

'Having the President meet with this charlatan is foolhardy,' he snorted across the Oval Office at Guenther. 'We know nothing about her. Hell, we don't even know for sure if she *is* a woman!'

Guenther, ever cool in the line of fire, turned patiently to his president. 'Al, there are times in a campaign when you look back on a missed opportunity and kick yourself hard in the butt. If we pass up this one, I can guaran-damn-tee you, we'll be kicking ourselves all the way to November. Look at what's happening right now. We got this upstart McGuire gaining in the polls—'

'Yeah,' Newcomb interrupted, 'after you let him get a toehold on us in New Hampshire by keeping us out of the primary for so damn long!'

Guenther ignored the jab. 'But look at where his support's coming from – the religious fundamentalists. The *millenarians*! They constitute twenty-seven per cent of the vote right now. They're the swing vote, Al, and they're McGuire's bread and butter.'

President Allen Moore was noticeably intrigued, to the dismay of his re-election committee chairman.

Guenther continued. 'We need something to separate McGuire from his voting bloc, and what better way to do it than with this gorgeous, sexy religious idol. A short meeting, a tasty photo op, front-page banners and TV coverage all over the place. And we fix it so McGuire can't even get close to her.'

'And exactly how do you propose to do that?' Newcomb challenged.

'Easy,' Guenther rejoined with a confident smile spreading across his wide, chunky face. 'WNN and the Mormons have to go through a lot of hoops to get their little lady into the country. Now, we can narrow those hoops, or we can eliminate them altogether, depending on how they want to co-operate with us. I've already got a message into Jon Feldman about this, and I'm just willing to bet he'll find a way to fit us into their schedule.'

'It doesn't—' Newcomb began, but the President waved him off.

'No, Brian, I like it,' Moore decided. 'We need to reach the millenarians somehow, and I know of no other way to do it. But let's be smart about it. A semi-private meeting. Nothing where the media can draw us into a controversy. Something warm and fuzzy, you know. Maybe in front of the fireplace here. But let's make sure we control things.'

Guenther could see that his commander-in-chief was starting to appreciate the potential here. 'How about we bring in a handicapped person,' Guenther mused, 'and see what she can do with him? Damn, wouldn't that be incredible if she could really cure somebody right here in the Oval Office, on national TV!'

58

The outskirts of Cairo, Egypt,
5.30 A.M., Thursday, 24 February 2000

Feldman had driven around for an hour, just to make doubly sure no one was following him. Heeding Jeza's admonition to come alone, neither he nor WNN was about to jeopardize their fabulous opportunity. Parking his Rover about a half-mile from the hill where he had last seen the prophetess, Feldman grabbed a travel bag from the back seat and walked the rest of the way at a brisk pace, keeping an eye on the sparse landscape around him.

Checking his watch, he ascended the slope right on time and arrived at the top to find the Messiah sitting cross-legged in her accustomed spot, in deep meditation.

Always appreciative of the opportunity to observe her, Feldman stood by, politely awaiting her attention.

Still engaged in her private thoughts, without looking up, she said in her cool, soothing voice, 'Come sit and pray with me.'

Feldman flopped awkwardly next to her on his designated stone and she held out her small hand to him. He swallowed it in his and closed his eyes to accompany her. After about five minutes he grew impatient and risked a peep at his companion.

She remained immobile and placid in her contemplations, eyes still shut, peaceful and calm. However, as if she could detect his glance, she spoke. 'Thank you for coming. What news do you bring me?' She opened her eyes now and turned to him with a welcoming smile.

Maybe he was starting to get used to it, but her gaze had less of its usual impact this morning. 'Good news, Jeza,' he responded, shaking his head quickly to clear it. 'How have you been?'

'Very well. You are well also,' she stated.

'Yes, I am,' Feldman agreed, smiling back. 'I've made arrangements for our trip, if you'd care to hear about them.'

'Yes.'

'We'll leave here Saturday, 4 March, at eight A.M. on a specially chartered Boeing 747. The plane's fully equipped with a private room for you. Shower, bed and round-the-clock room service from an on-board galley. We'll fly non-stop to Washington, DC, for a stay-over.'

He paused here. This was the one bottleneck he was not quite sure how to handle. As was his general solution, however, he resorted to the truth. 'Jeza, perhaps you're aware, but because you have no official identification papers, it's very difficult to get clearance for you to travel to other countries. In order to gain your admission to the United States, I was forced to make a small compromise. I hope you don't object.'

She said nothing, looking deep inside him with her unsettling eyes.

'The President of the United States would like to meet you. To have you visit him, have your pictures taken together, join him and Mrs Moore for dinner, and stay overnight at the White House. Would that be all right with you?' He held his breath.

'If that is what you wish for me,' she said without a moment's reflection.

Feldman was unprepared for so quick a concession and momentarily lost his train of thought. 'Uh, yes, wonderful. Well, that simplifies things so much. Thank you. Uh, then, the next morning we leave early for Salt Lake City and will arrive in time for you to make a noon appearance at the convocation. It's a bit of a hectic pace for you, but does that sound acceptable?'

'Yes. I thank you for your efforts.'

'There are a few other things that will be required of you, also, Jeza. For example, there are certain inoculations and vaccines you must have to ensure your health on your visit. This can all be done orally, simply by swallowing some medicines I've brought with me.'

Jeza accepted a handful of sealed pills, capsules and vials of fluids from him without comment, opened and arranged them all on the edge of her stone seat in front of her. She then picked them up and instantly popped them all into her mouth in one sudden, quick motion. Feldman was startled, expecting her to choke, and blinked away his surprise as she turned calmly back to him awaiting his next direction.

He laughed out loud, despite himself, and Jeza smiled back.

'Now, I need to take a quick picture of you.' He pulled out a Polaroid camera and snapped off a few shots. 'And I need to get you to read and sign a few papers.' He opened a clipboard and placed it in front of her, indicating with an X the lines she was to sign.

She made no attempt to read the documents, but immediately affixed her 'signatures', which, Feldman noticed with interest, were perfectly rendered Stars of David.

Returning the papers to him she looked questioningly into his eyes.

'That's about it for now,' he informed her. 'Is there anything you wish to ask?'

'No.'

'I've brought some sweet rolls and coffee with me if you'd care to join me for a little breakfast,' he offered, hoping to prolong the visit. He pulled a Thermos from his bag and opened the bakery box invitingly.

Jeza shook her head and sprang lithely to her feet. 'I thank you, but I am fasting and I must return now to the desert to complete my morning prayers.'

'Well then, I guess we'll see each other next Saturday, here, at the same time? Or' – he was fishing again – 'perhaps I could pick you up somewhere else?'

'I shall await you here at first light, nine days from this. May I call you by your first name?'

'Yes, yes, of course,' he replied, clumsily attempting to rise without the aid of his hands, which were occupied with coffee and sweet roll. 'Please call me Jon.'

'Thank you, Jon,' she said and, recognizing his encumbrance, she dispensed with the customary handshake.

Sitting back down on his rock to enjoy his breakfast, Feldman watched her striding spryly out into the wasteland, her robes and unruly hair flowing freely behind her. As she receded in the distance, he wondered where she went and what she did. The morning rays of sun sent up from the desert floor waves of heated air behind her, creating atmospheric distortions that shortly, he would swear, dissolved her into nothingness.

59

The Papal quarters, the Vatican, Rome, Italy,
11.12 A.M., Friday, 25 February 2000

Nicholas VI was standing at his study window, peering out over the colonnades of St Peter's Square. An exquisite view of Rome, yet it brought him no comfort this morning.

Arriving outside the Pope's quarters, Cardinal Antonio di Concerci could see his pontiff from the threshold, but halted, announcing his presence respectfully at the open doorway.

'Tony, please' – the Pope had been anxiously awaiting him – 'what word do you have of Alphonse?'

'Not good, Holiness,' the prefect replied, glumly. 'As you know, he's vacated his quarters without word. All his personal effects, and only his personal effects, are gone. Yesterday he emptied his Vatican bank account, and a Swiss Guard at the piazza saw him leave about seven-thirty this morning in a cab. He took with him three large suitcases and a foot locker. We're checking all the city hotels now.'

'I would suggest you try the airport.' Nicholas sighed heavily.

'You feel he's left the country?' the prefect asked.

'Yes, Tony. I believe he's pursuing his obsession to follow this false prophetess. You know how badly he wished to attend the forthcoming Mormon convention. Hearing that his Jeza would be making an appearance there, I'm certain, was more temptation than he could resist. Especially in his current agitated state of mind.' The Pontiff looked again out of the window, as if searching after his lost cardinal.

Frowning, di Concerci followed Nicholas's eyes with his own. 'I fear we will not easily be rid of this seductive impostor, *Papa*.'

Nicholas pivoted slowly and looked with troubled eyes at his prefect. 'Yes, I'm afraid our encyclical has not been well enough received. The allure of this woman is very compelling to many. We're encountering strong rebellion in the ranks – all over, not just in the United States.

'And it's not only our parishioners, Tony,' the Pope elaborated. 'We're losing priests, nuns and even a number of our bishops. The media pronounce last rites on us. Can you image what they'll make of Alphonse's defection if it comes to light? To lose a cardinal – a curial cardinal, no less!'

'Yes, Holy Father,' di Concerci commiserated, 'it keeps me awake at nights.'

'I, too, have difficulty sleeping. And when I do nod off, I have these tormented, recurring dreams that I cannot explain. In different forms I encounter this elusive presence. It abides near by, always around, yet always in the periphery. Disappearing a step ahead of me, just around the corner. A familiar shadow, only I can never glimpse its face nor make the proper connection to identify it. I believe God is delivering a sign to me, Tony, but I cannot yet read it.'

'An intervention from God would be most welcome right now,' the cardinal agreed. 'We're all praying for guidance.'

The Pope paused, observing his adviser closely. 'Tony, I'm about to ask an important favour of you.'

'Anything, Holy Father,' di Concerci pledged.

'I want you to go to this second interdenominational convention in America.'

Di Concerci's positive expression evaporated.

'Hopefully you can persuade Alphonse to return. But more significantly, I want you to gain a first-hand experience and assessment of this mysterious Jeza woman, this spellbinder who's entranced so many, including one of our very own Holy See. I've arranged for you to occupy a seat on the presiding panel. I'd like you and another cardinal of your choosing to represent the Curia at the convocation. Hopefully while you're there, you'll find Alphonse and return him to his senses.'

Nicholas placed his hands on di Concerci's shoulders. 'Bring Alphonse back, Tony. Bring him back. But more importantly, bring with you an answer to this spreading problem that grows more serious by the day.'

60

Mormon Convention Centre, Salt Lake City, Utah, 9.00 A.M., Thursday, 2 March 2000

Not unexpectedly, the Mormon organizers had been more than receptive to WNN's overtures. Jeza would be scheduled in whenever WNN wished, for as long as WNN wished. WNN would also have exclusive coverage rights for the entire convention, complete with scheduled TV time-outs for sponsorships and commercial messages, with the exception of Jeza's speech, which would be telecast live and uninterrupted.

Subsequently, the atmosphere for this much-vaunted Second Convocation of Interdenominational Religious Faiths of the Third Millennium was far different from the first. For one thing, thanks to the announcement of the new surprise guest speaker, the convocation had gleaned vastly more respect and world interest. Literally overnight, the Mormons were overrun with registration requests. In the first hour alone, after the mere rumour of Jeza's scheduled appearance leaked from a Washington, DC, radio station, the Mormons had received over 400,000 orders from all over the globe, by phone, fax, e-mail, and telegram, not including the massive in-person invasions of the Tabernacle Hall itself.

The 'Holy Bowl' was unquestionably an event of epic proportions. The excitement in the world religious communities was electric. And despite the sell-out, millions of rapturous pilgrims were still converging on the city by the Great Salt Lake.

So many people, in fact, that the governor of Utah was compelled to call out the National Guard to handle the unprecedented influx of pilgrims. Tent communities and soup kitchens were set up to accommodate the swelling numbers of homeless and afflicted who'd journeyed here just to be near their Saviour. Cars, mobile homes, trailers and RVs stretched for tangled miles along the major routes feeding into the area.

Out along the boulevards leading to the hall were street vendors, spiritual hucksters and religious entrepreneurs of all ilks, peddling everything from Jeza T-shirts, ashtrays and watches to animal-friendly Jeza veggieburgers. Even prostitution, virtually unknown in this Blessed City, had arrived with an opportunistic vengeance. To the outrage of the religious community, some of the more marketing-oriented streetwalkers were even dressed to resemble the prophetess herself, with wigs of wild dark hair, bright white pancake, dark blue contact lenses and white flowing robes.

Scalpers, it was said, were commanding up to $250,000 for a prime seat at the hall, willingly paid for by wealthy individuals with serious health problems, hoping for a miraculous cure. 'Jeza Feva' extended everywhere, as countless bumper stickers proclaimed. Churches, temples and mosques were setting up big-screen TVs on their altars and advertising the event on their outdoor marquees.

It was into this bizarre circus atmosphere that a tired and emotionally drained Cardinal Alphonse Litti descended from his transcontinental early morning flight. As a charter attendee of the first convocation and a member of the prestigious Roman Catholic Curia, Litti had been able to secure a coveted front-row seat on the convention hall floor, immediately in front of the stage, right behind the presiding panel. However, after this considerable expense, the cardinal had been left with little money for accommodation. He'd had to settle for a small room in a third-rate hostelry, several long blocks from the convention centre.

Following his cab ride from the airport, standing alone on the pavement in front of his hotel with his three leather suitcases and green seaman's foot locker, the disenfranchised cardinal took stock of himself. He had with him his sole possessions in the world. Four black cassocks with purple trim; two red-and-black cloaks (one light, one heavy); two red zucchetto skullcaps; six white shirts; six clerical collars; a black sweater; a pectoral cross; a crimson fascia; a purple sash; four sets of underclothing; and two pairs of black dress shoes, size seven and a half. Also, his valued collection of precious books and papers; miscellaneous personal effects and mementoes; photos of his parents and of his childhood.

Certainly, many cardinals had more and better possessions than he, Litti was well aware, but the cardinal had always taken his vow of poverty seriously. As a young priest, at his mother's side in the hospital when she was so sick with tuberculosis, he had promised St Jude Thaddeus, saint of the impossible, that if the good apostle would only spare his mother's life, he would give to charity half of any money he ever earned.

Although St Jude welshed on the deal, Litti forever kept his half of the bargain.

For the cardinal, this trip to Utah was, in more ways than one, a journey of no return. The entire package, convocation ticket, hotel, one-way plane fare, et cetera, had required virtually all of his life savings: the tiny inheritance from his father, God bless him; nickels and dimes squirrelled away from forty-eight years of faithful, low-paying servitude to his Church; the proceeds from his pawned cardinal's ring.

Where he would go from here, Litti had no idea. All that was left in his wallet was 626,350 litre – about four hundred dollars. But in his heart, he had the unwavering confidence that what he was doing was right. And for Alphonse Litti, that was wealth enough.

Also in town today was the Right Reverend Solomon T. Brady, DD. He'd arrived a little earlier, was staying at a substantially nicer hotel, and was in considerably better spirits than he'd been at the last convocation. While barely into his new televangelical fund-raising strategy, he could already forecast success. His twenty-four-hour, pay-per-call phone lines, with trained counsellors always available to accept calls and solicit donations, were operating at peak capacity. Things appeared to be back on track at the Universal Kingdom.

And, making his first appearance at the convocation, another TV minister was arriving in style. Rolling up to his four-star hotel in a purple stretch limo, complete with a showy retinue of beautiful people, was the elegantly dressed First Reverend Fischer of the Samaritan Leadership Council, who'd recently changed his forename from 'Richard' to 'Peter', to reflect his enhanced role as a 'Fischer of Men'.

Still condemning WNN's exposé as libellous, and still professing an intimate connection with the Messiah, Reverend Fischer was rumoured to have paid an outrageous sum for two front-row seats for himself and an attractive, puerile little blonde girl he referred to compassionately as 'my poor little orphan'.

61

The outskirts of Cairo, Egypt,
5.45 A.M., Saturday, 4 March 2000

For his drive out to the desert, Feldman had left extra early, plagued by the fear that this time Jeza wouldn't be awaiting him. It was a worry brought on by another of those nagging, perplexing dreams he'd been experiencing with such regularity.

Arriving at the familiar hill, he parked his Rover at the bottom and jogged quickly to the top, his heart racing more from anxiety than physical exertion. Disastrously, his worst fears were immediately confirmed. No Jeza. And with the dawning sun easily defining the flat desert horizon, she was nowhere to be seen across the vast panorama.

He began to explore the humiliation and financial loss this major *faux pas* would visit upon him and his company. The entire world was poised in anticipation of this great event, with Feldman the manifest master of ceremonies.

Refusing to fall dictate to his dream, he resisted calling for Jeza across the wilderness void. He'd simply wait and hope. He looked at his watch. Six A.M. First light. She had said she'd be here at first light. He folded his arms impatiently.

'Good morning,' a voice spoke softly behind him.

Feldman spun around in startled relief. This time she must have come up the same hill as he, behind him. He had simply assumed she'd arrive from the desert, that being the direction in which she'd left.

Embarrassed, he responded 'Hello' with a sheepish grin. 'You look great this morning!'

She smiled back.

'Did you leave your bags at the bottom of the hill?'

'I have no bags,' she explained simply.

Feldman wrinkled his brow and wondered how she managed to get by with nothing more than the clothes on her back.

'No matter,' he said, cheerily. 'God will provide. Or at least WNN will provide. We've got everything you'll need, from clothes to toothbrush. Are you ready?'

She nodded.

'Okay, then!' He extended his hand, she took it and they trekked down to his vehicle together.

'Have you ever ridden in a car before?' he asked as they made their way to a rendezvous point with the helicopter that would shuttle them to Cairo airport.

'No.'

'How about a helicopter or an aeroplane?'

'No.'

'You'll enjoy it,' Feldman assured her, although he had to wonder if this implacable lady ever really experienced true joy or pleasure. He'd never heard her laugh. And while she'd smile on occasion, it was usually fleeting and never exactly convincing.

The helicopter was a safety precaution. On the mere rumour that the Messiah would be departing from Cairo airport, crowds had jammed the public areas and gates for days. The easiest way to avoid any entanglements was simply to fly the prophetess over the crowds and deposit her at the plane.

WNN's clandestine arrangements for Jeza's flight, thanks to the full co-operation of the White House, had been well orchestrated. The chartered jet sat alone and undisturbed at a desolate area of the airport. But Feldman knew that a whole contingent of CIA security operatives were randomly scattered about in the immediate vicinity.

Other than four crew members and two stewardesses, Hunter and Cissy McFarland were the only other passengers Feldman and WNN had allowed on board. Feldman had felt that at least one woman from WNN's staff should be available if Jeza required some kind of personal assistance on the flight. Under normal circumstances, Cissy would have been an automatic choice. But given her widely known conflict with Hunter, it had taken an extraordinary effort from Feldman to convince the WNN hierarchy. And that was only after Cissy had trained her big green eyes on Feldman and sworn a blood oath that the Devil himself couldn't provoke her to another incident.

Feldman also had to wrest a solemn pledge from Hunter not to say or do stupid things during the trip that could possibly antagonize Cissy. But he realized that this was not an issue under Hunter's control. So the reporter had a few other worries to occupy his mind as the hatch to the jetliner was sealed and he and the prophetess took their plush seats near the mid-section of the fuselage. The jet was immediately cleared for take-off and they were soon hurtling down the runway off into a cloudless blue sky to begin their long journey to America.

62

The White House, Washington, DC,
7.20 A.M., Saturday, 4 March 2000

Over an early breakfast meeting in the first family's sun room, White House campaign advisers Brian Newcomb and Edwin Guenther were having a difference of perspectives about the day's presidential agenda. They'd already been informed that the prophetess Jeza was in the air and their ambitious plan was under way. The President, who had intended to join them, was delayed by a phone call and had insisted they start without him.

'This gambit had better pull in some major support from the millenarians,' Newcomb was warning as he attacked a plate of bacon and scrambled eggs, ''cause we're sure pissin' off the rest of the media by only allowing WNN to cover the dinner tonight.'

'It's all right here,' Guenther responded confidently, tapping his fork on the top of a large bound document. 'Five separate, independent research reports. This Jeza's so hot with the millenarians, all Al has to do is stand next to her and we're gonna pump his ratings seventeen to twenty per cent.'

'All the more reason we should have stuck to the game plan,' Newcomb pointed out. 'Bringing her in for lunch would have been just fine, but a formal dinner and reception? Overnight? There's too much time to kill. Too many opportunities for things to go wrong. We just don't know enough about her. Hell, I've heard reports she's a certified wacko. I mean, shit, the girl thinks she's a female Jesus Christ, for Chrissakes!'

'If she's wacko, she's no more wacko than some of the other religious nuts we've paraded through the Oval Office.' Guenther was not above talking with his mouth full. 'And none of 'em have done us an iota of good. Besides, a quick in-out isn't gonna get the job done. She's too damn important. Having her come all this way for a fast lunch and then packing her off again would make Al look like a superficial vote-panderer. Hell, the public thinks she's God, and we damn well better treat her like one!'

'I guess I'm getting cold feet,' Newcomb confessed, rubbing his face. 'Let's just make sure we keep Jon Feldman close. At least he seems to be able to exercise some control over her.'

'Yeah. He's a good man. Gave us everything we asked for.'

'Not that he had much choice, now did he?' Newcomb added, laughing.

Guenther laughed with him. 'The power of the presidency!'

'But I hear he did make one demand on us,' Newcomb mentioned.

'Oh yeah? What was that?'

'He made us promise we wouldn't put her on the spot or try to get her to perform any miracles.'

'Damn!' Guenther feigned disappointment. 'I was gonna have her take off twenty pounds around my middle and give me another four inches on the ol' sausage!'

They both laughed heartily.

63

The skies over the Atlantic,
10.10 A.M., Saturday, 4 March 2000

The large four-engined jet that WNN had specially chartered for this journey was the private property of a Saudi oil sheikh. In addition to offering plush, oversized leather seating, the jet had been converted to house a large forward stateroom with king-size bed, elegant dining room, and all the accoutrements of the incalculably wealthy. Feldman had been curious about how Jeza might react to all this indulgent extravagance, and saw the flight as a special opportunity to gain important insights into her nature. He was not disappointed. But he was surprised.

From the onset of the trip, he had been kept off balance by Jeza's inexplicable awareness and understanding of her surroundings. Intending to assist her with her seat belt as they had prepared for take off, for example, he found she needed no instruction. The same held true for adjusting her electronic seat controls, regulating her air-conditioning, turning on her overhead light, and manipulating the arm-rest dials to listen to music on her headset. She had handled all these things easily and perfunctorily, requiring no assistance.

Relatively early in the flight Feldman had also discovered, in attempting to point out some of the more notable sites and cities over which they passed, that Jeza was well up on her geography, too. After waxing professorial to her about various regions of the Mediterranean, he'd mistakenly identified the island of Sardinia as Sicily. She had casually corrected him, and he was suddenly aware, to his great chagrin, that all this time she'd been politely tolerating his amateurish stint as tour guide. Once again, he'd seriously underestimated this fathomless woman.

Ever mindful of his duty to WNN, and with the world desperate to know more about the mysterious Messiah, Feldman turned his efforts towards drawing Jeza into revealing discussions. With mixed results. At first, she answered most of his questions with a simple yes or no, and seemed preoccupied, uncommunicative. Given that there would be plenty of time and opportunity for him to attempt further conversation, he felt it best not to press, and finally allowed her some peace.

During this time, Hunter and Cissy dutifully kept their distance in the front seating section, allowing Jeza and Feldman privacy. Occasionally, and discreetly, Hunter would turn around and shoot a little footage of the prophetess with a zoom lens. While Jeza could not have avoided noticing some of these occurrences, she tolerated them.

It wasn't until almost five hours of flight time had elapsed that a clumsy but fortunate accident eventually opened the door to an anecdotal insight into the Messiah.

Well out over the Atlantic now, Jeza and Feldman were dozing in their seats next to each other. Cissy was curled up with a pillow and blanket beside Hunter, who'd been staring vapidly out of the window, bored.

Deciding that this was a perfect opportunity for some candid close-ups of the prophetess, Hunter slipped past Cissy and crept out into the aisle, stealing slowly towards the back of the plane. This was the nearest to the Messiah he'd yet dared venture since first being introduced to her.

Although he was absolutely silent in his approach, Jeza, like a cat, sensed him and shifted upright in a flash, freezing him with her ice-blue eyes. Feldman was jarred from his nap. He knew instantly what had happened, but had no idea how the Messiah would react to this rude intrusion into her valued privacy.

Before Feldman could decide what to say or do, Hunter recovered from her gaze, and searching to ad lib his way through the incident, clumsily blurted out, 'Miss Jeza, I was just wondering, uh, if you wouldn't mind, uh . . . showing me how you make yourself disappear in the middle of a crowd the way you do. I, uh, I won't tell anyone, I swear to God.' He winced at his profanity.

The panicked look on his face was so pitiful, Feldman cycled uncontrollably through flashes of embarrassment, fear and amusement.

From her seat down the aisle, Cissy McFarland was more certain in her emotions. She'd been watching all this develop with nervous curiosity, and now she buried her face in her pillow, mortified.

Through all of this, Jeza sat stone-still. Slightly frowning, her lips pursed, her emotions indiscernible.

At length she leaned forward in her seat and deliberately, slowly, drew an arm up in front of her until the full, hanging sleeve of her robe completely obscured her face, like a magician drawing a scarf over an object that was about to be vanished.

Hunter shrank back, apprehensively.

Suddenly she dropped her arm to reveal her head completely covered in a traditional black Islamic veil.

A childishly simple but effective little trick. To disappear in a crowd, all the Messiah ever had to do was to duck down, flip on her veil, and instantly render herself indistinguishable from the myriad of other similarly attired women around her. No one would be the wiser. And even if suspicious, no self-respecting Middle Easterner would ever consider defiling the confidence and modesty of the veil.

Hunter quickly nodded his understanding, thanked the Messiah effusively, and then hastened off to the rear of the plane to lie low for a while.

As he fled, Jeza slipped off her veil, exposing a slight smile. Feldman was relieved and pleased to see that the Messiah did indeed have a sense of humour. He turned to her, grinning.

'You know, it's only natural that people are curious about you, Jeza,' he opened. 'You're a very important person, and so little is known about you.'

'I am not important,' she said with a sigh. 'It is the Word that is important.'

'But you *are* important! If people are to believe your message, they must believe in *you*. That can only come from getting to know you.'

'The Word stands on its own,' she responded flatly. 'Little is known about the writers of the four Gospels, yet their words are immortal.'

Feldman leaned towards her and looked into the abyss of her eyes. 'Well, *I* would certainly like to know more about you, Jeza.'

She was inside his mind again. His soul. He felt suspended out in front of her, as weightless as a ghost. She sighed again, sounding disappointed. 'You have seen more than any other, nevertheless you must see more. Blessed are those who do not see, yet believe.'

Deflated and confused, Feldman sank slowly back in his seat.

Jeza closed her eyes to return to her sleep and softly murmured something that sounded to Feldman like, '. . . in your dreams'. Although he was certain he misunderstood.

About half an hour later, a flight attendant appeared before them to announce dinner, and to invite Jeza and Feldman to freshen up before convening in the dining room.

Hunter, returning to his seat from his self-imposed exile, spied Jeza coming his way as she headed for her stateroom. He withdrew into a corner, giving her a wide berth. But noticing this, Jeza walked over to him and asked if he and his companion would join her and Feldman for supper.

Feeling reclaimed, Hunter readily accepted.

From their first two meals on the plane, Feldman had learned that Jeza followed a very meagre and strict diet. When a flight attendant had brought them breakfast menus, Jeza had passed altogether and taken only water. At lunch-time, she had ignored the meat and poultry dishes to settle for a salad.

For her dinner, she had a raw vegetable plate and hard rolls, unbuttered. Which made it a little difficult for the others, who were tempted by, and ultimately succumbed to, gourmet appetizers, entrées and desserts. When asked if she objected to anyone having wine, she offhandedly replied, 'Christ Himself enjoyed wine,' but took none herself.

Not having had any personal contact with Jeza before, but with a long list of burning questions, Cissy cautiously attempted a query of her own.

'Excuse me, Jeza, I hope you don't mind me asking, but there's an issue you've raised several times, a point about which there's still much anxiety and concern in the world. Does your coming really mean that the Last Day is imminent?'

Raising a glass of water to her lips, Jeza paused and returned it to the table. She was quiet for a moment before responding. 'That there is at long last concern in the world over the will of the Father, I submit, is good. The purpose of my coming is to deliver the Word of God and to reveal God's plan for all mankind. I say to you that the destruction of the world can take many forms, and that mankind has brought upon himself God's judgment. A great trial is coming. And all will be revealed soon, at the appropriate time, and not before.'

This disclosure had a sobering effect on the gathering. A prolonged silence ensued and Cissy's remaining questions had suddenly lost their fire.

Finally, in an attempt to dispel the gloom and rekindle the conversation, Cissy asked, 'Jeza, you seem to lead such a hard life. No home, no possessions, no close friends. How do you manage?'

'You say I have no friends?' she responded, looking genuinely surprised. 'But everywhere I am, people open their hearts to me. I am generously offered shelter, food, clothing. And when I leave, I leave with friendship. I lack for nothing. How is my life hard?'

'But don't you ever get lonely?' Cissy persisted. 'Don't you ever long for companionship, a family, a normal life apart from all the turmoil and crowds?'

'I find peace in my meditation,' she responded. 'My mission is not to seek earthly gratifications. Each of us is here for a purpose. And in fulfilling that purpose, so do we achieve personal happiness.'

Feldman opened his mouth to ask an intentionally loaded question. A difficult, dangerous question he knew he must ultimately ask of this New Messiah. And then he reconsidered. Although sorely tempted, he dared not risk it now. Perhaps on the return flight, if and when they'd cleared all that lay ahead.

After dinner, Cissy offered to show Jeza some of the extensive wardrobe of beautiful clothes, shoes and accessories they'd assembled for her. She wasn't interested. 'I will wash my robe tonight and it will be clean and dry for the morning,' she decided.

'But what about shoes?' Hunter wondered. 'It's winter and cold in Washington!'

Jeza looked down at her worn leather sandals and appeared perfectly satisfied.

'Well,' Cissy enticed her, 'at least let me show you some of the nice new robes we have. You'll be meeting a lot of important people at the White House and you'll want to look fresh.'

Hesitantly, Jeza accompanied Cissy to her stateroom and they closed the door behind them.

'How about a round or two of HyperWar?' Hunter challenged his fellow newsman to a video game on the big-screen TV in the lounge. 'They've got a great set-up in here.'

While Cissy and Jeza were occupied, Feldman and Hunter did 3D battle in outer space. They became so engrossed, it wasn't until Hunter whirled around in celebration after destroying one of Feldman's Stellar Interceptors, that the men noticed the vision standing behind them. Hunter stopped and whistled. A beaming Cissy extended her hand to display proudly an uneasy, uncertain Jeza.

The New Messiah was clad in another simple, full-length white robe. But rather than coarse linen, this one was of soft, elegant fabric, far more stylish and attractive. Cinched at her waist with a simple gold cord, it was a well-tailored garment with a modest square-cut collar. Upon her tiny white feet were two new sandals with pretty gold side buckles.

But most noticeably, her thick, formerly untamed hair had been washed, trimmed slightly, and brushed smooth. It slipped like black, shiny silk down the sides of her face.

'She wouldn't allow any make-up,' Cissy complained.

She needed none.

Jeza had obviously been pushed into all this, and showed increasing discomfort at the appreciative stares and comments. 'I prefer my own robe,' she declared finally, starting to back away, but Feldman rushed to the defence.

'Please don't change,' he asked disarmingly. 'You look so fresh and revitalized! Once you see what the women wear in Washington, you'll be thankful!'

Jeza appeared unconvinced, but Hunter, attempting to lighten the situation, interrupted with another of his soaring non sequiturs.

'Hey, Jeza, I bet you've never tried this before,' he chirped. 'It's called a video game. Give it a shot, it's fun! I just disintegrated five of Jon's spaceships, no contest!' He turned and, with a quick flip of his hand-held control, sent another of Feldman's armada into oblivion.

Jeza again stared at Hunter with that incredulous, slightly frowning gaze he seemed to invite. Then, almost as an afterthought, she took the control from Feldman's outstretched hand, turned, and in one fell swoop, faster than the eye could follow, executed the complex manoeuvres necessary to annihilate Hunter's entire space fleet. She immediately handed the control back to the astonished Feldman, pivoted quickly, and with a slight, bemused smile on her face, retired to her room.

Hunter could only stare at the screen, mouth agape.

Jeza spent the remaining few hours before their arrival in her room, alone, meditating.

64

Salt Lake City, Utah,
8.00 A.M., Saturday, 4 March 2000

Cardinal Litti was up early in anticipation of yet another full day at the second convocation. He sat on the sofa in his hotel room, sipping tea and praying.

But in the middle of his thoughts, the cardinal was interrupted by a knock. Assuming it to be maid service, he quickly unlatched the lock and opened the door wide. But it was not the chambermaid.

'Hello, Alphonse,' a familiar but unwelcome voice intruded. 'May we come in?'

'Di Concerci! Santorini!' Litti gasped. 'What are you doing here?'

The two cardinals entered the room, despite the lack of an invitation.

'You're looking well, Cardinal Litti,' Silvio Santorini greeted his errant colleague.

'"Cardinal?"' Litti questioned. 'Do I still hold that title?'

'Of course,' di Concerci reassured him.

Litti asked the impossible. 'Can it be that you're here because Nicholas has re-evaluated my report?'

'No, Cardinal,' di Concerci said. 'We're here to observe the convocation, and also to talk with you about returning to the Curia. Perhaps we were too abrupt with you. Perhaps you should have been allowed to discuss your . . . interesting theories. If you'd be willing to come back with us at the end of the convocation, we assure you, you will have an opportunity to present your thinking. Come, let us go to breakfast together and we'll discuss all this further.'

Litti was not won over so easily and emitted a short, contemptuous laugh. 'Please spare me the patronage. The Congregation's encyclical on the New Messiah is written and disseminated. It's too late for my words to matter.'

'It's never too late, Alphonse,' Santorini promised. 'Please, reconsider.'

'Do you think I make my choices casually, Silvio?' Litti's face reddened with emotion. 'That I so simply give up fifty years of devoted service to my Church? Abandon my security, the only life I have ever known, to pursue—?' He fought back the tears that welled in his pained, sad eyes.

Knowing he was wasting his efforts, he calmed himself and changed the subject. 'You're here for the duration of the assembly? You'll stay to hear the Messiah speak?'

'We are here for the duration, Alphonse,' di Concerci pledged. 'I'll be representing the Vatican on the dignitary panel.'

'What!' Litti shouted, in disbelief. 'You try to prevent *my* coming, and then you steal the panel seat I want!' He turned and retreated to a window, needing to put distance between himself and these interlopers. On the horizon, the snow-capped mountain peaks stood serene and eternal against the azure heavens.

'Antonio did not steal your place, Alphonse,' Santorini attempted to reassure the wayward cardinal. 'The convocation made a formal request of the Vatican for an official representation on the panel. Nicholas was considering you when you forsook your position on the Congregation. You were *in absentia*. We didn't even know for sure that you were here until after we arrived last night.'

'I don't believe you!' Litti challenged. 'Nicholas denied my request to come here. Why would he reconsider?'

'Irrespective, Alphonse' – di Concerci sidestepped this – 'we're here to observe and evaluate this alleged Messiah, which is precisely what you wished of us all along.'

Litti turned to face his old adversary once more. 'Cardinal di Concerci, I caution you that you cannot possibly understand her message unless you adjust your perspective. You must listen with a virgin ear, feel with a pure heart, think with an unadulterated mind.

'Regretfully, in knowing you, Prefect, I must say that I have little hope for you in that regard. But if, after hearing the New Messiah, either of you find yourselves persuaded to my position by even a small degree, seek me out again and I will speak with you further. Beyond that, we have nothing more to say.'

With that, the two Vatican emissaries departed. Litti attempted to return to his prayer but was too upset.

In the elevator down to the lobby, Silvio Santorini rolled his eyes and shook his head at his colleague. 'He's exactly as you described him. Not at all himself. It's very sad. And potentially very embarrassing for us should he express his views to any of the media who hover constantly around us here. Perhaps, under the circumstances, it was not wise to allow Alphonse to retain his cardinalship. Should he speak out in public, he may be presumed to be representing an opinion of the Curia. Or at best, intimating a division in our ranks. It's dangerous.'

'I agree, my friend,' the prefect replied, 'but the Pontiff wouldn't hear of it. At least, not yet. Nicholas and Alphonse were once very close. Nicholas still holds out hope that our fractious cardinal will come to his senses. Personally, I've *never* found him to be sensible.'

Santorini nodded. 'Did you bring your virgin ears?'

'None that I would allow the words of this false prophetess to penetrate, I can assure you,' di Concerci quipped. And both men indulged in a brief laugh as they left the elevator and exited the hotel into the brisk morning air.

65

Dulles International Airport, Washington, DC,
2.15 P.M., Saturday, 4 March 2000

It was a bright and beautiful winter afternoon. Right on schedule, WNN's charter flight touched down on the outskirts of the US capital. The sight that greeted the deplaning party was spectacular – hundreds of thousands of screaming, near-hysterical people with flowers and signs and flashing cameras, amassed as far as the eye could see around the protected perimeters of the huge airport.

It would have been impossible to motorcade through this congestion and, as planned, the Moore administration had one of its presidential helicopters waiting close by to whisk the four travellers immediately off to the White House. All the immense crowd got in return for its extensive patience were a few glimpses of the Messiah as she intermittently appeared among the moving wall of Secret Service agents.

But there was no mistaking her. Her radiance set her dramatically apart from everyone else around her. Disappointingly to Feldman, Jeza had returned to the security of her old linen robe and tired, worn sandals. Her hair, however, looking considerably less unruly than Feldman was accustomed to seeing it, gleamed and bounced in the mourning sun as she and her party moved rapidly across the tarmac into the idling chopper, up and off to the South Lawn.

The welcome at the White House was even more ebullient. The crowds were larger still. Stretching all along Pennsylvania Avenue and its surrounding blocks were throngs of well-wishers, followers, the hopeful afflicted, the curious – as well as a few isolated groups of protesters who held absolutely no sway over this generally adoring crowd.

Throughout the cheering multitudes, colourful signs and placards

abounded, praising Jeza as Lord, citing scripture, predicting the end of
the world. And there was one banner that was particularly popular on
all three major network evening newscasts: 'Moore needs a miracle!'

Stepping out of the helicopter, Feldman took Jeza by the arm,
assisted her down to the pad and along a lengthy red carpet past a
full-dress colour guard, a gauntlet of ramrod-straight Marines with
drawn swords, a brass band and saluting Boy Scouts. The band,
Feldman noticed, was playing a familiar tune. He had to smile. It
was the same Sousa march Anne Leveque had hummed to him in
recounting her story of the dancing lamb.

Unfortunately, Hunter and Cissy wouldn't be able to stop and take
in much of this pomp and ceremony. Their responsibilities would be
to help orchestrate the WNN camera crews deployed in and around
the White House. And, with access to Feldman and the prophetess,
they hoped to provide a personal, more intimate coverage of this
historic event.

At the end of the military tunnel stood the President and First Lady,
the Vice-President and his wife, and countless senators, congressmen,
assorted VIPs, socialites, foreign dignitaries and high-ranking bureau-
cratic officials. Everyone was smiling profusely. Feldman looked over
at his companion and was impressed with the confidence and poise
she exhibited. None of this pageantry affected her in the slightest. She
seemed neither impressed nor intimidated. Merely curious.

Feldman took the outstretched hands of President and Mrs Moore,
and then those of the Vice-President and his wife. Exchanging quick
greetings, he immediately introduced them to the woman of the hour.
Jeza stopped, standing somewhat aback, and looked quizzically at
each of them.

Astounded at his stupidity, Feldman realized what was about to
happen and went into a sudden panic. He was too late. There
was nothing he could do now. Swooning, the presidential and
vice-presidential couples fell victim to Jeza's scrutiny.

Feldman rushed to the First Lady, who was close to falling. Secret
Service agents materialized spontaneously from nowhere, reacting in
alarmed, unfocused confusion, without direction or clue. The odd
event was captured live from every camera angle.

Fortunately, the presidential party recovered quickly. After a
few moments' composure and good-natured laughter, the President

greeted his special guest and the introductions moved forward. As they proceeded next towards the presidential mansion, Feldman leaned down and whispered in the Messiah's ear. 'Jeza, you may not realize what you're doing, but when you stare hard at people, you make them feel very uncomfortable. Can you control that at all?'

She looked up at him questioningly, said nothing, and continued along with the party. Moore was still shaking his head and mentioned something to his wife about helicopter fumes.

Moving into the main entranceway, the group took up position near the centre of the long corridor, with Feldman and Jeza situated between the first and second families. A receiving line developed and for the next several hours, Feldman and Jeza were occupied shaking hands and exchanging comments with an endless parade of the gawking privileged. Feldman noted with some relief that, while people meeting Jeza were still affected by her eyes, the consequences now seemed less severe, and shorter in duration.

He was not sure how the Messiah would take this extended imposition. He had never really explained to her the specifics of his arrangements with the White House. Just that she'd be meeting people, having dinner and spending the night there.

During the lengthy reception, he noticed that Jeza seldom smiled, although she didn't appear seriously put off, either. With the steady procession of people, he had no opportunity to enquire as to her physical or mental state. But he could catch snippets of her conversations.

At one point, the President asked Jeza her opinion of politics, and she responded, 'God and government are much alike: there is no peace for either because society continually fails to follow the laws set for it.'

Feldman was impressed to hear her speaking with foreign dignitaries in their native tongues. After hearing only a word or two of accented English, she had instantly grasped the correct language and, to the endless delight of the beneficiaries, responded in precisely the proper dialect. All carefully captured on videotape by the ever-vigilant Hunter and WNN camera crews.

One exchange proved particularly amusing. A rather prominent Washington defence attorney, whom Feldman recognized from the national news, stepped up to Jeza with an attractive young thing on the arm of his expensive suit. 'Miss Jeza,' he greeted the Messiah, 'I believe you and I have something rather significant in common with one another.'

Jeza stared at him without comment and he was momentarily staggered, grappling to hold his train of thought. 'You see,' he recovered, 'we, uh, we're both in the same business, you and I – the business of saving people.'

Jeza regarded him critically for a moment and then bluntly replied, 'Yes, but my means of salvation do not render people penniless!'

Significant laughter erupted from all within earshot, and the miffed barrister quickly slunk away.

There was yet one more of these strange interludes that Feldman took note of, the possible explanation for which he would not have until weeks later. One of the last people in line to greet Jeza was a very elderly, frail-looking, tiny little nun, even smaller than Jeza herself. Feldman recognized the lined and saintly face of Mother Bernadette, the world-famous 'Sister of the Silent Sufferers', renowned for her life of selfless, charitable work on behalf of the sick and destitute of Africa.

Looking hesitant but compelled, the trembling little nun took the Messiah's outstretched hand and kissed it, staring shyly up at her with imploring eyes. 'Sweet Lady,' she addressed the prophetess in a voice as small and ancient as she, 'I come to ask your prayers, not for myself, but for my poor, forgotten little babies who are ill and starving in a faraway land.'

Feldman watched Jeza's face turn troubled and her eyes moisten as she gazed into the little woman. Then, grasping Mother Bernadette by her thin shoulders, she leaned forward and whispered something into her ear. The nun's eyes grew large and a smile began to spread through the lines of her face like a wind rippling across the waters of a sea.

Jeza drew back and the nun asked excitedly, 'Today?'

The Messiah smiled and nodded.

Mother Bernadette could hardly contain herself. 'Right now?'

Jeza's smile grew larger and she nodded once more.

The nun made an awkward half-genuflection and the sign of the cross. Repeatedly bowing and thanking the prophetess, alternating between smiles and wide-eyed expressions of excitement and disbelief, the little nun backed away and quickly shuffled off towards the White House front door.

Feldman gave Jeza a questioning look, which she dismissed with a slight smile and a roll of her eyes, turning to greet her next visitor.

After the reception, Jeza and Feldman were escorted into the White House dining room as guests of honour at a two-hundred-seat dinner. Asked to render grace, Jeza raised her eyes, extended her hands to shoulder height in supplication and simply said, 'O Heavenly Father, Which created the sun, the rain and the earth to bring forth great bounty, bless this nourishment for our bodies, that we may also nourish our minds and our spirit.' There was a round of applause and appreciation which, to Feldman's mind, appeared to leave the Messiah uncomfortable.

After the final course and before the serving of desserts, the President rose from his seat, officially welcomed the Messiah to the United States, and then offered a toast to the 'most famous woman on the face of the earth'. Jeza did not join in the toast, but merely stared down at her virtually untouched plate, in what appeared to be abject embarrassment.

President Moore remained standing, and graciously asked, 'Jeza, I'm sure everyone here would love to hear some more of your intriguing thoughts. Would you care to say a few words?'

In a soft voice most could not hear, she replied, 'My message is of God, not of government.'

To which Moore responded, 'It's always been a cherished personal belief of mine that there's an important place for the spiritual in politics. And I can tell you with great assurance that your inspirational message here would be most appreciated. Certainly, government could only benefit from your insights.' Turning to include the body of seated guests, he added, 'Isn't that so, everyone?'

Feldman wasn't quite sure what Moore was hoping to accomplish here. But he suspected this was a ploy to solicit soundbites from the Messiah for future campaign advertising and commercials.

The response of the dinner guests was overwhelming. The entire assembly was on its feet, encouraging Jeza with unceasing applause and cheers. Understandably, an aura of expectation had engrossed the gathering all evening.

Jeza endured the attention with bowed head. Her sable hair, highlighted in a halo by the bright candelabras and crystal chandeliers, overshadowed her face. Feldman couldn't make out her expression.

The enthusiasm for a speech did not abate, however, and only when at last she rose did the appeased guests begin to quieten and take their seats. After all was complete silence, the Messiah lifted her head, and Feldman could see that she looked both tired and anguished. But this soon passed as she marshalled her energy and held forth in an assertive, authoritative voice that commanded full attention.

There was a murmur of appreciation and delight throughout the dining room as the rapt listeners quickly realized they were the privileged recipients of one of the Messiah's infrequent, celebrated allegories. It would later become known as:

THE PARABLE OF THE FARM AND THE OVERSEERS

At this time, Jeza came accordingly to a town in America called Washington, near the River Potomac, and here She was the guest at a great banquet. After the meal, the host, who was the high official of the land, said unto Her, 'Jeza, will you now speak to us?'

And Jeza was reluctant, for the affairs of government were not of Her concern. But the guests at the banquet beseeched Her and, not wishing to appear discourteous, She delivered to them a parable:

'There was once a good and honest man who left the safety of his home-town and went forth into the wilderness to seek his fortune. Over many years of hard work, this man built from the harsh land a large and bountiful farm. On his farm were plentiful tracts of golden wheat and barley and corn; and green pastures with great herds of fine cattle and sheep.

'Now it came to pass that the man grew old and died, and having no direct heirs, left his great farm to a young nephew who lived away in the town.

'The nephew, who was also a good and honest man like his uncle, had no knowledge of farming and decided that he must hire an experienced overseer to ensure the farm's continued prosperity.

'Soon, there came to him two shrewd foremen who worked at the farm and wished to improve their station. The first said unto the nephew, "Hire me to oversee your farm and I will safeguard your properties and increase the bounty of your grain fields twofold."

'And the second said, "Hire me to oversee your properties, for

I will see that your farm thrives, and I will double the size of your herds."

'Now the nephew was much impressed by this and said to them, "Each of you has experience in different ways. Therefore will I hire you both, and to both of you will I entrust the care of my properties. You shall share equally in control of the farm and in its profits. For four years shall you labour together to make the land productive, at which time I will return to judge your fruitfulness."

'The nephew then went away and left his farm in the care of the two men. But soon afterwards, the two overseers fell to quarrelling between themselves. The first said, "I will buy new equipment and hire more workers to enhance the grain fields." The second then said, "I will buy more cattle and sheep and open new pastures to improve the herds."

'And attempting to outdo one another, they borrowed large sums of money on the farm, each predicting that his harvest would return the greater measure of profit.

'But the first year the rains did not come. The fields grew parched and the crops withered. The pastures dried up and the herds declined. And the farm lost much money.

'The second year, each man, wishing to make up the losses of the first year, borrowed more money to install great watering systems. But in the summer, the locusts came and devoured the crops and the pastures, and again the harvest failed.

'The two overseers then said to one another, "We have much responsibility here and the pressure is great. We should be paid more for our burdens." And they therefore increased their wages.

'Each year thereafter, the two men likewise borrowed more money to assure their harvests and to raise their wages, but each year their ambition only served to reduce their yields.

'At the end of the fourth year, the nephew returned to the farm to find his once-golden fields of grain lying barren and fallow, and his prized herds ravaged, sick and dying. No more was the great farm prosperous, but the moneylenders were at the door, demanding payment.

'In great anger the nephew called the two false overseers before him, saying, "You were sworn to me to protect the land and double *its yield. Behold, this is how you repay me. The great farm is in ruin and its prosperity have you squandered!"*

'Yet each man accused the other, saying, "My judgment was sound and I would have fulfilled my promise had it not been for the foolishness of he whose profligacy has caused this loss!"

'But the nephew cast them both out, saying, "Foolish are you, but more foolish am I, for the master is responsible for the servant. Verily have I failed to honour the faith of my uncle, therefore have I lost all."'

And the guests at the banquet marvelled amongst themselves and asked of Jeza, 'What is the meaning of this parable?'

So in answering them, She said, 'The great farm is your nation. The nephew is your people. The two overseers are your Congress. As a nation is divided and corrupted from within, so is it the responsibility of its people to jealously guard over its command and cast out false overseers.

'I say unto you, great treasures require great vigilance. And he who fails to safeguard his treasures, so shall he lose them.'
(Apotheosis 23:1–48)

Concluding, Jeza bent towards Feldman and asked if she could now be allowed to retire for her evening meditation. The table was abuzz with reaction to her homily as Feldman conveyed her request to the somewhat befuddled-looking President. Moore immediately stood and escorted Jeza to a servant, who then led her away to her room upstairs.

Feldman smiled as he observed the controversy Jeza's sermon had fostered around the huge table. Some of the dinner guests, he noted, felt that the parable was a rebuke for the voter who failed to stay fully engaged in the governmental process. Some felt it was a condemnation of the two-party system, or the national budget deficits.

And others felt the parable was a not-so-veiled indictment of the current administration, which had suffered a recent series of graft and corruption charges. Fortunately, the ambiguity of the sermon would allow the White House spin doctors easily to deflect this interpretation, and the official assessment of the precarious evening was that, overall, things had gone well for the President.

Entirely exhausted, and facing an early departure for Utah with another demanding day ahead of him, Feldman soon excused himself also, adjourning to his room. He collapsed face down on his bed, kicked off his shoes and fell fast asleep.

It was nearly dawn when he awoke with a start from yet another nightmare. He loosened his tie and walked out into the hallway to stretch his legs. Across the way, the door to Jeza's room stood ajar. He tiptoed over, listened for a moment, and then rapped gently. No answer.

'Jeza!' he called softly through the crack. 'Are you awake?'

No response. He gently pushed open the door to reveal an empty, apparently unused bed. There was no light in the bathroom. He retreated into the hallway and wandered downstairs, where he found a night servant in attendance.

'If you're looking for the Messiah, sir,' the elderly gentleman said with some reverence, 'you'll find Her out in the Rose Garden. She's been there most of the night.' And he pointed the way.

Shoeless, Feldman padded over to the double doors and stepped outside into the chilly March morning. It was still dark, with only a trace of light breaking on the horizon.

His socks were soon wet on the dewy brick walk, and Jeza was nowhere to be seen. Exploring further along the hedges, Feldman turned a corner and could faintly detect a small form across the patio, crouched in front of a hedge.

As he drew closer, he saw that Jeza was half kneeling, half sitting on the cold ground. The upper part of her body was lying across the seat of a stone bench in front of a large dormant rose bush. Her face was buried in her arms and she appeared to be sobbing. Feldman rushed over and dropped to her side, placing a comforting hand on her back. Her robe was cold and damp. Her shoulders felt small and delicate.

'Jeza! What's happened? Are you all right?' He attempted to draw her upright and she did not resist. Gently, he turned her, smoothing back her hair to see her face.

Her eyes were closed, her brow creased, her lips compressed in a tight, bitter line.

'Jeza, sweet Jeza!' Feldman dried her eyes with his handkerchief and caressed her hair. 'What's happened?'

Drawing back from him slowly, she placed one hand on the stone bench and began to stand. Feldman rose quickly to assist her. He held her arm to steady her, but she seemed impervious to him, looking out towards the dawning sky, introspective and troubled, but no longer crying.

'My soul is sad unto death,' she said, hollowly. 'What must be is not of my will, but foreordained.' And without looking back, she gave Feldman's arm a tight squeeze with both hands and then slipped away from him, returning along the path to the house.

66

Salt Lake City, Utah,
8.00 A.M., Sunday, 5 March 2000

Cardinal Litti had been up since well before dawn, too excited to sleep. This was the day he'd been so anxiously awaiting. Showered and carefully shaved, he was dressed in his best cassock, best white shirt and clerical collar. Standing before the full-length mirror, he attempted to suck in the ample girth that strained his cincture, detected little improvement, and surrendered, laughing.

The cardinal was in a bright mood, if somewhat nervous. He realized that this day would see him witness his New Messiah, and would most likely determine for him the course he would follow for the rest of his life. He draped his red-and-black cloak across his shoulders and placed a spotless red zucchetto skullcap meticulously on his crown.

'Now,' he said to himself with appreciation, 'I'm ready to meet my maker!'

As it was his policy to preserve his previous remaining dollars, rather than take a cab Cardinal Litti elected to make the invigorating walk to the hall. It was a mistake.

Unlike on the previous two days, which had seen large but navigable crowds in the vicinity, today the turnout was almost impenetrable. It started in Litti's hotel lobby, which was packed with impatient guests. But worse, outside his hotel, the pavement traffic was elbow to elbow.

He regretted not reserving a ride, but certainly now getting one would be impossible.

Summoning his determination, the sturdy cardinal pushed out into the mob and began working his way slowly towards the towering Tabernacle Hall in the distance. His journey was made all the more difficult because Salt Lake City's Department of Crowd and Traffic Control had mounted a stubborn effort to keep all down-town streets open for the endless cavalcades of limousines and police escorts that constantly streamed by. To cordon off the roads, barriers had been erected up on the pavements, rather than down by the kerbs, abnormally narrowing the pedestrian access ways.

Even though the convocation didn't officially assemble until 10 A.M., Litti was experiencing growing concern about ever getting there. If the crowd was this compact blocks away, he couldn't imagine how congested it must be near the hall. Inching along, he hugged the barricades, as near to the street as he could get, hoping to snare a passing cab. But none that streaked by in a yellow blur paid him any heed. Finally, in desperation, he closed his eyes tightly and whispered a fervent prayer to Jeza, asking for deliverance.

When he reopened them, the cardinal found himself staring into the lens of a TV camera. A roving news crew from a US network had been cruising around doing man-in-the-street interviews. Having been unfairly shut out of the convention hall, as were all news media save for WNN, competing networks were reduced to developing collateral stories wherever and however they could. Spying the cardinal's vivid red cap and cloak from their mobile van, the opportunistic crew immediately pulled over. A real Catholic cardinal was a rare find in these parts, and they were obviously delighted with their luck.

'Can we trouble you for a few comments about Jeza for our viewing audience, Your Grace?' the reporter asked, smiling.

'My son,' Litti responded in his thick Italian accent, 'I fear if I delay, I shall be unable to make today's opening at the hall; the crowds are impossible.'

The news reporter was even more excited to have stumbled across a cardinal who would actually be in privileged attendance. 'I tell you what, Monsignor,' he said, lowering his camera, 'if you'll give us an interview and you don't mind riding in our truck here, we'll drive you down and make sure you get there on time.'

Litti grinned broadly. Yes, his faith in his Messiah was well founded.

67

Salt Lake City Airport, Utah,
10.17 A.M., Sunday, 5 March 2000

The jet carrying Feldman, Hunter, Cissy and their special envoy landed at Salt Lake City Airport right on schedule. It had been an uneventful flight, with Jeza spending the entire cross-country journey in her room. Sleeping, Feldman hoped, since she had apparently got none the previous night. He was concerned about her state of mind after her troubling display in the Rose Garden.

His worries were quickly alleviated, however, once she took her seat for the landing. She was herself again, looking fresh and calm once more. She even afforded Feldman a quick smile.

Safely on the ground, the jet taxied to a service facility somewhat removed from the terminal. Here, Secret Service representatives transferred the four passengers quickly and stealthily to a waiting helicopter for their last, short leg.

As they approached the huge Mormon Tabernacle Hall, Hunter called out to the others in amazement at the staggering sea of people far below them. 'Would you look at the crowd!' he exclaimed. 'There must be millions of millenarians down there!'

Jeza remained completely uninterested. Indeed, she'd made it eminently clear that she wanted no more of the display she'd been previously subjected to. Before leaving Washington, she had requested that there be no reception, no greeters, no visitors and no media to interrupt her meditation prior to her address. Feldman had placed a quick call to the disappointed Mormons to ensure this.

Made comfortable in a private suite in the upper levels of the great hall, Jeza appeared relaxed and composed.

'Why don't you lie here on the sofa and rest for a while, Jeza,' Feldman suggested to her. 'I'll slip outside to make sure all the arrangements are in order for your address, and I'll be back soon.'

She smiled gratefully, nodded, and sat quietly on the edge of the couch.

Leaving her suite, Feldman checked in with the Secret Service agents stationed outside to ensure she would not be disturbed. He then signalled a nearby Mormon aide and asked where he might have a discreet look at the Grand Auditorium. The aide led him to a mezzanine and into one of many private, glassed condominium suites overlooking the huge assembly. In addition to a panoramic eagle's-eye view, the condo offered plush seating, a large-screen TV monitor and non-alcoholic wet bar. About thirty of the 'beautiful people' were here munching hors d'oeuvres, enjoying boisterous conversation and laughter.

Stretching out in front of Feldman, the huge hall was set up like a rock concert, with elevated speaker's platform and lectern at one end, elliptically encircled by steeply rising stadium seating and fronted by a special celebrity section on the main floor. Just below the speaker's stage was a row of tables. Seated at the tables would be the VIP religious dignitaries who would be panelling a question-and-answer session after the address.

From his Mormon aide, Feldman learned that the expected attendance would include 64,891 clerics, priests, ministers, pastors, imams, rabbis and assorted other clergypersons of every stripe. Left unmentioned was the fact that there would also be many not-of-the-cloth VIPs, as well as invalids, the terminally ill and others who had bought, conned or cajoled their way into this celebrated appearance. A good number of attendees were decked out in formal wear and lavish jewellery, attired as if this were some great social event. The excitement virtually crackled in the air, like the anticipation before the entrance of a nominee at a national political convention.

Feldman's guide interrupted his sightseeing to inform him that it was time to return to Jeza's suite in preparation for her imminent introduction.

*   *   *

On the floor of the hall, there was some grumbling regarding the nature of the selection process for the VIP panel. Many attendees resented the fact that the Mormons were occupying three of the precious twelve seats. There was also considerable irritation that a Catholic cardinal, His Eminence Antonio di Concerci, who had not even been in attendance at the first convocation, had been seated on the panel.

The only Catholic cardinal who was present previously, Alphonse Litti, enjoyed a preferred position in the front row directly behind the VIP table, right next to another Curia cardinal, Silvio Santorini. Many voiced their suspicions about some sort of Vatican intrigue.

In truth, Vatican influence had played both a direct and an indirect role in the seating arrangements. Directly for di Concerci and Santorini, for whom the Vatican had applied considerable pressure and funding. Indirectly for Litti, whom the lower-echelon Mormon organizers had mistakenly included in the prime seating, assuming he was part of the Vatican package. Neither di Concerci nor Santorini was aware of the confusion until Litti had already been issued his seat.

The make-up of the final, controversial panel ultimately comprised three Mormons, an evangelical, two millenarians – including a representative of the Messianic Guardians of God – a Hindu, a Jewish rabbi, a Buddhist, a Muslim, a Presbyterian and Cardinal di Concerci.

As the appointed hour drew near, however, all differences were put aside and the attention of the audience focused entirely upon the staging area.

The main lights of the massive hall dimmed and two lone, concentrated, bluish-white spotlights shone down from different locations on the high rafters. One illuminated the podium, the other was fixed on a solitary tunnel behind the stage.

From the giant bells of the clock tower atop the hall, the sounds of high noon came tolling down. As the final reverberations died out, the crowd became animated. Two figures, one tall, one slight, emerged from the tunnel and, together, began ascending the ramp at the rear of the stage.

One spotlight followed them with its beam as the audience rose to its feet. When the two figures arrived on the stage, they paused. The audience gathered a collective breath, and then there was a discharge of thunderous applause, loud praise and cheering.

Feldman remained behind in the dark while the Messiah and spotlight broke away together to advance to the podium. As Jeza reached her position at the lectern, the volume of the crowd increased and the two spotlights converged to concentrate an intense, white aura of light about her. She stood there, alone and silent. Her hands were clasped easily in front of her; her face cast downward, in shadow.

The waves of adulation rolled over her, uninterrupted, for a full five minutes. But not all shared the enthusiasm. Two sombre-faced cardinals remained seated and silent through the entire welcoming.

The roar continued. In the dark periphery, Feldman took his place on the right side of the stage in a chair placed there for his use.

Immobile throughout this enthusiastic reception, Jeza waited patiently until an absolute silence had at last been attained. Finally satisfied, she lifted her head to take in the assembly. She studied it solemnly, carefully, for a time. Then, drawing in her breath as if gathering her resolve, she called out over the masses in a clear, ringing, angelic voice:

'In the name of the Father, I come to you. In the name of Truth, I come to you. In the name of Revelation, I come to you!'

She paused and the audience inched forward in its seats.

'I come to you with the Newest Testament in the fulfilment of God's will. A Testament which calls to each man, woman and child, alone and apart from all others. A Testament wherein you will receive the New Light – a light which shall lead you from the darkness.

'I speak to the spiritual leaders of the world; to those who would preach the way of the Lord to others.

'I say to you, look to the words of Christ as is written in Matthew six, verses five to eight:

"Again when you pray, you shall not be like the hypocrites, who love to pray in churches and synagogues and in public in order that they might be seen; but when you pray, go into your room and close your door. Pray to the Father in secrecy and the Father who sees in secrecy shall hear you.

"And in praying, do not imitate the words of others; be not like them. For your Father knows what you need before you ask Him!"'

Having quoted this scripture, Jeza dropped her head again and
deliberated for another long moment. Then her small white hands
tightly gripped the edge of the lectern, she stood upright, levelled her
magnificent gaze once more at the audience, and her voice assumed
a more portentous tone.

*'Amen, amen, I say to you: How shall you lead others when you
yourselves are lost?'*

The words echoed out across the sea of intent faces.

*'The New Light is upon you. You, the shepherds to whom God has
entrusted His sheep. So have you led them far astray. You, who
profess to tend your flocks, yet care less for its souls than the value
of its fleece.*

*'You, who preach loudly of the Bible, yet turn not to the Word of
God, but turn the Word of God to you. You, who recast the Lord's
meaning to your own end; to manipulate; to create guilt and shame;
to solicit money and favour; to launch strife and conflict and war,
and turn brother against brother.'*

Jeza had undergone an amazing physical transformation. Her face
was seared with emotion. The jaw muscles were taut, the noble brow
furrowed, the eyes damning. Her voice was a piercing cry, unsettling
in its self-righteous anger. With each stabbing slash of her accusatory
finger, the unfortunate, randomly targeted section of audience recoiled
and cowered.

*'You, who seek not truth, but justification. You, who speak one way,
yet live another. You, who pursue not life hereafter, but worldly
reward.*

*'The time of Revelation is at hand. To each of you who hears
my words, I say, behold and obey this, the true will of God:*

*'Go forth from this place, back to your churches and to your
synagogues and to your temples and say unto your congregations
as I say to you now: let all who would heed the Word of
God disperse and worship no more together. For only when
you are free of artifice, and only in the privacy of your own*

*heart will God reveal to you His true meaning and personal
message.*

*'Let all who would follow the New Way of the Lord look to the
written Word of God and to that alone for counsel and guidance.
Trust not in the opinion of others, nor in the teachings of the
world religions, for they are corrupted and cannot know God's
plan for you.*

*'To each child born is a separate way to everlasting life. And to
each child born is a holy knowledge to find the way. Look not to
your neighbour for your answer. Look inside your heart. For alone
must you labour to clear the obstacles in your path.*

*'You, who call yourselves spiritual leaders, hear the message of
the Lord that you may know His will and obey His command:*

*'From this day forward, speak no more of God's way, for you
know it not. Let the tongues of the clergy be stilled. Let the voices
of the theologians be silenced. Dispense with your hierarchies
and bureaucracies. Recall your missionaries and close down your
seminaries. Preach no more to any man, but return instead to the
world as penitents, seeking not the righteousness of others, but the
sanctity of your own souls.*

*'Let not another day pass before you have accomplished all these
things. For in your arrogance and hypocrisy have you angered the
Lord!' (Apotheosis 24:7–32)*

Finished, Jeza remained motionless at the podium. The assembly,
shocked beyond measure, sat numb and silent. Stung, humiliated,
deeply flustered.

Situated well back and high up in the stands, the Right Reverend
Solomon T. Brady, DD, was visibly shaken. The house lights abruptly
came up and slowly the crowd reacted. The woman seated to Brady's
right, a Protestant deaconess, was whispering to him, but the Reverend
did not respond.

'Tell me she didn't say we should dissolve our churches? Is that
what she really said?' Receiving no answer, she turned to her other
side and repeated the plea.

From his seat close to the stage behind the presiding panel, Cardinal
Alphonse Litti gazed up at his Messiah, tears flowing freely down his
fleshy cheeks. Several seats to the right of the cardinal, an inspired

Rabbi Mordachai Hirschberg, ageing leader of the ultra-Orthodox
Jewish sect of Hasidic Lubavitchers, inhaled deeply as if to thank
his God for having let him live long enough to witness the coming
of the true Messiah. Near by, First Reverend Richard-Peter Fischer
was flushed and sweating, grabbing at his right arm where a creeping
sensation of numbness had developed. And Jon Feldman had risen
from his chair, eyeing the distance between Jeza and the exit tunnel.

At the VIP table fronting the stage, eleven of the twelve panellists
had scrapped their culled list of questions and were searching about
desperately for a resolution to this unexpected dilemma.

Calm and collected in the midst of the confusion, Cardinal Antonio
di Concerci had maintained a hard, unwavering scrutiny of the young
prophetess. He, for one, was not about to let this appalling display
go unchallenged. The prefect realized someone had to seize control
of the deteriorating assembly. He addressed the microphone before
him with a question that arrested the rising bedlam.

'And by what authority do you assert to us the will of God?' he
asked loudly in his imperious, aristocratic voice. To ensure that he'd
been heard by all, as the noise quelled he repeated himself. 'By what
authority do you assert to us the will of God? What credentials do
you present to us?'

Jeza, who had been as immobile as a graven image, now looked
down in sovereign composure at her challenger.

'My authority is of the Father, as is self-evident in His words that
I speak. Your conscience confirms my credentials!'

Di Concerci didn't hesitate. 'Then I must wonder at both your
authority and your credentials, *Prophetess*.' The cardinal empha-
sized his pronunciation to establish his scepticism for the benefit
of the audience. 'Your words raise doubts and my conscience
senses little.'

'How can you understand if your heart is hardened?' she asked.
'Those with most to lose, give least!'

Unaffected, Jeza's inquisitor pressed his attack. 'You would have
that the Church no longer celebrate the Mass? You would halt the
sacraments? Deny spiritual comfort to the disconsolate, the sick, the
dying?'

Jeza looked annoyed. 'The Lord commands that you abolish
liturgy and ceremony, the trappings that distract people from His

true meaning. Abandon rites and rituals and devote this time to the service of man in the Lord's name!'

'But,' one of the Mormons on the panel pleaded, 'the sacred practices of our religions hold great meaning and comfort for our congregations. There would be much sorrow and confusion over the loss of our spiritual communality.'

'I say to you,' she responded quickly, 'there will be far greater sorrow for those whose souls are unprepared for the judgment of the Lord! Maintain your communality in charitable service to your fellow man, and interfere not with the communality of God.'

This talk of Judgment Day set the agitated assembly on further edge.

Nevertheless, di Concerci was not intimidated. 'You claim that it's God's will for the organized religions of the world to disassemble themselves and you cite the Apostle Matthew to support your contention that God wishes man to isolate himself in matters of spirituality. Your interpretation, however, contradicts Matthew eighteen, verse twenty, which says: "When two or more are gathered together in My name, I am in their midst."'

'By your very words do you prove me,' the Messiah responded. 'This passage praises *co-operation in the performance of good works in Christ's name* – and *not* communal prayer!'

Between each exchange, the angst flowed in tense conversation through the crowd.

The elderly, bespectacled rabbi on the panel summoned the courage to ask, 'My Lady, are you a prophetess? The only begotten Daughter of God? The Sister of Jesus and Muhammed?'

'I am as you say,' she responded.

He followed up, his voice quavering, 'Are you the true Messiah of the Jews?'

'I am the Messiah of the Jews and of all people, everywhere.'

Di Concerci thought he saw an opening. 'So, you proclaim to be the promised Messiah? How is it then that *nowhere* in the Bible is there ever to be found a prophecy pertaining to a *female* Messiah? You *are* female, I presume?'

There was anger in her voice. 'I am as God has made me. And the truth of who I am is indeed in the Bible. If you desire to find the truth, you must look with your heart, not your eyes!'

'Messiah,' the evangelical on the panel cried, 'I truly want to assist God in spreading His Holy Word. Is there no way I can continue my work?'

'In this manner shall you spread God's Word,' she replied. 'To all you meet, give the writings of the Koran, the Talmud, the Veda, the Avesta, the Old and New Testaments of the Bible – all the great spiritual texts of the world. God's message is in all of them. But do not interpret God's Word for others, for that is how the corruption begins.'

'Messiah?' It was the representative of the Presbyterian contingent. 'If there is to be no more collective study of the scriptures, no more theologians and no more dialogue among religious scholars, do we not limit man's ability to understand the mind of God?'

Jeza softened in her response. 'It is still possible for you to commune with your fellow man about the mind of God apart from the scriptures. Let the earth be your catechism. You were given this world, and in it, everything you need. Once you crawled upon its face, ignorant animals. Then God spoke to you and you began to grow. From this earth you fashioned clothes to cover you, fire to warm you, tools to ease your labour, and weapons to protect you from the wild beast.

'In this earth is everything you require to complete your journey. All the materials necessary to satisfy your physical needs. To heal every disease. To travel the stars. So, too, in all these wonders is everything you require to understand the mind of God. In your physics and mathematics. In all your sciences. All the secrets of heaven exist everywhere around you. Commune in *this* manner. And discover!'

Di Concerci narrowed his eyes at this surprising creature. She was certainly not what he had expected. While previously recognizing her to be a destabilizing influence on institutional religion, the prefect had considerably underestimated the magnitude of this influence. Standing here in her youthful vigour, so composed, so authoritative, she had summarily demanded no less than the immediate dismantling of two thousand years of sacred Christian heritage. This little slip of a girl!

He dared not concede the battle to her. He had to find a way to throw this apostate off balance. Pull her into controversy. Somehow diminish the divine stature flooding out from her to the world through these damnable TV cameras. He had to search for weaknesses.

'Jeza, you purport to know the will of God?' he tried again.

'I *am* the will of God!' she declared, the strong tone returning to her voice.

'Then tell us more of the will of God,' the cardinal began his gambit. 'You speak to us primarily in abstracts. Give us clearer answers to better help us solve the world's problems. Give us particulars.'

'When God speaks in generalities,' Jeza responded indignantly, 'man hears in specifics. When God speaks with specificity, man becomes obsessed with minutiae and ritual. God has already provided you with all you need to find your way. Look not to God to provide you with particulars. Look within yourselves. For each individual, there are individual answers.'

'But many issues are not merely individual, as you attempt to so simply portray,' di Concerci countered. 'You say the churches of the world should no longer define and interpret morality? Who then is to lead the charge on such things as human rights, the death penalty, euthanasia? Tell us, *Messiah*,' a contempt creeping into his tone, 'tell us God's will on *abortion!*'

Jeza cocked her head to one side and searched the cardinal's eyes.

But di Concerci did not waver. As she hesitated, the prefect's heart leaped. To his knowledge, she had never dealt with divisive, controversial, politically unsavoury issues such as this. He'd dragged her off her ancient biblical turf on to more contemporary, treacherous ground. A light smile played on his lips.

She looked down at him with an expression of anguish, and her first response was a mere whisper to herself which Feldman could barely hear:

'With encircling words shall they set their snares,' she breathed.

Then, in a louder voice, she answered his question to the entire assembly with an allegory that would become known as:

THE PARABLE OF THE ILLICIT CHILD

And the leaders of the opposition came unto Jeza thinking to entrap Her and discredit Her and do harm to Her in the eyes of Her followers, saying:

'Tell us, what is the will of God if a woman should take the life of her unborn child?'

And Jeza said to them:

'*Behold, a mother of three young children went forth alone from her home and was accosted by an evil man whom she did not know; and he took her by force and lay with her against her will.*

'*Now this man was caught and punished, but the woman conceived by him. And her husband, in rage and injured pride, admonished her saying, "Woman, you must remove this unborn child from you for it is not of your husband's seed; it is the seed of evil and uncleanness."*

'*But the woman would not, and her husband therefore rejected her and his children, and departed from them. And in the fullness of her time, the woman brought forth a female child and raised the daughter up in love and kindness as if she were of rightful issue.*

'*Now it came to pass that in the woman's later years she fell into ill health. And the three natural children quarrelled amongst themselves, saying, "Who of us shall watch after our mother? We have families now ourselves, and are burdened by many obligations."*

'*But the illicit daughter said unto them, "Did not our mother attend us when we were helpless? And did she not sacrifice for us that our lives would be fulfilling? So must we care for her now as she once cared for us."*

'*Yet the other children would not, and like the father before them, departed and contributed not to the care of the mother.*

'*Then the daughter who was the least of them went to the mother and took her in and nurtured her and cherished her and became a source of comfort and great joy in the mother's old age.*

'*Now, I say unto you, who was the true and blessed daughter?*'

But they would not answer her, and instead asked, 'Then you agree that it is wrong to take the life of an unborn child?'

And Jeza responded to them saying, 'It is for woman to decide, and it is not for man to judge her. Only woman, and she alone, in her deepest heart, can know the right way. For I say unto you, good can come from evil and evil from good. Therefore choose your way as if you would know the will of God, for indeed, the will of God is within you.' (Apotheosis 24: 41–58)

Di Concerci was stymied. By cleverly employing proverbs and archaic terminology, Jeza was able to project a convincing messianic image. It was this carefully cultivated demeanour that defied him, not her logic. His Eminence was not accustomed to conceding theological arguments to any man. Much less to a female, one-third his age. He refused to yield.

'Perhaps we would be less inclined to misunderstand you, *Prophetess*, if you were to speak in modern English rather than dated biblical constructs.' There was an edge to the frustrated cardinal's voice that even the disciplined di Concerci could no longer hide. 'Would you be so kind as to enlighten us about yet another perplexing issue?' His brows arched slightly with his next manoeuvre. 'The Bible tells us that homosexuality is abhorrent in the eyes of the Lord. Do you also condemn homosexuality?'

Jeza again regarded this austere Jesuit from her elevated perch. Again she paused, and again the cardinal's spirits rose.

'It matters not in what custom I speak,' she said. 'Truth is truth in any form. If your heart is to misunderstand, you will find a means.' Then, to the general assembly, she continued, 'I condemn nothing which God has created in nature.'

With surging confidence, di Concerci rejoined, 'But homosexuality is *un*-natural. It is counter to nature. It mocks the natural, sacred act of procreation and the continuance of the species, and is condemned clearly and often in the Bible!'

Jeza shook her head at him like a frustrated parent with a recalcitrant child. 'Does your celibacy not mock the natural, sacred act of procreation and the continuation of the species?' Then, turning to the general audience, she proclaimed in plain English, 'The homosexual is no more responsible for his or her condition than is the person born deaf, or blind, or lame. Homosexuality is as impassive to moral proscription as the dominance of one's hand.

'Homosexuals must find the Lord in their own way, mindful of the Word of God, holding true to heart, injurious to no other, protective of the innocent. Rather than being reviled, homosexuals must be left to pursue their path to God without the interference of the self-righteous.'

Di Concerci was appalled, as were a growing number of other listeners in the audience. For the first time, there were isolated catcalls and jeers.

'What about Armageddon?' the imam on the panel blurted out.

'Does your coming truly portend the fulfilment of the Apocalypse, as many say?'

Jeza's face darkened and she closed her eyes. The great hall grew deathly solemn and anxious as it awaited her response.

In a slow, sombre voice, the Messiah declared,

> *'Israel, O Israel, hear my words! Rising up among you now are the false leaders; the betrayers of the prophets. I say unto you, those who would deceive you are in your midst, and the time of despair is at hand. On the battlefield of the shamed shall hypocrisy meet itself. The two-edged sword, Ignorance and Arrogance, shall you wield; sibling shall set against sibling, spouse against spouse, child against parent. War shall you wage on every continent and in every city and in every house, and no family shall be left unscathed. Blood shall you shed in the streets and unto the very temples of the Lord. Death and sorrow shall turn light into darkness, and for three days shall perdition and confusion reign over the land. Even now, the armies assemble and the sides are drawn; the dark hour of dissolution is upon you!' (Apotheosis 24: 59–67)*

A fearful consternation was developing in the hall, and indeed throughout the world, where billions bore live witness to the dreadful prophecy. The imam who had broached this terrible prospect was horror-struck and trembling.

'Great Lady,' he sobbed despondently, 'is there to be no hope for us, then? Have we all failed Allah so' – he gasped – 'so completely? Are we then all to be *destroyed*!'

Jeza opened her eyes and examined the despairing man below her. 'Only those who embrace violence shall perish by it,' she said. 'Not by weapons but only through your faith shall you persevere. What is to be will be; and the word of the prophecy shall be fulfilled. Amen, amen I say to you, as man has broken his sacred covenant with the Lord, so shall the rock be cleaved; yet from the crevice, the seed of the new way shall sprout and flourish anew.'

Di Concerci had risen from his seat, his face flushed with indignation. 'This is simply too outrageous to accept,' he shouted. 'If you wish us to believe you, you must give us a sign. Prove to us that you are who you say you are!'

A hush pervaded the crowd once more.

Jeza looked tired and frustrated. 'You ask for a sign that you might believe,' she said heavily. 'And yet of your own followers do you demand unquestioned faith. I say to you, the only sign you shall receive shall be in the fulfilment of my words!'

Di Concerci started to challenge her once more, but she cut him short. Her eyes blazing, she slashed her right arm forcefully down at him, extending a judgmental forefinger and startling the entire assembly with the volume of her pronouncement: '*Thus be the will of God!*' she exclaimed. 'Woe to those who fail to hearken to His Word. Go forth now from this place, *and try no longer the patience of the Lord!*'

Exasperated and angered, but containing himself masterfully, the prefect recognized that any further efforts to repudiate this demagogue would be in vain. He knew now that he would have been much better served not entering into a debate with her. By default, her invocation of God in defence of any argument was a *fait accompli*. To his great dismay, di Concerci realized he had only managed to make the Church look worse in this confrontational exchange.

A few seats away from Cardinal di Concerci, an ashen Brother Elijah Petway rose on behalf of the Mormons to conclude the devastated proceedings. But before he could speak, a stout arm, draped in black and crimson, reached from behind and grasped his microphone.

Di Concerci was shocked to observe the energized face of Alphonse Litti. In a breathless, reverential manner, Litti announced himself. 'Most Holy Daughter of God,' he began, and di Concerci clenched his teeth. 'I am Alphonse Bongiorno Litti, a cardinal of the Curia and Magisterium of the Holy Roman Catholic Church. And I have a humble but urgent request of you.'

Jeza gazed down from her pulpit, an endearing look gradually replacing the anger on her face.

'Great Lady,' Litti continued, 'other than yourself, there is no more recognized spiritual leader in the world than the supreme pontiff of the Catholic Church, His Holiness Pope Nicholas VI. As a direct descendant of St Peter and leader of Christianity's oldest and most continuous religion, it's vital that the Pontiff meet you and hear your word. Would you allow yourself a personal audience with His Holiness?'

Di Concerci leaned forward quickly to protest into his microphone. 'Speaking as a member of the Curia *in good standing,*' the prefect said, 'I must caution that the Pope's schedule is a most pressing one, and I am uncertain—'

Litti would hear none of it. 'The Pope will not, *cannot* abdicate his responsibility to the faithful,' he interrupted. 'Nicholas cannot refuse to meet with a proclaimed Messiah who professes the revealed Word of God. It's the Pontiff's sacred obligation to hear this special lady, and to personally evaluate Her important message!'

Di Concerci dared not protest too strongly or risk portraying the Church as weak and fearful. And perhaps he should not be so hasty after all. Such a meeting, assuming this mercurial woman even accepted, might yet explore ways to defuse this dangerous development. Certainly, a proposed conference with the Pope would at least forestall the current dilemma. And it would buy time for Holy Mother Church and her associate world religions to regroup and counter Jeza's absurd self-destruct order – a command which many clergy in the audience were obviously taking seriously.

Responding directly to Cardinal Litti, without even acknowledging di Concerci, the Messiah stated flatly, 'Yes, I will come.'

68

Salt Lake City Airport, Utah,
6.19 P.M., Sunday, 5 March 2000

Feldman saw the reserved, pensive prophetess safely to her cabin in the jetliner where she retired for the rest of the day. Then, donning his trusted sunglasses and a baseball cap pulled low to conceal himself, he retreated with Hunter and Cissy to a concourse cocktail lounge to reflect. The mood of the patrons around them was gloomy. Ordering a round of beers, the three newspeople listened quietly to the TV telecasts as a tale of global distress unfolded before them.

From dozens of cities across the world, the reports were rolling in – all uncannily alike. There was a great religious schizophrenia in evidence. Despite Jeza's dictates, many people were flocking to churches, synagogues and temples desperately seeking solace, direction, hope. As often as not, they were met by angered ecclesiasts who were vigorously discrediting the Messiah and disputing her claims and prophecies.

Nevertheless, sizeable numbers of clergy were submitting heart and soul to Jeza's commands, forsaking their churches. Particularly the Catholic Church, which had been most notably embarrassed at the convocation. Many congregations and former congregations shared a common despair and assumption that the end of the world was rapidly approaching. Incidents of panic attacks, nervous breakdowns, suicides and mass hysteria were common, particularly in the West. The level of these incidents exceeded even those that occurred during the infamous Black Eve of the millennium. Outbreaks of violence, however, were relatively few.

The world was in a Great Depression certainly more definitive than any previously experienced. In those parts of the globe where Monday morning had already arrived, absences from private- and public-sector jobs were widespread, effectively shutting down many important industries and government services, throwing everyday life into turmoil.

Although WNN would actually return Jeza to Cairo, as she had requested, hundreds of thousands of people were planning pilgrimages to the Holy Land in anticipation of the Messiah returning to Jerusalem for Judgment Day, as the Bible predicted. Their arrangements, however, were frustrated by the shortage of booking agents and travel personnel, who had deserted their posts.

The deteriorating situation was a serious concern to governments everywhere. It was particularly uncomfortable for US President Allen Moore, who was now desperately seeking to distance himself from his recent house guest. On the TV above the bar, Feldman and his associates viewed Moore delivering a statement from the White House press room.

The President was reading from an index card: '. . . this administration had no forewarning regarding the content of this alleged prophet's message to the religious convention,' he said, his upper lip moist, his eyes having difficulty meeting the camera. 'Furthermore, we wish to stress that, in keeping with typical biblical stories, the colourful comments heard earlier today are most certainly meant to be allegorical and are not, I repeat, *not* to be taken literally . . .'

'Not very convincing, is he?' Hunter smirked.

'How can he be?' Cissy sympathized. 'There's no questioning what Jeza said in that hall. And if you happen to believe in her, you're quaking on your knees right now, ticking off the minutes till the Cataclysm.'

'I have to say,' Feldman interjected, 'some of her comments struck a chord with me. Like her points about man's obsession with religious trivia and rituals – those tiny pebbles theologians stumble over.'

Feldman vividly recalled what certain relatively minor distinctions between the Jewish and Catholic religions had done to disrupt his parents' marriage. Many times, as a frightened, clueless little boy, he'd intervened futilely in bitter quarrels over trifling issues. In the grand scheme of things, did it truly matter whether the proper day of Sabbath was Saturday or Sunday?

Not to mention his parents' great, classic bone of contention – whether or not Jesus Christ was, indeed, the promised Redeemer. This, too, was an inconsequential issue, Feldman had later come to decide. After all, the core principles of both the Jewish and Catholic faiths were the Ten Commandments, and since few on either side of the religious divide seemed to master even these simple, clear-cut tenets, he saw no point in arguing more abstract doctrine.

'Look how all the religions out there squabble among themselves,' he remarked, 'each claiming to be the one true faith. There's absolutely no way for the sincere, well-meaning worshipper of the world to really know for sure which religion, if any, is right.'

'Will the real God stand up?' Hunter snorted, irreverently. 'Where *is* the Supreme Waldo?'

Feldman shook his head and rocked back in his chair. 'Look, I know we're all supposed to be professional, impartial, hard-nosed journalists here, but can you guys continue to sit there and tell me this whole Jeza thing isn't starting to spook you just a bit?'

No answer.

'Think about it,' Feldman expounded. 'Beyond all those amazing capabilities Jeza got from the Negev lab, there's still a hell of a lot going on that doesn't quite compute. Just look at all the hundreds of afflicted people over the last two months who've claimed she's cured them. Some of them have been pretty damn convincing. It can't all be psychosomatic, can it?

'Then, there are those odd little things she seems to have prior knowledge about. On the plane ride over from Cairo, she warned me about upcoming turbulence before the pilot did, for Chrissakes!

'And have you ever wondered why it is WNN always happens to be in the right place at the right time? It's wearing a bit thin trying to explain everything as simply a bunch of bizarre coincidences.'

Hunter emitted a short laugh. 'It's a hell of a lot easier than explaining them as miracles.'

Feldman shot right back. 'You pile up enough coincidences, that in itself is a miracle.'

'Well,' Cissy admitted, 'I don't claim to have an explanation for all those things, but I do have a theory about this mission from the Father she's frightening everybody about.' She looked around to make certain no one could overhear her, and then cautiously lowered her voice. 'I think Jeza's reacting to a subliminal message Jozef Leveque planted inside her to help her handle the military infusion stuff. You know, a safety valve or protective default or whatever.

'I mean, wouldn't you do something to protect your child from that kind of brainwashing? And then later, when Jeza got mixed up with that Samaritan cult, she simply got Leveque's message confused with all the doomsday garbage they fed her. So now she thinks her mission is to prepare for an Apocalypse.'

'Jesus, I don't know what to believe any more.' Feldman groaned loudly. 'I've managed to live my whole adult life with this God thing shoved over in a corner. I couldn't make any sense of it. I'd look for God, but I could never see Him. I was fed up with all the bickering religions and their contradictory theologies and preachy gibberish. And now, I find myself pulling out all my confusions and dusting them off again.'

He took off his cap and ran his fingers through his dark hair. 'I don't know what's happening here, guys, but I have to tell you, there's *something* very strange going on, and it's starting to worry me.'

'Don't tell me you buy into all this scare talk about the Last Day?' Cissy asked, disbelievingly.

'No,' Feldman assured her. 'At least, not a biblical Last Day.' His face clouded. 'But if you look at where this whole millenarian movement is heading, certainly all the ingredients are here for one hell of a confrontation. What you call it, I guess, just depends on your perspective.'

'Well, I'll give you a videographer's perspective if you want one,' Hunter offered. 'This is a cataclysm, all right. A cataclysm of crap! Jeza is as crackers as they come. I agree with Cissy. Her brain is all twisted up from those mad scientist experiments they did on her. She really *believes* she's some sort of Messiah. And why the hell not? What else has she got? No parents. No family. No childhood. No sex life. Nothin'. Nothin' but bullshit illusions of grandeur, stuck in her head from some damn computer and those goddamn Samaritans.

'But I tell you what, whether she's responsible for her actions or not, if that little woman continues down the hell-bent path she's on, she's gonna find herself in a lot hotter water than she's already in. It's one thing to have a bunch of religious fanatics out to burn your ass. It's an altogether more serious deal to mess with the international conduct of business and nations. And the rest of the world aside, she's destabilizing the Middle East, man. She's threatening the oil lanes. And when you do that, you run afoul of the CIA and the National Security Administration – and a whole lot worse!'

This ominous observation was not a welcome insight for Feldman. He sighed. Despite his misgivings about Jeza, he could not deny a strange affection growing inside him for the woman he'd left resting alone in the aeroplane beyond. An admiration for her convictions, her remarkable poise and mysticism.

And also a great pity. He could not ignore the basic truth in Hunter's statements. Despite the technological marvel of her mind and her extraordinary abilities, she was, after all, only human. And sooner or later, she was going to have to come to terms with the unpleasant facts about her real nature.

69

Mormon Convention Centre, Salt Lake City, Utah, *7.09 P.M., Sunday, 5 March 2000*

Cardinal Alphonse Litti was not quite sure how to take all the attention. In only a matter of hours, he'd gone from relative obscurity to international acclaim. Suddenly, he'd become the official Exegete Extraordinaire in matters concerning the mysterious Jeza.

In the lobby of the Convention Hall, Litti was surrounded by hot lights, cameras, microphones and avid news crews, all crowding in to hang on his every word. What had initiated all this uproar were the predictions he had made in his pre-convocation TV interview. Litti had proclaimed Jeza to be a bona fide Messiah and flatly declared that she'd be calling for the abolishment of all organized religions as seriously flawed and failed institutions. When, out of hundreds of opinions televised, his proved exclusively and absolutely dead-on correct, the networks and the world at large took respectful and immediate notice.

'Tell us when and where the meeting between Jeza and the Pope will take place,' a newswoman shouted, jabbing a microphone into the cardinal's face.

'We're not sure yet,' Litti responded, perspiring under the lights and feeling a little overwhelmed. 'We're hoping for two weeks from today, possibly in Rome. I know that communications with the Vatican commenced a short while ago, immediately after the Messiah left the hall.'

'What about all this talk of Armageddon?' another reporter called out. 'You seem to know Jeza's mind better than anybody. Are we heading for doomsday?'

'I cannot claim to know the Messiah's mind.' Litti smiled, flattered by the overstatement. 'But I do feel I have somewhat of an understanding, an insight if you will, gleaned from careful reflection on Her teachings. I believe that a day of reckoning is imminent, just as She stated. The world has had two thousand years to absorb Christ's message and to respond properly to it. In that regard, unfortunately, we've failed badly.'

'So you're predicting all-out war, battles to the death, neighbour turning against neighbour, just as the prophetess stated?' yet another reporter asked.

'I predict nothing, and I truly don't yet know exactly what this "dark hour of dissolution" means. I hope we'll get more clarification during the Pope's audience with the Messiah.'

The questions continued, and for the time being it appeared that Cardinal Alphonse Litti would be a highly sought-after spiritual resource for a gravely distressed and confused world.

70

Salt Lake City Airport, Utah,
6.07 A.M., Monday, 6 March 2000

Jeza had been up early, before any of the others, well before the 7 A.M. take-off. When Feldman came yawning out of his cabin, he found her sitting cross-legged in her passenger seat, earphones on, eyes closed, hands folded in her lap, meditating.

Although he was quiet in his approach, no sooner did he draw next to her than she spoke. 'Good morning, Jon,' she said, her eyes still closed.

'Good morning, Jeza,' he replied. 'Did you sleep well?'

'Yes. And you?'

'Well, frankly, I'm having rather unusual dreams these days. It doesn't make for peaceful sleep.'

She opened her eyes and evaluated him soberly. 'This is not a time for peaceful sleep,' she said, and removed her earphones.

Feldman decided the Messiah was in a mood to talk this morning. 'May I join you?' he asked.

She nodded and he sat down expectantly in the seat next to her. 'Well,' he started, not really knowing where to begin, 'yesterday was quite a day for you.'

'Yes,' she said. 'And now we must prepare for yet another important day. You are making arrangements for me to meet the sovereign of the Roman Catholic Church?'

'That's in the works,' Feldman answered. 'Needless to say, WNN will be delighted to sponsor that trip, too. Our people are in direct contact with all three papal representatives at the convocation. We're hopeful of scheduling a meeting in two weeks, Sunday, 19 March, if that's acceptable to you.'

'Yes, I thank you,' she said, appreciatively.

Since she appeared a willing conversationalist at the moment, Feldman hoped to shed some light on a few topical questions.

'Jeza,' he ventured, 'do you know that your comments yesterday caused a great deal of unrest in the world? Particularly your prophecies about Armageddon. Many people are extremely upset. Some have even committed suicide.'

'Know that the future would bring far more deaths and suffering without my warnings,' she replied, some sternness edging her voice.

'Can you do nothing to prevent this Apocalypse from taking place?' Feldman refused to be discouraged from his line of questioning. 'Can't you just call it off? Forgive the people and give them another chance?' He was patronizing her, hoping to extract a more conciliatory statement that might help ease global tensions. 'Isn't that what Christianity is all about?'

'This is not of my will, nor of the Father's making,' she responded. 'What is to be is a conspiracy of man. Come of man's failure to hear the Word. The stubbornness and arrogance of man turn the truth such that good becomes evil and evil good. Just as an infection of the body must rupture to purge its poison, so must this festering wound be lanced that it may be cleansed and healed.'

This simile did not sit well with Feldman before breakfast. On the spur of the moment, and with considerable reservations, he decided it was time to brave a precarious topic – the same issue he'd almost broached on their flight over, but had decided not to chance prior to the convocation. However, in the face of the current tumultuous global conditions, he felt the gamble was worth taking.

'Jeza,' he asked, gingerly, 'what are your earliest memories of yourself?'

She looked thoughtful. 'My earliest memory is my first moment of awareness, the night of the white light and trembling earth when the Father breathed into me my soul, and delivered unto me His message.'

'Do you know anything about your parents?' Feldman asked. 'Where you came from?'

'I issue from God and man,' she said.

'Do you recall an explosion, Jeza, or perhaps a big fire *before* the night of the white light and trembling earth?'

'No,' she said, looking casually out of the window.

Feldman could not get a read on her. There was no emotion in her answers.

'Do you recall being found injured in a desert by a Bedouin couple?'

'No.'

Feldman paused, reflected, and decided to try a different approach. 'Jeza, you seem to have a great deal of knowledge about things with which you've never come into contact. Do you have any idea how you arrived at such knowledge?'

She turned back to face him. 'All that I know comes from the Father,' she replied.

Feldman pondered his next move carefully. His calculated intent here was to confront Jeza with the reality of her origins, and he fully appreciated the inherent hazards in this gambit. Regardless of how distasteful the exercise might be, it was his job. As a journalist, he had to seek out the truth.

He looked down at her childlike-yet-wise face as she stared intently up at him. An apprehensive crease appeared on her brow, as if she were anticipating him.

He opened his mouth, and then suddenly hesitated. For whatever reason, he simply could not bring himself to tell her who she really was. Exhaling, he blinked and turned away, disappointed at his sudden cowardice. He searched his mind, unsuccessfully, for an explanation. Perhaps he too readily recalled how his own personal world had once been similarly destroyed. He abruptly changed the subject.

'Jeza, how is it that your eyes have such an effect on people? Just by staring at someone, you seem to be able to render them light-headed and disoriented.'

'God looks at people through my eyes,' she explained, simply. 'And I see into their souls. I know their hearts.'

In demonstration, she focused intently on Feldman, and once more he underwent that familiar, discomfiting sensation of utter invasion, confusion and vulnerability. His soul lay naked before her. His cheeks reddened with embarrassment.

Her eyes slowly widened, and then narrowed with insight. Sadly she murmured, 'Behold the child who has borne the parents!'

Her face softened as she looked through him. She took his hands gently in hers. 'Know that the parent is responsible for the child, and not the child its parent. For you to have the capacity for mature love, your heart must first be emptied of its callow burdens.'

A bell in the compartment sounded and a crewman's voice announced take-off in twenty minutes. Interrupted, the Messiah dropped her thoughtful gaze and the hands of her flustered companion.

Badly shaken, Feldman hurriedly excused himself and returned unsteadily to his cabin. Inside, he shut the door and leaned against it, breathing heavily.

He simply did not know what to make of this strange woman. There was a great warmth, a feeling of powerful humanity that issued from her, drawing him irresistibly to her. And yet, this messianic power that she wielded, this spell that she cast over people, troubled him deeply. He could not understand or reconcile the contradictory attraction and anxiety her extraordinary abilities summoned within him.

71

The Palace of the Sanctum Officium, the Vatican, Rome, Italy, 11.51 A.M., Tuesday, 7 March 2000

The Congregation for the Doctrine of the Faith, with the Pope himself presiding, had been in uproar all morning. Although heated arguments had often wandered far from the main topic – the proposed Jeza visit – on that particular issue the Congregation appeared irreconcilably divided.

A learned, elderly cardinal from Latvia argued passionately, 'A meeting with this fanatical mystic is unthinkable! Impossible! It becomes a confrontation of supremacy, pitting our Holy Father against this parvenue charlatan in a public opinion contest over who has the greater divine authority. It is degrading.'

A stalwart Franciscan cardinal stood to offer his concurrence. 'Consider the implications: simply allowing the woman to come here serves to legitimize her. We must not sanctify her fear-mongering, nor should we reduce the sacred Basilica of St Peter to the level of a Mormon tabernacle.'

Another cardinal, a Jesuit from Malaysia, embraced the entire assembly with a gesture of his arms. 'This misguided, self-proclaimed Messiah is anathema to Holy Mother Church and to all organized religion. Look at the calamity she has brought upon us. All over the world our dioceses are in shambles. Our support and contributions evaporating. Our congregations deserting us. I implore you, Holy Father,' a tone of urgency entering his voice, 'do not subject yourself to this humiliation.'

'It's precisely because of the disaster we face that the Holy Father must hold audience with this Jeza,' asserted a young cardinal from the Roman diocese. 'Just as we are divided here in our own Curia over this issue, so, too, are the lost sheep of our congregations. This is our opportunity to assume a more assertive role. We must be seen as the unshakable standard-bearers around which the remaining faithful may rally.'

Another young cardinal rose in support. 'I wholeheartedly agree. I cannot abide some of the recommendations that I've heard here today. I cannot accept that our best course of action is to simply stand idly by, trusting that the passage of time alone will be sufficient to expose this false prophecy.

'Have we not learned from past experiences how powerful the allure of the Apocalypse is to many people? The Seventh Day Adventists are a perfect example. Their very existence is predicated on an imminent Second Coming. And yet, each time their proclaimed target date passes, the governing fathers merely invent a rationalization and set another date. We *cannot* allow this current emergency to continue unchecked. Pontiff, you must counter this woman. Personally and forcefully. Head on, with reason and the courage of our faith.'

Through all of this, Prefect Cardinal Antonio di Concerci had been sitting quietly, observing. He tapped the ends of his fingers together and waited for the Pope to have his fill of everyone's ventings.

Finally, Nicholas turned to the prefect. 'Antonio, will you also offer your opinion to our colleagues? You've had nothing to contribute as yet.'

Nicholas was well aware of di Concerci's perspective on the issue from their lengthy conversations of the previous day. This round-table discussion had simply been the Pontiff's failed hope of building a consensus.

'Yes, Holy Father. If I may also speak for Cardinal Santorini, who was present with me at the convocation?' And Santorini nodded his assent.

Di Concerci stood and extended his arms to the assembly. 'I don't believe anyone here needs to be reminded of the seriousness of the current situation,' he said in a relaxed and reasonable tone. 'In short, the harsh pronouncements of this self-proclaimed Daughter of God have created extraordinary antagonism and animosity towards all organized religions, not just the Church.

'Nevertheless, while all religions must face this common threat, Nicholas, with direct lineage to Christ, and with the consecrated authority to administer Christ's will on earth, is the only religious entity with the mandate to counter the problem.

'At first, I, too, thought this proposed meeting a mistake. However, it is now my fervent conviction that this challenge is a test from God. And a pre-ordained opportunity. If we can meet this challenge – if we can be successful in confronting this false prophetess, if we can deliver mankind from the irrationality and wanton emotionalism of this destructive millenarian movement, if we can restore spiritual order and peace once again to a world racked by panic and confusion – if we can accomplish all these things, we will have within our reach a goal towards which the Church has laboured ceaselessly for two thousand years: the ability to reunite not just the Christian faiths once again, but to convert *all* peoples. To bring *all* religions under the auspices of the one true Church!

'My fellow cardinals, it's our sacred duty as defenders of the faith to confront this, the greatest of all schisms. His Holiness *must* meet with the woman, Jeza. Here in the Vatican. Before God and the eyes of the world. And together, with your prayers and God's great blessings, Holy Mother Church will find a means to resolve the apostasy that has brought such anguish upon this planet.'

There was a moment of stillness in the palace auditorium. And then, from the hands of the Pope, a solitary clapping began. Joined by the young Franciscan cardinal. Then the monsignor from Latvia. Another cardinal stood, and another, and the applause became an acclamation as everyone in the entire hall, Nicholas also, rose to their feet to endorse the inspired objective.

72

WNN regional headquarters, Cairo, Egypt,
7.00 A.M., Thursday, 9 March 2000

Feldman, dreaming an unpleasant dream, was awakened by an itching nose and the melody of a soft giggle. Above him, captured in a shaft of cascading morning light, was Anke. Lying across his bed, she was dangling her long dark hair playfully across his face, laughing mischievously.

'Welcome back to earth, dream cadet,' she teased, and laughed again.

Feldman was overjoyed. 'Anke! Where did you come from?'

'It's been so long since I've seen you,' she said, 'I figured I'd play truant for a day!'

'I'm sorry,' he responded ruefully, rubbing his eyes, recognizing he hadn't spoken to her since leaving for the convocation.

'I'll forgive you,' she replied complaisantly, '*if* you tell me all about your visit to the White House.'

Feldman laughed and gathered her up in his arms. Without realizing it, the tensions and pressures of the last week had taken their toll on him. As always, his time with Anke restored him in a way nothing else could. They spent the rest of the morning together until a phone call forced Feldman back to reality. He had to leave her again and return to his office for what would prove to be another exceedingly long day.

WNN, he was informed, had not found the Catholics as easy to negotiate with as the Mormons. The Vatican was positioning itself as a reluctant participant in this proposed meeting between Jeza and the Pope, and was seeking to exercise complete and strict control. The meeting would not be a closed-coverage operation. At the Church's insistence, the affair would be open to all media. But WNN still held out hope for a prominent presence.

The date of Sunday, 19 March, at twelve o'clock noon at the Vatican, had been agreed upon. Just as Jeza had assured Feldman it would be when he had deposited her at her clandestine desert drop-off the previous Monday evening. But the Vatican had insisted that the prophetess arrive approximately an hour early to accommodate an involved procedural schedule; it also insisted that WNN arrange for the now-world-famous Cardinal Alphonse Litti to accompany Jeza and serve as her escort at the Papal Palace.

73

The Papal Palace, Vatican City, Rome, Italy,
2.09 P.M., Monday, 13 March 2000

As the Pope entered the room, Cardinals Antonio di Concerci and Silvio Santorini rose behind a table covered with stacks of reference materials, notebooks and documents. They were in the Pope's spacious, impressively decorated private library where Nicholas often met informally with his advisers and guests. For today's important presentation, the table and a number of large easels had been brought in and placed in front of the Pontiff's elevated receiving throne.

The large double doors of the library were closed behind him as Nicholas waved the two cardinals to their seats and quickly ascended the steps to his chair. The Pope was anxious about today's meeting. Anxious in general about his impending audience with the prophetess Jeza. He'd had more troubling dreams and second thoughts.

Di Concerci, as if sensing his pontiff's uncertainty, launched immediately into his introduction.

'Holiness, I'm pleased to inform you that we've concluded our investigations and the information we've uncovered far exceeds our expectations. As you will soon see, we now have everything necessary to implement a successful plan.'

The Pope nodded his approval, withholding his enthusiasm. Di Concerci motioned for Cardinal Santorini to begin. Santorini stood, moved to the first easel, and unveiled an enlarged colour photograph.

'This is the Leveque family, Pontiff,' di Concerci explained. 'Jozef Leveque, his wife, Anne, and their daughter, Marie. This photograph was taken some ten years ago, when the young lady pictured here was in her early twenties.' The Pope rose and walked down the steps to have a closer look. He placed his spectacles on his nose and peered intently at the picture.

Di Concerci continued. 'Shortly after this picture was taken, the daughter, Marie, was involved in an unfortunate incident in which she became the innocent victim of a tèrrorist bombing in Jerusalem. She was gravely injured, and although she survived, she was rendered comatose and remains so to this day.'

The Pope frowned as he examined the image of the smiling young woman. 'Appalling,' he lamented. 'Will there never be peace in the Holy Land? But I fail to see the association with the subject of today's meeting.'

As Nicholas turned away from the beaming young face, Cardinal di Concerci pointed back to it, refocusing his attention. '*Papa*, look again at the photograph. Do you not notice something familiar about the young woman?'

Nicholas returned to the photograph, leaned forward and squinted more intently at the image. His eyes suddenly widened and he exclaimed, 'Is this Jeza's sister? I see a resemblance!'

The prefect smiled. 'Clone is perhaps the more correct explanation. This is the woman whose ova were utilized to create the genetic double the world knows as Jeza. Just as was presented in the televised programme on Jeza's origins.'

'Amazing!' the Pope whispered in wonderment, staring at the face. 'But I'm confused. While this woman resembles the prophetess, the similarities are not that pronounced. They appear more familial than identical.'

'That is due, we understand, to the processes under which Jeza was gestated,' di Concerci explained.

The Pope nodded his understanding and returned slowly to his throne in a thoughtful state.

'We have everything we need to expose the truth, Holiness,' di Concerci asserted. 'A secret contact in the Israeli Defence Force has assisted us in providing full documentation. Also, we understand from WNN that Cardinal Litti has accepted our invitation to conduct Jeza to our welcoming ceremony.'

'Excellent.' Nicholas was feeling considerably better about developments. 'Describe for me the entire plan as you have conceived it, Antonio.'

'Certainly, Holiness.' Di Concerci took his seat again at the table and gathered his notes in front of him, although he did not refer to them. He began.

'Cardinal Litti, Jon Feldman and the woman, Jeza, will arrive at the Vatican heliport at approximately eleven A.M., Sunday, 19 March. They will be escorted on foot by Cardinal Santorini with a small contingent of the Swiss Guard and papal knights. They will travel through the gardens, enter and pass through the Sistine Chapel, view several of the cortiles and gallerias, and then will proceed across the square to the front of the basilica. They will then enter the basilica at approximately eleven forty-five and await your arrival. All this will be covered in its entirety by the various TV networks in attendance.

'During this walking tour, it will be Cardinal Santorini's objective to display to the woman some of the exquisite beauty and grandeur of the Vatican, and to imbue her with a sense of the historic religious significance represented in the culture of the Church. We wish for her to appreciate fully the inspiration of the great works of art commissioned by the Church through the centuries for the honour and glory of God.

'As Jeza, Jon Feldman and Alphonse are escorted by Cardinal Santorini through the front doors of St Peter's, the Julian choir will be in performance and the entire cathedral filled with all members of the papal court and representatives of all official religious orders.

'Jeza *must* be affected by the pageantry and majesty of the sacred cathedral. Obstinate though she may be, surely her heart cannot be so hardened that this great presentation of beauty and adoration will not move her. At such time as she has arrived at the tabernacle and been allowed to meditate over the sacred relics of Saints Peter and Paul, you will arrive, Holy Father.

'We will follow standard procedures for an official ceremonial audience. Cardinal Santorini will be announced to you first. He will ascend the stairs, you will extend your hand to him and he will kneel and kiss the ring of St Peter.

'Next Alphonse will be presented to you, you will extend your ring, and Alphonse will, no doubt, also kneel to kiss the ring. And then at last, Jeza will be presented to you. You will extend your hand once more and, God willing, she will follow suit, kneel and kiss the ring as well.

'Now let me caution you here, Holiness.' The prefect held up a restraining hand. 'When you look at Jeza, you will likely find her eyes quite unsettling. They are a most unnatural colour – a vivid purplish-blue – and they can have quite a vertiginous effect on the recipient at first. I suggest you remain seated and be prepared for a moment or two of discomfort. It will quickly pass.

'The significance of Jeza's participation in the kissing of the ring, of course, is to demonstrate to the entire world the supremacy of the papal throne, and Jeza's acknowledged subordination to you as dominant spiritual authority.'

'And what if she refuses?' Nicholas questioned.

'That will not divert us from our purposes,' di Concerci assured him. 'If at any point in time she becomes difficult or confrontational, we will simply move to the next phase of our plan.

'Our objective will be to secure a retraction from Jeza concerning her position on the dismantling of organized religion, at least regarding Holy Mother Church. As it's unlikely we will be successful in that regard' – di Concerci paused to retrieve an item from the table – 'we'll then proceed, with the entire world watching as witness, to confront her with *this*!'

The Pope leaned forward in his throne with great interest.

A hard glint of confidence in his eyes, Cardinal Antonio di Concerci held up a large brown book.

'Holiness, this is the unaltered, personal diary of Mr Jozef Leveque, the man responsible for the genesis of Jeza.' He paused to let this revelation settle.

'In this journal lies the *whole* story behind this strange woman and her mysterious powers. A tragic and, in many ways, a very moving story. A story of all-consuming love and obsession. Of a desperate, brilliant man, driven to reclaim that which only God has authority over; that which God had taken from him: the life of his only daughter.

'But most important' – di Concerci's face was burning with conviction – 'this diary is a full disclosure of exactly *what* our purported little Messiah truly is. Here in this diary, Holiness, are untold shocking details that WNN conveniently omitted from their TV documentary. Details that will surely convince the world that Jeza cannot be a prophetess, nor a Messiah, nor the Sister of Jesus.

'Contrary to WNN's report, Jeza's cognitive powers are not merely

the result of some passive memory-building process. The explanation
for her remarkable intelligence and abilities is entirely *inorganic*.
Artificial and ungodly. Composed of fabricated silicon microchips
surgically implanted deep within the hemispheres of her brain.

'*Papa*, this woman the world hails as the Daughter of God is,
without question, a diabolical impostor. The entire Jeza phenomenon
is a well-calculated, profane ruse developed by agents of the Israeli
Defence Force for some as yet undetermined purpose.'

The Pope's mouth dropped open in astonishment. The two cardinals
could not contain their pleasure.

'Wh-what are you saying to me?' Nicholas stammered.

'Pontiff, what I am pleased to report is that Jeza is *not* fulfilling some
divine mission conveyed to her atop those temple ruins on Millennium
Eve. But like a pre-programmed robot, she is nevertheless carrying out
some sort of secret mission. All of the proof is right here,' di Concerci
proclaimed, tapping his forefinger soundly against the hide of the
upraised diary. 'Irrefutable evidence that we will make amply clear to
the world media with enlargements of key passages. All documented
in Jozef Leveque's own hand.'

The Pope was speechless. He collapsed back into his chair with a
clenched expression of deep relief. After a moment's recuperation,
he shook his head in wonder and addressed the two cardinals, who
awaited his reaction with expectant smiles. 'You're telling me the
nightmare is over?' he breathed, the magnificent awareness seeping
into him. 'This dreadful nightmare is finally *over*?' The conclusion was
so sudden and anticlimactic, Nicholas could not immediately absorb
its full significance. He tilted his head back into the soft velvet support
of his throne and closed his eyes.

The two cardinals exchanged nods, beaming in silence.

The Pope recovered, wiped his eyes under his spectacles with a
handkerchief, and then asked, 'You must tell me, my amazing, beloved
Antonio, how did you possibly come by this godsend?'

'With a little intervention from the Almighty, Holy Father,' di
Concerci answered. '*And* a little persuasion from the Congregation
for the Doctrine of the Faith. As it turns out, the wife of Jozef Leveque
is a practising Catholic in Tel Aviv. After the panic in our world dioceses
from Jeza's announcement at the Salt Lake convocation, we received
a call from Mrs Leveque's parish priest. He had learned all about

the diary from a confession Anne Leveque had made to him some months prior.'

Nicholas was aghast. 'You mean to say, her priest betrayed the confidence of the confessional!'

'Under the circumstances, Holiness,' di Concerci pointed out, 'the pastor, in good conscience, felt the defence of Holy Mother Church a more than worthy justification. As did we cardinals of the Congregation. After all, that is our sacred consecration – to defend the faith!'

Nicholas nodded gravely, not entirely comfortable with this explanation.

'From the pastor,' di Concerci continued, 'we also learned that Mrs Leveque had subsequently lost possession of the diary to the Israeli Ministry of Defence. We were then able to secure the diary from a supporter inside the ministry who learned of our interest and acquired it for us.'

'Who is this mysterious supporter?' Nicholas interrupted.

'We may never know,' di Concerci responded. 'He will not identify himself.'

'I don't understand.' The Pope considered the point. 'Given all the negative publicity surrounding these experiments, why would the Israeli Defence Ministry allow such damaging details to emerge?'

Di Concerci cleared his throat. 'Defence Minister Tamin is not yet aware that we've acquired the diary. The individual who secreted the material to us is neither a friend of Shaul Tamin's, nor an advocate of this false prophetess Jeza. Moreover, considering the misery the defence minister has unleashed on the world with his miscreant experiments, none of us should be too distressed if Mr Tamin does not survive the pending scandal.'

'Still,' Nicholas complained uncomfortably, 'I do not like to see Holy Mother Church involved in such political intrigue . . .' He paused, weighing the issues. 'Nevertheless,' he said, finally relenting, the waves of relief rising from deep inside him to purge his conscience, 'I must commend the both of you on a truly miraculous, God-delivered reversal of fortunes.' He could not suppress his delight.

The two cardinals accepted their pontiff's gratitude with broad smiles.

'Now,' the Pope asked, 'may I request one last consideration of you, Tony?'

'Anything, Holy Father,' the prefect agreed.

'If Jeza refuses to accommodate our plans and it becomes necessary
to expose her, as I fear it will, I would not wish to see the papacy directly
involved in the accusations. While I will remain by your side in support,
I would ask that you personally conduct the indictments, given your
close knowledge of the particulars and your past experience with the
woman.'

'Gladly, Holiness,' di Concerci replied with a gleam of anticipation
in his eyes.

Nicholas leaned back in his chair and exhaled in soulful relief. 'It's
over, Tony?' he asked again. 'It's finally over?'

'Yes, Holiness.' Di Concerci smiled. 'It is.'

74

WNN regional headquarters, Cairo, Egypt,
10.14 A.M., Wednesday, 15 March 2000

Feldman gave the London *Times* article a thump with his forefinger
and dropped the newspaper to his desk, gazing at it thoughtfully. The
face of Mother Bernadette, the Sister of the Silent Sufferers, smiled
back at him from a photograph.

According to the story, the elderly little nun had recently won the
Virginia state lottery's powerball jackpot, worth some nine million
dollars. All of which she was devoting to save her precarious African
children's charity. An 'angel', she claimed, had whispered the winning
numbers in her ear.

Before he could give the matter any further thought, Feldman
was interrupted by a knock at his door. It was Cissy, arriving for
a meeting, bringing with her a new visitor and temporary house guest
of WNN. Feldman was summarily introduced to the smiling Cardinal
Alphonse Litti.

The reporter took an instant liking to the affable cardinal, finding him intelligent, warm and outgoing, with a good sense of humour and an engaging openness. In the course of their meeting, the cardinal was pleased to enlighten Feldman, Hunter and Cissy as to papal protocol and procedures, which Feldman would need to understand in his roll as co-escort. Cissy, much to her chagrin, had not received an invitation from the Vatican. However, the good cardinal promised to see what he could do for her, as well as for Hunter, whose position was also still undecided.

'You understand, of course,' Litti waxed effervescently, 'the Vatican is actually an independent, fully sovereign state, with the Pope serving as supreme and absolute monarch. It's the only such state in the Western world in which the governing ruler possesses unchallenged executive, judicial and legislative powers, all at the same time.

'Since Sunday's audience will be conducted as a formal reception of state,' he explained, 'there will be a full ceremony of the papal court, complete with pontifical procession, regalia and decorum. It's a beautiful and impressive presentation and I'm certain you'll enjoy it.'

'I guess I'd better have my tux cleaned,' Feldman quipped.

'Yes,' Litti responded, apparently unaware that Feldman was joking. 'Black would be appropriate.'

Out of the cardinal's sight, Cissy arched her eyebrows at Feldman and assumed mock airs. Feldman, who didn't own a tux, grimaced and made a mental note to get fitted for one the next morning.

Litti then proceeded to outline the general three-hour timetable for the visit, including a ninety-minute meeting set aside for Jeza and the Pope. The schedule was very precise, with a step-by-step itinerary the party would follow from arrival until departure.

Basically, it would appear that Feldman had no role to serve beyond that of observer. Which, while perhaps a bit deflating, was not unwelcome news to him. He was thrilled to be allowed such an intimate view of this auspicious event. As they concluded their meeting, Feldman took the liberty of asking a personal question of the gregarious cardinal.

'Your Eminence, I can't help but wonder what your objectives are in setting up this meeting between Jeza and the Pope. What do you hope to accomplish?'

'I have known Nicholas for over forty-five years, my son,' the cardinal told him, 'since my first days in Rome as a young seminarian. I assure you, the Pontiff is a good and honest man. He seeks the truth. And I firmly believe that once he has met Her and heard this truth directly from the Messiah, he will recognize it and he will accept it.

'It's my fervent hope that there's still time for another reconciliation between God and man. That's what's needed here. A rapprochement between God and His Church. Over the centuries, Holy Mother Church has drifted away from the truth. She's lost the full meaning of Christ's teachings. God is displeased and justly angered. But, as in the parable of the Prodigal Son, I'm convinced of God's eternal mercy and capacity for forgiveness. I pray that God might welcome back His Church if only Nicholas can be truly repentant and willing to accept the New Word of Jeza. That is my hope.'

75

The outskirts of Cairo, Egypt,
6.30 A.M., Sunday, 19 March 2000

This time, Jeza was already sitting there, waiting for Feldman. Again, she had no belongings or accessories to bring with her. Just her trusted white cotton robe, trimmed in red and purple.

On the short ride to where the helicopter awaited them for the shuttle flight to the airport, Feldman, wriggling uncomfortably in his tuxedo, mentioned to Jeza the formality of the Vatican reception that they would be attending. He had had no way of informing her prior to their rendezvous that morning, and once again he tactfully suggested that she consider a change of attire on the plane.

Jeza thanked him for his thoughtfulness, but declined.

As the helicopter lifted off and passed over the perimeter of the airport, Feldman could see in the early morning light that the multitudes converging for Jeza's send-off hadn't diminished any in size. However, there was a dramatic difference in the make-up of this crowd.

Prior to Jeza's performance at the convocation, these assemblies had been virtually unanimous in their support of the Messiah. Now, a substantial group of angry protesters were defiantly rejecting Jeza in the face of the dominant opposition. It required the Cairo police to keep the two factions from clashing with one another. This wasn't a situation unique to Cairo. It was happening all over the world. And some of the confrontations had been more than verbal. Violence was on the rise again.

Well out on the tarmac beyond the turmoil, the WNN charter jetliner sat waiting. An impatient, meticulously outfitted Cardinal Litti stood near by with Hunter and Cissy, for whom Litti had finally been successful in securing special invitations.

The cardinal's reaction on meeting the prophetess close up was priceless. He was a freshman on a first date with the senior prom queen, talking incessantly, gushing, fawning, stammering and hovering around her like an energetic puppy. Boarding the plane, he furtively asked Feldman if he might have the seat next to the Messiah, and the newsman generously agreed.

Feldman was amused by the display, and pleased to see that the Messiah was completely tolerant of, and gracious towards, her admirer. It was not that Cardinal Litti's conversation was boring or banal. Quite the contrary. He continually impressed Feldman as a very learned, engaging, insightful man. His philosophical and religious questions were intriguing and provocative. It was his unbridled enthusiasm that was so overwhelming. As Feldman observed laughingly to Hunter, 'Turn off the volume and you'd swear he's thirteen years old!'

During the flight, Cissy, Hunter and Feldman listened in rapt fascination as Litti plied the Messiah with a steady stream of theological curveballs. Feldman found one discussion, which focused on the complicated, long-troubled relationship between God and man, particularly interesting. It began with Litti asking Jeza how man was to be absolved of Original Sin if, with organized religion invalidated, there would no longer be any priests left to perform the ceremony.

Feldman recalled from his Catholic upbringing that Original Sin was an inherited, moral dishonour that all people shared at birth. It stemmed from Adam and Eve's failure to obey God's command not to eat from the Tree of the Knowledge of Good and Evil. In being cast out from the Garden of Eden, Adam and Eve and all their descendants had been denied access to heaven unless freed from Original Sin by a duly administered sacrament of baptism.

Jeza smiled and shook her head at all this. 'You are too steeped in your religion's catechism,' she chided Litti. 'Baptism, like many of the rituals of the Old and New Testaments, is a *symbol*, meant to serve as a physical manifestation of the spiritual. It *represents* the holy cleansing that takes place when the individual makes the conscious decision to reject sin and accept the presence of God.

'That this symbolism has assumed such importance fully illustrates why man must dissolve his communality of faith. Through the ages, the world religions have greatly misinterpreted the true message. They have placed too much emphasis on the act and the ceremony, rather than on the substance.'

'But,' Litti pursued his train of thought, 'how is the helpless infant to be freed from Original Sin? What of those children who die before they have the maturity to understand and accept God's presence? Are they for ever to be denied God's grace? Isn't baptism necessary for their salvation?'

Jeza shook her head again. 'The fallacy is in the doctrine of Original Sin. Do you think the Father so callous and unfair as to deny innocents the rewards of heaven for the actions of their forebears? The redemption that is promised in the Old Testament is to redeem each man from the consequences of his *own* transgressions, not those of his ancestors. Man, in ascending from the clay, in his progression towards godliness, requires the Father's instruction and assistance along the way. Christ came less to redeem man of sin than to show man the way.'

'You mean to say,' Litti said, dismayed, 'that all these centuries, the many faiths of the world have all been labouring under so many false precepts?'

'By no means are all the precepts of the world religions false,' she responded. 'Those principles based on the commandments and the *general* teachings of Abraham, Christ, Muhammed and the many great Messiahs remain valid. It is when the autocracies of religion have sought to complicate these principles that they err.

'The need for religions to elaborate on God's will is invariably founded in their need to control. By complicating the way, religions make themselves indispensable to those seeking salvation. The faithful are then tied irrevocably to their religions, falling prey to dictates and tithes.'

'Do you feel that *all* religions are failures?' Litti questioned.

'That religion which asks *nothing* for itself from its membership may call itself worthy,' the prophetess responded flatly.

However credible her theologies were, Feldman had to admit that this controversial young prophetess certainly knew her own mind. The lively discussion made the three-hour flight seem magically shorter.

Feldman had never been to Italy before, much less seen the famed Vicarage of Rome. Despite being apprised beforehand, he was nevertheless amazed at how tiny the little state appeared from the air. And fragile, given that it was now surrounded by an estimated crowd of four million people.

But on closer inspection from the shuttle helicopter, as they pirouetted down to the landing pad, he corrected the assessment of fragility. The Vatican was a veritable fortress, protected by massively thick and towering walls. Surrounding the Vatican, Feldman could see the excited faces of people waving and shouting and pointing upward. Some gestures, he noted, were not welcoming.

Settled on the ground, Cissy made a last-minute adjustment to Hunter's bow tie and everyone stepped out into the bright Roman morning. Greeting them at the end of a long gold carpet that extended from the steps of the helicopter to the end of the landing pad was a formal reception committee. It included a complement of twelve Swiss Guardsmen attired in colourful yellow, blue and red uniforms with gleaming metal helmets and breastplates, starched white neck-ruffs, and carrying long, iron-tipped halberds.

A sallow-cheeked, serious-looking man in regulation black cassock and crimson zucchetto skullcap was introduced by Litti as Cardinal Silvio Santorini. He was attended by a full complement of official papal chamberlains and knights.

The guardsmen presented the yellow-and-white papal colours, turned smartly on their heels, and the party began its long promenade towards St Peter's Basilica at the opposite end of the city. The entire length of the route they would travel was roped off on both sides by velvet cordage, behind which crowded hundreds of representatives of the international media, cameras flashing, videos whirring. Despite the temptation, no journalist dared cross the barricades upon penalty of instant expulsion.

To the on-going frustration and resentment of the world media, WNN continued to enjoy an unfair advantage. Not only did WNN provide live coverage alongside the other media from behind the barriers, but Hunter and Cissy, in the very cross hairs of the action, were also allowed to record the entire occasion on non-live videotape. Shortly, the world would be treated to yet another up-close-and-personal, ratings-topping WNN special.

From the start, Santorini took a prominent position on the Messiah's right, with Litti on her left. Although Feldman followed directly behind, he was unable to make out clearly all of the soft-spoken Santorini's monologue with Jeza. From time to time, he picked up on bits and pieces of a historical dissertation as presented by a well-seasoned professor. Each turn presented some exquisite antiquity, priceless sculpture or famous *objet d'art*, complete with accounts of its origins.

Always looming majestically before them, growing impossibly larger with every step, was the soaring majesty of St Peter's Basilica. Ultimately passing beneath the towering rear edifice, Feldman, truly humbled, could virtually feel 'the venerable presence of a spiritualism that stretches back, uninterrupted, to the dawn of Christianity', as Silvio Santorini so aptly put it.

But hardly had he reflected on this stirring abstraction than he, Jeza and their party were ushered through an unremarkable entranceway into a side building, leaving behind the Swiss Guardsmen, chamberlains, knights and a frustrated knot of journalists. As his eyes slowly adjusted to the darkened interior, Feldman was astonished to find himself in the celestial presence of Michelangelo's frescoed Sistine Chapel. He watched curiously as Jeza separated herself from her escorts and walked behind the altar to stare up thoughtfully for a moment at the fresco of the *Last Judgment*, a section of which was marred by a large crack, currently undergoing careful repair.

From here, the tour group was led outside again, through a series of art-adorned courtyards, and then back indoors through several museum halls of exquisite paintings, statuary and tapestries. Finally, they exited out into the sunlight and the vast magnificence of St Peter's Square. Catching up with them here were the media,

Swiss Guards and the rest of the knightly court they'd previously left behind.

As large as half a dozen football fields, the immense square was deserted, closed off at the bottleneck of the stately Bernini colonnades by rows of riot-geared police. Beyond the blockade, crowds of fervid onlookers massed all the way out to the distant banks of the Tiber.

The point where the Jeza party emerged on to the square was roughly midway between the colonnades and the imperial Basilica of St Peter. As they traversed the lengthy expanse of cobblestone, it was explained that this huge common had once been a spectacular Roman circus where, for sport, gladiators had fought to the death and early Christians were devoured by wild beasts. Indeed, it was in this very courtyard that St Peter himself, as an eighty-year-old man, had been nailed upside down on a cross to die agonizingly in the sun.

Awaiting them at the steps of the cathedral was a formal military formation of more plumed Swiss Guardsmen and assorted papal knights in full-dress regalia. One by one as they were announced, the military brigades snapped into a gauntlet of opposing columns leading up the stone steps into the cathedral. With Santorini still in the lead, Jeza and company ascended through the human tunnel, passed between huge white portals and ornate wrought-iron gates, and into the vast, sacred chambers of the world's largest church. The armed guards then collapsed in orderly fashion and fell in behind the group.

It was dark and cool inside, like a cave. And just as otherworldly. As he marched down the broad, open aisle, Feldman's mouth was agape. He'd never witnessed such splendour. The voices of the all-boy Julian choir wafted down from the lavishly embellished, vaulted heights of the loggias. If it had been the Pope's intent to impress his visitors, he'd most certainly succeeded. At least with Feldman and his WNN associates, who were visibly awestruck. The Messiah's perception, however, was indeterminable, her face impassive, her demeanour polite and unaffected.

As enormous as it was, the spacious cathedral's galleries were utterly filled to capacity with representatives of every conceivable Catholic religious order and declension. Perfectly civil in contrast to the milling crowds outside the Vatican gates, this was still a decidedly hostile assembly. Feldman noted more than a few glares of disapproval on the wan faces of the nuns and clergy. And now, sealed off from behind by the rear guardsmen, he found himself growing increasingly uneasy as he moved deeper into the ecclesiastical stronghold.

Directly ahead of the procession, rising to a height of eighty-eight feet, was a gigantic gold-bronze canopy supported by four colossal, spiralling pillars. The canopy was centred under the enormous, four-hundred-foot-high dome of the cathedral, sheltering below it the elevated platform of the High Altar itself. In front of the altar sat an empty throne awaiting the arrival of the Pope.

A lone cardinal, dressed in white and bright scarlet, stood tall and immobile next to the throne, his hands clasped behind his back. It was the redoubtable Antonio di Concerci, observing the approaching party with the cold, emotionless appraisal of a war-hardened general surveying his enemy before battle.

As Feldman drew near to the point of rendezvous, he was surprised to find, upon closer inspection, that what he had taken to be a railed enclosure in front of the altar turned out to be the dark passage to an underground chamber. He suddenly recognized this to be a section of the catacombs, the ancient altar that was the mystical repository for the bones of the first Pope of Rome himself. As he stared down into its sombre depths, Feldman felt a cold draught emanating.

Santorini continued around the railing and brought his procession to a halt at the steps leading up to the left side of the High Altar. Turning back to face his charges, the cardinal raised a palm as if to ward off any questions, lowered his head and eyes, and then folded his hands at his waist in prayer. Cardinal Litti followed suit.

Feldman noticed that Jeza had also closed her eyes in silent meditation. Not having much alternative, he and the rest of the party maintained their positions, patiently awaiting what was to come next. A few rows behind him, Hunter was busy zooming his camera in on points of interest around the basilica, and Cissy occupied herself with adjusting the sound levels of the choir on her portable digital recorder.

When the choir suddenly fell silent, Feldman took this as a sign that something significant was imminent. In a few moments, tall bronze double doors from a side sacristy opened wide with a heavy metallic *bong*. The choir erupted in a joyous hymn, the huge audience rose, turning as one in excited reverence, and the media pressed in as close as the cordons and stationed Swiss Guards would allow.

First to emerge through the bronze doors was the papal master of ceremonies in white-and-black robe, flanked by the procurators of the ecclesiastical colleges and two Swiss Guards. Behind them followed the Capuchin preacher to the Holy See, clad in dark brown. Then the papal father-confessor, dressed in jet black; after him, a series of monsignors in deep purple; a group of protonotary apostolics in white; and a chaplain bearing the papal mitre.

Next were six judges of the Rota and legal officials carrying candles, followed by two deacons, one Western, one Eastern; then abbots, bishops, archbishops and patriarchs, succeeded by two clergy with flower-bedecked staves; next came the entire College of Cardinals in brilliant crimson robes; after them, the prince assistant at the pontifical throne, dressed in black with silk hose and white lace fichu.

And finally, in gala uniforms of the court, came the papal chamberlains, who bore upon their shoulders the *sedia gestatoria* – the royal sedan chair – bearing His Holiness the Vicar of Rome, the two hundred and sixty-ninth successor of St Peter, Pope Nicholas VI.

The Pontiff was spectacularly arrayed in a flowing white robe of the finest silk, with short shoulder *mozzetta* of crimson velvet. Towering atop his head was a magnificent, three-tiered papal tiara, once the property of his predecessor and namesake, Nicholas V. It gleamed with burnished gold, set off by nearly one thousand rubies, emeralds, sapphires, diamonds and pearls.

Floating above the tiara was a white mobile canopy, held aloft by eight *monsignori*, as two privy chamberlains walked alongside with white ostrich-plumed *flabelli* on long poles. Behind the caravan, following with a satin pillow, was the dean of the Rota, whose responsibility it was to bear the heavy papal tiara, when not in use. Bringing up the rear was the papal majordomo, then a selection of other papal officials, and finally, the high generals of all the noble religious orders.

The elaborate, regal train manoeuvred slowly towards the High Altar as the Pope magnanimously bestowed blessings upon his adoring faithful and saluted them with small, wristy waves of both hands. As the sedan chair glided up to the altar, a mendicant scurried in from nowhere with gold-carpeted portable steps which he placed at the side of the carriage. Removing his unwieldy tiara, the Pope handed it down to the dean of the Rota for safe-keeping and awkwardly exited his sedan. The choir continued its glorious chants until the Pope had ascended the altar and seated himself on his throne.

There was a full three minutes of applause and subdued cheering before the Pope lifted his left hand slightly from the arm-rest and called for silence. Breck Hunter, with Cissy at his elbow, moved with impunity directly up to the side of the High Altar for an acolyte's-eye view.

As soon as the great cathedral had quieted, the papal master of ceremonies strode up the steps of the altar and bowed slightly to Nicholas.

'Holy Father, may we ask for your blessings upon our assembly?'

To which the Pontiff made an aerial sign of the cross in front of his heart and whispered Latin words.

'Holy Father,' the master of ceremonies continued, 'may I present to you Cardinal Silvio Santorini, who marshals today's delegation.'

Santorini mounted the steps and dropped to one knee before the throne as Nicholas extended his hand. Kissing the Ring of Peter, Santorini rose and descended on the right to the base of the steps, taking up a mirror reflection of his former position.

Standing next to the Pope, di Concerci's face was implacable. But behind his back, his clasped hands were locked in a tight grip. The Pope's state of mind was evidenced in the steady creasing of his brow.

'May I present to you Cardinal Alphonse Litti, escort,' the presiding master announced, and the stout cardinal made his way energetically up to the throne.

Just as di Concerci had predicted, Litti genuflected and kissed his pope's ring. Nicholas gave him a slight wink, and Litti rose with a broad smile on his face, descending to join Santorini. Over among the Pope's entourage, a chamberlain was readying an armchair, presumably for Jeza. He held off installing the chair on the altar until after the prophetess could be announced.

'Your Holiness,' the master of ceremonies spoke again, 'may I petition for your audience the Lady Jeza of Israel.'

So far, the Messiah had been indifferent to the ceremony, her head cast downward and off to the side, as if preoccupied. Di Concerci unclenched his hands behind him and lowered them slowly to his side. The Pope anxiously edged forward in his chair, his ring hand at the ready.

Watching all this develop, Feldman had wondered how Jeza would respond to this overwhelming display of pomp and power. He did not have long to wait.

Having chosen her moment, the prophetess slowly ascended the stairs. The Pontiff leaned forward expectantly, extending his arm at full length to the oncoming woman. Video cameras rolled and flashbulbs popped as the historic union impended.

Raising her eyes as she climbed, the Messiah fixed them, for the first time, on those of the Pope. There was blue fire in her glare and she unleashed its flame with full force. Despite di Concerci's warning, Nicholas was ill prepared for the searing effect. He was startled, gasped, and reflexively retracted his arm, averting his face, flinching and splaying his hands defensively in front of his eyes.

To the crowd of amazed onlookers, the Pope appeared intimidated, his reaction submissive. Instinctively, di Concerci moved forward to assist his pope, but Nicholas was recovering. The Pontiff took a furtive glance through his fingers at the prophetess as she reached the top level of the High Altar, pulling up short of the throne. Standing but a few feet away from the stricken Pope, Jeza looked down upon him, her head tilted slightly to the side as if carefully studying him.

The basilica had grown as quiet as the catacombs that mouldered beneath it.

'I do not come to venerate the Ring of Peter,' she exclaimed in a loud voice, placing her hands defiantly on her hips. 'In the name of the living God, I come to reclaim it!'

The Pope was taken completely aback. Alphonse Litti, anxious and distraught, had dropped to his knees at the base of the altar.

With a look of outrage, di Concerci attempted to intervene, but was it obvious that Jeza wasn't going to yield the floor. Her eyes flashing with passion, she cautioned the prefect back with an upraised palm, and with her other hand aimed an accusing finger at the confounded Pope.

'Your Church has broken faith with Almighty God,' she declared. 'It has betrayed the consecrated covenant of Peter. For two millennia has it abused the sacred trust of Christ. Through the centuries has it corrupted the Holy Scripture to its own selfish purposes in its lust for power and control. In its hypocrisy has it ruled its followers one way, yet secretly lived another. In its jealousy and intolerance has it muted and destroyed the holy men and women God has sent to enlighten it. In its arrogance has it ignored the Father's messages and warnings.

'And in its greed and pursuit of worldly materialism has it accumulated vast wealth at the expense of the destitute it was ordained to cherish and nurture.' She lowered her accusing finger slightly to target the Pope's hand.

'Of what value is this gold ring you would have me kiss?'

The Pope could not answer, he could only stare vapidly up at her.

'And of what value is a life?' she asked, but he failed to answer. 'If selling this ring would feed but one person, save but one life, would not its value increase a thousandfold? And if this ring would feed a thousand, would not its worth increase a thousand times a thousand?

'Has Christ not said in Matthew nineteen, verse twenty-one: "*If thou wilt be perfect, go sell what thou hast and give to the poor, and thou shall have treasure in heaven*"?

'Yet you, who call yourselves "God's chosen on earth", and "the One, Holy and Apostolic Church", have acquired vast holdings, surrounding yourselves with the richest concentration of treasures in the world!'

The Pontiff sat frozen on his throne, a look of deep hurt and shock on his face, unresponsive as Jeza spewed her venom before the entire world. With the Pope unable or unwilling to counter the attack, an alarmed-looking Cardinal di Concerci stepped forward to confront the prophetess.

'The Church is merely the custodian of these sacred treasures,' he pointed out angrily, assuming command in the glare of the unblinking cameras. 'The wondrous works of art that you see about you are revered religious symbols that have inspired devotion and prayer in the millions of worshippers who have meditated upon them over the centuries. The very creation of each of these masterpieces was itself an expression of devout faith on the part of the artist, undertaken for the honour and glory of God.'

This rally to the defence of the Pope released a pent-up frustration in the crowded galleries, and cries of 'Amen' and 'Alleluia' echoed encouragement to the Cardinal Prefect.

Jeza was not dissuaded. 'Do the starving, sick and naked of the world draw inspiration from your works of art?' she asked. 'Are the priceless pagan antiquities of the Greeks, Romans and Egyptians in your Museo Profano, your Museum of the Profane, also inspirational religious icons?

'And how do you justify the enormous wealth of the papal financial institutions whose great fortunes are stockpiled in deep secrecy? Or the vast holdings in real estate that you hoard throughout the world? I say to you, the Father values not goods, but goodness. He neither needs nor wants your tributes. The Almighty is neither insecure nor vain such that the trappings of mortal man can embellish Him!

'Did Christ seek wealth or glory? You acquire these adornments to enrich yourselves, not God. How can the towering structures you erect as places of worship be more inspiring than the cathedrals of the forests and mountains, or the altars of the open fields and valleys that God Himself has created for you?

'Behold,' she cried, throwing her arms wide and gesturing towards the vastness of the basilica. 'My house is the house of the faithful. Yet you have made it a temple unto yourselves!'

An increasingly furious and desperate di Concerci lashed back. '*Your* house?' he exploded in indignation, pausing for his point to solidify, then petitioning the cameras with imploring eyes. 'Are these not the ravings of a megalomaniac! This girl is self-righteous and utterly delusional. And so ill informed that she can focus only on the superficial and cannot see the greater good!'

Turning back to Jeza, the prefect declared, 'You are misguided, woman. Blind to the true purpose and goodness of Holy Mother Church. You do not know of Her extensive philanthropies. Her irreplaceable largess that feeds and clothes and tends and heals and educates and uplifts the suffering masses of the world. Her charitable missionaries, hospitals, orphanages, schools and benevolent organizations!'

Jeza turned her unwavering gaze on her opponent. 'It is not that I am unaware of the virtuous deeds of your Church,' she intoned. 'It is that I am unmoved. The good services you perform are but a fraction of what God has mandated of you, and a pittance of what your vast resources enable. God's patience grows thin!'

Cardinal di Concerci, whose patience had apparently also grown thin, nodded down to a frantic Cardinal Santorini, who slipped quickly away from the battle.

At long last, Nicholas VI stirred from his paralysis. 'Lady,' he called out falteringly, and Jeza, who'd been facing away from the throne, pivoted slowly to acknowledge him. 'I do not understand. I must tell you in all sincerity that our efforts in the service of the Lord have been genuine and faithful. Why do you single out the Catholic Church for such denunciation? How could the honourable efforts of so many dedicated people have disappointed God as severely as you represent?'

Feldman seemed to detect a slight softening in Jeza's expression, which, to this point, had remained deadly serious.

'If my words sound harsh to you,' she replied, 'it is only because you appear unable to grasp anything less.' She paused and sighed. 'I do not say that yours is the most misdirected of religions. There are many more which have led their followers further astray. Yet it is the Catholic Church that was the original vessel of Christianity, the first Church ordained by Christ to carry forward His Word. Therefore it is the Catholic Church that must bear the greatest responsibility for the wayward directions of Christianity. In failing to heed the pleadings of the Lord's messengers over the centuries, in failing to redress your abiding arrogance and materialism, the Catholic Church is responsible for causing the great schisms which divided Christianity into the countless fragmented sects now scattered across the lands.

'After two millennia and the many warnings of God's holy messengers, your time for reparation has passed. The Almighty is reclaiming that which He gave you. All that is left to you are your benevolent services in assisting the physical afflictions of mankind. Your spiritual authority is no more.'

In admonition, she raised her right forefinger in front of her face and called out loudly, 'In the name of the Living God, I command you to relinquish to the poor all that has been given you through the ages. Surrender up your vast wealth and possessions. Abandon your throne, disband your ministries, and preach no more your flawed catechism. Persist no longer in your stubborn ways. I warn you now for the last time, obey the will of God or be met with a just and devastating retribution!'

The Pope retreated in his chair, completely pale. Feldman, despite his personal discomfort at the scene, marvelled at the Messiah's undaunted mettle and defiance in the face of the overwhelming numbers and strength of her adversaries. She stood alone, with the possible exception of Cardinal Litti, who appeared helpless and lost at the moment. And yet, just as at the convocation, the prophetess had assumed complete control.

Feldman did not realize, however, that di Concerci was about to make a power-play. Cardinal Santorini had returned, accompanied by a papal chamberlain who carried a large, flat parcel covered with black drape. Concealed ominously in Santorini's hands was a large brown book.

76

The Basilica of St Peter, Vatican City, Rome, Italy,
1.17 P.M., Sunday, 19 March 2000

Prefect Antonio di Concerci had been anticipating this moment with coiled vengeance. Armed with his damning evidence now, he sprang on his opponent with the surge of a lion confronting a lamb.

'Jeza!' he called out loudly, jolting the entire assembly. 'His Holiness has welcomed you here as a guest, and yet you accost him with insults. He pays you homage, and you repay him with accusations. Despite this, he has sat here patiently, calmly enduring your censure. Censure for which you offer no substantiation. You accuse only with words! Words whose implications are hollow, false and filled with bitterness.

'You hold yourself out to be the only begotten Daughter of God, a New Messiah with the divine mandate to judge the long-standing religions of the world. And now you come to Rome, before the world's oldest, most revered institution of Christianity, to dare threaten the legacy of Christ's succession. With a few brief words and the wave of your hand, you would end a sacred, apostolic authority that extends, unbroken, back two thousand years directly to Christ Himself!

'For two millennia has the Church fought such oppression and persecution in many forms. And through the grace of God, we have always prevailed. Today, also through the grace of God, we shall prevail once more.' He moved towards her, his statuesque presence accentuated by her small frame.

'Jeza, as you have accused us, so are we forced to condemn you. But unlike you, we will support our accusations with complete and incontrovertible proof. Irrefutable evidence that you are *not* what you say you are. That you are not a Messiah, not a prophetess. That you are not of God. Rather, that you are a delusion and fraud of a magnitude the world has never before seen!'

With a theatrical flourish, di Concerci unfurled his right hand, designating with opened palm the cloaked item held by the chamberlain. 'Look at this photograph, Jeza, and tell me who these people are.'

The chamberlain quickly drew back the drape. Jeza's eyes had narrowed with intensity at this challenge, and she slowly shifted her glare from the Cardinal to the enlarged photograph that Santorini's assistant prominently displayed. There was much commotion in the gallery, as large sections were in a poor position to see the image. Feldman emitted an audible groan.

'Tell us, Jeza, who are these people?' di Concerci demanded once again.

Jeza said nothing. She neither moved nor showed any change of emotion beyond an initial frown of concentration.

'Perhaps I should enlighten you, Jeza,' the cardinal prodded. 'As the world will now see, there is far more to the story of your true origin than accounted for in that tabloid TV report. Let me begin by introducing you to your family. Your *real* family.

'The woman on the left in this photograph is your genetic mother, Anne Leveque. The woman on the right is your biological mother and identical twin sister, Marie Leveque.

'And the man in the middle is your creator. The person who invented you, Jeza, out of test tubes and biology and incubators. This is your true father. Your genetic father. The late Jozef Leveque, a brilliant bioengineer in the service of the Israeli defence minister, Shaul Tamin.'

Jeza's face steadily darkened, her invasive eyes poring over the image of the tall, white-haired man in the photo.

The prefect continued to press his advantage. 'Jozef Leveque is the individual responsible for your celebrated mental gifts. The man who filled your mind with vast stores of information – supposedly through some unique process of passive memory-building. However, that explanation is only partially correct. As we now know, there is a far more sinister secret behind this miraculous intelligence of yours.'

Di Concerci gestured dramatically towards Santorini. 'Here lies the truth, Jeza,' he asserted. 'In Jozef Leveque's own words, carefully recorded in this, his personal journal, until shortly before his death in the Negev laboratory explosion.'

Santorini obligingly held the diary up high over his head, rotating it slowly. With the media and audience gaping in wonder, he opened the book wide and quickly flipped through its pages. Hunter, who'd insinuated himself on to the second step of the altar, zoomed his camera in tightly on the journal while the prefect continued his indictment.

'As revealed here, Shaul Tamin's ambitions went far beyond the sacrilege of artificially gestating human beings.' Slowly and methodically, di Concerci began to circle the troubled prophetess, studying her intently like a predator salaciously savouring the death throes of its mortally wounded prey. 'This is an accounting of how your father created you, Jeza. Not in God's image and likeness, but after the pattern and scheme of some profane military blueprint. In this diary we finally learn the true objective of Tamin's sordid experiments: an ambitious plan to develop human computers for military applications. Supernatural soldiers. Robotic beings less human than machine. Blasphemous experiments of which you, Jeza, are the only survivor.

'The reality is, your father did not merely tamper with your mind, Jeza. In defiance of God, he endeavoured to alter *the very structure of your brain*! Surgically embedding deep within your cerebral hemi-spheres thirteen profane, man-made contrivances. Thirteen silicon microchips through which your artificial intelligence flows.'

Santorini now opened the journal to a two-page, hand-drawn, 3D illustration of a human brain. Throughout the image were distributed thirteen postage-stamp-sized squares.

With the waggle of a stern index finger, di Concerci attempted to direct Jeza's attention to the drawing, but she remained steadfastly focused on the image of her late father.

'It is this, these accursed microchips,' the prefect declared, 'which is the source of the stubborn delusions you now interpret as some

God-given mission. Contrary to what your adulterated mind tells you, Jeza, you are not the recipient of a divine calling. And contrary to what your followers may believe, the malignancy of that laboratory was not purged from you by a stroke of God's lightning on Millennium Eve. Sadly, this artificially implanted evil still resides deep within you.'

Feldman had known full well that sooner or later this climactic moment had to happen. That this innocent, unwitting young woman he had grown to admire and respect must one day confront the coarse, disturbing truth about herself. But he could not have imagined a more cruel or devastating end to her ministry. Here, in the stronghold of her enemies, centre-stage before the entire world.

His heart heavy, he prayed for a swift conclusion.

Mercifully, the prefect no longer directed his ruinous charges at the seemingly defenceless Messiah. Turning, he now appealed directly to the jury of converging cameras. 'People of the world,' he exhorted, 'it's time to bring closure to all of this turmoil, anxiety and conflict. It's time to accept for what they are the misrepresentations that have been perpetrated upon you. The visions that this confused woman sees in her mind, which she believes come from God, are in fact artificial images implanted for some sinister purpose about which even her father was kept in the dark.

'Finally, let it all now come to an end. Let all the fear and torment and anguish forever cease. This unholy plan, whatever its original intentions, is over. Sabotaged. Destroyed. Exposed. And all that's left from its ashes is this poor, defective test subject. This experiment gone wrong. This lonely, pitiful, deluded woman possessed of grandiose, messianic fantasies.'

He paused in his attack, allowing his audience to fully absorb the thrust of his damning exposé. After a moment's purposeful reflection, the cardinal took a deep breath, looked over at his victim, and then bestowed upon her a kind, benevolent gaze of reconciliation.

'I do not mean to be unduly cruel to you, Jeza, with these disturbing revelations. We can all appreciate now that you are not responsible for your actions. Nevertheless, the seriousness of the world upheaval and violence caused by your misguided message has demanded a complete and final climax to the madness.' He moved towards Jeza and extended both hands to her.

'Jeza, in the name of God, will you kneel with me now, here, together in Christ's holiest of churches, and pray with all of us for God's blessings and deliverance finally from this long nightmare?'

Jeza said nothing. She neither acknowledged her opponent, nor reacted in response to his overtures. Apart from her aggrieved eyes, which had been in constant motion over the displayed materials, she remained motionless.

After a prolonged silence, she ended her scrutiny of the evidence, gave her accuser a disdainful look, stepped backward away from di Concerci towards the centre of the altar, turned and directly engaged the main assembly.

Closing her eyes tightly, clenching her fists against her chest, she cried out at the top of her lungs, quoting the scriptures of the apostle, Matthew 23:27–28; 33–34:

'"Woe to you, Scribes and Pharisees, hypocrites! You are like whited sepulchres, which outwardly appear to men beautiful, but within are full of dead men's bones and uncleanness. So you also outwardly appear just to men, but within you are full of hypocrisy and iniquity.

'"Serpents, brood of vipers! How are you to escape the judgment of hell? Therefore, behold, I send you prophets, and wise men, and you receive them not, but persecute them and scourge them in your tabernacles."'

She opened her eyes but her voice maintained its rage and intensity. 'I say unto you, it matters not the origin of truth, whether it be implanted artificially, or whether it be inspired by God Himself. It matters only that it be truth.

'"There is nothing outside a man that, entering into him, can defile him; but the things that come out of a man, these are what defile a man. If anyone has ears to hear, let him hear."'

With these last words of Mark 7:15–16, Jeza made a sweeping turn to face the Pope, who had remained, all this time, in a quandary on his throne. Her arm extended above her, her forefinger pointed to the heavens, she called out in a loud voice, 'As good can come from evil, and evil from good, so now shall the truth be proclaimed:

'Behold, on this day, at this hour, of this moment, does God for evermore reclaim from this Church His keys to the Kingdom of Heaven. No more is your covenant with Christ. Dissolved is your bond with Peter. And now shall the rock upon which this Church stands, the foundation of the house of God on earth which has stood inviolate for two thousand years, now shall all be put asunder!'

Her raised arm came slashing down until her condemning finger was levelled directly at the centre of the High Altar. As it did so, there was a deep, resonating rumble that split the air. With a tremendous thunder, the huge, foot-thick centre stone of the altar cleaved in the middle and came crashing down, shattering and sending bits of small marble flying off the dais, skittering and spinning long distances across the polished floor of the basilica.

Instantly, the entire cathedral was in an uproar, but Jeza allowed no time for the dust to settle.

'Come, eyes of the world,' she announced to the astonished media. 'Come and bear witness to God's revelations of truth!'

She bounded down the steps of the altar, off towards the north sacristy door, leaving a flustered di Concerci and a dishevelled Pope in the smoke of her destruction. The Swiss Guard looked nervously towards the Pontiff and di Concerci for guidance. The media, caught totally unawares, scrambled to mount a pursuit.

Keeping up with the swift-moving Messiah was an impossibility for the live-coverage video crews, whose bulky broadcast cameras and equipment prevented rapid redeployment. But not so for the print media, who quickly joined in the chase. Feldman, Hunter and Cissy, who were among the few with entirely mobile video capabilities, nevertheless found themselves out of position, and had to struggle to catch up.

Feldman was completely overcome by what had just transpired. Hunter, panting along next to him, his camera and equipment haphazardly slung over his shoulder, looked at his friend in amazement. 'God,' he puffed, 'would you believe, right after the cardinal's vicious attack, I said to Cissy, "Only a miracle's gonna save that little lady this time!" God damn!'

And yet here they were, plunging headlong after this incredible woman once again, the entire momentum of events suddenly slammed into reverse, hurtling back in her favour. Not knowing where he was going, or why, Feldman's heart raced out of control in his chest. Not from exertion, but from excitement. His mind was reeling, frantically attempting to keep pace with his feet.

Back at the smouldering altar, amid the swirl and confusion, a stone-faced di Concerci grabbed his distraught pope's trembling arm to assist him from his throne. '*Papa*,' the prefect declared, 'I will direct the Swiss Guard to restrain her.'

'No,' his pontiff replied in a shaken voice, staring in the direction of Jeza's departure. 'Tell the Guard to stand down. We don't know what we're dealing with here, Antonio, and I don't choose to antagonize this woman any further. If indeed she's God's messenger, let her reveal her truths, whatever they may be. And let her leave us as quickly as possible!'

After exiting the great basilica, Jeza took a right turn past the Sistine Chapel and continued her northerly course into the grottoes, an area of the Vatican Feldman had yet to see. Hurrying beneath the scowling statue of St Andrew, she entered the long corridors of the Vatican Library, passed under the Torre dei Venti, the Tower of the Winds, and continued on through the Museum of the Profane.

She wheeled through the venerable halls at a surprising gait for someone of such small stature. As she and the winded troop following her neared the end of the corridor, their passage was blocked by a large bronze porticoed double door. The entrance was manned on either side by two stalwart young Swiss Guardsmen who, at the sight of the approaching crowd, reflexively crossed their halberds in front of the threshold. But, after a quick check on their radio phones, the guards, exchanging looks of disbelief, unlocked and unbolted the huge doors, stepped back into attention and reassumed their impassive stare.

'Oh my God!' Feldman heard an Italian-accented woman behind him exclaim in English. '*This is the Biblioteca Secreta! She's taking us into the Vatican Secret Archives!*'

77

The Vatican Secret Archives, Vatican City, Rome, Italy,
1.41 P.M., Sunday, 19 March 2000

Beyond these doors lay Bramante's Corridor, the first floor of what is the largest, least understood, most shrouded depository of knowledge in the world. This was the fabled Biblioteca Secreta, a suppressed papal mystery that traced its origins back to the first centuries AD, to the very presence of the four evangelists themselves.

An excited murmur from her followers surrounded the prophetess as she placed her palms against both huge doors and with one powerful thrust heaved them aside full force, crashing and jarring them violently against their stops. Before them lay the dust-laden vista of eras long passed. A murky, brooding milieu interrupted at regular intervals by parallel diagonals of sunlight cast from high windows. Across the barrel vaults of the lofty ceilings, mischievous imps and horned satyrs grinned down from faded murals.

Advancing into the musty dimness, Jeza pressed onward past innumerable aisles of fourteen-foot-high, hand-carved wooden bookcases. Stacked in monkish fastidiousness along the shelves were countless thousands of letters, autographs, calligraphies, original manuscripts, one-of-a-kind transcriptions, documents and codices of priceless, hidden, forgotten wisdoms.

A young newspaper reporter, in better shape than most of his colleagues, managed to overtake the racing prophetess. 'Jeza!' he puffed. 'Where are we?'

'We are among the dark secrets of the ages,' she announced, without looking at her pursuer. Blindly, she pointed down a passing aisle to her left. 'There, recorded in Hebrew, the original Gospels of Matthew and the lost Apocrypha of Thomas.'

She switched her aim to a high shelf on her right. 'Here, the missing

Gospels of James the Lessor.' She began a series of rapid, random spearings with her index fingers. 'The lost *Book of the Dialogue of the Saviour*; the last copy of the forbidden *Nekromanteia Echeiridion*; Thomas Aquinas's *Book of Denial*; the encrypted papal order for the execution of the Maid of Orléans; the complete library of the *Index Librorum Prohibitorium*; the journal of the Jesuit pogroms of the West Indies—'

Hunter, Feldman and Cissy could only fleetingly ogle the wealth of disintegrating manuscripts as they hastened along. Many of the bound volumes bore the rubricated coat of arms of the respective popes who reigned during their acquisition, with roman numeral dates embossed on the spines of the blanched and cracked bindings. Hunter stopped periodically with his camera to catalogue as many forbidden tomes as he could before dashing on to catch up with the group.

Jeza never slowed to consider her direction, but moved ever onward, around corners, through archways, leading her troop deeper and deeper into the bowels of the archives. Soon they arrived at yet another large bronze double door, sentried by a lone, dour-faced friar in brown robe sitting behind a desk. As the monk watched this strange posse bear down on him, his eyes grew wide and he anxiously rose to his feet and stepped protectively in front of the doorway.

Jeza trained her irresistible glare on him and demanded forcefully, 'Unbar the door!' Which he did, with nervous fingers and fumbling keys, without hesitation.

Drawing open the doors, the quaking monk admitted them down a long, broad flight of stone stairs. The expansive repository that awaited them at the bottom was of relatively recent renovation, its appearance open and contemporary. It occupied the basement deep under the Cortile della Pigna, the least accessible extremity of the archives.

Here resided the most private, jealously guarded reservoir of the Holy Roman Catholic Church. The enormous vault contained over fifty thousand metres of flat metal file cabinets, each drawer meticulously numbered and labelled. Within these drawers, whose latches were individually protected by an unbroken wax impression of the official papal seal, lay thirteen hundred years of detailed Vatican documents. Listed year by year, they held all surviving papal records, in succession, from the sparse materials of AD 692 up to the complete dossiers of the most recent calendar year, bearing the fresh red-wax stamp of 31 December 1999.

The files were arranged in endless rows, interrupted systematically by cubicles housing computer work stations with the latest in data-processing equipment. The highly classified materials and information stored here included all existing acts and documents relevant to the government of the Church. Everything from minutes of private papal meetings to copies of papal correspondence, privileged notes and messages, and all the working papers at the service of the Pope and his court.

Withdrawing to an open anteroom just inside the entranceway, Jeza moved to a large chalkboard at the far end. When finally the surviving news teams had collected themselves in front of her, she raised her hand and the gathering fell silent, save for heavy panting.

'To arrive at this place,' she began, 'you have passed through the ancient sepulchres of Christendom. Past the remnants of distant memories, some from the very days of the twelve apostles. Here lie the accountings of magnificent achievements, noble quests, great learnings, profound thoughts and wondrous enlightenments. The most ascendant accomplishments of history, to the credit of all mankind.

'Yet here also lie buried fearful secrets. Answers to dark, disgracing mysteries shrouded in time. Recorded among these forgotten ledgers are unholy deeds committed by Christians in the name of Christ. The untold persecutions of the Inquisition. The forced conversions and the merciless desolation of innocent aboriginal peoples. The full breadth of the misbegotten Crusades and the slaughter of the infidels. The persecutions of the eccentric and the abnormal. The executions of prophets and teachers, of blessed men and women sent by God, silenced as heretics. The cruelty of superstition, the baseness of jealousy, the treachery of self-preservation.

'Yet such tales of abomination are too distant to hold consequence now. These bones shall we leave undisturbed. Rather, I shall now set before you more befitting accounts of hypocrisy and greed. Of those who, at this very hour, hold themselves up to you as administrators of God's will on earth.

'You have been told that my words are hollow and carry no truth. You have been told that my charges of avarice and worldliness are without foundation. Behold, now shall you bear witness so that the will of the Father may be fulfilled.'

The prophetess turned to the chalkboard and began rapidly inscribing numbers and letters. At first there was confusion in the group as to what these rows of characters might mean. But directly, someone determined that this was a list of files, dates and drawers of specific data contained in this last archive. Dividing up assignments, teams branched off and began searching for the referenced contents.

'These drawers are sealed with the papal stamp,' one newsman called out after locating his designated cabinet. 'Isn't this illegal?'

'We're on a mission from God,' another called back. 'Break 'em. Break 'em all, for Chrissakes!'

Feldman, Hunter and Cissy scurried around the vault, tearing open seals to the designated cabinets, searching out specified documents and hurriedly videotaping the contents, not sparing time to read them. So preoccupied was he in his espionage, Feldman almost missed the fact that Jeza had finished her listings and was quietly leaving the chamber. He nudged Hunter and Cissy and the trio aborted their task to follow her, accompanied by a half-dozen other alert newspeople. They left behind them a dozen more, still busily occupied with their absorbing scavenger hunt.

The sentry monk at the top of the vault was nowhere to be seen. As they reached the exit of the archives, the two Swiss Guardsmen were anticipating Jeza and spied her with some relief. They swung wide the heavy doors in advance and let the Messiah and her following march through.

78

The Papal apartments, Vatican City, Rome, Italy,
2.25 P.M., Sunday, 19 March 2000

At first there was no response to his loud, anxious knock on the door. Then Cardinal di Concerci heard a muffled voice summon him into the papal quarters. Entering, the prefect found Nicholas VI sitting alone in his favourite armchair, staring out of a window overlooking St Peter's Courtyard.

The crowds outside the square had grown ever more boisterous in the short time since Jeza had delivered her scathing defrocking in the basilica. The police barricades strained against the massing hope for yet another glimpse of the Messiah. Although there'd been no public word for some time regarding the whereabouts of Jeza, since her helicopter had yet to leave its pad her supporters could assume she must still be here somewhere in the Vatican.

Indeed, her whereabouts was the pressing issue behind di Concerci's visit. The prefect was thankful to be admitted, having been told by the protective attendant nun that the Pope wasn't to be disturbed.

'Holiness,' the cardinal opened tentatively, 'I regret this intrusion, but there is a matter of some urgency.' Di Concerci had been hopeful that a little time alone would allow Nicholas to compose himself, but he could see that was not going to be the case. The Pope persisted in the same state of dejection he had carried away with him from the foot of the broken altar.

'*Papa*,' di Concerci tried again, and Nicholas finally turned a pained face to his adviser. '*Papa*, I know you are in no mood for more distressing news, but I must alert you, the Swiss Guard informs me that Jeza has gained entrance into the Biblioteca Secreta, and she has taken with her an entire mob of news reporters with cameras.'

Nicholas turned back to his window, said nothing, and placed his elbow on the sill, his chin in his cupped hand.

'Holiness, we must do something!'

'She has made us into her scribes and Pharisees,' Nicholas said to the window, ignoring the emergency. 'We are the hypocrites now. The barren ground upon which the seed has fallen and withered. God has deserted us, Tony. Jeza has turned everything upside down.'

'No, *Papa*, God has not turned against us, as you will soon see. But for now, we must deal with this breach of the archives. Who knows what this woman is up to? You must let me send the Guard to remove her.'

'I cannot set my hand against the will of God, Antonio. You saw what happened today. This only confirms the troubling dreams I've had of her.'

'It is *not* the will of God, Holy Father,' di Concerci stated adamantly, 'and I will *prove* this to you. But for now, Holiness, we cannot simply allow her to take over the city.'

'Do what you think best, Antonio, but I cannot deal with this right now.'

'Yes, Holiness,' the prefect said, satisfied. 'And soon, I will report back to you with additional information that I believe will help restore your hope.'

The Pope paid this no heed, returning to the spectacle outside his window. Di Concerci bowed and quickly took his exit.

79

The Vatican Gardens, Vatican City, Rome, Italy,
2.29 P.M., Sunday, 19 March 2000

Rather than retracing her steps through the bulk of the Vatican Museums, Jeza cut along a hallway and exited into the afternoon light of the Vatican Gardens. She maintained her steady clip, heading in what Feldman took to be the general direction of the helipad.

At length, as they neared the vicinity of the helicopter, Jeza veered off and entered the serene vista of the Lourdes Grotto near St John's Tower. Here Feldman spied the faithful Cardinal Litti, sitting quietly by himself on a bench, waiting for his lost Messiah. As he caught sight of her, his eyes grew large and he moved anxiously towards her, like a puppy greeting its returning master.

Jeza took the cardinal's hand and Litti dropped to his knees, kissing her knuckles, tears in his eyes. The prophetess smiled

down at him and raised him to his feet. Feldman, Cissy and
Hunter flopped to the grass and stretched out to regain their
breath.

Their rest was short-lived. Within minutes, a contingent of
ten Swiss Guardsmen came trotting down a path to confront
them.

'Lady,' the captain of the guard announced to Jeza, 'we have orders
that you are to accompany us to your aircraft and leave the Vatican
State immediately.' The Messiah did not protest, but willingly allowed
the corps to escort her away.

Feldman and company were not yet permitted to follow. At
halberd point, the guards insisted that all the media turn over any
videotape, photographic film, notes or other records made during the
'unauthorized, criminal break-in at the Biblioteca Secreta'.

Despite his concern, Feldman had to grin as Hunter, aided by
the distraction of the other loudly protesting newspeople, hastily
slid a tape out of his knapsack, pulled out the back of the
unsuspecting Cissy's gown, and deposited it deftly in her under-
wear. Yelping in surprise, Cissy quickly recognized the ruse and
suppressed the reflex to slug her partner. As she shrugged off
the jolt of cold plastic, Hunter surrendered two blank tapes to a
suspicious guard.

Finishing their search, the guardsmen released the group. Feldman,
Hunter and an indignant Cissy joined Cardinal Litti and the Messiah
on the landing pad next to the idling helicopter. While the remaining
news crews captured the send-off, Feldman and Hunter helped their
companions up into the passenger compartment. First the Messiah,
then the ever-faithful Cardinal Litti, and finally Cissy, displaying
a notably unflattering shape as she bent to duck through the
hatchway.

As the helicopter rose slowly from the compound, Feldman
observed an appreciably different complexion in the swelling crowd
outside the walls below. While there were still isolated pockets of
protesters pushing and shoving, the majority seemed to be solidly
supportive of the prophetess now. As the aircraft whirled up into
the blue Roman sky, Jeza's followers waved her off with wild
cheering and banners that read 'Jeza Is God', 'Jeza Rules' and
'Rapture Me!'

80

The skies over Rome, Italy,
3.14 P.M., Sunday, 19 March 2000

Aboard the helicopter shuttling back to Rome Airport, Feldman couldn't take his eyes off the incredible young woman who had just, once again, single-handedly upset global equilibrium.

But Jeza did not return his gaze.

Feldman's mind was churning, arranging and rearranging his perspectives on the events of the day. It was not difficult to imagine Jeza as the Daughter of God. She possessed such an imposing presence; an inner control and strength unlike anything Feldman had ever known. And those invasive eyes. They lent an air of infinite wisdom to her noble face.

And yet, there was that one nagging question that continued to trouble him. How did those bizarre, artificial devices she carried within her head factor into all this? He simply could not shake off his discomfort. There was something too unsettling, too ungodly about them to fit properly into this whole divinity scenario.

On the return flight to Egypt, Feldman could not rest. He sat by himself in the passenger compartment of the jetliner, Jeza having vacated her seat immediately after take-off to retire to her room. Before she'd left, Feldman had tried, unsuccessfully, to engage her in conversation, but she'd avoided him pointedly, appearing very tired and withdrawn.

Several rows away, Litti was sitting quietly, reading. Hunter was stretched out across three seats, snoring. Cissy was still in Rome. She'd stayed on temporarily to work with WNN Europe, rushing to completion a report on the Secret Archives expedition. As she had said her goodbyes at the airport and turned to leave, contraband video in hand, Hunter had patted her on the backside and advised her to keep his precious tape in a safe place. This time she did not resist the compulsion to punch him hard in the gut. If not admiring Hunter's style, Feldman had to appreciate his resourcefulness. He could only hope that some of the other media were also able to salvage their archival treasures.

As the captain sounded the bell for his passengers to return to their seats for the descent into Cairo, Feldman anticipated another opportunity to sit with the Messiah. But when Jeza left her cabin to take a window berth near the back of the plane, he found himself upstaged. The good cardinal proved too tenacious a suitor, grabbing the coveted aisle seat first.

And then, after arriving in Cairo, Litti continued to shadow the quiet, pensive woman, even insisting on accompanying her for their final helicopter commute to Feldman's car. Feldman assumed the possessive cardinal would insist on tagging along to Jeza's drop-off point, too. But thankfully the Messiah broke her long silence and commanded that no one but Jon Feldman could accompany her further. Extremely reluctant to be separated from his Saviour, Litti had to receive repeated assurances from Jeza that he would soon see her again. Feldman also placated the anxious cardinal by providing him with accommodation at a downtown hotel as a guest of WNN.

It was late when, at last, in his car on the way to deliver her to her desert retreat, Feldman finally had the Messiah to himself. Not quite sure how to broach the subject on his mind, he drove for a good while along the dry dirt roadway, incubating his thoughts in silence.

Suddenly finding himself closer to their destination than he realized, he slowed the Rover to regain some time. He stole a sideways glance at his passenger. Her face was turned away from him towards the full moon rising outside her window. Her ivory hands rested quietly in her lap.

'Jeza?' Feldman finally broke the stillness. 'Jeza, why did you choose *me* to conduct you on these journeys?'

She neither turned towards him nor responded.

'Why me?'

'Because I know your heart,' she answered after a long pause.

'Do you also know my mind?'

No reply.

'Do you also know I'm uncertain about you? That I have problems accepting who you say you are?'

Again there was a long pause. 'That does not matter,' she decided, still facing away from him. 'God's plan is set forth and His will shall be.'

'What about *your* will?'

'That you are in God's plan was not of your design nor mine. I chose you because I recognized you.'

'You recognized me?'

'From the moment I first saw you at the Mount of the Beatitudes.'

'You mean you recognized me from television?'

'No. When I saw you it was for the very first time. And I recognized you.'

Feldman was confused. Having arrived at Jeza's release point, he stopped the car.

'I don't understand,' he said.

The Messiah, still facing away, did not respond. Feldman shut off the motor and leaned forward in his seat to get a glimpse of her face.

He was stunned to see her crying. Eyes wide open, staring off towards the desert, a deep melancholy etched in her brow, her cheeks glistening with tears.

'Jeza, I'm so sorry! I didn't mean to hurt you with that stupid comment about not accepting who—'

She turned her large, dazzling eyes upon him.

'I know,' she responded softly. 'You have not.'

Feldman had never before experienced such a concentration of complex emotions as those that surged within him at this moment – empathy, protectiveness, desperation, yearning, emptiness, fear.

Love.

Before he was even aware of it, Jeza had slipped from the car and he realized he was about to lose her once again to the wilderness.

'No, wait!' he cried, fumbling with the door. Rushing to her side, he grasped her by the arms and pulled her towards him. She averted her face in an anguished grimace. Withstanding the tremendous temptation to embrace her, Feldman instead gently dried her tears with his handkerchief, took her hand in his and walked slowly with her up the winding hillside path.

She seemed very distant now, staring straight ahead mechanically, totally oblivious to the confusion of the man beside her. The closer they drew to the top of the slope, the more anxious he became, his eyes glued to her, his stomach knotted at the thought of her leaving.

At the crest she stopped to meet his gaze, her dark eyes reaching far inside him again. And the more he stared into that compelling visage, the more he was drawn into it.

'When will I see you again?' he asked her.

There was a troubling concern in her face. 'For a while you shall not see me,' she said slowly, 'and then in a while again, you shall see me.'

'But I want to be with you. I *need* to be with you!' Feldman pressed her, not liking the open-endedness of her answer.

The Messiah averted her eyes, turned and withdrew a few paces. 'It is not to be,' she said.

Feldman was staggered. He moved close behind her and gripped her shoulders. 'Please don't tell me that, Jeza. I couldn't bear the thought of that!'

She looked around into his turbulent eyes. 'Jon, there is a great void ahead of you. A wide chasm that you will confront alone. A long and difficult leap.' She turned to face him and took his hands in hers. 'And when you land on the far side, things will no longer be as they were.'

She squeezed his hands hard, her eyes filling with tears again, searching the depths of his soul. 'But at that moment, you must remember, the Father has His purpose. And while you cannot change what is meant to be, you will always have what once was. Remember. And remember that I hold in my heart a love for you that is eternal.'

Feldman could no longer control his emotions. He simply lost himself to her. To her sorrowfulness. To her sincerity. To her spirituality.

In tender, selfless, pure and loving devotion, he leaned down to kiss her.

But her eyes prevented him. They shocked him, numbed him in the darkness of their icy blue waters. As he reeled, insensate, she released his hands and he fell heavily to his knees. She stood there staring at him, tears reflecting moonlight from her cheeks. And then, like an illusion, she slipped away, disappearing quickly and silently into the night.

81

Na-Juli apartments, Cairo, Egypt,
10.00 A.M., Monday, 20 March 2000

Before Feldman had left on his trip to Rome, he and Anke had made arrangements to get together on his return to make up for lost time. It was a decision Feldman was regretting. His state of mind after the previous evening left no room for interpersonal associations. He desperately needed time alone. To rest. To reflect. To rebuild his damaged psyche.

Despite his best efforts, it was obvious to him the minute Anke arrived at his door that she sensed the distance. He was unable to convey the accustomed warmth and emotion in his greeting. His hug was fleeting, his kiss perfunctory. He smiled with his lips, but his eyes were far away. She closed the door behind her and placed her hands on his cheeks, searching his face for a clue.

He could not endure her scrutiny and turned away. 'I – I'm just not myself today, Anke. The effects of the trip, I guess . . .'

'Of course,' she comforted him. 'I can't imagine what it must have been like for you. It was more than I could handle just watching it on TV. We don't have to go anywhere or do anything special today. Come on, let's just sit down, relax and talk for a while. I have so many questions!' She took his hand and escorted him to the couch.

Reluctantly, Feldman acquiesced. He felt so unreconcilably guilty. Anke was such an amazingly vivacious and spirited woman. Such a positive force in his life. So full of optimism and happiness. So different from Jeza. Yet his romantic feelings for Anke had inexplicably gone into hiatus. *Is it possible that a man could love two such different women, so differently?* he wondered. Annoyed with the complexity, he closed his eyes and shook his head in a vain attempt to clear his mind.

Noticeably concerned, Anke sought to draw him out. 'Jon, what happened yesterday has really upset you, hasn't it?' She reached over and turned his face towards her to catch his eyes. 'Can you let me in? I'd like to help.'

He took her hand. Her soft fingers were slightly larger than Jeza's, but hardly as strong. *What am I doing with these absurd comparisons?* he berated himself. He laboured to meet her gaze, shook his head again, denying her.

'Anke, I'm sorry, I can't talk about it now. I've been through a lot. I just need to regroup a little.'

'Sure, Jon,' she accepted, reluctantly. 'I – I was just hoping you could fill me in a bit about all that happened with Jeza. There's so much I don't understand.'

'I have a feeling,' he continued to sidestep her, 'that a lot of your questions are being addressed right now. Why don't we see what the latest news reports have to say?'

Without waiting for an answer, eager to learn if any Vatican archival data other than WNN's had survived the Swiss Guards, he grabbed the remote control and switched on the TV.

Anke snuggled up to him, as if working to bridge the distance, but he remained preoccupied and the disconnection continued. Acceding to his strange behaviour, she sighed and settled back on the sofa. A little more removed from him this time.

The TV news report was chronicling world reactions to the previous day's events. Everywhere, more and more terrified, God-fearing people were polarizing into pro-Jeza or anti-Jeza alignments. Increasingly, the majority of Jeza supporters were rallying around the rising flag of the Messianic Guardians of God. Meanwhile, the opposition was dominated by their staunch arch-rivals, the Guardians of God. As the report elaborated, the current crisis was affecting all aspects of global society. The commerce and government of nations were crippled, falling apart, drifting, as many people simply cancelled life, hunkered down and girded themselves for the coming unknown.

Reports on the Vatican Secret Archives were all over the tube. But, as Feldman soon figured out, most of the purported exposés turned out to be bogus – rehashes of known Vatican scandals dating back centuries and masquerading as new revelations. Stories of papal intrigues: mistresses, illegitimate children, secret marriages, homosexuality, paedophilia, murder, graft and assorted corruptions. On and on.

Feldman pointed this out to Anke with irritation, and she looked at him quizzically, surprised at his uncharacteristic level of emotional involvement.

At last, his remote control found a channel with the report he was seeking. This was the genuine article. Although not a WNN production, the report credited WNN and other networks that had been successful in smuggling materials past the Swiss Guards.

In a spirit of unprecedented co-operation, these several news media had shared their spoils of precious information, assembling the scattered bits and pieces of the archival puzzle for a clearer, although incomplete, picture of Jeza's revelations. Feldman and Anke watched intently as, once again, Hunter's camera travelled down the musty halls of the Vatican Museum, chasing Jeza through the massive bronze doors of Bramante's Corridor while the announcer revealed the findings:

'. . . penetrating the veil of the mysterious, forbidden Secret Archives of the Roman Catholic Church. Records previously hidden from all eyes but those of caretaker monks sworn to lifetime vows of silence, now exposed to the world for the very first time.

'This first series of documents,' the announcer explained, 'is a collection of records detailing a portion of the Vatican's vast financial holdings.' And a number of accounting sheets were displayed in succession, with specific entries emboldened. The Italian was translated into English across the screen.

The columns displayed the assets of the Administration of the Patrimony of the Holy See – the Propaganda Fide. The viewer was taken quickly through the numbers, arriving ultimately at a bottom line of trillions of lire. Once this figure was established, the huge sum was converted to US dollars and displayed at the top centre of the picture. This financial figure was captioned 'Vatican Assets' and remained on the screen as a running tally while the report moved on to investigate other records.

Next came an analysis of the portfolio value of the Vatican International Bank, the Instituto per le Opere di Religione. This body of stocks, bonds, securities and notes also turned out to be substantial. But even more astounding was the production of a receipt substantiating large stores of gold bullion stockpiled by the Vatican at the US Fort Knox depository. The fabulous sums were added to the previous number.

'It's like a telethon,' Feldman observed.

Turning to an analysis of the Church's corporate holdings, the announcer apologized for the incomplete data, which nevertheless provided enough end-of-year financial statements to document trillions more lire in assets. The tally at the top of the screen grew ever higher.

Moving on, the announcer presented a compilation of financial records from thousands of Catholic dioceses, archdioceses, bishoprics and cardinalships around the globe; records of the Vatican's worldwide ecclesiastical and non-ecclesiastical real estate holdings that the Church had systematically and quietly accumulated over the millennia through third-party purchases, private donations, estate bequeathals and charitable gifts.

Next came an even more startling revelation. A fascinating account of a longstanding, on again, off again, direct and indirect involvement with the Sicilian Mafia. Cited were specific, significant financial contributions made by the Cosa Nostra through the years, which were demonstrated to have been accepted knowingly by the Church.

But, as the announcer pointed out, this odd-couple relationship grew more problematic. 'In a 1988 internal report from the Vatican Prefecture for Economic Affairs is the disclosure of major financial fraud involving several disastrous investments of the Vatican bank.

'It's shown that during the 1980s, the cardinal secretary of the Vatican Bank served in a personal capacity on the boards of several Italian companies in which the Vatican had majority holdings. Owning sizeable shares in two of these companies, and known to the Vatican at this time, was a Mafia-controlled entity called Finia CC.'

The report went on to explain how the Vatican had allowed Finia to pool their collective holdings for the purpose of acquiring shares of international companies through bulk stock transfers. Later, Mafia financiers manipulated these holdings into a complicated foreign exchange pyramid scheme in a hostile takeover attempt on the ailing insurance firm International Fidelity Trust of New York.

Ultimately, the venture ran afoul of the US Securities and Exchange Commission. But the Vatican, alerted beforehand by a sympathizer in the SEC, sounded the alarm to Finia, which then divested all relevant holdings before the investigation became public. The unfortunate companies and individuals who acquired the problem holdings, however, were left with massive losses and tangled legal actions which continued to the present day.

The reporter concluded this account by displaying a compromising Vatican file of dates and financial figures, including the names of Mafia individuals involved in the illegal transactions.

The revelations continued.

More records showed that, near the end of World War II, the Vatican had accepted from Nazi Germany many important art objects and other spoils of war. Included in this trove were more than 139 paintings, extensive collections of valuable jewellery and miscellaneous rare antiquities, rightful ownership of which was never questioned by Curia officials.

'Until now,' the announcer expounded, 'all of these valuables were presumed lost or in Russian hands. As detailed in these Secret Archive records, however, this priceless art collection is now known to reside in the private repositories of St Peter's Treasury.'

And on the topic of St Peter's Treasury, more disclosures. An incomplete cataloguing of some of the Vatican's prized collection of modern masterpieces: oils by Matisse, Chagall, Gaugin; watercolours and drawings by Klee, Kandinsky, Moore, Dali and Modigliani. All told, over eight hundred signed works by more than two hundred and fifty of the world's most renowned and accomplished artists. And beyond this, a fabulous wealth of statuary, tapestries, rare furnishings and artifacts of inestimable worth.

Although incomplete, the news report's final assessment of the Church's assets, as calculated on the tote board in US dollars, came in at an astronomical sum in the billions.

Feldman whistled in astonishment. He could only wonder what other surprises had been intercepted by the Swiss Guard and reconsigned to the dust and cobwebs of the Vatican's eternally mysterious Biblioteca Secreta.

The report ended and neither Anke nor Feldman spoke.

At length, Anke looked sideways at her companion and suggested, 'Maybe we should take our minds off all this unpleasantness.' She turned, slipped her hand slowly under his T-shirt, up his flat stomach to his muscled, furry chest. Caressing him slowly and lovingly, her fingers worked their way up to the tense muscles of his shoulders and neck.

But none of the familiar stirrings were there for him. He gazed back into her enticing eyes, and while he felt her sensuality, he couldn't return it. She kissed him, but his response wasn't heartfelt. She backed off.

Without sufficient nurturing, the interlude withered.

82

National Ministry of the Universal Kingdom, Dallas, Texas, *10.00 A.M., Thursday, 23 March 2000*

At the knock upon his door, the Right Reverend Solomon T. Brady, DD, rolled himself away from his mahogany desk and leaned back in his kidskin leather chair, a look of peace and contentment on his face. He ran a grooming hand through his perfect white pompadour and waited.

The magnificent burl-wood doors at the far end of his office swung wide and an attractive, well-dressed young woman entered the room, calling out across the expanse of marble flooring.

'Dr Brady, your ten o'clock appointment.'

'Thank you, Ms Conners,' the Reverend replied brightly to his new secretary, and the young woman stepped back to admit a gaunt, grey, spirited-looking gentleman with thick glasses and loose-fitting suit.

'How are you today, Walter?' the Reverend greeted his chief accounting officer with a warm grin.

The accountant returned the smile. 'Very well, sir, I must say!' He walked forward and placed on Brady's desk a thick report, the Universal Kingdom's latest income figures.

Brady didn't care to inspect it. 'Just tell me, Walter, in round percentages.'

'Well, sir, we're up nearly seventeen points. Your venture with the Mexican Jeza Hotline has proven a real winner. I have to tell you, I fully expect our next returns to post an all-time record.'

Solomon Brady's eyes glistened. 'Thank you, Walter. I'll go through the report over lunch and get back to you if I have any questions. Be sure to have Ms Conners give you a framed copy of the new Jeza Bible Study Centre architectural drawing on your way out. It's a marvel.'

'Yes, sir. I'm anxious to see it. I'll certainly do that. Good day.'

As his visitor exited, the clergyman swivelled his chair towards the window to view the rather deserted campus below. Despite the fact that enrolments were dramatically down, the Reverend's fortunes had never been better. He exhaled contentedly, looking ahead, beyond the Jeza era, to the next cycle where he would once again preside over a thriving divinity college and a burgeoning national – perhaps international – congregation. It was merely a matter of time. For those with foresight.

83

Palace of the Sanctum Officium, Headquarters of the Congregation for the Doctrine of the Faith, Vatican City, Rome, Italy, *9.00 A.M., Friday, 24 March 2000*

Cardinal Antonio di Concerci presided over a dispirited quorum of his congregation. To the prefect's side at the head of the table, in his accustomed velvet armchair, sat the Pope, looking pale, tired and distracted. On the other side sat four cardinal officials. The rest of the Curia were dispersed irregularly around the long table, sombrely conferring with one another in small groups. Several cardinals were not in attendance today, having resigned their positions in the aftermath of the past week's revelations, either because of complicity or indignation.

'I understand the Church is being investigated for international securities fraud,' one grim cardinal said to another.

'Yes,' his confidant replied ruefully, and added, 'We're also the subject of a criminal grand theft investigation. What problems poor Nicholas has inherited.'

They shook their heads forlornly.

Di Concerci, however, was surprisingly relaxed and collected under the circumstances. 'Your Holiness – ' He rose from his seat to open his address. 'And my distinguished fellow cardinals. God's blessings upon us that we may achieve the great purpose for which we are assembled here today.'

A chorus of solemn 'Amens' answered.

The prefect peered into the eyes of his colleagues assembled around him. 'As we are all painfully aware,' he framed the problem, 'our beloved Church is enduring the onslaught of its most formidable challenge since the Roman persecutions of the first century AD. Allegations have been raised that focus world acrimony upon us and jeopardize the very continuation of our sacred apostolic mission.

'Unfortunately, there are some parishioners throughout the world who are willing simply to accept everything they see and hear at face value; all too ready to abandon their faith in despair. Indeed, there are even clergy of this disposition. Some who once sat among us at this very table, who are not with us today.

'To them I say,' and he shouted this in a thunderous condemnation, jolting his audience, '*O ye of little faith!* God has sent us these travails to test us, to try our beliefs and to verify our true love of our Lord, Jesus Christ! Just as God tested Job and Isaac and the apostles and the holy martyrs who persevered in their faith down through the centuries under the most horrible of physical and mental afflictions Satan could visit upon them.

'Has our great religion endured all of this over the millennia only to resign itself suddenly, overnight, because of the acrimonious words of some unknown, untested girl? This Jeza? This self-ordained spokeswoman of God who preaches destruction and lashes out against us and all religions? I stand before you today to say that the Catholic Church will endure *only* if we truly believe in the power and the glory of our Almighty. I challenge each of you. Do you have the strength and the faith to persevere?'

The prefect was met with less-than-enthusiastic agreement.

'Do you have the strength and the faith to persevere?' he asked again, but did not wait for an answer this time. 'Because I come before you now with the most disturbing revelation of all. A revelation that will bring fear to your hearts and require *far greater* courage than has been demanded of you heretofore!'

He paused, satisfied now that he had their complete attention.

'Last Monday evening, in the aftermath of Jeza's attack, I entered, alone, the catacombs of St Peter's. I took with me this,' and he held up a copy of a small, very old and worn book with a faded burgundy cover.

'This is a fifteenth-century, hand-lettered Latin manuscript of the Gospel of St John. Once the property of Joan of Arc, this is the very testament that the Maid of Orléans carried with her in the breastplate of her armour as she rode into battle. The stains on these pages are of her own blood when she was once wounded in combat. A peasant girl, unable to read, Joan carried this Book of the Gospel as a sacred talisman to inspire her triumphs over seemingly insurmountable odds.

'Before the tomb of our first pope, I fell to my knees and invoked the sacred power of this Bible. I called upon our beloved Great Fisherman for deliverance from our enemies in this hour of darkness; for a way to preserve the legacy of Peter that has endured for two millennia. I prayed for the love of Jesus Christ, for the blessings of God the Father, and for the wisdom and guidance of the Holy Spirit.

'I prayed for an answer, and an answer was delivered to me.'

At this, even the Pope brightened somewhat. All eyes were upon the prefect in desperate hope.

'At the end of my prayer,' di Concerci told them, 'there suddenly came into the catacombs a brilliant light, and around me a resounding clap of thunder. I was momentarily blinded and deafened. In my shock, I dropped the testament. And from inside me I heard a voice as deep and ancient as the sepulchres. It proclaimed, "Behold your answer!" Instantly, I could see again, and before me I found my testament lying on the ground, in the consecrated dust of the martyrs, open to this page, chapter and verse.'

Di Concerci held the book in his outstretched hand, deferentially displaying it first to Nicholas, then rotating slowly for all to inspect. The Pontiff, and those close enough to translate the page heading, gasped as the cardinals further away leaned forward and appealed to their neighbours for an explanation.

'This is the answer given to me, gentlemen,' di Concerci announced to the agitated assembly. 'In the Apocalypse of St John the Apostle!

As you can see, this page shows the brown stain of the very blood of St Joan, martyr. Remarkably, the stain has highlighted all the verses of chapter seventeen of the Apocalypse, as well as a single passage from chapter two. *The other chapters and verses surrounding these bear no bloodstains whatsoever!'*

Di Concerci lowered the book slowly and adjusted it in front of him. 'Here, my pontiff and my fellow cardinals, is the verse that has been given us. And in this verse we find our special answer.' He translated from the Latin:

'*THE BOOK OF THE APOCALYPSE OF*
ST JOHN THE APOSTLE
Chapter 17, Verses 1–16

The Woman on the Scarlet Beast:

'*1 And there came one of the seven angels who had the seven bowls, and he spoke with me saying, "Come, I will show thee the condemnation of the great harlot who sits upon many waters, 2with whom the kings of the earth have committed fornication, and the inhabitants of the earth were made drunk with the wine of her immorality."*

'*3 And he took me away in spirit into a desert. And I saw a woman sitting upon a scarlet-coloured beast, full of names of blasphemy, having seven heads and ten horns. 4And the woman was clothed in purple and scarlet . . . 6And I saw the woman drunk with the blood of the saints and with the blood of the martyrs of Jesus. And when I saw her, I wondered with a great wonder.*

The Angel's Explanation:

'*7 And the angel said to me, "Wherefore dost thou wonder? I will tell thee the mystery of this woman and the beast that carries her which has seven heads and the ten horns. 8The beast that thou sawest was, and is not, and is about to come up from the abyss, and will go to destruction. And the inhabitants of the earth – whose names have not been written in the book of life from the foundation of the world – will wonder when they see the beast which was and is not. 9Here is the meaning for him who has wisdom. The seven heads are seven*

*mountains upon which the woman sits; and they are seven kings;
¹⁰five of them have fallen, one is, and the other has not yet come;
and when he comes, he must remain a short time. ¹¹And the beast
is moreover itself eighth, and is of the seven, and is the Evil One
and will go to destruction.*

*'"¹²And the ten horns that thou sawest are ten kings, who have
not received a kingdom as yet, but they will receive authority as
kings for one hour with the beast. ¹³These have one purpose, and
their power and authority they give to the beast. ¹⁴These will fight
against the Lamb, and the Lamb will overcome them, for He is the
Lord of Lords, and the King of kings, and they who are with Him,
called, and chosen, and faithful."*

*'¹⁵And he said to me, "The waters that thou sawest where the
harlot sits, are peoples and nations and tongues. ¹⁶And these peoples
will come to hate the harlot, and will make her desolate and naked,
and will eat her flesh and will burn her up in fire."'*

There was a low murmuring in the hall as the full meaning of this
rather abstract passage failed to take hold. Di Concerci looked up
at his colleagues with an expression of optimism and faith. 'And
now, Holy Father and my fellow cardinals, I give to you the divine
interpretation that was revealed to me in the catacombs.

'As you have realized for yourself now, Jeza is not as she claims.
Rather, verse by verse, see her for what she really is:

'Verses one to six: Jeza, the harlot of the beast – dressed in her
purple and scarlet-trimmed robe, holding herself above all the world
religions, consorting with presidents and rulers of nations, intoxicating
the masses with her blasphemous claims and preachings – she herself
drunk with power and vanity and world attention.

'Verses seven to eleven: the seven mountains are the seven hills
of Rome. The seven kings are sovereign popes of the Roman
Catholic Church. The five who have fallen are Popes Nicholas
I to V. The "one who is" is our Holy Father, Nicholas VI.
And the "seventh" is a pope yet to come. A pontiff who will
reign but for a short while. And the "eighth" is the Beast, one
who would be pope, an antipope, and one who will "go to
destruction".'

As di Concerci was acutely aware, his surprising revelations were creating a slow undercurrent of incredulity, amazement and excitement in the hall. He moved on.

'Verses twelve to fourteen: these are the things yet to come. A prediction of the struggle between the forces of good and evil. For a short while, the Evil One will seduce powerful people in support of a wicked cause. Those deceived will rise up in Armageddon – an armed struggle against the forces of good. But through the power of the Almighty and the Lamb of God, the apostates will ultimately be suppressed.

'And finally, verses fifteen and sixteen: those peoples over whom the harlot reigns will finally see her for the Evil One she is. They will rise up against her and destroy her. At last, the world will be returned to peace, and to the fulfilment of the apocalyptic prophecy in which Christ will reign on earth for a thousand years in a glorious new millennium.'

The entire gathering was dumbstruck, astounded at the significance of the prefect's revelations. Cardinal di Concerci had but one more correlation to drive home.

'The world has come to accept the name this woman goes by, Jeza, as a derivative of Christ's biblical name, a feminine form of the holy name Jesus. I tell you that while the name Jeza is truly of biblical origin, the world has grossly misinterpreted its source. For you see, the name of this false prophetess is not written J-E-Z-A, as is most commonly seen. It is, in fact, J-E-Z-E. A shortened, disguised form for her true and revealed identity – the name of the most reviled harlot, temptress and deceiver of the Old Testament, *Jezebel*!

'Jezebel! The infamous idolatress of the First and Second Book of Kings. The beautiful pagan girl who, for a short, disastrous time, also led the faithful astray in the worship of a false idol, the god Baal. Jezebel, the charlatan who, like her modern namesake, reduced the world to turmoil. Until at last, her evil was recognized and she was destroyed in just anger by her own people in accordance with prophecy.

'This new Jezebel, who now comes before us and brazenly demands that we end the sacred institutions of our Church and our religion, this Jeza woman is no prophetess. She is no New Messiah. No messenger of God. As was revealed to me in my holy vision, this Jeza is the realization of all the most dreaded and despised prophecies of the Book of the Apocalypse. Not the Daughter of God, but the Daughter of Satan. The incarnation of all evil.

'The Antichrist!'

The impact on the assembly was profound as these now suddenly apparent connections fell squarely into place.

'And lastly,' di Concerci announced in triumph, 'I will tie together all of this for you with the final quotation marked by the blood of Joan in the Book of Revelation, chapter two, verses twenty to twenty-three. This prophesies clearly how the new Jezebel has been sent from the Devil to tempt the modern world astray:

'"But I have against thee that thou sufferest the woman Jezebel, who calls herself a prophetess, to teach, and to seduce my servants, to commit fornication, and to eat of things sacrificed to idols. And I gave her time that she might repent, and she does not want to repent of her immorality. Behold, I will cast her upon a bed, and those who commit adultery with her into great tribulation, unless they repent of their deeds. And her children I will strike with death, and all the churches shall know . . ."'

The prefect closed the Bible and gazed solemnly into the pallid faces of his colleagues. 'God has visited upon us our most formidable test of faith in two thousand years. My fellow cardinals, the Judgment is at hand. The long-feared Antichrist, this Jezebel, is finally come. And we dare not falter in our responsibility to expose this evil. For if we fail, we will reap the consequences of the Apocalypse, too horrible to contemplate.'

The prefect turned to appeal personally to his deeply affected Pontiff.

'Nicholas. On behalf of our Lord Jesus Christ, on behalf of the Church, on behalf of two thousand years of custodial papacy in the protection of the Sacred Covenant of Christ, I beseech you to initiate an immediate order for the formal defence of the faith. I ask for the issuance of a decree *ex cathedra*, declaring and condemning Jeza as the true, revealed and confirmed Antichrist.'

The hall stayed absolutely quiet. Di Concerci remained standing, his arms folded, awaiting his answer.

There was a slight tremor to Nicholas's hands, which were clasped in front of him in a prayerful posture. His unseeing eyes were in rapid motion, his brow creased, his lips tightly compressed. At last his eyes ceased their incessant flitting, he blinked several times and took a large breath. Speaking softly and slowly, as if to himself, he replied, 'Without exception, this is the most difficult, spiritually disturbing consideration ever borne by a successor of Peter. For months this matter has lain heavily on my soul, and as I pray daily for the great weight to lessen, it only grows more burdensome.

'I have listened carefully to all you've revealed to us this morning, Cardinal, and I must admit that I find it quite compelling. I have little doubt the rest of our Congregation would agree with me.'

There was an immediate murmur of concurrence from the religious advisers around the table.

'However,' the Pope continued, 'this matter is of the utmost gravity, and I must tell you that I do not see clearly enough to render an *ex cathedra* ruling immediately.'

'Holiness,' di Concerci interjected with some alarm, 'only when you speak *ex cathedra* do you invoke the absolute and unquestioned infallibility that the faithful will demand in such a serious matter. You *must* feel the conviction to speak with certainty here or our holy mission cannot succeed. And we simply have no time to delay or I fear all will be lost!'

The Pontiff stopped his cardinal with an uplifted hand. 'I understand your concerns, Prefect. Nevertheless, before I pronounce an edict *ex cathedra*, a most solemn decision that could well unleash a premature Armageddon, I will retire to my chambers in prayer and meditation. As you have done, Antonio, I, too, will ask God for an unmistakable sign. And by six o'clock tomorrow morning, I will return to this hall and render my decision to the Congregation.'

With great restraint, di Concerci bowed to his pope's judgment. Nicholas rose heavily to his feet and the assembly immediately stood in respect, holding their positions until the Pope had left the room. After Nicholas had departed, the remaining Curia members followed, offering their congratulations to Cardinal di Concerci as they filed past, their spirits significantly uplifted by the prefect's amazing presentation.

Silvio Santorini remained to accompany di Concerci for the short walk back to their offices.

'Would you allow me to inspect the Bible of St Joan, Antonio?' Santorini requested, and di Concerci accommodatingly located in the ancient text the precise chapter and verse.

Santorini received the book reverentially and examined the holy relic with engrossed curiosity. 'In all my years with the Church,' he observed, 'I have never been so privileged as to experience a personal revelation. You are greatly honoured,' he said, bringing the yellowed pages close to his eyes to behold the sainted brown stains that highlighted the passages. 'You must have been frightened and deeply moved. What a boon to your faith!'

Di Concerci said nothing, continuing to gather and neatly store his papers in his attaché case.

Obtaining no answer, Santorini asked again, 'How did the experience affect you, Antonio?' He looked over at the prefect questioningly.

Impositioned by the stare of his friend's eyes, di Concerci finally ceased his housekeeping and met the gaze. 'I tell you this in the utmost confidence, Silvio,' and Santorini nodded his assent, 'I felt the need to add a certain drama to my announcement today.'

Santorini's astonishment was evident.

'Do not worry,' di Concerci reassured him, 'the bloodstains you see are genuine. And I did indeed meditate in the catacombs and was truly bestowed with the revelation. I merely offered the thunder and lightning as simple embellishments to help augment the message.'

The restored hope Santorini had previously felt was shaken. 'And the voice you heard, Antonio?' he asked. 'The voice of Peter?'

The prefect grabbed one of the smaller man's thin shoulders and gave it a heartening squeeze. 'That, Silvio, I assure you, was very real. I *did* hear the voice of the Fisherman, and the rest is exactly as I explained it.'

Santorini's faith was only partially salvaged.

Di Concerci smiled confidently, patted the side of his associate's shoulder and turned to close his briefcase, advising, 'Sometimes God's miracles are better appreciated with a little theatricality. I merely added a harmless garnish, nothing more.'

Detecting a hesitancy, the prefect turned to his colleague again, a stronger tone entering his voice. 'The Lord helps those who help themselves, Silvio. And I, for one, do not intend to sit idly by and watch my beloved Church disassembled by this insufferable freak of science. We must rally the troops for the war ahead of us. We must stay united in our cause and we must attack with deadly force.'

84

Shadow of the Pyramids bar and lounge, Cairo, Egypt, 10.17 P.M., Friday, 24 March 2000

'All right, that's it,' Hunter announced to Feldman, rotating on his bar stool to face his friend head on. 'I've been doing a monologue all evening. All I get out of you are yeahs, uh-uhs and maybes. What's going on, Jon?'

Elbows on the bar, his shoulders stooped, Feldman looked over glumly at his partner. 'Sorry, Breck, I'm not good company tonight, am I?'

'Hell, Jon, good company? You're not even *here*. You haven't been here all week, for Chrissakes. You haven't contributed a thing at a staff meeting since we got back from Rome. It's like you've lost all interest just when things are heatin' up.'

Feldman said nothing and resumed staring down at his drink.

'Come on, Feldman, for the last time, talk to me!'

The lanky reporter shrugged his shoulders and gave Hunter a sideways glance. Looking back down at his now-warm glass of beer, he mumbled, 'I'm in love with two women.'

'What!' Hunter cried, a large, insidious grin spreading across his rugged face. 'You're shitting me! You sly dog! Where the hell have you had time to—?' He stopped and the grin collapsed. 'Holy shit, Feldman. Jeza?'

Feldman nodded his head.

'Holy shit!' Hunter repeated himself. He paused for a few moments as if he needed to let the outlandish thought sink in. 'When did this happen?'

'It's *been* happening. But I guess it really materialized the night we flew in from Rome. I took Jeza back to the desert. We were alone together. I walked her up the hill to the drop-off point, we held hands, and—'

Hunter's brows arched.

'Nothing like that!' Feldman hurriedly clarified, reading Hunter's lascivious expression. 'Damn, give me a break, will you!'

Hunter's brows returned to normal. 'And now you think you love her,' he said. It wasn't a question. More like a restating of the circumstances in an attempt to absorb them. 'I don't know, bubba. Somehow I just can't see you and little Jeza settlin' down in suburban Cincinnati to raise a family. It just doesn't compute, man.'

'You don't understand,' Feldman attempted to explain, shaking his head. 'I don't exactly understand it myself. It's not just a physical attraction that I feel for her, I don't think. I mean, she's beautiful and all. But it's more than that—'

Hunter rolled his eyes. 'She's bewitched you, man. She's got her millenarian hooks deep in you just like all those other raptured suckers out there. Come on, guy, I don't mean to belittle you, but you're a hell of a lot smarter than that!'

Feldman took his glasses off, laid them on the bar and rubbed his eyes with his fingertips. 'God, Breck, I don't know. Maybe that's part of it. I really don't know what to make of her on that level. I mean, how do *you* explain what happened at the basilica?'

'You mean, do I believe there's some sort of divine intervention in what went on there? Hell, no!'

'Well then, how do you explain the altar stone? How in the name of God did Jeza know her way around the archives like that? How the hell did she know exactly where all that data was hidden? Explain that to me. Christ, she even knows things about *me* I never told anyone but my shrink.'

'I don't know about the altar stone, man, but finding her way around a bunch of musty old books is not exactly right up there with walking on water. How do we know Jeza didn't have knowledge about all that archive stuff programmed into her head by Leveque?'

Feldman was unimpressed and Hunter tried a different tack.

'Look, Jon, there are a lot of things about human nature we don't understand. Clairvoyance, mental telepathy. And as far as that altar stone goes, there are things like psychokinesis, telekinesis – moving shit around with your mind, for example. You know, like poltergeist phenomena, where pubescent little girls get all weirded out and mentally crash dishes and crap, and everyone blames it on mischievous ghosts.'

Feldman was still unimpressed.

'So Jeza pulls a few David Copperfields,' Hunter conceded, exasperation in his voice. 'That doesn't mean we have to get all Jesus-freaky and emotional and fall on our knees and everything. I mean, Jon, a few thousand years ago people worshipped the sun, for Chrissakes. This is the twenty-first century. If we can't explain something right away, we don't have to reach for the God handle.'

He smacked the bar, 'Shit, it's time people wised up. Society's been prey to faith healers and con artists ever since supersitition was invented. Religion's nothing more than a scam. A way to make money from the gullible. You know it and I know it. It's all a big con. The concept of God is psychological salve for the insecure. Santa Claus for adults.'

Feldman shook his head. 'Come on, Breck. All religions aren't scams. There are millions of people out there who're completely sincere in their beliefs and honestly trying to live their faiths.'

Hunter sighed impatiently, set his jaw and frowned at Feldman. 'Even if there are, Jon, the truth of the matter is, I just don't give a big ol' goddamn shit. I don't *like* religion. I find it boring and political and manipulative. I don't like the sanctimoniousness. And most of all, I don't like the goddamn rules.

'I *like* to sin! I like to do all the things they don't want me to do. I like to live the good life, and if that doesn't cut it, then God can just haul my ass off to hell when I die, 'cause I'm not about to change. Those goddamn millenarians out there are idiots,' he exclaimed, dismissing them all with a grand, sweeping gesture. 'A bunch of sheep trotting to the slaughter.'

Neither man said anything for a while. Feldman cleaned his glasses with a cocktail napkin and put them back on. At length, Hunter rested an arm on his friend's shoulder. 'What about Anke, Jon? What are you gonna tell her?'

'She already knows something's wrong,' Feldman moaned. 'She's tried to get me to talk to her about things, but Christ, I don't understand it well enough myself to make any sense to her.'

'Well, you sure as hell don't make any sense to me. Here you've got this fantastic woman any guy would die for, and you're ready to throw her over for a platonic relationship with someone who thinks she's the Daughter of God? I mean, face it, man, Jeza's got some bad wiring. Literally! She's a lab experiment gone wrong. A freak!'

Feldman swung around on his bar stool and grabbed Hunter's forearm hard, spilling his drink. 'If I ever hear you say anything like that again, I swear I'll kick your ass big time. Understood?'

It was unlikely that Hunter, who once entertained offers to play pro football as a defensive linebacker, felt any intimidation, but he realized he'd gone too far. 'You're absolutely right, buddy,' he backed off. 'I was way out of line there. I'm sorry.'

Feldman released his friend, scowled over his poor personal display, and reached for his wallet. 'Look, it's late. We've both had a little too much to drink. Let's just call it a night.'

Hunter screwed up his face quizzically. 'You're not pissed at me? I'm really sorry about shootin' my mouth off like that. I just don't want to see you go spoil a good thing like you've got with Anke. You'll never find another one like her.'

'No, I'm not pissed off. And you're right about Anke. She's one in a billion. I don't want our relationship to end up like all my others. I've just got some soul-searching to do, I guess.' He tossed some bills on the bar and they left in separate cars.

But Feldman didn't go home. Instead, he drove out to the desert and sat alone on his stone seat at the top of the hill where he had last seen Jeza. The same place he'd come alone each night for the past several nights, sitting quietly for hours, waiting, hoping.

85

The Papal apartments, Vatican City, Rome, Italy,
3.47 A.M., Saturday, 25 March 2000

Escorted by his ever-loyal Swiss Guard, Nicholas VI returned to his palace in the early morning dark, entered his private quarters and sat wearily behind his large desk. He'd spent the last fifteen hours abstaining from food and drink, alone in St Peter's Basilica, having ordered it sealed from all intrusions so that he might meditate in absolute isolation.

He had lain prostrate before the High Altar. He had knelt for hours on the cold stone of the catacombs in front of St Peter's tomb, beseeching his predecessor to speak out to him as the Great Apostle had chosen to speak to Antonio di Concerci. For eight hours Nicholas had fervently prayed, petitioning the Lord long and passionately for inspiration and guidance in this desperate time.

He had read and reread all the passages di Concerci had cited from the Book of the Apocalypse. Indeed, Nicholas had located three more very telling scriptural clues of his own in the Gospel of Mark, 13:2–23; the Epistles of Paul, 2 Thessalonians, 2:3–4; and from the Old Testament, the Book of Deuteronomy, 13:2–6.

Still, before he could bring himself to make this most serious and terrible indictment, Nicholas had pleaded for a sign. Something, *anything* that might illuminate this greatest of all enigmas.

Yet there had been nothing. Not even the whisper of a ghost nor the flicker of a vision to inspire him.

So he'd returned, reluctantly, to his quarters to continue his vigil. The most important decision in the history of Christendom, and he was to be bereft of spiritual guidance. The ultimate decision, and he must render it feeling such estrangement from his God. That potentiality staggered him.

But there was at least one thing more he could do. Though he had read it a dozen times before, he must consult, for the last time, the only modern source of divine revelation known to exist on the grave subject of the Last Day.

He retrieved the golden key from the chain on his cincture. He inserted it carefully into the lock on the vault of his desk. He turned the heavy tumblers, and slowly the thick wooden door clicked open. From within its large cavity, Nicholas retrieved a faded brown leather-bound portfolio and placed it carefully on his desk. Slowly he untied the leather thongs that secured it and laid open its heavy cover. Removing its hallowed contents, he spread a series of yellowed parchments gently across his desk.

The documents were letters, written in Portuguese, in laborious longhand. The first letter was dated 17 November 1929. The last, 23 November of the same year.

And each was signed Marie Lúcia de Jesus, RSD.

These were the original, famous Fátima Letters recording the prophecies of the Virgin Mary to three young shepherd children on a hillside in rural Fátima, Portugal, in 1917. The words had been written by the only surviving visionary, Lúcia, more than a decade after the events.

In these letters, Lúcia transcribed the celebrated Three Revelations – the Virgin's portentous words of foreboding and hope that were unveiled, one per letter.

The first two Revelations were well known to the world, even at the time Lúcia transcribed them. She had proclaimed them orally on several occasions after the miraculous visitations. It was the Third Revelation, however, the mysterious Last Secret of Fátima, about which the world had anxiously speculated for all these decades.

Indeed, the Last Secret was so confounding and dire that Lúcia, a mere child of twelve at the time she first received it, was told by the Virgin not to be concerned with its meaning or recollection; that Mary would return to her again some day to reveal it once more.

This the Virgin did on the morning of 23 November 1929. True to her promise, on this, the Virgin's last and most disturbing appearance to Lúcia, Mary conveyed once again the terrible Last Secret of Fátima, which Lúcia transcribed verbatim.

What made these Three Revelations unique and so important was that they were unlike most biblical prophecies, which were generally couched in nebulous symbolism. These predictions, if still somewhat mystical, were far more precise in their language and written for the immediate future.

Nicholas read once more all the letters, beginning with the earliest to determine any possible correlations in the three prophecies.

In the first document, Lúcia had detailed the celebrated miracles of the Fátima visitations, such as the day of the 'dancing sun', in which the sun is said to have wobbled in the sky above the Fátima hills, moving around mysteriously and ominously. This was authenticated by over a hundred thousand attendees, including formerly dubious, anticlerical members of the press.

And then, Lúcia went on to transcribe the first, well-known

prophecy. She spoke of the Virgin's sadness in contemplating the universal woes of the era. The continuing devastations of the Great War. The Russian Revolution, which, in accordance with the prophecy, began that very year. Also accurate were the predictions of the rise of godless communism and its long reign of terror and aggression.

The Virgin predicted the rise of Fascism and the horror of World War II. She correctly anticipated the Holocaust, famine, disease and widespread misery that lay ahead.

In the second letter, the Virgin had made a conditional promise. She had pledged the fall of communism in Russia and a period of relative peace and tranquillity in the world – if enough prayers were said for the conversion of Russia. Indeed, the Virgin's conditions were well met, and the promises of the second letter were fully honoured.

It was the last letter of the group that directly and specifically pertained to Pope Nicholas and the events of the present. The Secret Letter. The only one of the three held in strict papal confidence, its mysteries classified for more than seventy years now. Nicholas was the only living person to have read it.

Pius XI, in 1929, was the pope first presented with the letter. The response attributed to him was that he grew severely agitated, covered his face with his hands, and then cleared his office, decreeing that the letter would remain sealed for as long as he had control over it.

His successor, Pius XII, who served under Pius XI as Vatican secretary of state, was present when his predecessor was first presented with the letter. Witnessing Pius XI's traumatic response, Pius XII forever refused to read its frightful contents.

Pope John XXIII's reaction in 1958 was described by his attendants as traumatic. His ruddy face was said to have turned white, and he immediately consigned the letter to the locked privacy of his papal vault.

In 1967, Pope Paul VI, after reading the letter, made a controversial pilgrimage to Fátima. Controversial because Portugal was still a Fascist regime at the time, under the dictatorship of Antonio Salazar. The Pope's visit was interpreted as endorsing the regime and, although Paul VI knew the trip would cost him much support around the world, he could not be dissuaded from undertaking the journey.

At Fátima, as Paul VI recounted later, in gazing out over a crowd of more than one million – the largest crowd he would ever experience –

he had a vision of Armageddon. It was as if the masses were assembled for Judgment Day, he had said in awe. The letter remained sealed.

Pope John Paul I suffered the most devastating effect from the letter. Although the circumstances were officially denied, Nicholas knew full well the awful truth. One morning, scarcely a month after John Paul's investiture as Pope, he was found dead, the vault of the papal desk open, the infamous letter lying in his lifeless hand. The anxious attendant nuns who found him dutifully removed the letter with trembling fingers and returned it in confidence to its leather case and the privacy of the vault.

But it was Pope John Paul II, Nicholas VI's immediate predecessor, who contributed the most extraordinary anecdotal footnotes. On 13 May 1981, the anniversary of the first appearance of the Virgin at Fátima, Pope John Paul II fell victim to the bullet of an assassination attempt in St Peter's Square. That John Paul II survived the attack, he adamantly attributed to Our Lady of Fátima.

On the tenth anniversary of John Paul II's attempted assassination, the seventy-fourth anniversary of the Virgin's first appearance at Fátima, the Pope did something unprecedented in the annals of Catholicism. He consecrated his entire worldwide congregation to Our Lady of Fátima. In doing so, he dedicated all Catholics to pray for the fulfilment of the letter's secret stipulations, intimating that to do otherwise was to allow the realization of a very grim prophecy.

Nearly setting off a global panic, John Paul II declared: 'Repent and amend your ways, for the end of the world is nigh!' Standing alongside the Pope for the ceremony was an eighty-six-year-old Carmelite nun, Sister Marie Lúcia de Jesus, RSD, the last surviving visionary of Fátima.

The Pontiff's alarming prediction only served to darken the ominous, millennial cloud then looming on the horizon. In 1995, perhaps to reassure the faithful that mankind might indeed survive the dreaded transition to the next century, John Paul had called for 'a sacred Jubilee Year to begin at the commencement of the New Millennium, 1 January 2000'.

Yet now, with the 1 January deadline and the commencement of the new millennium behind him, Pope Nicholas was finding the Jubilee Year 2000 anything but jubilant. Stewardship of the troubling letter had passed to him. And however disquieting the letter's contents may have been to his predecessors, Nicholas bore the misfortune of being the pope to whom its revelations ultimately accrued.

It had all come down to him and this moment. With a deep breath and rapidly pulsating heart, Nicholas VI lifted the yellowed parchment to search once more for an answer in its strange message:

23 November 1929

These are the words of Our Blessed Mother, the Virgin Mary, which I, her humble servant, do faithfully record:

'*My sorrow is great and I am troubled deeply that little is done to end the deception and selfishness and misery in the world. Everywhere, the message of my Son is corrupted, and the spiritual is supplanted by the material. The patience of the Almighty is lapsing. My Son wishes to return but even now, His way is not made ready.*

'*Yet soon shall you understand that the time is near, as even you, the successors of Peter, shall know violence and injury and death in fulfilment of my prophecies. When these things happen as I say, so shall you remember my words and know that the time is nigh.*

'*But even now, it is not too late to repent and make right the way of the Lord. Return again to the scriptures given unto you by the Son of God. Hold carefully to the Word. Change your ways. Pray and do penance and raise your voice against pride and inequity.*

'*Do so and you may escape God's wrath. Yet two last prophecies do I bring to you – only one of which shall come to be. Whichever shall be fulfilled is by your doing, as the decision is still within your province to effect.*

The First Prophecy – The Desolation

'*If you fail to maintain your vigilance and keep faith with the Lord, then this First Prophecy shall befall you:*

'*The Almighty shall send His messenger bearing the sword of truth; and those who know the truth, by the purity of their hearts shall they also know the messenger. But woe be to you, hardened hearts, which fail to see and hear. For you who hold your head high with arrogance, so shall you stumble over that which lies conspicuous before you. Your people shall turn one against the other in bewilderment, accusation and rage. The Desolation shall commence and the sword shall smite you down and rend you asunder.*

'Death and abomination shall reign. The great shall be laid low and the mighty shall be brought to ruin, and that which you glorified will be no more. By the sword of truth, the one who is sent shall again attempt to make straight the way of the Lord. For it shall be that you are not worthy. And you who survive shall not share in the promise of the scriptures and in the Second Coming of Christ – nor shall your progeny nor its progeny, until the twilight of time.

'In the eleventh hour shall these things be accomplished as I have prophesied. And nothing that has been revealed can then be changed.

The Second Prophecy – The Glorious Reign of One Thousand Years

'Nevertheless, if you heed my admonitions and honor the Word, the promises of the scriptures shall yet be fulfilled. But be forewarned: a great test shall be set before you. Unto your midsts shall come the Evil One, in comely guise, to spread before you the sweet fruit of perdition.

'You must choose between the hunger of good and the gluttony of evil. Deception shall embrace you like the snake its prey; and you shall be struck where you lie unprotected; and all manner of confusion and turmoil shall assail you. But in the darkness of the night, the light of the Lord shall come to you. You shall be emboldened to confront the Evil One and to command the armies of God against the legions of Satan.

'And, in the darkest hour, the Saviour shall return in all His glory; and in His divine judgment shall He strike down the Evil One and divide the believer from the non-believer; He shall separate the righteous from the heretic; the allegiant from the apostate. And the unfaithful will He cast from Him for ever with the Evil One into the fires of eternal damnation.

'But you who are soldiers in the army of God, so shall you be

raised up. And you who are generals shall be exalted above all the hierarchy of heaven; you shall sit in jubilation at the Lord's right hand to rule the earth for one thousand years in the glory of eternal life.

*   *   *

'Thus I bring you hope for that yet to be. With the authority and power that has been vested in you, balance carefully the truth. Know that in the last days, good shall appear as evil and evil as good. But if the First Prophecy is to be, it shall be fulfilled before the turn of the millennium; and if the Second Prophecy is to be, it shall be fulfilled thereafter.

'Yet I caution you not to speak of these words to anyone. Such are the admonitions and the promises the Father makes to you, his anointed apostles, who are entrusted with His Word. Hear the truth and act accordingly, and that which is to be, shall be in your power to effect.'

As was revealed to me this 23rd Day of November, in the year of Our Lord 1929.

Respectful servant of God,
Marie Lúcia de Jesus, RSD

And there it was. The ultimate conundrum.

If this strange woman, Jeza, was as she said, a New Messiah, then the First Prophecy was being fulfilled. Mankind had failed God and fallen short of the Virgin's stipulations. Man would be denied, indefinitely, his promised reunion with Christ 'until the twilight of time'. And this angry Jeza, God forbid, heralded a period of divine punishment and desolation.

On the other hand, if the Second Prophecy was the correct one, then Jeza *was* truly the Jezebel, the Antichrist, and she portended a violent struggle between good and evil. Armageddon. After which would come the Second Advent of Christ and the beginning of the long-awaited One Thousand Year Glorious Rule. The fulfilment of the scriptures.

So which was she, Messiah or Antichrist? Was it to be desolation or a thousand years of bliss? In his final reflection on the letter, the Pontiff's choice had become no easier. There were certainly aspects of each prophecy that paralleled current developments, causing him to question any decision he might make.

Yet Nicholas had to feel that each pope in possession of this portentous Last Revelation, including Nicholas himself, had done everything within his power to meet the Virgin's requirements and to earn the blessings of the Second Prophecy. The major work of Nicholas's papacy, his Millennial Decree, was consecrated entirely to this purpose. Surely he and his predecessors had succeeded in meeting the Virgin's stipulations, just as the Church had succeeded before in ushering in the fall of communism in Russia.

Needless to say, Nicholas hoped with all his soul that di Concerci was correct. And there were subtle indications in the Secret Letter that supported the prefect's arguments. The passage in the second paragraph of the Second Prophecy and its reference to a 'snake', for example, was highly reminiscent of the Book of Genesis and the serpent in the Garden of Eden. This would tend to cast Jeza as Eve, seducer of Adam and precipitator of the fall of man. And this was the only section of the letter that might be construed as gender-reflective. But this was not a new inspiration to Nicholas. He'd considered this point before.

At length, he returned to more conclusive passages, the same passages he'd always relied upon each time he referred to this difficult document for guidance. He went back to the two phrases that appeared to hold the key. The only lines, in his estimation, which offered the foundation for a decision.

Referring to the First Prophecy, last paragraph, first line:

'In the eleventh hour shall these things be accomplished as I have prophesied.'

And buried in the second-to-last paragraph of the letter:

'But if the First Prophecy is to be, it shall be fulfilled before the turn of the millennium; and if the Second Prophecy is to be, it shall be fulfilled thereafter.'

So, assuming 'fulfilled', as translated from the Portuguese, meant 'concluded' or 'satisfied', then Jeza's appearance came after the deadline. Under this interpretation, if Jeza were the New Messiah, her work should have been completed *before* the millennial transition. This was why Nicholas had been able to breathe a short-lived sigh of relief on New Year's Day, despite the millenarians in his courtyard, the cracks in his fresco and altar, and the disturbing happenings in the Holy Land. If this view were correct, Jeza *couldn't* be the 'Anointed One'. She would have to be the Antichrist, meaning that the Second Prophecy was materializing and it was time to marshal the troops for the final holy war.

On the other hand, as Nicholas had painstakingly considered, 'fulfilled' *could* be construed to mean 'to put into effect', or 'to convert into reality'. Certainly, Jeza had come into being *before* the year 2000. She was 'converted into reality' on Christmas Day, in the eleventh hour of the last year. Adhering to this definition of 'fulfilled', the Desolation was at hand, and Nicholas knew that if he were to condemn Jeza, he would be guilty of denouncing the living messenger of God and opposing the will of the supreme being!

Then again, favouring the One Thousand Year Glorious Reign was the fact that the term 'jubilation' happened to appear in the last line of the Second Prophecy. Was there a connection with John Paul II's call for a 'Jubilee Year'? Had Nicholas detected a veiled clue, or was he merely being misled by a coincidence?

The ambiguity was maddening. Despite his intense prayers among the world's greatest wealth of religious icons, the Pope had yet to glean even the slightest sign from any source to which he'd turned.

'Enough!' he cried out in anger. 'My God, why have you forsaken me?'

If he had to make this dreadful decision alone and abandoned, then so be it. This was his conclusion:

While Jeza's physical arrival may have occurred prior to the millennial transition, unquestionably the essence of the First Prophecy was *not* fulfilled beforehand. She did not even become active in her ministry until *after* the year 2000. What was more important, to accept her as the 'Anointed One' was to become fatalistic and despondent, to accept the Desolation, to deny hope and the future of the world. Of man.

'My God!' The Pontiff dropped from his chair to his knees. Trembling, he leaned over the letter, rereading a passage upon which the first beam of dawn light had now fallen through his window:

'Whichever shall be fulfilled is by your doing, as the decision is still within your province to effect.'

God help him, the letter meant exactly what it said! He, Pope Nicholas VI, supreme representative of Christ on Earth – he alone was to decide! It was *his* faith that was being tested here!

'. . . And whatever you shall bind on earth shall be bound in heaven, and whatever you shall loose on earth shall be loosed in heaven.'
(Matthew 16:19)

The Pope moaned and crossed himself repeatedly. At last, with the first light of day, he'd been given his sign. Large, pent-up tears streamed down his cheeks as his whole body shuddered and heaved with the relief of his understanding. So, without realizing it, he had held the answer to this quandary all along. Whichever prophecy was to be fulfilled, the decision was *his*.

He thanked his Lord, rose unsteadily to his feet and, with fumbling hands, secured the Holy Letters in his vault. Taking a few more moments to compose himself, he headed straightaway to the Palace of the Sanctum Officium where the Congregation anxiously awaited his announcement.

86

WNN regional headquarters, Cairo, Egypt,
4.30 P.M., Tuesday, 28 March 2000

'Another wild-goose chase?' Bollinger assumed, as Feldman and Hunter entered the meeting room to join the bureau chief and staff for a discussion in progress.

'Yeah,' a disappointed Feldman responded. 'Jeza was long gone when we got there, but we took some footage of seventy-two people she allegedly cured.' The two men had just returned from a new Jeza sighting, only her second public appearance since the memorable Vatican episode. Jeza had been spotted first at an area orphanage the previous morning, and then earlier that day at a Cairo hospital where she was said to have healed an entire wing of AIDS patients.

The most interesting aspect, disturbing from Feldman's perspective, was that both times the Messiah happened to be in the company of a certain Cardinal Alphonse Litti. It would appear as though Feldman had been displaced as Jeza's preferred liaison. He decided she must have found his garish display of affection simply too forward. He mentally kicked himself.

'Still no word from Litti?' Feldman wondered.

'No,' Bollinger answered. 'The cardinal hasn't been back to his hotel room since Sunday morning.'

Feldman shook his head gloomily.

'And now, gentlemen' – Bollinger changed the subject to a more positive one – 'let me bring you two up to speed on the latest turn of events: while you and Hunter were out, WNN Europe notified us that the Pope is going to make an important announcement on Monday night, 3 April, at nine o'clock their time. The Vatican is inviting all the world media to St Peter's Basilica again to cover the message live, and they're granting WNN prime, front-row space. Additionally, they're also allowing us an exclusive live interview with their Cardinal Prefect di Concerci immediately following the address. Another WNN exclusive!'

'Rather accommodating of them, wouldn't you say?' Feldman observed, suspiciously.

'They're just ensuring themselves the biggest possible TV audience for their message,' Cissy declared. 'We're simply the network with the widest reach.'

'What's the address about?' Feldman wanted to know.

'A concession speech,' Hunter quipped.

'More likely a counter-attack,' Bollinger opined. 'Jeza tore 'em up so bad last week that half the world's Catholic parishes are in open revolt.'

'We don't know the specifics of the address,' Sullivan clarified, 'other than it concerns the Jeza situation, naturally.'

'The Vatican says it's going to be a major papal announcement,' Bollinger added, 'an *ex capita* decree, whatever that is.'

'You mean *ex cathedra*,' Erin Cross corrected him, suppressing a smile. 'And that *is* a major papal announcement.'

'Right,' Sullivan concurred. 'Erin, as our expert on religious affairs, perhaps you wouldn't mind enlightening Jon and Breck a little on the subject?'

'Of course,' she agreed pleasantly. '*Ex cathedra* is Latin for "from the Chair". It's a unique designation given to the most sacred pronouncements of the Catholic Church. *Ex cathedra*, which can only be invoked by the Pope, is extremely rare, employed solely for issues of faith and morals. When the Pope speaks *ex cathedra*, he's speaking from his papal throne, with complete infallibility.'

'Infallibility?' Hunter arched his eyebrows.

'Yes,' Erin elaborated. 'A pronouncement from the throne of St Peter in an *ex cathedra* capacity carries divine authority. The Pope's decision has the same binding effect on the faithful as if Christ Himself were speaking. All Catholics are required, on faith alone, to fully accept and follow the ruling, whatever it might be.'

'You mean,' Hunter questioned, screwing up his broad face in disbelief, 'if the Pope says that, uh,' and he searched around for an example, finally seizing upon Robert Filson, literally, by the lapel, 'if the Pope decides that Filson here is God, then all the billion-odd Catholics in the world have to bow down to him?'

Everyone got a laugh out of this except for Filson, who was visibly miffed.

'Well,' Erin explained, 'the Pope's not going to make an *ex cathedra* ruling on something as theologically spurious as that.' Hunter released Filson, who unruffled his jacket and glowered haplessly at the much larger videographer. Hunter paid no attention and Erin continued. '*Ex cathedra* is only invoked for serious religious purposes. In fact, I don't think there's even been an *ex cathedra* decree in my lifetime.'

'Excellent, Erin,' Sullivan commended her. 'Everyone, this is precisely the sort of background material I want refined into a feature story to preface Monday night's programme. Jon, you and Erin will be on loan to WNN Europe working as co-hosts for the programme. You'll fly back Monday morning.'

'What about Breck?' Feldman questioned.

'Sorry, Breck.' Sullivan turned to the clearly disappointed camera-man. 'WNN Europe will be using their local crews since it's a simple set production.' Hunter accepted this with a shrug of his big shoulders.

'Okay.' Sullivan got down to business. 'Let's collect our thinking and see what approaches we want to take in the coverage. Jon, how'd you feel about letting Erin handle the *ex cathedra* history and you take the wrap-up interview with the cardinal?'

'Sure,' Feldman agreed, conceding the logic of the decision.

Erin reached across the table and gave Feldman's hand an appre-ciative squeeze. Feldman acknowledged this with the briefest flash of an uncomfortable smile as Sullivan proceeded to engage the group in a discussion of strategies and research plans. This was all conducted without the benefit of Cissy, who sat back in her chair, curled up and withdrawn in a huff.

The circle deliberated briefly over a suitable format for Erin's history lesson, and then moved on to structure Feldman's interview. This subject, however, required some speculation regarding the content of the Pope's address.

'All right,' Sullivan said, 'I have my own suspicions, but what do the rest of you think the Vatican's up to with this *ex cathedra* business?'

'That's not too hard,' Hunter snorted. 'It's payback time. They're gonna do a number on Jeza and order all their Catholic followers to dump her, right?'

There was collective agreement around the table.

Particularly from Feldman, whose mind had been travelling this very route. 'The Catholic Church has no choice,' he said, reinforcing the consensus. 'Their survival depends on success-fully discrediting Jeza. They're going to take their best shot, and I'm afraid it could lead to a lot more world turmoil and violence.'

'If that's what we anticipate the Vatican's position will be,' Sullivan proposed, 'I'd suggest, in the interests of balanced reporting, that we be prepared to follow up the Pope's address with a critique. Assuming the Church will be leaning heavily on biblical scripture to debunk Jeza, this may be another area in which we need Erin's expertise.'

Cissy rocked forward in her chair to re-enter the circle. 'We're going to lose the audience with all these dry recitals!' she protested. 'We need to put the emphasis on Jon's interview with di Concerci. The cardinal is where the action is. He's hot media. Everyone's going to want to hear from the guy who took on Jeza twice and got his ass kicked both times. Besides, Jon can critique the Pope's speech with his questions to di Concerci.'

A volley of arguing ensued and Feldman held up his hands to make a point. 'As much as I'd like to carry the ball on this one, we've got to be realistic about what we're up against here. No doubt, the sole purpose of this proposed interview is to put a positive spin on the Pope's speech. It's a manipulation game. The Vatican's sending in their heavy hitter to deflect any criticisms we toss at them. And I'm certainly no match for a cardinal prefect of the Holy See. I can't go toe to toe with him in scriptural matters. And with all due respect to you, Erin' – he locked eyes with WNN's expert on religious affairs – 'I'm not sure you want that assignment, either.'

Erin's brow wrinkled at this and she pursed her lips, no doubt contemplating the thought of being humbled in the glare of international TV.

Cissy countered, 'Then let's level the playing field and give the world a real show. Let's bring in a strong counterpoint person to neutralize di Concerci. Jon can act as referee and provoke some high-charged debate.'

This gave everyone pause.

'I like it, Cissy,' Sullivan mused. 'Who do you have in mind?'

'I don't know just yet' – she back-pedalled for a second – 'but there are certainly plenty of good candidates out there. I'm sure we'll get someone qualified. If only we could find Cardinal Litti.'

Bollinger was cautious. 'We don't have much time, guys. And just any pro-Jeza millenarian won't do. We need a really first-class opponent.'

'A real biblical scholar,' Sullivan added. 'Someone highly regarded. And assuming we do find such a candidate, we'll need to be subtle in how we work him or her into the programme. We don't want the Vatican to become suspicious and quash our plans.

'Irrespective,' he concluded with a presumptuous smile, 'I suspect

Monday night at the Vatican should prove yet another ratings triumph for WNN.'

87

WNN regional headquarters, Cairo, Egypt,
9.12 A.M., Thursday, 30 March 2000

Feldman sat in his office, staring at a phone message from Anke dated the day before. *'Please call as soon as possible,'* it read. He knew full well he was long overdue in providing her with some sort of explanation. Only he had none yet.

An appreciated diversion, Cissy came strolling into his office with a self-satisfied grin on her freckled face and plopped herself down triumphantly on the cluttered couch. Feldman looked up from the note, questioningly.

'I did it!' she exclaimed.

'You did what?'

'I found him! The perfect antithesis to di Concerci.'

'You found Cardinal Litti!' Feldman's heart jumped.

'No,' Cissy responded, momentarily annoyed. 'Rabbi Mordachai Hirschberg.'

Feldman searched his memory in vain.

'Hirschberg's the current head of the Jewish Lubavitcher movement,' Cissy elaborated, sifting through news clippings she'd brought with her. 'He's a resident of New York City . . . he's considered one of the foremost scholars in the world on Old Testament scripture . . . he attended both Mormon convocations – and he was one of the first rabbis to recognize Jeza as the Messiah.'

'Sounds good,' Feldman concurred. 'Let's bring his name up at this morning's meeting and see if he works for everybody else. Is he available?'

Cissy's pleased expression deflated slightly and she bit her lower lip. 'I don't know yet. I had a brief conversation with him yesterday to broach the subject, and he's agreed to a teleconference call with me at three this afternoon. It's such short notice. I was hoping you'd sit in and help me convince him.'

'Sure,' Feldman offered without hesitation, and Cissy flitted away to prepare for the staff meeting.

A little before three that afternoon, Feldman accompanied Cissy to the WNN teleconferencing centre and together they settled at a table in front of a large TV screen and video camera for a conversation with the rabbi. Feldman was not quite sure what to expect from this reputedly mercurial, often confrontational religious teacher. In a moment, they were teleconnected to their party halfway around the world in Brooklyn, New York.

'Good morning, Rabbi,' Cissy opened as the grave, wise countenance of the Lubavitcher leader flickered up on the screen. The rabbi was a large, alert man of seventy-seven, with full white beard and hair, bushy white eyebrows, and deep-set eyes that sparkled despite the serious gaze.

'Good morning,' Hirschberg answered.

'I appreciate your willingness to come by our studio in New York to conference with us so early in the morning,' Cissy said, recognizing that the sun was not yet up in New York.

'It is not early for me, Miss McFarland,' Hirschberg replied matter-of-factly. 'I've been up for hours, as is my custom.'

'I'm glad to hear that, Rabbi,' Cissy replied. 'I'd like to introduce you to my friend and colleague, Jon Feldman.'

'Yes.' Hirschberg nodded politely to Feldman. 'Mr Feldman is a well-known figure to us here, and everywhere, I'm certain.'

'It's a pleasure to meet you, sir,' Feldman returned, not able to get a read on the rabbi's disposition yet. 'Do we find you in good health and spirits this morning?'

'Yes, Mr Feldman, you do,' the rabbi continued in a non-committal manner. 'At the very least, I'm always in good spirits. But I suspect you're not investing eighty dollars per minute of your company's money to make small talk with me. You wished to discuss the arrangements for my attending Monday night's telecast?'

Both Feldman and Cissy were caught off guard.

'You mean you accept our invitation?' Cissy could not mask her surprise and delight.

'Of course,' he responded as if there were never any question. 'I simply had to consult my doctor first. I have a slight medical condition. Nothing to be concerned about.'

'Wonderful,' Feldman quickly responded. 'We welcome your participation. May I ask you, Rabbi, what, in your opinion, will be the Vatican's strategy here?'

'There's no question in my mind that the thrust of this speech will be to discredit the Messiah and command the world Catholic community to reject Her as an impostor and false prophet. The decree *ex cathedra* will no doubt require the Catholic faithful to disclaim Jeza under penalty of mortal sin and excommunication.'

'How are you intending to respond to that proclamation, Rabbi Hirschberg?' Cissy asked.

'With prophecy, of course,' he replied. 'With the Word of God! You must fight fire with fire!'

'Begging your pardon, Rabbi,' Feldman interrupted. 'May I play devil's advocate for a moment?'

'Of course.'

'Couldn't it be said that the source of this entire Jeza controversy lies in an undue reliance on scripture? And on the completely inconsistent ways in which all these obscure prophecies are interpreted? Isn't the real obstacle for many people that the prophecies you rely on are simply too ancient and ambiguous to relate to?'

The rabbi nodded his head, impatiently tapping his fingertips together as if he'd anticipated this question all along. Then, compressing his lips tightly, he turned to a sheath of papers beside him, sorted through them, and held up a selected document. 'Can you make this out, Mr Feldman?' he asked.

'I can see what looks like a handwritten letter, Rabbi.' Feldman squinted at the screen. 'But I'm unable to read what it says.'

'This,' Hirschberg explained, 'is no ancient prophecy. This is a prediction made in 1937 by the great Hasidic holy man, Rabbi Haim Shvuli. It prophesies a war in the Middle East to be waged against Israel in the year 1990 by an Arab nation. According to Rabbi Shvuli, this war would involve the use of chemical and biological weapons, and involve attempts to bomb Jerusalem from the air. However, it predicts that the city would be protected by the Almighty. And note this most important aspect, Mr Feldman – Rabbi Shvuli proclaims that this war would signal *the beginning of the messianic era*!

'As you no doubt recognize, my young friend,' Hirschberg continued, 'Rabbi Shvuli was accurately describing the war with Iraq known as Desert Storm, anticipating it to the very year, *more than fifty years prior*.

'Bear in mind, Mr Feldman, that this prediction was made *eleven years* before the Jewish State of Israel even existed. Back when the Holy Land was under the complete control of the Palestinians. *Before* the true implications of this prophecy held any significance for the Jews.

'You see, even the creation of the Jewish State in 1948 foretold of the coming of the Messiah Jeza. The Old Testament predicted the destruction of Jerusalem by the Romans in AD 70, and the Great Exile of the Jews. Yet the scriptures also promised there would one day be a great "ingathering of the Jewish exiles". And that this ingathering would mark the long-foretold beginning of the messianic era.

'After two thousand years, that prophecy was fulfilled with the formation of the modern Jewish state, which brought about the ensuing mass immigration of Jews to Israel from their scattered, displaced existences all across the globe.

'But let me provide you with yet another current prophecy, Mr Feldman, as you require. In August 1990, two years before his death, in response to the Iraqi invasion of Kuwait that same month, *my* esteemed rabbi, Menachem Schneerson, delivered a special sermon here at our temple in Brooklyn. Regarding the Iraqi threat against Israel at that time, he predicted this.' Hirschberg selected another paper from his collection and held it up for Feldman to observe. 'Let me document this to you in a published copy of Rabbi Schneerson's very words: "*These events do not have to disturb the spiritual and physical peace of a single Jew because they are a preparation and preface for the actual coming of the Messiah.*"'

Hirschberg returned the paper to its place. 'Rabbi Schneerson went on to say that there would be no need for Israelis to acquire gas masks or stockpile food or gird themselves for attack. That Israel would never be truly threatened by this war at her doorstep. And that the advent of the Messiah was *imminent*!'

Cissy looked over at Feldman with raised eyebrows, denoting her approval. Feldman nodded his head in concurrence. This refreshingly contemporary, non-Christian perspective sounded like just the sort of solid rebuttal WNN had been looking for. Cissy had done well.

'Excellent, Rabbi,' Feldman commended him. 'I'd like to ask you to fax copies of these materials to us, if you will, so we can make some visual excerpts for the telecast. We're going to need persuasive material like this if we hope to counter the Vatican's position.'

The rabbi smiled for the first time. 'Somehow, Mr Feldman, I feel as if you've taken sides.'

This took Feldman aback for a moment, and his eyes flitted with internal conflict. He then levelled his gaze at Hirschberg and his brow creased. 'I'm not pursuing any personal religious convictions here, Rabbi. And I certainly have no desire to endorse one theological view over another. Quite frankly, I believe that the resolution to all this current unrest lies somewhere in the temporal world, not the spiritual. But I don't want to see any harm come to Jeza, either. And I support whatever can be done to balance the threat of a backlash against her.'

88

Cairo Airport, Egypt,
11.30 A.M., Monday, 3 April 2000

Late Monday morning, Erin and Feldman were shuttled to the airport and deposited aboard a small charter jet for the hop across the Mediterranean.

This was the first time Feldman had truly been alone in Erin's company, and it was not something he'd looked forward to with any degree of comfort. Nevertheless, aside from infrequent exchanges of pleasantries and a few requests of Feldman for his opinion, Erin remained completely absorbed in the project. For the duration of the three-hour flight, she kept her professional distance.

The two newspeople were met at the airport by WNN Europe staff and transported first to their downtown hotel to freshen up, then directly to the Vatican and the cathedral for prepping before the telecast. As he crossed familiar St Peter's Square, Feldman's sensations of queasiness increased.

Inside the ancient basilica, Feldman and a fascinated Erin Cross were escorted to the staging area, which, as promised, was ideal. It was positioned directly in front of the High Altar, and Feldman noted that the massive altar stone had been repaired or replaced. WNN's set was comprised of a huge Persian rug, four comfortable overstuffed chairs and a coffee table.

About 6.30 P.M., Feldman was informed that Rabbi Hirschberg had arrived. For the duration of the Pope's speech, Hirschberg would be secreted in a separate, reserved media section. He wouldn't be brought on to WNN's set until the interview with di Concerci was actually under way. Not knowing how the cardinal would react to WNN's ploy was yet another worry for the newsman's nervous stomach.

Feldman passed on a catered dinner, choosing to move to his chair on the set with his notes for a little quiet time. Instead, he found himself the object of a growing assembly of Vatican personnel, nuns and clerics who approached him with a raft of questions about the Messiah.

An annoyed WNN director was about to clear the set when, quite abruptly, Feldman's little audience went strangely quiet, came to wary attention, and collectively stared over the back of Feldman's chair towards some imposing presence behind. Turning around, Feldman was startled to find himself peering up into the implacable face of the tall, august Cardinal Prefect Antonio di Concerci himself. The cardinal had made an imperious, lone entrance in brilliant white cassock with crimson cape and matching skullcap.

Di Concerci said nothing, standing serenely, his hands folded behind him, his head erect, his unblinking eyes first scanning the gathering, then looking down at Feldman. Dumbfounded for a moment, Feldman quickly rose to his feet, extending his hand.

Without changing his demeanour, the cardinal slowly clasped Feldman's palm as the bystanders dissipated meekly into the background. Feldman was surprised at the strength of the grip and at the degree of control and power projected by the unnerving, analytical eyes. Eyes as expressionless, passionless as those of the marble statuary residing in the dark alcoves and musty labyrinths of the Vatican palace.

'It's a pleasure to finally meet you in person,' Feldman managed.

'Yes,' the cardinal said simply. 'I am early, I realize. However, I thought if I were to join you now, rather than in the middle of the announcement as was planned, it would prove less disruptive and I might be able to witness the Pontiff's address in its entirety.' He hastily added, 'If that's not an imposition, of course,' spoken with the presumption that it would not be.

'Not at all,' the reporter agreed, although uncomfortable with the idea of having to bear the prefect's critical scrutiny through the earlier parts of the programme. He doubted that the cardinal would appreciate certain aspects of WNN's background report.

'There is seating accommodation for you.' Feldman gestured towards several armchairs in a wing to the side of the set. 'And I'll have one of our staff explain procedures to you and assist you with your microphone. After the Pope has concluded his address, we'll break for station identification and commercials, during which we'll seat you next to me here for the interview, if that's acceptable.'

The prefect nodded. 'I trust you've found our arrangements for you comfortable?'

Overly so, Feldman was thinking, but responded, 'Yes, Your Eminence, everyone has been most considerate.'

The cardinal's eyes hardened. 'Good. Then perhaps your network will choose to be a little more compassionate in its treatment of the Church tonight?' Holding his gaze long enough to emphasize his point, the cardinal bowed slightly and excused himself to take a seat in the shadows.

As airtime approached, Erin Cross returned in the company of several solicitous Italian WNN brass who had been only too happy to serve as her Vatican tour guides. Charmingly, she disengaged herself and took her chair next to Feldman with a bright and cheery 'Hello!' It failed to raise his spirits.

A few minutes later, the couple were given their cue as an 'on air' light flashed red and the familiar WNN logo swirled on to countless TV screens all across the globe, immediately followed by the images of Feldman and Erin. An off-camera voice announced, 'Live from St Peter's Cathedral in Vatican City, here are World News Network correspondents Jon Feldman and Erin Cross.'

The camera cut to a close-up of a pensive-looking Feldman.

'Good evening, ladies and gentlemen,' he opened without his customary shy half-smile. 'We welcome you to WNN's special coverage of the first-ever live broadcast of a papal edict.

'Before tonight's address, WNN has prepared for you an informative documentary on this rare pronouncement of the Catholic Church, known as a 'decree *ex cathedra*'. Following the Pope's message, we ask you to stay tuned to WNN for an exclusive interview with the Vatican Curia's prefect of the Congregation for the Doctrine of the Faith, His Eminence Cardinal Antonio di Concerci.

'Now, with some historical background on tonight's papal address, here's WNN's expert on religious affairs, news correspondent Erin Cross.'

The camera widened to include Erin's arresting, smiling face.

'Thank you, Jon,' she said, tossing back her stylish hair.

'Erin, can you begin by telling us a bit about the principle of infallibility behind this *ex cathedra* decree? I presume this is a power originally bestowed by Christ upon St Peter, the first pope, and handed down to successive popes through the millennia?'

'No, Jon,' Erin answered. 'Actually the doctrine of infallibility only goes back a little over a century, to the year 1870, during the time when the Italian government was threatening to take the papal states away from Pope Pius IX.'

'The Pope owned states?' Feldman feigned ignorance, following their strategy of leading eventually into further Secret Archive information that WNN had yet to reveal.

'Yes. For more than one thousand years, the popes ruled huge kingdoms,' she explained. Slowly, the camera zoomed in on Erin to the exclusion of Feldman, turning the programme over to her. 'Until the late 1800s, the Catholic Church owned more than five thousand square miles of valuable landholdings in central Italy, protected by large papal armies and navies.' The camera cut away periodically to punctuate Erin's story with beautiful old cartographies of the papal states, interesting photographs, lithographs and illustrations of the papal armed forces. 'Land that the Catholic Church had long claimed was given to it by the Emperor Constantine back in the fourth century AD.

'The Church had at one time even produced an ancient contract, allegedly signed by Constantine himself, to prove this claim.' And a photograph of an ancient, yellowed scroll was displayed on camera. 'Only, as you can see from this 1998 memo recently recovered from the Vatican Secret Archives, the contract was a forgery.' The camera next revealed an internal Vatican memo, typed in Italian on official Curia stationery, with a section translated in English on the screen. Erin read: '". . . recent advancements in scientific dating techniques make it advisable to exclude the scroll (Constantine contract) from outside study. Modern analysis of the document could readily expose the parchment as having been generated five centuries after the royal seal it bears . . ."'

An oil painting of an imperious, bearded man appeared on the screen. 'In the spring of 1869, King Victor Emmanuel of Italy acted on long-standing suspicions about the legitimacy of the contract. In an attempt to finally unite his divided nation, he made a claim on the Vatican states.

'The reigning pope at the time, Pius IX, denied the claim and pronounced the Constantine contract "genuine by divine revelation".' Next to the painting of Emmanuel appeared the portrait of a severe-looking man in white and crimson, wearing the papal mitre. 'Pius declared that all popes possessed a God-given power of infallibility when rendering important Church decisions.

'In a desperate attempt to solidify his position, the Pope summoned the entire world College of Cardinals to Rome for an official synod to endorse his controversial new powers. In open balloting, in the midst of a raging lightning storm and under the equally intimidating glare of the Pope's scrutinizing eye, all but two of five hundred and thirty-five cardinals voted to grant Pius his wish.' The camera zoomed in on the piercing eyes of the Pope, then dissolved away to the contrastingly fresh face of Erin Cross.

'So,' Feldman enquired, as the camera zoomed wide to reinclude him, 'did all this effort help save the Pope his states?'

'Unfortunately, no,' Erin finished. Italy invaded anyway and the Pope's army was no match for Emmanuel's superior forces. After three weeks of bloody fighting, the stubborn Pius finally surrendered. Italy reclaimed the states and annexed them permanently, leaving the Pope the Vatican and a considerable number of other valuable landholdings within Rome, which the Church still owns to this day.'

'And a magnificent kingdom it is,' Feldman acknowledged, gesturing to the glorious artistry of the grand cathedral. In demonstration, the camera dissolved to shots of selected points of interest within St Peter's, and from many of the museums and halls of the Vatican. This was filler time to consume the brief interval before the Pope, who had now entered the basilica, could be installed on his throne.

The camera then dissolved back to Feldman, who announced, 'And I believe we're now ready to go to the throne of St Peter for the first-ever live *ex cathedra* address to the world. Ladies and gentlemen, His Holiness, the Supreme Pontiff of the Roman Catholic Church, Pope Nicholas VI.'

Off the air now, Feldman could feel di Concerci's eyes boring into the back of his head. He consciously avoided looking in the cardinal's direction, quite certain of the prefect's reaction to the exposure of yet another unpleasant archival secret.

89

The Basilica of St Peter, Vatican City, Italy,
9.00 P.M., Monday, 3 April 2000

The camera began a slow zoom into the face of Nicholas VI. The Pontiff sat relaxed on his throne, clad entirely in a white, caped cassock and white skullcap, a golden pectoral cross around his neck, a bright red fascia sash across his chest. On his nose were perched his gold-rimmed spectacles. Upon his lap he held a Bible and a series of typed papers that he was organizing.

This was not the same pope Feldman recalled from his previous visit. This pope was in control, deliberate and decisive. He exuded confidence and authority.

Speaking in English to reach the largest global audience possible, the Pope's words rang out powerfully across the cathedral, each syllable underscored by resonant echoes. 'Brothers and sisters of Christ,' he called forth in a strong voice, 'may the blessings of the Almighty be upon you and yours in these times of trepidation. For tonight, I come before you with a sacred proclamation which the entire world community of Christians has awaited for nearly two thousand years. A divine message that carries with it the gravest importance and consequences for all mankind.

'One week ago, God revealed to me the ultimate reason behind the disturbing events which we now face. As I was alone in my chambers, after a dark night of anguished meditation and prayer, the new light of dawn broke fresh upon me, and the Lord's purpose filled my soul. And what God disclosed to me that morning, I now divulge to you.'

The Pope's voice dropped to a hushed, awed tone. His eyes appeared to see beyond the camera, as if staring back to his miraculous vision. 'The menacing challenge that confronts us now, these times of wrenching spiritual conflict, these are the days of the supreme ordeal. The great trial of the Final Judgment. Armageddon!'

Instantly, the cathedral was rocked with delirium, but the Vicar of Rome was not to be deterred. One by one, Nicholas laid out all the compelling, scriptural premises leading towards the terrifying conclusions of his decree. Like overwinding a clock, the relentless logic of di Concerci's scriptural indictments ratcheted the nervous congregation to breaking point. And as the devastating arguments unfolded, Feldman, who'd been standing to see better above the forest of microphones fronting the Pope, felt all the blood drain from his face. He sat down slowly in his chair.

Further removed from the altar, in a special section reserved for media personnel, a trembling, perspiring Rabbi Hirschberg sat confounded, clutching his chest. He staggered to his feet and made his laborious way to a public rest room where he joined several other pale and perspiring clerics near the washbasins. Fumbling with his bottle of medication, Hirschberg was elbowed accidentally by a nauseous priest bolting past. The bottle pitched from his hands to the marble floor where it rolled elusively beneath a toilet stall.

Out in the basilica, the Pope was arriving at the climax of his address.

'I think it unnecessary for me to belabour these points any further,' he stated. 'By now, I would hope the truth is becoming abundantly clear to you. By now, you can see that the champion which opposes the Evil One, and which the Evil One is attempting to destroy, is certainly Holy Mother Church. And surely you also know the identity of the Evil One.

'You recognize the false prophetess who has risen up among us, working strange wonders and commanding you to abandon your faith, desert your churches, ignore the sacred traditions of religious community that mankind has so reverently cultivated since the beginning of recorded history.

'I do not need to tell you that the name of the Evil One is Jeza, or *Jezebel*, as the Book of the Apocalypse identifies her. But I do need to place yet another label upon her. A terrible title which must now also be apparent to you.

'I come before you tonight to pronounce a solemn decree *ex cathedra*, the first such declaration of the Catholic Church in decades. I come to you as the Supreme Successor of St Peter, invoking the infallibility of Christ in making a judgment of faith and morals binding upon all the faithful.

'I therefore decree to you, *ex cathedra*, that this woman, known to the world as Jeza of Israel, is *not* a New Messiah; *nor* a New Christ; *nor* a prophetess of God. Rather, that she is the False One of whom the Bible prophesies. She is the enemy of truth and the greatest of immoralities against which the faithful have been preparing for two millennia. She is the Great Antagonist, the Profane Seductress, the Harlot of Babylon—

'*Jeza of Israel is the Antichrist!*'

With that terrifying pronouncement, the pent-up, visceral desperation and hysteria that had been coiling ever tighter since the turn of the millennium was suddenly released. The cathedral disintegrated into uncontrolled panic and disorder.

'We must rally together the army of God!' the Pope exhorted his troops over the bedlam. 'We must oppose this Jeza in every manner possible, fighting this evil to the death, body and soul, with every ounce of our strength until the Lord Jesus Christ comes in Judgment to relieve us!'

Feldman buried his face in his hands as the huge basilica reverberated with soulful agitation. Why he had not anticipated this Antichrist ploy, he did not know. It was, perhaps, a predictable next step in such a ruthless, relentless war of one-upmanship. And sadly, as this bizarre, seesaw battle lurched towards its finale, it appeared that the Church had just dealt the Messiah a staggering blow.

Feldman was appalled and furious.

And worried. Not only was more world conflict now inevitable, Feldman also knew that Jeza's life was in serious danger.

Presiding over the disrupted cathedral, the Pope endeavoured to regain control. He accomplished this masterfully by invoking the promise of Christ's 'One Thousand Year Glorious Reign', commanding the crowd to calm themselves immediately to receive a special 'atonement' blessing. Desperately dependent on the Church for survival now, the faithful responded in short order, with fearful compliance.

Amid the myriad emotions coursing through him, Feldman was dimly aware of a presence to his right. In preparation for the forthcoming interview, a WNN assistant had seated Cardinal di Concerci in the empty chair next to him. The reporter, flushed with anger and amazement at what he'd just heard, turned to face the prefect's characteristically unwavering gaze. A gaze edged this time with the slightest tinge of victorious self-satisfaction.

Feldman did not wait for Nicholas to finish his benediction, nor for the cameras to switch over for the live interview. Reeling from the *ex cathedra* pronouncement, he confronted the cardinal.

'Do you have any idea what you've done?' he cried out. 'Your Church has just set the entire world on a bloodletting. A rampage! This decree of yours is a death sentence for Jeza!'

Erin Cross, who'd been sitting to the other side of Feldman, engrossed in the Pope's startling edict, was jolted back to reality by the spontaneous eruption at her side. She laid a placating hand on Feldman's arm, to no avail.

As if dealing from a position of superior strength, the prefect responded calmly and dryly. 'That's a surprising observation coming from a representative of WNN, given that your network is singularly more responsible for the rise of world tensions than any other factor.'

WNN's directors and camera crews, caught completely off guard by the untimely start of the interview, were all facing in the opposite direction, towards the Pope. Frantically they came about, making confused, self-absolving gestures to one another, undecided as to whether they should interrupt the imbroglio and restart the interview, or simply pick up the altercation in progress. But the look on Feldman's face told them there was no going back. Cameras were hurriedly swivelled into position, lights switched on, cables kicked out of the way, boom microphones lowered. Erin was waved off the set to leave the two combatants alone in the ring.

'It doesn't matter any more who's responsible for world tensions,' Feldman snapped as the cameras zoomed in on his taut face. 'What matters is that you're in a position to quell the violence. Instead, you call for Armageddon! Just consider the incredible human suffering this will cause.'

The cardinal didn't hesitate. 'If it's God's will that there be human suffering, then it's hardly within the province of the Church to interfere.'

The newsman was astonished. 'Surely it isn't God's will for there to be more violence and senseless killings?'

'Neither you nor I can presume about God's intent, nor sit in judgment of it,' the prefect declared with finality. 'Do you think that Lot of the Old Testament understood God's annihilation of Sodom and Gomorrah? Or that Noah could fully comprehend God's anger as the rising floods inundated all the peoples of the world? It's not man's place to question the workings of the Almighty!'

Feldman was no match for di Concerci, and he knew it. His outrage had caused him to charge prematurely into this battle, unarmed, unthinking. Anxiously, he searched beyond the glare of lights for his tag-team partner, but Mordachai Hirschberg was nowhere to be seen.

Feldman parried. 'Your turning one man against another isn't an act of God. No one has authority to do that.'

Di Concerci reclined in his chair, in complete command. 'Mr Feldman, the *Church* is an act of God. The Church, with all its human flaws which your network is so fond of pointing out, is, nevertheless, God's instrument on earth; established personally by Jesus Christ to guide the faithful and to instruct them in the ways of the Lord.

'If you were to fully appreciate this, you'd realize that the decree *ex cathedra* is not a political document. It was not uttered in defence of property or position, as some will no doubt claim. It's the result of intense spiritual meditation, consecrated by Divine Revelation.'

As the cardinal spoke, Feldman grabbed a notepad from the coffee table, frantically scribbling: 'Where's the Rabbi? Get him *now!*' and passing the note off-camera to a stagehand.

'God has spoken to His Church, Mr Feldman, directly and clearly,' di Concerci continued. 'And the decree, however disquieting it may be, is very much the will of God.'

Feldman's face had steadily darkened and he was starting to sound strident. 'Even presuming the decree *is* the Will of God,' he argued, 'is it necessary for man to carry out God's retribution? I thought "Vengeance is mine, sayeth the Lord" was a pretty decent concept, myself.' He ransacked his mind, sorting through his limited store of scripture. 'What about "Love thy neighbour as thyself?" and "Thou shalt not kill!" In branding Jeza the Antichrist, the Church has just condemned her to death. How can you live with that knowledge?'

'You let appearances blind you to the diabolical truth, my young friend,' the cardinal replied, a look of sincere concern developing on his face. 'What more cunning ruse could Satan concoct than to fashion his messenger in the form of an attractive young woman? A seemingly innocent, defenceless woman. Yet a woman with amazing powers of magnetism, oratory and authority. A woman who can look inside your very soul and understand everything about you – your weaknesses, your sympathies, your vulnerabilities.' His eyes bored into Feldman's with accusation and his voice inflected knowingly: '—*how to seduce you and manipulate you!*'

This observation stopped the reporter cold. With effort, Feldman was able to shake off the disconcerting images the prefect had so forcefully planted. But he realized he had little reserve left. He could no longer sustain a theological argument. Without the rabbi, he had only one hope for reversing the seemingly inexorable direction of this lopsided debate. Inhaling deeply, he gained control of his anger, squared his shoulders to the camera and turned his resolute eyes on the world of frantic viewers glued to their TV sets.

'In my entire career as a reporter,' he declared clearly and forcefully, 'I've never once attempted to interject my own editorial opinions into my work. Unbiased news coverage has always been at the core of everything I value as a journalist. But tonight, in the light of what I've just witnessed, I cannot remain passive any more. I can no longer sit here and let the fate of this innocent woman, Jeza, and her followers, turn on the provocative, false, self-serving charges being levelled against her.

'Obviously, I'm ill equipped to argue scripture with this learned cardinal here. I have no formal religious background. But there *is* one relevant skill I bring to this debate: my knowledge and expertise as a trained observer. I'm a reporter. A professional journalist, experienced in seeking out and recognizing the truth. And in exercising that one qualification I do have, I'd like to make an important observation to all of you who've been watching these disturbing proceedings.

'By a remarkable stroke of fortune, I've had the opportunity to assess Jeza more closely and personally than any other human being alive, beginning with her very first public address nearly three months ago. With that unique and privileged perspective, I feel I'm more qualified, by far, to define her than any of her accusers.

'I can solemnly attest to you that *none* of the arguments advanced by the Vatican tonight ring true. None of them spring from direct observations of Jeza. They are all theoretical. Academic. So much theological speculation.

'None of these arguments serves to evaluate Jeza in the fairest, most credible way possible – from time spent with her; watching her gentleness with children; her kindness with the elderly; her sensitivity and generosity to the poor and the ill and the helpless. None of these arguments takes into consideration the warm, heartfelt response she elicits from people with whom she's directly shared her message.

'I must tell you that the Jeza I've seen is a very different Jeza from the one this pope and cardinal paint for you tonight. The Jeza I've come to know and appreciate isn't evil. She's not deceiving, cunning or hateful. The Jeza I know is loving and empathetic. A very sensitive person, deeply upset by the hypocrisy, self-righteousness, materialism and politics that she sees permanently fixed in the structures of the world's established religions—'

Boldly interrupting, di Concerci regained the camera, directly addressing the world audience himself. 'You must bear in mind that Satan is the master defrauder! He speaks in compelling half-truths to achieve his ulterior purposes. While it may appear that Jeza serves a higher purpose in exposing the human failings of our world religions, to what end is this? Not true reformation. She doesn't seek to "clean out the temple" as Christ did. She seeks to *destroy* it. To destroy religion as we know it! Look at the results of her work. Is the world a better place? Are people more moral? Happier? Better off than before her coming? Most certainly not!

'Indeed, when you look at the pervasive deterioration that's occurred in the world as a result of her brief ministry, you see the dangerous cunning and true genius of Satan. And that's why it is clear, beyond any question, that the Second Coming is upon us. Circumstances are so hopelessly degenerated, there is only one person with the power and the glory to restore this earthly community to normality again. And that person is most certainly *not* Jeza!'

Feldman's eyes implored the camera for reason. 'I cannot sit here and tell you that I know for certain whether Jeza is or is not sent from God as some new Messiah. In all my time and dealings with her, I still don't know the answer to that great question. But what I can tell you is what I firmly believe in my heart. And that is this: *at the very worst*, this isolated woman is not someone deserving of all the hatred and violence that's been stirred up around her. *At the very worst*, she's nothing more than a well-meaning, intelligent, tragically deluded human being. Not some sinister, diabolical creature, but a truly unique, extraordinary person – an innocent victim, robbed of her childhood, separated from her family, denied her humanity and her identity. Misguided and caught up in a charade that casts her in an impossible role. A tragic role with dire consequences for herself and for all mankind' – anger surged in his voice and he pointed accusingly at the cardinal beside him – '*if* you listen to this man!'

He consciously composed himself, appealing directly to the camera once again. 'All I ask of any of you is one very reasonable and simple request: I ask only that you wait. That's all. Just wait. Do nothing. Take no actions, make no decisions, just wait. If God is indeed calling down His Judgment on us, it will all become very apparent soon enough. Without any man-made violence and bloodshed to obscure it.'

'It's apparent already!' di Concerci came storming back, his eyes flashing.

'It is *not* apparent!' a faltering, breathless voice from off camera vehemently insisted. 'The Final Signs are not yet in evidence.'

Requiring the assistance of two WNN staff members, a deathly pale, afflicted but determined Rabbi Hirschberg made his way slowly to his chair. Feldman would have been relieved if it hadn't been for the rabbi's alarming appearance.

'Rabbi!' He leaped to his elder's assistance.

'It's all right now,' Hirschberg asserted with a grimace, gingerly taking his seat and motioning Feldman back to his. 'We have more important concerns at the moment.'

Feldman was not reassured, but hesitantly acceded to the rabbi's wishes. 'Ladies and gentlemen,' he announced to his world audience, 'may I introduce to you the distinguished biblical authority and spiritual leader of the Lubavitcher movement of Hasidic Jews, Rabbi Mordachai Hirschberg.'

If the prefect was surprised by this unannounced intruder, or if he felt more challenged by an adversary with worthy credentials, it didn't show. Di Concerci curtly nodded his acknowledgment of the rabbi, who warily returned the gesture.

Despite his apparent infirmity, it was obvious that Hirschberg was not about to shrink from his mission. 'I must tell you, Cardinal di Concerci,' he rasped between breaths, indignation replacing discomfort in his face, 'in all candour, while I respect your pontiff and his office, I am appalled by what I've heard here tonight. I must concur with this young man's observations. There's no need to escalate the confrontation. Why can't you do as Mr Feldman here suggests? Why can't you simply wait and let the predicted Final Signs of your Apocalypse manifest themselves before you condone this destructive course of action?'

Di Concerci allowed a dramatic pause, letting the cathedral subside into absolute stillness before responding. 'Because, my good rabbi,' he stated in an unwavering voice of conviction, 'the Final Signs *are* in evidence.'

'Rubbish!' Hirschberg scoffed. 'There are many critical signs not yet revealed. Where is the mark of the Devil? You and your pope have rashly labelled Jeza the Antichrist, the handmaiden of Satan! Yet, I defy you, show me the Devil's brand on Her! Your Book of Revelation calls for the mark of the beast to be clearly visible on the Antichrist. Where does Satan hide his accursed seal?'

Di Concerci leaned forward and narrowed his gaze at his defiant rival. 'The mark of the beast is to be found *precisely* where the prophecy says. On the *head* of the Antichrist. If you look closely at video taken of Jeza at the Mount of the Beatitudes, you will notice, entirely visible under her hair, on her scalp, the burns left from Satan's fingertips where the Evil One ordained her. She's been claimed by the Devil. She *is* the anointed Antichrist!'

The rabbi was stricken. 'These are *not* the marks of Satan!' he gasped. 'My God, man, what you speak of are simply the abrasions left on the poor lady from the electrodes She was forced to wear during Her cruel gestation! You twist things to your designs.'

'I twist nothing,' the cardinal maintained. 'It is *you* who rationalizes.'   Hirschberg was not about to concede. 'There are other, far more critical Final Signs you conveniently ignore,' he insisted. 'You have yet to identify for us the signs for the battle of Armageddon! Your pope claims that we are on the eve of the Judgment. But where, I ask you, are the armies of Gog and Magog, the prophesied armies of Armageddon? Where are these signs?'

Di Concerci pursed his lips in constrained triumph. Turning to the camera, he reached for a blank tablet of white paper on the coffee table in front of him. 'May I bring to the attention of my esteemed colleague,' he said, writing an unseen word on the pad with a large-nib marking pen, 'a rather conspicuous observation which has apparently gone unnoticed by him?'

The rabbi spread his hands out in front of him and arched his eyebrows questioningly.

'Rabbi,' di Concerci said, 'you've just made reference to the Apocalyptic armies of Gog and Magog.'

'Yes,' the rabbi confirmed, disdainfully. 'These are two important signs of Armageddon still left to be revealed. In the prophecy of the Old Testament, Ezekiel 38 and 39, Gog is the ruler from the land of Magog who will attack Israel in the battle of Armageddon and who will be met with destruction. Likewise, the names Gog and Magog appear again in your Book of Revelation, chapter twenty, verse eight. This time representative of *two* separate entities of Satan, the two wicked armies of the Antichrist.'

Di Concerci gleamed with certitude. 'Is it lost on you, Rabbi,' he asked pointedly, 'that the names of the two major factions currently opposing each other over the issue of Jeza's divinity are known as the Guardians of God and the Messianic Guardians of God, respectively?'

Hirschberg fell back in his chair as if a thunderbolt had struck him.

The prefect continued with the obvious. 'When broken into their separate acronyms,' he said with self-satisfaction, turning his pad so that both Hirschberg and the camera could see the two phrases he had written, 'the *G*uardians *o*f *G*od and the *Me*ssianic *G*uardians *o*f *G*od reveal the two apocalyptic names of the Book of Revelation, G-O-G and M-E-G-O-G – or Magog, if you will.

'These are the armies prophesied to descend upon Jerusalem from the north, from the ancient mountains of the city of Megiddo, Israel.' He wrote again on the tablet. 'In Hebrew, "H-A-R" means "mountain". Therefore, you have "Har Megiddo", or "h-A-R-M-E-G-I-D-D-O-n". That is, "Armageddon" as we all now know it.'

Hirschberg slumped further in his seat. Feldman's knuckles were white as he gripped his arm-rests.

'And now,' di Concerci said, turning sideways to face Feldman full on, 'let me call your attention to another bit of conveniently ignored information of which you should also be aware. As you now know, your Jeza carries within her brain a number of sophisticated neuromicrochips which provide her with a variety of spectacular functions.

'Let me remind you that one of these chips – and I have personally studied the descriptions recorded in the Leveque diaries – one of these chips happens to be a very advanced communications transmitter-receiver.

'As explained by Jozef Leveque, this unique microchip is powered by the normal electrochemical currents of the brain, and was designed to both *transmit and receive* messages in a form of silent telepathy.'

The cardinal waited for these facts to sink in. 'I submit to you that all your *prophetess* need do is cock her head in the proper direction and she can send out or tune into messages on any radio or microwave

frequency; send and receive messages via satellite; enter and peruse
any computer database she chooses, any time she desires, for any
information she wishes. The world's entire computer network is her
brain, Mr Feldman. Jeza can access any intelligence, all of mankind's
collective knowledge, whenever she wants, merely by *thinking*.

'All of which explains her seemingly omniscient mind. And also
explains how Jeza was able to penetrate the Vatican Secret Archives
so effectively. She knew all about the papal records in the Biblioteca
Secreta because these records had all been entered into the Vatican
computer files.'

Which would also explain, an astonished and deflated Feldman had
to admit to himself, how Jeza could have known of his early childhood
trauma – by accessing the computer records of his therapist.

Di Concerci did not pause to savour his masterfully executed
performance. He pressed on to his final point. 'Even more disturbing,
gentlemen,' he said, his demeanour growing intense and his voice taking
on an ominous timbre, 'is the greater probability that your so-called
Messiah is not in full control of her thoughts or actions. Rather, I
suggest to you that she is still the recipient of special instructions being
fed to her through the cerebral receiver she carries in her head.

'She is, I submit, a living robot. A cybernated slave, obedient to
the dictates of evil forces. Not a messenger of God, but a messenger
no less. *A messenger sent by individuals from within the Israeli Defence
Ministry!* Jeza and her secret overseers, whoever they may be, are
agents of the Devil.

'What the world confronts here, my well-meaning friends,' di
Concerci asserted with bombast, 'is the ultimate perversion of
deus ex machina. Jeza is *not* the innocent, benign entity that
appears to you in the deceptive guise of a sweet young girl. She
is indeed *the Antichrist*. The False One! Whether she be man-made
or hell-sent, the major signs of the apocalyptic prophecy are now in
evidence.'

There was no time for rebuttal, the period of programming
allotted to WNN by the Vatican having now lapsed. Not that
Feldman or Hirschberg had any defences left to counter the
totality of these arguments. Both men could only slump in stunned
dejection as Erin hastily re-entered the set to rescue the sign-
off.

90

Vatican City, Rome, Italy,
10.53 P.M., Monday, 3 April 2000

Standing on the wet, mist-swept cobblestones of St Peter's Square, Feldman watched the ambulance work its way fitfully through the throngs massed beyond the Vatican gates. Mordachai Hirschberg was being taken to a near-by hospital, suffering from acute angina.

Feldman felt guilty not accompanying him, sending along WNN personnel instead. But the rabbi wasn't the only one whose heart was ailing. The events of the evening had left the reporter deeply pained and anxious. Declining dinner invitations from his European associates, he stood aloof and preoccupied near his shuttle van, impatiently awaiting a ride to his hotel, a hot shower and the blessed relief of sleep.

The sound of clicking heels approached from behind him and he felt a consoling arm lightly encircle his waist. 'You were absolutely chivalrous tonight, Jon,' Erin commended him, drawing close. 'I'm really proud of the way you went up against that cardinal.'

He glanced around, snorted, and returned to scanning the crowd. 'A hell of a lot of good I did,' he complained caustically. 'Jeza's completely vulnerable now. God knows how long she'll survive this.'

'You and the rabbi did everything you could,' Erin assured him with a squeeze. 'How could you know what the Vatican had up its sleeve?'

'They outfoxed us,' Feldman acknowledged. 'Di Concerci set us up perfectly, holding those damned Final Signs in reserve till the end, and then ambushing us. We walked right into his trap, we just . . .' He trailed off, suspending his upturned hands out in front of him in a gesture of utter futility.

'Look, Jon, we just need to fall back and regroup. We'll think of something. Another special report, maybe. But right now, you have to take your mind off all this. You're all tensed up. You haven't eaten a thing all day.' Her voice assumed a tone of maternal lecturing. She moved around in front of him, tossing her hair, insinuating herself between his still-outstretched arms until he could no longer avoid her eyes. 'What you need is a nice hot meal and a good stiff drink!'

He shook his head, pulled back and turned aside, but she moved with him.

'We're going to find us a quiet little trattoria where you can relax,' she coaxed, 'have some dinner—'

His retreat backed him into the side of the van, which jarred him out of his incognizance. Grasping her firmly by her shoulder, he held her at arm's length. 'No!' he declared brusquely, glowering at her.

She appeared hurt, turning away, staring at the ground. He immediately regretted his behaviour. He gave her a quick, apologetic pat on the back and his voice softened. 'Erin, forgive me. I didn't mean to yell at you like that, I'm just very upset right now.'

Still averting her eyes, she nodded her acceptance.

'Listen,' he suggested, pointing over to where a large number of newspeople were evading the drizzle under the eaves of the great cathedral. 'You've got a dozen WNN brass dying to show you the city. It's a good career move. Go on and enjoy yourself.'

She turned back to him, the mist gathering in little beads on the fringes of her hair, reflecting the lights of St Peter's behind her like strings of pearls. There was the glint of a new awareness in her eyes.

'You're really taken by that woman, aren't you?' she ventured, searching his face closely. 'She's gotten to you, just like the cardinal said . . .'

Feldman avoided her gaze.

'I'm worried about you, Jon,' she breathed. 'I'd like to help.' But her expression was one of intrigue, not compassion.

Feldman returned to his hotel room. He slammed the door behind him, immediately stripped off his clothes, wadded them in a ball and threw them in a corner of the bathroom as if they were contaminated. Standing under the cleansing water of a long hot shower, he sought to rid himself of the evening's seamy residue.

He finished, wrapped a towel around his waist, and flipped another over his head to rub dry his hair. Stepping out of the bathroom, he walked blindly into the next room, intending to switch on the TV and look in on how the world had reacted to this last incendiary telecast. Instead, he tripped headlong over a surprise obstacle.

He sat on the floor, rocking back and forth in pain, swearing and rubbing his stubbed toes. Peering out from under his towel, he saw a carpet strewn with ice, along with a tripod stand, a toppled silver ice bucket and a full magnum of champagne with a note attached. Snatching off the envelope, he shook it open and read the card:

Let's celebrate! Erin.

She had obviously made these arrangements prior to the telecast. He tossed the card aside and grabbed the bottle. Popping its cork he ducked back under his towel as it sprayed the room with effervescence. Once the eruption had subsided, he turned on the TV and sat back down on the floor, amid the melting ice and champagne dew, swigging directly from the large bottle.

The latest reports were not comforting. The *ex cathedra* decree had been taken to heart by substantial numbers of viewers. There was, however, no word yet on Jeza or her current whereabouts.

Pointing accusing fingers at each other, both the Guardians of God and their bitter rivals, the Messianic Guardians of God, now had added impetus for their desire to annihilate one another. Each was firmly convinced that their counterpart was the prophesied army of Satan. Additionally, Feldman learned, millenarian leaders of both camps were mobilizing their forces, urging their fanatical followers to begin an immediate return to the Holy Land for the now imminent Second Coming.

The reporter watched the scenes of uncontrolled religious fervour with renewed alarm. It was the New Crusades, he thought to himself, forlornly. He rose to his feet with the intention of eliminating some of the liquid he'd consumed, but found himself suddenly light-headed. Sitting back on the bed, he beheld in his hand a half-empty bottle. The intensity of the news reports, he decided, had reduced him to a state of oral fixation. He'd been gulping champagne as if it were spring water.

Once his equilibrium was stabilized, he righted the stand, inserted the ice bucket back in its cradle and replaced the bottle. The exertion made him nauseous, lack of food taking its toll.

He placed his glasses on the nightstand, dropped his towel to the

floor and crawled naked under the cool sheets of his bed. With his
face buried in his pillow, he fumbled around the headboard for the
light switch and plunged the apartment into welcomed darkness.

He slept deeply for an extended period before slipping into yet
another dream. This time, he was out alone in the desert night, a
wandering nomad. Lost, lonely, and confused. And desperately tired.
He staggered and fell in exhaustion, face down in the dust. There was
suddenly a bright light in front of him and he looked up to encounter
the ethereal visage of Jeza, suspended above the ground, floating,
arms outstretched, silhouetted by a massive full moon, her robes
extraordinarily long and billowing around her. She was speaking to
him, but he couldn't understand her.

At the same time Feldman was aware of a red cast to the desert
sand in front of his face, as if the sun were dawning behind him. He
looked up and Jeza, too, was bathed in a rosy glow. She gazed past
him in the direction of the light. He rolled on his side and looked
over his shoulder. But it wasn't the sun blazing behind him, it was
the meteor – large and churning hellfire, barrelling straight for him.
He was transfixed.

The meteor struck him, but he felt nothing. There was a loud ringing
like a phone, jangling, pausing, jangling again. A shower of sparks,
brightness all around him, and a feeling of confusion and helplessness.
Reflexively, he flipped over on his back, holding one hand out in front
of him to protect himself, hiding his face in the crook of his other elbow.
Someone was softly calling his name. And finally he realized that this
was just another dream. He relaxed and removed his arm from his
face to open his eyes.

He was in his hotel room. But he was not awake. There, floating in
the air, in the dark just beyond the end of his bed, was the glowing
figure of Jeza. Larger than life. More lustrous than life. Her arms
were outstretched to him, her robe open, revealing a divine, surreal,
phosphorescent nakedness.

'Jon,' she called to him again. He rose on his elbows and tried to
focus his near-sighted, alcohol-dulled eyes on the apparition. Jeza
stepped out from space on to his bed and descended to her knees,
straddling him.

This was *not* a dream! He could feel the motion of the bed as she
rolled downward, her weight upon him, her bare breasts brushing his

chest. She enfolded him, caressing his face with her warm, soothing, moist hands. He could feel her wet lips enveloping his.

Dropping from his elbows to his back, he pulled away, reached up and clasped the shimmering face in his hands. This was certainly Jeza's tousled mane of dark hair. This was Jeza's gleaming brilliance, if considerably brighter in candlepower. But this was *not* Jeza!

'Love me,' the voice whispered to him.

He withdrew his hands and his palms glowed in the darkness. 'Erin?' he gasped incredulously.

'Love me, Jon,' she cooed again.

'Erin, what are you doing? How'd you get in here?'

She leaned down, nuzzled his neck and began slowly to wrap herself around him. 'Just lose yourself to me. Let yourself go.'

Grabbing her wrists tightly, he unwound her, casting her off forcefully as she collapsed beside him in reluctant resignation. The bedsheets were stained with luminescence.

'Dammit, Erin! How the hell did you get in here?' He flipped on the lights and retrieved his glasses.

Lying on her side, her head resting submissively on her outstretched arm, her hair in her face, she was silent for a moment, and then said with a curt sigh, 'I told the desk clerk we were married.'

Exasperated, Feldman grasped the edge of her robe to cover her unselfconscious nakedness. 'Jesus! What could have possessed you to do something as crazy as this?'

She dispelled the hair from her face with an upward puff of breath. 'If you haven't noticed, Jon,' she said, rolling her eyes up at him, '"crazy" is the prevailing disposition of the world these days. A little inoculation of crazy is exactly what you need to deal with all this.'

'What I don't need are more complications in my life,' he snapped, irritably. 'Please, just leave.'

'There don't have to be any complications,' she assured him, inching closer. 'No one needs to know anything.' She rose on her elbow and leaned towards him again. 'I can take you far away from all this turmoil,' she whispered softly. 'I can be any woman you want me to be. I can clear your mind and unburden your soul. And all you have to do is just give yourself to me. Just let yourself go,' she purred as her robe fell away once more and her painted breasts glistened up at him pointedly.

It wasn't the sensuality but the notion of surrender itself that was alluring. His psyche, wearied by weeks of relentless emotional expenditure and frustration, longed for escape. To weightlessly, aimlessly free-float in the ether of irresponsibility. He said nothing, allowing the concept to fill him.

'I understand what's troubling you,' she declared, her confidence growing with his indecisiveness. 'The way you took on that cardinal tonight. The way you defended her against him. She's seduced you, hasn't she?' Erin sat upright to engage him directly, her eyes narrowing with the certainty of her prosecution. 'You're infatuated with her. You've come under her spell. She's compromised your relationship with Anke and you don't know what to do!'

Cornered by the truth, Feldman remained silent.

'I can help.' She advanced persistently, running the fingers of one hand lightly across the sculpted pectorals of his chest. 'I can break that spell, if you'll let me.'

It was ironic to him. Throughout his entire life he'd always abandoned his relationships whenever they became difficult or complicated, finding quick solace in the arms of someone new. Now, enmeshed in the most complicated of triangles with Anke and Jeza, he refused to escape.

Brushing Erin off, he concluded the issue decisively. 'No. You *don't* understand. You can't begin to understand. Whatever my problems, no one can help me with them. Now, Erin, I'm telling you for the last time – leave!'

She sighed heavily, drew her legs into her body, and spun neatly out of bed to her feet, facing away from him. Without looking back, she lamented, 'We could have been so perfect together. The quintessential media couple . . .' Her voice dropped, she girded her robe about her and slipped away to the door, quietly letting herself out.

Surveying the room before he turned off the light, Feldman noted the chair at the end of the bed on which Erin had been standing. He shook his head sadly, hit the switch and watched smears of luminescent paint signal their presence randomly about the room: on the doorknob, in ghostly footprints across the carpet to his bed, in a handprint on the receiver of his desk phone, all over his sheets, all over himself. He shut his mind and fell back on his pillow, numb.

91

The Oval Office, Washington, DC, 9.30 A.M., *Wednesday, 5 April 2000*

Edwin Guenther, presidential campaign manager, and Brian Newcomb, Democratic Presidential Re-election Committee chairman, rose respectfully and solemnly as the forty-third president of the United States entered the Oval Office.

Smiling faintly, Allen Moore motioned them back into their chairs and took his seat behind his desk. This morning, the day after Super Tuesday, the normally youthful-appearing President looked much older than his fifty-six years. Yesterday had been a disaster. Of the nine states holding presidential primaries, not one supported the incumbent. It was a landslide for Moore's tenacious opponent, Billy McGuire.

'A tough night, eh, boys?' The President broke the uneasy silence.

'Yessir,' Guenther responded glumly.

'I don't see how we can give credence to yesterday's results when only eleven per cent of the electorate shows up to vote,' Newcomb volunteered.

'Is that what the final tally was?' Moore sighed.

'Yeah,' Guenther confirmed, 'and only seven per cent turned out in California. Now what the hell kind of primary is that?'

'The most expensive ever conducted,' Newcomb calculated.

'There's gotta be a way we can invalidate the returns based on insufficient voter turnout,' Guenther suggested. 'I've got the attorneys working on that now. Given the unprecedented national crisis, I think we've got grounds to—'

Moore held up a hand to stop the turning wheels. 'No.' He shook his head. 'That wouldn't change things. Look at the polls. We've been dropping steadily since early March.'

'Ever since the Jeza fiasco,' Newcomb icily finished the thought.

'So what would you have us do, anyway?' Guenther spat out. 'Have Al get born again and make him suck up to the anti-Jeza far right like that craven opportunist McGuire?'

'It's a little late for that,' Newcomb spat back. 'You know McGuire got the Confraternity of US Catholic Bishops to endorse him. Hell, the Church even *ordered* their flocks to the polls to support him.'

'They were leaning that direction anyway.' Guenther's corpulent face was turning a fiery red. 'It was as much McGuire's anti-abortion stance as it was the Pope's decree.'

Newcomb started to respond, noticed Moore's crestfallen face and thought better of it. 'Al,' he tried to sound encouraging, 'it's a long way to the convention. And with the political climate in such an uproar, hell, a lot can happen between—'

Moore held up his hand once more and forced a dim smile. 'No, gentlemen, please. Enough's enough. The writing's on the wall. McGuire has a two-to-one margin of delegates already. He's leading in fourteen of the twenty states left. I talked it over with Susan last night. It's a doomed effort, boys. It's time to pull the plug.'

Guenther and Newcomb shot looks of hurt disbelief at their president. Although Moore's decision should now have seemed inevitable, neither campaign manager was truly prepared to accept this incredible turn of events – the most decisive rejection of any sitting president in the history of the union.

'At two o'clock this afternoon,' Moore informed them, 'I'm holding a press conference to announce my withdrawal.'

'Al, please,' Guenther pleaded, '*anything* could happen between now and the convention. Or even *during* the convention. You can't abandon the party to the likes of McGuire!'

'I'm sorry, Ed.' Moore stood up to make his decision final. 'To be quite frank, it's not so terribly hard for me to give up the responsibility of this office. Nothing makes sense to me any more. I feel like I've completely lost any handle on the nation. And I pity the poor bastard who inherits the social nightmare out there. I'm beginning to think that woman is right. Maybe it is the Last Day.'

92

Na-Juli apartments, Cairo, Egypt,
9.39 P.M., Friday, 7 April 2000

Returning to his apartment after a long day, Feldman found the tape
on his answering machine completely filled. This time, however, there
were no calls from Anke. There was an assortment of unimportant
business messages, and then an almost continuous series of short,
anxious calls from the resurfacing Cardinal Alphonse Litti.

The cardinal left no number, but claimed it was important he reach
Feldman, gave the time of his call, and added that he'd keep phoning
every hour, on the hour, until he connected.

Litti was perfectly prompt. At ten o'clock sharp, the phone rang
and Feldman heard a familiar, welcome voice. 'Jon, thank God I've
found you!'

'Hello, Cardinal. How have you been? *Where* have you been?'

'That's not important right now, Jon. Let's just say I've been
meditating and studying and learning from the Messiah.'

'How is Jeza?' The concern in his voice was apparent.

'She's well, Jon. We've had to keep Her hidden as much as possible
with circumstances as dangerous as they are, you know. Not that we
can do so for long. She has this uncanny knack of slipping away when
She has a mind to.'

'Yes.' Feldman smiled drolly. 'I've experienced that a few times
myself. When can I see her again?'

'Shortly, Jon, I suspect. I don't know Her plans exactly, She's rather
mysterious in that way. But that's the reason I'm calling you. I – She –
needs your help.'

Feldman's heart kicked.

'Jon, I have to rely on your complete confidence here.'

'You know you can, Alphonse.'

'Jeza wants to leave Cairo and return to Jerusalem. I need your help to smuggle Her back.'

'Jerusalem? Why? It's too dangerous. All her enemies are there. Everyone who thinks the world's about to end is converging on Jerusalem for a front-row seat. It's safer here in Cairo.'

'She has to be "about Her Father's business", as She says. Whatever the Almighty might be asking of Her, I don't know, but She's determined to return, one way or another.'

'You realize, Alphonse, WNN's still blacklisted in Israel. All our facilities up there are seized and we're not allowed back in the country.'

'Please, Jon, I have nowhere else to turn!'

'Did Jeza ask you to contact me?' He held his breath.

'She doesn't know I'm calling.'

Feldman sighed.

'She's intending to leave within the next week or two, I believe,' the cardinal continued. 'She doesn't want me along, says it is too dangerous. But I insist that you also make provision for me.'

'Okay,' Feldman agreed. 'I'll see what I can do. How can I get back in touch with you?'

'I never know where She'll lead me next, Jon. Just tell me when and where, and I'll contact you.'

Feldman did so, hung up and immediately placed a call to Sullivan. A short time later, he was phone-conferencing with Bollinger, Hunter and Cissy, developing a plan of action. While still going over a few details with Cissy, he heard a knock at his door. Begging her indulgence, he laid down the phone, rushed over to the door, flipped the latch, shouted, 'Come on in!' and dashed back to the phone.

Looking over his shoulder, he saw the slender form of a young woman dressed in a full-length trench coat, white beret and matching scarf, her head tilted downwards. Signing off, he replaced the receiver and turned to meet his visitor.

When she lifted her head, he gasped. *Anke!* She looked tired, her eyes red-rimmed, her fine jaw set in determined anger. She folded her arms and leaned back against the door, closing it.

'Anke,' he whispered, the guilt welling up inside him.

She said nothing, staring at him through steely eyes.

'Please. Come in. Let me take your coat.' He approached her, combing his hands through his hair in a haphazard attempt to make himself look more presentable.

She didn't move.

'Anke, I know you're upset with me, and I don't blame you, the way I've neglected you—'

'How understanding of you, Mr Feldman,' she snapped, and he pulled up short at the unaccustomed sharpness.

He tried again, opening his arms to her. 'Sweetheart, I'm not sure what to—'

She wasn't listening and cut him off flat. 'I can lose my patience with you, Jon,' she hissed through clenched teeth. 'I can lose my temper. My mind, even. But the *one thing* I never thought I'd lose is *my respect for you*! If you owed me nothing else, Jon Feldman, you owed me honesty. I would have stood by you through hell itself. But *this*! This is so, so' – she began to cry – 'so *cruel* of you.'

Feldman was beside himself. 'Anke, I never meant to hurt you.'

He moved towards her again, but she held him at bay with a fierce glower, her anger cauterizing her tears.

'Since you seem incapable of the truth, let *me* take the initiative to be straightforward with *you*.' She closed her eyes tightly, as if squeezing out her response. 'I know what's going on, Jon. I – I know there's someone else.'

He sat down numbly and heavily on the couch.

'What I don't know,' she continued, 'is why you didn't have the decency to be truthful with me. I just can't walk away without knowing that. After all we shared, after all we meant to each other, why didn't you respect me enough to tell me the truth instead of just letting me hang on like that? How could I have misjudged you so badly?' The tears came again.

'Anke,' he pleaded, 'I don't know how to explain this. I *do* love you. I want to work things out. In my mind, *and* with you.'

'You have such an incredible ego,' she flashed at him. 'There's nothing left to work out. Do you think you're so irresistible? That I have such little self-esteem that I'll just accept this in you? Honesty isn't something I value lightly, Mr Feldman. You can't just lose and redeem faith with me so casually!'

Feldman was heart-stricken. 'But Anke, nothing really happened.

It was more of a . . . spiritual thing. I honestly don't know how to explain it. It was so . . . *beguiling*.'

'Jon, don't make this any worse, and don't insult my intelligence. I know the two of you spent the night together.'

Feldman was more confused than ever. He shook his head, stood up and tentatively approached her. 'Anke, please, I don't know what you're talking about. I'm telling you the truth.'

'And you're going to tell me she was never in your hotel room, I suppose?'

'No, Anke, she wasn't. Honest.'

She lowered her head in despair. 'Jon, for your information, I called your room in Rome Monday night – early Tuesday morning, I should say.' She turned away from him and faced the window. 'After watching you battle that cardinal on TV, I couldn't sleep. I – I just had to talk to you. I wanted to tell you how proud I was of you.' She choked with emotion. 'I was so touched by what you tried to do. You were so, so . . . *gallant*.

'I tried to reach you for hours. The international lines were tied up with all the turmoil. And then finally, when I do get through to your room, *Erin* answers the phone! She was whispering, but I recognized her voice. I couldn't say anything, I just hung up.'

Feldman's mind churned, failing to assimilate this puzzling information.

Anke wheeled back on him with accusing eyes. 'I called the front desk to make sure I had the right room. The desk clerk told me that both Mr and *Mrs* Feldman had checked in. Then I had them switch me to the room they had listed for Erin Cross. There was no answer.'

'You're talking about *Erin*?' It finally sank into Feldman's head. Taking off his glasses and covering his eyes with his hand, he shook his head. 'No, Anke, you've got this all wrong.' He collapsed slowly on to the couch again. 'Please, come here and let me explain everything to you, from the beginning.'

'Why, Jon? So you can spin me more tales and cause me more hurt?'

'No, Anke,' he said sadly, looking her squarely in the eyes. 'So I can tell you the whole truth. While you've got a right to be mad at me, it's not for the reasons you think. Please. For everything we've meant to one another, at least hear me out.'

She faltered for a moment, then stiffly took a seat in a chair as far from Feldman as was available. Crossing her arms and legs, she glared distrustfully at him.

'First of all,' he bent towards her, his hands spread imploringly, 'let me tell you the whole story about Erin . . .'

And he started at the beginning, relating the early flirtations and his initial suspicions about the woman. Then he described their trip to Rome. How he purposely declined dinner with Erin after the debate, and went instead to his room to shower and turn in without supper. How in an effort to assuage his frustration over the disastrous telecast he foolishly drank the champagne Erin had sent to his room.

He was exceedingly embarrassed and uncomfortable recounting the bizarre seduction sequence. He watched Anke drawing herself up in her chair, tucking her legs under her, appalled. When he arrived at the part where Erin confessed how she got a key to his room, she began to relax.

'All I can figure,' he explained, 'is that you must have called after Erin had entered my room and before she aroused me—' He flinched at the choice of words and hurriedly corrected himself. '— before she woke me. Maybe after drinking all that champagne I was sleeping a little more soundly than usual and she simply got to the phone before I heard it.

'But Anke, I swear, as soon as I recognized her, I made her leave, so help me God! Nothing happened, honest.'

Anke's eyes narrowed in sudden awareness. 'But you just told me Erin was *never* in your room,' she said, suspiciously. 'You can't seem to keep your stories straight, Mr Feldman!'

Feldman sighed and shook his head. 'No,' he said heavily. 'You're confusing issues. I wasn't referring to Erin.'

Anke, who had been gravitating towards the edge of her chair, came to an abrupt halt and retreated again, dumbstruck. 'You mean there's someone other than Erin?' She looked crushed.

Feldman nodded his hanging head.

'Please tell me it isn't Cissy!'

'Christ! No, no, it's not Cissy.'

Anke studied him for a moment. And then her eyes grew increasingly large. Softly and slowly she exclaimed, 'Oh my God!' She rose to her feet and looked down at the tortured Feldman. 'Don't tell me.' She

began to amble slowly around the room. 'Oh my God!' she cried
repeatedly.

Feldman peered up at her from under heavy brows.

At length, she stopped her pacing, sat down next to him and placed
a hand on his shoulder. 'Jon, do you . . . do you love her?'

He bit his lip and glanced furtively at her, his face contorted with
confusion. 'I honestly don't know. I feel *something* very strong for
her. But it's, it's not like what I feel for you. I mean, it's – God, I
don't *know*! I feel very loving and protective towards her.'

'And you don't feel that way towards *me*?' Anke asked, hurt.

Feldman looked over at her, puzzled, then realized what he'd just
said. He scrunched his face. 'No, no, that's not what I mean at all.'
He shook his head and looked away. 'I don't know what I mean any
more. It's not a romantic love I feel for her, I don't think. But – I'm
trying to be completely honest with you – I *do* want to be with her.
I *do* miss her.'

He turned back to her again. 'I don't know how to explain any of
this. I've never felt this way before. I want to be entirely straight with
you because, despite what you think, I *do* respect you. Very much. I
wouldn't hurt you for the world, but of course, I know I have. And
I'm truly sorry for that.

'You see, I feel as if I'm tied to you *both*. I miss you *both*. I care
about you *both*. I *worry* about you both. I want to be with both
of you.

'Yes,' he decided. 'I love you *both*!'

Anke dropped her hand from his shoulder like a dead weight. 'This
is unbelievable,' she exhaled as she stood again.

She wandered around in small circles once more, mulling it all over,
while Feldman stared after her in a hopeless quandary. Finally she
stopped and looked down at him. 'Well, Jon, I don't know if this has
occurred to you or not, but you simply *can't* have us both. You're
just going to have to figure this one out for yourself. I've had all the
insanity I can take.' She headed for the door. 'I'm leaving.'

Feldman sprang to his feet and grasped her arm from behind. 'Anke,
please, I don't know what to say, but I've told you the truth.'

She turned around and looked up into his disturbed, grey eyes. 'I
know that, Jon.' She was crying again. With her fingertips, she gently
touched his cheek. 'I'm not angry with you any more. And, certainly,

I can understand why you feel so drawn to Jeza. She's, she's so . . . But Jon, I just can't see it bringing you any happiness.' She took her hand away, stretched to kiss him softly on the lips, then moved away.

Opening the door latch, she gazed back at him, her face a mask of resigned defeat. 'You're a very special person, Jon. I love you. I always will. It was so perfect with you. But this! How do I deal with this?' The emotions came surging back. 'How do I compete with a . . . a *goddess*!'

She rushed out of the door. Feldman started after her, calling, but she paid him no heed. Fleeing down the stairs and into her car, she was gone.

93

Meeting chambers of the IDF Command Centre,
UVDA Israeli military airfield, southern Negev,
10.37 A.M., Saturday, 8 April 2000

An uncomfortable Intelligence Commander David Lazzlo sat next to a solemn ex–Chief of Staff General Mosha Zerim. The two men were in tense conference with fellow officers of the Israeli Joint High Command, now under the auspices of the newly appointed chief of staff, Senior General Alleza Goene.

The general had taken his time in arriving at the unpleasant crux of this meeting. Finally putting aside other business, he sat back in his chair and folded his powerful arms across his chest.

'As you know, gentlemen,' he addressed his colleagues, 'before taking a leave of absence, it was Defence Minister Tamin's last official act to designate me chief of staff. I would like to re-emphasize that this action was not intended in any way to slight the irreproachable service of General Zerim.' He nodded casually towards the ex-chief of staff, who held his grave composure.

'The decision was simply a matter of logistics. Given the current state of affairs in Israel, the defence minister felt that my veteran war-command experience might prove invaluable. As part of Minister Tamin's directive, General Zerim has been reassigned to command the northern divisions.'

Lazzlo stole a sideways glance at the implacable Zerim.

Goene continued, 'I am making further reassignments, as well.' He turned to Lazzlo. 'Commander, given our current difficulties with security breaches, you will be relinquishing your responsibilities as head of intelligence operations, effective immediately.'

There was a murmur of surprise from the other attendees in the room.

Lazzlo's face flushed red with anger. 'You have no authority to remove me from command!' he barked. 'Only the defence minister or the Knesset can take such actions.'

A smile of contempt formed on Goene's lips. 'I am not removing you from command. But in the absence of an acting defence minister, I do have the authority to redirect your command.'

Lazzlo stopped short, his irate objections dying in his throat.

'From this point forward,' Goene ordered, 'General Roth will assume responsibility over intelligence operations. And you, Commander Lazzlo, will now take charge of our defence forces in Jerusalem. As you no doubt recognize, you are being entrusted with the IDF's most sacred responsibility – to protect the Holy City and its sacred shrines from the growing factions of millenarian extremists.'

What the commander no doubt recognized was that Goene was placing him in the middle of the most impossible, incendiary situation ever to confront the Israeli Defence Force.

The general leaned forward and his eyes narrowed. 'This will be a rather more challenging assignment in the light of the recent Leveque diary revelations, wouldn't you say?' He paused to let his insinuation register, and then stood up, signalling an end to the meeting.

Lazzlo and Zerim left together, engrossed in conversation, marching sombrely across the tarmac to the helicopters that would ferry them to their new assignments.

'They have to be on to us, David,' the general decided.

'No,' Lazzlo assured him. 'If Tamin felt we were personally responsible for smuggling the diary to the Vatican, we'd be looking at a court martial, not a mere demotion. Trust me, I was thorough about the leads I planted. They're convinced it was the work of some unknown staffer, caught up with an anti-Jeza sect.'

'Regardless.' Zerim's anxieties were not allayed. 'Our plan to put an end to Tamin and his accursed Negev experiment has misfired on us. If anything, Israel is worse off than before. Although Tamin may be physically out of the picture while the Knesset investigates him, he still exerts control of the IDF through Goene – and I fear that madman more than I do Tamin.

'David, we failed in our efforts to neutralize this damnable Jeza threat. Instead of discrediting her with the Leveque diary, we only served to create more worldwide division. Now millions of fanatics are descending on Jerusalem to engage each other in the battle of Armageddon.'

'Yes, my friend,' Lazzlo reluctantly agreed. 'And now it's become my responsibility to try to stop them. God is poetic in His justice, isn't He? I'm about to reap the consequences of my involvement in all of this.'

94

WNN regional headquarters, Cairo, Egypt,
8.00 A.M., Monday, 10 April 2000

The office operator sent a phone call through to Feldman's desk and the newsman took it expectantly.

'Good morning, Cardinal.'

'Hello, Jon, how are you?'

'Fine.' Feldman spared him his true feelings. 'I think we've got things squared away for you.'

'Excellent. Bless you!' Litti sounded relieved and grateful. 'What's your plan?'

'Well, I've got us a car and a dependable, professional driver. Cardinal, you're going in under cover as an Egyptian diplomat *en route* to the Palestinian peace talks in Hebron. Jeza will pose as your daughter. You'll wear a turban and Jeza must keep a full veil on at all times. We have papers and credentials and everything you'll need. It should work fine if you leave the talking to the driver and stick to the few Arabic phrases we'll give you. Once we make it safely across the border, we should be able to make our way to Jerusalem without a problem.'

'Okay. Excellent.'

'And one other thing . . .'

'Yes?'

'Breck and I are travelling with you as your attachés.'

'Do you think that wise, given your troubles with the Israelis?' Litti said, concern in his voice.

Feldman tried to sound reassuring, 'We'll be disguised too, Cardinal. Don't worry, no one's going to recognize us. Besides, Egyptian officials don't travel without their attachés, and I don't trust anyone else to handle this. Even our driver won't know who you and Jeza are.'

Litti was hesitant, but coming round. 'Well, all right, if you think that will work . . .'

'When do we leave?' Feldman asked, looking forward to seeing the Messiah again.

'Saturday morning, I think,' Litti said. 'I'll call and let you know as soon as I can determine exactly when and where.'

95

Ali'im Projects, West Cairo, Egypt,
6.00 A.M., Saturday, 15 April 2000

At the appointed time and location, the reporters arrived in a long, dark stretch limo, complete with tinted windows, Egyptian government seals on its side and a burly, no-nonsense Arab chauffeur.

As they turned down the last row of modest white adobe houses, they encountered the cardinal pacing the dirt road, anxiously awaiting them. Feldman was about to scold him for parading around undisguised when he noticed the distraught look on the cardinal's flushed face.

'She's gone!' Litti yelled, rushing up to the slowing car.

Feldman was aghast. 'Gone? When? Where?'

Litti held his hand over his heart, short of breath. 'When I awoke, our hosts told me that Jeza had disappeared last night after I retired for the evening. She gave instructions that I not be awakened, and She just left! No one will say where, but I'm certain She's headed for Jerusalem. This is so reckless of Her!'

'Goddammit!' Hunter blurted out his disappointment. 'I say we make a run for Jerusalem anyway. If she's headed there, maybe we can catch up with her on the way. It's worth a try, 'cause if she's left Cairo, our work here is shit-canned any- way.'

It crossed Feldman's mind that this was no way to speak in front of a Catholic cardinal of the Holy See, but the reporter was too dispirited to raise the issue. 'You're right,' he agreed, taking a last look around the sleepy development. 'Let's do it.'

Litti climbed inside and the limo sped off down the dirt road towards the Israeli border.

'Can you tell me how you found Jeza, and what's been happening with her since I last saw you?' Feldman asked as they began getting into their disguises.

Litti nodded. 'You know, when I returned to my hotel after our trip to the Vatican, I thought I'd never see Jeza again. Three days of prayer passed and I heard nothing. Then, on the fourth morning, I was sitting in my room meditating and I felt this overwhelming compulsion to go to the window. I looked down on the street and was suddenly seized with ver- tigo. When I regained my balance, lo and behold, there was Jeza, four floors below, standing on the pavement, staring up at me.

'I went down immediately and, without saying a word, She led me through the streets to the outskirts of Cairo and a small encampment of Bedouins. That's who She stays with in the desert.

She moves around with them and their herds, living in tents and teaching.'

'Do they even know who she is?' Feldman wondered.

'Oh my, yes,' Litti confirmed. 'They have portable TVs and radios they take with them everywhere they go. They're totally devoted to Her. She's cured several of them of serious illnesses.'

Feldman nodded his understanding. After all, it was Bedouins who had first discovered Jeza in the desert after her escape from the Negev disaster. In a sense, they were her first family.

'So,' Litti went on, 'Jeza invited me to live and travel with her and the Bedouins, which I've done now ever since. We roam all about this region, visiting different locales where Jeza stays at the home of a local inhabitant, preaches, performs an occasional miracle, and then we move on.'

'And you're still convinced that Jeza is the true Messiah?' Feldman questioned.

'Absolutely!' Litti exclaimed without hesitation. 'Quite certainly She's a Messiah. Just as Jesus was. She's the only begotten Daughter of God, here on His special mission.'

Adjusting Hunter's turban to hide his blond hair, Feldman gave Litti a sideways glance. 'Other than dismantling organized religion and causing untold world turmoil, just what is her mission, exactly?'

The cardinal looked disappointed. 'Jon, tell me, after all you've seen, you still do not believe?'

'I don't know what to believe, Cardinal,' Feldman admitted. 'I see a lot of strange occurrences with messianic overtones that could have many different explanations. Including satanic, if you're inclined to interpret the scriptures that way.'

Litti's face saddened. 'Jon, other than during the last few weeks when I've been blessed to know Her, you've spent more time observing Jeza than anyone else. What have you seen? What does your heart tell you?'

Feldman looked chagrined. 'It's so confusing, Alphonse. I find her incredible. I love her kindness, her conviction, her strength, her beauty, her courage. These are the godly things I see in her. But then I see all the destruction and pain and suffering that are a result of her coming.'

Litti leaned back, thoughtfully. 'Have you ever considered, Jon, that sometimes God's business can't always be love and kindness? God is like the good parent raising a beloved child. He must strike a balance between affection and discipline, applying both, in proper measure, as appropriate. There's as much love in the chastisement as there is in the embrace. To let bad behaviour go unpunished is to ruin the child.'

'That's a rather condescending perspective,' Feldman observed.

'In comparison to the perfection of God, man *is* an infant,' Litti maintained. 'Nevertheless, Jeza says that it's God's will for mankind to grow and mature and ultimately become independent of God. But that the road we're taking has swerved away from His path and has become circular. She says we're no longer growing. That we're stagnating in the current religious environment.'

'So God means to chastise us by ending the world? That goes a little beyond corrective discipline, wouldn't you say?'

'It's true, She's warned that Armageddon is upon us. But that doesn't mean we're all going to die. Perhaps some will be taken up, body and soul, into heaven and eternal life.'

'The Rapture, huh?' Hunter identified the familiar doctrine.

'Or perhaps' – Litti remained undaunted – 'Christ will come again, and together He and Jeza will separate the good from the evil and rule side by side for a thousand years of blissful heaven on earth.'

'But what about Cardinal di Concerci's charges – the signs?' Feldman questioned. 'How do you explain the signs? And if Jeza isn't the Antichrist, who is?'

Litti smiled with self-assurance. 'Remember Jeza's admonitions about interpreting scripture? These signs are Cardinal di Concerci's perspectives. They do not prove Jeza is the Deceiver. Who's to say what form the Antichrist will take. Or even that it's one person and not an entire group of people? Admittedly, Jeza does not fit the conventional notions of how a Messiah should look or act, but we'll only understand God's purpose once His plan is fully revealed to us, if then.'

'Surely you've asked Jeza what's going to happen?' Feldman asked.

'Yes, I've asked Her. She'll only say that the Dissolution is near and that all She has foretold will soon occur. Indeed, if She does return to Jerusalem, She'll be setting into motion the last prophecies of the Apocalypse. I have an ominous foreboding in that regard. As if we may already be in the Last Days.'

96

Mount of the Ascension, Jerusalem, Israel, *9.17 P.M., Saturday, 15 April 2000*

It was well after dark when Feldman, Hunter and Cardinal Litti rolled up to the small hillside villa WNN had reserved for them on the western side of the Mount of the Ascension. Crossing the border had actually been less difficult than the trip to Jerusalem. The roads north were choked with pilgrims, militants and military convoys, and there were signs of destruction and outbreaks of violence continually along the way. Once, shots had even been fired at the trio's car when they refused to stop for a group of marauding Gogs.

Upon arrival, they found Jerusalem little changed, yet entirely different. Many of the buildings damaged in the earthquake more than three months ago were still in a state of disrepair. Apparently there had been too much civic disturbance to attend to these details. The famous Golden Gate of the Old City, Feldman noticed, was still partially disassembled, covered with scaffolding, many large stones stacked on pallets around its base.

The millenarian shantytowns, which were now separated into pro-Jeza and anti-Jeza sections in a futile effort to restrain the incessant quarrelling, had grown to prodigious proportions outside the walls of the city. Israeli military were everywhere, and the crowded markets were rife with altercations.

The hillside villa Feldman and company would occupy was not too far from where he and his associates had witnessed the night of the millennial transition. It was closer to the bottom of the mount, with a balcony that faced towards Jerusalem this time, offering a splendid view of the Old City.

Concerned about Anke's safety in these uncertain conditions, Feldman attempted to contact her at both her Jerusalem town house and her Tel Aviv apartment, getting nothing but a voice recorder. He left a contrite message, promising to call again soon, but gave no number, not daring to disclose his whereabouts.

97

Mount of the Ascension, Jerusalem, Israel,
8.58 A.M., Sunday, 16 April 2000

In this dream, Feldman was clinging naked to the trunk of a lone, skinny tree at the top of an otherwise barren hill. He was hanging on for dear life, only a wisp above the snarling jaws of a pack of vicious yellow curs. They were hellhounds. Filthy, matted fur. Crimson, crazed eyes. Maws slinging the foam of hydrophobic madness. And Feldman's grip was loosening, his vulnerable, exposed bottom inching ever closer to those snapping fangs. He hiked himself up again and again, but with each enervating effort his fingers cramped a little sooner and the cycles grew shorter.

From somewhere off in the distance, he could hear Hunter's voice calling enthusiastically, 'Hey, everybody, get a load of this! Where's my camera!'

Feldman came to, panting, safe in his own bed, his fingers still desperately clutching the rungs of his headboard. Hunter's voice rang out again. 'Hey, you gotta see this – you won't believe it! Hurry!'

Rolling out of bed stark naked, Feldman staggered to his feet, grappling with glasses and pants. Hunter was still hollering, and Feldman made it a duet when he caught himself with his zip. Swearing and stumbling from his room into the glaring light of a gorgeous spring morning, the newsman squinted to spy Hunter out on the balcony. Telephoto video camera in hand, Hunter had been joined by the dishevelled-looking Cardinal Litti, who was also overcome with excitement.

'Jon!' The cardinal beckoned Feldman with a repetitive, circular motion of his forearm. 'Look!'

Shading his eyes with his hand, Feldman leaned over the balcony and peered out towards the bottom of the Mount. A caravan of Bedouins on camels and mules was winding its way from the desert around the base of the Mount of Olives along a dirt path into the city. In reception, a crowd was gathering near the Old City walls. From a near-by shantytown, people were scurrying out on foot to meet the arriving travellers.

At the forefront of the caravan, a small, lone figure, mounted on a mule, was being led along by a walking nomad. Even at a distance, it was obvious from the sharp contrast of dark hair and white skin who this celebrated rider was. Feldman fished a pair of binoculars out of a duffel bag and zoomed in on the spectacle.

'I'm an idiot!' Litti declared to himself, smacking his forehead repeatedly with the butt of his hand. 'A complete fool!'

Hunter was too absorbed in his camerawork to react. Feldman responded without removing the binoculars from his eyes. 'How do you mean?'

'She's fulfilling prophecy again!' Litti exclaimed. 'Following in the footsteps of Christ and fulfilling an Old Testament prediction. Do you know what day this is?'

Still unable to take his eyes away, Feldman shook his head, smiling to himself as the prophetess passed among the cheering throngs towards the city.

Litti chirped, 'It's Palm Sunday, of course!'

Feldman's smile broke into a broad grin as he revelled in Jeza's triumphant return to the Holy City. The steadily expanding crowd of spectators was jubilant, dancing, singing and shouting, liberated in joyous celebration.

But momentarily, Feldman detected a disruption on the periphery of the crowd. Training his field glasses on the disturbance, his grin abruptly vanished. 'Hunter!' he called to his friend, concern edging his voice. 'Look to the left.'

Hunter panned his camera and immediately picked up the source of Feldman's alarm. Unquestionably, the initial gathering of well-wishers had been composed of pro-Jeza supporters. It would appear, however, that word had quickly spread to the opposition camps, and a sizeable contingent of vigilantes was now converging on the crowd. As yet, there were no Israeli soldiers or police in sight to protect the defenceless caravan. Fighting had broken out, and two cars of armed guerrillas were ploughing through the panicking masses, heading in the direction of the Messiah.

Litti emitted a groan and Feldman's grip tightened on his binoculars. At this distance there was nothing they could do. The attackers would reach their quarry in a matter of seconds, long before the three men, unarmed though they were, could have scrambled down the hill to Jeza's defence.

They watched in desperation as the caravan began to scatter. The hysterical crowd pressed against Jeza's mule, forcing it off the path to stumble sideways, clumsily, towards the walls of the Old City. Jeza turned to see the approaching vehicles, which apparently had also spotted her. A passenger in one of the cars rose up through an open sun roof and rested a rifle on the top of the jostling vehicle.

Feldman's heart was racing. Jeza was trapped against the walls and the scattering throngs were yielding to the oncoming vehicles. Pressed back to the Golden Gate, the desperate Bedouins hurried Jeza towards the pallets of stone stacked under the construction scaffolding. But this limited cover had already been claimed by scores of frantic people. With nowhere else to go, Jeza slipped off her mount and stood to face her adversaries. The car was well within rifle range now and the sharpshooter leaned forward, taking aim.

Calmly, Jeza turned in Feldman's direction. Through his binoculars, it appeared as if she were staring directly into his eyes. He could not watch this, and he buried his face against his shoulder.

The sound of repeated rifle fire popped in the distance.

'Oh my God!' Hunter cried, and Feldman clenched his fists in bitter anger. 'Son of a bitch!' Hunter shouted and Feldman slumped to his knees.

'She disappeared!' Hunter bellowed in glee. 'She escaped!'

This failed to register on either Feldman or Litti.

'Hey, guys.' Hunter wouldn't spare them a glance, but he thumped the cardinal on the top of his head. 'It's okay. Get up. Look!'

Unbelieving, Feldman and Litti rose slowly and peered out over the edge of the balcony. They saw that the attacking car had pulled up near the pallets of wall stone and that the occupants were out, investigating the rubble under the scaffolding.

'What happened?' Feldman gasped, his voice barely audible.

'She squeezed in through a gap in the wall they're repairing,' Hunter explained in wonderment. 'She's so small, she just slipped through a tiny opening there and left them all sucking air.'

'I'll be damned,' Feldman exhaled.

'Another miracle, more or less,' Hunter decided.

98

Mount of the Ascension, Jerusalem, Israel,
8.18 P.M., Monday, 17 April 2000

Hunter's riveting footage of Jeza's escape through the Golden Gate was delivered out of Jerusalem by special courier that morning. By evening, WNN had yet another ratings triumph.

Worldwide, the repercussions of the report were devastating. Pro-Jeza forces, outraged at the brutish attack on their defenceless Messiah, railed against their opposition through a long and bloody night.

In Jerusalem, however, the situation was quickly contained by the IDF, which had mounted a tight security ring around the Old City. The Ben-Miriam government, despite adamant IDF opposition, had allowed Jeza sanctuary inside the walls. Although the administration would have preferred Jeza not to re-enter the country at all, she was, arguably, an Israeli citizen. Indeed, despite the shocking revelations of the Leveque diary, many Israeli Jews, particularly the Lubavitchers and Orthodox sects, and even some members of the Knesset, still supported Jeza as a holy person, if not the promised Messiah.

The new head of the Jerusalem IDF, Commander David Lazzlo, had implemented a successful policy to lessen tensions. He had ordered that all perpetrators of violence in Jerusalem be arrested and transported to the city of Afula, approximately one hundred kilometres to the north. Two large, internationally funded UN holding centres had been established there – a separate internment camp for each of the two opposing factions. The effort had been helpful in removing some of the most aggressive and dangerous militants.

Feldman and Hunter had box seats to the entire operation. Nevertheless, without their visas, not secure seats. Before Alphonse Litti had left them on Palm Sunday morning to seek out his Messiah in the Old City, the good cardinal had pledged not to abandon his reporter friends. Good as his word, he'd dropped by briefly on Monday afternoon with the welcome news that he'd been reunited once again with Jeza. She was safe, well hidden within the city, protected around the clock by legions of staunch supporters.

After the cardinal left, with evening drawing near, Feldman joined Hunter out on the balcony in the spring twilight. Below them, the effects of their Palm Sunday video could be seen in the unbroken streams of pilgrims migrating into the area. The numbers had easily doubled.

'Jesus, there must be millions of them!' Feldman marvelled to Hunter, who'd been studying the crowds through binoculars. 'I thought the IDF would've had better success sealing the borders.'

'Even with the UN helping now,' Hunter contended, giving his field glasses a rest, 'the Israelis don't have the manpower to deal with this. When you believe you're about to face your maker, like all these poor bastards do,' he inclined his head towards the endless droves, 'it's gonna take a hell of a lot more than a few roadblocks to stop you.'

They leaned together against the rail for a while, observing in silence the mass procession. 'Just think,' Hunter reflected, 'all that fanaticism converging from all over the globe, funnelling into this one, sorry little spot. Yep, we're headin' for one hell of a confrontation. And once again, you and me got a bird's-eye view.' He turned to go inside. 'Too bad we don't have a programme of events. I get tired just sittin' around, waitin' for something to happen.'

'Maybe we do have a programme,' Feldman ventured.

The cameraman paused. 'How do you mean?'

'Remember what Alphonse said about Jeza fulfilling biblical prophecies?'

'Yeah?'

'Maybe there's another way to look at that. What if she's *emulating* Christ?'

'Well, we all want to be more Christ-like, now don't we?' Hunter responded sarcastically, his curiosity abating.

'No.' Feldman screwed up his face. 'I mean, what if she's *copying* what Christ did? You know, paralleling his life. Like her Palm Sunday entrance into Jerusalem yesterday. Like her Sermon on the Mount. Her miracles. Her flight into Egypt. Her parables. The whole shtick! I mean, it isn't identical exactly, but it does follow the general pattern.'

'The only real pattern I see,' Hunter pointed out, 'is that she seems to arrange her appearances to occur at the worst possible places at the worst possible times to create the most possible havoc!'

'Stay with me on this for a minute,' Feldman appealed. 'Let's just assume that the Samaritans convinced Jeza that she's a New Christ, right? So that's who she's modelled herself on. And she's got this incredible microchip communications technology in her head that gives her instant access to all the scriptures and prophecies. So she studies the Bible and when she needs direction she simply refers to the life of Christ, like a road map.'

'Okay. Your point?'

'The point is, if she's using scripture for direction, what's her next move?'

'I don't know, I missed Bible school.'

'Look at the calendar, Breck. What's 21 April?'

'I give up.'

'Good Friday, man! You know, the Crucifixion?'

This stopped Hunter cold and he gaped at his friend. 'They're gonna nail her to a cross?'

Feldman shook his head rapidly. 'No, no, not literally.' But then, in a spasm of alarm, he caught himself. 'Hell, I don't know!'

Hunter began to formulate the logic. 'So that's what's bugging Litti now. He knows what she's up to. She's biding her time until Friday to turn herself over to the Gogs to be crucified. Self-martyrdom so she can fulfil her destiny. Sick, man.'

Feldman's head was reeling with abhorrent images. 'The Gogs may be fanatical enough to execute Jeza, but they wouldn't dare cruci—' He couldn't bring himself to say it. 'They're too smart for that!' he insisted. 'That would be playing right into her hands – the final validation of all these Christ parallels. It's self-defeating.'

'Unless,' Hunter countered, 'they're really convinced she's the Antichrist. Then a crucifixion is poetic justice. Payback for the cruel way Christ was executed. Retribution. I mean, there are certainly enough crazies out there, I wouldn't put anything past 'em.'

Unwillingly, Feldman had to accept this reasoning. 'Holy shit,' he whispered, and both men sank slowly to sitting positions side by side on the rail. Feldman put his hand to his brow, thinking. 'We've got to get into the Old City, Breck. We've got to get Jeza out of there.'

Hunter was wagging his head. 'No way, man, the Israelis have it sealed up tight. The only way you can get in now is with a residency photo. And they'll only issue 'em to people like Litti who were already inside the walls before the crackdown.'

'It's going to take a helicopter, then,' Feldman concluded.

'Nope.' Hunter shook his head again. 'Restricted airspace. The Israelis would shoot down any unauthorized aircraft before you could even get close. Look' – he offered Feldman his field glasses – 'they've got artillery and troops stationed everywhere now. They're prepared for Armageddon.'

Feldman rejected the binoculars. 'Dammit, then we've got to get the Israelis' co-operation. We've got to get our visas restored!'

'Agreed.'

'I'm calling Sullivan to see if he's made any progress. Maybe our concerns about Friday will give him a little more incentive. And let's hope we get a visit from Litti tomorrow. We're going to need him.'

Hunter nodded, started to rise, then had a last misgiving. 'But what if Jeza refuses to leave?'

Feldman bit his lip.

And then a wry grin played across Hunter's face. 'On second thoughts – three big, grown men; one little girl. I think we've got all the persuasive tools we need.'

Feldman looked thoughtfully at his friend. 'You may want to reconsider that approach, old pal. Let's not forget what she did to that altar stone!'

99

Mount of the Ascension, Jerusalem, Israel, *10.11 A.M., Tuesday, 18 April 2000*

Arriving as promised for his morning visit, a troubled Cardinal Litti could not contain his anxieties.

'Something's in the air, my friends,' he began, his voice heavy with concern. 'The Messiah sent me to the Israelis with a special request. She wants permission to broadcast a public speech at the courtyard of the Wailing Wall this Friday afternoon.'

Feldman and Hunter exchanged confirming glances.

'What did the Israelis say?' Feldman wanted to know.

'I met with a Commander David Lazzlo,' Litti explained. 'He said he'd get back to me later today, but he indicated that the IDF might allow us to hold the assembly as long as we agree to a quid pro quo. Jeza would have to require our followers to lay down their weapons and forgo any further violence. But that's a non-issue since she's been appealing for that all along, anyway.'

Feldman looked perplexed. 'I don't get it. Letting Jeza make a public appearance in the middle of this powder keg is insane. It'll only lead to bloodshed. Why would the Israelis risk it?'

'Jeza is safe as long as she remains behind the walls of the Old

City,' Litti pointed out. 'Her support is solid inside. Outside, the
IDF has completely secured the walls. And, thankfully, most of the
truly militant extremists have been removed to internment camps in
Afula now.'

'So what's the purpose of the speech, anyway?' Feldman asked.

'Jeza won't say.' Litti sighed. 'Just that, once again, She has Her
Father's unfinished business to attend to.'

Feldman considered this for a moment. 'Alphonse, I don't have to
tell you what day Friday is.'

Litti's furtive eyes answered for him.

Feldman gripped the cardinal's forearm. 'We're concerned about
her safety, too. And we have an idea. A plan to rescue her.'

Litti looked up at Feldman questioningly.

Grinning, Hunter stole Feldman's news. 'WNN is talking with the
Israelis right now about a plan to get the both of you out of here. The
Israelis would like nothing better than to defuse this time bomb. And
with your help, maybe we can pluck the two of you off to someplace
where it's a little more stable.'

The cardinal wagged his head at them. 'You don't understand.
There *is* no hiding from what's coming. It's not just Jeza's safety I'm
concerned about.'

Feldman and Hunter's excitement abated.

'Do you remember' – Litti alternated back and forth between the
two newsmen – 'how Jeza escaped Her attackers on Palm Sunday
morning?'

Both men nodded.

'She fled *through* the Golden Gate. And do you remember the
prophecy about the Golden Gate?' He answered their blank stares.
'It's foretold that in the Last Days, the Messiah will enter the Old
City by way of the Golden Gate. This will be another final sign of
the imminent Judgment.'

Dimly, Feldman recalled hearing this somewhere, and his stomach
knotted.

'Until the earthquake,' Litti elaborated, 'the great Golden Gate
had been sealed up for centuries. The Muslims had walled it up as
insurance against the scriptural warning. But Jeza has defied them
all. She's fulfilled another Last Prophecy.'

'And you think Friday is D-Day?' Hunter asked.

'What more appropriate day for the Lord to return than on the anniversary of His death?' Litti reasoned.

Even Hunter's tanned complexion paled at this notion.

'Is there anything else that draws you to that conclusion, Cardinal?' Feldman questioned.

'Only in how I interpret the Messiah's mood,' he said. 'She's even more pensive and sad of late. She eats little and devotes an inordinate amount of Her teaching to eschatological themes.'

'Scato—?' Hunter tried.

'Eschatological, Breck,' Feldman finished for him. 'Judgment Day stuff.'

Hunter blinked.

Feldman's face took on a grave cast. He reached over and touched the sleeve of the cardinal's cassock. 'Alphonse? Will she leave with us if you ask her to?'

'No, Jon, I'm afraid not,' he replied with resignation. 'She's determined to make Her appearance on Friday, and I dare not interfere with Her in that regard. She follows the Father's Will.'

Feldman's shoulders slumped and his brow wrinkled in frustration. After a moment's thought he brightened slightly. 'Well, then, will she leave *after* her appearance?'

'I don't know.'

'Here's what I propose,' Feldman said. 'We get the Israelis to provide a helicopter at the site, on stand by, ready to lift off. Immediately after her speech – or at the first sign of trouble – we bundle the two of you aboard and get you the hell out of there. Agreed?'

Perhaps a trifle more comforted, Litti looked over at his earnest young friend. 'It's such a blessing sometimes *not* to believe,' he said, and patted Feldman's arm. 'Agreed. And I can only pray that you're right and I'm wrong. But if not, I pray instead that we'll all be chosen to join the Lord in paradise together.'

Hunter smiled dourly and extended his hand. 'Well, Padre, just in case I don't make the shortlist, it was nice knowing you. You're the only religious dude I ever liked.'

Litti took the big man's hand and gave Hunter a fatherly smile. 'It's never too late to repent, my boy. I think God would be proud to have you on His side.'

100

Mount of the Ascension, Jerusalem, Israel, 8.44 A.M., Thursday, 20 April 2000

The phone rang. It was Sullivan.

'Good news, Jon. They've reinstated our visas.'

'*Yes!*' Feldman shouted, setting aside the New Testament he'd been leafing through for clues to Jeza's plans.

'They're letting a limited number of us back into Jerusalem, but they're not releasing our office headquarters yet,' Sullivan qualified. 'I have visas for you and Hunter, and I'll be leaving for Jerusalem with Arnie, Cissy and team one shortly.'

'Excellent.'

'The Israelis are also allowing Jeza to make her public address,' he added. 'It's set for two-thirty, Friday afternoon. They're erecting a large platform for her now near the north end of the East Wall, and they're shielding it from all sides with blast-proof glass for protection.'

'Good. What about the helicopter?'

'The Ministry of Defence has agreed to provide an army helicopter on stand by to evacuate Jeza and the cardinal after the speech, or in the event of an emergency. They'll place it as close as feasible to the stage and will fly the two of them directly to Cairo, assuming Jeza's willing to go. We've made arrangements for the UN to take custody of them in Cairo in the hope of getting asylum in Switzerland.'

'And you've arranged for Hunter and me to be with her for the speech and evacuation?'

'Well, not exactly. The IDF doesn't want us – especially you – involved in the operation. They want to handle the entire mission themselves. And the Israelis aren't permitting any media on the stage or in the helicopter. In fact, we don't even have access privileges to the Old City at this time.'

'I don't like the sound of that, Nigel,' Feldman fretted. 'Having the IDF involved makes me edgy. Goene's chief of staff now and he's hardly better than the Gogs. I've got a bad feeling about this.'

'It's all we have at the moment, Jon.'

'And why the hell aren't they letting us in for the speech? All the other media will be there.'

'They claim space is at a premium and that all secured camera sites have already been allocated.'

'That's bullshit!' Feldman vented. 'Goene's screwing with us.'

'I presume you've heard that there's been a major uprising at the internment camps in Afula?'

'No.'

'The militant Guardians of God revolted and broke out. They attacked an arms depot outside Megiddo where they captured a large cache of weapons. And now they're advancing on the second internment camp of the Messianic Guardians. At this time there are about a hundred thousand well-armed vigilantes. The UN and Israelis have both sent forces to try to stop them.'

'My God, the armies of Gog and Magog!' Feldman breathed.

'It appears so, doesn't it?' Sullivan concurred. 'So you can see, the administration has larger problems at the moment than finding us seats for tomorrow. But we'll continue pressing the issue.'

Signing off, Feldman switched on the TV to view developments on the revolt. He consoled himself with the knowledge that, at least, Jeza and Litti would now have a means of escape.

At four o'clock, Feldman finally received a call from the cardinal. There was considerable commotion in the background.

'Things are quite tense in here, Jon,' the clergyman shouted over a bad connection. 'I've had trouble getting a call out to you. The Gogs keep cutting the lines. I presume you've heard that the speech is on?'

Feldman affirmed.

'Well, the Messiah is in seclusion, meditating, and everyone is convinced that tomorrow is the Last Day. People have already staked out their spots in the courtyard and are staging vigils throughout the entire Old City. It's elbow to elbow all the way to the platform. Oh, by the way, they've set up a helicopter pad.'

'Right,' Feldman confirmed. 'They've promised us a chopper. It'll be there prior to the speech, and if at any time you and Jeza appear to be in danger, the Israelis have instructions to evacuate you immediately. Regardless, they're going to pull the two of you out as soon as the speech is over. You'll be flown to Cairo, and then, hopefully, to Switzerland.'

'Good, Jon. I've asked Jeza if she'd consider leaving the city after her assembly – I didn't tell her what we had in mind, exactly – and she simply said that it wouldn't be necessary. That's not a no, is it?'

'Not from my perspective,' Feldman concluded.

'What about you and Breck?'

'Well, so far we've got our visas, but the IDF isn't allowing us into the Old City yet. We're still hoping to get a berth inside the courtyard or on a rooftop somewhere to video the speech. Nothing's definite, but it doesn't look like we'll be joining you on stage or for the evacuation.'

'Will you be meeting us in Cairo, then?' the nervous cardinal asked.

'I'm not sure, Alphonse. If we can get down there quick enough, yes. But we don't want to delay your departure. We don't see Cairo as exactly a safe haven, either. But in any event, we'll be joining up with you at the earliest possible time.'

Feldman was pleasantly surprised to hear the clergyman speaking positively about the future. Perhaps even Litti was straying from his doomsday bent. 'Try to get some sleep tonight, Alphonse,' he urged, 'you'll want to be fresh for tomorrow.'

'It will be difficult with the all-night ceremonies that are planned, but I'll try. You do the same. I'll call you tomorrow morning if possible. If not, best of luck to you. And God bless you for your efforts. We'll see each other soon, I'm certain.'

'It's been a pleasure, Your Eminence.' Feldman felt a tightening sensation in his throat. 'Please be very careful tomorrow. I'm not real comfortable with some of the Israeli military behind the evacuation, so stay on your toes.'

Four hours later, WNN team one rolled up to the mountain villa in an RV, shy one member. Erin Cross, Feldman was told by a pleased Cissy, was feeling ill and wouldn't be joining them.

A short time thereafter, Feldman received a strange phone call. The voice on the other end was hauntingly familiar.

'Hello, Mr Feldman. I'm with the Israeli Defence Force.'

'How did you get my number here?' Feldman asked, alarmed and annoyed.

'Oh, I've known of your whereabouts from the time you arrived on Saturday night,' the caller responded, non-threateningly. 'But don't be concerned, you're in no trouble. You're completely safe.'

'Do I know you?' Feldman enquired. 'I know your voice.'

'Well, it's been a while since we've spoken, Mr Feldman. Last time, I believe you were in a hurry to leave Israel.'

Feldman made the connection. He immediately softened his tone. 'I never had a chance to thank you, sir. You did us a great service. We're all very appreciative.'

'No thanks necessary,' the voice assured him. 'And now I'd like to perform yet another service for you. I've made provisions to get you inside the Old City for tomorrow's affair.'

'Outstanding!'

'Well, not entirely. The location I've been able to set up for you isn't the best. It's a little removed from the stage, but it will give you an unobstructed view. With a telephoto lens, you and your videographer, Mr Hunter, should be able to make do.

'Unfortunately, I can only make arrangements for the two of you. You both will need to meet representatives of the IDF near the Dung Gate by twelve-thirty tomorrow afternoon. Look for a Corporal Illa Lyman. She will provide you and Mr Hunter with the necessary papers and escort you to your designated position. Once there, please do not leave your area under any circumstances until after the speech is concluded.'

Feldman was scribbling this information in his notebook. 'I'm very indebted to you, sir. Now, please, can you tell me your name, and why you've taken these risks to help us?'

'You'll pardon me, but I would prefer to maintain my low profile for the time being.' He hung up.

'Who was that?' Hunter wanted to know, looking up from the TV.

Feldman grinned. 'Oh, just some more divine intervention, I would say.'

101

Mount of the Ascension, Jerusalem, Israel, *6.03 A.M., Friday, 21 April 2000*

Feldman had slept fitfully and wasn't spared his typical allocation of strange dreams, the last of which woke him.

A soft, gloomy light infiltrated the living room where he lay on the floor in a corner on his bedroll. The only one yet stirring, he slipped on his pants and tiptoed through a minefield of sleeping bodies out on to the balcony. In all directions, the surrounding countryside was coated with pilgrims as far as the eye could see. He thought to himself that this must have been what it looked like to the pharaoh as the Israelites gathered for their exodus to the promised land. He prayed that history wasn't repeating itself.

Because no more people would be admitted into the Wailing Wall commons, which was already filled well beyond capacity, enormous-screen TVs had been set up in several strategic places outside the Old City where mass viewing of Jeza's speech would be possible. Large speakers sat at intervals atop the huge walls, facing out to every point of the compass. If not able to see her, at least the multitudes would be able to hear this much-anticipated address to the world – Jeza's first direct speech to the general public since her initial appearance at the Mount of the Beatitudes.

It didn't look to be a pretty day. Although the sun had broken, it was overcast and there was a strong breeze coming out of the east.

Good, Feldman thought to himself, surveying the threatening clouds. *It sure wouldn't hurt to put a little dampener on today's events.*

For the rest of the morning, Feldman, Hunter and the WNN staff worked on their preparations for the upcoming telecast. After a final equipment check, the crew assembled in the front room to give the two

men their send-off. It was as if he and Hunter were soldiers leaving
their families for the front. The accustomed frivolity and irreverence
were gone. The solemnity of the handshakes and hugs he received
told Feldman that, despite the secular convictions his associates had
been touting, millenarian fears had crept in.

They left in a car with Bollinger driving, slowly picking their way
down the mountain road through the dense crowds. The closer they
drew to the Old City, the slower the going became. At length,
they reached the Dung Gate, so called for the heaps of rubbish
and horse manure once piled here by the Romans and Byzantines
during ancient times.

Bollinger pulled over to the side to assess the situation. 'Anyone
see a female corporal anywhere?'

'I see IDF soldiers manning the gate over there, and they don't seem
to be letting anyone in or out,' Hunter reported, angling around in his
seat to better inspect things. 'But I don't see a female soldier yet.'

'We've got five minutes.' Feldman checked his watch. 'They said
twelve-thirty, let's not get nervous.' This was hypocritical advice.

'I hope you brought your raincoats,' Bollinger cautioned, glancing
up at the sky. 'It looks like we could get some weather. Maybe this
damned drought is about to break.'

'Yeah, nice day for a Judgment, eh?' Hunter opined.

'Or a Rapture,' Feldman added.

At precisely 12.30, a new group of soldiers pulled up to relieve the
old. The officer in command was a no-nonsense, capable-looking
young female with dark hair and eyes to match. She saluted the
departing soldiers and stationed her fresh men in front of the gate,
machineguns drawn.

Feldman slid out of the car, grabbed his equipment bag and leaned
back in through the side window. 'Okay, Arnie, I'll check this out.
If all goes well I'll signal for Breck. We'll keep in touch by cellular
phone once we're settled inside.'

'Check.' Bollinger gave him the thumbs-up. 'Be careful now. I don't
have to tell you it could get rough in there.'

Feldman returned the gesture, smiled grimly, and trotted over to
address the corporal. In a few minutes he was receiving papers and
waving Hunter to join him.

After repeating the formalities with the cameraman, the corporal picked up what looked like an empty coffee can and, along with three soldiers, silently escorted the two newsmen through the huge gate. Once inside, the reporters could see, high above the dense crowd, a platform erected at the north-eastern end of the plaza, flush against the great East Wall. Unfortunately, Feldman and Hunter were being led in the opposite direction.

'I don't suppose there's any way we might influence you towards a better location?' Hunter suggested to the young corporal, flipping the corners of a large bankroll. Without losing her stride, she looked first at the money, then at Hunter, pulled the bolt on her rifle, and silently continued on her way.

'Maybe I should've offered my body,' Hunter whispered to Feldman, loud enough for the corporal to hear.

It was slow going through the standing-room-only crowd of chanting, singing, praying millenarians. The entire quadrangle was a sea of mixed cults, ethnicities and ages. It reminded Feldman of the eclectic crowd he'd witnessed the night of Millennium Eve, only the mood here was considerably more intense.

Passing out of the plaza into the heart of the Old City, the party crossed several narrow alleys, turned down a side street, and then stopped in front of what appeared to be an old four-storey warehouse. It bore on its door the same bold yellow signage, in multiple languages, that appeared on the other buildings near by: 'Roof access prohibited as of 4.20.2000 by order of the IDF. Violators subject to immediate arrest and imprisonment'.

The corporal withdrew a key from her breast pocket and unlocked the door. 'Up here,' she said, motioning with the muzzle of her gun towards a dark, dank stairwell. Her adjutants stood aside to guard the entryway and the two newsmen accompanied her up four flights of wooden stairs all the way to the rooftop. Swinging open a door, they stepped out into a cool breeze.

'The roof is bad over here.' She gestured with her gun to her left. 'So keep to your right and you'll be fine. The street-level door locks from the inside, so you shouldn't be disturbed. When you finish, let yourself out as you came. There are no toilet facilities.' She dropped the coffee can on the roof. 'Use this as necessary and carry your waste away with you. Any questions?'

'Will you be back to walk us home?' Hunter flirted.

She looked the big man up and down with a raised eyebrow and snorted, 'I would rather experience doomsday!' Both Hunter and Feldman burst out laughing, appreciating the break in the tension.

This was not shared by Corporal Lyman, who wasted no time ducking back into the darkness of the stairwell.

Hunter hooked a thumb in the direction of her departure. 'From the Goene school of charisma,' he smirked, and began unloading his equipment.

Feldman walked out towards the edge of the roof in the direction of the stage to survey the scene. He saw that their building was connected directly to the one in front of them, one storey below them, and that this was connected to the building in front of it, and so on. From the look of things, the two newsmen could work their way from roof to roof to the very front row of buildings at the perimeter of the huge quadrangle. If the opportunity presented itself. Beyond the rooftops, directly adjacent to the stage, Feldman was comforted to see a military helicopter resting on its pad.

As the mystery voice on the phone had promised, the stage in the Wailing Wall plaza was certainly visible from here, but it must have been a good hundred metres away. All the other news crews were far better situated on the periphery of the plaza, either on the surrounding walls, or on the tops of buildings at the edge of the open common. No one was set as far back as WNN.

'We're not going to get any decent audio from up here,' Feldman said, stating the obvious.

'No,' Hunter agreed. 'Headquarters will just have to fall back on simulcast audio from some other network, like we anticipated. But hopefully, you and I'll be able to hear her speech. They've got a decent sound system set up on the stage.' He pointed over at the series of horizontal, two-foot-by-eight-foot speaker boxes placed on their sides along the front of the platform.

'What do you make of the empty rooftops out there?' Feldman asked. He guessed he was standing on the sixth row of buildings back from the edge of the plaza, and was surprised to see that there were no spectators on any of the roofs in front of them. The view-path was deserted.

Hunter dropped a camera case and walked over next to Feldman. 'Hmmph. Bad roofs, like the corporal told us? Or maybe security. See how we look down a bit on the platform from up here? That would make it easy to lob a rocket or grenade over the top of the glass shield. All the windows facing out on to the square are probably stationed with militia. But I don't know why the hell they couldn't have gotten us a little closer, anyway.'

'I guess we're lucky to be here at all,' Feldman conceded.

Hunter pulled up a tripod and positioned his camera on top. 'Yeah, only I don't like the angle. I'm too low. I can't get you and the speaker's platform in the same shot.'

Feldman walked over to squint through the lens. 'What do you suggest?'

'Well, with all the open access in front of us, maybe we should just try moving a little closer?'

Feldman considered this for a moment and then observed the large number of Israeli military stationed around the perimeter areas. 'No,' he sighed. 'If we get kicked out of here, WNN will be completely dark on this whole event. We'd better play it safe.'

Hunter peered around and fastened his gaze on the higher roof of the building behind them to their left. 'Up there,' he proposed. 'Let me see what it looks like from up there. You hand the camera up to me.'

Before Feldman could object, Hunter was off. 'Watch out for the roof,' he called after him.

The new position worked perfectly, Hunter decided. He could hold Feldman full-frame and then adroitly zoom in over his shoulder, directly into the stage and speaker.

'I don't like the look of those clouds,' Feldman observed, casting his eyes up to the sky. 'You're target practice if a lightning storm kicks up suddenly, you know.'

'No problem. I'll skinny offa here slicker 'n shit if I have to,' Hunter assured him. 'Come on, give me a hand with the rest of the stuff.'

As the appointed hour for Jeza's appearance drew near, Feldman made one more attempt to reach Anke on his cellular phone. This time he got through, only to encounter the answering machine. He left a detailed message about where he was, phone numbers and how he might be reached later. He pleaded with Anke to contact him soon, given that he might be leaving for Switzerland that night. Frustrated, he snapped shut the phone and returned it to his pocket.

And then, without warning, the two newsmen were suddenly alerted to Jeza's presence by the eruptive excitement of the crowd. From nowhere, it seemed, the prophetess had appeared on the platform, unannounced, and was taking her place on the stand behind an array of microphones. In a panic, Hunter scrambled up to his perch on the rooftop. Feldman, captivated by her arresting image once more, had to force himself to turn away from the vision and return to his work. He took his place below and well out in front of the cameraman.

'How's my audio?' he called into his wireless lapel mike.

'Fine,' the word came back through his ear-set. 'Hold for a sec while I clear our signal.'

Feldman's ear-set went quiet momentarily, and then Hunter's voice crackled back. 'Okay, we've got a green light. Go ahead and do your intro and just ad lib until she starts her speech.'

That could take a while, as the crowd showed no intention of diminishing the volume of its wild welcome. Feldman, his back reluctantly to the stage, brushed his coat, cleared his throat and addressed the camera. He got a hand cue from Hunter and began.

'This is Jon Feldman reporting live for WNN from historic Wailing Wall Square in Jerusalem. As you can see from the masses of faithful celebrating behind us here, this is a major event in the continuing story of the young visionary who calls herself Jeza.'

As he opened his mouth to take his next breath, a huge cry welled up from the crowd. He turned to see Jeza raising her hands behind the transparent blast shield in what he assumed was a greeting to the crowd, or perhaps a plea for quiet.

The roar for Jeza was deafening now. It rose up from within the square and set off a chain reaction along the encircling hills of Jerusalem, blackened with the presence of five million witnesses to this supreme event. Jeza stretched her arms out to the crowd and finally, like the aftermath of an explosion, the cacophony rumbled to absolute stillness.

At length she lowered her arms and spoke out in a loud, authoritative voice that projected from the loudspeakers and echoed across the landscape of the Holy Land.

'In the name of the Father, I come to you!' she began in her well-known entrée. The crowd erupted again, but she forged on, not encouraging their interruption. This time her speech was in English only, as if she had too much to say to belabour her delivery. The crowd immediately quieted again.

'I have spoken to you of the liberation of the soul,' she called out in a commanding voice. 'I have spoken to you of the need to abolish your dependence on others for spiritual instruction that you may arrive at your own meaning of scripture. And I have warned you to leave your churches and temples and mosques and to abandon your religious leaders, as the direction they give you misleads you from God's truths.

'Today, I bring the Final Word that you might understand.' She paused and took a deep breath, as did the crowd.

'In the beginning, God prepared for you great blessedness,' she continued. 'A unity of heaven and earth and life eternal. It was God's plan, then, that all mankind should forever share in the glory and joys of paradise. But man was not ready for this great gift. In pride did mankind fail to recognize the sacredness of this unity. Of his own free will, man rejected God.

'And so came the fall from grace, when God divided life from death, and the earth from the heavens, and humanity from divinity. And man was banished to roam the wilderness, lost and alone.

'Yet even after the fall, God prepared a plan of redemption so that one day you should again partake completely in the wonder of His divine perfection. This plan did God set before you in the visions of the prophets. And in the messages of the Messiahs did God further reveal His intent:

'That man should learn and grow in the ways of the Lord, and work towards the day of the Final Judgment when the worthy might again be allowed to experience the unity of God in life. God left man with the promise that, at the Judgment, He would come again to reign with the righteous on earth. Until that time, only through death would man be reunited with the Almighty.

'But man has been slow to prepare himself for Judgment. He has been wayward in his journey towards righteousness. He has misunderstood and ignored the messengers of God. He has foundered and struggled in his understanding of God's intent.

'Thus have I come to you to carry forward the Word so that you may at last find your way back to the Father. For only in knowing the Word shall you close the abyss which separates you still.

'In the Word shall you recognize the enduring disharmony *that divides you from yourselves*! Hear the Word and understand. For, behold, I am the Anointed Messenger. I am the New Meaning. I am the final chapter of the New Testament . . .

'I am the Book of the Apotheosis!'

With this ringing declaration, the turbulent, brooding clouds above the prophetess were rent by an enormous shear of lightning. The multitudes dropped to the ground in abject terror as the earth reverberated from the deafening, apocalyptic peal. But Jeza was unfazed and unblinking.

'I speak to you of the great iniquities that prolong your fall from grace,' she called out to them as the thunder faded and the cries of alarm escalated. 'I speak of the ungodly separations of man from humanity!'

Collecting themselves and calming under the Messiah's continuing sermon, the masses regrouped and refocused.

'At the fall from grace,' she pressed on, 'God ordained the separation between Himself and mankind. Yet, after the fall, man took it upon himself to create further divisions, unnatural and prideful in their conception, and blasphemous in the eyes of the Lord. In these unnatural divisions, man first chose to set himself above his mate, separating himself from woman, whom God had created as equal and counterpart.

'Over the millennia, man has sought to lend sanction to this wrongful division by corrupting the very Word of God. In the Book of Genesis, chapters two and three, woman is portrayed as secondary in creation; subservient to Adam; the perpetrator of Original Sin; the seductress who tempts Adam to taste of the forbidden fruit, thereby bringing about mankind's fall from grace.

'I say to you, the debased meaning of this book is the foremost of the many corruptions of the scriptures. These passages were first given to you as a holy message of the general and of the symbolic. Yet has the true meaning been abandoned, reduced to the specific and the literal.

'Be it known to all that, in the true progression of life on this earth, it was the female form that came first. In the beginning, God created the primitive organisms. And in His design, He created them female one and all. Cell begetting cell, female begetting female.

It is only later in time that maleness emerges, male issuing from female.

'And it is only later in time that man, as the hunter and protector, surpasses woman in strength and prowess. And then deigns to wield his powers to hold dominion over woman. Yet, when woman attempts to offset lesser strength with greater wit, she is condemned for her cunning.

'In the writings of the Bible and in all ancient scriptures, the symbol of woman suffers from the biased pen of man. Over the ages, these false meanings have been used to sanctify the enslavement and abuse of woman. Throughout the millennia, man has denied woman access to her true spirituality and religious authority, holding her in spiritless submission out of arrogance and stubbornness and jealousy and insecurity.

'Look about you in your midst,' she called out, arcing a reproachful finger over the crowd. 'See among you the many women still bound by doctrine to conceal themselves behind long veils, their value discounted, their presence and importance diminished.'

There was an uneasy stirring in the crowd as the reclusive female subjects of Jeza's observations were made conspicuous.

'Look to the hypocrisies of the Western religions,' she continued. 'And look to the successor of the Apostle Peter of the Roman Church who refuses woman control of her body in propagation; restrains her status within her house of worship; denies her blessed fulfilment in the performance of the sacraments.

'Be it known that, through me, God shall deliver woman from her spiritual bonds. For now, through me, does God give to man a new law. A separate, new Commandment by which all men shall live.

'I say unto you, sons of Adam, hear and obey the Will of God:

'"*Thou shall honour woman as thy equal; and thou shall cherish her in unity with thy fellow man.*" (*Apotheosis 25:15*)

'Thus be the new Law of God to man in keeping with the others by which you are already bound.

'Therefore shall you return to the scriptures to right the inequities. Wherein you discover passages of abasement, do as I direct you: where you find male, write female; and where you find female, write male. And read again the Word in this New Way, woman learning confidence and man selflessness, in even measure.

'I command you, woman, throw off the spiritual shackles that encumber you. Put aside your veils and your false shame and rise up – not against man, but next to man, in balance.

'Yet I admonish you, woman, do not harbour in your heart bitterness nor resentment towards your counterpart. For these are empty passions that will divide your further. But rather, accept your partner and understand the forces of the ages within him, as he must strive to understand you. Together, work towards resolution and harmony whereby you and all your children may ascend towards godliness and the exaltation.'

As if exhaustion had overcome her, the Messiah seemed to wilt slightly, dropping her chin to her chest, placing her right fist against her heart, and lapsing into silence.

The masses took this opportunity to wonder and conjecture among themselves. Noting the absence of any referrals to an imminent call to Judgment, many of the faithful began to take heart in what they had just heard, hoping Jeza's message might conclude without incident.

But the prophetess was not quite through. Gathering her resolve once more, Jeza squared her shoulders, lifted her face, which appeared even paler than before, inhaled and began anew.

'Now I speak to you of the larger separation of God and man,' she cried out, jolting everyone to rapt attention once more. 'I speak to you of the last and greatest separation which distances man from himself.'

Her small hands gripped the edge of the lectern and her brow knitted with the effort of her convictions. 'In the Book of Genesis, chapter four,' she continued, 'is this separation revealed. Yet again has the figurative been corrupted to the particular, and the rightful meaning lost.

'This passage of scripture is the telling of Cain and Abel, an allegory in which is hidden the larger meaning of man's most damning secession. It is the story of the self-betrayal. Of man turning against his fellow man; violating his own humanity; denying his brother sanctity and life in an act of ultimate disloyalty.

'So abhorrent is this sin that God marked Cain and his kind with a sign so that all might know and reject them. Yet have you also corrupted this meaning. You look to find the mark of Cain in the physical dissimilarities of those who differ from you.

'But you are mistaken. The mark by which you shall know Cain is not a physical sign. It is not in the colour of his skin, nor in the features of his face, nor in a brand upon his body. The mark is in his actions. By his words and deeds shall you know him. *Enmity* is the mark of Cain. Hatred of fellow man. A mark that is to be found evident among all peoples, in all places. It is the enduring trait of evil that divides you most from yourselves. Until you remove this mark from you, you shall not achieve the unity to know God.

'For two millennia have you had this clear and certain message from the prophets who preceded me. Yet still you continue to use your differences as justification for inflicting sorrow, suffering and death upon your brother. Still you divide yourselves by race, by creed, by colour, by age, by station, by wealth, by possessions, by every and all differences you can distinguish among one another.'

Jeza pulled back and angled her head away slightly, biting her lower lip and glowering off to her side in building rage. Then she turned once more to her audience, unleashing her pent-up fury. 'And now do you dare mock God's Word and debase His messenger by abusing and destroying each other *in my name!*'

Through his binoculars, Feldman could readily perceive tears filling her eyes. This was the same tortured face, the same unbridled passion he recalled so indelibly from the Millennium Eve video of Jeza atop the ancient temple steps.

'Why do you not listen?' she cried, looked down, shook her head in dejection. 'In this I give you no new Commandment. For one who came before me has already given it to you. It is the Perfect Law: I say unto you, "Love your neighbour as you do yourself; and unto others do as you would have them do unto you." In this law, therefore, are contained all the other Commandments governing man's conduct towards man. In this law is the Word to guide you back to the unity you have lost.'

She paused again to stare deeply, intently, into the crowd. And even at this distance, Feldman thought he could detect a glimmer of hope restoring some of the resplendency to her anguished face.

'I look into your individual souls,' she spoke in a virtual whisper, 'and I see the remnants of the sweet innocence bequeathed each of you by God at your birth; a most perfect and precious treasure that now lies lost and forgotten, concealed beneath the sediments of injury and suspicion. Where once you looked with wonder and excitement upon the world about you and filled your hearts with hopefulness and elation, now you withdraw to build walls about you and gird your defences, distancing yourselves from your neighbours, removing yourselves from contact and understanding and commitment.

'But I say to you, you must reclaim the vision of your youth. You must each see again through the eyes of a child so that you may recognize in the face of your enemy the child that also lies beneath. You must learn again to see all men as God sees them. Even your enemy must you love and safeguard as if he were your cherished flesh and blood, for surely he is that to the Father.

'Do this in your own way, of your own free will. Do this with utter faith and trust, and with absolute love. Do this without resentment or regard for sacrifice or cost. Abandon your concerns to the Father and know that the Father, in turn, will nurture your souls and release unto you the bounties of heaven that He has long promised to bestow. This you can and must do, for even as you evolve in body, so also must you evolve in mind and soul to attain the balance that is unity.

'I say again, the great separation of man from God is the greater separation of man from himself. Therefore, you shall not be worthy of unity with God until you achieve the unity of your own spirit. Thus is the way by which you may lift yourselves up. Through God, you can yourselves become as God – the ultimate expression of your evolution. And only in this way shall you come to know God and achieve His final perfection: *the Apotheosis!*'

She paused again and the raging, roiling sky hesitated with her, holding its gusty winds in abeyance momentarily as she raised a warning finger.

'Heed my words, O Children of Israel!' she cried, her face assuming a more solemn countenance. 'For God's displeasure with you is great and His anger just. Even now the Great Trial is upon you, and none can halt what is to be: *the Tribulation comes, and the dark hour of your Dissolution is at hand!*'

'Dammit!' Feldman heard Hunter curse through his head-set.

Feldman, who'd taken a seat atop an air vent out of Hunter's camera range, lowered his field glasses and glanced back over his shoulder at his partner.

Hunter was pointing in the direction of the stage, irate. 'There's some late-arriving ass setting up his video equipment right in my line of sight! Look!'

Sure enough, about four buildings up, directly in their visual path, a cameraman was belatedly, hurriedly piecing together a tripod and video camera. Feldman trained his field glasses on him.

'Hell!' he called up to Hunter. 'He's one of ours! Look at his jacket!'

On the back of the interloper's coat was a bold WNN emblem.

'Can't you shoot over him?' Feldman suggested hopefully.

'Barely. I can get a shot, but he's definitely in the foreground. I'm calling Bollinger to see if they can shut him down. Sullivan must've gotten additional clearance, but a hell of a lot of good it does us now.'

While Hunter attempted unsuccessfully to reach the field crew, Feldman retrained his binoculars on the fiery orator. She looked as if she were drawing to a close now. And the audience was getting increasingly edgy and uncomfortable with this awareness.

The unrest was greatly exacerbated by a steady ingathering of low-hanging, green-black stormclouds undulating tempestuously overhead. Feldman was surprised that there'd been only limited lightning so far, but an outburst appeared imminent. This ugly celestial display was more than ample evidence to all gathered that the fulfilment of the Apocalypse was at hand.

Jeza raised a palm to silence the crowd, and then, sweeping her arm across the entire gathering in a giant benediction, she cried out in a loud voice, '*It is finished!*'

The Messiah stepped down and away from the podium and stood there, her head bowed solemnly, her arms held straight at her sides, her fists clenched as if she were summoning her resolve. After a lengthy pause, she then raised her forlorn eyes and moved out from behind the shield, walking very slowly and deliberately in a direct line towards the front of the platform. As she cleared the shield, the wind, coming at her back, caught her hair and garments, billowing them out around her in a wild display.

As she moved steadily towards the right front side of the stage,

Hunter smoothly panned his camera after her. But her path carried her directly behind the newly arrived WNN cameraman, completely obscuring his view.

His shot ruined, Hunter swore under his breath and focused his camera tightly on the meddler in an attempt to identify him. Instantaneously, he screamed into his microphone. 'Holy shit! Feldman! He's got a gun!'

Feldman, his ears throbbing in pain, frowned up at the crazy, flailing figure of his partner silhouetted against the backdrop of angry sky. Hunter was waving frantically at him from atop the roof, jabbering incoherently into Feldman's ringing head. Finally, the sounds coalesced into recognizable words.

'Goddamn, Feldman, *he's got a gun*. The cameraman – *look*!' He pointed with both arms.

Feldman spun and squinted towards the suspect.

'Feldman!' Hunter was fumbling to divest himself of his equipment. 'For God's sake, *get him*!'

At last, the message was conveyed. Feldman was off and sprinting across the rooftop in a mad frenzy, hurdling air ventilators and leaping frantically from level to level. Any concerns about decayed roofing were forgotten.

He could still hear Hunter in his headphones, urging him onward, 'Hurry Feldman! *Hurry!*'

In a matter of only seconds, Feldman had ascended what he thought was the last rooftop, and accelerated instantly to top speed. In his jarring, panicked sight, he spied the sniper looming before him. And suddenly realized, when it was too late, that the gunman was on an entirely different building, separated from Feldman by a yawning chasm of alleyway.

Suicidal though it appeared, Feldman had absolutely no hesitation. Reaching the end of his roof, with an irate surge of power he launched himself, his hands clawing the air, his legs bicycling. He soared high over the abyss, landing forcefully on top of the gunman with terrific impact. Everything went sprawling and Feldman spun to a dazed stop. Both men briefly lay motionless. Then, dizzily, Feldman raised himself on one elbow, shaking his head, working desperately to clear his vision.

He was aware that the sniper was also stirring, groaning and staggering to his feet in an attempt to escape. Still in a fog, Feldman lunged towards blurred legs tottering by. They were thick, strong legs, but he wrestled them down.

Now the anticipated rash of lightning split the sky in continuing, stunning flashes that whited out the entire panorama. Below the struggling duo, the assembly recoiled and cowered in unbounded fear, their screams nearly as deafening as the ensuing thunder.

His head clearing now, Feldman stared into the glaring dark eyes of a large, powerful man. A mask was drawn over the bottom half of his face, exposing only the fierce, snake-vile eyes of a merciless killer. The man swore at Feldman in what sounded like Italian, drew back and lashed out with a vicious kick to Feldman's shoulder. The newsman's glasses went flying and he fell back, wincing, but managed to roll his legs back under him and regain his feet.

So did his opponent. Feldman had unknowingly come between the sniper and his escape route, an exterior stairway leading down to the alley. The man, arms at the ready, approached menacingly. Unskilled in the martial arts, Feldman mimicked his foe, crouching and clenching his fists.

It had little of the desired effect, as the gunman, unintimidated, swung hard with a left cross, catching Feldman a glancing blow to his chin. What the reporter lacked in combat skills, he made up in anger and courage. As the arc of the blow turned the sniper past him, the reporter coupled his hands and brought them down hard on the back of the man's neck. Crying out in pain, the enraged gunman faltered, recovered, and threw himself bodily into Feldman, crashing him to the roof, knocking the wind from him.

Before Feldman could regain his breath, the man kicked him again, hard in the ribs, propelling the reporter to the edge of the building. As he was kicked once more in the stomach, Feldman's feet slid backward over the roof, and suddenly he was dangling by his fingertips, three storeys above the street.

The sniper stood over his helpless prey, a look of cruel triumph in his eyes. With the surly clouds swirling sickly green overhead and the wind whipping his oily, dark hair, the gunman slowly raised his boot to crush Feldman's tenuous grip.

But the gunman's look of victory instantly dissolved into glazed bewilderment as something heavy smashed against the side of his head, sending him reeling across the roof. A strong hand grabbed Feldman by the wrist, hauling him up to safety. It was Hunter, his broad face flushed, his breath coming in puffs.

'What kept you!' Feldman gasped.

Hunter gave his friend an intolerant glare. 'Oh, about thirty feet of open air, three storeys up! How the hell did you get across that!'

Feldman put a loving arm around his friend in exhausted relief. 'God knows, Hunter, God knows. Was I in time?'

'Shit, I don't know, I was too busy chasing after your kangaroo ass.'

They looked out worriedly over the plaza to find the stage a swarm of millenarians, police and militia. Jeza and Litti were nowhere in sight, and the helicopter was gone. Lightning and thunder were crashing overhead and large raindrops began to fall. The crowds in the plaza and beyond continued their screaming and panicking in complete disarray.

From across the roof of an adjacent building, a troop of Israeli military came storming up, brandishing weapons.

'Relax, guys,' Hunter called to them, 'my man here did your job for you!' The gunman was still out cold, a very nasty gash bleeding from the side of his head. A splintered camera tripod lay next to him.

As the military took the sniper into custody, a suspicious sergeant-major began to confront Hunter and Feldman. But a familiar voice intervened.

'It's okay, Manny, they're clean.'

Feldman recognized Corporal Lyman, their female escort from earlier that day.

Hunter smiled. 'I knew you'd be back.'

She ignored him and told Feldman they were free to go.

'What about Jeza?' Feldman asked. 'Is she okay?'

'I don't know,' the corporal answered. 'We couldn't see.'

It was pouring now, and a very large spike of lightning flashed near by. Corporal Lyman, her face streaming rivulets of water, motioned the two men to leave. 'Quick, off the roof. Lightning!' Neither man had to be warned twice. On their way, Hunter stooped quickly to snatch up Feldman's bent glasses.

As they found their way down a stairwell and out into the alley, Feldman gaped up in wonder at the airspace he'd so recently vaulted.

It had to be nearly thirty feet across. He shuddered and Hunter grabbed him to hurry him along. Feldman recoiled in pain, which Hunter failed to notice.

'Come on, we got to get my equipment before it's ruined,' he yelled into the driving wind.

'I'm not letting you go up there in this storm,' Feldman shouted back as he hobbled after his partner through the streets.

'I want to get the videotape!' Hunter yelled over his shoulder. 'I left the camera running!'

Ordinarily much fleeter than the big videographer, Feldman, hurting from the effects of his leap and the pummelling, could barely keep up. On reaching their building, neither man remembered that the door was locked from the inside. Without hesitation, Hunter smashed it open with a mighty foot.

Reaching the top of the stairs, despite Feldman's pleas, Hunter forced open the door and fought his way towards the elevated roof where he had left his camera. Feldman halted at the doorway, then braced himself to follow, ducking low to ward off lightning, praying they'd make it through.

The camera, however, was no longer visible. Whether it had been struck by a bolt or blown away, they couldn't be sure until Hunter scaled his way up the wall. Meanwhile, Feldman gathered the remaining gear and dumped it through the door into the dry corridor.

Hunter was soon by his side, holding a wet and damaged camera.

'The wind blew it over!' he yelled, pushing Feldman through the doorway. 'It's soaked. I sure as hell hope we got a usable tape in here.'

They shook as much water off things as they could, and Feldman tried to contact Bollinger over his cellular phone. He got nothing but static. Meanwhile Hunter began hooking the camera up to a small monitor. Miraculously, it appeared to be working, and he rewound the tape.

'What?' Feldman was amazed. 'You're going to try to review the tape right here?'

'Why not?' Hunter said. 'We're not going anywhere for a while, are we?'

The screen flickered, the image twisted, flipped, fought to balance itself, and then locked into a discernible picture. The image was Jeza speaking on the platform, so Hunter scanned the tape on fast forward until the point where she stepped away from the podium. He then reduced the speed to a crawl.

Once more, Jeza's immaculate image transfixed them. Gracefully, she began gliding towards the right front side of the stage, the camera following her. It was as if she were looking directly at them the entire time, her face composed, purposeful. The sniper started to come into frame now, a fuzzy blur in the bottom right foreground. Momentarily, Jeza's image was entirely obscured by the gunman, and Hunter's camera centred on the man's back, rolling into focus. The white letters 'WNN' showed plainly on his jacket. And then, haltingly, the sniper began to move away from his camera and the butt and scope of a rifle came clearly into view.

'See!' Hunter remarked. 'He's got the gun built right into the camera! Probably attached the scope and stock once he got it up on the roof.'

The image underwent a few spasms and then settled down again. 'Yeah,' Hunter indicated, 'here's where I left the camera running to chase after you.'

They moved in closer as the events continued to unfold.

'Look, you can see Jeza again!' Hunter exclaimed as a hazy image in white rose up in the right side of the frame, off in the distance. 'It looks like she's standing on something in the foreground of the stage. It's too out of focus to see.'

The sniper, however, was in perfect focus. In slow motion, he looked up from his sight, made a slight adjustment to something on his rifle, looked up again, and then hunkered back down behind the gun.

'What's she doing?' Hunter wanted to know as the cloudy image appeared to widen.

'She's stretching out her arms,' Feldman offered. 'Kind of like she's embracing the crowd, or giving a blessing or something.'

The sniper bore down on his scope.

'God, hurry, hurry!' Hunter was muttering to himself, as Feldman mouthed the same words.

Suddenly, from the upper right-hand corner, a blurred shoe emerged on the screen, and in the next few frames Feldman came barrelling down on to the gunman as the unfocused image of Jeza backed out of the picture.

Hunter began to cheer in jubilation, but Feldman placed a stifling hand on his friend's shoulder. 'Wait!' he commanded. 'Back it up a few frames and freeze it.'

Hunter did so, reversing the action until Feldman's legs were eliminated from the screen once again.

'Stop!' Feldman ordered. 'Hold it right there!' He squeezed Hunter's shoulder as if it were a remote control. 'Now, take it back and forth quickly between the two frames.'

Hunter saw what his friend was pointing at, and his face fell. There, out in front of the camera-gun, for the span of only one frame, was the briefest wisp of smoke before the wind immediately removed it.

'He got off a round,' Hunter confirmed in a hushed voice.

Advancing the tape, they could see the blurred image of the Messiah, arms still outstretched, receding from view.

'Jon, that doesn't mean she took a hit,' Hunter declared as Feldman slowly rolled back on his haunches away from the monitor, staring blankly at the floor.

While they both sat in silence, the video played on, showing bits and pieces of Feldman's battle as the fight drifted back and forth, in and out of view. Neither Hunter nor Feldman paid any heed until Hunter finally noticed the obscured image of a helicopter rising in the screen.

'Hey, Jon! It looks like maybe they got her out of there!'

Feldman took heart at the possibility. 'I've got to know, Hunter,' he said at last, attempting to get to his feet and falling back in pain on top of his friend.

'Whoa, pal!' Hunter saw the agony on his face. 'You okay?'

Feldman pulled up his trouser leg and a badly swollen ankle answered.

'Jesus! You hurtin' anywhere else?' He looked at Feldman's face closely for the first time and was surprised at the swelling jaw and blackening eye.

Feldman held up a puffy right hand. 'And my ribs and my shoulder.' He flinched as Hunter poked his enlarged ankle.

'You aren't goin' far on this. And look at it out there. All hell's breakin' loose.'

Gale-force winds and torrential rains were tearing at the window of the stairwell. The entire building was vibrating. The lightning was virtually incessant.

'Well,' Feldman said, 'I'm not going to stay here and get electrocuted. I've got to find out what happened to her.' He slid himself up the wall, this time making it to his feet.

Hunter shrugged, pulled the tape out of the player, stuck it inside his shirt and lent Feldman a hand.

Out in the storm, soaked to the skin, they hobbled along, arm in arm through the rain-whipped, deserted streets. Less than an hour earlier, this entire area had been standing room only. Now, eerily, the city was totally devoid of life.

'Well, if this *is* the end of the world,' Hunter shouted into Feldman's ear, 'looks like we're in for another Deluge!'

Feldman didn't respond, concentrating on his torturous progress as they made their way slowly out of the city, past the pitifully inadequate tent shelters of the millenarians, and steadily up the Mount of the Ascension to their villa.

At the door, an aghast Robert Filson beheld the spectacle of the two drenched newsmen. 'Jesus! We thought you guys were dead!'

Hunter lowered Feldman gently to the floor at the bottom of the stairs. From the rooms above, the voices of Cissy, Bollinger and the others came calling down.

'Oh my God, you guys look awful!' Cissy wailed, as Bollinger and Hunter assisted Feldman up the stairs. They settled the injured newsman on the couch, and Cissy returned with towels. She hurriedly began blotting Feldman dry, causing him to cry out in pain.

'Easy on him,' Hunter cautioned. 'He's pretty beat up.'

'Jeza!' Feldman shouted from behind the towel Cissy was dabbing over his face. 'What happened to Jeza?' He pulled the towel away and immediately located the TV, which was on and functioning despite the storm. Although not the best-quality picture, the news clip of Jeza was far clearer than the blurry image Feldman had watched on Hunter's monitor in the musty stairwell.

The room was deathly silent as the two reporters witnessed a full accounting of the episode they had only glimpsed before.

The video was from a different angle. As Hunter had surmised, upon reaching the edge of the platform, Jeza had stepped up on to what appeared to be a loudspeaker box. She stood there, elevated in front of the crowd for a few moments, and then stretched out her arms wide, holding them slightly above her shoulders. She was staring out beyond the crowd, unblinking in the wind, her face composed, the gnarled clouds swirling overhead. Her mouth formed several unintelligible words.

At the final moment, she smiled. Sweetly. Innocently. Her skin radiant, her eyes brilliant, deep blue and shining. The way Feldman would always remember her best.

And then the impact of the bullet drove her backward off her stand into the waiting arms of her disciples and the ever-faithful Cardinal Litti. Lying in their embrace, her eyes slowly closed and a bright red patch grew large upon her chest.

Hunter stood and left the room. Feldman hung his head and sobbed.

102

Mount of the Ascension, Jerusalem, Israel, *2.12 A.M., Saturday, 22 April 2000*

Feldman sat alone on the villa balcony, staring out into the still city. The rains had continued steadily until precisely midnight, then stopped suddenly, as if turned off by a switch. Now the clouds had dissipated and the stars emerged timidly, one by one, on a moonless, immaculate night.

For the moment, there were no throngs in the streets. No shouting. No violence. Ironically, it was peaceful and quiet in the Holy Land. The millenarians were all stilled, huddled in their tents and shelters, unable to get at each other due to the considerable flooding and oppressive mud.

And Feldman had never felt so despondent.

Thankfully, his associates displayed considerable respect for his feelings, granting him the distance he needed. Only now had his emotions quelled enough that he could reflect back on the TV coverage of the cowardly assassination.

Jeza had been evacuated promptly in the Israeli military helicopter and flown directly to Hadassah Hospital a short distance away in north Jerusalem. She was pronounced dead on arrival. The body was being held under tight security by a full division of the Israeli Defence Force. The Israeli Prime Minister, Eziah Ben-Miriam, had announced a day of mourning and called for a special session of the full Knesset as soon as the roads were passable. There would be hell to pay over the botched security job, it was said.

Feldman found appalling the incessant stories of mindless, vengeful rampages across the planet that marked Jeza's passing. Finally, succumbing to acute exhaustion and his painful injuries, he escaped into the kind mercy of sleep.

Hours later, Feldman woke to a clear, sunlit morning, the air washed clean by yesterday's torrent. Turning painfully to his right, he was surprised to find Hunter slouched in a chair next to him, sleeping. The villa woke early, and yawning cohorts strolled out from their various nests to enquire about the two newsmen's well-being.

Cissy brought out coffee and bakery goods, and checked Feldman's temperature with a cool, soothing hand. 'We've got to get you to a doctor this morning and have you looked at,' she said, trying to sound like a Jewish mom. 'You may have a broken bone or two.'

He smiled, nodded, and she placed his glasses on his nose, having remedied their crookedness.

The phone rang and Filson yelled out from the living room, 'Hey, Jon, feel like talking to someone from the Israeli Defence Force?'

Feldman pained himself attempting to set down his cream cheese bagel safely. 'Ouch! Damn!'

'Is that a yes?'

'*Yes!*'

Filson brought out a phone and Feldman recognized the voice of his mysterious acquaintance.

'Mr Feldman, I trust I'm not calling too early.'

Feldman detected a tenseness in the voice that had not been present before. 'No. I didn't get a chance to fully express my appreciation for your help yesterday.'

The voice hesitated for a moment and then responded simply, 'Yes.'

'What can I do for you, sir?' Feldman asked.

'I need to see you, Mr Feldman. This morning. Immediately, if possible.'

'Where are you?' Feldman enquired, unsure that he was fit to travel.

'This must remain absolutely confidential,' the voice insisted. 'There's considerable danger involved.'

'You have my word,' Feldman pledged.

'I'm at Hadassah Hospital. I'll send a helicopter for you. And I'd also like to invite your associate, Mr Hunter, if he'll be kind enough to bring his camera.'

'Can you tell me what this is all about?' Feldman asked, amazed to learn that this call was originating from behind the walls where the Messiah's body now rested.

'I'm sorry, I can't say anything more over the phone. All I can do is assure you that you'll find the trip here worthwhile.'

Putting aside his discomfort, Feldman didn't hesitate further. 'We can leave whenever you wish. We're located on the—'

'Yes. I know where you are.'

'Of course.' Feldman shook his head knowingly. 'We'll be ready.'

Hunter looked over with questions in his bloodshot eyes.

'It's confidential till we're in the air,' Feldman explained, 'but you and I are going for a little helicopter ride. And you'll need your equipment.'

Hunter grimaced and rolled out of his chair with a grunt.

The helicopter was hardly on the ground thirty seconds. From under a grey-and-blue flight helmet, one of the air crew looked familiar. It was Corporal Lyman, the female security guard from the Dung Gate. She nodded soberly to the two newsmen, and they nodded back.

Both men and their equipment were quickly hauled aboard and swept airborne. The hospital, located on the northern, more open side of the city, was but a short distance away. Feldman could see a thick crowd of millenarians already congregating outside the tall, stone perimeter walls. The rain and mud hadn't discouraged them for long. A thin row of Israeli guards kept them at bay.

'Look.' Hunter pointed inside the grounds to where patients and medical staff were being loaded aboard military transports. 'It looks like they're evacuating the hospital.' He duly recorded the scene on videotape.

The two newsmen were met on the roof heliport by four armed military, who carried Hunter's equipment for him as the cameraman assisted the ailing Feldman. Awaiting them inside was a trim, middle-aged man in the military uniform of an Israeli Defence Force commander. The officer was of medium height, with a tired, strained face, and troubled blue eyes.

He extended a right hand to Feldman, which Feldman had to grasp with his left. 'Commander David Lazzlo,' he introduced himself. 'A pleasure to meet you.' But there was no pleasure in his voice.

'Likewise,' Feldman returned. 'This is my associate, Breck Hunter.'

'Certainly.' Lazzlo took the big man's hand. 'Please come with me, gentlemen.'

Patiently allowing for Feldman's restrictive injuries, Lazzlo escorted them down a long hall to an office area, where he invited them inside, offering them a seat and closing the door.

'Can you tell me, Commander,' Feldman asked, 'is Cardinal Litti here, and is he okay?'

'Yes to both questions, Mr Feldman. And if you like, you'll be able to see him shortly. However, I'm afraid we don't have much time, and I really must press forward with several issues.'

'By all means,' Feldman assured him, settling stiffly into his chair. 'It's your show.'

Lazzlo looked grim. 'Very good. Gentlemen, let me just inform you from the outset that, for what I'm about to disclose, I could be shot. And if either of you are caught with the information I'm giving you, it could cost you your lives, as well.'

'Caught by who?' Hunter wanted to know.

'Let me explain this from the beginning and it will make much more sense to you,' Lazzlo responded. 'First, let me tell you that I'm a twelve-year veteran of the IDF, for the last four of which I was in charge of intelligence operations, until just recently.

'Let me also say that what I'm about to tell you will no doubt upset you greatly. It upsets *me* greatly, as there are many things in which I've been personally involved that I now know were terribly wrong. I only ask that you withhold judgment and hear me out completely.'

Hunter and Feldman looked at each other and agreed.

'I will confess to you up front that I was well aware of Defence Minister Tamin's secret Negev laboratory experiments. However, beyond the IDF high command and the scientists who worked at the institute, no one else knew the true nature of what went on there. Tamin had to make damned certain that neither the Ben-Miriam administration nor the Knesset were ever apprised of the facts. Experimental procedures, such as the neurochip implantations and intelligence infusions, are forbidden by the Israeli constitution unless sanctioned first by the Israeli Medical Board. Which, of course, these weren't.'

'Do you mind if I take notes, Commander?' Feldman requested, fumbling with a pen and notepad.

Noticing his bandaged right hand, the officer smiled dryly. 'It doesn't look like that's a viable option for you. You can record this if you wish. I'm no longer concerned with the consequences.'

'And why is that, Commander?' Feldman asked, as Hunter fired up his camera.

'You will learn soon enough.' Lazzlo kept control of the agenda. 'There's been much speculation regarding the actual cause of the Negev Institute's destruction. Let me tell you, as the chief investigating officer, I was unable to come up with a definitive answer.

'I can at least tell you what it wasn't. It was not sabotage, as some of the media have claimed. The destruction was caused by a projectile originating from beyond Israel's borders, due east. It wasn't a missile. At least not of any conventional design we've ever seen. There was no detectable propulsion system or warhead. We know that the projectile was a solid, superheated mass, approximately two feet in diameter at its widest, composed of forty per cent iron, six per cent nickel and fifty-four per cent silicates, weighing approximately one quarter of a ton.

'The most logical explanation we could arrive at is that the projectile was delivered by a super-cannon, such as Iraq had been developing at one time before your country kindly destroyed it.'

'What about the meteorite theory?' Hunter wanted to know.

'We could not rule that out,' Lazzlo admitted. 'The consensus at the Defence Ministry, however, was that the projectile was intentionally created to resemble a meteorite in its composition as a means of disguising its true design. Nevertheless, we've been unable to discover any trace of a cannon or other delivery system that would explain the phenomenon better than the meteorite theory. When we determined that the Negev explosion was, at worst, a random attack and not an invasion, we changed the focus of our concern.

'In light of the subject matter of the experiments, Shaul Tamin was desperate to prevent a leak. His priority became damage control. At the time, we believed all physical evidence and any compromising records had been destroyed in the explosion. All the scientists involved were dead – with the exception of Mrs Leveque, who we thought could be easily intimidated into silence, and a few lower-level lab assistants who knew little.

'Everything appeared so neatly contained, and then suddenly you broke with that survivor story. At first, Tamin resisted the idea that one of the test subjects might have escaped the blast. But later, when your Japanese witnesses positively identified Jeza as the survivor, he had no choice but to take action.

'Tamin viewed Jeza's survival as both a liability and an opportunity. While she posed a threat as living proof of his experiments, she also presented Tamin with the prospects of recovering the priceless Leveque microchips she carried inside her. The last chips of their kind in existence. Their value for medical applications, alone, was astronomical – military uses notwithstanding. Tamin intended to recover them, whatever it took.

'And then came your bombshell. Your *True Origins of the New Messiah* telecast. Tamin was furious! As you know, WNN continues to bear the consequences of airing *that* story.'

'We've had our suspicions,' Hunter acknowledged, sarcastically.

Lazzlo nodded contritely and moved on. 'After your report, the microchips were considered secondary. Tamin was desperate for his political survival and simply wanted Jeza out of the way. But of course, by that time she'd become too much an international icon.

'As you know, Tamin's outrageous proposal to take Jeza into "protective custody" was a disaster, causing demonstrations all over Israel and the world. The Ben-Miriam government was coming under intense political pressure from many influential Jews, both here and abroad, who subscribed to the belief of Jeza as Messiah. The numbers in the Knesset calling for Tamin's resignation were rising and his political base was dwindling.

'And then, miraculously, it looked as if our problems had vanished. Jeza fled the country and the threat appeared to be subsiding. The respite was short-lived, of course. After her fearful pronouncement at the second Mormon convocation, the flood of millenarian extremists began anew. Radicals on both sides of the Jeza issue poured into Jerusalem, anticipating the return of Jeza and/or Christ, and the fulfilment of the Judgment Day prophecies.

'Israel was haemorrhaging again. I and another in the high command decided to take drastic steps to defuse the nightmare Tamin had brought down upon our country. Covertly, we leaked the Leveque diary to the Vatican in the hope that the unholy truth about Jeza's microchip implants and secret military entanglements would discredit her to the world. Yet with her incredible performance at the Vatican, she was able easily to defeat our tactics.

'And then suddenly, with Israel already stretched beyond its limits, Jeza reappeared in Jerusalem. The IDF could not hope to deal with the emergency for long, despite assistance from many international agencies, including the UN. We knew something decisive had to be done. The attitude became "Jeza or Israel". We could no longer coexist.'

Feldman saw an apparent contradiction. 'I don't understand. Then why, when Jeza returned, did you provide her with such protection? With all the fierce anti-Jeza sentiment that had developed by that time, I would have thought Tamin and Goene would have opted simply to step back and let the Gogs destroy her. Instead, you surrounded the Old City with troops and protected her.'

'The situation was much more complicated than that,' Lazzlo explained. 'For one thing, if we hadn't taken action to control the opposing factions, the resulting civil war would have ravaged the Holy City and every sacred shrine within it. Religiously and politically, the IDF couldn't allow that to happen. But more importantly, we couldn't afford to have any *Israeli* involved in a violent act against Jeza. Our tiny nation could never have survived the world repercussions. So while Tamin concluded that Jeza had to be eliminated, the liquidation had to come from a politically acceptable source.'

Feldman's stomach soured at the image of the cold, calculating mentality behind this scheme. But his desire to know the entire truth overrode his revulsion.

'The solution arrived at,' Lazzlo continued, 'was to position the IDF as champions of peace. The IDF would protect the prophetess and begin separating the two warring factions, to the best of its abilities. But the idea was to be *selective* in protecting Jeza.

'The IDF would defend the Messiah from any and all sects that might pose political problems for Israel should Jeza come to harm at their hands. Meanwhile, the IDF – specifically, my former Department of Intelligence operations – would identify the sects and conspiracies that best suited our purposes. Ideally, those with Arabic origins. Once we selected the appropriate conspiracies, it was simply a matter of allowing one to succeed. Indeed, there were many ingenious plots uncovered.'

'I assume that's why you were so accommodating in allowing Jeza's Good Friday sermon – to facilitate an assassination attempt?'

'Exactly,' Lazzlo admitted. 'Even to the point of providing a blast shield and an evacuation helicopter so it would appear we had done everything reasonable to protect the Messiah. Good-faith efforts to reduce any internal or international recriminations.'

'You knew' – Feldman was restraining himself, but the veins in his neck betrayed his anger – 'that a professional sniper would have no problem striking Jeza when she finally emerged from behind the screen. That's why you were so careful to keep the media off the stage and to clear the rooftops for him.'

'And to enlist you and Mr Hunter as witnesses,' Lazzlo added.

Feldman was stunned at this revelation. 'We were a part of the plot?' he blurted out, incredulously.

The shame in Lazzlo's face was apparent. 'We went to the additional lengths of having the assassin furnished with a WNN jacket so you couldn't possibly miss him. We knew when and at what gate he would be entering the Old City. When he presented his falsified credentials, he was informed that it was mandatory that he wear a media identification jacket, and we supplied him with one of WNN's. He was even escorted to his position directly in front of you to ensure he'd be completely conspicuous.'

'So the gunman was a Muslim Gog?' Feldman wanted to know.

'No,' Lazzlo said. 'Although at first we were concentrating on several Arab extremist groups, in the final analysis we settled on a Mafia operation.'

'Mafia?' Feldman was puzzled.

'Yes. One of the plots we uncovered had direct Mafia ties. Probably a reprisal for Jeza's Secret Archives revelations about the Vatican–Finia CC scandal. At any rate, the Mafia's scheme proved simpler and more ingenious than any of the others. The camera-rifle was perfect. And we were able to assemble an extensive file on the sniper – a man with a record of success and a reputation for sharpshooting accuracy. His MO was always to fire several rounds to the upper torso in rapid succession, resulting in fatal wounds to the heart and lungs. That was perfect for our purposes because, of course, Tamin and Goene did not want the neurochips damaged, if at all possible.'

'And you wanted us to witness, if not record, all of this so that the gunman could be arrested, identified and convicted,' Feldman concluded for him. 'With an obvious trail and documented Mafia ties, the IDF would be entirely in the clear.'

'Precisely. Security personnel were positioned to arrest the assassin in short order. We had all his escape routes cut off. However, you nearly upset our plan single-handedly, Mr Feldman. No one anticipated your superhuman leaping abilities. If that first shot had not been perfect—'

Lazzlo paused and his face clouded as darkly as those of his companions.

Feldman had heard enough. Not bothering to mask his anguish and disgust, he rose stiffly to his feet. 'I'd like to see Jeza, one last time,' he requested.

'Certainly,' Lazzlo allowed. 'But I must caution you, we do not have much time. Immediately afterwards, if you will bear with me, we have just a few more things of some importance to discuss.'

Feldman agreed.

'While I make arrangements for your visit,' Lazzlo said, 'perhaps you'd care to see the Catholic cardinal?'

'Litti?' Feldman's face lightened slightly. 'Yes, please.'

Awaiting Feldman and Hunter in a room in another wing was a reasonably composed Cardinal Alphonse Litti. Feldman felt a surge of warmth on seeing him again.

Looking tired, but maintaining control, the cardinal hugged him like a long-lost sibling. Despite the pain, Feldman accepted the embrace without complaint.

'Jon, thank God! It's so good to see your face. But you're hurt.'

'It looks a lot worse than it really is, Alphonse,' Feldman replied. 'It's good to see you again, too.'

Litti repeated the ceremony with Hunter, who affectionately patted the cardinal's back.

'Things have turned out quite differently from what any of us would have anticipated, haven't they, my friends?' Litti said as he offered chairs to his visitors, holding his precarious emotions in check. 'Quite frankly, I just never thought God would allow this to happen to Her.'

'I know, Alphonse,' Feldman responded, admiring the clergyman's brave front. 'It just doesn't seem possible that she's gone.'

They were all three quiet for a moment, pursuing their independent memories.

'Of course,' Litti sighed, 'She knew this was to be, all along.'

Feldman looked at him.

'She prophesied this many times,' he continued. 'Only I misunderstood. I saw things from an entirely incorrect perspective, the way *I* wanted to see them. How very presumptuous of me. Such befalls one who dares anticipate the mysterious ways of the Lord!'

Hunter reacted to this, breaking a long silence. 'It certainly looked to me like she was aware of what was coming. It was as if she knew that gun was waiting for her and just walked right into it.'

'Yes,' Litti agreed. 'And of course in retrospect it's all very clear. She never intimated a joyful ending to her journey.'

Feldman dropped his head and his voice. 'Alphonse, was she – was it – quick?'

The cardinal clasped Feldman's good hand in both of his and squeezed it gently. His face took on the cast of a man at peace with his vision of God. In a hushed voice he said, 'It was very quick. She was dying as She fell into our arms. She lay there quietly, so incredibly beautiful. So brave, and so noble.'

Litti shut his eyes and tilted his head heavenward in spiritual transport. 'She simply closed Her eyes and the life left Her. I could actually feel it. As if a great weight were lifted from Her. There was a trace of a smile on Her lips, I thought, and She was gone.'

He paused for a long period and then opened his eyes. They were tearful.

Feldman's jaw was taut, his eyes seeing into the past. 'And then the Israelis came to your aid?'

Litti nodded. 'The Israelis were wonderful. They came right up and took Her from me and rushed us both into the helicopter and flew us directly here. The Messiah was in the emergency room in a matter of minutes. But of course it was too late.'

'Alphonse?' Feldman had one more thing he must know. 'Right before the end, as she stood there, she whispered something. Do you recall what her last words were?'

The cardinal looked thoughtful. 'I can't say, Jon. In fact, I don't actually recall Her saying anything after She left the podium.'

Feldman nodded, disappointed. 'Where is she now, Alphonse?'

'She's still here, Jon. They have Her in a separate vault in the morgue. There's some question as to the release of the body and who holds claim. They're attempting to contact Mrs Leveque, I understand. I was afraid they'd try to conduct an autopsy. Fortunately, Jewish law makes that very difficult, although in murder investigations they generally can receive permission from the rabbinical court. But I have no intention of allowing such a desecration. I've demanded temporary custody until tomorrow morning.'

Feldman knitted his brow. 'Why tomorrow morning, Cardinal?'

Litti stared at him as if the newsman were from another planet. 'Jon!' he chided. 'Tomorrow morning, Jeza will be restored to us. It's Easter Sunday. The Resurrection! You must have faith!'

Feldman squinted hard at the clergyman and nodded again. Lazzlo appeared at the door. Standing, Feldman bent towards the cardinal and compassionately gripped his arm. 'Alphonse, I'd like to pay my respects to Jeza now. Would you please excuse us for a short while?'

Litti looked searchingly into his friend's eyes. 'When you see Her, you will know. You must believe, Jon. You must believe!'

As they left, Feldman turned to Hunter and they exchanged sighs.

Proceeding at a respectfully slow pace, Commander Lazzlo led Hunter and the struggling Feldman along a corridor to a service elevator guarded by armed security personnel. He pressed the last button for the lowest level of the hospital.

As they descended, Feldman stared at the officer, a concern rising in his mind. 'I presume the plan was to retrieve the neurochips under the guise of an autopsy?'

'Yes.'

Feldman swallowed hard and asked, 'Has that been completed yet?'

'No,' Lazzlo answered. 'I've defied Tamin and Goene and blocked the post-mortem, which is why we have little time left. They consider me in mutiny. An armoured division is on its way as we speak.'

Exiting the elevator past a row of guards, travelling through several corridors past still more guards, they turned into a large morgue filled with columns of small metal doors along two facing walls.

Feldman felt ill at ease and his palms began to sweat. They advanced through this room into another corridor that ended in a single large metal door, very much resembling the entranceway to a bank vault.

Lazzlo paused ahead of them. 'Would you care to be alone with her for a few minutes, Mr Feldman?' he offered graciously.

Feldman looked to Hunter, who nodded solemnly, barely able to meet his friend's gaze.

Lazzlo pulled open the large door and Feldman hesitated, then entered. A cold wall of air met his face, and felt refreshing under the circumstances. The door closed behind him and he needed a moment for his eyes to adjust to the dim indirect lighting.

The room was completely bare save for a lone table at its centre and security cameras in opposing corners of the ceiling. The table was completely covered in a white sheet, under which was the unmistakable form of a small female. A dark stain showed conspicuously above the breast area.

Feldman approached slowly, with the heaviest of hearts. He halted next to the still form and bowed his head in prayer. After a minute, he summoned his courage and nervously, tenderly, drew back the sheet.

It was too much for him and the tears flowed freely from his unblinking eyes. He found her every bit as noble and precious as she had been in the full bloom of life. Yet the lustre was gone. Her skin no longer glowed, but now manifested the eternal grandeur of white marble.

He stared at her for a long time, his mind churning with images and memories. He realized he was overstaying his visitation, but he couldn't tear himself away, knowing this would be the last time he would ever be with her again. He ran his hands through her soft hair and then gently replaced the sheet.

Lazzlo and Hunter patiently awaited the reporter as he emerged from the room. Feldman had composed himself, but he could tell from the men's expressions that his face bore the evidence of his experience. He was not embarrassed.

Lazzlo gestured to Hunter. 'I've already asked Mr Hunter if he cared to view the remains, and he has declined. Perhaps you'd allow me a few more moments of your time, Mr Feldman?'

'I also have more questions to ask you,' Feldman replied, solemnly.

'Of course.'

'First, I want to know why you bothered to warn us about Goene's raid on WNN back in January.'

Lazzlo stared at the floor. 'While you may find this hard to accept, Mr Feldman, I was truly attempting to help you. Let me just say that I, and another within the IDF high command, were becoming increasingly concerned about the devastating effects Tamin's Negev experiment was having on our country. Our world!

'We could not oppose Tamin directly. He is a powerful man with many influential friends. We had to work secretly to counter him. His order for your arrest, for example, was simply a personal vendetta. All the IDF needed to do in response to your *True Origins* broadcast was to eject WNN from Israel. I tried to accomplish what was necessary without putting innocent people behind bars.'

'Again' – Feldman wagged his head – 'I don't understand. In trying to help us, you resist Tamin and Goene, but you willingly participate in this cowardly murder.'

Feldman was amazed at the rapid deterioration in Lazzlo's demeanour. Like a deflating balloon, he shrunk in both stature and poise. 'Please understand, Mr Feldman, that I do now recognize the full weight of my actions. And while I understand I can never make atonement for what I've done, what there's left for me to do, I am doing.'

The reporter almost felt sorry for the commander.

'Please also understand,' Lazzlo attempted to explain, 'that at the time, I truly believed our actions were in the best interests of Israel. I bore Jeza no personal malice. I merely thought her another of the countless deranged fanatics who have plagued this city for four millennia. Only this time, the fanatic happened to have a global following which threatened our nation, and perhaps our world.'

Feldman could no longer withhold his empathy, recognizing that in the past he himself had harboured precisely the same fears. The newsman placed his good hand on the officer's shoulder. 'If it's any consolation to you, Commander, I feel certain Jeza would forgive you. I think I knew her well enough to say that.'

This had a positive effect on Lazzlo, who searched the reporter's face carefully. 'That means more to me, Mr Feldman, than you can possibly know.' His composure returning, he gestured down the hallway. 'But come, I have something else to show you that I trust you'll want to make public. Mr Hunter, you'll need your camera.'

As they exited the room and headed back down the corridor to a side laboratory, Feldman had one last question to ask.

'What about those claims that Jeza was controlled by that neurotransmitter chip? Was someone communicating with her? Or exerting some sort of influence over her?'

'I'd like some satisfaction on that one, too,' Hunter added. 'The way she sacrificed herself to that gunman yesterday. She walked to the front of that stage and just offered herself up, like she was under someone's spell or in a trance or—'

'I'm about to answer that question for you now,' Lazzlo replied.

They entered a glass-doored room and an elderly gentleman in a white lab coat stood to greet them.

'Gentlemen,' Lazzlo introduced them, 'this is the head of forensic medicine here at Hadassah. Dr Goldberg, could I trouble you, please?'

As if he'd performed this duty several times before, the doctor moved spryly to a large screen on the wall, darkened the room and flipped a switch. Hunter turned on his camera to record the demonstration. Illuminated instantly on the screen was a transparent, multicoloured image of a full-sized human body, laid out horizontally on its side.

Feldman looked at the fascinating image, curious as to its relevance.

'Dr Goldberg,' Lazzlo asked, 'can you explain what we're looking at here?'

'Of course, Commander,' Goldberg responded, and moved in front of them to the centre of the screen. 'Gentlemen, what you're viewing is an Enhanced Position Emission Tomography of a human body. An E-PET scan, if you will.

'You'll notice that all internal organs of the body are completely visible.'

'We'll have to take your word on that one, Doctor.' Feldman made their lack of medical knowledge understood.

'Now,' the doctor began manipulating controls under the screen, 'we're advancing to the cranial area, and I'm magnifying the image and rotating it so that you can see all angles and aspects of the cerebellum. Can you see?'

Feldman and Hunter nodded dumbly, watching the revolving anatomy.

'Now, tell me,' the doctor said, like a professor leading a student, 'what do you notice?'

The two newsmen studied the image for a moment, baffled. 'I don't know, Doctor,' Feldman finally admitted. 'Am I supposed to see something unusual?'

'No,' the doctor answered. 'As a matter of fact, this is a completely normal brain in every way.' He flipped another dial at the bottom of the screen and then stepped away to allow a clearer view.

Magically, the rotating skull started to change, to fill in, to gain features, to become whole – a complete human head and face. A full-colour, three-dimensional image of a young woman with tousled black hair and alabaster skin.

Feldman gasped as the enormous implications began to sweep over him. He said nothing, his eyes orbiting the peaceful, sleeping face. Finally, in a soft voice, he asked, 'This – all of this – is Jeza?'

'Yes,' Lazzlo said, 'down to the minutest detail. Even to the whorls of her fingerprints. This procedure was undertaken last evening as a preliminary to an autopsy.'

The doctor reversed the image sequence to expose, once again, the internal aspects of the cranium. 'As you can see,' he pointed out with a pen, 'there are no internal microchips. No wires. No electrodes. No artificial anything. Simply a natural, normal, healthy human brain.'

'No,' Lazzlo corrected him. 'Not exactly human.'

Hunter whispered to himself, 'I'll be damned!'

Staggered, unable to take his eyes off the fantastic image, Feldman had to sit down.

The doctor continued his demonstration, scanning down the body to reveal the internal organs of the chest cavity. 'You'll notice here,' he indicated with his pen, 'a single invasive trauma of the cardiac muscle . . .'

But Feldman was no longer paying attention. He was trembling inside. Aloud, to himself, he played out his thoughts. 'Then Jeza *wasn't* the main test subject of the Negev laboratory, after all. She wasn't even an enhanced subject. She was the control. The unaltered daughter. The pure, untouched one. Which means . . . that all di Concerci's arguments are false. Which means . . . that none of Jeza's knowledge or abilities came from the infusion process, or telecommunications with computers, or any of that. Which means—'

His mind reeled and he lapsed into virtual catatonia. He did not begin to recover until Lazzlo, who'd left the room momentarily, returned to thrust a sealed envelope into his hands.

'Here,' Lazzlo said. 'Here's everything you'll need to indict the entire IDF command – Tamin, Goene, me, all of us. These are intelligence documents and internal memos exposing it all – the corruptions, the conspiracies, the cover-ups. And I've also included a full CD disk of the Messiah's E-PET scan for complete authentication of what you've just seen.

'Now, I'm afraid it's time for you both to leave. Goene has called on his troops to take this hospital and rid Israel of a traitor. An advance of helicopters from the Negev base is due here any minute, and I can assure you, they'll stop at nothing to acquire Jeza's body.

'But of greater concern,' he warned, 'even larger numbers of anti-Jeza forces are approaching Jerusalem from the north. They've been met by our northern army division several miles outside the city and a bloody battle is under way as we speak. I don't expect General Zerim can hold them long, and certainly this hospital will be their next target.'

The dazed look in Feldman's eyes changed to one of sympathy for the doomed officer. 'What are you going to do now, Commander?'

Lazzlo paused and calmly faced the reporter. 'I'm going to stay here, Mr Feldman,' he said evenly, 'and defend my Messiah.'

Hunter placed a hand on the officer's back. 'What's the point? That sounds like suicide. Why not evacuate and take Jeza's body with you in the helicopter? We can get asylum for you somewhere, I'm certain.'

'You don't understand,' Lazzlo replied, his face hardening. 'You see, I – *I personally* – am largely responsible for what happened yesterday. The commission of the most deplorable crime in two thousand years.

I conspired in the death of my Messiah. The most grievous sin against God. The sin of all sins.

'With all my heart I must believe that Jeza will rise tomorrow, here in Jerusalem, as scripture foretells. And I must also believe that I will be given the opportunity to kneel before Her and plead personally for Her forgiveness. Protecting the sacred temple of Her body is now the only hope my eternal soul has left. *I cannot leave!*'

Feldman inhaled deeply. 'I wish you well, then, Commander.' He extended his good hand. 'You have my word I'll air this information as quickly as possible.'

'Thank you, Mr Feldman.' Lazzlo gripped the reporter's hand with both of his. 'And you too, Mr Hunter.' He repeated the gesture with the videographer.

'Commander—' Feldman paused on his way to the door. 'I have to take Cardinal Litti with me.'

'By all means, do,' Lazzlo urged them. 'As you've no doubt noticed, we've almost completed the evacuation of the hospital, but the cardinal has refused to leave. Take him, but hurry. You *must* see to it that the information you carry, especially the PET scan, is made public immediately. Perhaps the truth can stop the madness.'

With that, Lazzlo left the reporters to resume his defence preparations. Feldman stashed the precious package of evidence inside his shirt and a guard escorted them to the room where they had left Cardinal Litti. They found him on his knees, in prayer, a small snapshot of the Messiah on the chair in front of him.

'Alphonse,' Feldman called to him, 'we're leaving.'

The cardinal placed a hand on the chair and rose slowly to his feet. 'Will you return at dawn to join me for the Resurrection?' he asked, bestowing a smile of perfect tranquillity.

'No, Alphonse, you don't understand.' Feldman grabbed him by the shoulder. '*We're* going. All of us. You, me, Hunter. Two crazed armies are converging on this place and all hell is about to break loose. Let's go while we can!'

Litti shook his head steadfastly. 'No, Jon. It's you who don't understand. There is no safer place to be. I tried to tell Commander Lazzlo that he's wasting his efforts with his defence measures. Do you really think God would let anyone interfere with the culmination of His Great Purpose?'

As if to underscore Feldman's argument, they suddenly heard the alarming report of automatic weapon fire outside, and then the sound of a small explosion. 'Alphonse,' Feldman pleaded, leaning close and looking hard into the clergyman's eyes, 'I don't know what God's intentions are, but we can't wait any longer. You have to leave with us. *Now!*'

The cardinal's response was a look of absolute conviction.

'Gentlemen!' their guard yelled from the doorway. 'We must go!'

Hunter grabbed Feldman's biceps. 'Come on, man, you're wasting your time. If we don't get out of here now, that package will never see the light of day.'

Saddened and frustrated, Feldman encircled the portly cardinal with his one arm and hugged him tightly. 'God protect you,' he said.

'And God protect you, my good friend,' the cardinal replied.

Feldman released him and exited the room, making his way cumbersomely down the hall with Hunter's support. By the time they reached the roof, the two newsmen realized they'd missed their window of opportunity. The air was acrid with smoke. Bullets were zinging everywhere around them. Despite this, the helicopter remained at high throttle, its pilot faithfully awaiting his passengers, the unwavering Corporal Lyman crouching alone inside the doorway, fiercely waving them on.

Upon spotting the reporters, the pilot revved the engine to full speed, the two men hurled themselves through the open door, the helicopter lifted off and tilted forward, swung ninety degrees around, and soared out quickly over the rear of the hospital. The pilot purposefully held the craft low to avoid offering a silhouetted target against the bright blue morning sky, but it was of little help. The chopper quickly took several hits to the undercarriage, pitched sharply to the right, and then was immediately jarred by a heavy impact just above the right side of the cockpit. Black smoke began pouring into the cabin.

There was a flurry of Hebrew from the pilot and Lyman screamed repeatedly to Feldman and Hunter to fasten their seat belts, which they'd yet to locate. In the thick smoke and turbulence, it was a futile effort. The chopper was vibrating and lurching badly, yawing alarmingly to the right. Feldman slid against the bulkhead and felt the strong hand of Hunter seize him by the arm.

He knew they were going down.

103

A deserted field, Northern Jerusalem,
9.22 A.M., Saturday, 22 April 2000

Feldman didn't remember the crash. As he came to, sputtering and coughing, he felt a cold, thick wetness on his face, partially obstructing his breathing. When he was able to clear his head and eyes, he realized he was lying on his side in a thick gruel of mud. Looking back over his shoulder, he spied the crumpled, smoking ruins of the helicopter, its tail elevated in the air, its rear blades still spinning. The crack-up could have been worse. There was no fire. The leaking fuel he smelled had not yet ignited.

Somehow he had been thrown clear upon impact, landing about twenty-five feet from the wreckage in a deep bed of mud left over from the heavy rains. As his reasoning came back to him, he was gripped with a frantic concern for Hunter and the two crew members. Crawling in the muck, oblivious to his injuries, he slogged his way back to the helicopter, calling out for survivors.

A large foot and a small groan emerged from a cavity beneath the shattered fuselage. Sitting down in the quagmire, Feldman placed his feet against the frame, lodged the protruding foot under his left armpit, grasped the calf with his left hand and pushed hard with his legs. The body budged towards him, slightly. Feldman worked his grip up to the knee, and with a few more such efforts, the bloodied form and face of Hunter appeared.

Feldman sucked the mud from a finger and pulled open one of Hunter's closed eyelids. There was movement underneath.

'Breck!' he called out. 'Can you hear me?'

The videographer growled in pain.

'Come on, Breck, wake up. I've got to get you away from this thing before it blows, and I need your help.' In the mud, and with his pre-existing injuries – as well as any new, undiscovered ones he may have just incurred – Feldman was incapable of enough leverage to move the big man any further.

Hunter's eyes finally peeked open and he grimaced up at his friend. 'Shit!' he said.

'Are you hurt bad? Can you move?'

'My right side is killing me, but if you can roll me over on my left, I think I can side-stroke on outta here,' he replied with a scrunched expression. 'How about the others?'

Feldman pulled himself up the fuselage to a standing position and looked around. The aircraft had fallen in a sparsely populated residential part of the city, in an open area approximately one or two kilometres north of the hospital. The newsman could see in the distance several people on foot labouring to reach them through the soggy field. Apparently the pilot had been attempting a forced landing here, but was unable to maintain control. The front of the aircraft was completely crushed and buried in the mud. It was obvious to Feldman that the pilot could not have survived.

Working his slippery way hand over hand around the upright tail section, he found an open door on the opposite side of the wreck. Peering inside, through the shadow and lingering smoke, he spied the back of a blue-and-grey flight helmet with dark hair spilling out beneath. He climbed through the doorway and slid down the deck to the still form of Corporal Lyman.

Carefully he attempted to work his good left arm underneath her when he felt the mass of warm blood. Leaning over to get a better look at her, he recoiled in horror to find the far side of her helmet crushed like an eggshell. He pulled back in shock, a creeping nausea pervading him, and let the limp body slip slowly from his grasp.

Outside, voices were audible. Feldman had no time to linger over his emotions, he had Hunter to consider. As he clambered in agony back up the side of the deck to look out of the door, a scraggly, bearded face confronted him with a pistol.

'What is this?' it said, in thickly accented German.

Feldman's heart sank. At least, he realized, the man was not an Israeli soldier. Remembering the important information he carried, he pressed his injured hand against his stomach. The package was still there, thank God, if not ruined by the crash and wetness.

'Please, I'm unarmed,' Feldman said.

'Gogormagog?' the guerrilla asked.

'What?' Feldman did not understand German.

'Are you Gog or Magog?' The question came slower. 'Are you for Jeza or against Her?'

Feldman finally comprehended. But not knowing which hands he'd fallen into, he hedged. 'Uh, I'm uh, I'm a reporter. Jon Feldman, WNN News,' he said, and wiped the mud from an ID card he retrieved from his vest pocket.

The eyes of the militant suddenly widened, and the man blurted out cheerily, 'Jon Feldman! My good friend Jon Feldman! I did not recognize you with the mud.'

Assisting the newsman from the wreckage, the German called out to his colleagues. 'Ya! Look, we have my good friend Jon Feldman, from World News Network!'

'My associate is injured,' Feldman appealed to his captor. 'Please, help us!'

'Ya, Jon! You remember me?' the strange man asked. 'Friedrich Vilhousen, from Hamburg! We meet at the Negev laboratory the night of God's Hammer!'

Unsure, Feldman was not going to jeopardize his good fortune. 'Of course. Am I glad to see you! We were just shot down by the Israelis. You've got to help us!'

'Ya! We help you. Come.'

Feldman was glad to see that Hunter had wriggled his way to a safer distance and was now sitting up, conversing with two of Vilhousen's three men.

'So which are you, Gog or Magog?' Feldman asked apprehensively as the German assisted him with a supporting shoulder.

'Magog, of course!' came the welcome reply. 'We are here for the Armageddon! The Gogs are coming to attack us and take Jeza's body. They think we are going to fake the Resurrection by stealing her away. But we will defeat them as the Bible predicts.'

Although there was a little colour in Hunter's face now, it was obvious he'd taken a nasty hit. At the very least, he had serious gashes on his right thigh and temple which the Magogs were attempting to bandage.

'Can you help us get back to our headquarters?' Feldman pleaded.

'We have some extremely important news about the Messiah that we have to get out of here.'

'Ya, ya, but look. We have trouble.'

Feldman swung around, peering up into the air where Vilhousen was pointing. Swooping over the buildings behind them and heading directly towards the crash site was an Israeli military helicopter.

Hunter saw it, too. 'Damn, Feldman. Get the hell out of here!'

Feldman looked to his friend, then back at the charging helicopter, then to his friend once more. 'No, I'm not leaving you. Not that I could make it anyway. Not in this mud, not in my condition.'

Over Hunter's protests, Feldman unbuttoned his shirt and extracted the limp package. He grabbed Vilhousen's arm hard with his right hand, despite the pain.

'Friedrich, listen to me,' he implored, his eyes boring into the German's. 'This package is a message to the world about Jeza. *An extremely important message!* You *must* see that it's delivered to WNN, to Nigel Sullivan at 419-A Mount of the Ascension, *immediately*! Do you understand? *Everything* depends on this! Do you understand?'

Dumbfounded, Vilhousen accepted the package, nodding, his eyes wide with the import of his responsibility.

Reaching up with discomfort, Hunter also waved a videotape at the perplexed German. 'Here, I saved this. You might as well take it, too.'

'Go!' Feldman shouted, sending the German on his way with a hard push. 'Hurry, *fast*! 419-A Mount of the Ascension. Nigel Sullivan. Don't fail us. Don't fail Jeza! *Hurry!*'

Vilhousen and his men took off arduously through the slime as the chopper circled once and then closed in.

'Damn it, Jon!' Hunter yelled at his friend. 'You can't entrust that information to them. You've got to go, too!'

Feldman trudged slowly and painfully over to his partner. 'Sorry, guy, but I can barely walk under the best of circumstances. I'd never make it in this muck.' He shaded his eyes against the sun and the oncoming gunship, concern growing on his face. 'And I'm not so sure Vilhousen will, either.'

At the sight of the fleeing Magogs, the helicopter hovered indecisively between investigating the downed craft and chasing the escaping men. Suddenly it pivoted towards Vilhousen's band and a high-calibre gun erupted from the undercarriage, discharging a volley of bullets and kicking up sprays of mud around the scattering guerrillas. One of the shots found its mark and a man fell headlong into the mire.

Frantically, Feldman began waving his arms at the helicopter and pointing at the wreckage.

'The bastards!' Hunter yelled. 'Did they get our messenger?'

'No,' Feldman detected from his higher vantage point, holding his breath. 'Not yet!'

But the helicopter finally decided against pursuit and swung back around to settle in alongside the two newsmen. Feldman flopped back down next to Hunter.

'How bad are you, Breck?' he asked.

'I don't know. I've got triple vision, my ears are ringin' like an alarm clock, and my leg's got a crater in it. Not too bad, I guess.'

Three Israeli military had reached them now, pointing rifles in their faces. 'You will come with us,' one said. It took four men to lug the cumbersome Hunter into the helicopter's bay. Two other Israelis carefully inspected the downed wreck, shook their heads back at their comrades, and then returned to the chopper for take-off.

Feldman and Hunter were stripped of their IDs and not allowed to talk as they were flown directly to an IDF command centre across Jerusalem on the western side of the city. They were shoved roughly into a large barracks and hauled up before an office door where, despite their condition, they were made to wait, precariously supporting one another.

Finally, the door to the office opened and the prisoners were admitted into the malevolent presence of their old nemesis, Senior General Alleza Goene himself. Seated next to Goene in a red-leather wing chair was another man. A short, slightly heavy-set individual, perhaps sixty years of age, with neatly combed grey hair. He was dressed in an expensive business suit. Although they'd never met, Feldman recognized him instantly.

The guards held the two reporters firmly at attention by their upper arms.

'Well!' Goene looked up from his conversation, not unpleasantly surprised at the newsmen's bedraggled appearance. 'We're not looking so high and mighty today, now are we?' he sneered.

Feldman and Hunter glared back silently.

Goene gestured to the man next to him. 'Gentlemen, allow me
to introduce you to Israel's esteemed minister of defence, Shaul
Tamin.'

Tamin did not bother to rise. He sized up the newsmen with a
methodical, imperious stare, scrutinizing them through cold eyes
under heavy lids.

'Your ambition has no conscience, does it, gentlemen?' Tamin
remarked, speaking in a resonant voice with little accent.

The reporters eyed him warily.

'Thanks to your illustrious reporting,' he continued, 'Israel is about
to confront Armageddon. I trust you're proud of your work?'

'We're just a couple of journalists trying to do our jobs, Tamin,'
Feldman replied dryly.

'Journalists?' The minister sniffed. 'Ah, is that how you characterize
yourselves? Endangering Israel's national security; inciting riots and
rebellion; creating a worldwide climate of fear and despair – all in
the name of good journalism! I see. What consummate professionals
you are.'

Hunter shook himself free of his guard. 'And I suppose you two
are just a couple of loyal patriots, aren't you? Plotting the gutless
murder of a defenceless woman, all in the name of good politics.
What consummate *bastards* you are!'

Feldman grabbed his friend's arm in warning.

Goene's self-satisfied leer evaporated, but Tamin betrayed nothing.

'Well,' the minister said after a moment's pause, 'let us see how well
your investigative talents have served you today.' He stood, smoothed
his suit jacket and walked around to the front of the desk, perching
himself lightly on the edge, facing the mud-caked reporters.

'I have but a few quick questions of you relevant to the security
of the State of Israel,' he stated matter-of-factly. 'If you will address
these issues completely and honestly, I'll have your injuries attended
to and see to your immediate release. You do look in pain.' He sounded
genuinely concerned.

Hunter stood a little straighter and folded his arms.

'Now,' Tamin demanded, 'I'd first like to know what you were both
doing at Hadassah Hospital.'

'Visiting a sick friend,' Hunter responded.

Goene pushed his chair back from his desk. 'You are not in the safety of your newsroom now, my smartass friend!' he growled, but Tamin held up a palm to the general and Goene restrained himself.

'I'll ask you once more,' the minister said calmly. 'Why were you at Hadassah?'

'You see,' Hunter began again, and Feldman elbowed him in the side, to no avail, 'I was thinkin' about gettin' myself a circumcision so's I'd have something to remember Goene by—'

Goene's face turned red with rage and he signalled a guard, who immediately struck Hunter in the base of the spine with the butt of his gun. The videographer went down hard, and when Feldman attempted to assist him, his guard grabbed him by his injured arm and forced him upright.

Feldman shouted at Goene with loathing, 'You cowardly son of a bitch!'

'Your turn.' Goene pointed to Feldman, and Feldman's guard raised his rifle, threateningly.

From between clenched teeth, Hunter spared his friend. 'We went to view Jeza's remains.'

'Hunter, *no!*' Feldman hissed.

'We've got nothing to gain from hiding the truth,' Hunter groaned. 'Just tell them!'

Goene relaxed a bit in his chair and Tamin nodded his head with satisfaction, staring down at Hunter with a distant, detached expression.

'Did Commander Lazzlo invite you?' the minister asked.

'Yes,' Feldman answered, reluctantly taking over.

'And he flew you in by helicopter early this morning?' Tamin did not look at Feldman, but continued to stare at the crumpled Hunter with the blank, uninterested face of a bureaucrat.

'Yes.'

'Did you view the remains?'

'Yes.'

'And at that time, had the body been autopsied?'

'No.'

'How do you know?'

'Because, as I said, I viewed the body.'

'That is not definitive,' Tamin declared flatly.

'And I viewed an enhanced PET scan of her.'

This seemed to have Tamin's full attention. He turned to Feldman with a trace of emotion creeping into his voice. 'That's a preliminary to an autopsy. Then a post-mortem *was* performed!'

'No. They halted the process after the scan.'

Tamin looked shrewdly at the newsman. 'They halted the process? Why?'

'Because they discovered from the scan that there were no microchips in her brain after all.'

Goene leaped to his feet, enraged. '*You lie!*' He motioned again to the guard and Feldman went down with an excruciating blow to his lower back. His entire body was racked as if a jolt of electricity had passed through it.

From somewhere beyond the periphery of his agony, he could hear Hunter swearing profusely. Tamin chastised Goene. 'That's enough, General, I'll handle this in my own fashion first.'

As the waves of pain subsided, Feldman detected someone's presence near by. It was Tamin, kneeling down close to his face.

'Mr Feldman, I apologize about that. I don't believe the general thinks you're being completely honest with me.'

Grimacing, Feldman spat back, 'I'm just telling you that I saw nothing unusual in the scan. I'm no physician!'

'Of course. So you say you saw the internal images of her brain, and there were no indications of any microcircuitry or wiring?'

'That's right,' Feldman exhaled, gingerly testing his limbs, which felt numb and tingly.

'How do you know the microchips hadn't already been removed, or that you weren't viewing the brain of some other body?'

Feldman pulled himself up on one elbow and glowered at the minister with restrained hatred. 'Because the scan was comprehensive. It was seamless. It covered the entire body from all sides and angles in three dimensions. And it showed every internal organ, taking us inside the body, layer by layer, to view everything at whatever magnification we chose. Without question, it was Jeza's body I saw.'

'But how can you be certain the chips hadn't already been removed?'

'I got a close-up view of her face and skull. At the very least, I would have seen incisions. She was completely normal. No incisions, no chips. Nothing!'

Tamin rose to his feet, reflecting on this, and walked back to lean against the desk again.

'He's lying!' Goene cried. 'They're in collusion with Lazzlo. I'm certain it was Lazzlo who tipped them off about the January raid. And most certainly it was Lazzlo who leaked the diary to the Vatican. He's been conspiring against us all along, playing both sides of the street. And now the traitor has the chips, and these bastards are in on it with him!'

As if armed with a new thought, Tamin walked back to stand over the two prostrate men.

'Did Commander Lazzlo give you anything that you took with you from the hospital?'

'No,' Feldman lied.

Tamin bent towards him, his hands on his knees. 'Think carefully,' he cautioned. 'Did anyone give you a package of any kind? An envelope? A magazine? Anything?'

'Nothing!' Feldman asserted.

'Do you know the whereabouts of the microchips?'

'I'm telling you,' Feldman protested, 'there are no microchips!'

Tamin straightened once more and turned away towards the door. 'Yes. And I suppose Jeza's ability to speak a hundred different languages and her vast wealth of knowledge are simply manifestations of her divinity? Correct?'

Feldman said nothing.

Goene moved to Tamin's side. 'We're checking out the other casualties from the crash and the helicopter itself right now.'

The minister nodded. 'Very good, General. The prisoners are yours. If they're concealing the chips, I want them found. Do whatever is necessary.'

Tamin left and Goene turned towards his prisoners with an expression of absolute supremacy. He grinned sinisterly as he addressed his guards. 'Take them below. Strip them completely and have every square millimetre of their clothing unravelled thread by thread. Take apart their shoes, their watches, everything. Search their bodies. Every crevice, every orifice. I want them under constant guard. Feed them emetics and run their vomit through a sieve. Give them laxatives and check every bowel movement to the last particle for the next twelve hours. Whether or not you find the chips by dawn tomorrow, take them into the courtyard and shoot them as spies. Then incinerate their corpses. And I expect complete discretion!'

He walked over, dropped to a squatting position and leaned low above the two broken, disbelieving men. His mouth spread wide in a brutish sneer. 'In the final analysis, gentlemen, I should think that the sword is, in fact, mightier than the pen. Wouldn't you agree?'

104

Dyan IDF military base, Jerusalem, Israel,
4.13 A.M., Sunday, 23 April 2000

Feldman and Hunter sat naked and cold on the wet floor of their cell, clutching their knees tightly, trying to maintain body warmth. It had been a long, disgustingly unpleasant and humiliating night. In addition to their untreated wounds, both men were suffering from extreme dehydration as a result of their repeated purgings.

Even in this lower-level, windowless dungeon, they could hear the sounds of military engagement emanating from outside. The heavy prattle of gunshots had been incessant, all night long.

'How are you holding up, Breck?' Feldman called out from between his knees.

No answer.

He turned to observe his cellmate, who was hunkered next to him in a tight, brooding ball. 'Come on, guy,' he encouraged, 'you gotta snap out of it. Why don't you channel your anger into helping me find a way to get out of here?'

'Cause we ain't gettin' outta here, man,' came the snarling answer. 'At least not alive we're not.'

'That's the spirit!' Feldman berated him.

'Goddammit!' Hunter's pent-up rage broke loose. 'I swear to God I'd give my immortal soul for just five minutes with that goddamned son of a bitch Goene!'

Feldman sighed, hard pressed to offer any meaningful solace under the circumstances. 'Come on, man, it isn't worth—'

'Goddamn that son of a bitch!' Hunter roared again, pounding the cell floor with a powerful fist. 'I swear to God, Jon, if we get out of this, I'll hunt that bastard down if it takes me to the bowels of hell. And so help me God, I'll kill him!' He looked up at God through the ceiling of the cell. 'Just give me one chance – that's all I ask – and you can have my damned soul. Just one chance!'

Hunter's raving had attracted the attention of one of the guards. 'Shut up i⅃ there or I'll turn a hose on you!' he snapped.

'Please,' Feldman pleaded, 'can somebody tell us what time it is?'

'A quarter to five,' the guard called back.

Sunrise – and the firing squad – were rapidly nearing. Once more, Feldman tried to penetrate the guards' resolve. 'Any chance we could get some hot coffee and a blanket now? You know we don't have anything hidden on our bodies. And there's sure as hell nothing left inside us any more!'

The two guards, who were seated at a table outside the cell, exchanged looks. There was a rumbling of conversation and a couple of old, dirty linen sheets were tossed into the cell. A few moments later, two cups of steaming brew were slid through the bars. Swaddled in their sheets, the two men shuffled stiff-leggedly over and bolted down the coffee, gratefully thanking their keepers and begging for more. Their pleas were granted, along with two hard rolls. Their last requests, Feldman presumed.

His musings were quickly answered. As they finished their meal, the moment they'd been dreading arrived: multiple footsteps hurrying down the stone stairs, keys jangling. The sounds of their approaching executions.

105

Hadassah Hospital, Jerusalem, Israel,
4.47 A.M., Sunday, 23 April 2000

Cardinal Litti knelt on the hard, cold concrete floor outside the vault where Jeza's body lay in state. Like matching bookends on either side of the closed vault door, two immobile, armed Israeli sentries were posted to ensure that her body remained undisturbed through the long night.

In response to Litti's incessant begging, Commander Lazzlo had finally relented and allowed the cardinal access to the restricted area. Litti had been here since dusk, in prayerful observance, faithfully awaiting the anticipated Resurrection. The long vigil hadn't been easy on the poor man's old bones. The ageing cleric felt cramped and chilled and deeply fatigued. But he was only too pleased to suffer these minor inconveniences. To witness this ultimate triumph over death and evil was the greatest honour God could bestow upon man.

Yet, as the hour of dawn now drew near, Litti grew increasingly nervous. Throughout the night, with muffled gunfire and violence raging above him, the cardinal had held steadfastly to his certitude about the Messiah. This despite nagging doubts deposited into the far reaches of his soul by a cunning Devil.

Litti's only other distractions came from Commander Lazzlo, who stopped in occasionally between breaks in the offensive outside. Sharing Litti's heartfelt hopes about the Resurrection, the officer kept abreast of the situation.

This visit, however, was not social. The cardinal heard a commotion advancing down the hall and a flushed Lazzlo rounded the corner with several of his troops. 'Your Eminence, I'm sorry,' he panted, a look of distress creasing his face. 'The Gogs have breached the west wing. You must leave now until we secure the corridor.'

Litti turned white with alarm. 'Leave now? It's unthinkable! We're so close to dawn!'

'I realize, Cardinal, and I share your feelings, but if we don't secure this corridor, there may be no Resurrection. The Gogs aren't like Goene's forces. They want to destroy Jeza's body. They'll use explosives. You must leave until we can secure the area again. I'll have you back as quickly as possible. We still have half an hour till dawn.'

Lazzlo motioned to the guards at the door and they grasped the desperate Litti under his armpits, assisting him to his feet. 'I beg of you, Commander!' the cardinal wailed, but it was too late. Lazzlo was off and running towards the west wing with his men.

Indeed, Litti and his escorts had barely made the stairwell when an explosion coursed through the halls. The cardinal said a prayer as the support walls of the substructure vibrated menacingly.

106

Dyan IDF military base, Jerusalem, Israel, 5.15 A.M, Sunday, 23 April 2000

Outside Feldman and Hunter's cell, there was an excited exchange of Hebrew between the guards and the four soldiers who'd just arrived. The animated discussion continued for several minutes.

Above them and outside, they could hear a great deal of troop movement, but the sounds of battle had ceased. Then, abruptly, one of the guards unlocked Feldman's door and announced flatly, 'You're free. You're being released.'

Unceremoniously, Feldman and Hunter were liberated as the four soldiers trotted off and the guards hastily began gathering up personal belongings as if they were vacating the premises.

'Please,' Feldman implored. 'What's going on?'

Without looking up from his packing, one of the guards explained,

'We are under martial law. The Knesset met in emergency session earlier this morning and the IDF has been dissolved. A warrant has been issued for the arrest of Defence Minister Tamin and General Goene.'

'Waaahooo!' Hunter yelped with joy.

'What are they being charged with?' Feldman asked.

'Treason, conspiracy and complicity to murder, among other things, I'm told. The both of you were ordered to be released by direct command of the Knesset. Goene and Tamin have fled. We've been ordered to surrender the base and submit ourselves for review.'

Astounded at their timely reversal of fortunes, Feldman and Hunter stumbled upstairs to the first floor, down the main hallway and hobbled for the nearest exit. Caked with dried mud, blood and filth, still clad in nothing but their soiled linen sheets, they stepped out of the barracks into the bright rays of a gorgeous sunrise.

Out on the grounds, resident troops were assembling and lining up in submission to new superior officers. Freshly arriving military teams and vehicles were pouring into the base in a flurry of activity.

'I can't believe it's over,' Hunter breathed.

'Something tells me it's not,' Feldman answered.

Directly in front of the reporters, a commanding officer, whizzing by in a jeep, spied Feldman and yelled to his driver, who slammed on the brakes and reversed up to the doorway. The officer barked an order in Hebrew to a platoon and the two newsmen were instantly surrounded.

'God!' Hunter moaned. 'Not again!'

But this time, instead of a cell, the two men were taken to the base infirmary where they were given fluids, a hot shower and a hot breakfast. Their injuries dressed, they were administered antibiotics, supplied fresh clothing, and quickly ushered before the desk of the commanding officer who'd discovered them.

Upon seeing his visitors, the officer dropped his paperwork, barked an order into an intercom, stood and extended a hand to both men. They declined the civility.

'What the hell's going on?' Hunter demanded. 'You've got no right to hold us here.'

'We're American citizens,' Feldman added.

The officer, his hand still outstretched in rejected greeting, nodded his head understandingly, and motioned them to chairs.

'You're not under arrest,' he told them, taking his seat again. 'You're merely being held in temporary protective custody pending a call I've just placed. I expect a response any moment.'

Calming down somewhat, Feldman asked, 'Do you mind telling us what's happening?'

'I don't have all the details,' the officer informed them, 'there's a lot of confusion right now. But I will tell you everything I know.'

The two newsmen accepted their chairs and the commander continued. 'As I'm sure you're aware, the whole city has been at war for much of the last twenty-four hours. Thousands have been killed. The heaviest fighting has been around Hadassah, where the hospital was under a three-way siege all night. It began when General Goene's men attacked yesterday morning.'

Feldman's jaw tightened with the recollection. Hunter's hands curled into fists.

'Commander Lazzlo's troops were able to hold Goene off throughout the day, with help from pro-Jeza resistance forces outside the hospital. Then, about eight-thirty last evening, the anti-Jeza forces responsible for the Megiddo massacre broke through our defences on the outskirts of northern Jerusalem and advanced on the hospital. They began attacking *everybody*, indiscriminately. In the darkness, it was hellish confusion.

'Goene brought in reinforcements, but refused to shell or bomb the hospital. We know now that he was after the Leveque neurochips and didn't want to risk destroying them. So the whole engagement settled into a long running battle throughout the night. About four A.M. WNN telecast a special news report with the information you'd smuggled out of Hadassah.'

Feldman and Hunter both raised fists of triumph at the news that Lazzlo's damning evidence had got through.

'But apparently,' the officer resumed his explanation, 'the Ben-Miriam administration had been directly notified much earlier by your network and had called an emergency session of the Knesset in the middle of the night. Based on the evidence of Commander Lazzlo's internal documents, the IDF was placed under direct order of the Knesset and warrants were issued for the arrest of the entire IDF high command, including Tamin and Goene. When the arrest orders came down, Goene abandoned his troops and fled, and his forces were then pulled back from the hospital.

'That left an opening for the anti-Jeza forces, which stormed a wing of the hospital and broke through. Soon after that, however, the anti-Jeza forces suddenly called off their attack, presumably reacting to your network's report. Lazzlo and his regiment are still barricaded in the hospital and Prime Minister Ben-Miriam is attempting to negotiate with them right now.'

'Where are Tamin and Goene?' Hunter wanted to know.

'We're not sure. Tamin left his estate even before the warrant was issued, warned by some of his cronies, no doubt. He was reportedly picked up by Goene in an IDF helicopter, destination unknown. Right now there's no further word on either of them.'

Hunter nodded his head. 'So that's why we're in protective custody. You think we're still in danger from Tamin and Goene?'

'Partly,' the officer acknowledged. 'Prime Minister Ben-Miriam diverted my troops here to secure this base. My orders were to ensure your safety and to notify the administration as soon as you were able to—'

He was interrupted by a voice speaking in Hebrew over the intercom. Looking up, the commander announced, 'Gentlemen, this is the call I've been expecting. It's for you, Mr Feldman. Prime Minister Eziah Ben-Miriam wishes to speak with you personally.'

The officer rotated the phone in front of Feldman and punched a flashing button. The reporter lifted the receiver.

'Hello.'

'Hello, Mr Feldman,' the Prime Minister greeted him. 'I'm greatly relieved to know you and your associate, Mr Hunter, are safe and well. We've been very concerned about you.'

'We appreciate your efforts on our behalf, sir. You no doubt saved our lives.'

'Unfortunately,' Ben-Miriam noted soberly, 'we were too late to save many good men and women who've been needlessly lost in this senseless fighting. And that's why I want to speak with you. The State of Israel needs your assistance one last time to bring an end to this unnecessary bloodshed.'

Feldman took a deep, apprehensive breath and answered Hunter's inquisitive look with a frown. 'What is it you need, Prime Minister?'

'Mr Feldman, we are, at this very moment, attempting to negotiate a peaceful settlement to the Hadassah stand-off. Commander Lazzlo will not surrender to our troops and we fear a bad outcome. The commander refuses to deal through anyone but you and Mr Hunter. You're the only individuals he trusts. I know you've both been through an ordeal, but we simply have no other recourse, it appears.'

107

The skies over Jerusalem, Israel,
9.55 A.M., Sunday, 23 April 2000

'What do you think Lazzlo wants?' a restless Hunter asked, as he inspected his military-issue camera on the helicopter ride back to the hospital. 'A taped statement before falling on his sword?'

'Maybe he just wants us to monitor the surrender to ensure the safety of his troops,' Feldman hesitantly replied, avoiding the supernatural subject neither man chose to address.

Passing over a division of Israeli military encircling the hospital, the helicopter touched down on the roof and the newsmen were quickly taken back to Lazzlo's basement bunker, positioned strategically near the morgue facility. Lazzlo was waiting outside the door in the hallway, leaning against a wall, his arms crossed, looking as exhausted as his visitors. He dismissed his guards so that he could be alone with the reporters.

'I'm deeply grateful that you came, gentlemen,' he began, his face dark and downcast. 'Especially given what you went through after your last visit.'

'Is Cardinal Litti safe and well?' Feldman asked with concern.

'Yes. He's resting comfortably now. Last night was rather hard on him, too, I'm afraid.'

'I'm sorry for the loss of your crew in the helicopter crash,' Feldman offered. 'They were brave soldiers, both of them.'

'Yes.' Lazzlo paused with a look of deepening sadness. 'You did not know, of course, but Corporal Illa Lyman was my daughter. My only child.'

Feldman looked over at Hunter, whose face was a grim mask. 'You have our deepest sympathies, sir,' he managed to say through a constricted throat. 'She saved our lives. If it weren't for her and her pilot, we would never have gotten that vital information out to the Knesset.'

'Unfortunately,' Lazzlo recovered his composure, 'the lives of many good people have been lost on all sides.'

'That's very true, Commander.' Feldman found his opening. 'And now, don't you think it's time, at last, to close the book on all this senseless tragedy?'

'Yes,' Lazzlo agreed. 'That's the reason I asked you here again. There's one thing more I need you to document before I'm finished. After which, I'm prepared to – to surrender.'

There was a spiritless look about the commander that made Feldman uncomfortable.

'Please, come with me,' Lazzlo directed, and led them once more to the vault room. He stopped, instructed the sentries to stand aside, and then motioned Feldman and Hunter through the large metal door, which was standing ajar.

Peering into the dimness of the vault, his heart palpitating, Feldman was not entirely surprised to find the room empty. Jeza's body was gone. There was nothing inside but the table upon which she had lain and the sheets that had covered her.

Feeling short of breath, Feldman stepped back out of the room and searched the commander's face carefully. 'Where is she?' he asked in an uncertain voice.

'I don't know,' Lazzlo replied softly. 'We've checked the hospital thoroughly. She's not here.'

'Did anyone witness her Resurrection?' Hunter asked. 'Or actually see her alive?'

'No,' Lazzlo admitted. 'No one was present when it happened, and no one's actually seen Her. This time, unfortunately, I haven't any conclusive evidence. But I do have something rather interesting to show you.' He pointed up to the corners of the ceiling where two security cameras watched with unblinking eyes.

Feldman's eyebrows arched with aroused interest.

The men returned to Lazzlo's office where two video monitors were set up.

'I have for you the two separate views from each of the security cameras in the room,' Lazzlo explained, and started both tapes. Two pictures of a draped female form materialized in surreal black and white – the same image from opposite angles, one on each monitor.

'You'll notice,' Lazzlo pointed to the lower left corner of the two screens, 'each tape has a date and time code so that you can tell exactly when events occurred.'

The date and time showed '4.23.00, 3.17:24'.

Lazzlo then advanced both tapes together and the time jumped rapidly ahead. He slowed the speed to normal at 5.14:30, advising, 'Now, watch closely.'

At exactly 5.14:54, there was a brilliant flash in the room, blinding the cameras and creating a lasting whiteout on the screen. Meanwhile, the time clock ticked slowly onward. Finally, at 5.15:46, the camera lenses cleared and a normal picture resumed. Only the image had changed. The sheets on the table were thrown back, the door was ajar, Jeza was gone.

'Is there any audio with this?' Feldman enquired.

'No,' Lazzlo replied. 'These are standard security cameras.'

Lazzlo replayed the tapes, slowing the motion to further emphasize the last frame before the image was obliterated by the light. 'From this angle,' he pointed to one monitor, 'you can see the door. You'll note that it appears secured. The flash of light begins *while the door is still closed!*'

The reporters were well aware of this point.

When the tape had played through again, Feldman shot a questioning look at his partner.

Hunter frowned, shaking his head numbly. 'Well, it can't have been a power surge; the time clocks function continually throughout the entire sequence. The disturbance, whatever it was, had to have been some sort of intense light.'

Both Feldman and Hunter fell quiet.

Finally, Feldman broke the silence. 'When did you first notice her missing, Commander?'

'Not until about twenty minutes past the hour,' Lazzlo told him. 'A wing of the hospital had been breached by the anti-Jeza factions, and we poured all our spare manpower into it, eventually turning them back. I had to pull our guards from the morgue and surrounding halls and evacuate Cardinal Litti to the east wing.

'When my soldiers returned, Jeza's body was gone and the room was just as you saw it. We touched nothing and the guards were immediately reposted in front of the door.'

'Wait a minute!' Hunter interrupted. 'If the hospital was penetrated, isn't it possible someone got in here and stole the body?'

'I can't say that it's not possible,' Lazzlo admitted. 'But to my knowledge, no one got through our defences. Even assuming we were penetrated, they would have had to pass our lines one more time to escape. A difficult enough feat without the burden of carrying a body with them. And then, there's still the matter of the disturbance of light on the security tapes.'

'If somebody did get in,' Feldman suggested, 'maybe he was able to open the door to Jeza's room an undetectable amount, insert a bright light—'

'Yes, there are other explanations,' Lazzlo broke in, looking at Feldman as if there weren't. 'Regardless, I ask that you and your associate document all the evidence you find here before others that come after me destroy or distort the truth, intentionally or otherwise. You have credibility with the public. They'll trust whatever data you collect. I also want you to take possession of the two security tapes.'

'Of course,' Feldman agreed.

While Lazzlo collected the tapes and Hunter took video of the morgue vault, Feldman stepped away into his own space, retracing the events of the past few days. He could not come to grips with the circumstances. Shaking his head, engulfed in the confusion of things profoundly unfathomable, he finally tabled his thoughts and returned to the situation at hand.

'Commander,' he said, accepting the tapes from Lazzlo, 'what can we do to assist you in your negotiations with the government?'

Lazzlo regarded him with a rueful smile of resignation. 'There's nothing more you can do for me now, my friend. My fate's already decided. I must face the consequences of my actions.' He sighed heavily. 'It no longer matters. I was too late to ask for the Messiah's absolution. The authorities can do what they wish with my mortal body. It's a higher authority that concerns me.'

'I guess you know that Tamin and Goene have disappeared?' Feldman mentioned.

'They haven't disappeared,' Lazzlo stated matter-of-factly. 'The administration just doesn't know where to look for them.'

'And you do?' Hunter stopped his videotaping and walked over to Lazzlo.

'I have a very good idea. Goene and Tamin have likely headed to the southern Negev. Goene knows that territory extremely well and he has access to military caches of vehicles and supplies stockpiled in the desert. They'll abandon their helicopter and try a land escape into Egypt tonight, after which they'll have no difficulty smuggling themselves to France or Spain.'

'Goddammit,' Hunter barked, slamming the desk with his palm, his face red with anger. 'I'm not about to let those two bastards get away scot-free! I want you to show me on a map exactly where they are, Commander.'

'*No way!*' Feldman objected immediately. 'It's all over for us, Breck. It's up to the Israelis now.'

'It may be over for you, pal, but it sure as hell ain't over for me!' He locked adamant eyes on his partner. 'I'm trading the commander's info to the Israelis for a seat on the bus. I'm gonna be there when they bring those sons of bitches down!'

Feldman returned the cameraman's gaze, frowning. In all their time together, he'd never seen Hunter so unrelentingly hate-filled. So unwaveringly resolute. After a long pause, he sighed and turned to Lazzlo. 'Commander, do you still want me to assist with negotiations for the transfer of power here?' He purposefully avoided the term 'surrender'.

'I trust no one else.'

Feldman turned back to the stubborn cameraman, shaking his head. 'I've got a bad feeling about this, Breck.' He sighed again. 'Okay, pack up your camera, we're heading for the Negev.'

108

The Papal quarters, Vatican City, Italy,
4.51 P.M., Sunday, 23 April 2000

Nicholas VI had remained in seclusion for the greater part of the weekend. He'd emerged in public view only twice. The first time, to conduct Good Friday services. The second, to preside over Christianity's most important religious celebration, this morning's open-air Easter Sunday Mass at sunrise in St Peter's Square. It had rained during the entire service, and it was raining still.

In the three weeks since the Pontiff's *ex cathedra* decree, Nicholas had grown increasingly depressed over the escalating discord and bloodshed in the world. The situation had caused him to put a distance between himself and his Curia, and in particular Antonio di Concerci. Apprehensive and agitated, the Pontiff had spent hours alone in his study, in front of his TV, obsessed with the steady streams of disturbing news issuing from the Holy Land.

His anxieties had begun in earnest a week ago with the unexpected return of Jeza to Jerusalem. The bizarre parallels with Christ and Palm Sunday had caught the Pontiff completely off guard. As had the prophetess's miraculous escape through the Golden Gate, the messianic implications of which had not been lost on him. Yet he had steadfastly refused to watch Jeza's portentous Good Friday sermon, having sternly warned the faithful to avoid her message as 'deceitful words of Satan'.

The news of her death had come to Nicholas as he was praying in his quarters. A chamber nun informed him. Nicholas had immediately gone to his television and watched the continuing replay of the shocking assassination. Despite his convictions, he had found himself stunned and disturbed by the pathetic, heartless murder. He'd reflexively begun a prayer for the repose of Jeza's soul, until it occurred to him that this was inappropriate. Instead, he offered his prayers for the souls of the countless victims falling to the worldwide religious civil war of Armageddon that currently raged across the planet.

Nicholas fully anticipated the Judgment to begin this morning. Yet, returning in disappointment from his Easter services, the Pope was hit with the unsettling PET scan revelations. Jeza's mind was unaltered! He calmed himself with the knowledge that, while perhaps this news refuted di Concerci's argument about Jeza being controlled by IDF radio messages, it did nothing to discredit Nicholas's doctrine that Jeza was the product of a more sinister, supernatural force.

But the day's disclosures were hardly over. Later that morning, the Pontiff was distracted from his thoughts by a breathless announcement of the *Resurrection Tapes*. He was riveted once more to his TV screen, his hands clasped tightly together as the sequences of Jeza's purported rise from the dead played out in front of him. His respiration rate escalated and he began to perspire. How could God ask him to endure any more of these assaults on his convictions?

'No!' he cautioned himself, aloud. 'My faith is being tested!' He would not succumb. He rose and walked decisively to his window where, outside, the sun was finally starting to break through the clouds.

The Pontiff studied the sky long and carefully for any signs that the Son of God might now be making His appearance. While there was still no indication, there was yet another ray of sunshine on the horizon. On his TV, Nicholas overheard a report that the cataclysm of world turmoil was at last waning. The majority of millenarians appeared to be pausing in their violence long enough, at least, to reconsider their positions in the light of this latest, ambiguous information about Jeza.

As much as he'd anticipated and prepared for the Second Coming these past weeks, even Nicholas would welcome a stay of execution. He sighed, feeling the pangs of his self-imposed confinement. He longed to walk in his Vatican gardens once more. To smell the flowers and sweet air after the cleansing spring rain.

He forbade his Swiss Guard to accompany him. Stepping outside his palace, the Pope realized that this was the first time since his coronation that he'd walked unencumbered in his kingdom. It was liberating. His unhurried afternoon stroll through the grounds took him past all the great, beloved treasures of religious art, architecture and priceless beauty that two thousand years of Christianity had bestowed upon him and his Church. He lingered delightedly among his possessions for hours, unrecognized without his standard retinue about him. With dusk approaching, he slowly began to wend his way back towards his quarters.

The sky was completely clear now, and before he retired, the Pontiff decided he would take this rare opportunity to enjoy one of his favourite panoramas. There was no more beautiful a view of Rome than that from the ancient papal observatory at the top of the Vatican's lofty Tower of the Winds.

Entering the ground-level museum building, he was greeted by several pale-complexioned clerics who were surprised from their quiet studies to see their monarch without his customary guards. Nevertheless, they were cheered to find the Pontiff out and about again.

Nicholas was wearied by the hard climb up the tower's steep, spiral stone stairs. At the top, the winded Pope happened upon a young archivist monk who looked shocked beyond measure to encounter his sovereign in this manner.

The friar had been seated on the floor, re-creating on a sketch pad inscriptions and drawings from the venerable walls of the old observatory. Astounded, the monk scrambled to his feet and bowed low, turning crimson in the face. 'Holy Father, pardon me, I had no idea you were coming here this evening.'

Nicholas placed his hands on the sides of the nervous man's cheeks and gently guided him to an upright position. 'Not at all, my son, you have nothing to be concerned about. My visit was unannounced. I was walking past and simply decided to come up for a quick view of my Eternal City. I used to come here often when I was a young priest in the service of Pope John XXIII. Please, don't let me interrupt your work.'

'No, Holiness,' the monk demurred. 'What I do is of no consequence. I'll leave and allow you your peace.'

Nicholas was touched by the man's deference, and smiled. 'Tell me, my son, what is your name?'

'I . . . I am Pietri Dominici, Your Holiness. I'm an archivist in the museum, here to document the information left on these walls centuries ago when the tower served as the Vatican's astral observatory.'

Nicholas found the company of this unassuming young man a

refreshing contrast to the pomp and politics of his entourage. 'Please, stay and keep me company for a while, Pietri. I won't hold you from your work long. Tell me, what have you learned from your research here?'

'Well,' Dominici reflected on his studies, 'as you can see on this wall here,' and he pointed to an inscription, 'these are calculations regarding the movement of the stars and planets, dating from the late 1500s, I suspect. And here,' he indicated a rather involved drawing of the sun and seven planets in elliptical orbit, 'is an illustration of the solar system visible with the primitive telescopes of the day.'

'Ah, wonderful!' the Pontiff said admiringly. 'And what of these figures over here?' He gestured towards a series of numbers in columns.

'Those, Holiness, date from about 1580, and are some of the early calculations in the preparation of the famous Gregorian calendar, the computations for which were developed right here in this observatory.'

'Amazing!' Nicholas exclaimed. 'Who would have believed at the time that, four hundred years later, this tower would still stand and Pope Gregory XIII's successor would come here to gaze out upon the third millennium!'

'Of course,' the monk added light-heartedly, 'you'll need to visit me again next year to do that.'

Nicholas was confused. 'How do you mean, my son?'

'Well,' Dominici smiled, 'although the world doesn't celebrate it this way, the *true* turn of the millennium won't occur until 1 January of next year—'

All the colour immediately drained from the Pontiff's face. 'What did you say!' he demanded.

The monk stepped back. 'Holiness, please, I did not mean to offend you! I—'

'Explain to me what you mean!' the Pope shouted, grabbing the hapless friar by the front of his brown robe.

His eyes bulging from their sockets, the quaking monk searched the Pope's face, as if looking for a clue to the meaning of this inexplicable display. 'H-holy Father, forgive me, I merely mean that in terms of the calendar, we are only now completing the one thousandth year of the past millennium. The first year of the third millennium does not begin until the year 2001.'

The Pope's grip had loosened and he stared past the humiliated monk, out across the tiled rooftops of his Eternal City. '*Of course!*' Nicholas whispered to himself, in shock. '*I knew this!* How could I have closed my eyes to something so obvious!'

The friar continued his explanation, trying to redeem himself. 'Just as the number twenty completes a full score, and the number twenty-one would begin the next score, and . . .'

But Nicholas was no longer listening. As the significance of this revelation fully enveloped him, he released the poor, frightened monk, slowly collapsed against the wall and slid to the floor, his eyes glazed.

At the sight of this, the friar became hysterical. He dropped his notepad and pencil and fled screaming down the staircase for assistance.

Before help could arrive, Nicholas had recovered enough to begin a lumbering, lurching retreat down from the tower. He met a flow of would-be rescuers rushing up from below, but they stopped immediately at the sight of him and stepped aside, flabbergasted, as he pressed past. At the bottom of the staircase, Nicholas confronted a bevy of flustered, well-meaning nuns and priests gathered in unfocused confusion. He did not look at them, but waved them off and staggered down the hall, moving persistently onward.

Vehemently, Nicholas threw open the main doors of the museum and exited into the night air. He trudged relentlessly on, heading towards the Basilica, a desperate group of Vatican personnel following in halting disarray. Pushing past the astonished guards at the front gates of the cathedral, Nicholas entered the quiet sanctuary. St Peter's was still full of worshippers this Easter Sunday evening, all of whom were quickly overcome by the unexpected distinction. But for those directly in the path of the distraught Pope, the exhilaration was cut short by the anguished, wild look on the Pontiff's face.

The baffled faithful recoiled in disbelief as he brushed by. Oblivious to the commotion he was causing around him, Nicholas approached the gaping maw of the catacombs leading to the tomb of Peter. He staggered to a standstill in front of the railing, swaying from exertion and emotion. Panting, his arms trembling beside him, he glared down into the silent depths, calling out in a booming voice that shook the entire basilica.

'*Why?*

'Why? Why? Why?'

He waited for an answer, but there was none. He leaned on both hands against the railing, breathing less rapidly now. Shifting his gaze upward to the High Altar, and in a more subdued, broken voice, he moaned, 'There have been worse popes! There have been popes less sincere, less conscientious, less faithful. Why! Where have I failed? Where have I earned Your disfavour?'

Still no answer.

In frustration, he blared down once more into the catacombs, 'Simon Peter!' And the words resonated endlessly. 'Hear me, Peter! I want no more of it!' And then in an impassioned voice of resignation, '*I want no more of it!*'

With that, Nicholas tore the papal ring from his finger, holding it aloft where the light of the altar candles caught it in golden gleams. 'I give it all back to you, Peter,' he wailed. 'The burden, the agony and the mystery, I return it all to you!' Pausing for a moment, he then hurled the ring into the blackness of the catacombs below, where it clanked and clinked and chimed off the stone steps in its descent.

The bewildered onlookers had drawn close in dumbfounded silence to witness this unprecedented exhibition. Nicholas, sweating profusely, spun around on them suddenly, catching them by surprise and sending them scattering. Taking no notice, the aggrieved Pope stumbled off down the main aisle, through the gates of the cathedral, and out once again into St Peter's Square.

A large gathering of the Vatican population had already collected there. In short order, word of the crisis had circumnavigated the city, and Nicholas's final, laboured leg through the square to his papal quarters was through a gauntlet of shocked, embarrassed but irresistibly curious onlookers. It was all the desperate Swiss Guard could do to clear a path for him.

While the screams of ambulances drifted closer, the white, perspiring Nicholas finally entered his apartments and arrived at his chambers, sending his attendant nuns into abject panic at the sight of him. Inside the sanctity of his library at last, he locked his door and faltered to his desk. Dropping heavily into his chair, he laid his head down amidst his books and papers, closing his eyes to the incessant pounding at his door.

Having never had to cope with such an emergency, the distressed chamber nuns required ten minutes to locate a key to the Pope's quarters. Several anxious cardinals and the resident papal doctor, a napkin still around his neck from his interrupted dinner, slowly, cautiously, edged open the large wooden doors.

'*Papa?*' one cardinal ventured timorously, looking around, unable to spot the Pontiff immediately.

Nicholas did not even lift his head. 'Leave me and lock the door! I command you!'

The cardinals stared at each other, and then expectantly at the doctor. The physician gave them an uncomfortable, searching look and cleared his throat. 'Holy Father,' he croaked, 'we are concerned that you have taken ill. You do not seem yourself.'

Nicholas bolted upright in his chair. 'I am *not* myself!' he cried out, clenching and unclenching his fists on the desk in front of him, his face a contorted mask. And then, overwhelmed, hanging his head with grief, he moaned tormentedly, 'My self is lost to the ages now. I am reduced to a metaphor, a – a *Caiaphas!*'

His fury welling again, he bellowed, '*Leave me now!*'

There was a scurry of footsteps and the door creaked shut.

Nicholas buried his face in his hands. 'My God, my God!' he lamented repeatedly. His phone rang and he slashed out furiously with his arm, sending it crashing to the floor, a shower of papers fluttering down after it.

His eyes were feverish, his face red and wet. Shaking badly, his hands fumbled for his waist fob. Locating a large, golden key, he jabbed it at his desk vault, missing the lock badly several times until he penetrated the keyhole. The tumblers turned, the vault door sprang open, and Nicholas grappled the faded leather portfolio from its dark haven on to the top of his desk. He tore the securing thongs from their stitchings and threw open the heavy cover, revealing the familiar contents of faded parchments.

More deliberately now, he cleared aside the top parchments with ungainly sweeps of his hand until he arrived at the page he sought. Praying for a miracle to deliver him, with shaking index finger he followed the handwritten passages to the lines:

'. . . *those who know the truth, by the purity of their hearts shall they also know the messenger. But woe be to you, hardened hearts, which fail to see and hear. For you who hold your head high with arrogance, so shall you stumble over that which lies conspicuous before you.*'

And . . .

'. . . *if the First Prophecy is to be, it shall be fulfilled before the turn of the millennium; and if the Second Prophecy is to be, it shall be fulfilled thereafter.*'

Disastrously, Nicholas had accepted at face value Pope John Paul II's call for 'a sacred Jubilee Year to begin *at the commencement of the New Millennium, 1 January 2000.*' He had overlooked the now conspicuous fact that the year 2000 – and not 1999 – was, indeed, the last year of the old millennium.

Despite how the world might celebrate its coming, in truth the new millennium had not yet arrived. A point which even Nicholas, isolated though he might have been in his ecclesiastical ivory tower, had surely been aware. Yet, somehow, fatefully, he had suppressed that knowledge. The dark passages of the Secret Letter reconfirmed the Pope's dread convictions. It was the *first* prophecy that had been fulfilled. *Jeza was the Messiah*!

Nicholas's lips contorted in a grotesque grin of disbelief and betrayed hurt. He began to laugh, tears flowing from his eyes. Leaving the yellowed page where it lay, he pushed himself up from his chair and staggered away from his desk. The vault key, still in its lock, tore free from the Pontiff's fob, but Nicholas was impervious.

'*My God, my God!*' the Pope ranted as he passed the threshold of his room, and those with their ears against his door jumped back in fear.

Collapsing on his bed, Nicholas could feel the pressure of his blood surging within his veins. He rolled over on his back and attempted to calm himself, but the sound of his chamber door closing alerted him to someone's unwelcomed presence.

'*You!*' the Pope gasped, turning to discover the dark shape of Antonio di Concerci slipping quietly towards him. Nicholas rose up on one elbow, the exertion and anger showing like fire in his face. 'What counsel do you bring me now, Cardinal Adviser?' he cried. 'Do you come to fill me again with more of your misconceptions and your schemes?'

Halfway to the Pope's bedside, di Concerci stopped. Frowning, he raised his hand to his chin and said nothing.

'The truth is there!' Nicholas pointed to his desk with a badly trembling hand. 'I did not want to see it. I allowed my vision to be clouded by power and pride and stubbornness and fear!'

The prefect's eyes followed the direction of the Pontiff's finger to where the yellowed papers lay.

'What do I do now, my cardinal prefect?' The Pope's anxious voice grew louder and more strident. 'Where do I go with my soul now? Will you share with me my failure and my shame? Will you stand at my side now before the Lord's throne?' Nicholas contracted his shaking fingers into a fist and bellowed out in desperate rage, '*Will you defend me to God for the murder of His only begotten Daughter!*'

With these last words, the Pope was overcome with searing pain. He stiffened and pitched back on to his bed, hands fluttering convulsively at his side, eyes turning upward in his head. He shivered there, alone, in unbridled torment. And then, in a long, slow, pained gargle, he exuded his final breath.

Through all of this, the prefect had stood immobile, a deep furrow impressing itself ever further into his brow. He backed slowly away from the bedchamber, making his way quietly to the Pope's desk. Picking up the letter, he read it carefully, stopping only once to glance over at the still form on the bed.

When finished, Cardinal Prefect Antonio di Concerci gathered up all the parchments, carefully slipped them inside his cassock, and then moved to the Pope's side to feel his wrist for a pulse.

Finding none, he stepped back, paused, then exited the room to summon the papal physician.

109

Somewhere over the southern Negev desert,
6.34 P.M., Sunday, 23 April 2000

A thousand feet above the desert floor, in one of six Israeli night reconnaissance helicopters, Feldman, Hunter, a pilot, co-pilot and two military police were racing towards the supply depot Commander Lazzlo had identified for them earlier.

Feldman's plan had worked perfectly. Eziah Ben-Miriam's government had a number of sensitive issues to resolve quickly, and Jon Feldman held two of the keys. He could deliver Ben-Miriam a speedy and peaceful surrender of the Hadassah, as well as the whereabouts of Israel's most wanted: Goene and Tamin.

And all Feldman had required in return was:

First, complete clemency for Commander David Lazzlo and his loyal troops. They had, after all, performed a great service for Israel. In defying Goene, they had defended the Messiah's body and delivered to the world the sacred truths that stopped Armageddon. Moreover, Feldman had argued, if the government accepted the premise that Jeza was risen from the dead, any pending murder charges would have to be dropped anyway.

And second, acceding to Hunter's demands, Feldman had insisted that he and the cameraman be allowed to accompany the Israeli search team to record the capture of Goene and Tamin – assuming it wasn't already too late. The interminably slow negotiations had cost Feldman precious hours.

As the reporters' aircraft cleared a small cluster of mountains, the pilot signalled that they were coming up on the depot Lazzlo had targeted as a probable hideout for the two fugitives. Through the windshield of the craft, in the fading twilight, it was impossible to see much. But the scene was eminently visible in the eerie green glow of the cockpit's night-scanning screen.

It would appear that Lazzlo had been correct in his suspicions. Feldman could easily distinguish the parked form of a single Israeli military helicopter in front of what looked to be a large rock formation with a door in it. 'There.' The co-pilot identified the craft, tapping the screen with his forefinger.

But it was soon apparent they'd arrived too late. A quick ground inspection showed the depot deserted and truck tracks heading to the south-east, towards the least guarded area of the Egyptian border. Also as Lazzlo had surmised.

'We should have intercept any moment,' the pilot promised, taking them back up into the sky and away. That proved to be an optimistic projection. An hour later, the tracks having dissolved in rocky terrain, the squadron had split up, hoping to detect the heat of the escape vehicle's engine on infrared sensors. But they came across nothing except a few carloads of millenarians working their way towards the new sacred shrine of Jeza's Resurrection.

'There's no way they could have made it to the border yet,' the pilot informed his passengers. 'I'm going to swing around and check out that Bedouin encampment we passed a few kilometres back. Maybe they've seen something.'

A few minutes later, they crossed a rise and came upon a sprawling camp. 'Probably about a hundred and fifty to two hundred Bedouins, all told,' the pilot estimated, gauging from the size of their large, circus-like tents. 'We'll put down far enough away not to disturb their flocks too much.'

They dropped into a flat bluff about fifty metres downwind, the helicopter's prop kicking up a blinding dust storm. As the blades slowed and the clouds settled, an assembly of about forty rough-hewn men with rifles slowly materialized in the darkness, just beyond the swath of the rotor. One of the Israeli militia slid out of the helicopter, approached the nomads with his arms in the air, chatted for a few moments and then came trotting back at a fast clip.

'Sir,' he called in to the detail officer, 'they've got them both right here! Caught them about an hour ago. Recognized 'em from TV reports. They claim Jeza spent time with their clan once, and they're real unhappy about what happened to their Messiah. Say they're gonna peel Tamin and Goene alive.'

The sergeant gritted his teeth. 'The hell they are! Call in the other choppers. I want two standard attack deployments behind that dune over there,' he began to order, but Feldman offered an alternative.

'Sergeant, if they watch TV, maybe they'll recognize me, too. They'll know I was a friend of Jeza. Maybe I can reason with them.'

Hunter elbowed Feldman hard in his sore side and whispered, 'No! Let 'em shred the bastards!' He was dead serious.

Feldman ignored his partner and the sergeant acquiesced.

Indeed, Feldman was immediately received with great ceremony and fanfare. The nomads knelt before him and touched the hem of his trousers, calling him 'Apoutü', or 'Apostle', as he was quickly informed by the military translator. He found this most uncomfortable, particularly with Hunter recording the episode.

He learned that this tribe of Bedouins was also well acquainted with 'Apoutü' Litti, who'd spoken often and highly of Feldman. The tribal leader was eager to accommodate the famous newsman, bestowing several choice goats and camels upon him.

Provided with an avenue of exchange now, Feldman succeeded in trading on his prestige, goats and camels for the persons of Goene and Tamin. The two were delivered, bound hand and foot and gagged.

As all this transpired, Feldman, who'd been keeping a stealthy eye on Hunter, observed the big man moving menacingly towards the captured pair. Quickly darting out in front of him to block his path, he grabbed the cameraman's shoulder. 'No, Breck!' he warned. 'You know I can't let you.'

Hunter stared at his friend as if seeing him for the very first time. Feldman could detect the battle going on within his partner, and for a time couldn't be sure of the outcome. But at length, Hunter blinked.

Feldman stared hard into his eyes. 'You take your revenge with your camera, Breck, not your fists. Swear to me?'

Hunter hesitated, turned his frowning face aside and scowled down at the ground. He finally nodded.

Only then did Feldman step aside. Hunter moved in with his camera to catch every humiliating particular as the former IDF minister and his general, both now dressed in civilian attire, were deposited unceremoniously in the dust at his feet.

Pressing in tightly on Goene's red, seething face, Hunter carefully
documented the capture. 'So nice to cross my pen with your sword
again, General,' he gloated with smouldering hatred. 'You sorry
bastards are gonna look damn impressive on tomorrow's news, rollin'
around in the camel dung there!'

The instant his gag was removed, Goene lurched himself into a sitting
position and appealed desperately to his former Israeli subordinates.
'They have the microchips! This is all a conspiracy. Set us loose, it's
not too late to recover the chips! The technology belongs to Israel!'

Hunter drew himself upright, shaking his head and glancing over
his shoulder at Feldman. 'Stupid to the bitter end,' he observed. As
he turned back to the defiant general, Hunter's rage boiled to the
surface. 'When you gonna get it through that dense shit inside your
skull that there *are* no chips. You let them shoot her for *nothing*, you
bastard! And a hell of a lot of good those microchips would do you
now, anyway. You turds are gonna spend the rest of your miserable
lives makin' little rocks out of big rocks!'

Tamin, his face as white as the full desert moon high in the clear sky
above them, had nothing to say. The two prisoners were untied, immediately handcuffed, and then carted off to the waiting helicopter.

Feldman turned his weary, relieved eyes to his partner. 'Feeling a little better now?' he asked, enjoying a smile of self-satisfaction himself.

Hunter did not return the smile. 'Give me just a few minutes of
personal "sensitivity training" with those sons of bitches, then I'd feel
better.'

Feldman and Hunter were allowed to ride back on the helicopter
with the prisoners, who were manacled to the bulkhead. Two Israeli
militia accompanied them, along with their pilot and co-pilot.

The Bedouins shouted and raised their rifles over their heads in
victory as, one by one, the helicopters lifted straight up into the starry
skies of the desert night. Feldman watched the celebrants recede quickly
below him, and had just begun to settle comfortably into his seat when
he was startled by a cry from the guard next to him. As he turned, a
firearm discharged and the soldier slumped to the deck, a red splotch
spreading next to the pouch of his empty shoulder holster.

Just as quickly, the second guard across from Feldman was hurtled
backward against the bulkhead by a gunshot to the chest and fell
lifeless next to his comrade. Goene – smoking revolver in one hand,

uncoupled handcuff dangling from the other – confronted the two unarmed newsmen.

'Standard Israeli issue,' he smirked, dropping the cuffs. As the frantic co-pilot groped futilely for his sidearm, Goene coldly squeezed off another shot. The unfortunate victim bucked forward and crumpled against the cockpit. The pilot immediately brought the helicopter around, screaming a distress call into his head-set.

'Hold it steady or I shoot you where you sit!' Goene shouted up to the pilot, who quickly complied. Tamin, still manacled to the metal frame, could only watch with wide eyes and rising spirits.

In smug vengeance, Goene turned on Feldman. 'Now you!' he growled, motioning the reporter to his feet with the gun.

Hunter started from his seat, but Goene negated the move by grabbing Feldman and jabbing the gun in his neck. The tough war veteran was powerful, maintaining a vice-like grip on the reporter's injured arm. Not removing the gun, and carefully monitoring the frantic Hunter, Goene pulled Feldman roughly to the door in the back of the cabin, releasing him only long enough to unfasten the lock and turn the handle.

'For God's sake, Goene,' Hunter pleaded, 'he just saved your life back there. Those nomads were gonna slice you to pieces.'

Goene's response was to cock his revolver. Stepping back from Feldman, the general placed the muzzle between the reporter's eyes with a triumphant look. 'You've crossed me once too often, my arrogant young upstart,' he hissed. 'But now I shut your big mouth for good. No last prayers for you. *I* have the last word!'

With burning vindictiveness, the general kicked open the door, and Feldman, staggered by the violent rupture of atmosphere, grasped on to a rib of the fuselage with his good hand, bracing himself against the outrushing torrent. The wind howled around him and he stared down at the desert floor a thousand feet below.

'Now,' Goene declared with victorious finality, 'I send you to join your false Messiah – *in hell!*' With the speed of a striking cobra, the general lashed out with his gun and struck Feldman hard on the temple. Instantly, Hunter launched himself at Goene, but was too late. The soldier spun and planted a foot hard into the semi-conscious Feldman's stomach, propelling him out of the door into the open sky.

110

Shrieking in savage rage at the loss of his friend, Hunter unleashed the full fury of his hatred, driving the general's thick body violently into the bulkhead, jarring loose the revolver.

But the war-hardened soldier proved as resilient as ever. Recovering quickly, he began attacking Hunter with a punishing barrage of martial arts. As they pounded and heaved each other across the cabin, Hunter's most pressing concern, beyond the danger of flying out of the open door, was to deny Goene his pistol. The gun remained at large, skidding and bouncing unpredictably about the deck, narrowly eluding Hunter's grasp several times as the pilot desperately plunged the helicopter towards the ground.

An anxious Shaul Tamin, one arm still manacled to the bulkhead, attempted to snare the gun with an outstretched foot each time it rattled by. Missing it, he'd turn his attention to Hunter, connecting on occasion with a vicious kick.

Yet slowly, the former linebacker's superior strength and endurance were gaining the upper hand. He at last caught Goene with a stunning uppercut. As the general toppled to the deck, Hunter leaped for the revolver. His fingers were just closing on the handle when the aircraft suddenly set down with a jarring thud and the gun hopscotched away once more, sliding neatly into the waiting hand of the snarling Goene.

Hunter winced as the report of successive gunshots thundered inside the cabin. It took him several moments to realize he'd somehow emerged unscathed. Opening his puzzled eyes, he spied the limp form of Goene lying face up on the floor, mortally wounded, blood spurting out of three holes in his chest. From the front of the helicopter, the pilot, his face ghastly pale and sweating, clutched a smoking pistol. A despairing Tamin let out a groan.

Cautiously, Hunter approached the motionless body. He placed a boot on the general's slack forearm, bent down and tore away the gun. Goene, stubborn till the last, was clinging to life, but barely. His mouth gaped open in shock, his breath came in shallow gasps as he focused on the big cameraman looming above him.

Hunter, panting from exertion, glowered down at his despised adversary. He narrowed his eyes, searching for signs of remorse in the bitter, weathered face. There were none. Instead, Goene's lips began a slow curl into his vile, contemptuous, detestable sneer.

All the raw emotions of pain and loss Hunter had endured at the hands of this ruthless man came seething up inside him. He raised the gun and his finger encircled the trigger. But as he glared with primal hatred into the leering eyes of his enemy, he suddenly halted, staggered by an utterly extraordinary vision. There, appearing in the face of this despicable creature, was the unmistakable image of a lonely, frightened, abused little boy.

Hunter gasped and the gun slipped from his fingers. While the pilot and Tamin stared in astonished disbelief, the big man dropped slowly to his knees. He paused, his hands trembling, and then carefully, tenderly, Hunter gathered Goene up into his arms, gently cradling his head, stroking his temple, comforting and consoling the dying soldier through his last battle.

111

Somewhere over the southern Negev desert,
9.44 P.M., Sunday, 23 April 2000

Feldman was falling. Floating in the air on his back, drifting down through the desert's cool night sky. His eyes were closed and there was no sound but the rhythmic whoosh of air and a distant chorus of angels.

With great effort, he opened his eyes to the purple sky overhead. Staring back at him, the moon lorded full and enormously pale. From its shimmering face, there arose the growing shadow of a celestial form, falling even faster than he, racing down after him in a tunnel of white light.

It was Jeza. Jeza unlike he'd ever seen Her. Even more godly, if possible, than before. Transformed. Transfigured. Her skin shining like burnished gold. Her robes flowing outward in tongues of flame. Her hair as black as pitch smoke, sweeping freely, gracefully away in endless plumes.

She swooped down and soared above him, gliding in, hovering, manoeuvring close. She was scant inches away now, staring far into his soul once again.

Ever so slowly, a smile began to form on her exquisite face. Softly, sweetly. It was satiating. Divine. Gazing up at her in enraptured fascination, Feldman was drawn once more into that demanding, honest, sapphirine clarity.

To a place where the origin of all mysteries resided. To a place where his amorphous conflicts and confusions could no longer elude him. He comprehended now the intense, disruptive, deeply moving emotions he'd been feeling towards this incredible being. Those unfamiliar, unexplored stirrings She had awakened within him.

They came from the *soul*. The supernatural love of man for the deific. That irresistible, inescapable, eternal yearning to bond with one's supreme parent. A holy longing for spiritual unity.

And clearly now, he also understood that the great affection he held for Anke sprang from the *heart*. The natural love of man for his own kind. A human compulsion for emotional and physical unity.

The balanced equation.

No longer were his passions interknotted and chaotic. At long last, he was at peace with himself.

Softly, the Messiah whispered, '*Mors vita est.*' Death is Life. And he realized she was repeating her last words.

His as well.

He wasn't fearful. He had grasped the fuller meaning of her words: to unleash the greatest potential of life, you must first overcome the constraining fear of death. An awareness that set a brilliant wave of energy coursing through his mind. A New Light that illuminated his way.

Although he could accept his fate, there was still one truly large regret he would carry with him. If only he could have seen Anke once more. To tell her what he knew now. To hold her in his arms one last time before letting her go for ever.

Feldman could sense the ground hurtling towards him. He shut his eyes, waiting, but there was no impact. Just the continuing, rhythmic whoosh of rushing air. Cautiously, he hazarded a squint.

He found himself lying in a hospital bed. In a quiet, private room, filled to capacity with floral baskets and bouquets and good wishes. At the foot of his bed, asleep in a chair, slouched a snoring Hunter, the source of the whooshing.

Outside, the sun was either just rising or setting, Feldman couldn't be sure. In a corner of the ceiling across his room, a WNN newscast was in progress on a suspended TV, its volume muted.

He felt disoriented and, at the same time, amazingly lucid. Attempting to sit up, he was surprised to find an arm in a cast and his chest and ankle heavily wrapped. However, surprisingly, he wasn't in much pain.

He fumbled for the bed control, pushing a button to elevate his head and shoulders to a more upright position. Blinking his eyes, he wondered what he was doing here. Or, more specifically, why he was still alive. *It's another miracle*, he thought to himself. *Jeza swooped down and She saved me.*

Thirsty, he whispered in a weak, cracking voice, a little hesitant to awaken his sleeping friend, 'Hey, Breck? Could I have some water, please?'

Hunter snorted and looked up with a bleary, muddled expression. 'Huh? Yeah, sure, man, hold on.' His eyes suddenly snapped wide, his jaw dropped and his face lit up. 'Jon, my God, you're back!'

Feldman smiled and the cameraman wrapped him up in his big, lanky arms. It hurt.

Seeming to recognize this, Hunter controlled himself. 'Thank God!' he cried. 'We didn't know if you were ever gonna wake up! This is incredible! Just incredible! I gotta call the others!'

'Breck, wait,' Feldman stopped him. 'First, you've got to tell me what happened!'

Hunter pulled back, his face flushed with emotion, his eyes watery, and he poured Feldman a shaky glass of water. 'Yeah, right. Sure, sure. Well, uh, do you remember anything?'

'The last thing I remember was Goene smashing me in the face and kicking me out of the helicopter. And then I sort of had this vision of Jeza coming to say goodbye to me.'

'A little prematurely.' Hunter grinned.

'So how come I'm not dead?'

Hunter shook his head. 'Jon, you fell square on to one of those Bedouin tents. It cushioned you like a giant airbag. Broke your fall and saved your life. You busted some bones and got a concussion – from Goene's sucker punch or from the fall, or both. Either way, you've been unconscious. No one could say if you'd ever come out of it. I mean, the entire world is outside your window, prayin' for you!'

Hunter walked over to the drapes and pulled them aside briefly. The sun was a trifle higher on the horizon now, so it was dawn. Despite the hour, the entire landscape beyond was filled with people. Many were slumbering on blankets and in sleeping bags in the open air, or in tents. But many were awake and holding quiet vigil with lighted candles in the diminishing shadows. They reacted with excitement to Hunter's fleeting presence at the window.

Across the room, the silent TV displayed a video of thousands of millenarians packing up and heading out of Jerusalem. A wider shot showed steady streams of them merging into vast caravans snaking their way along the roads out of the Holy City. Israeli soldiers were smiling to the cameras as they directed traffic. Near by, groups of celebrating Arab women were shown laughing, waving their veils above their heads in liberation. A headline font on the screen read, 'Holy Land Returning to Normal'.

'How long have I been out?' Feldman asked.

'Five days,' Hunter informed him.

On the TV, a scene of celebration in Times Square looked as if the Yankees had just won the World Series. A huge bonfire roared in the middle of an enormous crowd. Under a sign bearing the initials 'NRA', bucket brigades of cheering people fed an unending supply of empty rifles and pistols, knives and assorted weaponry into the blaze.

A headline banner on the screen read: 'National Rifle Association Changes Name to National Resistance to Arms'.

'Five days?' Feldman was amazed.

'Yeah, we've been taking turns watching over you.'

'We?'

'Me, Cissy, Alphonse and Anke. I had the morning shift today.'

'Anke? Anke was here!' Any pain Feldman had been experiencing was gone.

'She's still here,' Hunter explained. 'She's been here since about three o'clock Monday morning. Came as soon as she heard the news. She and Cissy are in a room down the hall now gettin' some sleep. They're wasted.'

'I've got to see her!' Feldman insisted. 'Just as soon as she wakes, okay? It's very important!'

'No problem, man, she's certainly gonna want to see you. But how about I get the doctor now?'

'Wait a minute!' Feldman stopped him. 'First tell me what happened with Goene and Tamin.'

Hunter sighed and sat back in his chair, shaking his head soberly, looking off into space. 'Tamin is in an Israeli prison awaiting trial. Goene is dead.'

Noticing Hunter's unusually sombre expression, Feldman nodded slowly, a tightening in his throat. Tentatively, he asked, 'And how did he die?'

'The pilot shot him. Saved my life . . .'

Relieved, Feldman started to pursue the issue further but noticed Hunter's strange, disturbed expression, and thought better of it.

There was a report on the TV of a priest being interviewed by a news correspondent in front of a moving van. Across the screen a headline read: 'More Church Closings'. The video cut away to show people packing boxes in the sacristy and moving furniture out. The segment ended with the pastor locking the front door of the church.

At that moment, Alphonse Litti, breezing into the room to relieve Hunter, drew up short in joyous surprise. He was beside himself, grabbing Feldman and hugging him repeatedly and excitedly.

'Thank God, Jon! You've been restored to us, just as Jeza promised!'

'Jeza?' Feldman returned the embrace as well as his disabled arms would allow. 'You saw Her?'

'Yes,' Litti beamed. 'She told me yesterday morning . . .'

Feldman inhaled.

'. . . in my dreams!' Litti added.

Feldman exhaled. But he turned his disappointment into a smile.

On the TV, he was surprised to catch a video clip of Hunter and Litti shaking hands with Prime Minister Eziah Ben-Miriam, accompanied by the Lubavitcher rabbi, Mordachai Hirschberg, Commander David Lazzlo in civilian attire, and a hesitant-looking Cissy McFarland. A font read: 'Israel Commits Funds for International Jeza Studies Centre in Jerusalem'.

His eyes wide, Feldman pointed to the screen. 'What's this, guys?'

Litti and Hunter turned together and reacted with proud smiles. 'That's right, Jon,' Litti responded. 'Breck, Rabbi Hirschberg, former Commander David Lazzlo, Miss Cissy, all of us decided we wanted to work together to spread the message of the New Way. To proclaim Jeza's words. Her truth.'

Feldman gaped in amazement at the big cameraman. 'Breck? Breck, you a missionary?'

'Not a missionary,' Litti corrected him. 'Simply a "disseminator of information". We're going to establish a centre here in Jerusalem, dedicated to facts and information associated with Jeza. A college of Her works and wisdoms. An archive of Her message.'

Feldman was beyond astonishment. He examined intently the self-conscious face of his long-time friend. 'I don't believe it! Breck, a minister! But didn't Jeza command no churches, no preaching?'

Hunter wagged his head. 'I'm not gonna be a minister, Jon. An administrator, maybe, but this isn't a church. We're not gonna interpret Jeza's scripture. We're simply gonna spread Her gospel. And we're gonna spread the other scripture books as well. The Bible, the Koran, the Talmud, all of 'em. Only, we're gonna fix all the corrupted passages exactly like She instructed. And we're gonna assemble all the video records I have and make a collection of Jeza's complete tapes, available for anyone who wants 'em. Free!

'Although,' he added, turning to Litti reflectively, 'we might want to consider a few corporate donations to help defray . . .' Catching Feldman and Litti's reproachful looks, he broke into an apologetic grin. 'All right, so no sponsors. But anyway, Cissy and I, we're gonna go on the Internet with everything, set up a communications system – modems, faxes, the whole nine yards. It's gonna be great!'

This was something Feldman would never have anticipated of Hunter the Hedonist. 'And Erin?' he asked.

'She's got herself a new job now.' Hunter turned, picked up the TV control and switched channels.

There she was, preening charismatically up on the screen, tossing her hair above the byline 'Erin Cross, UBN Morning News Anchor'.

Feldman smiled and nodded his head. 'And what about you and Cissy now?'

Hunter shrugged and grinned. 'She doesn't exactly trust me yet, but she says she's willing to try me out on "a probationary basis". We'll see. Anyway, we've got big plans for the centre. And we want you to join us, too.'

Litti stood beaming next to Hunter, nodding his encouragement.

'*Me?*' Feldman gasped. 'I'm a reporter. What would I do?'

'You could narrate our videos,' Hunter suggested. 'Give inspirational talks about Jeza. Answer all the questions people will have about what She's like, your personal experiences with Her, stuff like that. Jon, you're one of the *choosen!*'

As he shook his head at all this, yet another news report caught Feldman's eye. 'Worldwide Cessation of Hostilities', the headline read, and the screen displayed a series of supporting film clips with the banners: 'Rwandan Hutus and Tutsis Declare Truce'; 'Serbs, Croats and Muslims Form Alliance'; and 'Castro Addresses US Congress'.

Next on the screen appeared an image of clean-up crews in Belfast, Northern Ireland, shown clearing the streets of riot debris left over from the Easter weekend Cataclysm. The camera cut to an historic meeting between former arch-adversaries, headlined: 'Rapprochement Between Ex-Catholic and Ex-Protestant Leadership'.

'Amazing!' Feldman exclaimed with delight.

'Yeah,' Hunter acknowledged brightly, following Feldman's eyes. 'Stuff like that's happening all over the place. Lifelong enemies befriending one another. Sudden, unprovoked, random acts of kindness between total strangers, breakin' out all over the globe. Everywhere, charitable contributions goin' through the roof. It's incredible!'

Litti could not contain his excitement. 'Yes, Jon, it's unbelievable. Over the last five days there have been no recorded hostilities occurring between countries anywhere in the world! Imagine that! Not one! Absolute peace! Nothing like this has ever happened before! You need to be a part of all this, Jon!'

'Guys,' Feldman said, attempting to subdue his friends' enthusiasm, 'you don't need me. The entire world is converting to Jeza.'

Litti shook his head. 'No, Jon. Unfortunately, the world still looks at Jeza through many lenses. There are large factions which continue to see Her as a delusional woman – just another of the endless false prophets who've plagued the Holy City over the centuries. And mark my words, although the Church may be crippled, it is far from finished. With Antonio di Concerci taking command as Pope Nicholas VII, you can be assured the intrigue will continue.

'But our new movement does enjoy great support among many of the Christian communities of the world. Also, we can count among our ranks the large majority of the Jewish faith, including the State of Israel, which now officially embraces Jeza as their promised Messiah. And, with several Arab nations accepting Jeza as a new prophetess – if not the daughter of Allah Himself – we finally have the basis for a balanced, lasting peace here in the Middle East. A great foundation on which to establish and build our Centre for the New Way.'

Feldman sat back in thoughtful reflection. He was utterly thrilled by all the wondrous energies and positive developments suddenly at work in the world about him. At long last, after all the turmoil, conflict, hatred and anguish, perhaps now mankind was prepared to change. Ready to seize the moment. To unleash the belated spiritual and social potentials this once-in-two-thousand-year opportunity afforded.

After two millennia of watching man drift further and further astray, God had sent us a message. An all-important 'spirituality check'. He'd sent a Messiah to remind us, once more, of the great love and self-sacrifice we humans are capable of. To remind us, indeed, of God's great love.

Feldman used to wonder where God was. Why he couldn't find Him, why he couldn't see Him, no matter how hard he tried. And now he knew.

It's all in *how* you look at Him.

Seeing God is something we all knew how to do once, and somehow managed to forget a long, long time ago. To see God is simple. It's exactly like Jeza said. We must look with the eyes of a child. Not straining and forcing and prying at God with the crowbars of theology. But relaxedly, with innocence and wonderment and faith. Like experiencing the three-dimensional images of a child's magic-eye picture book.

God is easy to find because He's everywhere. But mostly, Feldman realized, God is within. And that's where it's best to look for Him. In one's own personal temple. The church of the self.

Feldman smiled. Maybe this time God's message would take. And maybe now, at some distant point in the future, man would yet give a worthy accounting of himself when he is finally summoned for that consequential Last Day.

Feldman broke away from his vision to look closely into the eyes of his good friends. 'Your Centre for the New Way will help ensure that none of us ever forget Jeza's message,' he told them, endorsing their plans, 'but I'm afraid I can't be a part of it. It's just not the right way for me.'

Hunter sighed and Litti nodded his reluctant understanding.

'Certainly we're wrong to try to influence the way you choose, Jon,' he admitted. 'You know we'd love to have you with us. But whatever it is God wants from you, that's between you and Jeza. And only you can determine what that is.'

A doctor, alerted to Feldman's regained consciousness, wanted the room cleared while he gave the newsman a thorough examination.

Feldman called after his friends, 'Don't forget, when Anke wakes I need to see her right away!' Hunter gave him an okay sign and left with Litti to inform the world of the miraculous recovery.

While the physician disconnected Feldman's intravenous tubes, and tapped and poked, the reporter sat back in his bed, thinking how he might best frame his forthcoming apology to the woman he loved.

On the TV, there appeared a story about the US presidential campaign, and Feldman turned up the volume. The commentator was reporting on the utter collapse of Democrat Billy McGuire's presidential candidacy. A 'Draft Moore' movement was under way, although the incumbent was described as unavailable, and said to be more interested in pursuing a personal, non-political 'New Way' of his own.

Turning to a local Israeli channel, Feldman saw that a conglomerate of American evangelists had arrived in Jerusalem, led by someone named the Right Reverend Solomon T. Brady, DD. They intended to petition for franchise rights to a US Centre for the New Way, to be constructed in Dallas, Texas. The Reverend wanted to call his proposed establishment the Brady University Jeza Studies Institute. Feldman winced, muted the volume again and closed his eyes.

Once more he slept. This time, his dream was both pleasant and real. Anke had arrived at his bedside, gently stroking his hand, tears in her big brown eyes. And when he woke, if she had any further doubts about his true feelings for her, his reaction dispelled them completely.

'Anke, Anke, Anke!' he cried, and enveloped her with his encumbered arms. He kissed her repeatedly, unable to satiate his feelings. 'I'm so sorry! So very, very sorry!'

While this was not the eloquent apology he'd rehearsed and now forgotten, Feldman's sincerity was indisputable. He drew himself up in bed, anxious to explain himself better. 'Anke,' he began, 'I want you to know that my feelings for Jeza and my feelings for you, they're totally different, they're—'

She stilled his lips softly with her forefinger, smiling, and whispered, 'Jon, Jon. It's okay. I know.'

They remained caught up in their tender intimacies until a familiar voice at the door cleared its throat.

'Well,' Cissy nonchalantly interrupted, 'I guess this means you two are back together again?' The elated gleam in her eyes betrayed her emotions, and Anke generously moved aside to make room for another teary-eyed reunion.

After telling Feldman how awful he looked, Cissy wiped her eyes with his sheet and informed the couple that there were special guests waiting to see them. Two people she thought they'd be particularly pleased to see.

Feldman nodded, and Cissy returned to the doorway, motioning to the visitors outside.

A well-dressed, elderly woman with silver hair and a glowing smile peered hesitantly around the door and trilled, 'Hello!'

Feldman and Anke instantly recognized Anne Leveque and returned her greeting, inviting her to enter. But as she did, Feldman's heart faltered and his delight immediately changed to disbelieving shock.

Following shyly behind Mrs Leveque, holding the older woman's hand, her face and eyes downcast, was a small, frail, pretty-looking woman with blue eyes, pale skin and dark hair. For a brief moment, Feldman was electrified with the misconception that this was Jeza. And then, his heart racing, he realized who this timid little woman was.

'Marie!' he whispered in awe.

The resemblance was startling, but certainly not exact. Marie was older than Jeza. And while attractive, she hadn't Jeza's perfection. Nor her eyes or luminescent complexion. But Marie's was a sweet and endearing face. And when she was introduced, her smile was engagingly, entirely Jeza's.

'When? How?' Feldman stammered.

Beaming, Mrs Leveque stood behind her daughter and gently drew her in, wrapping her arms around Marie's tiny waist. 'Good Friday afternoon,' she said, placing her cheek on Marie's head, her eyes starting to water. 'I was in my home,' she explained, 'watching my Jeza give her last speech, live on television. Then there was that awful moment when she was struck down, and all the announcers were saying that she was shot. I could not bear the pain of another loss. I just slid from my chair to my knees, rocking and crying, begging God, pleading for Him please not to take away my child from me again.

'And then, suddenly, I heard a voice calling behind me, softly, "Mama, Mama, Mama."' The poor woman could no longer contain herself and she began sobbing heavily as Marie looked up, squeezing her mother's hands with a consoling smile. 'God took my Jeza, but He restored to me my Marie.' Mrs Leveque composed herself, gazing adoringly down at her daughter. 'He returned her to me, in His great love and forgiveness, completely and wholly as she was before the accident.'

Feldman could only stare in wonder at the incredible scene.

In the corner, on the TV, an image of Feldman was flashed up on the screen along with the headline 'Newsman Recovers!' Simultaneously, Hunter and Litti re-entered the room just as a growing tumult arose from outside the window. The crowd below was reacting to the news, cheering and shouting.

'Your public,' Cissy announced to Feldman, bowing and extending her arms to the window.

Coming upon the surprising sight of Marie Leveque, Hunter and Litti skidded to a halt in utter bewilderment. While they were introduced and brought up to speed, Feldman tried out his legs, Anke on one side, Cissy on the other, making his unsteady way to the window on his sore ankle.

Spotting him, the crowd erupted. There were hundreds of thousands of people camped out across the hospital grounds, spilling out into the bordering roadways. All facing the newsman's window, they were pressing forward, calling out, waving, displaying signs and celebrating Feldman's wondrous recovery.

The reporter was moved. 'They've all been watching and waiting here for me?' he asked in disbelief.

'You're an important link to Jeza for them,' Alphonse Litti said, coming up behind him to admire the crowd. 'You've had a special relationship with the Messiah, a closeness that, I confess, even I envy.'

A placard below, held as high as the unseen author could stretch, read: 'Jon, You Are Jeza's Chosen'. Another said, 'Show Us the Way!' And still another proclaimed: 'She Is Risen!'

Spying the ex-cardinal at the window with Feldman, the crowd's excitement intensified.

Feldman gazed without focus into the distant Israeli hills, waving abstractedly to the celebrating throngs, as Anke watched him, intently, silently.

Fearful that his energies were being overtaxed, the doctor returned to clear the room. The visitors were forced to offer their abrupt farewells, but Feldman wasn't about to let Anke go. As the room emptied, he grasped her by her arm and held her back.

'Anke,' he said earnestly as they held hands, locking eyes, attempting to see into each other's hearts. 'Everything is much clearer to me now. Clearer than ever before. I know what I want from life. And I know now that I could never be happy without you.'

She didn't respond immediately, taking time to consider more than just his words.

'I love you,' he whispered.

'Sweetheart, I love you, too,' she finally said. 'But during these past strange days, I've had lots of time to think. And things are much clearer to me now, too. I know our love for each other is very important, but it isn't a complete answer. It's only a beginning.

'Look at all you've been through. Look at all the incredible experiences you're holding inside you. Look at what's going on right now outside your window. Jon, you've got to deal with this first. For my own peace of mind, I need to know exactly where all this is taking you. I need you to tell me where *you're* heading before we can decide where *we're* heading. Maybe we can get there together, and maybe we can't. But I need to have the facts so I can decide for myself.'

Feldman nodded and looked away towards the window. 'You're right, Anke. I know I have to do something with all this. I have to deal with it somehow. But not in the way that Breck and Alphonse are. I'm a journalist, not an archivist. Maybe I have been chosen, but I intend to have a say in what I do with that responsibility. And I know now that that's perfectly okay with Jeza, that's part of Her message. *I* get to determine my own way. I do need to unburden, but I'll do it in the way any self-respecting journalist might. I'm going to *write* about it. I'm going to commit everything I've experienced to paper.'

Anke followed his eyes out of the window and nodded with growing appreciation and approval.

'I can do my part to spread the gospel of the New Way,' Feldman explained, 'transcribing all the experiences and revelations I've been privy to. But Anke, I don't want to be without you any more.'

'Is this a marriage proposal, Mr Feldman?' she asked with feigned suspicion.

Attempting to kneel to make this more formal, Feldman put undue weight on his injured foot. He groaned in pain, releasing Anke's hands just in time to avoid pulling her down to the floor with him. Despite the hard landing, he did not evade the question. 'Yes, yes!' he moaned. 'Will you marry me?'

Assuring herself that he was okay, Anke stepped back, restraining a smile. She pursed her lips and began a careful assessment of his bandaged body. 'Well, I can't say that's exactly my idea of a romantic proposal,' she declared.

He grimaced up at her, rubbing his ankle, still hoping for a positive response.

Frowning now, she put her left hand to her chin and stroked it with thumb and forefinger. 'I don't know about this marriage thing, Mr Feldman,' she vacillated. 'You look like damaged goods to me. I wouldn't want to find myself stuck for the rest of my life with defective merchandise.'

He broke into a grin. She helped him to his feet and he placed his good arm around her shoulders.

'So,' she changed the subject, 'how are you going to write this story, anyway? As memoirs? As a biography? Autobiography?'

Feldman sighed, impatient over her coy avoidance of his proposal. 'I'm not sure, exactly. I haven't had a chance to think it through yet. I'll probably write it as some sort of journal.'

'Good!' Anke approved his choice. 'A journal's the perfect vehicle for telling Jeza's story the way She'd want it to be told. It'll help you stay more objective and keep personal interpretation out of it.'

'What's this!' Feldman rejoined with a smile of amazement. 'Is this the same woman who once heckled me about my reporting being too objective? Is this the same woman who called me a human word-processor, who said I should inject more personal opinion into my journalism? Well, well, well!'

She screwed up her face in amused irritation and gave him a disparaging look. 'There's nothing more obnoxious than a man who thinks he's right all the time!'

'Hey,' he cautioned her with raised eyebrows and mock superiority, 'are you forgetting that I'm a recipient of divine revelation?'

She narrowed her eyes at him and leaned in close. 'This is going to be an interesting marriage, isn't it, Mr Feldman?'

He drew closer still, narrowing his eyes back at her. 'Yes, ma'am,' he prophesied, 'I believe it is.' And he kissed her.

Outside the window, the cheering swelled, rose up and spread across the greening spring landscape of the Holy Land.